I0722463

The Kauai Sea Adventures

Books 1 – 3

The Kauai Sea Adventures

Books 1 – 3

A Funny Thing Happened on the Way to Miami

Dagger Quest

Caribbean Counterstrike

Bravely and Faithfully

by

Edward M. Hochsmann

Copyright © 2022 by Edward M. Hochsmann

Paperback ISBN-13: 978-1-956777-94-9

Hardback ISBN-13: 978-1-956777-02-4

All rights reserved. Edward M. Hochsmann asserts the moral right to be identified as the author of this work. No part of this book may be reproduced in any manner whatsoever without written permission except in the case of brief quotations embodied in critical articles and reviews and properly attributed to the author. This assertion likewise extends to all named characters in this book and the concept of USCGC *Kauai*, none of which may be used in other works without the written permission of the author. For permission requests, write to the author, addressed "Attention: Permissions" at info@edwardhochsmann.com.

Edward M. Hochsmann
PO Box 286
Shalimar, Florida 32579-0286
www.edwardhochsmann.com

This novel is entirely a work of fiction. The names, characters, and incidents portrayed in it are the work of the author's imagination. Any resemblance to actual persons, living or dead, events or localities is entirely coincidental.
Designations used by companies to distinguish their products are often claimed as trademarks. All brand names and product names used in this book and on its cover are trade names, service marks, trademarks, and registered trademarks of their respective owners. The publishers and the book are not associated with any product or vendor mentioned in this book. None of the companies referenced within the text have endorsed the book.

Table of Contents

DEDICATION

This book is dedicated to my wife and sons, who provide the love and support that gets me through each day and every effort I face. It is also dedicated to the Coast Guard, the oldest continuous seagoing service of the United States, and its complement of supremely skilled, committed, and courageous professionals. They stand the watch and lay their lives on the line every day to save others, defend the homeland, protect the environment, and promote maritime commerce.

Semper Paratus

Prologue

Captain Jane Mercier, U.S. Coast Guard, Chief of the Office of Response for the Seventh Coast Guard District, received a phone call she had been dreading for several weeks from Captain Nathan Worley, Commander of Coast Guard Sector Miami. The patrol boat USCGC *Kauai* was en route to her homeport in Miami; her Alien Migrant Interdiction Operations patrol cut short by a fatal mishap. Two migrants were dead, several injured, and the boat's second-in-command and senior boatswain's mate were also severely injured and medically evacuated.

"Jane, I have no choice. I have to yank him," Worley said, referring to the cutter's commanding officer. "Is there anything you can do to help me with a quick replacement?"

"What about the XO?" Mercier asked, referring to *Kauai*'s second-in-command or Executive Officer.

"We had to medevac him for a head injury. Besides, you know he isn't up to it."

"Yes, I know," Mercier said. *Kauai* had been on their mutual radar for several months, with material discrepancies and adverse personnel actions well above the norm. They had sent a "fixer", a Chief Machinery Technician named James Drake, known for his ability to ferret out and solve problems, replace the chief on board, and privately provide a report on the command. Drake's account had been shockingly frank—the boat was in a downward spiral only a change of command could fix. Mercier and Worley had been working through the administrative details to make that happen quietly when the incident had forced their hand.

Kauai was an Island Class Patrol Boat, 110 feet long and displacing 168 tons, with a crew of fourteen enlisted and two officers. The last of her class built, and among the last few still serving with the Coast Guard, *Kauai* was scheduled for decommissioning within two years. The issue with the command presented a dilemma—should they invest in repairs and the disruption of a relief for cause, or just call it a day and move up the decommissioning?

Drake's report also said the hull was in good shape, and he could turn around the engineering department with a bit of help. Mercier was reluctant to throw *Kauai* away early because the boat had been upgraded with a prototype of the automated main gun installed on the new patrol boats and the hull had plenty of life left. For a replacement commanding officer, she had her eye on a lieutenant in her department named Sam Powell, working through the command center controller syllabus after a successful command tour on a smaller eighty-seven-foot coastal patrol boat. The need to replace the injured executive officer was unexpected, and she would have to scramble through the recent list of screened officers to find an available replacement.

Sam was stunned when Mercier pulled him into her office a few minutes later and ordered him to report to Base Miami Beach and assume command of *Kauai* as soon as the Sector Commander relieved his predecessor. But, like any officer of his high caliber, he said "aye, aye" and carried out his orders. Within two weeks, Mercier had identified and transferred in the new second-in-command, Lieutenant Junior Grade Ben Wyporek.

Sam and Ben's job was to restore the ship and crew to operational readiness as soon as possible. This they did within a few months, despite the damage from mishap and the critical morale problems their predecessors had left behind. After the restoration period was complete and a few operational wins were under their belt, Sam and Ben pivoted to building the crew's esprit de corps.

Kauai's crew became Mercier's special project, and Sam was surprised with how easily they could swap out the few irredeemable troublemakers and slackers for top performers. Given their proximity to decommissioning, he had feared *Kauai* would become a dumping ground for malcontents. Over time, the combined efforts of Mercier directing high-caliber personnel into the crew, Drake's wheeler-dealer skills with maintenance and parts, and Sam and Ben's leadership acumen brought *Kauai* to a peak of operational competence and readiness unimaginable a year earlier.

A Funny Thing Happened on the Way to Miami

A BEN WYPOREK ADVENTURE

EDWARD HOCHSMANN

Edward M. Hochsmann

A Funny Thing Happened

on the Way to Miami

Lieutenant Junior Grade Benjamin Wyporek, US Coast Guard, was an hour into a fifteen-hour drive from Little Creek, Virginia, to his new duty station in Miami, Florida. He was tremendously excited about the new job he was heading for and almost as excited to leave Virginia for sunny Florida on this frigid January day. He should have waited a couple of days for the weather to moderate. There had already been freezing rain this morning, but this was an emergency transfer. His new unit had already waited nearly two weeks, but it couldn't be helped. He was the Communications Officer on his previous ship, which meant he had custody of beau coups classified publications and hardware, all of which had to be inventoried and page-checked before he could be relieved and detached. That took precious time, leaving little to spare for waiting on the weather. So, he drove along white-knuckled in his white Camaro, well under the speed limit on the two-lane state roads forming the shortest route from Norfolk to Interstate 95, and alert for any issues on the road ahead.

It had been only ten days ago when he learned of the new job. He was knee-deep in the usual drudgery of Communications Officer duty in U.S. Coast Guard Cutter *Dependable*'s

Cryptography Office. He did not hear the ringer on the ship's phone in the adjoining radio room and was startled when the Operations Specialist poked his head in and said, "Mister W., XO on the phone for you."

Ben's heart sank. The Executive Officer, better known aboard ships as the "XO," had never been a bearer of good news in Ben's experience. XO calls typically included dreaded phrases such as: "Are you aware...." "Why did/didn't you...." or "I had occasion to inspect your division spaces today...," none of which resulted in a positive outcome for him or someone in his division. He pulled the Crypto Office door closed and took the phone. "Lieutenant J.G. Wyporek, ma'am." A month after his promotion, he was relieved he had finally gotten out of the habit of answering "Ensign Wyporek," a source of amusement among his peers in the wardroom, as the officer's mess was known aboard ship.

"Ben, I need to talk to you right now, please."

Wow. No preamble; just get down here. Ben's heart descended another couple of levels. This had the makings of a severe ass-chewing, and he would not help himself with the next sentence. "Ma'am, I have the safe open and crypto laying out, and I'll need a couple of minutes to get it squared away."

"Yes, yes, of course. But get down here as soon as you're done."

"Yes, ma'am."

Ben hung up the phone and strode back to the crypto room. He took a deep breath and replaced everything in the safe, checking thoroughly around the room to ensure he left nothing out before closing the drawer and spinning the dial. Making a mistake with classified material was the worst form of unforced error a junior officer could make. Regardless of the added ire it cost him with the XO, he was determined not to become one of "those guys."

He left the radio room, hustled through the corridor toward the ladder, and bounded down to the next deck to reach the XO's stateroom. There was no need to knock. The door was open, and the XO looked up as he arrived. "Come in, Ben, and close the door, please." After he did so, she said, "Have a seat," and motioned to the spare chair by her desk.

Hmmm. Not an ass-chewing. He would be braced-up at attention. *What the hell is going on here?* "Yes, ma'am?"

"I have some good news for you, Ben. How would you feel about an XO job on a one-ten?" she asked with a smile.

Ben, a twenty-three-year-old graduate of the Coast Guard Academy, had been aboard *Dependable* for eighteen months and was due to transfer in the summer. He had hoped for a commanding officer job on an 87-foot patrol boat, but those went to Deck Division officers, not Communications/Electronics weenies like him. With the 110-foot patrol boats, referred to as one-tens, being phased out and their larger replacements having a full lieutenant as XO, his hopes he'd have a shot at command cadre in the next tour were fading fast. "I would feel great, ma'am. Is there something I need to do I haven't done already?"

"You misunderstand. How would you feel about getting the job right now? There's a mid-season opportunity, and your name has come up."

Did I hear that right? What's the catch? Uh-huh. It's probably one of the boats three thousand miles from civilization up in Moose's Balls, Alaska. "Still sounds good, ma'am. Dare I ask which boat?"

"*Kauai*, in Miami."

No way! Chasing drug smugglers in the sun and calm seas instead of puking my guts out measuring fishnets while counting the days until sunrise! "It just got upgraded to awesome, ma'am. Not looking at a gift horse in the mouth, but this is rather sudden. Did something happen to the current XO?"

"That's the downside. *Kauai* just had a serious mishap. The XO's been taken off on a medical disability, and they have relieved the Commanding Officer for cause."

Yep, there it is. If that boat wasn't a hot mess before, it sure as hell will be now. "Um..."

"Before you reply, let me fill you in on things. I was on the phone with the captain heading up response in the 7th District—she's ramrodding the replacement rather than going through the normal process because they need someone down there yesterday. The mishap and the relief are on the old CO. He was one of those rare cases of a Captain Bligh slipping through the cracks. She says the crew's a good bunch, just a little downtrodden right now.

"Anyway, the new CO is there, and he's the best one to right the ship. I haven't met him, but I know of him, and everyone I trust says you *want* to work for this guy. So, do you have any questions before I pin you down for an answer?"

"Yes, ma'am. I'm in, but am I right for a turnaround job? Kicking ass and taking names is not my forte."

The XO smiled again. "The last thing *Kauai* needs is another screamer. 'Ass-kicking,' as you call it, is a tool every officer should use when needed to get something done in an emergency. Officers who think it's the only tool don't last long—they have nothing left in a real jam. *Kauai's* former CO just provided a spot-on example of that truth.

"You and your division have done extremely well under a very demanding schedule the last year. The chiefs and petty officers trust and respect you. They like working for you, and it's not because they think you're a soft touch. Your quiet competence has not gone unnoticed upward either; that's why you got the call. You are the right man for the job."

Ben was staggered by the revelations he was appreciated both down and up the chain of command. He knew he was a skilled ship handler, far better than average, but he was nowhere near as aggressive as the other junior officers in the leadership dimension. Ben thought that might be a disadvantage and considered changing, but decided he just couldn't bring it off. He was getting the job done without being a dick, and that is how he wanted to keep it.

"Thank you, ma'am," he said. "If you think it's right, that's good enough for me. Where do I sign up?"

Ben turned over the Communications Officer job and sundry to other junior officers on *Dependable* with breakneck speed. He arranged the shipment of those possessions that would not fit in the Camaro, which was pretty much all of them. Finally, with great satisfaction, Ben was able to invoke the Soldiers and Sailors Civil Relief Act to cancel the lease on the hideously expensive apartment in Virginia Beach he'd been talked into by an ex-girlfriend. The big day came, and he pushed off, despite the weather. Next stop, Miami.

A few miles past Newsome, Virginia, a large green pickup pulled up behind him and started tailgating. Ben wanted to throttle the driver for doing something that stupid under the existing conditions, but settled for slowing even further. This drew several honks on the pickup's horn and an obscene gesture from the driver when traffic allowed him to pass. *Go to hell, jackass! I've got your number.*

Ben watched the pickup speed off to repeat the tactic on a small SUV driving a couple hundred yards ahead. This time, it didn't work out so well. The pickup mistimed his passing of the SUV, veering back into the right lane too soon. The SUV driver jigged right to avoid the pickup, hitting the road's soft shoulder, then over-corrected, crossing the road and smashing into the guardrail. After penetrating the barrier, the car came to rest, teetering on the edge of a cliff-like embankment. As Ben pulled over to see if he could help, he dialed 911 with the Camaro's voice-activated Bluetooth.

"Nine-one-one. What is your emergency?"

"This is Lieutenant Junior Grade Benjamin Wyporek, U.S. Coast Guard. There has just been a single-vehicle accident two miles west of Newsome on state highway 761."

"Understand single-vehicle accident. Are there injuries?"

"Unknown, I am just pulling up now."

"Understood. Please stay on the line and let us know what you find."

"Will do," Ben said as he pulled to a stop and grabbed his phone. The scene that awaited him was surreal, with the SUV's front half over the embankment's edge, hanging in space with a sheer forty-foot drop. The guardrail was pierced and blocked both passenger doors. With the driver's airbag deployed, he couldn't see much other than that the driver was female and not moving. The car's back end was drifting slowly up and down. *Holy shit! Talk about flipping a coin and having it land on its edge!* As he approached the vehicle, he could hear a child softly crying. Ben grabbed the hatchback's top and put his full weight on it to bring the rear down. He was not a large man, five-foot-ten and 165 pounds, but his weight was enough to ground the vehicle's rear wheels. Ben breathed a relieved sigh and then called, "Hello, can anyone hear me?"

"Yes, I can hear you!" said a young child's voice.

"Hello, my name is Ben. What's yours?"

"Dierdre!"

"Hello, Dierdre. Are you hurt?"

"No, but my mommy is. She won't wake up!"

"I understand. Is there anyone else in the car besides you and your mommy?"

"My little brother, Sean. He won't wake up either!"

"OK, Dierdre. I know this is very scary, but I need your help. I need you to stay where you are and not move around. Do you understand?

"Yes, I understand!"

"Super. Now I need to talk to someone on the phone so that they can get help for us, but I'm staying right here with you. OK?"

"OK!"

Ben pulled out his phone and whispered, "Operator, are you still on the line?"

"Still here, Lieutenant."

"Alright, we have a single-car crash with airbag deployment. The driver is unresponsive. There are two passengers, both children, one unconscious. The car has penetrated the guardrail and is hanging over a steep embankment. I am standing on the rear of the vehicle to keep it from going over the edge. I can't enter the vehicle to check injuries or remove the occupants."

"Copy all, Lieutenant. We'll get you help as soon as it's available."

"As soon as it's available? How long will that be?"

"Estimate forty-five minutes."

Ben was appalled and barely able to continue in a whisper. "Forty-five minutes? Have you been listening to me? This thing's about to go over a cliff with two kids in it!"

"Lieutenant, we are working a dozen emergency cases right now with the weather. I'm sorry, but that's the best I can do."

Ben ground his teeth and said, "OK, make it as soon as possible. While I have you on the line, copy down this license plate number: Virginia IG5B17. It belongs to a green RAM pickup, and that's the asshole who caused this accident and then ran off."

"Copy all. I'm sorry, Lieutenant. We'll get someone there as soon as we can."

"Understood. We'll be here." He hung up the phone. "Dierdre, how are you doing, honey?"

"I'm OK!"

"Alright, the people on the phone are sending help, but it's going to take a little while to get here."

"I'm getting cold, Mister Ben!"

"I know, honey. I'm going to get you out of there soon, but it's very important you stay in your seat. OK?"

"OK!" After a brief pause, she asked, "Mister Ben, are you a policeman?"

"Sort of. I'm a Coast Guard officer. That's like a policeman who rides on ships."

"Oh. Do you like it?"

"Yes, I do. Very much. What would you like to be when you get older?"

"I want to be a soldier like my daddy. Mommy doesn't like that. She wants me to be a doctor."

Yeah, don't they all? "You have a lot of time to decide. I'm sure you'll pick a job that makes you happy." Ben continued this banter to keep the child's mind off her predicament. It also helped with his own—his hat and gloves were still in his car, and he keenly felt the twenty-five-degree temperature's effects on his fingers and ears. After fifteen minutes, which seemed like hours to Ben, another car pulled over, and a man jumped out.

"How can I help?"

"Do you have any sandbags or other heavy stuff we can use to weigh down the car?"

"No, nothing like that."

"You have something I can use to pry open the rear door?"

"I have a tire iron."

"Get it. And get my hat and gloves out of the front seat of the Camaro, please!"

"Roger that!"

Ben was sure the relief he felt after putting on the hat and gloves was psychosomatic, but it was palpable nonetheless. "Thank you!" he said to the man. "There are two kids in there, along with the driver. We're going to get the kids out, and we'll put them in your car. Looks like I'm lighter than you, so I get to be the one to go in. I need you to take over holding down the rear end. I'm Ben, by the way."

"Tom. I've got it," Tom said, grabbing on with clear relief that he was not expected to climb into a car hanging over a cliff.

Ben stepped off, flexed his arms, legs, and fingers, and then picked up the tire iron. He tried his best, but the door wouldn't budge. Finally, he said, "I'm going to have to break the window." He made his way to the guardrail and looked in the passenger window. A small girl buckled into one of the passenger seats next to an infant car seat. He knocked on the window and, as she looked over, said, "Dierdre?"

"Mister Ben?"

"Yes, honey. I'm going to get you and your brother out, but the door is jammed, so I'll have to break the window. Do you understand?"

"Yes, Mister Ben!"

"OK. Can you reach over and cover up Sean with that blanket, please?"

"Like this?" she asked as she pulled the blanket across the top.

"That's perfect! Now, I want you to turn away and cover your face with your hands, like this." He covered his face in a demonstration.

"Like this, Mister Ben?" She covered her face and turned toward the door.

"Perfect again! I need you to stay just like that until I tell you to stop. OK?"

"Yes!"

Ben returned to the rear of the vehicle. He looked at Tom and said, "Are you ready?"

"Let'r rip!"

"Alright, Dierdre, now there's going to be a big crash when I break the window. So you know when to expect it, I'll count down from three to zero and hit it on zero. OK?"

"OK!"

"Good girl, keep your face covered now. Three, Two, One!" He swung the tire iron as hard as possible and shattered the window on the first try. The child involuntarily screamed at the impact. He used the tire iron to clear the glass around the edge, and said, "All done, Dierdre. I'm coming in now."

"OK!"

Ben crawled in the window and moved to a position behind the passenger seats. He reached down and unbuckled Dierdre's seat belt, and she looked up and hugged him. "OK, honey. You sit here for just a second while I get Sean out. OK?"

"OK. Thank you, Mister Ben!"

"Not at all." He reached down, unhooked the seat belt, and pulled the child seat into the rear of the SUV. "OK, honey, time to go." He took Dierdre's hand, led her to the back, lifted her out the window, and lowered her to the ground. He did the same with the car seat and climbed out himself. He leaned on the car and turned to Tom. "I've got it. These kids must be hypothermic. Get them into your car to warm up."

"On it," he said, picking up the child's seat. "Come on, Dierdre, I'm Tom. Let's get you in my car to get warm."

"Yes, sir. Bye, Mister Ben."

"I'll see you in a little while, Dierdre."

As Tom returned from placing the children in his car, a second and third pulled over, and three more men jumped out and came to the SUV. Ben looked around at each of them, and a quick mental calculation derived he was still the lightest of the group. "Thank you for stopping. We have enough weight now to go for the driver. You guys, climb on the back, please."

They nodded and grabbed onto the rear of the SVU as Ben climbed back into the window. He made his way carefully past the passenger seat and felt the woman's carotid; she had a strong pulse. He then took the Leatherman tool off his belt and pulled out the knife. From his cutter flight deck training, he knew you cut the seatbelts to avoid entanglement when you pulled someone out of a crash. As he leaned over to make the first cut, the car shifted abruptly. *Shit, Shit, Shit!* He froze, his heart pounding in his chest. *OK, I finally found something I hate more than being in a confined space—being in a confined space about to fall off a cliff!*

"You need to hurry, Ben!" Tom called.

No shit, Sherlock! "Roger that." He completed cutting the belt, then punctured the airbag. As soon as the bag deflated enough, Ben dragged the unconscious woman into the passenger seat. The car shifted again with a grinding noise.

"Hurry up, Ben! The roadbed's crumbling!" Tom said.

Ben dragged the woman into the back, climbed out the window, turned to Tom, and said, "Help me lift her out!" He and Tom each reached under one arm and pulled the woman through the window. They carried her clear as the other men jumped off the car. It teetered for a moment, then toppled off the edge, followed by a loud crash.

Ben stared at the hole in the guardrail for a few seconds, then looked at the second new vehicle, a large SUV. "Let's get her into the back of your SUV so we can keep her warm until EMS gets here." Tom and Ben carried the unconscious woman to the SUV. Then Ben took out his phone and redialed 911.

"Nine-one-one. What is your emergency?"

"This is Lieutenant Wyporek. I called in an accident west of Newsome."

"Yes, Lieutenant. I am the one who talked to you earlier."

"Good. We got everyone out of the car alive before it went over the cliff. Everyone is in a vehicle with heat. The driver and one child are still unresponsive. How long before we can expect to see EMS?"

"It will be at least fifteen minutes for police and half an hour for EMS."

"OK, where is the nearest ER to this location?"

"Stand by." After a few seconds, the operator came back on the line. "OK, Lieutenant, the closest ER to your location is the Marysvale Medical Center in Marysvale, thirteen miles away. Follow 761 east for ten miles, then turn left on 872. You'll see the hospital signs as you enter Marysvale."

"Roger. Tell the state police we're a convoy of three vehicles led by a white Camaro."

"Will do. Please stay on the line so I can follow your progress, Lieutenant."

"OK." He turned to the other men. "Tom and, I'm sorry, I didn't get your name?"

"Keith."

"Keith, glad to know ya," Ben said as he shook the man's hand. "It'll be at least thirty minutes before an ambulance can shake loose, but we can get these folks to the ER ourselves in twenty. Any objections?"

As Tom shook his head, Keith said, "Hell no, let's roll."

"Roger that. Follow me."

The men returned to their vehicles and started east on the highway. Five minutes later, the operator came on again.

"Lieutenant, are you still there?"

"Affirmative."

"There's a state police car waiting for you two miles ahead of your present location, and they'll pick you up for an escort."

"Roger that, thank you. Tell them I'll flash my lights when I see them."

"Will do."

They came over a hill a few minutes later, and Ben saw a stopped police car ahead. He flashed his headlights, and the car's vehicular beacon came on as it pulled onto the road ahead of them. "Operator, state police escort in place."

"Roger that, Lieutenant. Do you need any other assistance?"

"No. Thanks for the help."

"Good luck, sir. I'm signing off." The call hung up. The rest of the drive was uneventful, and on arrival at the hospital, Ben pulled into parking while the other two vehicles pulled up to the ER entrance.

As Ben arrived, Dierdre climbed out of the car and ran over to hug him. "Mister Ben!" He picked her up and carried her into the ER as Tom followed with the child in his car seat.

"This way, please," a nurse in scrubs led Ben and Dierdre into one of the intake areas. "Are you the father?"

"No, just a good Samaritan."

"Then you'll have to leave."

"No!" Dierdre began crying and hugged him tightly. "Don't leave me, Mister Ben!"

Ben quickly said, "Nurse, I'm a Coast Guard officer. The girl's mother is unconscious. Can I stay with her until next of kin arrives?"

"Oh, I didn't know. I suppose it will be all right. You must step out when we do an examination, of course."

"No problem." He put Dierdre down on the bed, pulled up a chair, and held her hand. "So, young lady, this has been quite a day!"

Dierdre fell asleep thirty minutes later. Ben covered her with a sheet and pulled up the bed rails as a state trooper appeared and beckoned him to come out. Ben stepped just outside the room to give his statement while not disturbing the sleeping child. When they finished, the nurse returned with a woman in tow.

"This is the child's aunt. I have to ask you to leave now, sir."

"I understand." He turned to the woman. "Is Dierdre's mother going to be OK?"

"Yes, she's coming around now. She has a severe concussion, and they will keep her overnight, but she should be fine."

"That is good news." He turned for a last look at Dierdre. "She's an extraordinarily brave girl. Would you tell her I said so and goodbye for me, please?"

The woman nodded and replied, "I heard what you did for my sister and the children. I was hoping you could stay for dinner tonight."

Ben shook his head. "I'm sorry, ma'am, but I have to get to Miami and report to my new unit as soon as possible."

The woman nodded sadly and offered her hand for a handshake. "I'm sorry too. Goodbye and good luck, sir."

After the woman turned and entered the room, Ben nodded to the nurse. As they walked, she said, "There's a reporter outside looking for the story."

Ben stopped in his tracks. "I don't want any dealings with the press. Do you have a side exit to the parking lot?"

The nurse returned a quizzical look. "Sure. This way, please."

Ben exited through the side door and hurried to his car. A few moments later, he was on his way again, this time sticking with the four-lane U.S. 58 to Emporia to pick up I-95 South. When he stopped for fuel and supper in South Carolina, he called the number for his new CO to report his progress. A female voice answered the phone. "Hello?"

"Ma'am, this is Lieutenant J.G. Wyporek. May I speak to Lieutenant Powell, please?"

"Of course. Hang on, please." Then, a male voice came on the line.

"Powell here."

"Sir, this is Lieutenant J.G. Wyporek. I am en route, but there was an accident, and it set me back four hours."

"First things first. Are you OK?"

"Yes, sir. I was a witness and pitched in to help out a bit. No injuries or damage here."

"OK, that's a relief. Look, I can't *order* you around until after you report in, so I'll *ask* that you keep yourself safe and heave to at a hotel no later than twenty-two hundred tonight. Naturally, I'm looking forward to meeting you and getting you in the game, but I'd much rather see you safe and ready in the afternoon than knocked out and bleary-eyed at zero-eight-hundred."

"Very good, sir. Shall we make it thirteen hundred then?"

"That will be fine, and if anything else comes up, don't feel obligated to push it. Just call me to let me know. Stay safe, and I'll see you tomorrow afternoon."

Around 9 p.m., fatigue set in, and he pulled over for the night at a hotel near Brunswick, Georgia. Unlike most hotel stays, he was asleep almost as his head hit the pillow on this occasion. He was up and on the road by 6:30 the following day and arrived at Coast Guard Sector Miami a little after noon.

His first impression of *Kauai* was very positive: clean and orderly, with an alert crewman manning the quarterdeck. Lieutenant Powell came out at once to greet him. His handshake was firm and warm. "Welcome aboard, Lieutenant! Your reputation precedes you, and I'm delighted you're here. What's your preference, Benjamin or Ben?"

"Ben, sir."

"Excellent. Come in, and let's talk."

Talk they did for over three hours. It was a relief to find that Ben's former XO was right—Powell had no intention for either of them to come down hard on this crew. The previous CO was an arrogant tyrant and a bully who had all but broken them. He *had* broken the XO. If the mishap hadn't physically crippled the man, he would have been relieved as psychologically unfit. Powell's program was quiet rebuilding and encouragement, one that Ben could sink his teeth into.

After Ben changed from his service dress uniform into his utilities, Powell took him around the ship to meet the crew. Chief Machinery Technician James Drake, the senior enlisted crewman, showed him the engine spaces. It amazed Ben that a six-foot-four, broad-shouldered man like Drake would want an assignment with such tight spaces as a patrol boat, but discovered later he enjoyed the autonomy it afforded him. He struck Ben as one of the "good" chiefs, who could be relied upon to keep the engines running *and* take care of most people-type problems before they came to the officers' attention.

The other crewmember Ben found notable was Operations Specialist First Class Emilia Hopkins, known as "Hoppy" among the crew. She was tall—Ben's height—about ten years older than him, and carried herself with a quiet confidence that seemed surprising, given the boat's history. Hopkins was extraordinarily knowledgeable about everything on the bridge, and Ben expected to learn a lot from her in time. She had also greatly impressed Powell. He told Ben privately that Hopkins had saved the boat during the mishap after the former CO's blundering and, with Drake, had kept the crew intact and functional through the transition.

Ben's worries about the crew and his fitting in were gone at the end of that first day.

****

Three weeks after Ben reported aboard, the Sector Commander arrived for an impromptu visit. Ben was called forward at a muster of all hands and, to his great surprise and intense embarrassment, was awarded the Coast Guard Commendation

Medal for saving Dierdre and her family. Later, he learned that her father, an Army lieutenant colonel, had put him in for the award after hearing the story. When the ceremony and heartfelt congratulations from the crew had passed, Powell pulled him aside.

"You 'helped out a bit,' I seem to recall you saying. Mind telling me what you consider helping out a lot?" he asked with a raised eyebrow.

"I might have understated my contribution some, sir."

"Right. Well, if you pull any more Captain America stuff in the future, would you let me know, please? I'd like to sign the award nomination myself," he said, putting his arm around Ben's shoulder as they went inside the boat.

Dagger Quest

Main Characters

Benjamin "Ben" Wyporek, Lieutenant Junior Grade, U. S. Coast Guard. Ben is the Second-in-Command or "Executive Officer" of the Coast Guard Cutter *Kauai*. He is young for an officer, but his demeanor and experience have earned the respect of the professionals around him, and although he is firm in his job, he never lets his position go to his head.

Dr. Peter Simmons is a field agent with the Defense Intelligence Agency. He has a talent for deception, which has led to his success as a DIA field agent, but is the antithesis of Ben's ethos. Simmons also has a risk-seeking bent that borders on pathology.

Samuel "Sam" Powell, Lieutenant, U. S. Coast Guard. Sam is Ben's boss and Commanding Officer of the Coast Guard Cutter *Kauai*. Sam is one of those people who is the total package - knowledge, judgment, experience, and "people sense." He was raised in a wealthy family and was being groomed to become another Wall Street "Master of the Universe" when a clash with his father led him to abandon that path and enlist in the Coast Guard. He is over ten years older than Ben, but despite this and their different backgrounds, they are best friends.

Emilia "Hoppy" Hopkins, Operations Specialist First Class, U. S. Coast Guard. She is close in age and a lot like Sam in terms of competence and professionalism, and they have as strong a friendship as people in their respective positions can. She has enormous respect and an exasperated affection for Ben, who reminds her of her late husband. Although a straight arrow, she is not afraid to forego convention in highly unusual circumstances.

James Drake, Chief Machinery Technician, U. S. Coast Guard. The senior enlisted member of the crew and the classic father figure among the enlisted and, to some extent, Ben. He is the quintessential "operator" and has what amounts to an underground network of fellow CPOs from whom he can acquire technical help, equipment, and "intel." His background is somewhat mysterious, but he is "connected" up to the senior officer level of the Coast Guard.

Arthur "Art" Frankle, Senior Case Officer, Defense Clandestine Service, Defense Intelligence Agency. Frankle is a veteran field officer, instructor, and mentor to many younger agents. He is approaching retirement age and considering moving from the field to a less "kinetic" post as an instructor or administrator.

Select Technical Terms

Afterdeck	The top deck behind the ship's superstructure
Airedale	Slang word referring to aviation personnel
Bridge	Control center for the ship
Conn	Position controlling the course and speed of the ship
Coxswain	Position controlling the operation of a small boat
CO	Commanding Officer (Ship's Captain)
DoD	Department of Defense
DoJ	Department of Justice
Foredeck	The top deck forward of the ship's superstructure
GQ	General Quarters (Emergency Stations)
Helm	Position controlling steering of the ship
IC	Intelligence Community
IR	Infrared
Knots	Nautical Miles per Hour
OOD	Officer of the Deck – watch position in charge of ship operations (Usually synonymous with "Conn" when the ship is underway)
Port (side)	To the left when facing forward on a ship
Puma	RQ-20 Small Unmanned Aerial Vehicle
Quarterdeck	The entry point for the ship when it is moored
RHIB	Rigid Hull Inflatable Boat
ROE	Rules of Engagement
SAROPS	Search and Rescue Optimal Planning System
Starboard (side)	To the right when facing forward on a ship
Steerageway	The slowest speed at which the ship can be steered
Stern	The rear end of the ship
UAV	Unmanned Aerial Vehicle
WILCO	Brevity code meaning "Will Comply"
XO	Executive Officer (Second in Command)

"A few armed vessels, judiciously stationed at the entrances of our ports, might at a small expense be made useful sentinels of the laws."

Alexander Hamilton

U.S. COAST GUARD
1351

Deployment

Contiguous U.S. Air Defense Identification Zone (ADIZ), thirty-five nautical miles east of Key Largo, Florida
02:02 EST, 10 January

It was the most dangerous period in East-West relations since the Cuban Missile Crisis in 1962. The previous decade and a half had seen the military ascendency of the Russian Federation and the renewal of its economic prospects dashed by the collapse of the oil markets. The subtle influence of so-called "Green Parties" in Germany had completely closed down the country's nuclear power capacity, making the largest consumer of energy in Europe completely dependent on Russian natural gas, not only for heating but also for electrical power generation.

The military adventures against Georgia in 2008 and Ukraine in 2014 had convinced Russia's revanchist president that NATO and the European Union were unwilling to risk war, even in the face of the most naked aggression. He began a long campaign to restore Russia to its "natural" borders, using means ranging from economic coercion to outright military threats to intimidate the smaller nations along Russia's periphery. With the West riven by political strife, he felt there would be no better time to wring out concessions to bolster Russia's military security. He would start by establishing a land corridor through Poland and Lithuania to the Russian enclave of Kaliningrad on the Baltic Sea. Kaliningrad was of enormous military and economic importance to Russia, being its only year-round ice-free seaport on the Baltic Sea. It was also vulnerable to counter-coercion from the West, as any land traffic between the enclave and Russia would have to pass through at least two other countries. That vulnerability needed to be fixed.

Russia's president dusted off the playbook that had worked so well before in Georgia and Ukraine. This involved fomenting unrest among the ethnic Russians toward the Polish and Lithuanian authorities, moving substantial military forces to conduct "exercises" in the Grodno region of the Russian puppet state of Belarus, and threats to curtail or cut off oil and natural gas supplies to the West. Given time, the broad political, economic, military, and psychological pressures would force the West to shrug and deliver another bloodless victory to Russia.

This time, it did not work.

Poland and Lithuania were far more homogeneous and nationalistic than the Russia-adjacent regions of Ukraine and Georgia and, unlike those states, were governed by relatively progressive and uncorrupted regimes. Also, unlike those states, Poland and Lithuania were not unaligned countries far from Western military centers. These were *NATO* countries with solid internal lines of defense and communications. A trustworthy and professional military cadre might have pointed out these basic first principles and dissuaded the Russian president from this effort. But like his distant predecessor Josef Stalin, he had purged the officer corps of no-men, preferring the loyalty of yes-men to competence.

The governments of the West came together solidly and quietly on the issue so as not to panic their populations or trigger financial collapse. The senior military officers in the West also conveyed a strong and unequivocal message to their Russian counterparts. A single Russian aircraft, tank tread, or soldier's boot crossing the Polish or Lithuanian borders would unleash a decisive counterattack on *all* Russian conventional forces across the theater. And if they thought firing nuclear weapons was an option, the West would ensure there was nothing left of Russia but a sad story, regardless of the cost.

That threat convinced even the bellicose president to move toward disengagement, but there had to be a show of force for internal purposes. Russian Long-Range Aviation units carried this out. TU-95 Bear Bombers launched from Siberia to the edge of U.S. airspace over the Bering Sea in the West. In the East, TU-160 Blackjacks flew from Caracas, Venezuela, to the U.S. Gulf Coast, and TU-22Ms Backfires from San Antonio de Los Baños Airfield southwest of Havana, Cuba, to the U.S. Southern Atlantic Coast. The Russians made no secret that these aircraft were carrying nuclear weapons—it was the purpose of the show of force. The U.S. Air Force dutifully intercepted and flew formation on the bombers with fully armed fighter aircraft. This was not the usual "poking the bear" operation, and both sides were on high alert during the bomber flights.

Formation flying carries a much higher risk of collision, particularly among tired, scared men and women flying at night around foreign aircraft with different flight procedures and communications protocols. It was not a surprise that a U.S. F-16 interceptor and a Russian Backfire "bumped" in the Air Defense Identification Zone. What was a surprise was that the collision triggered the drop of the bomber's Kh-47 Kinzhal hypersonic missile. As the crew of the bomber and the fighter's pilot fought to regain control of their respective aircraft, the missile's rocket engine ignited after it had dropped fifty meters, quickly accelerating it to its maximum speed of twelve times the speed of sound. The disabled F-16's wingman promptly fell back, locked his fire control radar on the bomber, and called his controller.

"Flash, Flash, Flash, Rondo Two, Bogie has launched, repeat strategic missile inbound!"

"Rondo Two, Plaintree, confirm strategic missile launch!"

"Plaintree, Rondo Two, confirm strategic missile launch heading west! Rondo One and Bogie collided, followed by launch. I am locked on to Bogie now. Request weapons free!"

"Rondo Two, Plaintree, hold and standby!"

"Roger. Break, break. One, this is Two, come in!"

"Two, One. You've got this one. My hands are full right now.

"One, Two, roger."

"American fighter, this is bomber. Launch is accident! Missile not arm! Repeat, launch is accident, missile not arm!" It was the bomber crew calling on the UHF distress frequency.

"Bomber, maintain heading, airspeed, and altitude. If you deviate, I will destroy you. Acknowledge!" *Go ahead and try to run, you son of a bitch!*

"American fighter, this is bomber. I comply."

"Plaintree, Rondo Two, I am in contact with Bogie. They claim the launch was accidental, and the missile is unarmed. Over."

"Two, Plaintree, do you have a visual on the missile?"

"Negative, Plaintree, it's long gone."

"Rondo Two, roger. Weapons tight. Direct bogie to RTB. Follow until you hit the Cuban ADIZ, over."

"Rondo Two, roger, out." He switched to the emergency frequency. "Russian bomber, this is the American fighter. You will execute a slow right turn to a heading of two three zero. Acknowledge."

"American fighter, I am turning right to two three zero."

The two aircraft completed a slow turn to the southwest, the F-16 trailing the larger bomber. The infuriated F-16 pilot was struggling to keep from pressing the fire switch as he listened to the steady growl of his sidewinder missile lock-on tone. *This bastard just launched a NUCLEAR MISSILE, and we are letting him go? WTF!*

On the ground, the alert went out instantly to the Supreme Headquarters Allied Powers Europe in Mons, Belgium, North American Aerospace Defense Command (NORAD) at Peterson Space Force Base in Colorado Springs, and Strategic Command at Offutt Air Force Base near Omaha. NORAD activated defensive systems, but it was for naught—the Kinzhal, Russian for "Dagger," flew so fast that its shock wave generated a plasma cloud that made it invisible to radar. Even if the missile could be tracked, nothing could fly fast enough to catch it.

The lack of indications and warnings of other offensive activity by the Russians lent credence to the claim that the launch had been accidental. They would know whether the missile was deliberately targeted and armed within ten minutes—the time it would take for the missile to exhaust its fuel. At that point, everyone could either breathe a sigh of relief or prepare for the next phase of the destruction of human civilization.

Sailing Vessel *High Dawn*, Gulf of Mexico north of the Florida Keys
02:07 EST, 10 January

Heinrich Köhler eyed the slowly approaching beach of the island through the night vision ocular. *A few hundred meters to go, then the final turn into the wind, and we anchor. Nearly done.* He confirmed his estimate using the hand-held GPS unit—283 meters. It would be close enough to the beach for short boat trips but not so near that an unexpected squall could put them on the beach. After coming so far, he would not be undone by a rookie blunder drawing the attention of the American Coast Guard or some other helpful do-gooder. Not with a metric ton of cocaine and one hundred kilos of fentanyl on board.

The two thousand three-hundred-mile trip had begun a little more than two weeks earlier for Köhler. His employers dispatched him and two assistants to take charge of the *High Dawn*, a beautiful sixty-five-foot cabin sloop in Greenwich, Connecticut. The yacht's owners were a Wall Street power couple who had lately made some abysmal market choices and needed quick cash. They made the fatal mistake of contacting his organization through one of their dodgier clients in hopes of a one-and-done trip to South America and back to clear their debts with no one the wiser. They were quite adept at working the system to clean up dirty cash and carefully and completely planned that aspect of the operation. Unfortunately, their skills in white-collar crime did not provide insight into the realities of the underworld of narcotics smuggling.

Köhler could not believe his luck when the two insisted on making the trip "to keep an eye on things." He feigned a mild annoyance and then acquiesced to the demand to keep them on the hook. From his perspective, the situation could not have been better: two wealthy gay men on a Caribbean vacation on their new yacht with a dour German captain and two crewmen provided the perfect cover for the trip down. It also obviated the need to dispose of them in Connecticut, risking discovery and failure before the journey began. The men's insistence on making the trip bought them an additional week of life. Their usefulness ended after the onload and departure from La Guaira, Venezuela, when they just became another liability. Both were quickly and efficiently disposed of at sea.

The organization took a substantial risk with this trip, concentrated in a single load rather than dispersed over several vessels. Köhler had sold them on the idea a year before—use their radar masker and decoy vessels to get a single large load through at small risk rather than accept the almost certain loss of some portion of the product in many, smaller loads. Operational security was the critical factor for success. They would not go into any port or marina. Eight terminal points for the trip were selected among the less traveled but accessible locations in the Florida Keys. All were reconnoitered just before nightfall, and the status of clear or occupied had been broadcast by radio "in the blind." Köhler himself would select the final destination and call it in once the *High Dawn* was anchored and secured.

With only a few minutes before anchoring, now was the time to go live and get things moving. After checking that Paolo was in position on the bow to release the anchor, Köhler turned the helm over to Jaime and ducked into the cabin to retrieve the satellite phone to make the call. He had to weave around the massive stacks of cargo in the cabin to get to the storage cabinet. He powered it on and verified he had a good signal link. It was the last act of his life.

Jaime and Paolo had a brief glimpse of a bright light approaching at over 3.5 kilometers per second, just long enough to turn their heads before the impact. Like Köhler working below in the cabin, they never knew what hit them.

Water, like all liquids, is virtually incompressible. A supersonic shock wave moving through the water is a solid wall for all practical purposes. This one broadsided the *High Dawn* with the equivalent effect of dropping the boat onto a solid surface from sixty feet in the air. The three men were stationary at the event's outset—the boat itself was "thrown" into them by the impact, killing them all instantly.

The *High Dawn* herself was laid waste. The shock wave crushed the starboard side of the hull. The mast stay on the port side snapped, and the mast itself was toppling over the starboard side, its attachment point to the deck shearing. Then the air shock wave hit, lifting the mast clear, snapping the starboard stay, running rigging, and the electric cable to the masker array. It was swept into the sea, along with Jaime and Paolo's bodies and anything else not fastened to the deck.

Köhler's command had become his tomb, rapidly filling with water from hundreds of cracks in the hull. Ironically, the priceless cargo was undamaged in the disaster, packaged in bales sealed in plastic and close-packed in any available space inside. The positive buoyancy of the bales would provide enough floatation to keep the boat from sinking for days as it sped off into the Gulf of Mexico with the residual momentum of the impact.

Two hours later, well past the expected time the *High Dawn* should have reported in, calls went out to the onboard satellite phones, then the crew's cell phones, and finally, in the clear on marine band radio. The alarm went out when no answer was forthcoming, and the organization began deploying resources for a covert search. The loss of this cargo would be a significant hit to the bottom line. Both inside and outside the organization, those responsible would pay dearly if it could not be recovered.

USCG Cutter *Kauai*, eleven nautical miles southeast of Fort Jefferson, Florida
09:43 EST, 13 January

Ben

Benjamin "Ben" Wyporek, Lieutenant Junior Grade, U.S. Coast Guard, was coming up on the halfway point of his Officer of the Deck, or OOD, duty in the eight a.m. to noon Forenoon Watch. In that role, he supervised the watchstanders, kept the vessel on course and speed and clear of other vessels, and was the captain's representative. The workload stayed low when *Kauai* carried just enough speed to hold heading and position against the light winds and currents in the area. She held a position near a known drug smuggler rendezvous. These were locations where "mother ships" carrying sizeable amounts of cocaine and other illegal products off-loaded to small, fast vessels for the final run to shore in the Florida Keys.

The watch had been quiet so far and somewhat boring, an unfortunate characteristic of sentry operations. Ben was grateful, at least for the comfortable weather. The temperate and dry days of January were the best time to be in the Western Florida Keys, at least for a born-and-raised northerner like Ben. Far preferable to July and August, when the only respite from the sweltering heat and humidity came from the torrential downpours of the scattered squalls that popped up during the day.

Even the seas were kind today—no swell, and the small waves stirred by the light winds gave the patrol boat a gentle rocking motion. The downside of January patrols was that weather systems often pushed down from the north with winds that stirred up moderate wave action. They were not a problem for larger vessels, but on smaller boats like *Kauai*, the choppy pitching and rolling they caused made even mundane activities such as eating and sleeping a challenge.

Kauai was a Coast Guard cutter. She was an Island Class Patrol Boat (D Class), one hundred ten feet long, weighing 168 tons, with a crew of fourteen enlisted and two officers. She was old, pushing twenty-five years of age on a design intended to last only fifteen. The Coast Guard had retired many of her older sisters, but *Kauai* was still alive and serving. Ben glanced out the rear window and saw the reason: Chief Machinery Technician James Drake walking toward the cradled rigid hull inflatable boat, called "the rib" for its acronym RHIB, with a junior petty officer in tow.

Drake got the title of "Chief," being the only chief petty officer on *Kauai*, was the senior enlisted member, and was the oldest man on the boat at forty-four. He was the finest chief petty officer Ben had ever known, both for the mastery of his trade and his leadership among the crew. Unlike the more legendary members of the chief petty officer ranks, Drake never shouted at his juniors. Six-foot-four and physically imposing, he only needed to lean in on someone to command attention. Ben wondered whether the junior petty officer with Drake had committed a minor blunder or if he was just doing on-the-job training. Most of the skills Coast

Guard technicians gained came from hands-on instruction on the job, and Drake took this responsibility seriously.

Drake looked after his officers as well. Occasionally, Ben had voiced a concern and soon found the problem had been corrected. He suspected Drake had dealt with many other issues before they even came to his attention. It went both ways. When Drake sensed Ben's uncertainty regarding an important decision, he often asked a respectful but pointed question. Sometimes, Drake pulled him aside and said something like, "You know XO, if I were you, I'd...." Ben always took the advice and never regretted it.

Five-foot-ten with an average build, Ben was personable and much more intelligent than his mediocre grades at the Coast Guard Academy suggested. He was among the crew's younger members, just past his twenty-fourth birthday. Ben had aspired to join the military since grade school, and his liking of naval history led him to apply to both the Coast Guard and Naval Academies. The Coast Guard offered an appointment first, and he accepted and never looked back.

Ben was the junior of the two officers on board, the executive officer or just "XO" by title and second in command. Besides standing the occasional watch, he oversaw the administrative needs of the cutter, including the reports, supplies, and financial accounts. Also, he preserved the crew's health, morale, and discipline, sometimes a grueling task on a surface unit as small and busy as *Kauai*. Yet, he was luckier than most officers in his position. There were no formal disciplinary actions in his year on board, and the only chronic troublemakers had rotated off to other units.

In the quiet times on patrol, such as this watch, Ben's mind often wandered back to his transfer to *Kauai*. His assignment resulted from good luck, although he wasn't sure of that at the time. Eighteen months into his first assignment on the large cutter *Dependable,* the ship's XO told him of the offer of an early rotation for the position on *Kauai*. She explained this opportunity was the perfect bird in the hand—with the number of one-tens dwindling, his chances for an XO job in his next assignment were fading fast. Needing no further encouragement, he took the job.

Lieutenant Samuel Powell greeted Ben on his arrival, having taken command two weeks earlier. The sector commander had fired their predecessors following a serious mishap, and Ben worried he was walking into a fiery mess of poor discipline and morale. Much to Ben's relief, Sam did not expect him to "whip" the crew into shape; they just needed to offer clear direction, stability, and encouragement. They set out to build *Kauai* into a successful team and shake loose the specter of failure that had brought them there. Within a few months, they had done just that.

Ben liked and appreciated Sam from the outset. An inch taller than Ben with a slim, athletic build, Sam was a Mustang—a former chief petty officer in the Operations Specialist rating who had completed Officer Candidate School and received an officer's commission. At thirty-five, he was second only to Drake in age among *Kauai*'s crew. Ben thought Sam was the most open and approachable officer he had ever met, possessing a ready, but not mean, sense of humor. He was not a pushover and insisted on decorum on the Bridge and in official situations. Still, Sam ensured the crew understood he stood by them if they worked hard and played by the rules.

It surprised Ben to learn later that Sam graduated from the University of Pennsylvania's prestigious Wharton School and came from a wealthy family. Children from that world rarely opted for the rigors of military life, particularly as enlisted personnel. When they were both on the Bridge, he worked up the nerve to ask Sam about his choice one quiet evening.

Sam dropped his head for a second, then looked up and said, "My family asked that question in shocked disbelief." After a brief pause, he said, "Let's just say I had to make a choice between two teams. One had people who'd let someone they know die just to make more money, and the other had people who risk their lives to save people they'd never met." He smiled. "The Coast Guard was the best call I ever made."

"Me too, sir," Ben had replied with complete sincerity.

Ben completed another round of scanning for targets by radar and binoculars when the alert sounded on the satellite channel used for communication with the operations center in Miami.

The message read, in plain language: "To *Kauai* from District Seven Operations Center: detach at once from the current mission and proceed to latitude 25 degrees 6 minutes north, longitude 81 degrees 8 minutes west for search and rescue on a disabled sailing vessel. The target is suspicious—a possible drug smuggler—and *Kauai* is to contact the Coast Guard maritime patrol aircraft 2303, the on-scene commander. Acknowledge."

This is more like it. Ben thought as he typed the latitude and longitude into the navigation system. *Drugs and search and rescue—buy one, get one free!* He picked up the phone to call Sam and report the development.

"Captain speaking."

"Sir, OOD here. They have detached us for SAR, disabled sailing vessel, potential drug target spotted by an HC-144. I read zero-six-seven true at one hundred-two miles. We should have comms from here if he is high enough."

"Very well. Make the turn and bring up full speed. I'm coming up now."

"Very good, sir." Ben hung up the phone and gave the orders to the helmsman. Sam entered the space a few moments later, and Ben announced, "Captain on the Bridge."

"Carry on, please." Sam returned Ben's salute. "Let's see if we can talk to them."

"Yes, sir." Ben dialed up the plane's frequency on the control console, then returned to his usual position, monitoring *Kauai's* progress while listening to the radio conversation. "We're up now, Captain."

"Thank you." Sam picked up the handset. "Two-three-zero-three, one-three-five-one on uniform in the green, over."

After a brief pause, the Coast Guard plane responded, "One-three-five-one, zero three, roger, read you lima-charlie in the green, over."

"Zero-three, five-one, we are on the way, ETA three and a half hours. What do you have for us?"

"Roger, it's weird. We have a large cabin sloop that's a total mess. The main deck is awash with heavy damage to the deck structures, and the mast is gone—nowhere in sight. No persons on board or bodies are visible."

"Copy main deck awash—is the vessel sinking?"

"Negative, vessel is upright and stable. The hull's trashed, but something's keeping it afloat. Could be sealed contraband."

Sam paused as he pondered the plane's report. A full load of drugs in sealed plastic packages could keep a small sailing vessel afloat, even with extensive damage. But that much product was worth a fortune—the owner's abandonment of it made little sense. "Roger, can you find the cause of the damage?"

"We got as close as possible and have good camera footage. No apparent weapons damage, no sign of vessel collision. It could be storm damage, but I've never seen it like this. It is just—weird. We will send the camera video to you when you get closer."

"Roger that. Any other traffic nearby?"

"Negative. Radar is clear, and nothing visual to the horizon."

"Roger. Can you hang in until we arrive?"

"Affirmative. Orders are to hold here until you're on scene."

"Zero-three, five-one, roger, see you in three and a half, out." Sam replaced the handset and stepped over to Ben. "This is a helluva thing. It must be dope keeping her afloat, but it doesn't figure them abandoning it."

The problem intrigued Ben. "A storm could have washed them overboard, but there haven't been any big storms around here since last October, Captain. Maybe a waterspout or rogue wave?"

Sam stared out across the bow, rubbing his chin. "Maybe. It's strange the mast is nowhere around. The stays and running lines should've kept it nearby. Like the man said, weird. Let's go in heavy on this one, XO, full law enforcement load-out. I want Chief to go along too and give that boat a check-up close before anybody sets foot on it."

"Yes, sir."

"Get Hoppy to relieve you in a couple of hours. I need your eyes on that boat with no distractions when we approach."

"Will do, sir."

"Besides, I want my best driver with the conn when we head into weirdness." Sam winked.

Operations Specialist First Class Emilia "Hoppy" Hopkins was a fast-tracker in her rating. Although that rating covered a wide range of skills, her primary responsibilities aboard *Kauai* included navigation, communications, and operational systems. She was an outstanding ship handler and the go-to OOD for any dicey situation. A thirteen-year veteran of the Coast Guard and above the cut for chief petty officer, she would pin on the coveted promotion this summer on rotation from her E6 billet aboard *Kauai* to an E7 billet elsewhere.

Like Ben, Hopkins was tall—five-foot-ten, and a fit, thirty-three-year-old, widowed mother of eleven- and nine-year-old sons. She shared a house with her mother, who cared for the boys when she was at sea. Sam liked and felt a kindred spirit with the warmhearted and professional petty officer, but, as captain, he had to take care not to let it show. His wife Joana followed no such restraint—she and Hopkins were the closest of friends. Ben shared Sam's admiration for Hopkins and often leaned on her for help with operational issues or advice for dealing with the crew.

"Boss, I'm crushed!" Ben faked a distressed expression at the implied slight on his competence. He knew it was the right call—Sam needed him to have his full attention on the problem instead of focusing on keeping *Kauai* from running into anything. Also, he had to admit Hoppy *was* a better driver than he—hell, she could give the skipper a run for his money.

As Sam went back below, Ben returned to his OOD duties, the watch less quiet than a few minutes ago. The engines were roaring at full power, with a brisk twenty-eight knots of wind produced by the full-speed run and intermittent loud thumps as *Kauai*'s hull cut through the occasional wave.

**USCG Cutter *Kauai*, Gulf of Mexico, fifty-six nautical miles northeast of Key West, Florida
12:03 EST, 13 January**

Ben

Before approaching the target vessel, *Kauai*'s crew went to Law Enforcement Stations. All topside personnel donned body armor and helmets. The gunners uncovered and loaded the fifty-caliber machine guns, and a carbine-equipped sharpshooter took position on the Flying Bridge above the main Bridge. The video downloaded from the plane did not yield any insights, just a full-round view of a wrecked boat. There was no hiding place topside, and both officers were sure the interior was uninhabitable to anyone not using scuba gear. Still, Sam did not take chances with his crew and his ship. After a slow approach from the south with all eyes on the target, Hopkins brought *Kauai* into the light westerly wind about fifty yards up sun and "parked" using throttle and rudder.

The RHIB was hoisted in position at the edge of the port main deck. Besides the coxswain driving the boat, it held the three-person boarding party led by Boatswains Mate First Class John Bondurant and Chief Drake. Bondurant was the senior boatswain's mate, leading the deck department aboard *Kauai* and supervising the other two boatswain's mates, the gunner's mate, and the three junior seamen. He was typical for a mid-grade boatswain: an expert coxswain, competent OOD, and smart law enforcement boarding officer. In his early thirties, Bondurant was an inch shorter than Drake, but even more broad-shouldered. His duties with *Kauai* were demanding, but at least he was home with his family a lot more than on other tours on larger cutters. He was relatively new, arriving at the unit shortly after Sam and Ben took over, but he fit in nicely and liked the crew.

Although Bondurant was the senior coxswain, his tasking to lead the boarding party meant his subordinate, Boatswain's Mate Second Class Shelley Lee, had charge of the boat. Lee was also a skilled boat driver and OOD and, being the only other female aboard *Kauai*, berthing mate with Hopkins. Lee was twenty-five years old and small for a boatswain's mate, barely five-foot-three, but a superb athlete.

Once the boat crew and the boarding party had boarded the RHIB and were secure, Lee reported by radio, "*Kauai, Kauai-One*, boat ready for launch."

"Launch the boat," Sam replied. After the RHIB had lowered the remaining six feet into the water, Lee detached the hook from the lift frame and guided it clear. Firing the engine, she moved the boat smoothly away from the cutter's side.

As the RHIB arced to the left to clear *Kauai*'s stern, Sam walked back to the starboard side of the Bridge. Ben had kept his eyes on the wreck during the launch. "Nothing to report, Captain," he said, sweeping the target with his binoculars.

"Right," Sam said, then radioed. "*Kauai-One*, *Kauai*, circle the vessel at least once at twenty yards. If satisfied, approach and board from the south."

"*Kauai*, *Kauai-One*, WILCO, out," Lee replied. Although Drake and Bondurant were both senior, Lee commanded the boat and reported to the captain as coxswain. The RHIB completed a slow turn around the wreck, with no one aboard seeing anything of concern. "*Kauai*, *Kauai-One*, nothing seen, closing for boarding now, over."

"*Kauai-One*, *Kauai*, roger, out," Sam answered, not taking his eyes off the scene.

The RHIB moved alongside the wrecked sailboat, allowing the three boarding team members to jump on and spread out. After Drake boarded, Lee pulled the RHIB back to a safe observation position.

"*Kauai*, LE-One, nothing in sight, but I believe there's a dead body somewhere," Bondurant stated via his voice-activated headset. "I'm pulling the hatch now." While the team's junior member moved to a cover position with his shotgun, Bondurant lifted the hatch. "Oh, goddammit!" he said, recoiling from the opening.

"LE-One, *Kauai*, report status, over," Sam ordered.

"Uh, *Kauai*, LE-One, sorry about that, sir. We've got a floater, pretty ripe. Standby."

Ben grimaced as he watched Bondurant don a surgical mask from his kit and add a stroke of VapoRub. "Floater" was Coast Guard slang for a human corpse made buoyant by trapped gasses generated during decomposition. This was a drawback of the operational Coast Guard: sometimes, the "R" in SAR meant recovery instead of rescue. It wasn't just the terrible smell of a decaying human corpse—it was knowing what that smell *was* that got to you. At least you can mask the odor with a pungent ointment.

Bondurant nodded when he finished, and the other team members took similar action. Drake stood back with his hand covering his mouth and nose until handed a mask and ointment container. "OK, proceeding," said Bondurant, moving back to the hatch. He stepped down through the opening and disappeared. After two minutes, he returned to the main deck.

"*Kauai*, LE-One, I have a report."

"Go ahead, One," Sam said.

"Roger. Just the one body. Lots of product down there—looks like it's the only thing keeping her afloat. The cabin's full of water. I couldn't see shit, er, excuse me, sir. I would say she took a hell of a whack. The starboard side's smashed in. I'm goin' to let Chief look around if you've no objection."

Sam paused before replying. "OK, tell Chief he can have a look if he's sure it's stable. But call the RHIB over first. If things turn bad, you guys bail immediately. Clear?"

"Roger, sir. Also, I cleared the junk hanging over the transom. The boat is the *High Dawn* out of Greenwich, Connecticut."

"Copy one, continue."

Ben called the infirmary. "Doc? XO here. There's a dead body on the boat. Please break out a body bag and stand by. Thanks. Bye."

Sam stepped inside and picked up the handset to radio the circling plane. "Zero-three, five-one, we've got it. Thanks for hanging around for us. For your records, the target's name is the *High Dawn,* and the home port is Greenwich, Connecticut. No registration numbers are visible, and documents are inaccessible at this time. Over."

"Five-one, zero-three, roger that, *laki maika'i, hoa aloha!*" The technician on the plane knew Sam from earlier encounters and that his last assignment was a patrol boat in Hawaii.

"*Mahalo hoa*, out," Sam replied with a slight smile.

After about fifteen minutes, Bondurant called again. "*Kauai*, LE-One, Chief is done. He says we might as well get off this tub. It's not safe to leave a prize crew on board."

"LE-One, *Kauai*, roger, board the RHIB and return to ship. Tell Chief to come to the Bridge as soon as he's on board."

"*Kauai*, LE-One, roger, out."

Sam turned to Ben. "Send Doc with Smitty and Lopez to recover that body. Make sure they get a thorough safety talk before they leave and have masks ready."

Ben saluted. "Very good, sir." He went below to arrange things. The recovery team swapped with the boarding team in the RHIB. The boat set off again, and Ben and Drake headed to the Bridge.

After exchanging salutes, Drake started his report. "Captain, I'm not sure what we can do. No point trying to dewater. The starboard side is crushed inward. You can also forget about towing her—I'm sure she'll break up if you try it."

"Crushed? The deck's intact. What do you think hit her, Chief?" Sam frowned.

"That's just it, Captain. It couldn't have been a collision. There's no dent of any kind. It's like, well, it's like the hull slammed flat against a wide stone wall, except that it didn't leave a mark."

"What?"

"I checked over the side; no scratches or mars on the paint, just cracks from the impact. It's like somebody set off a big bomb beside her, but there's none of the scorching or residue you'd expect to see. The only time I've ever seen hull damage like this was when they tried that airdrop of the new oil skimmer, and the chutes separated—smacked down from a thousand feet. And it gets weirder, sir." Drake paused.

"Do tell."

"The mast was yanked right off. Bolts sheared up, and the stays snapped right above the deck. That's why it's not dragging alongside. It's just gone, blown away." Drake wiped his forehead. "That body we found? I figure he was inside when it hit, or he'd been blown off too. It's too bloated to be sure, but it wouldn't surprise me if he just got smashed around inside the cabin."

Sam leaned back against the rail with a furrowed brow. "So, you're telling me you think this boat was dropped from a great height?"

"No, sir. I'm sayin' the damage looks like that other boat. I don't see how it could have happened, but that's what it looked like."

"Great." Sam shook his head. "Can't tow it. Can't just sink it because of the dope. I guess it's time to call the boss. Thanks, Chief."

"Yes, sir." Drake saluted and then turned to leave.

Sam started a "chat" on the command net with the District Operations Center in Miami to report their findings and seek further orders. By the time Health Services Technician Second Class Michael "Doc" Bryant and the two junior enlisted crew members returned with the body, he had the answer he expected:

"Standby in the vicinity of the subject vessel and await orders."

"XO, surprise, surprise. Our orders are to await orders. OOD, stay within five hundred yards of the wreck. Call me right away if anything changes. Resume the at sea watch, please."

"Yes, sir," Hopkins replied, turning to check the radar while Sam and Ben left for the afterdeck.

"Doc, you got anything for me?" Sam asked Bryant when he reached the afterdeck. Bryant provided routine medical services and was the EMT aboard *Kauai*. A slight build and bookish manner with steel-rimmed glasses hid a quiet intensity gained as an Army medic in Afghanistan before he transferred to the Coast Guard. He had good-naturedly shrugged off the "Army grunt" jokes in his first days on board. The jokes stopped when the crew saw Bryant in a tropical blue uniform with his Army Combat Medic Badge on his pocket and the Silver Star and Purple Heart topping his rows of ribbons.

Bryant replied, "Sorry, Captain, we almost needed a strainer to pull him out of the cabin. I figure he went down at least three days ago, based on decomp, but you'll need a lab to get anything definite. We ought to get him on ice, or we will have to vent the bag. Any chance we'll be heading in soon?"

Sam frowned. There was no cold storage aboard beyond two large kitchen refrigerators. "Sorry, Doc, we're to standby until further orders, and yes, I told them about the body."

"So be it, sir." He turned to Ben as Sam returned to the Bridge. "XO, I still need to do the workups for your annual. I can clean up and be ready for you in half an hour."

"Um, yeah, I'll be a bit busy for a while. Let me get back to you." Ben waved his hand dismissively, turned, and started walking forward to catch up with Sam.

"You have to let him take your measure eventually," Sam whispered.

"Sir, the best you can hope for from any physical exam is not getting fired. I'm in no hurry to take that chance."

Sam turned. "Something I should know about?"

"No, sir. Just a personal tic. I'll take care of this in the next dockside, Scout's honor." Ben grinned.

Sam returned a sad smile. "Mmmm, yeah."

Investigation

USCG Cutter *Kauai*, Gulf of Mexico, fifty-six nautical miles northeast of Key West, Florida
17:32 EST, 13 January

Ben

Ben returned to the Bridge twice for command net chats since completing the boarding operations on the *High Dawn*. The first entailed calling Drake up to give detailed, plain-language descriptions of the condition and damage to the hull of the wrecked sailboat. The second had good news and excellent news: the excellent news was the Clearwater Air Station had dispatched an MH-60T "Jayhawk" helicopter to pick up the body. Also, the buoy tender *Poplar* would arrive in thirty hours with specialized gear to recover the wreck. The news relieved Ben: they had already been underway for two days when diverted to the new mission. Even if refueled and restocked on-scene, a continued stay would be progressively more unpleasant. He was heading for a quick meal when Sam stepped into the room.

"Hey, Number One, we just got a secret immediate message; care to stroll up with me for a read?"

Ben grimaced. "Secret and immediate—either of those words is normally attached to 'another good deal.' I expect they mean a squared or even higher order of good deal together."

Sam chuckled. "Courage, son. That's why they pay us the big bucks!"

Secret messages were rare for *Kauai*, and the contents were astonishing. Besides picking up the body for transport ashore, the Jayhawk from Clearwater would deliver a Dr. Peter Simmons of the Defense Intelligence Agency. After the hand-off of the *High Dawn*, *Kauai* was to proceed independently and provide all services Simmons needed *as practicable* under a National Defense mission code. The message also addressed the sector command at Key West with orders to give any support *Kauai* required as a priority.

"Holy shit, Skipper!" Ben exclaimed. "Keeps getting weirder with this boat."

"You said it." Sam grinned. "What *will* they do next?" He glanced at the clock. "That Clearwater bird will be here in forty-five minutes. Brief out Bondurant and have him detail the deck crew for helicopter ops."

"Will do, sir. I suppose I'll have to room with this DIA guy."

"Yes. Sorry, Number One, but besides the VIP aspect, I don't want a spook hanging around with the crew."

"Oooo-kay. Sounds like you have some experience. Is there something you're not telling *me*, boss?"

"Me, no. But I was raised to distrust intel types, and nothing I've experienced as a blue-suiter has changed that bias." Sam finished with a neutral facial expression. "No need to worry about it, and just remember, he's no one's buddy."

"Very good, sir." Ben took the hint.

The helicopter arrived five minutes early, but the reception crew was in place and ready. Bondurant supervised the operation on the afterdeck and had been thorough in his briefing. He was pleased to see the crew members were safeguarding against the aircraft's strong downwash of air as it moved over the deck with the DIA man lowering on the hoist cable. The man slipped out of the hoist harness on gaining footing with the deck and started walking forward. Bondurant's shouted warning to wait could not be heard over the engines and rotors. When the man crossed from directly under the helicopter, the ferocious wind struck him down like he'd been tackled from behind. Once the aircraft moved clear of the patrol boat, Bondurant crossed over and helped the man upright and then forward to the superstructure. "Are you OK?" he shouted over the aircraft noise.

"No injuries but my pride, thank you. Wow!" the man shouted back. "I have some gear coming with the litter. Should I go back and help?"

"No, you stay here. They'll be disconnecting the litter to load the body, anyway. Wait while the helo pulls back again," Bondurant received a thumbs-up from his charge. The helicopter was returning, a weighted nylon "trail line" dangling just above deck level. The deck crew grabbed the line and kept it tight to keep the litter from swinging as it lowered. When it was under control on the cutter's deck, they disconnected the cable, allowing the helicopter to move clear again. Bondurant tapped the man's shoulder and gave a thumbs-up. The man nodded and walked over to retrieve a large canvas bag the deck crew had taken out of the litter. He then moved forward, flipping a wave at Bondurant as he passed. When he met Ben at the bottom of the ladder, Bondurant turned back to the afterdeck, shaking his head. "Dumbass!"

"Dr. Simmons, I'm Ben Wyporek, executive officer," Ben said. "Welcome aboard."

"Thank you, Lieutenant," Simmons replied. "Where can I go to get out of your way?"

Ben gestured toward a crewman standing alongside. "Petty Officer Guerrero here will escort you to my stateroom, and you'll be staying there while you're aboard. Please stay there until we finish. Then, the CO would like to chat."

"Excellent, I'll just be hanging out there then." Simmons slung his bag, and after he and Guerrero disappeared inside, Ben returned to the Bridge.

"Passenger secured, sir," Ben said when he stepped up to Sam as he watched the crew loading the body into the litter.

"Thank you," Sam answered, keeping his eyes on the deck.

Bondurant reported the litter loaded and ready, and the helicopter returned to a hover beside *Kauai*, completing the pickup in a little over two minutes. The litter disappeared into the cabin, and the aircraft picked up speed and climbed. "Five-one, two-three, we are flight operations normal, en route Clearwater, out."

Watching the aircraft's flashing anti-collision light fading into the distance, Ben recalled the recent meeting with the Miami plane and said, "They aren't much for talking, I guess."

"Helo drivers are generally all business, the 60-drivers especially so. Not sure why," Sam replied. "OK, OOD, please, secure from flight quarters, set normal at-sea watch."

"Yes, sir," said Hopkins.

Sam turned. "Right, XO, let's grab a drink and deal with your new roommate."

****

"Welcome aboard, Doctor." Sam stood to shake Simmons's hand when he and Ben entered the cabin. "Please have a seat." They sat in the cramped room, Sam sitting at his desk, Simmons in the spare chair, and Ben on Sam's bunk.

"Thank you, sir. I appreciate your accommodation, particularly Ben's generous sharing of his room with me," Simmons replied. Simmons was almost the quintessence of nondescript: five-foot-nine, average build, a plain face, with his brown medium-short hair and scruffy goat beard, a sharp contrast with the close-cropped and clean-shaven officers. His casual dress—a well-worn polo shirt, jeans, and topsiders—also set him apart from his hosts' dark blue utility uniforms. His age was obscure, but Ben guessed it was the early thirties.

"Not a problem. I was a little surprised to run into a DIA man called 'Doctor.' Are you an MD?"

"No, I have a Ph.D. in Astrophysics."

Sam's eyebrows raised. "Really? That's more surprising than the 'Doctor' part. OK, let's get down to business. I'm sure you know that we are ordered to support you in whatever your mission is out here. Unfortunately, this is a pickup game, and we haven't received any details. I need you to explain what's going on so we can give you the best service."

Simmons rubbed his forehead and replied, "I'll do what I can, Lieutenant, you see—"

"Captain." Ben interrupted.

"I beg your pardon?" Simmons's hands froze.

"The correct address for commanding officers aboard their ships is 'Captain,' regardless of nominal rank."

After a few seconds locked in a stare with Ben, Simmons smiled and continued. "Forgive me. As I was saying, *Captain*, my work here is highly classified, and I've limited discretion on what I can share."

"I understand. Please continue," Sam said, his face devoid of expression.

"Thank you. Several research facilities detected an unusual event in this vicinity a few days ago, and we investigated. We've been on the lookout for unusual items correlating with the observations. This wreck you've discovered qualifies."

Sam leaned forward. "What sort of *event* are we talking about?"

Simmons crossed his arms and sat back. "I can't go into details on the different theories in play here. We have readings on one set of sensors that don't line up with the observations on the remaining relevant sensors. We're trying to figure out if there's an issue with the technology or if we are seeing something new and possibly dangerous. Either way, I'm sure you can understand the urgency here."

Sam leaned back. "OK, if the 'event' *is* tied to that wreck, does it pose any hazard to the crew?"

Simmons waved his hand dismissively. "No, no, no. I assure you, if we thought that was the case, you'd not be here right now. The patrol plane you relieved took a thorough scan of it with everything they had, and they'd have detected any significant chemical or radiological hazards. The final assessment pends the autopsy on that body, but we don't think we'll find anything. I've brought some field test equipment with me just to make sure. If you don't object, I'd like to examine anyone who went over there with the help of your medical technician."

"Certainly. XO, can you see to that, please?"

"Yes, sir." Ben nodded.

"I also need to visit the wreck myself as soon as possible. I've some other measurements I need to do right away," Simmons continued.

"It's dark now. I can close to twenty yards, and you can work from there. A boarding must wait until daylight. That will be..." Sam turned and consulted a piece of paper on his desk. "Zero-Six-Forty-five tomorrow morning."

Simmons frowned. "Captain, that will *not* be satisfactory. I have to take physical samples of the hull and cargo and do interior measurements—twenty yards might as well be twenty miles. It's necessary to get these readings immediately to develop a course of action."

"I'm sorry, Doctor, but it's risky enough to send a boarding party to a wrecked vessel, and I won't do it in the dark."

Simmons's eyes narrowed. "Captain, you obviously haven't gotten the memo. This is a question of national security, and I insist you put me on that vessel at once!"

Ben started to stand up, unconsciously closing his fists, before Sam rested an arm on his shoulder. Ben sat down.

Sam turned to Simmons. "Doctor, we need to get something straight right now. Only one person aboard can *insist* on anything, and you're looking at him. My orders are to act independently and cooperate with you *as practicable*. They don't relieve me of my primary responsibility for the safety of this ship and its crew. You'll need to give me a lot more than 'the pointers don't line up' before a night boarding onto a sinking vessel falls within my threshold of calculated risk. Now, anything else you care to share with me?"

"No, *Captain*, not now."

"Very well. How about you go with the XO to check our boarding crew, and we'll get you over there by first light?" Sam nodded his head toward the door and then turned back to his desk. After five seconds of Simmons sitting in astonished silence, Sam said without turning, "Was I unclear that you've been dismissed, Doctor?"

Ben stood and motioned to the door. "Sir, this way, please."

He started to follow Simmons when Sam asked, "XO, once he's settled in with Doc, can you come back here, please?"

"Very good, sir."

Ben met Simmons in the passageway. "Please follow me, sir."

"Fine," Simmons replied coldly. "I'll need some testing equipment from my case."

"At your service, sir." Ben returned an icy grin. Simmons ducked into Ben's stateroom and returned carrying two small cases. "This way, please." Ben turned to lead him to the mess deck where Bryant, Drake, and the other personnel who had boarded the *High Dawn* had assembled.

"Guys, this is Dr. Simmons of the Defense Intelligence Agency," he began. "We're here to help him check some things that impact national security, so it's important. We think that wreck out there may be involved, so we will hang around here while he does his stuff. Now we're pretty sure there's no danger from that thing, but just to be absolutely sure, Doc here will help him run a few medical tests. Questions?"

Drake stepped forward. "Sir, it would help to know what's going on. What does a wrecked drug boat have to do with national security?" he asked, looking between Ben and Simmons.

"Chief, you said yourself there's something queer in that boat's damage. Well, you got someone's attention. As for the other stuff, I'm told it's well above our paygrade, so we'll do our jobs without knowing every detail. Not the first time, right?" He smiled at Drake.

"No, sir, I reckon not."

"Okay, it's not the preferred situation, but we'll make the best of it. Rest assured, the CO and I are on this, and we'll pass anything on when we can. Meanwhile, Dr. Simmons here is as VIP as it gets, and I expect you to treat him right and help him out whenever and however you can. Am I clear?" Ben finished, looking at Drake.

Drake smiled. "We've got this, XO."

"OK." Ben turned to Simmons. "Petty Officer Bryant here will help you. If you need anything, call me."

"Thanks," Simmons replied. "I'll see you shortly."

Ben made his way back to the cabin and sat at Sam's invitation.

Sam turned to face him. "That could have gone better. What's your impression so far?"

"He's an arrogant dick," Ben replied. "Who the hell does he think he is?"

"I understand your feelings, but I think we need to cut him some slack. I suspect he's not here for his charm and personality. It's because he can handle whatever needs to be done. Also, I can understand his agitation at having to wait. Something damned important must be happening to be diverting two cutters and laying on special flights. To sum it up, I believe he has a legitimate concern with whatever is going on here, and he's probably dead on his feet with fatigue."

Sam's response after the earlier tense meeting surprised Ben. "Sir?"

"Look at his eyes. He says this started a few days ago, and I doubt he's slept since then. That load, on no sleep, would make anybody punchy."

"I guess I missed that. I was ready to kick his ass for how he was talking to you."

Sam smiled in return. "Thanks, XO, but I can take it. I hated to take him down that way, given what I think he's going through right now, but we needed to settle who's who in this particular zoo. When we're done, I want you to take care of him. As soon as you can persuade him to get some rack time." He checked his watch. "He's got about eight hours before we can put him on the wreck. Convince him he might as well sleep as sit around and stew."

"Yes, sir, I'll try."

Sam patted him on the arm. "Stout hearts." Assuming his uncanny impression of the actor Patrick Stewart, he finished, "Make it so, Number One!"

Ben returned to the mess deck to find Simmons and Bryant processing the last crew member, and he sat to wait for them to finish. After a few minutes, Simmons started packing his gear, and Bryant walked over to Ben.

"XO, I have *got* to get me one of those," he said, jerking his thumb toward Simmons. "Do you know it screens for 103 different toxins and can turn around the results in five minutes?"

"Doc, I expect there isn't enough money in the entire Seventh District, much less the boat's checkbook, to buy something like that, but I'll certainly ask. Thanks for taking care of this. See you later." When Bryant moved off, Simmons finished and turned to Ben.

"Lieutenant, I'm happy to report you have a slime-free crew as far as I can tell. There are still a few tests running, but I'm not expecting anything from them." Simmons rubbed his forehead and wiped his eyes.

Ben leaned in and said sympathetically, "When's the last time you've had any sleep?"

"I can't remember. A couple of days, I guess."

"Hey, there's nothing to be done until dawn, and that's eight hours off. You should try to get some rest."

"Yes, I suppose I should yield to the logic of the situation. There's no chance the captain will change his mind?"

"Not a chance in hell." Ben smiled.

"OK, the timely dew of sleep, now falling with soft slumb'rous weight inclines our eyelids," Simmons conceded as he started toward the passageway.

"What's that, Shakespeare?"

"No, friend, Milton," Simmons replied, shuffling along in trail behind Ben.

USCG Cutter *Kauai*, Gulf of Mexico, fifty-seven nautical miles northeast of Key West, Florida 06:03 EST, 14 January

Ben

"Dr. Simmons? Dr. Simmons?" Ben knocked on the locker next to his bunk, now occupied by his temporary roommate. Simmons shot upright and grasped at the location he had left his bag.

"Whoa, whoa, take a second!" Ben said. "I locked your bag in the armory, and no one will mess with it."

Simmons's confused and desperate expression faded at once, and he put a hand to his face. "Sorry, occupational hazard," he mumbled. "How long was I out?"

Ben's heart rate was returning to normal—he had seen no one appear that wild-eyed. "A good six and a half hours. We'll be putting the RHIB over in about half an hour, and I thought you might like a bite of breakfast and coffee."

"That'd be amazing, thank you." Simmons's face twisted into a rueful smile. "I take it you saw the contents of the bag?"

"Yes, that's a lot of firepower." After seeing Simmons to his bunk earlier, Ben lifted the case, saw the pistol and Uzi submachine gun, and locked it in one of the ammunition lockers. "We can't have weapons just lying around. We'll return them to you when you leave."

"Not what I'd prefer, but I suppose it would be futile to protest, right?"

"Not even a day onboard, and you already have us figured out." Ben grinned.

"Let me splash my face for a jump-start. How's the food here?"

"It's not the jazz brunch at the Court of Two Sisters, but it'll do." Ben tossed him a towel.

"Pity, I would fancy a mimosa right now," Simmons said as he caught it.

✱✱✱✱✱✱✱✱✱✱✱✱✱✱✱✱✱✱✱✱✱✱✱

Ben and Simmons arrived on the afterdeck and met Sam coming down the ladder from the Bridge. Simmons carried a smaller bag of instruments, and he and Ben were donning flotation gear for a visit to the *High Dawn*. The wreck was visible in the pre-dawn twilight, one hundred yards away.

"Good morning, Doctor," Sam said. "I hope you had a good night's rest?"

"Indeed, Captain. And I topped it off with an excellent breakfast and coffee—your man does a splendid job." Simmons smiled.

"Outstanding. I'll pass along to Chef that his lofty Yelp score is safe." Culinary Specialist Second Class Thomas "Chef" Hebert

53

was one of Sam's aces in the hole in terms of morale. Born and raised in New Orleans, Hebert apprenticed in a small family-owned and run restaurant in the Vieux Carré before enlisting in the Coast Guard. Sam contributed funds, and Drake scavenging to support his more "exotic" condiment and equipment needs. The result was high-end restaurant-quality meals for the crew when underway, a significant plus in the otherwise spartan existence on a patrol boat. As for Hebert, he loved the work, relished the appreciation he received, and, best of all, got to shoot a fifty-caliber machine gun in his General Quarters billet.

"He can count on four stars from me," Simmons said. "Thank you also for the loan of your XO. I can use the help with these instruments." He turned to Ben. "Although I'm afraid you might find it tedious."

"I'll live," Ben said.

After a briefing from Boatswain's Mate Third Class Jenkins, the boat coxswain, and a brief ride, Ben and Simmons boarded the *High Dawn*. When the RHIB had pulled off, Simmons commented, "That kid is into his job—the most thorough and enthusiastic safety brief EVER."

"It's his first solo sortie as a coxswain. Bondurant is leveraging a low-stress op to give him time on his own with the boat." He smiled as the RHIB pulled away to make practice approaches on *Kauai*. "He's psyched, but Bondurant is nervous—he subbed in on the OOD watch just to keep an eye on him."

Simmons paused in assembling his equipment to glance at the white-painted cutter. "Dad hands the keys over to his son. Almost sounds like a regular family."

"It is." Ben nodded. "They mess around and get on each other's nerves, but when things go crazy, nothing gets between them."

"Hmmm, must be nice." Simmons nodded, returning to his work. "Can you give me a hand here? We'll start with laying sensors...."

Ben and Simmons worked over the boat for four and a half hours, laying and moving tiny electrical sensors, cutting samples from the hull and metalwork, and measuring, measuring, measuring. Helping with the interior measurements was the worst experience in Ben's life. Crawling through the dark, flooded, crowded cabin on a vessel on the verge of sinking evoked almost debilitating claustrophobia. This fear, combined with the revolting thought that the confined space once enclosed a rotting corpse, resulted in a struggle even to think, much less complete scientific tasks. Ben's relief on returning to the open air of the *High Dawn*'s main deck was extreme.

At last, Simmons related he had finished, and they could start gathering up the equipment. Ben inquired, "So, what's the verdict? Is this what you're looking for?"

Simmons nodded while continuing his packing. "Definitely. You are looking at the effects of a powerful shock wave that began underwater close to the surface. The hydraulic shock crushed the starboard side of the hull. This lurched the boat to the left, snapping the mast shrouds and throwing at least one guy into the scupper here, killing him instantly—there are blood and skin fragments around there." He pointed at a narrow draining channel in the deck. "The air shock wave impacted right after that. It tore away the mast and cleared anything loose off the deck." He pointed at a metal fitting on the deck. "Look at the mast step here. The pin's bent, and the fork sheared to the left."

Ben eyed the twisted deck fitting, pondering the force that could do that. "It wasn't a bomb?"

Simmons paused and looked up at him. "No. Any chemical explosive close enough to do this would leave trace residue, if not actual burn scoring. A nuclear device would leave a radiation signature and heat damage. Besides, we'd detect any nuclear detonation." He looked down to finish packing his gear. "And to anticipate your next question, I know what this is, but I can't tell you about it. I *can* say we must find the event's location as soon as possible." He glanced at Ben, noting his raised eyebrow. "Hey, I know this sucks being kept in the dark, but I have my orders. I'll be reporting in right away, and I'll see if I can get them to loosen up, at least for you and your CO."

"That would be an excellent idea if you don't want this operation to turn into a major goat rope."

"I'll pass that along. When can we start back to Key West? I need to get resources organized."

Ben checked his watch. "*Poplar* should arrive in eighteen hours, figure a couple of hours for the hand-off, and then four hours to motor down to Key West."

Simmons shook his head. "OK, sorry I came across as such a douche last night, but I'm not exaggerating. We can't wait another day to start on this. Can't you just leave it with a marker on it?"

This time, Ben shook his head. "No way. There could be a couple of tons of product here. On the street, that's more than a hundred million bucks. We can't leave it unattended for a second. We can try to get a patrol boat out of Key West to relieve us. That'd cut our wait time in half."

Simmons nodded. "We need to do that right away. I'll call in the request from my end as well. And I'm done here; you can call Billy Budd to come pick us up."

Ben turned away to call over the RHIB and report to *Kauai*. *Billy Budd? WTF?*

USCG Cutter *Kauai*, Gulf of Mexico, fifty-seven nautical miles northeast of Key West, Florida
14:27 EST, 14 January

Sam

Ben, Simmons, and Sam sat in Sam's cabin with the door closed. Not a situation the latter liked when underway. Sam had called Sector Key West and convinced an irritated senior duty officer to launch his ready patrol boat, the eighty-seven-foot cutter *Skua*. She was still more than an hour from the rendezvous, but Hopkins was on the Bridge, passing information to her captain to hasten the transfer.

Simmons shunted off to the foredeck on their return to *Kauai* to make a private call by satellite telephone while Ben briefed Sam. Simmons still could not share any information with the officers, and it was clear the limits frustrated even him.

"Captain, believe me, I'm getting sick of this situation, too. If you're in it, you should be in all the way, but they told me flat-out no deal."

Sam nodded. "I understand, and we'll continue to do the best we can. But you need to know that if we run into a critical situation, you may face a choice between following those orders or completing the mission. So, what can we do in the meantime?"

"It's been three and a half days since the event, and I imagine that wreck could drift a fair distance."

"There's a strong current in the Florida Straits, the foundation of the Gulf Stream. There's a clockwise current called the Loop in the center of the Gulf. Between the Keys and Tampa, it gets confused."

"Well, we're sure whatever happened occurred somewhere within a thirty- by sixty-mile ellipse centered about twenty miles east of Key West."

"Really? OK, you can forget Key West and Boca Chica as someone would have seen it. You can also discard anything south of the Keys. The Gulf Stream would've swept up this hulk, and it'd be off Jacksonville by now. That leaves the northern shores of the Keys. Don't you guys have any Keyhole satellites or spy planes you can search with?"

Simmons grimaced. "Believe me, everything, and I mean EVERYTHING, available has been sweeping this area for the last few days and has come up with bupkis. It seems like it'll come down to a close examination of the ground to find disturbances on the shore. Even if we had squadrons of aircraft, we don't want to draw the attention."

"From the Press?" Ben asked.

"Yes, and others. We have special unmanned aircraft we can stage locally, but they're not fast, and we need to cut down the search area. You guys are good at this search and rescue stuff; surely, you have planning tools that can help."

Sam shook his head. "We have a computer suite called the Search and Rescue Optimal Planning System, or SAROPS. It's good, but it *forecasts* the position of a target based on the time and place of the event, using known winds and currents. We can't use it to figure out where a target *was* three days ago."

"Um, Captain?" Ben interrupted.

"Yes, XO?"

"There *is* a way to use SAROPS for this. A few of us looked at an application of SAROPS for hindcasting a vessel's position at the academy. We thought it might be useful for forensic work…."

Sam leaned forward. "I'll be damned. Did it work?"

"We got an 'A,' but it didn't go anywhere as far as I know."

Simmons was now interested. "How does it work?"

Ben shifted in his seat. "The captain's right. SAROPS can only project forward, but you can pick a set of feasible launch points in the past and let SAROPS run them out to the present using historical wind and current data. Then you can build a probability field and do a Bayesian search. We can knock down the possibilities to a workable list."

"I like it." Simmons beamed. "Let's start. Where is this SAROPS?"

"Um, hold on there, Doctor," Sam said. "We are a patrol boat. We don't have SAROPS here. They'll have it at the Sector Office in Key West, and we can run it there."

"Besides," Ben piped up on seeing Simmons's face fall, "There's a lot of front-end work to do, identifying potential start points and setting up the post-processing models. It'll take a good five or six hours at this end, anyway. We'll gather the information on our way down and hand it over when we moor. After a few hours of batch runs, we can drop the results into Excel, and we're done."

Sam smiled. "You believe you can do this, Ben?"

"If I can get Hoppy's help with the electronic charts, no worries, sir."

Sam clapped him on the shoulder. "Make it so then. Well done, Number One!" Ben stood, made his way past Simmons out of the compact room, and closed the door. After Ben left, Sam turned to Simmons. "OK, now for the hard part, Doctor. Once we decide where to search, what are we searching *for?* If half of Space Command is bore-sighted on this area and can't find anything, what do you expect from an obsolescent Coast Guard patrol boat? You mentioned something about unmanned aircraft?"

"Yes, Captain." Simmons sat back. "I have a team equipped with two upgraded RQ-20 Puma UAVs—they have a payload package specialized for this and an associated analysis team."

"Analysis team?"

"Yes, they have advanced portable tools for image processing and analysis. They were all standing by at Homestead in case we found something. When I called in before, I directed the UAV drivers to meet us at Key West. They should be waiting when we arrive, and they can set up the aircraft to fly in an hour."

"Doctor, you're crazy; look at this boat! We don't have the space for takeoffs and landings."

"Captain, the Pumas are hand-launched and stressed and sealed for saltwater landings—no launch and recovery equipment are needed. The control antenna is shoebox-sized, and you can mount it in any clear spot. The GCS, excuse me, Ground Control Station, is a large laptop with a Bluetooth link to the antenna."

"Hand-launched? And it can carry a payload that's more effective than reconnaissance satellites? How big's a Puma?"

"It's not that small. It has a nine-foot wingspan, but a reasonably fit crew member can launch it by hand. As far as the sensors go, they wouldn't be worth a damn in low earth orbit, but from five hundred feet, they can image individual grains of sand."

Sam relaxed. "OK. We can shake out another couple of bunks. I guess I'll have to deal with two more of your guys hanging around the crew."

Simmons grinned. "Not my guys, your guys. This team is two aviation petty officers from the Coast Guard Air Station at Cape Cod."

"The hell you say! The Coast Guard's running an Intel UAV program?"

"No, Captain, the Coast Guard was researching low-cost, low-footprint, maritime surveillance technology. The Puma was an army and special ops land-based program, but the Coast Guard recognized its handiness and did research and testing up in New England. You can see its usefulness for keeping persistent surveillance on restricted areas. So, your guys provide a portable aircraft with good speed and endurance and are nearly silent in flight. My guys invest big black ops bucks to provide payload miniaturization and hardening. Voila! You have a nifty maritime tactical recon stealth bird."

"It will be a pain in the ass, but I'll admit I'm curious to see flight ops on a PB. Anything else I need to know?"

"What's your weapons status?"

Sam tensed again. "Up and running with a full ammo load. What's your interest in that? If you expect a fight, you need to tell me, regardless of security restrictions."

"Captain, I'm not gunning for a fight, and I don't expect one. But, we have a wrecked sailboat with hundreds of millions of dollars worth of drugs on board. Don't you think the owners might search for that boat and maybe wait near the spot we seek?

"We won't be going in anywhere without knowing the ground—that's one reason we have the UAVs. I also have my guys back on land keeping an eye out, so I don't expect any surprises. Nevertheless, given the circumstances, I believe we can't have too much firepower."

"Doctor, you're right on the edge of my envelope without providing me the full story on this. If I get a whiff of bullshit from you, this operation ends at once. Is that clear?"

"Quite clear, Captain."

"Very well. If you'll excuse me, I need to be on the Bridge for transferring custody." They both stood up, and Sam continued, "You can follow me if you like, just stay out of the way, please."

"Captain, you'll never know I'm here." Simmons stepped out of the cabin.

"Yeah, I wish," Sam muttered under his breath as he climbed up to the Bridge.

Skirmish

USCG Cutter *Kauai*, Moored, Trumbo Point Annex, Naval Air Station Key West, Florida
20:36 EST, 14 January

Ben

The handoff of the *High Dawn* went without a hitch. Sam simply had to brief the *Skua*'s CO on the events to date, since the crew had removed no contraband or documents from the vessel. Within an hour of the smaller cutter's arrival, *Kauai* was charging toward Key West at her maximum continuous speed of twenty-eight knots.

It was Bondurant's turn for the mooring, and he had no difficulty bringing the cutter to rest alongside the dock. However, *Kauai* remained under quarantine until completing a drug sweep. The boarding team and Ben and Simmons's coveralls had been bagged and sealed on their return from the *High Dawn*, and the inspection team took and signed for these items. Next, a drug-sniffing dog came aboard to tour all the spaces. Except for an embarrassing moment involving Simmons's equipment bag, this, too, went without incident. An hour and a half after mooring, the inspectors officially "de-quarantined" *Kauai* and departed.

The UAV team, waiting on the dock since *Kauai*'s arrival, reported to the patrol boat after the inspection team left. The senior member, Aviation Electronics Technician First Class Erich

"Fritz" Deffler, introduced himself and his teammate, Aviation Electronics Technician Second Class Michael "Mike" Morgan, to Ben and Drake. Then they discussed their gear and planned activities. Drake took charge of settling the newcomers, while Ben returned to the Bridge to collect the electronic files needed for the SAROPS runs. As he passed the cabin en route to his stateroom, Ben could hear Sam on the phone with his wife, Joana. He poked his head in, waved, and mouthed, "Hi, Jo!"

Sam held up a finger to wait. "Pardon me, my dear, but the executive officer has interrupted to respectfully offer his greetings to the captain's spouse. Yes. Very well." Sam held the phone down. "The captain's spouse sends her compliments and suggests the executive officer should find a nice girl and settle down."

Ben grinned. "My respects to the captain's spouse, and if she can find someone as classy as her to introduce to the executive officer, he would commence ring-shopping forthwith."

Sam relayed the message and received a response. He held the phone down again and said, "The captain's spouse's response is: 'Aww!'"

Ben flipped a casual salute and continued to his stateroom. The exchange was only half-joking—Ben thought Jo Powell was one of the finest women he knew. A freelance computer graphics artist working from home, she was smart, gracious, funny, and drop-dead gorgeous. She was the perfect match for Sam, and despite his reserved demeanor, he was obviously crazy about her. Social events with a CO were usually an ordeal. Dinners and cookouts with the Powells were relaxing and pleasurable. They and their two kids, whom Ben also adored, were like his family.

Jo shared their story with Ben during the first of those gatherings. The couple's fateful meeting took place while Sam attended Officer Candidate School in New London, Connecticut. He had befriended a young University of Connecticut graduate named Eduardo Mendez and mentored him through the rough spots of officer candidate training. In gratitude, "Eddie" invited him to dinner with his parents and sister Joana in Gales Ferry on their first liberty. His sister, a few years his senior, lived at home while attending Eastern Connecticut State after completing an enlistment as a Navy Mass Communications Specialist. Jo said

Eddie related later that Sam had smelled a setup and tried to beg off, but Eddie managed to guilt him into attending.

Sam was hooked about halfway into that first dinner. At least, that's what he told Jo. Jo claimed it took two dates before she was all in. Jo said she was ready to swap vows upon Sam's completion of OCS. However, they agreed to put it off for a year to finish her degree, and Sam could find his feet as a commissioned officer. He was lucky enough to hook a billet on a large cutter in Boston for his first post-graduation assignment and be nearby for those rare occasions when the ship was in homeport. A year later, they married in her family's church, with Eddie standing up as Sam's best man.

Reaching his stateroom broke him from his reverie, and he stepped in to grab Simmons. "I'm heading over to the sector office now. Care to tag along?"

"You know I do. How'd it go with your girlfriend?"

Ben's jaw clenched, "If you are referring to Petty Officer Hopkins, please say 'Petty Officer Hopkins' or 'Hopkins' or 'Hoppy' or even 'Emilia.' Never refer to her as 'girlfriend' or 'girl' anything again to anyone here, especially me, clear?"

"Shit, I'm sorry," Simmons was genuinely embarrassed. "I swear I didn't mean any disrespect. Far from it. She's one of the most professional people I've ever met."

"OK, OK. Come on, let's roll."

Once off the ship and walking toward the sector building, Ben said, "About your ill-phrased question, we did well. We have twenty-three potential spots where a boat like that could anchor and be within reasonable reach of an offload point."

"Is twenty-three good?"

"It's a good start."

"What's well begun is half done."

"More Milton?" Ben asked.

"No, Horace. I thought I'd spare you the Latin version."

"Thanks for that. If you'll pardon me, I'm a little surprised hearing all this poetry talk from an astrophysicist. I thought you guys were all about quarks and comic books."

Simmons smiled in the darkness. "I'd like to take offense, but I was at Princeton with several guys who were exactly like that. It's actually a question of biology."

"Biology?"

"Yes. You see, if you'd like to have a second date with a pretty English Lit grad student, you better bring more to the conversation than Stress-Energy Tensors and Stan Lee."

Ben laughed. "That's all right. Did it work? Did you get a second date?"

"Yup."

"Care to elaborate?"

"Nope. You have a clearance, but no 'Need to Know,' sorry."

Ben chuckled again. "Touché." When they stepped into the sector building, he said, "OK, let's see how much pushback we get from the watch supervisor." After passing through security, the watch supervisor, a chief operations specialist, shuttled them to a room with several workstations. A man in civilian clothes greeted them when they entered, and the chief introduced him as Jim Rossetti, a civilian employee and the sector's resident SAROPS expert. Ben put him in the picture with a brief explanation of the problem.

"We can run five separate threads of SAROPS simultaneously," Rossetti explained. "But I have to hold one open in case we get a search mission."

"You do?" asked Simmons. "On a weeknight like this?"

Rossetti glanced at Ben and rolled his eyes. "Doctor, we have more than a thousand response cases per year in this sector alone. We're actively working two now, and a dozen are open. I'd say it's almost certain that we'll have at least one more new one before morning."

"Sorry, I'm new to this."

"Perfectly OK. Hey, at least it's not Miami—they have more than double our load."

"So, best case," Ben interjected. "We've six cycles of runs plus set up time. When do you think it'll wrap up?"

"I already have a batching macro setup. Figure about sixty to ninety minutes per cycle end to end. I think we can have the last runs complete by 05:30, 06:30 at the latest."

"OK, let's get on it," Ben said, handing him the disk. "Everything's in one file."

"Thanks. Hang around for a minute while I get this loaded and make sure there are no hiccups; then, I can cut you loose." After a few minutes of typing, he said, "OK, everything looks good. You got a number I can call when they finish?"

Ben jotted down *Kauai's* in-port number and handed it to Rossetti. "We'll see you later." He turned to Simmons. "I'm heading back to catch some z's. You coming?"

"No, I'll hang here and catch up with the outside world." To Rossetti, he said, "Can you spare an office with a landline?"

"Sure, right out the door, then second door on the right."

"Thanks." Waving to Ben. "See you later, friend."

Ben returned the wave. "See you back here at 5:30-ish." He then excused himself to return to his ship. After a brief walk, Ben arrived at *Kauai* to the familiar odor of diesel fuel. Drake never procrastinated with the readiness of the engineering department, always setting up refueling first. Ben waited for him to look over from whatever he was supervising, then asked, "How's it going, Chief?"

"Halfway through, sir," Drake replied. "I have the Cape Cod guys billeted. I put Deffler with Joe and John and Morgan with the non-rates."

"Good. Thanks for that. Anything else going on?"

"Nothing to hold up sailing, sir."

"Roger that," Ben said and then walked on board. After taking a quick turn around the decks to check things, he stopped by Sam's cabin. "Captain, the SAROPS runs are working. Probably be wrapping up around 05:30."

"Fine," Sam said. "Is our new aviation detachment settling in OK?"

"Yes, sir. Chief put the first class in with Williams and Bondurant. Unfortunately, his buddy will slum with the non-rates."

"Them's the breaks." Sam nodded. "OK, I know you're tired, but I'd like to hold a strategy meeting as soon as possible. Can you get the department leads together, please? Make sure Williams, Guerrero, and the aviation lead attend too."

"Will do, Captain."

About fifteen minutes later, Sam strode into the mess deck after being called down by Ben for the meeting. The assembled crew stood up, and Sam waved his hand. "Relax, please." After they resumed sitting, Sam sat at the head of the small table. "OK, guys, it's late, but we need to get a plan together for tomorrow. Oh, and the inconvenience of this extended patrol will be reflected as usual in your pay." The group chuckled, and Sam looked over at Drake. "Chief, what have you got?"

"We are topping off with fuel and water now. I'm replacing the generator air filters. Should be wrapped up in a couple of hours. Ready for sea, sir."

"Thanks, Chief." Sam turned to Bondurant next. "Boats, what say you?"

"Captain, Connally just left on Emergency Leave with his dad's passing, but we're solid in spite of that, and we have no equipment casualties."

"Thanks, Boats. Hoppy, what's up in Ops?"

"Captain, I have just loaded the latest SeaWatch software patch, and I'm running a diagnostic right now. The radar and comms gear are all up and available."

"Thank you, and I have good news: I'm doubling the size of your department. If anyone here hasn't heard, we've picked up our own aviation detachment: two Aviation Electronics Technicians from Cape Cod and their pair of UAVs. Petty Officer Erich Deffler here is the senior, and he'll be reporting to Hoppy. Petty Officer Deffler, welcome aboard. Do you go by Erich?"

"Thank you, Captain. Most people call me Fritz."

"Great, I'll ask you to tell us a little about your aircraft shortly. XO, how are we doing?"

"Captain, I've just been over to the sector office, and our SAROPS runs are proceeding. They'll wrap up by 0530, and I'll have a good list of investigation sites an hour later. Chef and Junior are out getting dry stores and the refrigerators restocked. I'm sorry, but we had to go on the economy for this one—I didn't want to wait for the commissary to open tomorrow."

"Can't be helped," Sam said. "I'll sign whatever exigency forms you need."

"Thank you, sir. The crew's in good shape, with no medical issues. As Bondurant mentioned, we sent Connally off to help his family. Chief's been collecting for flowers from the crew." He nodded to Drake.

"Hit me up when we're done, Chief," Sam said.

"Right, sir."

Ben continued, "We'll be turned around and ready for sea in about three and a half hours, sir."

"First rate. OK, everybody, I know you're wondering what the hell is going on here. Mr. Wyporek and I are in the dark too. What I do know is this: that boat we boarded took a huge whack from something that landed right next to it. They sent an astrophysicist, so I'm guessing it must be some sort of rare meteorite. It lit off plenty of screens, and they all point somewhere between here and fifty miles east. Now XO and Hoppy churned through the charts and came up with a list of every spot in this general area that boat could have anchored when 'the event,' as our passenger calls it, happened a few days ago. We are using the SAROPS computer software to…. What's the word, XO?"

"Hindcast, Captain."

"Thank you. 'Hindcast' to ditch the impossible spots and rank the ones left. If you want a detailed explanation of the geeky-mathy stuff that makes it work, I'll refer you to the XO. Anyway, we'll use that list to guide our search. Fritz, I'm told your UAVs have the latest gear and should be very helpful to us for this job.

"Now, the bad side. As you also know, that wreck is chock full of dope. A street value of a hundred million plus is likely, and you can't get that much product without investing lots of cash. I think you can see where I'm going here. The owners are not likely to be satisfied just writing it off on their taxes. In fact, they might look right where we'll be searching for that space rock."

Sam let that set, watching the assembled crew exchange concerned glances. "I don't think they'll be foolish enough to take a crack at us. But better safe than sorry. Gunner," he looked at Gunner's Mate Second Class Guerrero. "We will exercise the main gun and fifties tomorrow, with live rounds, if we can get clearance in the warning area. Sound good?"

"Hell, yes, Captain!" Guerrero grinned.

"Sweet. Hoppy, after we break up, I want you to see if you can get us one of the warning areas for at least four hours starting about 13:00 tomorrow."

"Yes, sir."

"OK. It's easier said than done, but try not to worry about this. We'll have eyes in the sky to prevent surprises, and we can beat anybody dumb enough to try taking us on. I'm sharing this because you deserve to know the risks. When I get anything, I'll pass it along. Any questions?" He scanned the table and, getting no response, continued. "OK, Fritz, tell us about our new air force, and, by the way, we're pleased to have you here."

Erich Deffler was a thirteen-year veteran and an experienced crew member on all Coast Guard fixed-wing aircraft types. He had jumped on the opportunity to pilot UAVs. After a rigorous training course, he was among the first in the Coast Guard to pass the FAA examination for Small UAV pilot. He took part in the flight testing the Coast Guard's Research and Development Center conducted at Air Station Cape Cod and on several cutters. This was his first independent deployment, and he was psyched. In his mid-thirties, he was six-foot-one and thin with thick, slightly graying black hair, deep blue eyes, and an angular face.

"Not as pleased as we are, sir." Deffler smiled. "We're in the season at the Cape with only two kinds of weather: butt-ass cold alternating with snow!" He paused while a few of the attendees chuckled. "We have two new Pumas with us. They have a special electronics payload I've trained on but never operated. Since you're heading out to the warning area tomorrow, can I ask for the opportunity to launch one of the birds? I need to check for glitches with the payload and antenna blind spots."

"You read my mind." Sam nodded. "I was going to ask you for a show."

"Yes, sir. It is amazing hardware. The resolution is wicked good on the camera, and we have a laser designator built in. It's hand-launched and sealed for saltwater recovery. I'm sorry to say we haven't come up with a practical way to recover aboard a patrol boat yet, so we'll need your small boat to do the pickup."

"Not a problem. Will you want your man in the boat, or are you OK with one of us knuckle-draggers doing the pickup?"

The phrasing of the question startled Deffler, but he quickly recovered. "Captain, we can do it whichever way you want."

Sam smiled. "We'll let him show us how, at least the first few times."

"Righto, sir," Deffler continued. "In theory, we can launch from any clear space on the weather decks, but I recommend the main deck forward of the gun. It has the best aspect clearance and likely the best relative wind. I'll need to mount the antenna in a prominent place. It has a Bluetooth connection to the control station, so I won't need to run any cabling if it's within fifty feet."

"I'll see to the antenna placement, Captain," Drake said.

"Great. We'll try putting the control station on the chart table for now," Sam said. "How much space will you need, Fritz?"

"Oh, not much at all, sir. It's just a laptop and a USB joystick."

"OK, it seems like we can make it work. What can it do for us?"

Deffler beamed. "Sir, the camera is hi-res with a hyperspectral imaging capacity. We can scout locations as well as having eyes-on. Sometimes it's even better because the hyperspectral can pick up traces we wouldn't normally see. We can get into a narrow waterway or cove and save you a risky transit or long small boat ride. We can even provide target designation for the gun."

Sam noted Williams's impassive face and folded arms. Williams was the Electronics Technician on *Kauai*—he worked and maintained the fire control station for the main gun and was territorial on this subject. "We'll check it out tomorrow, but it sounds good. Anything else we need to know?"

"No, sir. That covers it."

"Right, anyone else?" Sam looked around the table. "OK, let's plan on stations manned by 11:45 and underway at noon tomorrow. Thanks everybody, and good night." They all stood when Sam rose and left the room, with Ben a few steps behind him.

Hopkins stepped over to Deffler, hand outstretched. "Fritz, I'm Emilia or 'Hoppy' if you like."

Deffler shook her hand and smiled. "Glad to meet you."

"Likewise." Hopkins smiled back. "I'd like to meet on the Bridge at 08:30, and we can go over placing your equipment and do some dry runs. I'd also like to chat about tactics."

"I'll be there." He nodded.

"OK, see you in the morning." She turned and left the mess deck, along with Deffler and the remaining crew.

USCG Cutter *Kauai*, Moored, Trumbo Point Annex, Naval Air Station Key West, Florida
05:43 EST, 15 January

Ben

"XO, XO?"

"Yes?" Ben opened his eyes to see Pickins, a non-rated watchstander, leaning over him.

"You have a phone call, sir, line two."

"Thank you." Ben swung his legs off the bunk and reached for the phone on his mini-desk. "Wyporek here."

"Hi Lieutenant, Jim Rossetti. Your runs completed successfully, and I saved the output for you."

"Outstanding. Is Dr. Simmons there?"

"Uh-huh. He's wearing a ditch in the carpet waiting for you."

"I'll be there in ten."

After a quick electric shave and comb, Ben jogged over to the building and the analysis office. "Good morning, Doctor, Jim. Shall we work some Bayesian magic?"

"When did morning ever break, And find such beaming eyes awake? Dazzle us with your analytical wonders, Lieutenant," Simmons smirked.

Rossetti stared at Simmons, then turned to Ben with a tired "Is this for real?" look before holding out an external data drive. "Here is the output you requested. Mind if I watch you work through this?"

"No problem." Ben sat down at the workstation. "I'll explain as we go."

After cranking the data through formulas on Microsoft Excel, Ben eliminated eleven possibilities and divided the remaining twelve between "more likely" and "less likely" candidates. After more work, he identified the best search plan based on the

SAROPS data. "... And you see here, the remaining probabilities update as we eliminate each candidate."

"Very nice." Rossetti nodded. "Can I keep copies of those spreadsheets?"

"Sure. I'd appreciate it if you could print out a copy for me while we're here."

"No problem."

The day was bustling on the Coast Guard base when Ben and Simmons walked to *Kauai*'s mooring. "So, get any sleep last night?" Ben asked.

"A couple of hours head down in between phone calls. Interesting developments have occurred, both in my dark domain and yours of sunlight and truth."

"For instance?"

"I got a report on the body you guys found. The cause of death is 'Generalized Acceleration Trauma,' meaning his injuries were consistent with a hundred-foot fall onto a pile of rocks. The time of death is unknown, but the decomp suggests it's contemporaneous with the event. No ID from CODIS, but we're still working it through Interpol."

"OK, not unexpected. Anything else?"

"Yes, I have arranged for us to access the highway camera recordings on U.S. 1 between here and Key Biscayne. Unfortunately, the only place we can view them right now is the Monroe County Sheriff's Office downtown."

"Ah, what's this 'us' and 'we' shit? *Kauai* will sail in a few hours for workups on the guns and those toy airplanes of yours. The executive officer isn't just sitting around when operational preps are underway."

"Understood, but this could be an important piece of the puzzle. I'm sure your captain wants all the information he can get."

"What's so interesting about highway footage?"

"Presuming this boat is linked to the event, we might see some evidence that can help us narrow down the location further."

Ben stopped and turned toward Simmons. "Alright, maybe I'm a bit slow here. What exactly do you hope to see on the camera footage? Some kind of vehicle?"

Simmons frowned and said, "No, something else."

Ben put his hands on his hips. "OK, Doc. You have to do better than that. The CO will ask me why I need to take the time to go downtown and stare at video footage when I should be helping with sailing preps. Right now, I don't have a good enough answer."

"Very well. The, um, *effect* that we are looking for generates a bright light. If it passes one of those cameras, we should see a brief illumination of the highway. Hopefully, we can follow the effect from camera to camera until it does not present anymore. That should help narrow the search."

"Interesting. I'm not sure you'll be able to convince the CO."

"Ye of little faith. I can be very persuasive, you know." Simmons winked and smiled.

Ben shook his head. "Dude, you're on your own."

Sam

The pair's return to the patrol boat elicited a mixture of reactions. The success of the SAROPS analysis pleased Sam, and he directed Ben to meet with Hopkins to plan the sequence of exploratory visits. Simmons's requisitioning of his executive officer for investigative work was another matter. After dispatching Ben, Sam took Simmons for a private talk in his cabin. "I don't like coughing up my XO when we're prepping for a hazardous operation, Doctor. You must have other assets here you can call."

"Captain, we keep a light footprint on the ground for operations this classified. We roll in the FBI and the rest, and we'll blow the lid off the entire thing. Ben's levelheaded and smart—I'm sure he'll be fine. Besides, wouldn't you rather have Ben with eyes on than me skulking around on my own?" Simmons smiled slyly.

Sam *did* prefer having one of his people monitoring Simmons's activities. Still, he could not comprehend Simmons's sense of urgency for a matter that seemed trivial and irrelevant to their mission. Also, something hidden behind the too-pat story and the agent's maddening expression worried him, so he temporized. "Tell me, if this thing is so damn secret, how will you keep a lid on it flashing a DIA badge?"

Simmons nodded. "Yes, that would normally be a problem. Fortunately, besides being DIA guy Dr. Peter Simmons, I'm also Investigator Douglas Pearson of the Florida Department of Law Enforcement. My people handled the groundwork with the locals to reduce curiosity."

"What about Ben?"

"We don't have time to build a legend around him, so he goes in clean. The cover is there's a maritime element that needs Coast Guard involvement."

This whole deal put Sam on edge. He wanted to put an end to it, but his thoughts returned to his orders: *provide all services he needed as practicable.* He knew Ben would have front-loaded any pre-sailing tasks requiring his direct attention, so Simmons's demand was *practicable.*

Sam relented despite his misgivings, made worse by the reptilian smile he wanted to wipe off the agent's face. "Very well. We sail in...." he glanced at his desk clock. "Four and a half hours. I want you both back on board in four. You can take the government vehicle. But Doctor, I don't like this. If you haven't picked up on it already, let me speak plainly here. Besides being an indispensable part of this crew, Ben's a close friend of mine. If anything happens to him because of you, I'm likely to react *irrationally.*"

Simmons's smile faded to a blank expression. "Yes, Captain, I'm familiar with your personal history."

Sam's face darkened. "That will be all, Doctor. I'll see you here within four hours."

Monroe County Sheriff's Office, 5525 College Road, Key West, Florida
08:28 EST, 15 January

Ben

Getting access to the camera footage involved the usual appeasement of officious clerks in the different departments governing interagency cooperation, information technology, and security in the main office. Afterward, they had to drive to a second office that actually housed the archive. It took the better part of two hours to get into the technology center and in front of the console where the archived footage could be retrieved and viewed.

A clearly bored technician sat next to them and operated the viewing equipment. "Anything, in particular, you guys want to see?" he asked around a wad of gum he was chewing.

"Yes, I would like to start at the first camera on U.S. 1 south of Key Biscayne, then work our way south. We're looking for the footage recorded between one-thirty and two a.m. on the 10th of January."

"OK," the technician said, then went to work on his keyboard. After a minute, he said, "KB-South is coming up now." He nodded toward the screen that showed a darkened highway bridge with the lights of passing vehicles every few minutes.

After about ten minutes of staring at what was essentially an unchanging picture, Ben asked, "Is there any way to speed this playback?"

Before the technician could answer, Simmons said, "No. The effect will only last a few seconds, and we can't afford to miss it. Once we get a good time reference, we can narrow down the time frame on the other cameras."

"Right," Ben replied, trying to keep the irritation out of his voice. The passive watching continued for another five minutes, then a sudden flash of light briefly lit up the scene. "Whoa! Did you see that?"

"Pause it!" Simmons said. After the technician hit the pause button, he added, "OK, run it back thirty seconds, then forward at one-quarter speed, please."

"OK," the technician said as he worked the playback controls.

The scene repeated, and Ben could see on the slower playback that the illumination was not the general flash it appeared to be at full speed, but a progressive brightening and then darkening, moving toward and passing the camera. Ben glanced at Simmons, who was grinning while jotting down the time.

"Now, we're in business," Simmons said. "Let's see the next camera south, same date, start at one-forty-eight."

They carefully reviewed the footage of the thirteen cameras between Key Biscayne and Boca Chica, noting the passing effect on the first seven. After screening the last one, Simmons stood and said to the technician, "That'll do-er. Thanks, friend."

"Yup," the technician said between pops of his wad of gum.

Ben and Simmons turned their visitor badges in at the front desk and walked to the car. After they were seated, Simmons asked, "OK, Lootenant. So, we know now that there is no need to look at Marathon or points east."

"That helps some."

"Yes, indeed. Feel like breakfast on me? I haven't eaten since last night."

"There's a Denny's on Roosevelt."

"Excellent! We should have plenty of time for the best of American fare."

"Right," Ben started the car.

A short time later, the two men finished their coffee at the restaurant, and Simmons gave Ben a hard look. "How much experience have you had with tactical driving?"

Ben choked on a small mouthful of coffee. "What?"

"It's a simple question. Have you had any training in tactical driving?"

"No. Why?"

"I need to get something together. Did you notice the four-door following us?"

"No. Since the base?"

"Since the sheriff's office, actually. I wasn't sure at first, but after the second stop, I knew for certain. Don't worry. We will make this work. I need you to walk to the restroom and hang out while I work through the checkout line. When I'm number two in the queue, you step out to the car and bring it up front. Once I get in, just do as you're told, and we'll be fine. OK?"

Ben nodded, stood up, and strolled to the washroom. After two minutes, he peeked out and saw Simmons stepping into the second position in the checkout line. Ben strode through the restaurant and scanned the parking area while walking to the car in the bright sunlight. Again, nothing stood out, and he wondered if his companion was seeing things. He pulled the car up and parked in front of the restaurant. Half a minute later, Simmons emerged and sat in the passenger seat. Putting on his seatbelt and pulling his sidearm, he said, "OK, let's move. As you leave the parking lot, take a right on Roosevelt. Nice and easy, just like before."

"OK," Ben nervously glanced at the drawn pistol. After turning on Roosevelt, he noticed another car emerging a discreet distance behind them. "That them?"

"Yep. Now, bear left and follow Roosevelt. When we make the curve to the right, get in the left turn lane for Overseas Highway, like we are going to continue on U.S. 1. Remember, nice and steady, just like we don't have a care in the world."

Ben complied, rolling to a stop in the turn lane behind two other turning cars.

"OK, now for the interesting part. When the light changes, creep up, and when you have a clear path, head straight at the intersection and floor it. Start sounding the horn and keep pumping it. You will want to shift right as soon as possible—you'll be hanging a right on Flagler. You got all that?"

"Yes."

"Now take it easy. We will be fine. I want you to slow down before the turn on Flagler. We can't afford to roll this thing, OK?"

"OK." Ben nodded stiffly. The light changed to a left turn only, and when the car ahead cleared their path, Ben jammed the accelerator and swerved right to pass through the intersection. Their tail jogged out of the turn lane in pursuit two seconds later.

"Horn! Hit the horn!" Simmons shouted, his head turned to track the pursuing vehicle, and Ben complied. "OK, OK, slow down for the turn."

Ben slowed and veered right onto Flagler with a screaming of tires and modest fishtailing as he straightened on the new path. Their pursuers also swung in behind them from Roosevelt a few seconds later.

"Floor it! We'll be hanging a right on Tenth in ten blocks, same tactic. Keep hitting that horn!"

Ben stayed on the horn, dodging through traffic at speeds approaching fifty miles per hour.

"Counting down," Simmons said, "Fourteenth, Thirteenth, twelfth, Eleventh, slow down and prepare to hang a right, NOW!"

Ben executed another tire-squealing turn and straightened out, heading north on Tenth, gunning the engine and leaning on the horn.

"Stand by to hit the brakes!" Simmons shouted. "Steady, steady, NOW, hit the brakes!"

Ben stood on the brake pedal, tires shrieked, and the anti-lock braking chattered. After skidding to a stop in the middle of the street next to a large lagoon, Simmons shouted, "Get down!" He opened both doors on his side of the car, using the rear door for cover.

Ben dropped behind the seat as their pursuer began screeching to a stop. Suddenly, there was a tremendous crash with the sound of tearing metal, followed by a large splash. Simmons shut the doors and said in a normal tone, "OK, let's roll. Back to the base, nice and easy."

Ben shot up and saw several figures in combat gear with guns drawn running forward from an SUV stopped in the middle of Tenth Street. The car chasing them was coming to rest upside down in the lagoon. "WHAT—THE—HELL!" he shouted at Simmons.

"Come on, friend, we need to move it. It's handled. We're clear now, so stay law-abiding all the way, please."

Ben stared at him for a few seconds, then pressed the accelerator. The engine raced briefly, and then, with shaking hands, Ben shifted into Drive.

"See, you're a natural," Simmons said with a smile. "You didn't even realize you shifted into Park."

Revelation

**Secure Compartmented Information Facility, Coast Guard
Sector Key West, Key West, Florida
11:17 EST, 15 January**

Ben

Ben sat silently next to Sam, looking straight ahead while stealing the occasional furtive glance at him. Sam sat quietly, also staring straight ahead, drumming his fingers on the table. They had been waiting in this state in the dim, windowless room for about two minutes while the Sector Security Watch fetched Simmons from the office he was using. Ben's hands had finally stopped shaking; it relieved him to see. They were still shaking rather noticeably when he reported to Sam aboard the ship on their return from Key West town. It was his first experience with post-adrenaline surge effects.

Sam had listened to the report without comment, then brought both hands down on his legs with a jarring slap. "Right. Let's go." They left the ship, pausing at the quarterdeck to reserve the sector's Secure Compartmented Information Facility. Sam's gaze fixed forward in steely determination on the silent walk over. Ben had not seen this side of his friend before, but he knew there were times he should keep his yap shut, and this was one.

After a knock, Simmons entered with the security watch. Sam nodded to the petty officer. "Thank you, that's all."

"Yes, sir," the petty officer mumbled as he exited and closed the door.

"Sit down, Doctor," Sam said. Sam leaned forward after the other man had complied, fixing Simmons's expressionless gaze with his own. "I will recap the morning's activities for you, Doctor, based on the report I received from my XO and some personal inferences," Sam began with a stiff formality. "After you left this base, you went to the Sheriff's office to gather information. You detected unknown persons trailing your car at some point in that journey. Is that correct?"

"Yes, it is."

"You withheld this information from my officer until you had completed a leisurely breakfast. After that, you had my officer lead those individuals on a high-speed car chase, ending with their vehicle being upside down in a lagoon off 10th Street. Is THAT correct?"

"Essentially correct, yes."

"You know what I think, Doctor? I think this entire exercise was a setup. I think you found out someone pretty bad was lurking around here, and you decided to take them out. This investigative mission was a bullshit pretense to go on the hunt. You dragged your coat around until they picked up on you. Then you took in a meal. Not because you wanted breakfast and coffee, but to give your thugs time to set up their thugs in an ambush. What do you think of my hypothesis?" Sam glared across the table at the agent.

"The investigative mission was not a ruse. I needed to see those archives. I didn't know the opposition was here, but when I picked up on the tail, I recognized an opportunity to change the gameboard, and I took it. That's my job."

Sam's face flushed with anger. "Doctor, you dragged my officer, unarmed, without his permission or even knowledge, into a life-threatening situation. Instead of calling in law enforcement, you forced him into violations of the law and put his and innocent civilian lives at risk. You had your sidearm out at the end. You were expecting a gunfight if your little bumper car ploy didn't work, weren't you?"

"Yes, but that was an unlikely possibility. This isn't our first rodeo, Captain. We practice and execute these tactics regularly, although not domestically. You should get hold of yourself here."

"I told you what to expect if you needlessly put my people in harm's way!"

"Aw, come on, Captain. It was well-controlled and successful. Your man came to no harm. In fact, he did well. He's a military officer who signed up to take risks, not your little sister."

Sam's mouth clamped shut, and he stood up. Ben followed and said, "Captain?" When Sam shoved the chair backward, closed his hands into fists, and started around the table, Ben grasped his arm and held him back. "Sam!"

Sam turned and blinked at his name, seemingly seeing Ben for the first time. He gave Simmons one last glare, then yanked the chair forward and sat down firmly. He took a breath to steady down and said, "Doctor, you just crossed the last line with me. You are out one patrol boat."

Simmons's smug smile continued. "Perhaps true for you, *Lieutenant*, not me. It seems you've forgotten I'm in charge of this operation. One phone call from me, and you'll be on the beach."

"Perhaps, but I don't think so. Anyway, *Kauai* will be out of it."

"Nonsense. They'll just move up your copilot here. I have a national security priority...."

"You obviously don't have a good grasp of what it means to command a military vessel," Sam interrupted. "Sure, if we were in the middle of a critical operation and I dropped dead, Ben would succeed to command. The operational commander would weigh the risks and then decide whether to continue or abort the mission. But one thing is certain: after the first mooring line goes over, *Kauai* will be offline until a new CO is appointed and installed. Make your phone call. Whether I'm in or out, the result will be the same."

Simmons's smug smile faded when he realized his poker hand was not as strong as he thought. "OK, stalemate. How do we move on?"

Sam sat back and cocked his head slightly. "You have one chance here: build trust by coming clean. We're in this SCIF to give you cover to spill on the whole scenario without compromising security. You give me the whole story on this, convince me it's complete and truthful to the last nit-noid detail, and maybe, MAYBE, you can also convince me to continue this excellent adventure. Otherwise, you might as well start packing."

The "stalemate," as Simmons described it, lasted another sixty seconds. He and Sam glared at each other, with Ben wishing he were *anywhere* else right then. Finally, Simmons blinked. "Fine, I hope you guys can keep this between us because I will be in deep trouble just sharing it with you."

"I understand," Sam said. "You have our word that nothing you say here will go any further. Right, XO?"

"Understood, Captain."

"Gentlemen, I am reluctantly reading you in on a top-secret operation under code word JUBILEE. Are you familiar with the term 'Broken Arrow'?"

Sam leaned forward. "If memory serves, that refers to a lost nuclear weapon. Please tell me I'm wrong."

"Alas, no," Simmons replied with a completely blank expression. "That is the correct reference to what we are dealing with here."

Ben felt a sudden icy chill and gaped at Sam, who returned a similar look of disbelief. "Bullshit!" was all Sam could say.

"Captain, I get I'm in a hole with you guys credibility-wise, but this is not a ploy or a cover story or any other weaselly spy trick." Simmons looked from Ben to Sam. "This is the real deal."

"OK," Sam began. "Let's pretend we would believe anything you tell us right now. And, by the way, that's a stretch, given you have consistently denied we were facing any radiological hazard. Where did this nuke come from?"

"To begin, we are not sure there is a nuclear weapon."

Sam snorted with disgust. "There is, or there isn't. How can you not be sure either way?"

"Because the weapon is Russian. We *are* sure they launched the weapon. We just don't know if it was carrying a conventional or a nuclear warhead."

"I don't believe it," Sam said. "The Russians attacked the United States? How could they cover up something like that?"

"It was an accident, Captain, not an attack." Simmons looked at Ben and asked, "You are aware of the current tensions in the Baltic?"

"The Russians are hammering the EU for a land corridor to Kaliningrad again. So what? Belarus may be a Russian puppet, but no one thinks Poland or Lithuania will cough up any territory. This is not Georgia or Crimea—Poland and Lithuania are both NATO. Any incursion by the Russians would trigger World War III."

"True, but it does not preclude some good old-fashioned saber-rattling. Here, a combination of Russian exercises in Grodno, Belarus, just over the Lithuanian and Polish borders, and some provocative flybys of our Air Defense Identification Zone in the Southeast by their Long-Range Aviation assets staging out of Cuba and Venezuela. One of their Backfire bombers got a little too close and triggered an intercept by F-16s out of Homestead. One thing led to another, there was a bump, and then an uncommanded launch of one of their Kinzhal hypersonic missiles."

"Holy Shit!" Ben exclaimed. "How did they keep that out of the news?"

"The missile did not hit any targets, on land anyway. There would be no hiding that—the vehicle's kinetic energy alone has the impact of a four-ton bomb, even if the warhead doesn't detonate."

Sam interrupted. "Take that kind of impact, a launch from a target we were not only tracking on radar but had eyes on, and the best you can do for a position estimate is a thirty-by-sixty-mile ellipse? What the hell?"

"Our pilots lost sight of it a few seconds after launch, and there's no way to track a Kinzhal on radar. The missile flies so fast that it generates a plasma cloud that absorbs radar energy," Simmons explained. "That's what caused the bright light we saw on the traffic cameras. Our non-radar sensor coverage is very sparse in the Keys. From Ben's and my efforts at the sheriff's office, we know it passed Marathon, but did not reach Boca Chica."

For Ben, the chill was passing. "OK, no explosion, no global nuclear war, and the missile vaporized on impact. What are we doing here?"

"That's the thing," Simmons answered. "The *vehicle* likely shattered, but the warhead has to survive the impact to operate correctly—it is almost certainly intact. Which leaves a live bomb packing an explosive power somewhere between one thousand pounds and five hundred thousand *tons* of TNT waiting to get tangled in someone's fishing trawl or anchor chain."

"OK, Doctor." Sam leaned back, folding his arms. "Let's say I believe what you have just told me. Answer me this: why us? Why isn't this place crawling with Army and Marines or the sky dark with search aircraft? Who thinks an aging Coast Guard patrol boat with a couple of toy airplanes is the right tool for this job?"

"Good question. You can't sortie forces like that on a moment's notice when everyone is already bore-sighted on Europe. Even if we could, we'd just draw attention to something we must keep quiet at all costs.

"From whom?" Ben asked.

"From everyone. Imagine the panic that would result if it got out that the U.S. government was hunting a lost nuclear weapon in the Florida Keys. Or the outrage when the public got wind of the Russians launching a nuke our way, even if we could prove it was an accident. This isn't the early 1960s, when the President could ask the publishers and network heads to help calm things down. They'll be stoking the viewers for ratings and mouse clicks until we declare war or have an insurrection. It's difficult to see how we *don't* end up in a nuclear exchange.

"You can see why you're ideal for this. You guys have a low-key footprint, and your presence where we will search is not considered unusual. Also, by all accounts, your crew is very sharp."

"What do you mean, 'by all accounts'?" Sam asked.

"You are highly regarded by the authorities. When we contacted the Coast Guard and asked for high-quality patrol boat support, they stuck with you."

Sam smiled ruefully. "Has it occurred to you we just might be the most expendable?"

Simmons feigned a distressed expression. "Good Heavens, I never thought of that!"

"And who were the guys who chased us? Russian agents?" Ben asked.

Simmons's smile faded. "No, those guys aren't with the Russians, and their presence is real bad news."

"Huh?" Sam said. "You're telling me a potential live nuke in our backyard is not the *worst* news? Who are we talking about here?"

"It's my day job at the agency. In short, they're the owners of the dope you interdicted. As you said, that amount of product would be worth a fortune. When that load dropped out of sight, the bad guys started searching hard. No mention of a large bust in the news media convinced them some rival organization must have snatched it. According to my sources, they've combed every harbor and marina within five hundred miles searching for it. I'm sure they had people keeping watch on every law enforcement group—federal, state, and local—and they're probably rolling up a big body count of their rivals gathering intel. Unfortunately, their watch at the Sheriff's office must have spotted me—I'm proud to say that I'm well-known to them for good reason. They've put together we have the boat, and something unusual is happening if I'm poking around. That little set-to this morning was a ham-fisted try by their local B-Teamers to grab and squeeze me for information. It didn't work out well for them."

"Drug cartel?" Sam asked.

"More of a transnational criminal organization. They informally call themselves the '252 Syndicate,' from February 25th, 1991, the date the Warsaw Pact fell. Founded by the worst the KGB, Stasi, Securitate, Sigurimi, and other Warsaw Pact secret police goon squads had and staffed with ex-agents and mercenaries with no wars to fight. They fund themselves through drug smuggling, human and weapons trafficking, extortion, and anything else that produces large profit margins. This mob's smart, well-equipped, and absolutely ruthless. That's another reason we wanted you guys, the Coast Guard, I mean. The Navy doesn't do law enforcement, and it may come to that before we finish."

Both officers sat in silence, processing what they had just been told. Sam finally broke the silence. "So, you have assets in the area, but I guess you have to presume that they'll draw in the TCO forces if they're observed."

"Yes, that's about it. We can flail around on a hard-target ground search, but we'd lead the 252s right to our target. As you can imagine, the last thing we want is for them to get hold of a nuclear weapon."

"So," Sam continued. "It's our job to prowl offshore with the UAVs and appear conventional."

"Yes, but we'll probably need a close look at some locations with your RHIB."

Sam leaned forward, putting his hands on the table. "And if we run into these guys, we can expect a fight?"

"Not necessarily. They don't want to start a war with the U.S. government. Bad for business, you know. However, if we corner them or get between them and something they want, they won't hesitate to shoot it out with us."

Sam sat back. "Is our operational commander aware of all this?"

"Select Coast Guard individuals are read-in, your Commandant, the Area Commander, and the Seventh District Commander and Response Chief."

"Forgive me, Doctor," Sam said. "I'll need to verify my chain of command is OK with things as they stand now. Since Captain Mercier is read-in, I'll get on a secure line with her."

"If you must, but remember, the details are compartmented information, and you can't discuss that on an ordinary secure telephone."

"Understood." Sam turned to Ben. "XO, can you call down to the District and arrange for a secure phone call with Captain Mercier, please?"

"Yes, sir," Ben replied, rising and heading out the door. Captain Jane Mercier was the officer in charge of response for the Seventh Coast Guard District. She was responsible for the better-known Coast Guard missions of search and rescue and law enforcement in South Carolina, Georgia, most of Florida, the

Bahamas, and Puerto Rico. For now, she was also Sam's boss, and his and Ben's fates rested in her hands.

It was a short walk to an empty desk and phone. After logging on to the computer, Ben looked up Captain Mercier's number in the global directory and dialed her number. She answered after three rings.

"Response, Captain Mercier."

"Good morning, ma'am. This is Lieutenant J.G. Ben Wyporek, XO of *Kauai*."

"Good morning, Ben. What can I do for you?"

"Ma'am, we are in Key West and have hit a sticky part in our mission. My CO, Lieutenant Powell, requests an opportunity to get some clarification over the STE."

"No problem. Give me five minutes to close up and get down to a secure space. I'll call you. I presume you'll be in the SCIF?"

"Yes, ma'am."

"All good. Talk to you in five."

"Thank you, ma'am," Ben said, then hung up and returned to the SCIF.

"I talked to Captain Mercier, sir," Ben said as he sat in front of the STE telephone. "She'll call us here as soon as she gets to her STE."

"Good. Now, Doctor, would you mind giving us the room, please?" His expression conveyed: *this is not a request.*

Simmons stared at Sam in astonishment. "Very well." He stood and walked out without another word.

After the door closed, Ben asked, "Sir?"

"I expect an 'inside baseball' talk with the captain. I don't want her holding back because our favorite spook is in the room."

"Yes, sir." Ben nodded.

"What do you think of this, really?"

"I don't know, sir. I can see the argument for staying lean for the sake of operations security, but just us? That's cut to the friggin' bone!"

"I agree. It's possible, I guess, but I need a lot more than a professional liar's word before I believe enough to continue on this one."

"I'm sure the captain will clear it up for us, skipper."

"Maybe. I wouldn't count on it, though."

The secure phone rang after a few minutes, and Sam activated the speakerphone. "Sector Key West, Lieutenant Powell speaking."

"Good morning, Sam. Jane Mercier here. What can I do for you this morning?"

"Yes, good morning, ma'am. You're on speaker with just my XO and me in the room. I'm sorry to bother you, but I need to verify that you are up to speed on developments before continuing the operation."

"OK, please go ahead."

"Ma'am, Dr. Simmons has told us about something related to this mission he claims I can't discuss over an STE. I'll just refer to it as 'X.' Do you know what I'm referring to, ma'am?"

"Yes, I do."

"Ma'am, I'm unsure how to put this. Is it for real?" After a few seconds of silence, Sam asked, "Captain, are you there?"

"Yes, Lieutenant, I'm here. I'm trying to figure out the best way to answer your question. Let's just say that several highly placed people believe it's real enough and issued orders accordingly. You are at the tail end of that chain of orders. Do you understand me?"

"Yes, ma'am."

"Good," Mercier said. "Was there anything else?"

"Yes, ma'am. It gets worse. A TCO has gotten involved, and they took a shot at grabbing Simmons and my XO this morning."

"Shit! Are you all right, Ben?"

"No worries, ma'am," Ben replied.

"They're both fine, ma'am," Sam interjected. "Simmons's people negated the immediate threat, and we are safe for now."

"I'm relieved to hear that."

"Ma'am, these guys don't screw around, and there's a genuine possibility of high-caliber use-of-force if we tangle with them. I'm sure there won't be time to get a Statement of No Objection when that happens."

"So, you're asking me for a blanket SNO? You know I can't give you that."

"No, ma'am, I'm not asking for a blank check, but you need to understand I will do whatever I need to do to protect my crew. Given that, should I continue this operation?"

"Your orders stand, Sam. All the 'But, sirs' have been said, believe me. I appreciate this is not what you wanted to hear, but I expect you and your crew to do your duty. In this case, that means you cooperate with Dr. Simmons to the maximum extent possible within the current rules of engagement until further notice. Clear enough?"

"Yes, ma'am. Sorry again to bother you, but I needed to be sure I understood the expectations. Thank you, ma'am."

"Not a problem. I understand your concern, given the new players. Keep your crew and ship safe. If there's nothing else, I'll wish you good luck."

"Thank you, ma'am. Goodbye." After turning off the phone, he turned to Ben. "Your thoughts?"

Ben's head swam at the implications of the conversation. "My God, Skipper! She thinks it's bullshit, too!"

"Mmm. And yet, we have our orders. Can you invite the good doctor back in, please?"

"Yes, sir." Ben blinked and then stood up to retrieve their passenger.

After Ben returned with Simmons and sat down, Simmons gazed at Sam. "Well?"

"Standard rules of engagement apply. We need a Statement of No Objection for the use of force unless it's self-defense. That means, Doctor, if your bad guys do not present an immediate and credible threat of lethal force, we need to get permission to shoot first. Is that understood?"

"You mean to say that given what I told you about these creeps, you will give them the first shot?" Simmons was aghast.

"No, what I'm saying is if they're not offering an immediate threat, I will call it in. If they come after us or pull out a weapon of any kind, I'll blow them right out of their socks."

"That works for me." Simmons nodded.

"I'm delighted to hear it. OK, XO, let's thank our hosts and get going before I come to my senses."

Workups

**USCG Cutter *Kauai*, Gulf of Mexico, fifteen nautical miles northwest of Key West, Florida
14:08 EST, 15 January**

Sam

Sam had put the shakedown of the Puma system first on the list after they reached the weapons exercise off Key West known as "Whiskey-174." Sam had seen testing of the larger ScanEagle unmanned aircraft system on the large National Security Cutter he served on before he attended officer candidate school. The ScanEagle needed a catapult for launch and a catch wire system for recovery that occupied a significant part of the cutter's flight deck. That experience had led to his doubt any UAV system could work on a unit as small as a patrol boat.

Thus, Sam continued to expect Deffler's junior counterpart Morgan to set up some sort of launcher on *Kauai*'s foredeck. Morgan assembled the aircraft while Deffler ran through control checks on the GCS. Ben was on the foredeck, observing the setup and launch. Finally, Deffler announced, "Pre-flight checklist complete. Request Green Deck for UAV launch."

Sam looked at Bondurant, who had the OOD, and received a shrug in return. He made a mental note to work out a formal procedure later. "Very well, Green Deck, launch when ready."

Deffler spoke to Morgan through the headset. "Green Deck, Mike. Let me know when you're ready for the count."

Sam glanced down and watched Morgan pick up the UAV by its fuselage just under the wing. At his ready report, Deffler activated the battery-powered engine into idle and began his countdown. "Launch in three, two, one, now!"

To Sam's astonishment, at the count of two, Morgan drew his arm back like a javelin thrower and threw the aircraft into the air, releasing on "Now!" with the engine coming up to the loud buzz of full power. The aircraft arced downward slightly when it cleared the rail on *Kauai*, then started a slow climb over the water.

Sam shook his head in amazement as the small aircraft continued its ascent. The ScanEagle had cost millions of dollars in ship alterations and had mostly disabled the flight deck of the cutter when operating. The Puma took two crewmen for the launch, and Morgan had already picked up his gear and left the foredeck. Deffler started his planned flight pattern to check for any communications blind spots caused by the ship's superstructure and radar interference.

Deffler "mapped" signal strength and quality in every direction for about an hour and noted the dicey locations. Afterward, Deffler brought the aircraft back to put the cameras through their paces. Bondurant delighted in bringing *Kauai* up to a brisk twenty-four knots and putting her through a series of quick turns and reversals. The Puma remained in a steady orbit through it all, its camera doggedly locked onto the gyrating patrol boat.

The quality of the images sent from the aircraft impressed Sam. Even from one thousand feet of altitude, the resolution was sharp enough to read the quarter-inch lettering on the warning labels of the life raft canister. "Deffler, you need any more dedicated time? I would like to get going on the gun shoot before we lose the light."

"All set, Captain. If you don't object, I'd like to keep the bird up to do shot spotting."

"Good, I'd like to see that too." Sam nodded. "How much endurance do you have left?"

Deffler smiled. "Oh, a good four hours if we're frugal, maybe three if we get fancy."

Sam pondered what "get fancy" meant, but put it aside for the moment. "OK, OOD, let's set Condition One for gunnery exercise, please."

"Yes, sir," Bondurant replied. He picked up the microphone for *Kauai*'s public-address system and announced, "Now, General Quarters, General Quarters, set Condition One for gunnery exercise." He then pulled the handle on the GQ alarm, starting a twenty-second repeating gong sound. Crew members began moving briskly to their GQ stations, putting on helmets and survival gear and, with the topside personnel, light body armor. Ben quickly appeared and relieved Bondurant as OOD, allowing him to leave for his GQ station on the boat deck.

Sam watched the quick transition of his cutter from peacetime cruising to combat-ready with satisfaction. He hid a smile while he saw Hopkins patiently helping Deffler get into his battle gear. Simmons had brought his own body armor but wore a loaner helmet and survival vest. Typically, during GQ, Sam would not have had visitors on the already crowded Bridge. However, he wanted Simmons to have a good understanding of *Kauai*'s combat capability, and Deffler was piloting the airborne Puma.

"OOD," Sam called over as Ben settled in and completed a radar check and circle round with the binoculars. "When the fantail station reports manned and ready, have them launch targets at two-minute intervals."

"Very good, sir."

The targets Sam referred to were small wooden boxes containing an inflated beach ball and rigged with a stone weight on one side and a plastic flag on the other. The ball would hold the box afloat even with leaks, and the weight would keep the flag upright, improving the target's visibility. Drake supervised the construction of a dozen targets this morning to prepare for the shoot.

"Captain, the first target is away," Ben announced after the deck crew dropped the first target buoy off the stern of the boat.

"Thank you. Hold this course until the last one goes over, then give me a wide turn course reversal to starboard. Put us about five hundred yards off, parallel to the target line at five knots. We'll take the first six with the twenty-five millimeter. Then close to one hundred yards to finish the others with the fifties and small arms."

"Very good, sir."

Sam glanced across to see Hopkins huddled with Deffler at the UAV control station while the latter tracked the targets with the Puma. "XO, a word, please," Sam called as he stepped out onto the Bridge wing.

"Yes, sir?" Ben said when he caught up.

"XO, I'd like you to get in some shooting with an M4 and pistol, at least two mags each."

"Very good, sir. May I ask why?"

"Our guest implied we would need to go ashore, despite our newfound air capability. When that happens, I'll need you to keep an eye on him, but you'll be properly equipped this time. I think it's been about six months since you've been to the range?"

"More like eight."

"Ever shoot the M4 on automatic?"

"No, sir, the range monkeys wouldn't have it."

"Do it today." Sam nodded. "I want you comfortable with that weapon in all modes."

"Yes, sir." Ben grinned. "This secret agent gig has perks."

"Before you get too giddy, think beyond the sale a bit."

"Sir?"

Sam fixed on Ben's eyes. "I'm making sure you're ready to use them because your life may depend on it."

"Yes, sir."

****

"Surface action starboard," Sam declared. "Target is the floating buoy bearing zero-eight-five relative."

Kauai armament included the latest model twenty-five-millimeter chain gun—a testbed installation of the new versions fitted to the latest ships. Williams controlled *Kauai*'s main gun from a compact control station on the Bridge. Its electro-optical and infrared gun sights and gyro-stabilization made it deadly even in rough weather.

"Target identified, target confirmed, on target and tracking," Williams announced, with the gun's electro-optical gun sight centered on the target buoy. Although challenging to see with the naked eye from five hundred yards, Williams had no problem tracking the target with the gun sight.

"OOD, is the range clear?" Sam called over to Ben.

"Affirmative, Captain, no surface or air contacts."

"Deffler, is the UAV clear?"

"Affirmative Captain, the UAV is overhead." Deffler locked the aircraft's camera on the target buoy.

"Very well. Batteries release, commence fire."

"Firing," Williams toggled off the safety and tapped the trigger. The gun responded with a sharp BANG, followed by the clank of the chain loader and the rattle of the spent cartridge ejecting on the deck. Williams pitched the first shot short, using a "walking up" technique with three single shots, then a "fire for effect" quick burst of three rounds of high-explosive incendiary shells, all detonating on impact.

"Damn!" Deffler exclaimed when the target on his screen exploded in a bright flash. The others on the Bridge turned to look at him, and he said, "Sorry, sir!"

Williams shook his head and turned back to his screen. "Airedales!" He declared under his breath before, more loudly, "Target destroyed."

"Check fire," Sam declared. "OK, let's make sure it's not a fluke. Shift target to next target float bearing zero-eight-zero relative."

Williams slewed the gun sight to the left to acquire the new target and then activated the target lock. On the foredeck, the gun barrel traversed a few degrees to the left and then crept up and down as its gyro stabilizers compensated for *Kauai*'s gentle pitching and rolling. "Target identified, target confirmed, on target and tracking."

"Commence fire," Sam repeated, and six rounds later, another target disintegrated. "Check fire. OK, I'm a believer. Williams, let's try infrared targeting only on the next two."

"Yes, sir." Williams brought up the infrared targeting system, but struggled at once. The infrared sight keyed on differences in temperature and the overcast skies and time since launch had rendered the target almost indistinguishable from the surrounding water, temperature-wise. Finally, Williams settled and locked the sight on a barely discernable smudge, announcing, "Target identified, target confirmed, on target and tracking."

Sam had noted his fire control expert's difficulty with a bit of concern. "Commence fire."

Williams tried the same technique as before, pitching the first round into the water about fifty feet short. Unfortunately, the hot incendiary tail and explosion from the round distracted the infrared gun sight and broke its lock on the target. "Crap! Oh, sorry, sir, target track lost, reacquiring." After a few seconds of jiggling, he brought the smudge representing the target buoy into lock again. "Target reacquired." This time, he aimed for a direct hit. "Firing." Another bang and another target lock break. "Target track lost, shot unobserved," Williams reported with discouragement.

"Shot fall five meters right and twenty long," Deffler reported from the chart table. Again, all heads turned to him. "Captain, recommend illuminating the target with the UAV—it's tuned to the Mark 38's infrared gun sight."

Sam looked from Williams to Deffler and then replied, "Why not? Permission granted. Let's see if it works."

Deffler worked his console, announcing, "Unmasking, target illuminated."

Williams noted a bright dot on the infrared screen and locked on it. "Target identified, target confirmed, on target and tracking."

"Commence fire."

Williams selected a three-round burst on this try. "Firing." The three shots within 1.5 seconds were followed almost at once by the detonation of the target.

"Target destroyed," Williams and Deffler announced simultaneously.

"Check fire," Sam ordered. "Very nice. Let's use the designator on the next two. Shift target to the next buoy bearing zero-eight-five relative. UAV, illuminate the target."

Deffler slewed the Puma's camera to the next target, locked on, and activated the illuminator. "Target illuminated."

Williams noted and locked on to the bright spot, selecting another three-round burst. "Target identified, target confirmed, on target and tracking."

Sam noted the briskness of the acquisition and ordered, "Commence fire." Three more quick shots were followed by another "target destroyed" announcement from the two technicians. After they repeated the process on the next target, Sam ordered, "Ceasefire." He glanced at his technicians. "OK, now we know we can use the infrared sight against a relatively cool target if we can illuminate it. We'll need a standard procedure for that. Hopkins, will you coordinate that in the follow-up, please?"

"Will do, Captain," Hopkins replied.

"OK, secure the twenty-five," Sam ordered. "Let's close to twenty-five yards for the rest of the shoot, please."

"Very good, sir," Ben replied, then issued the orders to the helmsman.

The boarding team members blazed away at the targets with carbines and pistols for about an hour. Hopkins relieved Ben as OOD to allow him to join in for the last twenty minutes. The targets still afloat were dispatched with the fifty-caliber machine guns to give Seaman Lopez and Hebert some experience. Although not as impressive as the main gun, the fifties still made quick work of the target buoys.

Sam secured the shoot at 17:15 to give the shooters a chance to gather the spent cartridges from the decks and help the gunner's mate clean the weapons. In the meantime, Sam directed the RHIB launch to recover the Puma. The RHIB sat idling off *Kauai*'s starboard quarter as Deffler brought the aircraft down, cut the engine, and flared it for a gentle splashdown between the two vessels. The RHIB motored to the Puma within a few seconds, and Morgan carefully lifted and secured the aircraft in the boat.

As the RHIB returned for recovery aboard *Kauai*, Ben turned and picked up his weapons and "sack o-brass" and headed toward the main deck. When he passed Simmons, the latter asked, "Got a minute? We need to review tomorrow's plans."

Ben held up the weapons. "I got clean-ups. I'll be with you in about half an hour."

Simmons frowned. "You don't have people for that?"

Ben stared coldly in return. "I suppose I can order one of these guys to clean my weapons—if I was a complete *dick,* that is. Excuse me." Ben continued down the ladder as Simmons turned to see Sam had watched the exchange.

"Your officer is quite the egalitarian," Simmons remarked.

"That's what makes him effective. Fieldstripping and cleaning your weapon after a shoot, tedious as it may be, is an important part of maintaining familiarity and qualifications. Ben knows that officers shirking their duty negatively affects the crew and wouldn't do so unless he had a damn good reason. I've seen plenty of JOs who believe their shit doesn't stink and wouldn't think twice about dumping this work on the junior crew. None of them made a difference to the unit or the mission like Ben has."

"Yes, I see." Simmons smirked. "I hope he can find time for other 'duties' soon."

"Don't worry, Doctor," Sam turned to leave. "He handles all pains-in-the-ass with equal diligence."

USCG Cutter *Kauai*, Gulf of Mexico, fifteen nautical miles northeast of Key West, Florida
20:17 EST, 15 January

Ben

"XO, got a minute?" Sam called out as Ben walked by the cabin.

"Yes, sir." Ben stepped aside as Hopkins moved out.

"Thanks, Hoppy," Sam said. "I appreciate you getting that turned out so quick."

"Not a problem, Captain. Goodnight," the petty officer replied, nodding to each man as she walked off.

Sam looked at Ben. "She came up with standard language for the UAV launch and gunfire spotting. We won't stumble around next time."

Ben glanced out the door sadly. "Figures she'd nail that. It will suck to lose her."

"Tell me about it." Sam shook his head equally sadly. "I won't have her turning down chief, though."

"Damn straight." Ben nodded. "You wanted something, sir?"

"Yes, yes. I wanted to ask what our guest is cooking up for us."

"Oh, he just wanted to go over the visit sequence."

"Right. And how's it going with you two?"

Ben sat back. "Skipper, I'm trying my best. But every time I start warming up to him, he pitches another 'Asshat, Esq.' card, and I want to kick his ass. Or step aside and let you kick his ass." He finished with a slight smile.

Sam closed his eyes and shook his head. "Not my finest moment. Sorry to drop you in the middle of that."

"It's OK, sir. Although the last thing I expected after our adventure this morning was to be compared to a little girl."

"Oh, he wasn't doing that. He aimed that shot squarely at me. I owe you an explanation. Please close the door."

Ben complied and then sat down. "Captain, you don't owe me any explanations."

"Maybe, but you will get one, anyway. You've been curious about my background and patient enough not to ask questions, and this morning's lunatic episode provides an excuse to come clean with you. So, sit back, relax, and let me sate your curiosity."

In the close quiet of the cabin, Sam began describing his early adolescence as the elder child of a Wall Street financial "Master of the Universe." His home was a mansion twenty miles from Manhattan in Essex Fells, New Jersey. Private schools, tutors, and lavish parties dominated his memories when he and his sister Gabrielle, three years his junior, grew up with their devoted mother, Danielle. His father, James, typical of the financial class, spent his weeknights at an apartment close to work downtown and returned to his family on the weekends. Although not close to his father, he was aligned with him in affection for his mother. Her death in a car accident when he was twelve blew both their worlds to pieces. His father coped by throwing himself into his work with increasing devotion, while Sam turned to his sister and a family friend, a retired Navy SEAL named Robert "Bobby" Moore.

James hired Moore to protect the family when Russian organized crime elements put the squeeze on some of his colleagues. Moore did not come cheap, but he brought a retinue of supremely skilled and dedicated former special forces acquaintances who quickly "negated" the threat. When Sam asked him how he managed it much later, Moore responded he had explained the situation to them in a language a Russian could understand and left it at that. Sam's father discovered Moore possessed many valuable skills beyond physical security and kept him on to help manage his personal life. Moore stepped readily into the void created by the death of Sam's mother. He became a multi-hatted head of security, household majordomo, and general "fixer," keeping things running while the family coped with and eventually overcame the grief of their loss.

With time and nearness, Sam and Moore forged a strong personal attachment. Moore admired Sam's quick mind, innate sense of duty, and the fundamental goodness of character fostered by his mother, and Sam was in awe of the older man's experience and talents. Both shared an exasperated affection for Sam's sister Gabby, whose charm and blossoming beauty matched the independent streak often found in a family's younger child. Under the distant oversight of his father and close mentoring by Moore, Sam matured into an outstanding student, both academically and athletically.

After high school graduation, Sam entered Wharton's Financial Engineering program. Sam thrived there from the intellectual challenge, despite the conflict between the intensely competitive culture and his natural tendency to team up with people. He finished at the top of his class and was accepted into the MBA program. He was moving inexorably toward following his father into the family firm when he confronted the event that changed his outlook and purpose in life.

As Sam progressed through undergraduate studies at Wharton, Gabby matured into a beautiful, social young woman.

Intelligent in her own right, she had no intention of following her brother into the family business and opted for a fine arts track at Princeton. She met and fell in with Paul Griffith, a scion of the family of one of her father's business competitors and classmate of Sam at Wharton. Paul was popular, handsome, and rich, and Sam had run into him periodically since they were young children. Growing up, Sam grew aware something was "off" about Paul, gradually distancing himself despite their shared background. By the time they completed their undergraduate work together at Wharton, Sam had seen enough inside and outside the classroom to conclude Paul was an undiagnosed sociopath.

Sam was appalled by Gabby keeping company with someone he regarded as a toxic, if not dangerous, personality and made no secret of it. Gabby, tired of living in her big brother's shadow, was having none of it. Paul sensed the conflict and played on it. He lacked any genuine interest in Gabby, but she was socially useful, and the knowledge he twisted up "straight-arrow" Sam by staying with her made it a win-win. Even Moore couldn't shake the hold Paul had on the young woman—he had to settle for suggesting he would not take it lightly if anything happened to her. The implied menace had no effect on the privileged young man.

The event Sam and Moore dreaded came to pass on a late fall weekend as Paul and Gabby were driving home from a party. He indulged heavily in alcohol and party drugs, and even Gabby was terrified as they sped through the night. Unsurprisingly, he missed a turn and rolled his Porsche down an embankment and into a tributary of the Raritan River. Paul glanced at his unconscious companion as the car filled with water and then bailed.

By an incredible stroke of luck, the accident happened in front of two off-duty Coast Guard petty officers on their way home from a unit gathering, who pulled off and immediately sprang into action. Passing Paul as he climbed the embankment, the two men paused briefly to ask if anyone remained in the car. Not getting a response when the young man fled, one plunged into the freezing water to get to the vehicle, while the other called 911, then waded in to help extract the stricken young woman. Both performed CPR until relieved by paramedics, who transported the unconscious but living victim to the local emergency room.

A thoroughly alarmed Bobby Moore roused Sam, and the two sped to the hospital, James joining them from Manhattan an hour later. The three men sat together in frightened silence in the waiting room for over four hours while the neurosurgery team did their evaluation and response. When the doctor emerged, he reported they had put Gabby into a medically induced coma until her brain swelling went down, but the prognosis was good. Near weeping in relief, the men agreed to take shifts standing by, with Sam remaining for the first watch while Moore escorted his father home.

Gabby's youth and good health paid off. Within a day and a half, she regained consciousness and went home in three. Although reasonably fit, she had no memory of the accident or even the party. After seeing her safely home with temporary live-in medical care, Sam and Moore began inquiries into the accident and the actions law enforcement intended to take.

Paul vanished for several days, then reappeared, completed unscathed. Sam was convinced he hid out to make sure whatever party drugs he had taken were clear of his system before encountering the police. A cursory investigation resulted in misdemeanor reckless driving charges for Paul, and he escaped with a fine. It was rumored Paul's father had dealt with issues like this before and had contacts in the local police and district attorney's office. Paul's father quietly made right on Gabby's medical costs, and, as far as he and James were concerned, the matter was closed.

Sam was furious at this result. He had taken the time to visit the Coast Guard station where the two petty officers were stationed to thank them and offer them a reward, which they politely refused. They told Sam of the events that night, including the driver fleeing the scene. After learning they had contacted the police the following day to offer statements and been summarily rebuffed, Sam was convinced the fix was in.

His anger only increased after a confrontation with his father. Sam was astounded he would go along with a slap on the wrist for the man who had recklessly put his daughter in mortal danger and then abandoned her to die. James was not unfeeling about the incident. But, in his view, more significant business issues were at stake, and he told Sam to put the matter behind him. He then left the task of calming down his son to his trusted adviser Moore and returned to work, a decision that only added more strain to a fragile relationship between father and son.

The situation simmered for several weeks. Sam and Paul returned to their studies at Wharton, but did not share any classes where they would cross paths. Finally, a chance meeting occurred outside the library. Sam nodded at Paul in passing, and Paul took it as a sign of acceptance and submission—an enormous mistake. Sam couldn't remember what Paul had said, only that after he said it, his world went red. By the time Sam was pulled off, Paul was on his way to the hospital with two broken ribs, among other injuries.

It took all the "fixer" juice Moore had to keep Sam clear of a felony assault charge. Paul and his father agreed not to file charges after Moore arranged the payment of Paul's medical bills and made subtle threats about Paul's known drug use and other activities.

On the other hand, James was apoplectic at his son's behavior and threat to the family business. In a showdown shortly afterward, he told his son in no uncertain terms to "get with the program" or get out.

The ultimatum proved the final straw for Sam. He hated the cutthroat environment of high finance presented by his father and school, but strove to succeed out of a sense of duty to his family. This incident made it clear to Sam that business came first and family a distant second in this world. He often thought of the two men who saved Gabby's life after the accident. They hadn't hesitated a second to plunge into a freezing river to rescue a young woman they'd never met from a sinking car. *That* was the world Sam wanted to join.

After a sleepless night and a long talk with Bobby Moore that didn't dissuade him, Sam visited the Coast Guard Recruiting Office in Philadelphia. He completed the required entry forms and tests and signed up to report to recruit training at Cape May the following January. The recruiter could not believe what he had in hand between Sam's aptitude test scores and top-of-the-line undergraduate degree. He frankly explained that Sam would have an excellent chance of acceptance to OCS or even a direct commission as a finance officer if he were to apply. He just followed protocol in this, as highly educated recruits could be problematic when they found enlisted life less intellectually challenging. Sam insisted, and the recruiter accepted his application for enlistment and administered the oath. Sam chose Operations Specialist for his desired rating. His test scores and background qualified him to go straight to the Operations Specialist A-school on graduation from boot camp without the usual period as an apprentice seaman.

January came, and the farewell was a hard one. James failed to appear, refusing to talk to Sam until, as he told Moore, "he returns to sanity." The thought of not having Sam close at hand depressed Gabby. They had grown closer since the accident and his fight with Paul. Although fully recovered physically and getting back in rhythm at school, she still had mild post-traumatic stress and occasionally leaned on him for support. Sam assured her he would keep in touch and that Moore could get word to him in any emergency.

Bobby Moore was another hard farewell. Moore did his best to talk Sam out of joining at James's request. However, he was privately relieved he failed and proud the boy he had helped raise was stepping up for service. He assured Sam that Gabby would be looked after, and he'd work on his father as best he could, providing Sam relief that at least the home front was well-covered. Moore drove Sam and Gabby down to Cape May on that fateful day. There, the young man joined a sizable group of apprehensive young people making tearful goodbyes from their families and moving to a new phase in life.

Gabby turned out all right. She finished school, met and married a decent man, and set up a successful art studio in Manhattan with her father's financial help. Sam had to give his father credit: he really stepped up to become more engaged and supportive of his daughter after Sam's departure. Moore continued in his role as Sam's surrogate father and family overwatch. He remained a close and trusted friend to this day. In fact, Jo and Sam named their first child after him, Robert Eduardo Powell.

****

Ben sat back in wonder as Sam finished the story, deeply moved by his friend's trust in sharing some truly private parts of his life. He found it difficult to think of something to say that didn't sound trivial by comparison. After a brief pause, he asked, "Whatever happened to Paul? Did he stir up any more trouble?"

Sam smiled grimly. "Bobby went harder at him on the second try and applied some 'Russian grade' menace. He stayed well clear of Gabby and me since then. The big merger planned with Griffith's company fell through, which pissed Dad off even more. But it worked out better in the end since their company tanked in the subprime lending catastrophe. The last I heard, Paul and his father fled the country with a bag of cash and the Securities and Exchange Commission hot on their heels. Good riddance."

Ben nodded and scratched his head. "Sir, it sounds like everything worked out great. So, what's the continued beef between you and your father?"

Sam shook his head. "No beef on this end. Dad's been invited to every event, and we made every effort to let him know he's welcome in our lives. His prime beef is he can't accept that someone of my 'breeding' and education would want a job among the hoi polloi, making a hundredth of what I can working for him. I think there's a bit of grudge nursing too since, in his view, I told him where to stick it right after he went to the mat to keep my ass out of jail." He smiled ruefully. "I'd agree he had a legitimate gripe back then. Pride can be an ugly thing sometimes, and I don't exclude myself from that indictment. Bobby is still hard at it. Maybe someday he can get us back together."

"Amazing, and what about Gabby?"

This time, Sam looked down sadly. "Things have cooled off with Gabby. She's still part of that world, and she and Jo never took to each other. They put on a brave show for my sake, but it's a strain on both of them when they're together, and we try to avoid it."

"Sorry, sir." Ben frowned in sympathy.

"That's the way it goes. You can see how that's still an open wound for me. The good doctor surprised me enough this morning to generate a psychotic break." He smiled maniacally. "But I'm much better now!"

Ben rocked his head back and laughed. "Roger that, sir. I'll put your Prozac dose back in the safe then. I'll keep Doc Simmons's on hand for a while, though." He winked, then stood and extended his hand. "Thanks for sharing all this, sir."

Sam stood and grasped Ben's hand in a firm shake. "It was easier than I thought. Thanks for hanging in there while I bared my soul. Trust is vital for us, Ben, particularly now. I want you focused on the job and not worrying that I will go postal and throw our guest overboard."

As Ben turned and stepped out, he said, "Yeah, get in line, Boss."

Seizure

**USCG Cutter *Kauai*, Gulf of Mexico, nineteen nautical miles northeast of Key West, Florida
07:01 EST, 16 January**

Ben

"All hands, set Flight Quarters Condition One, clear the foredeck for UAV launch," Ben announced through the ship. Flight quarters on *Kauai* proved to be a low-key operation compared to his previous ship. On *Dependable*, the activities associated with launching a helicopter and standing by in case of crash and fire tied up dozens of crew members for hours. Ben watched as Morgan walked out with his toolbox, one of the seamen following with the separated Puma fuselage and wing. Turning aft, he saw the ready boat crew moving to stand by the RHIB if the immediate recovery of the aircraft was needed. He turned back inside when Deffler arrived from his check of the ground control antenna and set up the control station.

Ben pulled and reviewed the laminated card Hopkins had prepared the previous night and completed the pre-flight checklist. Ben put the card back in its holder and picked up his binoculars to make his final survey of the area around the boat. Returning inside, he called Sam to let him know checks were complete for launch.

"Very well, OOD, carry on," Sam said.

"Very good, sir," Ben replied. Simmons had arrived and pulled up a stool next to Deffler for the flight. The two consulted using the annotated chart extract Hopkins had provided, showing the likely anchorages on the first two targets. After a brief time, Deffler paused and touched his earpiece.

"OOD, Flight Control, pre-flight checks complete, request Green Deck for UAV launch," he announced.

"Very well, Green Deck."

"Yes, sir. Green Deck, Mike," Deffler spoke into the headset. "Let me know when you're ready for the count." He activated the battery-powered engine. "Standby, three, two, one, launch." The Puma arced over the side and began its climb. "Flight operations normal, camera operating, climbing to three hundred."

About forty minutes later, Bondurant appeared on the Bridge to make his rounds in preparation to relieve Ben of the OOD for the Forenoon Watch. When satisfied with his understanding of the current situation, he stepped up to Ben. "XO, I'm ready to relieve you. Do you have anything to pass?"

"No, Boats. Just monitor our aviation detachment there. Expect they'll bring the bird back about 11:00."

"Got it. I relieve you, sir," Bondurant stated with a smart salute.

Ben walked over to the chart table, where Simmons and Deffler gazed at the video displays. Simmons looked up after a moment. "Heading down for some sleep, friend?"

"I wish. Hopefully, I can coax Chef to turn out one last breakfast ration. Then it's on to my three least favorite things: paperwork, paperwork, and paperwork. Will you be sitting there watching the screen all day?"

"From time to time. Frankly, I don't expect to discover anything this way. The previous searches would have picked up whatever we see. We'll have a better chance letting the analysis team's machine learning algorithms paw through the imagery. They will process the visual and hyperspectral in half-hour blocks."

"You don't have machine learning on the earlier stuff?"

Simmons shook his head. "No, the resolution's too low, and the atmospherics are problematic. The clouds and junk in the air confuse the algorithms."

"Right. How do you plan to get the imagery to the analysts? You have satellite comms through that thing?"

"Not exactly," Simmons replied, his voice dropping. "Also very hush-hush, please. We have a High-Altitude UAV doing communications relay throughout this operation, and they are getting the imagery at the same time we are through high-bandwidth UHF."

"Wow. OK, I'm off. Can I send anything up for you guys? Coffee?"

"No, I'm good," Simmons turned to Deffler. "Fritz?" and received a head shake in reply as the airman concentrated on the screen. "Thanks anyway, friend. See you later."

"Later," Ben replied, turning to leave.

A couple of hours afterward, Ben and Sam were going over the drafts of operational reports in the cabin when the phone rang, and Sam hit the speaker button. "Captain."

"Captain, OOD here, could you come to the Bridge, please, sir?" Bondurant's voice came from the speaker.

"On the way." Sam hit the hang-up button, and he and Ben stood up to make their way to the Bridge. Half a minute later, they arrived and walked over to Bondurant.

"Captain on the Bridge," Bondurant announced.

"Carry on. What have you got, OOD?"

"We have a visual on a surface contact heading slowly in this general direction, sir. It appears to be a sloop under sail, but it is not showing up on radar."

Sam frowned. "Show me."

Bondurant led the two officers to the SeaWatch console and pointed at the screens. "Lookout picked it up first. Then we locked on with the camera. You can see it's definitely under sail and hull-up. I would say nine thousand yards right now. But check out the radar plot: nothing. And nothing's wrong with the radar. You can see we have a good trace on Snipe Point here." He pointed at the screen.

Sam picked up his binoculars and trained them on the bearing. After a brief search, he picked up on the distant object, barely visible through the haze, a small vessel under sail. "Can they see us, you think?"

"If they have radar, yes, sir. Otherwise, I doubt it in this haze."

"Hmmm. XO, what do you think?" Sam whispered, keeping his eyes on the boat through the binoculars.

"Captain, a few days ago, I would have shrugged and said, let's check it out. After yesterday's adventure, I'd rather send the UAV in first."

"Agreed. Doctor, could you come here, please?" Sam called across the Bridge.

"Yes, Captain?" Simmons said when he stepped up.

"Doctor, take a look." Sam handed him the binoculars. "We have a large sailboat that's not showing up on radar. Do you know anything about this?"

As he peered through the binoculars, Simmons replied, "Definitely not." He handed back the glasses and looked Sam in the eye. "I presume you'd like the UAV to go investigate before we close on it."

"I would indeed, Doctor. Can you break off the survey, or do we need to launch the other bird?"

"We're at a good breakpoint. Fritz, what's the fuel state?" he called over.

"One plus five-five."

"OK, bring her up to one thousand and head her back this way. Get the Ghost ready."

"Cool! Turning to three-three-five, leaving three hundred for one thousand."

"Ghost?" Ben asked.

"Compass Ghost System. It's one of our spook add-ons to the basic aircraft. I'll wait until it's almost overhead to switch on so you can get the full effect."

"OK, I'm breathless in anticipation," Sam said wryly. "OOD, let's keep a parallel course and match speed with the target as best you can. Put the radar on standby. Except for the UAV, full emissions control—I'd like to stay undetected for now."

"Yes, sir." Bondurant issued the orders to the helmsman and selected the settings on the console.

The three men stood outside a few minutes later, watching the UAV approach from the southeast. The nine-foot-wide aircraft was small but very visible against the cloudy sky at one thousand feet. Simmons turned to Deffler, "Stand by, Fritz. OK, gentlemen, you have the little bird in sight?" Seeing nods in return, Simmons said, "Now, Fritz."

Suddenly, the aircraft vanished before their eyes. "Damn!" Ben exclaimed, and Sam startled and then brought the binoculars up to his eyes.

"Wait, OK, I can just barely make it out. XO, still not seeing it?"

"No, Captain," Ben said in wonder. He glanced at Deffler, now smiling at the three men.

"Welcome to Compass Ghost," Simmons stated. "There are sensors on top connected through a processor to LED projectors on the wings and lower fuselage. It eliminates the underside shadow with an approximate representation of the sky's color and brightness. It's not invisibility, but it's close. Under these conditions, with a solid overcast, performance is optimal. It's still pretty good against a clear sky, but it's not as effective when there are scattered clouds."

"Doctor, I'm impressed," Sam admitted. "Does it affect the performance of the aircraft?"

"It knocks about ten percent off the maximum airspeed and maybe twenty percent off the endurance if we leave it on for the entire flight. The cameras and designator are unaffected."

"Wow!" was all Ben could say.

"Captain, if I may?" Simmons asked Sam, receiving a nod in return. "Fritz, your contact is about two-seven-five degrees at four-point-five, but that's an estimate. We need a distant, then close survey," he directed.

"Roger that, going wide."

"Doctor, even if it's made of fiberglass or composites, we should be able to get a primary radar return on that sailboat from this distance," Sam began. "Do the people you tangled with yesterday have a, well, whatever the correct scientific term for a radar cloaking device would be?"

"Captain, I have never seen anything like this, but I'm not in on everything. I do agree with you. It's far more likely this one is a non-Russian. If you'll allow me to send a burst transmission through the VHA-UAV antenna, there's a chance I could get some useful info from my guys."

"Very well, you may go ahead, Doctor. I expect you to share everything you get back."

"Absolutely, Captain!" Simmons smiled and ducked back inside.

"Should we set the LE Bill or GQ?" Ben asked.

Sam shook his head. "Neither. Let's check out this guy first. We've plenty of time either way, and I'd hate to call one, then jump to the other." He turned to Ben and smiled. "It'd make me appear indecisive."

"Sir, the UAV has the target," Bondurant said, poking his head out the door.

"Thanks, OOD, I'm coming," Sam replied, and he and Ben turned to enter the Bridge.

Ben and Sam stood behind the seated Deffler and Simmons, the former working the flight controls and the other controlling the camera.

"Still about two miles out," Simmons said. "We're powering down to slow flight now to reduce the noise signature. They should be unaware it's up there."

The vessel was a large, black-hulled sloop under a single jib and mainsail, making about three knots in the light wind, with no one visible.

"Remarkable," Sam replied. "Get a read on the crew first, followed by a close examination of the mast and deck. Whatever they're using to mask their return, I'd like eyes-on before they figure out we're here. Any chance you can scan for crew or weapons?"

"Only visually."

"That'd still be useful. I don't suppose you heard back on your inquiry."

"No, I'm afraid not."

Sam turned back to the screen. "Let's see what the bird finds. OOD, can you come over here, please?"

"Yes, sir." Bondurant walked over to the UAV station. He glanced at the screen and nodded approvingly. "Marlow Hunter 50AC. That's a sweet ride. Captain, that's at least half a million dollars worth of boat. There should be plenty of information available if we call it in."

Sam nodded. "Agreed, but I still want a good look before canceling emissions control. How big a crew do you need to handle one of these?"

Bondurant was puzzled by his CO's caution, but shrugged and went along. "It can be handled solo, sir. That's a Marlow Hunter specialty, but it's a handful for just one."

"Coming around port side, sir," Deffler interrupted. "There's a name on the aft quarter."

"Zooming in," Simmons added. "Okay, it's the *Sunrise Surprise II*. Homeport Clearwater. One person is visible in the cockpit, and no weapons or contraband are visible.

"Examining the mast now. Normal, Furuno radar. Wait a sec. Hello there!" He zoomed in on an egg-shaped object mounted on top of the mast. "I don't believe this comes with the standard package."

Sam and Ben both joined Simmons in gazing at the object. Finally, Sam broke the silence. "Assuming that's what's obscuring the radar image, how would it work?"

"I can think of several possibilities, Captain, but it's hard to figure anything that small containing the hardware needed. Suggest we file that one under 'maybe' and move on."

"Very well. Complete the survey, please."

"Yes, sir." Simmons returned to the screen. After a few minutes, he called out again, "Survey complete, Captain. We have good imaging of everything. Still only one person visible, a white male, age appears to be early twenties. No weapons visible."

"Very well. OOD, discontinue emissions control, take the radar off standby, and set an intercept course at ten knots. Who's up for Boarding Officer today?"

"Guerrero, sir."

"OOD, let's set the LE Bill, but I believe I'll let the XO earn some of his pay today. Once Hopkins relieves you, I want you to hang around and get a feel for the risk based on the pre-board interview. If you think you need to bump Lee and take the boat, I'll approve it."

"I'm sure she'll be fine, Captain."

"Thanks, carry on, please." Sam turned to the chart table. "Deffler, keep your eyes on that boat; sing out if anything changes. XO, Doctor, come with me, please." Sam led the way out to the Bridge wing, and Bondurant announced setting Law Enforcement stations over the PA system.

Turning around after closing the door, Sam addressed Simmons first. "Doctor, I am convinced that there's more to this boat than meets the eye. If he is carrying a load of drugs like the other boat, what's the probability your hyperspectral camera would pick up something?"

"Pretty much one hundred percent, Captain. Even sealed, the camera would pick up a trace. If a dog can smell it, the camera will see it."

"So, if they are not carrying a load, they would have no reason to mount a vigorous defense if we try to board them, correct?"

"It would be foolish of them, Captain. They know that you've reported in. Even if they took us out, they'd lose big time. We'd slap a terrorist label on them and anyone they associated with and, best case, that'd be game over for most of their revenue stream. Worst case, they know we have a history of pursuing cop-killers to the ends of the Earth. There's a remote chance this is some psycho they don't have a handle on, but that's unlikely. No, I believe this might be a pickup boat for moving product off the *High Dawn*. That presupposes this *is* their boat and not another rich kid out to get laid."

"Very well." Sam turned to Ben. "XO, I want you to take this one because you're up to speed on everything, and I need someone who can think on his feet. I want a thorough look inside, but I don't want this to get ugly. I wish we had a way to check for hidden compartments without knocking a bunch of holes in her."

"You've got it," Simmons interrupted. "I have a hand-held X-ray backscatter recorder among my gear I can lend Ben here."

"Doctor!" Sam smiled. "I may revise my opinion of you yet. Can you train this young man on its use in the next fifteen minutes?"

"It's switch-on, then point and shoot. You get the image in real-time, and it records." Simmons grinned. "Even an Ops Research grad can handle it."

Ben rolled his eyes. "Thanks, Doc."

"Don't mention it." Simmons winked. "Just don't drop it overboard, please. You wouldn't believe how expensive it is!"

"All right, XO, gear up, please." Sam nodded.

"Very good, sir. OK, Doc, let's get some tech on."

Sam

Hopkins had relieved Bondurant after *Kauai* had completed the turn toward the sailboat and came off emissions control. Williams manned radar and communications during law enforcement operations, allowing the OOD to focus on ship handling and safety. After a few minutes, a radar target track coinciding with the sailboat's bearing and range popped up on the SeaWatch system.

"Captain, OOD, they appear to have shut down their masker," Williams commented. "Range sixty-eight fifty and bearing consistent with the visual target."

"Very well. Now we know."

"Captain, I have a second POB coming up into the cockpit," Deffler called. "Appears to be female based on dress or <ahem> lack thereof. I, uh, do you want me to continue scanning and recording, sir?" he added, glancing at Hopkins and shifting on his stool.

Sam observed Hopkins turning away to hide an amused grin and suppressed one himself. "Yes, Deffler. They know we're here and watching. Your job is to maintain situational awareness— keep it so."

"WILCO, sir." Deffler wondered where the boundary between close observation and leering lay.

Sam caught Hopkins's eye and nodded to the starboard Bridge wing. Once out of sight and earshot, he turned to her and smiled.

"I appreciate you're enjoying the hell out of this, but I need him on the top of his game. In a minute or so, wander over and reassure him he's not looking at a sexual harassment violation."

Hopkins affected a downcast expression. "Aw gee, Captain, I never get to have any fun!"

Sam turned back and raised his binoculars to watch the sailboat. "Yes, it's the monstrous burden of command, so get used to it, Chief-to-be. Carry on, please."

"Yes, sir." Hopkins smiled and turned back inside.

****

After a briefing and instruction on the operation of the x-ray scanner, Ben and Simmons returned to the Bridge, the former wearing his boarding equipment and the latter in his personal body armor. They went straight to the chart table to check the UAV feed. The picture invoked a "Yowsa!" from Simmons and a stoic silence from Ben. There were still only two people visible on the boat: the male handling the wheel and the bikini-clad female lounging on the foredeck. *Kauai* had come around and paralleled the sailboat's course about two hundred yards distant.

"Any changes besides the fresh face?" Ben asked Deffler.

"No, sir. And I've had eyes on since you left."

"I bet you have!" Simmons quipped, drawing scowls from both men. After two seconds, he continued, "She's a bit underdressed, don't you think?"

"All right, knock it off," Ben said with irritation.

"No, I'm serious. It's cloudy and cool right now. Why walk around quasi-nude like that when she knows we're here?"

"Because she's a tease? How would I know?" Ben said.

"Think about it. The radar masker switches off, and she pops up on deck looking like a centerfold right afterward. The 'evade detection' plan didn't work, so it's on to Plan B. Be very careful over there, friend."

Ben gazed at Simmons's face and saw actual human concern. "I get what you mean. Thanks."

Ben turned and walked over to Sam. "Captain, I'm ready to begin the interview."

"Very well, XO. Carry on, please."

"Yes, sir." After setting the radio frequency to Maritime Channel 16, he picked up the handset. "Sailing Vessel *Sunrise Surprise II*, this is the United States Coast Guard, Channel 16, over." No response. Ben repeated the call with the same result. After two more unsuccessful attempts at contact, Ben hung up the handset. "No joy, Captain. Recommend close to one hundred yards and use the loudhailer."

"Very well. OOD, close to and maintain one hundred yards from the target vessel."

"Yes, sir," Hopkins replied and gave the orders. After they had closed the distance, she said, "Holding at one hundred yards, Captain."

"Very well," Sam replied and nodded to Ben.

Ben activated the loudspeakers. "Sailing Vessel *Sunrise Surprise II*, this is the United States Coast Guard. Contact me on VHF-FM Channel 16 immediately." After a brief pause, Ben repeated the hail and finally saw movement in the sailboat's cockpit.

"Coast Guard, *Sunrise Surprise*, what do you want?" said a male voice on the radio.

"*Sunrise Surprise II*. This is the Coast Guard. Reply with last and next port of call, please," Ben said into the radio handset, keeping his eyes on the vessel through his binoculars.

"And how is that any of your business, Coast Guard?"

Ben grimaced. "*Sunrise Surprise II*. This is the Coast Guard. You are a U.S. vessel sailing on the High Seas. The Coast Guard may make inquiries, examinations, and inspections and enforce federal law on all U.S. vessels on the High Seas. Now I'll ask again, and you will reply. What are your last and next ports of call? Over."

"Fine. We are out of Clearwater, heading for Key West."

"*Sunrise Surprise II*. This is the Coast Guard. Thank you. How many people do you have onboard? Over."

"That's it, Coast Guard, inquire into this!" said the voice with an accompanying gesture from the man in the sailboat cockpit.

Ben turned to Sam. "Captain?"

Sam nodded in return. "That's it, indeed. Pull him over, XO." He turned to Williams at his SeaWatch station. "Williams, start a Command Net chat with the Ops Center. Tell them we are preparing to board a less than-fully compliant US-flagged sailboat named *Sunrise Surprise II*, homeport Clearwater, FL, and give our position."

"Yes, sir."

Ben turned back and activated the blue flashing "law enforcement light," turned the siren on for ten seconds, then returned to the radio. "*Sunrise Surprise II*. This is the United States Coast Guard. You will stop your vessel immediately for boarding and inspection. Acknowledge, please, over."

After a pause, the voice replied, just as angrily, "I don't think I have to do that, Coast Guard!"

Ben took a breath, straightened up, and keyed the headset. "Captain, this is a lawful order, not a request. You will stop your vessel immediately and prepare to be boarded. Failure to comply violates U.S. law, which will make you subject to arrest and your vessel to seizure. Acknowledge, please."

Through the binoculars, Ben watched the woman on the foredeck jump up, sprint aft, and engage the man in a lively discussion. When Ben saw the man pull his arm back as if to strike her, he transmitted, "This is the Coast Guard. Acknowledge my last transmission!"

The man hesitated, then lowered his arm. "Fine, Coast Guard, I'm taking in the sails, but I'm also going to contact my lawyer over this!"

Ben turned to Sam. "Did you see that, sir?" Receiving a nod in return, Ben continued, "If you've no objection, I'd like Lee in the boarding party."

"Great minds, XO. By all means. Bondurant, I want you on Coxswain, please. You OK with Jenkins handling the crane for this one?"

"Absolutely, sir."

"Excellent. I think we're about done here. Go get your people ready." Bondurant saluted and departed, and Sam turned to Ben. "XO, this one will be tough. After seeing what that guy did, I get how you feel, but I'm sending you because I know I can count on you to keep hold of the big picture." Ben nodded, and Sam continued, "I'll back you whatever you decide to do, but make it solid. Don't let him goad you into a mistake. OK?"

"Captain, prepare for some world-class 'counting to ten' unless he makes another move at that woman or one of our people."

"Just right. Off you go—play it cool and play it safe."

"Very good, sir." Ben saluted and left.

Sam turned to see Simmons watching him from across the Bridge. When their eyes met, Simmons nodded, then returned to his work with the UAV. Sam returned to the window with his binoculars and addressed Hopkins, "Status, please, OOD."

Hopkins recognized the heightened concern Sam hid and replied in a quiet voice, "Captain, the target vessel has heaved to with sails furled. We are maintaining position one hundred yards north. The ship is at LE stations, awaiting launch request from the boat deck. UAV is performing covert overwatch at one thousand feet. District operations center has been advised and is standing by on Command Net chat." She gave a slight, sympathetic smile. "You have everything covered, sir."

Sam turned to Hopkins and smiled. "Thanks, Hoppy."

Ben

"Hey, XO, you slumming with the little people today?" Seaman Lopez joked. Another recent addition to the crew, Juan "Lope" Lopez was the senior among the non-rated crewman of the cutter's deck force. He was a Southern California native, hardworking, reliable, intelligent, and somewhat quiet, except, obviously, for the occasional joke. Lopez was waiting for a slot to open at the Maritime Law Enforcement Specialist School in Charleston, South Carolina, to fulfill his dream of becoming a full-fledged law enforcement officer.

"Well, Lope, I occasionally venture down to the nether reaches to see how the other 'haff' is getting by," Ben responded in his best upper-crust accent. After waiting for the chuckles to subside, he snapped into professional mode. "OK, guys, here's the deal. No weapons or contraband in sight, but keep your eyes open. As far as we know, only two people are on board, one male and one female. I've got this boarding because the master has a bug up his ass about stopping, much more than usual. We're still checking for safety and compliance, but I consider this a medium threat, so stay sharp. I think we will get a lot of abuse over there, but I want you to keep your cool and let me take it for you." He nodded toward Lee. "Shelley, the reason you're along instead of driving the RHIB is I think the female POB may be taking some physical abuse. I don't know for sure, but it looked close to that during the approach. I want you to evaluate and, if necessary, find out if she wants us to take her off."

"You've got it, sir." Lee nodded with a grim expression.

"Good. Don't push it. We're not relationship counselors, but if it seems like there's an actual problem, give me the high sign, and we'll deal with it. Finally, the female is wearing very brief swimwear. Do NOT get distracted," He gave Seaman Smith, the fourth boarding party member, and Lopez his sternest expression. "Copy?"

"Yes, sir," both men answered with slight smiles.

"Anybody have questions?" Ben asked.

"Yes, sir," Lee piped up, smiling now. "What's with the bag?"

"Ah, yes. Dr. Simmons has loaned me one of his toys. It's good at seeing through walls, so I can get a peek without drilling holes if there are any hidden compartments. Let's keep that to ourselves, please. I don't want to stir this guy up any more than he already is. Any other questions?" Seeing nothing but shaking heads, Ben concluded, "OK, let's do it. Remember, stay cool and see something say something." He turned to Bondurant. "Boats, we're ready when you are."

"OK, XO, everybody, follow me," Bondurant said, stepping into RHIB alongside the rail and up to the center console. The rest of the boat's crew and the boarding party followed, and when they were secure, Bondurant gave a thumbs-up to Jenkins at the boat crane control and announced, "Ready for launch."

"Bridge, Boat Deck, RHIB is manned and ready for launch," Jenkins said into his headset. After a moment, he said, "Cleared for launch, swinging out." After moving the boat clear of the side, he lowered it to the water. He watched Bondurant start the engine and then veer off toward the sailboat. "Boat away, Boat OK," Jenkins transmitted as he recovered the cable.

Bondurant brought the RHIB around the sailboat, with everyone onboard alert for anything suspicious. The sailboat's two occupants were sitting on the deck forward of the cockpit, having mustered reluctantly at Ben's request over the radio. Satisfied, Bondurant looked at Ben, "Looks OK, XO."

"Right. We'll board on the stern steps aft of the cockpit. Smith, you're first. Get on board and cover the rest of us. Lee, you're second. Head to the bow and cover from there. I'll go next, and you bring up the rear, Lopez. I'll do the standard walkabout to check the lights and stuff, and then I'll head below with the camera. Lopez, I'll have my hands full with that, so I want you to stay in sight and cover me. Silent routine, everybody, unless you see something. Let's get a discreet radio check, please. Lee?" Lee responded by clicking her transmitter twice <click, click>. "Smith?" <click, click>. "Lopez?" <click, click>. "OK, Boats, we're ready to go in."

Bondurant swung the RHIB in a wide loop and brought it to a stop with the center console, even with the boarding step. Ben said, "Now." All four boarding team members were on board and moving to their positions within five seconds, and Bondurant backed the RHIB out to a safety and cover station. Ben stepped up to the male passenger and announced, "Captain, I am Lieutenant Junior Grade Benjamin Wyporek of the United States Coast Guard. I am here to conduct a safety and compliance inspection. Thank you for your cooperation, and we hope to have you on your way shortly. Before we start, I need to confirm that you two are the only ones on board, correct?"

"Correct," came the curt reply.

"Thank you. Is either of you carrying any weapons right now? Sir?" The male shook his head in response, and Ben turned to the woman. "Ma'am?" The woman looked up and shook her head. The expressionless face behind narrow sunglasses and the absence of any marks on what was a mostly uncovered body made Ben question his original concerns about abuse. He looked at Lee, who arched an eyebrow, shook her head slightly, and then turned back to watch the woman. "Thank you. Sir, I'll need to check your registration and your IDs. Where might I find them, please?"

"They're all in the Nav drawer. I'll show you...." The man started to get up.

"Sir," Ben held up his hand. "I need you to stay where you are, please. I can find them if you tell me where to look."

"Fine. In the drawer under the main panel."

"Thank you. Wait here, please." Ben ducked into the cockpit, found the drawer under a panel of switches, and located the boat's registration certificate and two driver's licenses. He noted the registration lined up with the description and display numbers on the boat and passed the names, addresses, and driver's license numbers to Williams to check out, although they appeared correct. Several life jackets were sitting beside the door to the main cabin. Check. Ben found the switch labeled "NAV LTS" on the panel, flipped them on, and then popped back out of the cockpit. Once on deck with an unobstructed view of the subjects, Ben nodded to Lee. "Lee, can you check the nav lights, please?"

Lee nodded in reply and glanced at the boat's navigation lights. "Port nav light on and correct, starboard nav light on and correct, sir."

Ben checked the functionality of the stern light himself, then flipped the switch off. Check. Popping up to the deck, he addressed the man, "I will need to go down into the cabin to check your sanitation device and test for fuel vapors, sir. Are there any hazards I should beware of, slippery decks, that sort of thing?"

"You're not going to be poking around our stuff without me down there," the man said with increasing menace.

"Sir, I will need you to stay on deck here while I complete the check for your safety and mine."

"Like hell, you fucking fascist!" The man jumped up and stepped forward.

Ben stepped backward, putting his right hand on his sidearm, holding up his left hand, and announcing, "Stop there, sir!" He noted that the other boarding party members had drawn their Tasers and held them behind their backs. "Now stay exactly where you are, please," he continued. Ben locked eyes with the man, who had stopped, his hands shaking at his sides. "Hey, I get this isn't how you want to spend your day, but when I step aboard a vessel, my duty is to conduct a complete inspection. This includes checking for safety and sanitation compliance, for which I *will* need to go down below. Mister, I will do my duty. While that's going on, you can sit quietly right there or sit in restraints on board that big white boat. What's it going to be?"

The man stood silently for a few more moments, holding Ben's gaze with clear hatred. Then the woman made a throat-clearing sound. The man glanced at her briefly and sat down. "Fine, but you'll be hearing from my lawyer."

"That is your prerogative, sir, and thank you again for your cooperation." He scanned at the other boarding party members and gave the "hold in place" signal, receiving a nod from each. Ben returned to the cockpit and picked up the bag, waiting until he was out of sight to pull out the backscatter scanner. After a brief tour around the cabin, he activated the device and recorder as Simmons had shown him and began scanning the bulkheads and decks. He spent a few minutes going through mundane items like stored clothing and foodstuffs, then came upon an image of an oddly shaped electronic device behind a forward panel. Several circuit panels and other solid-state components were visible, along with a cable leading to the mast. He directed the scan beneath the device, looking for other components and connections, and his heart nearly stopped.

The image on the screen showed, below and disconnected from the device, four brick-shaped objects connected by wires to a smaller, cell phone-sized object. Pretty much how you would expect a bomb to appear.

Ben shut down the scanner and took a few deep breaths. If this was a bomb, it could explode when he opened a panel or disturbed something else in the cabin. It could also have a remote trigger worked by a sailboat crewmember or be on a timer running down right now. Ben carefully retraced his steps to the after part of the cabin and keyed his microphone. "Everybody stay real steady and silent and take a breath." He paused briefly. "There appears to be an explosive device fixed to the hull. We will do a coordinated takedown of both POBs in case one of them has a remote detonator. I need Smith to step behind the male POB and Lee to stay where you are behind the female. When I step out of the cabin and get their attention, bring up your Tasers. If either of them so much as twitches before I get them cuffed, you tase them immediately. Lee, you take the female. Acknowledge silently, please."

Two clicks sounded in his headset.

"Smith, you stay on the male, acknowledge," Ben said, receiving two clicks.

"Lopez, I want you to step down into the cockpit and draw your sidearm, but keep it at your side and out of sight. If a POB gets away from a tasing, you take them down, acknowledge."

"Click, click." Through the open cabin door, he watched Lopez step down slowly into the cockpit, then draw and charge his pistol, careful to keep it low and beyond the view of the main deck. "OK, guys, I'm coming up now. Standby." Ben secured the scanner in its bag, then stepped into the cockpit to Lopez's left. He gathered himself, stepped up onto the main deck, and announced, "Ma'am, Sir, I need your attention, please." Both turned to him, and he paused briefly while Lee and Smith brought their Tasers to the ready. "I am sorry, but I have to place you under arrest for...."

At this moment, the woman growled and lunged forward, the move followed instantly by the pop and buzz of Lee's Taser and the woman crying out. The man's arms shot over his head. "Don't shoot! Please don't shoot!"

Lee was already fastening handcuffs on the stunned woman, and Ben did the same for the now-crying man while Smith covered him with the Taser. Ben nodded at Lopez, who holstered his pistol and came up to take over. Satisfied the two people were safely subdued, Ben keyed his microphone. "*Kauai-One*, LE-One, return at once for pickup of six. Break, Break, *Kauai*, LE-One, over."

"LE-One, *Kauai*, report," Sam's voice responded.

"*Kauai*, LE-One, I have detected what I believe is an explosive device concealed in the hull. I have placed the POBs under arrest, and we are evacuating now. I had to order non-lethal on the female POB, over."

"LE-One, *Kauai-One*, this is *Kauai* actual, do not acknowledge, cease all transmissions, carry out evacuation, and return to ship."

"Radios off, everybody, and don't touch anything," Ben ordered, turning to see the RHIB approaching the sailboat's stern. "Smith, you go in first and keep overwatch. Grab the scanner bag on the way and treat it *carefully*, please. Lopez, you help Lee with her prisoner and board next. I'll follow with this man. Board as soon as it's safe."

"Don't hurt me, please!" The man's voice was pleading and markedly different from the arrogant prick of minutes before. "It's her, not me. I was just hired to drive the boat! It's her, man!"

Ben shook his arm, "Quiet! I'll hear what you have to say when we get aboard the cutter. Zip it until then!"

When Bondurant nudged the RHIB to the cockpit steps, Smith jumped aboard with the scanner bag, followed by Lee and Lopez carrying the semi-conscious, handcuffed woman between them. Ben tugged the cuffed man to his feet and led him to the RHIB, holding him upright as he stumbled on board. "OK, Boats, let's go," Ben said and sat beside his prisoner.

Bondurant nodded and eased the engine control back, pulling the RHIB away from the sailboat. He slammed the control forward at twenty-five feet of distance, turning toward the cutter as the boat picked up speed. After half a minute, he pulled alongside *Kauai*, preparing for the hoist back on board.

Sam stood at the ladder's base with arms folded when the RHIB hoisted even with the main deck. "Well done, XO!" He clapped Ben on his shoulder. "You and your people OK?" Sam's expression showed deep concern.

"My heartbeat is back below a hundred, I'm happy to say, and the rest are fine." Ben smiled. "How do we handle these two, sir?"

Sam's face relaxed, and he whispered to Ben, "Let's split them up. I want them both under armed guard and manacled at all times. Doc is standing by in female berthing to check the woman out, after which I want her strip-searched. Have Lee do that. I'll have Bondurant relieve Hoppy so she can help."

"Yes, sir. I'll have Smith take the other one to non-rate berthing with Guerrero to do the same. Our tough guy crapped himself when I mentioned the bomb on board, so the strip search won't be fun."

Sam grinned back. "It'll be excellent practice for when they have their own kids."

"Yuk, and you can quote me on that, sir," Ben stepped aside when Lee and Lopez approached with the still-staggering female. "I guess we won't need your counseling skills after all, Shelley."

"Ya think, sir?" she puffed as they stumbled past.

After they passed, Sam asked, "Now, what did you see?"

"I'm pretty sure I saw the masker, or whatever you call it. It's behind the paneling in the berthing area. Didn't see much, a general shape and features that make it appear electronic with a cable leading to the mast. The bomb is right under it. It looks like four M112s strung together with a small box that I'm guessing is the detonator. There might be others. I beat-feet when I saw that one."

"Good call—five pounds of C4 would have done the job for sure. Simmons put in a call for their bomb disposal team on alert up at MacDill Air Force Base and a relief prize crew to take custody of the boat afterward. The sector folks will bring them out in a Medium Response Boat as soon as they get down here. In the meantime, we stand by at a safe distance. We're back on emissions control until we get a safe signal from the bomb techs. Let's get the interrogations done ASAP. I want to offload the prisoners on the sector boat."

"Yes, sir. You want me to handle both?"

"Yes, but break off when the boat arrives. You'll need to brief the bomb techs on what you found and where."

"Yes, sir." Ben looked down. "About that, sir, it could have gone badly without the scanner the Doc loaned us." His head came up eye-to-eye with Sam. "He didn't have to, you know. I don't imagine his bosses would be too keen over him sharing the details on that thing, much less letting me haul it around on a chancy boarding."

"Yes, I get that," Sam said with a wry grin. "I find myself on the horns of a dilemma—deeply grateful to him you're safe, while I'd personally get a big lift out of throwing his ass overboard. I suppose I must lean on the net positive and try to tolerate him for the sake of the mission."

"You remain an unyielding source of strength and inspiration to me, Captain. I'll do my best to keep him out of your hair."

"Do that." Sam turned back to the ladder to head up to the Bridge.

Defusing

**USCG Cutter *Kauai*, Gulf of Mexico, nineteen nautical miles northeast of Key West, Florida
12:02 EST, 16 January**

Ben

As Ben approached the Female Berthing room, Bryant pulled him aside. "I completed the check-over of the female detainee, sir. She's not showing any aftereffects of the tasing, a couple of bruises when she went down, but nothing actionable. However..."

"However?" Ben asked with raised eyebrows.

"However, we need to be very careful with this one, and by careful, I mean armed guard out of reach. I've seen this type before in Iraq and Afghanistan."

"Suicide bomber? Must be one hell of a bomb vest."

"No, sir." Bryant shook his head. "This is the type that recruits and launches suicide bombers, smiles at you until you turn your back, and then...," He drew his finger across his throat. "I got these out of her hair and a fake scar on her hip." He held up an evidence bag with two needle-like metal objects.

"A *fake* scar? No way!"

"Way. New one for me too, believe it or not. Fortunately, Doc Simmons briefed me on what to watch for before I started. I hope you don't mind, sir, but I told Shelley and Hoppy to hold off on the strip search. She might be hiding stuff where I can't go, and honestly, they're not trained to find what she might have. I promise you she's not secreting explosives or a detonator anywhere, and that should do until she's ashore with the intel guys. In the meantime, she's double-cuffed, wrists and ankles around the bed frame, and I strongly recommend you NOT uncuff her before the marshals arrive."

"OK, thanks Doc." Ben shook his head. "Between bombs and spies, this place is getting hazardous to my health."

"On that subject, XO, when are you coming down for your prelims?" Bryant asked, his face empty of expression.

"All this, and you're still hung up on my physical?"

"Yup. This is what I do, sir."

"OK, OK, let's set it up during the next home port stop."

"OK, sir. But I *will* hold you to that," Bryant said, turning away.

Ben turned to the door of the berthing area and knocked, announcing, "XO."

Hopkins opened the door and stood aside as Ben entered the small room. The female detainee sat on the bottom bunk, arms and legs encircling the corner post with her hands and ankles zip tied. She now wore a set of prisoner coveralls over her brief swimwear and canvas shoes. She was stunningly beautiful and turned to Ben with long dark brown hair and deep blue, almond-shaped eyes that should have been attractive, but chilled him to the bone. The moment reminded him of a tiger he once shared a stare-down with through a zoo window. Hopkins and Lee stood in opposite corners of the room, out of reach of the prisoner. Ben looked at Hopkins. "Anything?" Receiving a head shake in return, he turned to Lee. "Lee?"

"Nothing that I would share in mixed company, sir," Lee replied, keeping her eyes on the prisoner.

"OK. Miss," He glanced at the ID taken from the sailboat—Laura Treblinsky. "Treblinsky. Did I pronounce that right?" Ben paused, received the same cold, silent glare, and continued reading from the "Miranda Crib Card" boarding officers carried with them. "Ms. Treblinsky, I have placed you under arrest on suspicion of violating Title 18, United States Code, Section 844. You have the right to remain silent. If you give up that right, anything you say can and will be used against you in a court of law. You have a right to an attorney and have them present whenever you are questioned. If you cannot afford to hire an attorney, one will be appointed to represent you before questioning if you wish. You may decide at any time to exercise these rights and not answer any questions or make any statements. Do you understand these rights I have explained to you?" Silence. "Having these rights in mind, would you wish to talk to me about these charges?"

The woman's icy stare remained fixed. "Lawyer."

Ben returned the blankest expression he could muster. "Am I to understand that you do not want to answer questions or make a statement without an attorney present?"

A half-smile appeared on the woman's face. "You're not as stupid as you appear, *Lieutenant Junior Grade*. Now, why don't you just fuck off and take the dykes with you? I don't like how the short one is undressing me with her eyes."

Ben turned toward Lee with a raised eyebrow. "My goodness, Petty Officer Lee! You aren't undressing the prisoner with your eyes, are you?"

"Definitely not, sir," Lee smiled, patting her Taser. "Just hoping for a reason to give her another zap."

Ben turned back to the woman. "See, no offense meant. Ms. Treblinsky, I regret our efforts do not seem to rise to your expectations, but you'll be glad to know that your stay with us will end shortly. I'll be stepping out to interview your companion, but if you change your mind about talking, one of these petty officers can fetch me."

The smile on the woman's face became broader and, if possible, colder. "Not happening, *dick*!"

Ben smiled, nodded to the petty officers, then turned to the prisoner. "Good afternoon, ma'am," he said, then turned and stepped through the door, closing it behind him. Simmons waited out of sight beyond the door. Ben looked at him and shook his head. "Holy Shit, Doc! What the hell is *that*?"

"Friend, my educated guess is *that* is a Next-Generation Sparrow, formerly of the Russian SVR, now working either freelance or full time for our TCO foes. You can bet on that ID being bogus. We'll see if her biometrics pop when we get her back ashore." He glanced back at the door to the berthing area. "Will your people be OK in there?"

"Worry about her," Ben replied as they turned toward the mess deck. "They both understand the situation, and if she makes a move or does anything off-key...." He snapped his fingers. "They'll take her down or out, as needed. Like I said, family."

"Gotcha. You know, my people would just keep her knocked out until we had her in a secure facility."

"Must be nice. We still have to play by the rules here."

Simmons smiled back sadly. "Yes, I don't envy you guys. I watched your CO having to send you in with one hand tied behind your back this morning—it was eating him up."

Ben stopped and faced him. "Good. Keep that in mind. Doc, I get that you have an important mission, and you're focused on that. I'm grateful to you for sharing the scanner. It probably saved our lives. But you're still in the hole with me for the crap you pulled on him yesterday. He's the best man I've ever known. Get it? We're the good guys here. Make us want to trust you."

"Touché. I'm genuinely sorry about that. I was furious at him for being so obstinate without considering that he did not understand the stakes—very poor judgment on my part. At least now you guys are in on everything, and I can stop being so cagey. May I ask the favor of a clean slate?"

"I'll grant it, but that's just me, and it doesn't automatically extend to the captain. He's down with the mission, but I'd keep my distance when possible if I were you."

"Thanks for the consideration and advice." Simmons nodded, extending a hand that Ben shook. "I'll try to keep on the undark side of the force. OK, let's interrogate the Cowardly Lion."

Clarence "Hawk" Rodin, the male detainee, was as effusive in his interview as "Laura" was reticent in hers. Ben had to threaten to gag him to enable reading his rights and offered him the Miranda Waiver, which he readily signed. Rodin was an itinerant deckhand on yachts in the Tampa area. The most beautiful woman he had ever seen approached him and paid a fantastic amount of money to captain the *Sunrise Surprise II* wherever she needed. When they sighted the approaching Coast Guard cutter, she had offered him a fifty percent bonus on top of non-monetary benefits to make like one of the rich assholes who typically hired him. She hoped he would intimidate the boarding officer into moving along without thoroughly searching the boat. He insisted the display of the physical threat during the interview was part of the scam. Knowing they weren't carrying any drugs—he'd checked, and who carries drugs *south*, anyway—he jumped at the opportunity.

Ben wrapped up the interview when the word passed the Sector Key West boat had arrived. As Ben and Simmons moved toward the main deck, Simmons asked, "What do you think?"

Ben shook his head. "He's either the greatest actor of our times or a complete doofus. They might charge him with accessory on 844, but it'd be a stretch to prove. He keeps cooperating, and he'll probably walk."

Simmons nodded. "That was my sense, perfect patsy."

"I guess we'll see. I'm not sure of anything on this crazy mission." They walked out on the main deck as the sector boat moored alongside *Kauai*. Within two minutes, the bomb disposal team leader climbed the ladder onto the main deck, followed by his deputy. He recognized Simmons and crossed over with a smile and hand outstretched.

"Pete, goddammit, I might have known you were hip deep in this one!" he said as they shook hands.

"Chief, it's great to see you; sorry it's about work." Simmons smiled back. He gestured to Ben. "Matt Kemper, Chief EOD Technician, U.S. Navy, Retired, this is Lieutenant J.G. Ben Wyporek. He's XO here and found the bomb."

Kemper shook Ben's hand. "Glad to meet you, sir, and that you're still in one piece." He turned to his subordinate. "This is Ken Davis, my deputy, and the man who'll be going after the device if we take it on."

As they finished shaking hands with Davis, Simmons asked, "Matt, you guys got on the scene in a hurry. Were you down here already?"

"No, a stroke of luck. When the call came, the Coasties had a Herc in the training pattern at MacDill. They full-stopped on the next landing to pick us up. An hour later, we're rolling off at Boca

Chica. You must have juice. It would have taken a week to get a lift from the Transportation Command."

"Yeah, we're saving the world, one sailboat at a time."

"Dedication, very inspiring." Kemper nodded. "Now, tell me about this bomb."

The four men retired to the mess deck. Simmons replayed the video capture from the scanner, and Ben described the sailboat's interior in detail. Kemper nodded and asked the occasional question. He pulled up his laptop and opened two files. "We got these plan views from Marlow Hunter, showing the basic design of the boat and some options. Lieutenant, which one looks closest to you?"

Ben scrutinized the three plans, trying to translate the lines on the screen to what he remembered seeing on the boat. Finally, he pointed at one drawing. "That one is closest."

Kemper nodded. "Alrighty then. The robot can't complete the disarm. We'd need the big one, and there isn't room to maneuver it. I'll send the mini in to drill holes and get a good peek with the camera. Then we can weigh the risks." He turned to Simmons. "Pete, I gotta tell you I will need powerful persuadin' before sending one of my guys in that box to clip wires."

Simmons nodded. "Chief, we're sure that rig's a self-destruct for some new stealth technology that we really need to get our hands on. We've seen it work—that boat was invisible to this cutter's radar until they switched it off."

Kemper whistled and shared a glance with Davis. "OK, you're on. If it looks like we can take it after the close inspection, we'll try it. Now, Lieutenant, you said the woman was making a move when you took her down. Did it seem like she was going for a detonator?"

"I thought so. She could have been reaching for a weapon or taking a shot at knocking me overboard for all we know. By that point, I didn't want my people sitting on top of a bomb while I went searching for answers."

"Definitely the right call, sir." Kemper nodded. "We will send Wally the robot in for a scan around the top deck to find what she was so eager to grab. Pete, I like this scanner of yours, and we will have one of those 'tater-to-taters' about that when we finish here.

Howsomever, I would like to use it for a top to bottom on that boat before we go. Are you down for that?"

"I'll even run it for you if you're sure it won't set the thing off."

"Naw, if it was sensitive, the Lieutenant would've set it off." Kemper winked at Ben and smiled. "These things are a compromise between doing the job and making sure it doesn't trip on you before you need it to do the job. That means they're rarely that sensitive. The last thing these guys want is for this gizmo to self-detonate when the boat bumps into a buoy or sails past a destroyer with the fire-control radar energized."

The four men continued the discussion for another twenty minutes. They completed a plan of action, after which the two bomb technicians made their way back to the sector boat. Simmons and Ben walked forward to exchange some gear. While they walked, Ben inquired, "Doc, I'm at a loss, but I didn't want to come across as a newbie. What's a 'tater-to-tater'?"

Simmons chuckled. "Matt Kemper is not just one of the best bomb disposal experts in the world. He can spin eggcorns and malaprops that would put Yogi Berra to shame. He meant 'tête-à-tête.'"

Ben laughed as much from the release of tension as the joke. "That one's going into the hall of fame!"

****

Much to the relief of Hopkins, Lee, and Sam, the sector boat also brought three members of the Marshal's Service to take custody of the prisoners. Once they were signed over, the women returned to work.

Shortly afterward, Sam and Ben stood together on the Bridge wing, watching the RHIB maneuver slowly around the *Sunrise Surprise II,* while Simmons and the two bomb technicians performed x-ray scans in the preliminary survey. Sam preferred not to expose any of his crew, but the response boat was as large as the sailboat and too heavy for the close work needed. Ben glanced at the afterdeck to see Bondurant watching the operation intently. Bondurant had been preparing to take the sortie himself when Lee walked up and reminded him *she* was supposed to be coxswain today. The sight of the diminutive Lee standing on her toes to press home her point to her full-foot-taller superior had evoked a broad smile from Ben. Lee's blood was up after a two-hour faceoff with the hostile and dangerous prisoner, and she was not settling for standing around quietly afterward. Bondurant eventually raised his hands in surrender and stepped back with a smile as Lee donned her helmet and led the crew and three passengers aboard the RHIB.

"*Kauai, Kauai-One*, external scanning complete, no other devices visible. Request approach outboard of response boat for passenger transfer. Over," Lee's voice came over the radio. Sam turned to Hopkins and nodded.

"*Kauai-One, Kauai*, cleared for approach and moor outboard of response boat," Hopkins responded.

"*Kauai, Kauai-One*, roger, out." The RHIB swung away from the sailboat and settled on a course back to the Coast Guard boats. A short distance away, Lee turned the RHIB's heading almost parallel to the two connected vessels and then slowed it to a soft bump and stop against the sector boat. The boat seaman and engineer fastened lines to the larger vessel's deck cleats, after which Lee turned to Simmons and the two bomb technicians and said, "Go!" After the three men had scrambled onto the sector boat, Lee shouted, "Let go!" Her two crewmen unhitched and retrieved the lines. A brief thirty-five seconds after contacting the sector boat, the RHIB swung clear to take up its rescue station between the cutter and the sailboat.

Simmons and Kemper shook hands with Davis aboard the sector boat and then climbed the ladder to *Kauai*'s main deck while the latter remained behind. After dropping off the scanner, they walked to the Bridge to confer with Ben and Sam. The sector boat headed for the sailboat with Davis and the robot.

Kemper set up his laptop on the chart table, opened his communication module, and set it to speaker mode. "Okay, Ken, we're set up. Light off when ready."

"Roger, Boss, coming on now."

Two windows popped on the laptop screen. "Gentlemen, welcome to Wally-vision," Kemper announced. "The top screen is the wide-angle scanning camera, the lower left is the fore/aft chassis cameras, and the lower right is for the scope camera." He leaned over the comms module and said, "Long view looks good, Ken. Let's check the close-in."

The wide-angle camera was obscured, then quickly refocused on Davis's comically twisted face. "How's this?"

Kemper smiled. "Good resolution of some major butt-ugly. Make it stop, please!" The picture returned to a distant view of the sailboat. "Ah, much better." He hit the mute button. "For luck, we like to start all our ops with a little levitation." Sam's mouth opened and closed silently, Ben turned away to hide a smile, and Simmons stared back, completely poker-faced.

The picture became jerky as the sector boat pulled alongside the sailboat, and Davis and one of the boat crewmen lifted the robot aboard. "Wally's onboard. We're pulling back fifty meters," Davis called through the comms module. "OK, in position, beginning wide scan."

The plan had the robot survey the top deck of the sailboat and secure anything resembling a detonator. Davis would return briefly to move the robot down to the sailboat's cabin since it couldn't "climb down" independently. After closely inspecting the bomb with the robot's cameras, Kemper would decide whether Davis could risk a hands-on disarm.

The robot's pass on the top deck found a canvas bag with objects resembling a pen and a cell phone. Kemper held his breath as these were deposited in the robot's lead-lined steel holding box. If either was broadcasting a continuous signal, the box would interrupt it and detonate the bomb. The box snapped shut. "No boom. I guess we're still in business." Kemper smiled. "OK, Ken, move in for repositioning."

The sector boat returned to the sailboat, and Davis and the seaman carried the robot down to the cabin level. The sector boat had pulled back to a safe distance, and the robot repeated the inspection process in the cabin.

Finally, the moment of truth arrived, and the robot stopped in front of the panel concealing the bomb. Davis had the robot drill a hole in the panel and insert the articulating camera to look inside. After a thorough interior inspection of the entire panel and seams for booby traps, Davis turned the camera on the bomb.

"Boss, it seems like they're playing it safe with this one—nothing hinky in sight. I am OK doing the clip."

"Stand by, Ken." Kemper selected mute on the comms module and turned to Simmons. "Pete, you and I know Ken can't work in there in the Bomb Suit. We'll be mopping him up with a sponge if this goes south. I need convincin' this is a no-shit national security deal and not some egghead science project."

Simmons locked eyes with Kemper. "Matt, I've been there. I know what I'm asking Ken to do, and I'd do the job myself if I could handle it. It's a big ask, but we've got to get hold of that masker."

Kemper held the stare for another ten seconds, then turned back to the comm module. "Ken, you are cleared to go. If anything goes one nanometer out of whack, you run like hell, clear?"

"Roger, Boss, you don't have to tell me twice. See you later."

"Not if I see you first. Good luck, whackjob." Kemper punched the mute button again. "We'll be going radio silent until he's done, just to play it extra safe. Nothing left but sit back and listen to the noise in my brain," Kemper said with a wry smile. As if on cue, the video feed from the robot cut off.

"Can we bring you up a mug of coffee or something, Chief?" Sam asked.

"No, thanks, Captain." Kemper stood up and closed the laptop. "I may take you up on that later. Excuse me, please, sir." He picked up the comms module and walked out onto the Bridge wing to watch the operation.

Ben asked Simmons, "On the other side? You've done this yourself?"

"Yes, I have a few times." Simmons nodded. "In the field, sometimes you're your own bomb disposal. I'm still breathing because Matt was talking me through the other end of the phone. I'd rather be the one working the bomb than have his job." He nodded toward Sam and started outside to join Kemper. "Your CO knows what it's like, I'm sure." He walked out silently to stand by Kemper and put his hand on his friend's shoulder.

Ben and Sam shared a look and followed.

****

"All safe, Boss," Davis's voice came over the comms module. "And I did another sweep. No surprises."

Holding the rail, Kemper put his head down for a few seconds, then stood up straight and pressed the transmit button. "Roger, pack it up. First one at Willie T's is on me." He turned to Simmons. "Your show now, brother."

"Thanks, Matt. Next time we catch up, I'm buying for everybody."

"You better believe it." Kemper nodded and turned to Sam. "Captain, that coffee offer still good?"

"Definitely." Sam offered his hand. "Dr. Simmons can show you to the mess deck. I need to stick around here, so I'll bid you a safe journey now."

Kemper shook his hand firmly. "Thanks, Captain. You've got a wonderful ship and crew here." He turned and followed Simmons down.

Sam turned to Hopkins. "OOD, recall the RHIB, please. We might as well get it stowed before the sector boat comes back."

"Yes, sir," Hopkins responded and continued inside the Bridge.

Within an hour, the makeshift conclave broke up. In the freshening westerly breeze, the *Sunrise Surprise II* was under sail, heading north for MacDill Air Force Base in Tampa. The sector boat with the prisoners and bomb disposal team motored down to Key West. *Kauai* headed southeast for the next round of reconnaissance. Sam had agreed to launch the Puma for a short sortie and quick surveillance of Resolution Key, the next on their list.

The aircraft returned a little before sunset, and Simmons had asked for a meeting with Sam and Ben afterward. The three men retired to Sam's cabin and gathered around Simmons's laptop for the discussion. "Captain, I need to ask if we can go ashore on Resolution Key tomorrow morning."

"I don't see that as a problem, Doctor. As I recall, there's good water to the west of the island's northern tip. Did the Puma turn up something?"

"It's probably nothing, but there appears to be human activity up there—a small shack with signs of recent habitation. If someone is there, I'd like to talk to them."

"Um, don't you think if somebody is there and they saw something, they would report it?" Ben asked.

"Think about someone who would live in those conditions and ask yourself if you believe they might fit that old cliché of 'because you didn't ask.' It's a long shot, but we need to check all the boxes on this."

"I agree, Doctor." Sam nodded. "Plan on taking the XO and Seaman Lopez with you. I want the Puma to do a security sweep and then maintain an overwatch while you are ashore. I don't expect trouble, but I'm into playing it safe these days. Once you're done, it can continue the recon. When we break up here, please sit down with Hoppy and Fritz and gin up one of your geeky-mathy optimized Op Plans for tomorrow. I'm sure the Doctor here would appreciate our trying to make up some time we lost today."

"That I would. Thank you, sir." Simmons smiled.

"Okay, this was quite a day." Sam sat back, scratching his close-cropped hair. "XO, before you get head-down with Ops and Air, I'd like you to do a wellness check of the rest of your boarding party. The adrenaline's worn off by now, and they might be a touch wound up. I'd do it, but the only answer I can get when I ask how someone's doing is 'Awesome, sir!' I figure they'll be a little franker with you than they'd be with the Old Man."

"Yes, sir." Ben nodded.

"Holler if I need to pitch in."

"Awesome, sir!"

"Dismissed, wiseass!" Sam threw a crumpled ball of paper in Ben's direction as he and a grinning Simmons stepped out the cabin door.

Reconnaissance—Sea

USCG Cutter *Kauai*, Gulf of Mexico, Off Resolution Key, Florida
07:56 EST, 17 January

Ben

Kauai idled a quarter-mile off the northern tip of Resolution Key, with Lee putting in a turn as the OOD. This morning, the driving was dull, occasionally goosing the idling engines to hold position and heading in the calm air and slow current. A small shack and a beat-up old pickup truck were visible on their arrival. An older man in a straw hat had emerged carrying fishing gear when the Puma completed its circuit and assumed overwatch. The man waved on seeing the cutter, then began fishing on the chair. Satisfied there was no apparent hazard, Sam had green-lighted the launch of the RHIB to put Ben, Simmons, and Lopez ashore for an investigation.

Bondurant was the coxswain of record this morning, but Jenkins was breaking in for landing operations. Landing operations could be tricky, and Bondurant would never pass up an opportunity to give his junior boatswain hands-on training. Ben, Simmons, and Lopez were sitting forward, ready to jump off when it nudged the shore. They were landing one hundred yards from the shack to avoid disrupting its resident's fishing and get a look at the ground. Bondurant whispered coaching instructions as

Jenkins steered into a soft bump when the prow touched bottom. The three passengers turned and, getting a thumbs up from Jenkins, jumped into the shallow water. The boat floated free, and Jenkins backed it off the beach.

As they waded ashore, Simmons said, "Your man is settling down nicely. That was only the second most thorough safety brief I've ever had."

As the coastguardsmen smiled, Ben replied, "Yes, we're riding the asymptote down to the 'Yeah, blah-blah, don't get hurt' version."

Simmons chuckled and then stopped, scanning the sand inland of the high tide ridge. "Hang on a minute, guys. Check out these impressions." He crouched down and peered hard, tilting his head back and forth. "What do you think?"

Ben shrugged silently, but Lopez spoke, "The track is too wide for that Toyota." He nodded toward the pickup truck. "More like a big SUV or Hummer. They dismounted there and walked to the tide line. From the tracks, I'd say two, maybe three guys."

"Yes, indeed!" Simmons responded, with Ben looking at Lopez in surprise. "Notice the vehicle tracks move inland instead of toward the shack. Let's file that one away." He turned and continued toward the shack, Ben and Lopez following.

"Lope, I never considered you the Sherlock Holmes type," Ben said.

"You should update yourself, XO. Doyle's great, but Deaver and Cornwell are the thing for modern detecting. Back in LA, a police detective and his wife took me on in the foster program. He turned me onto the books and took me on some ride-alongs. It stuck."

"Steer me to some good ones when we get back to Miami." Ben looked over at the shack as they started toward it. The old gentleman was seated in a beach chair under a canopy extending from the front. He had his straw hat off in the shade, and Ben guessed his age to be between sixty-five and seventy, with long, scraggly gray-white hair and an equally pale walrus mustache. The older man saw his gaze and waved, which Ben and Lopez returned.

"Gud'day fellers!" the old man said with a smile as they approached. "Whadda y'at?"

"Um, good morning, sir," Ben began as he tried to place the accent he heard. "I'm Lieutenant Junior Grade Ben Wyporek, U.S. Coast Guard, and these are my associates: Seaman Juan Lopez and Investigator Doug Pearson. We're investigating a boat accident around here a week ago and wondered if you might have seen anything."

"Oh, I bin round since just after Boxing Day." The older man nodded. "I always come down dis time a'year to warm up in me pally's place here. Pally and me swap—he comes up for a break in me cabin when it's burnin' hot down here, and I come down when it's cold enough to skin ya up home. Yup, I was out here a week back, didn't see nuttin'. A few fish cops come round in a big SUV, but dem's the only folk I seen. No boats, no time except yours dare," he said, nodding toward *Kauai.*

"Sir, you're from Canada, I take it?"

"*Newfoundland*, 'Olyrood." The man huffed up.

"Sorry, sir, no offense meant. Do you mind if I see your passport, please?"

"It's on de cuddy inside de door." The man pointed. "I hopes you don want my arse outta dis nice chair right now?"

"No, sir, if you don't mind, Seaman Lopez will peek in and grab it for you." Ben nodded at Lopez. He ducked into the shack, returned with the booklet, and handed it to Ben. The photo inside was a cleaner, slightly younger version of the older man. Ben read aloud, "William Witson, 23 MacKenzie Ave, Holyrood, Newfoundland and Labrador. Did I say that correctly, sir?"

"That's Newfound-LAND, son, spot-on wi tother."

"Thanks, Mr. Witson. Is that truck a rental or on loan from your friend?" Ben noted the entry stamp in the passport dated December 27th.

"Ya can call me Bill if ya like. Dat's my pally's truck. He loans it t'me when I comes down. Ya can look round it if ya likes."

"You don't mind?" At his nod, Simmons turned and walked toward the vehicle.

"Naw, anyting for the law." Turning toward Lopez, he continued. "I'm 'bout to have an eye-opener, son. Care to join in?" He reached for a beer in the cooler beside the chair.

"Thank you, sir, but it's a little early for me." Lopez smiled back. "Besides, I don't want to be drinking in front of the lieutenant." He winked conspiratorially.

"Ha! I dies at you. Where you from, son?"

"East Los Angeles, sir."

"Cally-fornia? I bet it never gets cold dare."

"Not like Newfound-*Land*."

The light conversation continued while Simmons searched through the truck and shack. He caught Ben's eye and shook his head almost imperceptibly as he returned. Ben nodded equally subtly and then brought the conversation to a close. "Sir, thank you very much for your time and cooperation. I wish you a pleasant visit and good luck with the fish."

"Tanks, Leftenant." Witson smiled and nodded. "You take care, and long may your big jib draw."

Ben called for the RHIB as they walked down toward the pickup point, and it nosed in as they arrived. Lopez held the bow just short of grounding while the other men climbed in, then pushed off and swung himself up. Jenkins backed the boat off, turned, and headed for *Kauai*. Ben turned to Simmons, speaking loudly over the engine. "Wow, that was some accent. I could barely make him out. I usually have more trouble telling someone's Canadian." He waved when he noticed the older man watching them.

Simmons smiled. "They're rather insular in Newfoundland. It wasn't even part of Canada until 1949. Still, you probably wouldn't have noticed with someone younger."

"Nothing interesting with the pickup or shack?"

"Nothing I could see. The truck is registered in Hialeah. It's big enough to carry survey equipment, but there's no evidence of it—only some receipts for food and beer. I got the registration information and VIN. Only clothes and junk in the shack."

"I'll send that and the passport info in and see if we get any hits, but it looks like a bust."

"Perhaps." Simmons paused and glanced back at the shack receding in the distance. "Still, I'm keeping this one in my pocket while we check the others."

Old Bill watched the RHIB make its way toward the patrol boat and raised his beer exaggeratingly in return for the wave from the young lieutenant in the shade of his makeshift porch. He smiled again and returned to fishing.

USCG Cutter *Kauai*, Gulf of Mexico, twenty-four nautical miles east-northeast of Key West, Florida
17:32 EST, 17 January

Ben

Kauai sped westbound for a return for refueling in Key West. The remaining survey areas were completed by launching both Pumas on independent flight plans with staggered launches and recoveries. Simmons and Deffler had worked a double shift, pre-processing the data for the image analysis to follow.

The crew cycled through an exquisite meal by patrol boat standards of mahi-mahi with coconut rice and mango salsa prepared by Hebert as the day's catch. During the Puma sorties, the lookout spotted a floating raft of seaweed, and Bondurant recognized the opportunity and persuaded Sam to stop for an impromptu fish call. As Bondurant expected, the area under the seaweed raft teemed with dolphinfish that began a feeding frenzy when the first line hit the water. Hebert had a dozen large specimens within thirty minutes and began planning the feast.

Ben sat across the table from Drake and Simmons, the latter shaking his head in wonderment. "My God, this is incredible. How do you keep this man? I couldn't get a meal like this for under a hundred bucks back home."

"In a big, fancy restaurant, he'd just be another guy at the stove, working under a puffed-up asshole. Here, he's the king and gets to work a machine gun in his spare time. The skipper and Chief keep him fixed up with all the fancy spices and tools he needs," Ben said, holding up a piece of the fish. "He's also seriously appreciated."

"He damn well better be!" Simmons responded. Catching Hebert's attention, he said, "*C'est fameux, Maître Cuisinier. Je me regale!*"

"*Merci beaucoups, Monsieur Professeur!*" Hebert mocked a sword salute with his spatula.

Simmons renewed his attack on the helpless fish. Ben glanced at the other end of the table where Hopkins, Deffler, Lee, and Williams were dining and sharing a relaxed conversation. Williams, as usual, expounded on a perceived atrocity of modern government, with Lee nodding and Hopkins patiently waiting for her chance for rebuttal. Deffler sat quietly and seemed to focus more on Hopkins than the conversation going on around him.

"Now, Hoppy. I think providing free school meals, that is, taxpayer-funded meals encourages poor behavior. I mean, if you're not held responsible for providing for your own kids, where does it stop?" Williams said.

Hopkins shook her head sadly, as she often did during similar table debates. "Joe, it isn't a question of trying to hold parents responsible. I doubt the decision would affect someone like that either way. You have to think if they're letting their kids go hungry, it's because they can't do anything about it, or they don't care. The government won't change that behavior by withholding food. It comes down to stopping children from going hungry. I'm sorry, but I just can't get worked up against stopping that."

"Aw, c'mon, Hoppy." Williams turned to Deffler. "Hey Fritz, help me out here."

Deffler smiled but continued gazing at Hopkins. "Sorry, sailor, can't help you outta this one. A guest like me should maintain a strict non-interference policy regarding the hosts."

"Airedales!" Williams scoffed, shaking his head.

Ben chuckled and returned to his conversation. He looked across at Drake and asked, "Chief, what happens with you, I mean, after we decommission? Are you going to move on to the Fast Response Cutters?" He referred to the new class of patrol boats replacing the one-tens.

"No, XO. I'm a PB guy to my bones. Not interested in Mini-Me's."

Ben's fork paused halfway to his mouth. "Mini-Me? Where'd that come from?"

Drake sat back, signaling the delivery of some deck-plate philosophy. "Think about that boat—four officers, so full of electronics and other gear, you can't even turn around. They jammed everything electronic you'd find on a two-seventy into a hull half the size—like they were going for a miniature Medium Endurance Cutter. Thus, Mini-Me."

Ben guffawed. "Chief, is it that bad? Wouldn't you like not needing to grind out replacement parts after every patrol? You'd have more than three guys working for you and not have all the EO paperwork."

"XO, I enjoy having a nice tight engine room crew I can run. And as for paperwork, that's why I have *you*, sir!" He paused while the other two men chuckled, then continued. "Naw, this is my twilight tour. I reckon I'll go out with the old girl and maybe hire on at a marine repair shop."

"Yeah, I don't doubt it. Just don't bail before I move along, please. You know, it's all about me."

"Don't I know it, sir." He turned to Simmons. "So, Doc, any luck with finding the space rock?"

Simmons swallowed. "Alas, no, the quest for the Holy Grail continues, and I'm hoping this last batch of imagery will bear fruit for us."

"I don't get it. A rock ginormous enough to cave in a boat ought to be easy to see."

"On the contrary, Chief. The impactor is likely quite small. Remember, speed is the big part of the kinetic energy of an object. An impactor ten feet across, hitting the Earth at a typical meteor's speed, would produce an explosion comparable to the Hiroshima atomic bomb. We're lucky most burn up in the atmosphere. I believe the water kept it from vaporizing, but whatever was left probably shattered. No, we're searching more for the effects of the impact, breaks in the patterns of the shore and seabed. That's why we crank the imagery through computer algorithms. They can pick up on anomalies too subtle for humans to see."

Ben hated the deception Simmons perpetrated on Drake, despite understanding and agreeing with the necessity. Still, he had to admire the skill Simmons displayed in his almost casual obscuration of the genuine nature of their mission. Ben tried not to think of how the crew would react if they learned the truth. He glanced at his watch. "Sorry, guys, gotta shove off for the entering-port brief."

Simmons turned to him. "As many times as you've been to Key West, you still need detailed briefings?"

"Doc, every mooring is unique. Tides, currents, and lighting effects can change daily or hourly. Try figuring things out while bearing down on the dock, and you add another dent on the hull. Chief wouldn't like that." He nodded to Drake.

"No, that wouldn't make my day." The look Drake gave told Ben the older man knew he was not hearing the truth, at least the *whole* truth. Ben kept his face impassive and nodded to Hopkins, inducing her to excuse herself from the table and follow him forward.

****

Having wrapped up the brief, Ben had started his usual mental preparation for the ship-handling effort to come in two hours when Sam beckoned him over. "Our guest has requested a confidential meeting to discuss the next steps. Meet you in the cabin in five minutes?"

"Yes, sir."

A few minutes later, Sam, Ben, and Simmons were sitting in their usual places in Sam's cabin with the door closed. Sam looked at Simmons and said, "OK, Doctor, you have the floor."

Simmons nodded. "Thank you, Captain. Image processing is continuing, but we have done all the seaborne reconnaissance we can. I need to get with my people to coordinate some deeper dives on land. If you don't object, I'll be moving ashore when we return to Key West."

Sam glanced at Ben, then back to Simmons. "Am I to infer that our role in this mission is ending?"

"No, sir. We know that missile landed in the water, although not where yet. Until we locate it, there's still an important maritime part to this effort. I have to ask you to stay nearby and be available."

"Very well, Doctor. Until our orders change, we'll continue on the mission. What do you envision us doing?"

"I need you to be the maritime response force in the event we locate the target. It'll mean being underway in a standby position north of the Keys, and we can work out a geographic point that would allow the best average response time."

Sam nodded. "That's doable, provided you remember, this is a patrol boat, not a large cutter, and that after three days underway, I need to go in for a fuel break."

"Understood. This should be resolved by then. There's one more thing." He looked at Ben. "I'd like to take Ben with me to serve as an advisor."

"You're joking!" Sam said with astonishment. "Do you realize what you're asking? What if we end up tangling with the Russians or the TCO thugs? You want me to risk going into a fight without my GQ OOD?"

"Hear me out." Simmons held up his hand. "It's a lot to ask, but consider the risks if I have to decide about your role without your knowledge or experience. No one on my team understands *Kauai*'s capabilities and limitations. I could easily put your guys, my guys, or both at unnecessary risk through sheer ignorance. Wouldn't it be better to avoid a jam than to fight our way out of one?"

Sam shook his head. "Even if I were to agree to that view, even if I believed I could assume that risk for my crew and ship, what about Ben? He's not trained for this kind of work. You cavalierly hung his ass out before without a by-your-leave or apology."

"Captain, I take exception to your characterization of that event. We had the risk under control. Now we have three teams available in support instead of one. And that's just my guys. I've heard the FBI, DEA, and ATF are moving in now that we've got terrorists, drugs, and bombs in play. We're covered far better than before." He paused, glancing at Ben. "I understand what I'm asking of you, and I wouldn't just throw you in the blades. Too much has happened on this trip,"

Sam stared at Simmons without speaking. After half a minute, Sam turned to Ben. "What do you think, honestly?"

Ben felt an icy ball forming in his stomach, the memory of his fear in the car chase still fresh. After a brief pause, he replied, "I'll go along with whatever you decide, Captain."

"Not good enough, dammit!" Sam shook his head. "I need to know if you can do this. If not, it's your duty to tell me here and now. This plan is way above and beyond the call. If you aren't confident in success, I'll put a stop to it, and nothing more will be said." He looked at Simmons. "By anyone!"

Ben blinked and swallowed. He glanced at Simmons, then back at Sam. "I'm in, sir. Let's finish this thing right. But I have one request before we commit."

"Name it."

"Chief Drake is already on to something out of whack on this patrol, and Hoppy will cover for me while ashore. They need to be read in to do it right. And, Captain, you need the job done right. That's what it will take to make me confident."

"Agree a hundred percent." Sam nodded and turned to Simmons. "There you go, Doctor. That's our *sine qua non*. Take it or leave it."

Simmons's mouth opened and closed, and his face hardened. "All right. But those two are it, agreed? I'm already way over my quota on this."

"Agreed. Now you get how I feel."

"Do you want me to read them in or be in the room?"

"No. I know my people and how much I can share. I want them to be able to ask questions and speak frankly without you fidgeting in the room." He looked at Ben. "We'll brief them in the sector's SCIF after securing from mooring stations. Are you going to be OK taking her in? Remember, you're still 'under oath' here."

"I can cut it, Captain. Hell, I can use the distraction at this point."

Sam nodded. "Fine. I guess there's nothing else to say, except, God help us all." He stood and offered his hand to Simmons.

Surprised, Simmons stood and shook Sam's hand firmly. "Thank you, sir."

Trumbo Point Annex, Naval Air Station Key West, Florida 20:41 EST, 17 January

Ben

Sam and Ben walked over to the sector building after preparations for another sortie. Drake and Hopkins had preceded them, having completed the refueling and setting up the charts for the departure, respectively. Ben was used to periods with little banter when hanging around with Sam—friendly as he was, no one would call him talkative—but this silence was thunderous. Ben was sure his CO was having second thoughts about this decision. Finally, Ben couldn't take it anymore. "It will be OK, sir. We've plenty of backup, and we have to see it through."

Sam continued staring straight ahead as he walked on through the darkness. "Do we? Why us? If this were real, it should be the biggest deal ever. All Hands on Deck. Yet, it's just us and an unknown number of men in black. We depend on a man who lies for a living. You heard the captain. She as much as said, 'Yeah, it's BS. Just follow your damn orders.' Now I will have to sell the mission to Chief and Hoppy without letting on that deep down, I think it's a load of crap." He glanced over at Ben as they passed under one of the pier lights, noted the grim expression, then smiled, put an arm around his shoulder, and shook it gently. "Sorry, XO, this is new for me, and I needed to vent a little. Odds are we'll come through this with the bosses scratching their heads and the rest of us laughing our asses off that a looney-toon Ph.D. bamboozled them." Both men smiled as they arrived at the sector building.

Drake and Hopkins, already waiting in the SCIF, stood up when the two officers entered. "Sit down, please," Sam said as he closed the door, and both complied while Sam and Ben joined them at the table.

As Sam opened his mouth to speak, Drake interrupted. "Captain, you're here to tell Hoppy and me that the ops we've been on for the past few days are not a space rock hunt. Also, we've somehow gotten mixed up with dangerous people, and the worst is yet to come." Seeing the two officers glance at each other, he continued, looking straight at Ben. "XO, you need to stay away from spying, politics, and poker tables. You can't even be in the room with someone bullshitting without breaking out in tells."

Ben blushed, and Sam chuckled out loud. "Now, Chief, while we ponder whether that is a virtue or a shortcoming for our brave XO, why don't you tell us what you think you know."

Drake turned to Sam. "We come across a drug boat with a kind of damage I've never run into before. Next thing, we're diverted from our patrol, and some IC-type drops out of the sky and takes over. XO goes with him to check something out and comes back as shook up as anyone I've ever seen. The next day we stop a yacht with stealth tech being run by a no-shit evil villain lady and set to blow itself up. The finale was that session on the mess deck. Dr. Spook spun this bullshit story about a goldilocks meteor—big enough to smash the hell out of that boat, but not so big that anybody would notice." He looked at Ben. "Sir, you couldn't handle sitting there while you knew that dude was lying to me. And that *is* a virtue in my mind, by the way."

"Right, Chief," Sam began. "We've had to keep the crew in the dark because the information is sensitive. Well, the situation has changed. We need to read you and Hoppy in if we are going to complete this mission. But before that, you need to accept what I'm going to tell you is as classified as it gets. If you disclose this information ever, you, and likely Mr. W and me, get thrown into Leavenworth. Chief, Hoppy, what do you say?"

"Yes, sir," Drake responded. "Let's have it."

"Understood, Captain." Hopkins nodded.

"OK," Sam began and then related the story behind the mission, including the possibility they were dealing with a loose nuclear weapon. Drake and Hopkins listened throughout with rapt attention, Drake nodding periodically, and Hopkins, silent and still with eyes growing wide at the big reveal of the hunt for the nuke. He withheld his and Ben's doubts about the truth of the worst assumption—sharing those would do more harm than good. "So, here we are. Any questions?"

Drake leaned back in his chair and shook his head. "Captain, if anyone else had told me that tale, I would've thrown the bullshit flag, and that would be that. Sorry to put you on the spot, but do *you* believe there's a loose nuke out there?"

So much for holding back. "Chief, I honestly don't know. If I had to lay a bet, it would be no. But I think it's at least possible with all the weird stuff going on here. We must run down that possibility. Regardless of what I believe, we have lawful orders, and we will carry them out."

"Thanks for the straight talk, sir. I'm with you." Drake nodded. He paused, turning to Ben. "Besides, I have the human truth detector here backing you up."

Sam turned to Hopkins. "Hoppy?"

Hopkins looked back and forth at the two officers. "OK, Captain. This takes getting used to, but your word will do for me. My question is, why tell us now? What's changed that we suddenly need to know?"

"The investigation has shifted from sea-based to shore-based. Dr. Simmons will continue processing the imagery data obtained on the UAV flights. He will work with his own team members to follow up on leads on the ground the UAVs couldn't pick up. We'll remain in the vicinity to provide support since the vehicle, however it's armed, landed in the water." Sam looked at Ben. "We'll also provide a liaison to Dr. Simmons to keep us in the loop and offer expertise on what a one-ten can do and what it can't. Mr. Wyporek has volunteered, so I'll be leaning on you two a lot more while he's ashore. Hoppy, you will take over the XO's operational duties. We will stand easy in terms of LE patrolling because we're short-handed and have to stay on station if needed. Chief, you get the admin burden. I need you to look after the crew even closer since I'm down a set of eyes."

Drake turned to Ben. "XO, haven't you been around long enough to learn not to volunteer for stuff?"

Ben mustered his best smile. "C'mon, Chief, good sleep, hotel showers. What could go wrong?"

"Permission to speak freely, sir?" Hopkins interjected, and Ben did not need a psychology degree to tell she was furious.

"That's why we're here." Sam nodded.

Hopkins turned to Ben. "Sir, with all due respect, are you out of your damn mind? Pardon my French."

"Take it easy, Hoppy." Ben appreciated her feelings but was surprised by her vehemence. "I'll be going in eyes open, and we'll have plenty of backup."

Hopkins wasn't backing down. "Sir, you're not trained for this. It's not Russians that scare me. Frankly, I think that part's pure BS. It's that lying piece of crap Simmons and his drug gangs. You've just told me he dragged you into what could have been a firefight. He did it with no notification and probably no more thought than he gave to if he wanted OJ with his eggs. You weren't in the room staring down that bitch for two hours, like Shelley and me. And I wouldn't trust Simmons any more than I would trust her. Don't do this! Please, Captain!"

Ben was about to speak, but remained quiet when Sam held up his hand and leaned forward. "Emilia, can you do this job?"

Her mouth opened and closed, and then she looked down. "Yes, sir. You know I can."

"Very well. Your concerns are well-founded. Please believe that Mr. Wyporek and I have discussed them and others at length. Bottom line: the mission and many lives could depend on clear and correct language at the right place and time." He turned to Drake. "What about you, Chief? Let's have it, no holding back."

Drake shook his head. "Sorry, Captain, but I'm with Hoppy. I don't trust anyone who lies right to my face. Ever. Are you sure you want to gamble Mr. Wyporek's life with this guy, not to mention ours?"

A slight smile softened Sam's expression. "OK, I'll admit that I'm not the good doctor's biggest fan. But recent experience has moved this decision from the gamble column to the one labeled 'calculated risk.' I can assure you I'll be reassessing that risk constantly as we go along, and the XO will too. We're done if either of us sees anything that changes the game. You've *my* word on that."

Drake's grim face did not change, but he nodded. "OK, sir. I can do the job for you."

Sam relaxed and leaned back. "OK, guys. Mr. Wyporek always gives it to me straight, even when he knows I won't like it. I depend on him for that, and I'll depend on you to do the same, please. Anybody got anything else? No? Let's get'r done then."

They all rose together and stood awkwardly until Drake broke the tension. "Captain's the last one on and the first one off the boat, sir," he said with a smile and a motion toward the door with his right arm.

****

Ben changed into casual civilian clothes and picked up a weapon "Go Bag." It contained an M4 Carbine, Sig pistol, several ammunition magazines for each, body armor, and a combat first aid kit Bryant had put together at Sam's request. He turned the keys to the locked files over to Sam and then met Simmons on the mess deck. The agent gazed at the ship's crest mounted on a plaque on the forward bulkhead. *Kauai*'s crest comprised the escutcheon of the Kingdom of Hawaii over a fouled anchor with the ship's motto, *Fortiter et Fideliter*, across the bottom.

"Ready, friend?" Simmons asked as he approached. At Ben's nod, he glanced once more at the plaque. "'Bravely and Faithfully.' That's a damn good sentiment for a unit that has your back."

Ben stared at the plaque and was slightly embarrassed that he had never looked up the Latin phrase. "Yes, I suppose it is. Shall we?"

Sam, Drake, and Hopkins were waiting on the pier by the entry port when the two men approached. Sam shook Simmons's hand and nodded. "Good luck, Doctor."

Receiving a blank expression from Drake, an icy glare from Hopkins, and no offer of a handshake from either, Simmons said to Ben, "I'll meet you over at the car." He turned and walked off along the dock.

Ben turned back to his shipmates and shook first Sam's, then Drake's hand. Sam's grip was firm and prolonged, and he smiled sadly on letting go. Drake's was equally strong, and he held Ben's eyes and nodded as he looked down on the young officer.

At her turn, Hopkins pushed his hand aside and hugged him hard, whispering, "Be careful, sir."

"Um, I will," came his stunned reply.

After she released him and stood back with the others, Ben picked up his bag, faced Sam at attention, received a nod in return, and turned to leave the boat.

After watching Ben get in the car with Simmons and drive off, Sam turned to Drake and Hopkins. "Ready for sea, Hoppy?"

"Yes, sir."

"Chief?"

"Ready for sea, Captain."

"Very well. Let's set mooring stations and get going." Sam returned their salutes and turned toward the ladder to the Bridge, followed by Hopkins as Drake turned toward the Main Space hatch.

Introductions

**U.S. Route 1, six miles West of Marathon, Florida
22:13 EST, 17 January**

Ben

One of Simmons's teammates provided the car they rode in from Key West. In it, they found the car keys, directions, and a key for a room at an off-brand hotel in the Key town of Marathon. The two men shared little conversation while Ben drove through the darkness. He was still processing his two enlisted shipmates' astonishing reaction to his acceptance of the mission while Simmons engaged in cryptic mobile phone communications. Simmons broke the silence about fifteen minutes before their arrival.

"That was some sendoff. For you, I mean, not me. Although it surprised me that your captain's farewell to me was the warmest."

"The bomb-defusing operation gave him cause to recalibrate. He sees the best in people, even those who give him ample reason not to. The other two think you're playing us and are uptight about my going off with you."

"And this surprises you?"

"The being played part or the other?"

"The latter."

"Kinda. I'm the XO. The arrangement I have with the skipper is that he's the smiling backslapper, and I'm the crabby nitpicker.

I don't seek opportunities to be a dick. But I will do it when the hair or uniform pushes outside the regs or spaces need policing."

"You often get on Hopkins or Drake about that stuff?"

"Are you kidding? Never."

"So, you're not there to keep them toeing the line. Do you offer expertise to them to help them do their jobs?"

"It's usually the reverse."

"Really? It doesn't bother you on some level to ask your inferiors for help?"

Ben glanced over at him and then returned to the road. "Are you trying to pick a fight with me right now?"

"Why would you say that?"

"They are not my *inferiors*; they're my subordinates. I have authority over them because I'm the XO, not because I'm *better* than them. Shit, I've learned plenty from both of them."

"Do all Coast Guard officers think like you?"

"No, not all of them."

"So, let's continue down your path a bit. You think the world of your CO, correct?"

"He's the finest officer and man I've ever known."

"Would it surprise you to learn he feels the same about you?"

Ben was at a loss for words and glanced briefly at Simmons again.

"Well?" Simmons pressed.

"There's no way he told *you* that!"

"Friend, I remind you he was about to rip my head off for putting you in danger the other day. I've been poking him regularly since I arrived. The only time he went beyond a contemptuous brush-off was when I said unkind stuff about you. Given your regard for him and his regard for you, is it that surprising the people who work for you feel the same?"

Ben continued to stare forward. "Are we there yet?"

Simmons chuckled. "Ben, I'm sorry to put the microscope on you, but we will be mixing up with real out-of-the-box stuff soon. I won't have time for explanations or pep talks when things get weird. I know your background pretty well—my outfit has access to that kind of information. You don't have any tactical experience other than your car ride with me the other day. The point of all this psychobabble is you will do OK, whatever happens, get me? A bunch of top-shelf people not only like you but trust you. That means something."

"You should keep in mind that car chase scared the shit out of me."

"I congratulate you on your sanity. Fear in those situations is normal, and fear is always useful when it informs your decisions. Fear's only a problem when it *dictates* your actions."

"Right. Thanks for the pep talk, Obi-Wan. Are we there yet?"

"Almost there, young padawan." Simmons chuckled. "You'll need to know a few things about my team before we arrive; it'll make things smoother in the introduction."

"Shoot." Ben was relieved his psyche was finally out of the spotlight.

"Besides the processing team, we have specialists for dealing with our TCO opponents and any new Russian 'friends.' Once we knew the other side was in the game, they deployed forward to cover the analysts. Art Frankle is the lead. He's an old agency hand, *my* mentor, or 'Obi-Wan,' as you put it. Lashon Bell is his partner, not much on conversation, but one of the best tactics guys you'll run into. Now, on the processing team, we have Steve Newsome, who keeps comms up and is quite a code monkey. He also takes care of our resident genius, Victoria Carpenter, who's amazing at pattern recognition and math. She can glance at a full-page matrix and not only tell you the determinant, but any notable quirks in the data. Also, she has a mild form of what used to be called Asperger's Syndrome but is now more kindly referred to as being 'neuro-diverse.' She does not have OCD, but her frankness is jarring at first."

Great, Ben thought. *I'll bet she looks like Velma from the Scooby-Doo cartoons, only geekier and neurotic to boot.* Aloud, he asked, "Um, I never met anyone like that. Any triggers or issues I need to worry about?"

"Nope. Just roll with it and don't take anything she says too personally—she calls it *precisely* as she sees it, no sugar-coating. Oh, and if she has anything arranged in her workspace, don't mess with it. It won't set her off or anything; it'll just distract her."

"Right," Ben said, thinking, *you just can't make this shit up.*

Conch Inn, Room 118, Marathon, Florida
23:23 EST, 17 January

Ben

The agents working with Simmons had booked three adjacent rooms, and Lashon and Steve had swept them thoroughly for microphones and cameras. The hotel was mostly vacant in the offseason and a little shabby. However, its single floor and row of rooms made it ideal for security. Ben and Simmons occupied the center room, which doubled as the command center for the group since the rooms on either side provided a screen against any would-be eavesdroppers.

Simmons's team had gathered in the center room on the notification he and Ben were a few minutes out. He gave the prearranged knock sequence, opened the door, and led Ben inside. The greetings were led by Victoria, who was, to Ben's great surprise, a beautiful, petite young woman with pulled-back auburn hair and large aquamarine eyes in a heart-shaped face. She hugged Simmons and said in a surprisingly husky voice with a midwestern accent, "Hello, Peter! I am very happy to see you." She turned to Ben with a smile. "You are Lieutenant Junior Grade Wyporek?"

Holy crap! Even her voice is incredible. Breathe, boy! Ben took a breath and played it as cool as he could. "Yes, I am. I am very pleased to meet you. You can call me Ben if you like."

"Why would I like to do that when your name is Benjamin?" Her smile faded.

"Some people like to call me Ben because it's shorter to say, but I like how you say 'Benjamin,' so I would be happy if you called me that."

A slight smile lit up her face, which Ben thought was one of the loveliest he'd ever seen. "Good. We have been working all day and ordered pizza. Mine is a thin crust with pepperoni and green peppers. Would you like some as well?"

"Victoria, I can't think of anything I would rather do more right now."

"That's good." She then abruptly turned, walked behind one table, sat, and began typing, gazing at the screen.

OK, there it is. Ben directed a puzzled glance at Simmons and got a shrug in return. He then turned and greeted the rest of the team. The pizza arrived about fifteen minutes later. Ben sat back and munched a piece of Victoria's favorite while he listened to the team update each other on the events of the past days, sneaking glances at the lovely young analyst whenever he could.

Frankle, the senior member and coordinator of the team, led the discussion. He was the oldest and presumably the most experienced of the group, with graying, close-cropped hair and a pair of reading glasses perched down on his nose.

"You did well setting up out here. We're out of sight, but still in the loop," Frankle said as he sipped a bottle of Heineken. "FBI, DEA, ATF, seems like half the DoJ has descended 'covertly' on Key West to assess the threat. So far, they're all focused on the drugs and bombs, nothing going on regarding either that stealth kit your folks found or the 'other thing.'" He glanced at Ben.

"He's read in." Simmons nodded. "Has the usual turf war kicked off yet?"

"Boy, howdy. Our guy says the leads for the FBI and the DEA almost came to blows. Bottom line is that the word is out, though not officially, that we bagged two narco-terrorist boats. Also, they are turning over every rock in Miami and Key West, looking for contacts and accessories. With the spotlight on those places, we believe we are in a clear spot between them.

"The bad news: that operative you guys nailed on the sailboat got away."

"What?" Ben nearly choked on a mouthful of pizza.

"Yep. She got a call off before you put her in the bag. Anyway, the marshals taking her to lockup got bushwhacked shortly after leaving the Coast Guard base. One dead, one fifty-fifty. They may have killed or wounded an attacker, but nobody was left behind. We got a hit on the biometrics and this gal's real bad news, an assassin, actual name Valentina Petrova, drummed out of the Russian SVR because she was too psycho even for them. Our 252 opponents attract cross-wired types like her."

Simmons saw Ben's face and interrupted, "Don't panic, friend. Now that she's graduated to federal cop killer, her face will be everywhere. She knows her only chance to stay alive is to exit this country as fast as possible."

Frankle nodded. "True. Hell, her own people might have grabbed her just so they could knock her off before she made any deals. A man can hope, anyway."

Simmons weighed in again. "She's connected with that first boat. Any Intel why they took a chance running a load that big? Seems like a big gamble. I mean, that loss has to hurt, even for them."

Frankle nodded. "Yeah, it has people scratching their heads. It may be a rogue element in the organization, or they thought they had the juice in place to keep people quiet."

Ben piped up, "They may have tested it in dry runs or smaller loads. I'm sure you guys know how lean our coverage in the Deep Caribbean is these days. The hardest part's getting through the passages, but they can hide in the commercial traffic if they're radar-masked. It's hard enough to see them when they aren't masked."

Frankle nodded. "Makes sense. But drugs are you guys' problem, you and DEA. Anyway, they're on it, so we're standing off the boat investigation unless there's overseas work to do."

"Have they done any testing on the radar masker we found on the second boat?" Simmons asked.

"A little. So far, it's invisible to the Coast Guard surface and aircraft radars. They plan to run it against high-end DoD models when they start serious testing. It's spooky. Drugs are nasty, but it's the other stuff they're running that scares me."

"No kidding. OK, let's talk about our little caper here. Victoria, can you come here, please? We need you to talk about what you found."

"Yes, Peter," she said, pushing back from her console and moving to join the group.

"Ben and I went ashore on Resolution Key because of evidence of human activity. There was no joy on the warhead, although I think the 252s looked in there. As far as I can tell, the rest of our aerial surveys have shown nothing positive in the areas we believe the missile could have crashed. We're handicapped because we don't have any baseline imagery for comparison."

"That's not true, Peter," Victoria interrupted. "Besides Resolution Key, there were vehicle tracks on seven other islands among those surveyed. The imagery revealed the tracks were likely from the same vehicle that explored Resolution Key."

"Interesting," Simmons said with a slight, contemplative pause. "What does that suggest to you, Art?"

"Our 252 friends are as clueless about where their boat got hit as we are. Do you think they were playing this on the fly? Why do that when they can just push aside anyone they run into? It's what they always do."

"Yes, in the Balkans and South America, where nobody gives a shit about a few more bodies. Here, the heat comes quickly and heavily if they knock off innocents. There isn't enough bribe money to make *that* go away. Better to avoid trouble—check on their pre-scouted spots and, when they find one that's clear, call in once they anchored." He paused briefly. "That's too bad. My hopes that the 252s will lead us to the landing site are fading."

"Mmmm, yeah," Frankle said, peering over his glasses between Simmons and Bell. "So, what's the plan?"

"Maybe we'll be fortunate, and Victoria's work will produce a definitive answer." Simmons glanced at the woman and received a nod in return. "However, we have to assume it's legwork again. Art, please tell me you got hold of the National Park Service stuff."

"Yes and no. We have the digital form of the most recent survey maps for the area. Many are PDFs, so image comparison won't give us much. Back to ground-pounding for us."

"About what I figured. At least the maritime constraint bounds our problem a bit. I suggest we split the load. Tomorrow, Art, you and Lashon take the easternmost four areas here." He pointed at the larger scale chart. "And our young coastguardsman and I will take the western areas. We'll be looking for signs of unusual shore erosion, recently flipped wood, or anything that points to a micro-tsunami that the impact might have generated. And we'll have the ground sensors."

"Long shot finding anything," Bell said, entering the conversation.

"Agreed. But we'll be down to that if Victoria's efforts don't bear fruit. Speaking of which, Victoria, once your runs are complete and you wrap up your initial analysis, I want you and Steve to pack up your gear and head back to Maryland. We're done with the UAV surveys, and we're spread too thin here to provide you two with adequate cover with all the bad guys running around. We'll hook up again once you're plugged in back in Bethesda."

"I understand, Peter," Victoria replied somewhat sadly. She turned to Ben. "I wish we had more time to work together, Benjamin."

Ben's heart jumped. "Well, Victoria, we have a few hours, don't we? Can I pitch in?"

"No." Victoria glanced back at the computer work area. "Everything is batch processing right now. However, I read your paper on the SAROPS project that provided the basis of your search strategy. There were several flaws and shortcomings. Would you like me to tell you about them?"

Ben blinked and opened his mouth in surprise, then noticed over her shoulder that Simmons was watching him with a slight smile. He consciously dialed down his ego. "Of course, Victoria. I'm always looking for ways to make progress."

"Oh, good." For the next five minutes, she explained everything from a suboptimal choice of prior probabilities to grammar and punctuation errors. When she finished, she asked, "Do you see how you could have improved this?"

"Yes, I do, Victoria," Ben said, trying to recover from the intellectual beating he had just taken. "I hope you aren't disappointed in me, considering I'm not the mathematician you are. Also, there were many demands on my time when I wrote that." He had to admit to himself that he was heartily sick of school and just going for "good enough" on the project at that point in his Academy tenure. He never dreamed it could come back to bite him with an attractive woman.

"I'm not disappointed." She nodded. "Very few people are as intelligent as I am. I hope you are not sad. Sometimes, it is hard for me to tell."

"On the contrary." He smiled warmly. "You can never go wrong being honest with me."

"Oh, good. In that case, I like you. Very much."

"Despite my inferior scholarship compared to you?" Ben teased with a smile.

"I am not bothered by that. You are very handsome and a hero." She nodded.

"Oh, ah, thank you," Ben blushed and stammered. "I'm not a hero."

"I do not understand." Victoria's smile disappeared. "You received the Coast Guard Commendation Medal for saving three lives last year, and you just arrested a dangerous criminal."

Ben had started stammering again when he saw Simmons over Victoria's shoulder, giving a thumbs up and mouthing silently, "Take the win."

"No, Victoria, it's my mistake. I just never thought of myself as a hero."

"Well, you are." Her subtle smile returned. "Will you tell me about your life as a Coast Guard officer, please? All I know is what I could read in the official records."

"Certainly. Is there any place you would like me to begin?"

"Yes. Please tell me the story of how you saved the mother and her two children. It was noted in your citation for the Coast Guard Commendation Medal."

"How do you know about that?"

"When Peter learned he would be working with *Kauai*, he was curious about the officers in command and asked me to pull your records."

Ben glanced at Simmons with a raised eyebrow. "That explains some things." After receiving a wry smile and shrug in return, he turned back to Victoria. "It was a matter of being in the right place and time, I guess. I was driving down from Virginia to my new job on *Kauai*, and the weather was pretty bad, with icy roads. A jerk in a pickup truck nearly ran me off the road when he passed me and did run that family off. The woman lost control and punched through a guardrail right in front of me. You should have seen it—their minivan was hanging half off the embankment with a sheer forty-foot drop. I came up and stood on the rear bumper to keep it from going over until help could get there. It was freezing cold, and the emergency services were two-blocked with calls."

"Sorry to interrupt, Benjamin, but what does 'two-blocked' mean?"

"Oops. Sorry about the jargon. It means they were super busy. It would have been more than an hour before they could get to us. I was pretty worried because the lady and one child were unconscious, and there was a real danger of hypothermia for everyone. Fortunately, some guys pulled up to help, and we got them all out and to the hospital ourselves."

Victoria flashed the most alluring smile Ben had ever seen and said, "There must be more to it than that, Benjamin."

Ben shifted nervously and said, "I did have to enter the vehicle to pull them out."

"You climbed into a wrecked vehicle hanging over a cliff to save people you did not even know? Why would you do that?"

"It was a calculated risk. With the other three guys hanging on the back, there was more than enough weight to balance mine when I went inside. Besides, I was talking to the little girl inside the whole time, and I couldn't leave her and her family to freeze to death...or worse."

"That was a courageous thing to do, Benjamin. Does it make you uncomfortable to talk about it?"

Ben smiled back. "Normally, it would. But it seems OK when I'm talking about it with you."

"Oh, good! Please tell me more about your life."

"You might find it boring from here—you've just heard my most exciting story."

"No, no, no. What you do is so different from everyone else, and everything about your work is new and interesting to me. Please continue."

Ben plunged into a lively discussion, answering detailed questions for the better part of an hour. Although he enjoyed himself in the conversation with the beautiful, attentive analyst, the effort of ensuring everything he said was logically consistent and idiom-free was more fatiguing than he realized. Eventually, even Victoria noticed Ben was flagging.

"You look exhausted, Benjamin. I am tired too. I think it is time we went to bed."

"What?" Ben sputtered, eyes wide. Victoria pulled back in alarm at Ben's apparent shock.

"You're right, Victoria," Simmons intervened with a grin. "Why don't we head to our rooms, and we'll pick it up again in the morning."

Nice going, dumbass! Ben thought tiredly. *You've managed to scare off the nicest girl you've ever met. Did you really think she would invite you into the sack after a couple of hours of conversation?*

Steve stood up and shuffled to the door, with Frankle and Bell close behind. Victoria stood up and checked the monitor for the model's progress. Then she walked over and hugged Ben, which he happily returned.

"I am glad we had time together, Benjamin." She smiled with a warmth that made Ben's heart jump again. "Good night."

Ben stared briefly at the closed door and turned to Simmons. "Holy shit, Doc! I did not see *that* coming."

Simmons patted the young man on the shoulder. "A sudden bold and unexpected question doth many times surprise a man and lay him open."

Ben tilted his head. "Doc, I can't even guess where that bit of poetry came from."

Simmons smiled. "Not poetry, Francis Bacon. You know, you're alright, coastguardsman. Get some sleep. We roll at dawn!"

U.S. Route 1, twelve miles west of Marathon, Florida
06:47 EST, 18 January

Ben

Ben and Simmons were en route to their first investigation scene, the former driving while the latter confirmed overwatch with *Kauai* on Simmons's radio. The image parsing runs had not yielded any definitive insights. As Simmons suspected, success in finding their lost warhead would come down to close inspection on the ground in the locations rated the most probable.

Steve and Victoria had packed up quickly, and the goodbyes were brief and heartfelt. It delighted Ben to find Victoria even more beautiful in the morning.

"Will you come and visit me in Bethesda?" she said to Ben as he placed her case in the car.

"Yes, I'd like that very much. But it might be some time. I can't leave the area while *Kauai* is operational or in readiness, you understand."

"Yes, I know," she said wistfully and then kissed him on the cheek before getting in the car and driving off. Frankle and Bell followed a minute later—with no word on the escaped assassin or any of her associates, Simmons took no chances. They would follow at a discreet distance to Homestead, where the technician and analyst would board an agency plane for the flight to Montgomery County Airpark in Gaithersburg, Maryland, and home. The two agents would then hit their search areas on the return trip.

Observing his young companion lost in thought as they drove to their first destination, Simmons asked, "She's quite a girl, isn't she?"

"Victoria? Yes, I have to say, I've never met anyone like her. Is she, I mean, are she and Steve?" He paused.

"No, Steve has a partner, and even if he didn't, he'd probably be more interested in you than her."

"Oh. So, she's unattached?"

"Correct. As you might expect, a relationship with someone like her is an enormous challenge. She's had a few, and none ended well." Simmons gazed hard at him. "Hmmm, I feel compelled at this point to ask you your intentions."

"Yeah, right."

"No, I am totally serious here."

Ben glanced over, one eyebrow raised over the sunglasses. "You're totally serious, eh? What are you, her father?"

"*In loco parentis.* Just think of me as a kind of big brother with a loaded Uzi."

"You've got to be kidding. She is an adult, after all."

"Yes, but a very unusual adult. She struggles to read people and can't pick up on malicious intent. Hence, she's the perfect mark for whatever slick operator comes along. She's also a beautiful young woman with access to highly classified stuff. It means she needs looking after."

"Excuse me, but isn't 'slick operator' part of your job description? How did someone like this fall under your protection? You don't seem the type."

"Fair question." Simmons nodded. "I met her when she was a very precocious thirteen-year-old. She was the younger sister of my fiancée. Their parents were dead, and Julie, my fiancée, was raising her. Her condition was just starting to be noticeable then, and she was in an accelerated special needs program."

"Was? You two break up?"

"No. Unfortunately, she died just before we were to be married."

"Oh, I'm sorry."

"Yeah, me too. Anyway, I regarded Victoria as my little sister by then. So, I took care of her until she graduated, and when I went with the agency, I snagged an analyst position for her. She's been invaluable with analysis work across the board. So, there's plenty of us watching after her now, but I'm the principal."

"I see. So, you and your buddies will beat me up and send me to Guantanamo if I have the nerve to call on her?"

"If you intend to get in a quick lay and hit the road, you can depend on the beat down. I don't think you'd do anything that low, but I've only known you a couple of days."

"I don't know how to respond to that."

"Right. Unlike her, I'm super good at reading people. I wouldn't be alive now if I weren't. I can see you are falling for her, and that's not surprising, given her looks and how disarming her personality is. In case you're wondering, her attraction to you is not an act—she's incapable of guile. To her, you are a handsome, intelligent, and kindly hero around her age, someone she would naturally be drawn to. If she comes to believe you reciprocate that admiration, she *will* fall for you. Hard."

"That'd be bad because...?" Ben was getting a little annoyed at the implied slight of his character.

"Because being with her takes work. How did you feel last night, just talking to her?"

"It was nice. At first, I felt like I did in the speech lab while trying to learn German in high school, but I was getting in the rhythm toward the end. This morning, it felt natural, not a big lift."

"Yet, it was a lift."

"What do you want from me, Doc? I like her, and I want to get to know her. She's different, I get that, and the usual rules don't apply. I've had relationships before, and the ones where I got dumped were because I couldn't read the code. Now, here's a wonderful woman who is unencrypted. I want to try that. How do I avoid an 'extraordinary rendition'?"

Simmons chuckled. "That's a good one. Hey, from what I've seen, you're one of the good guys. Your associates' quality and high regard for you do you credit. My belief your near-pathological honesty would make you a failure in my line of work strengthens that assessment. I believe you'd be great for each other. But she is neuro-diverse. She is now what she will be forever—she won't be 'getting better.' So, while you discover whether that's what *you* want, and what you want *is* important, I just want you to be careful with her. Because if she develops a strong attachment and you end up dumping her, it'll be traumatic. All finer feelings aside, it'll disable her for quite a while, and our team can ill-afford that these days. What I ask is, to use your term, be unencrypted— explain the process and don't 'woo' her until you're sure she's the one."

"OK, I get it. You've got my word that I'll take it slow. I won't have much opportunity before this PB tour is over, anyway."

Simmons nodded. "Time and distance can work for you. Email her. None of us use social media for obvious reasons, and she relishes getting personal messages."

Ben smiled. "Doc, I can't tell if I'm being encouraged or discouraged here."

"You two together would be a great thing. You two passing in the night would be status quo—not great, but OK. You two breaking up is a tragedy to be avoided. That clear enough?"

"Crystal. It looks like we're coming up on the exit."

"Right." Simmons pulled out his radio. "X-ray One Delta, Uniform Two India. Over."

"Uniform Two India, X-ray One Delta, go ahead," Deffler's voice replied.

"X-ray One Delta, arriving at the first site now. Over."

"Two India, roger, completed a perimeter sweep with negative contacts. Over."

"One Delta, roger, please assume overwatch, will advise when we're complete. Over."

"Two India, WILCO. Out."

Simmons placed the radio back in his pocket and glanced at his laptop. "OK, there's a place to park about a half-mile down. The anchorage you ID'd is a quarter-mile from there."

"Roger that." Ben kept the car on the hard-packed sand path. A minute later, he sighted the clearing and pulled the car over to park.

Simmons looked at the laptop and said, "OK, there are a few spots we need to check out, but a general sweep of about two-hundred-fifty yards north and south of the potential anchorage." He closed the laptop and climbed out. He grabbed a long cloth bag out of the trunk and followed Ben through a gap in the foliage to the long, vacant beach.

The two men started at the south end, spread out about five yards, and strolled northward, turning over any driftwood they found to see if the top weathering was as expected. Simmons took a four-foot-long sensor pole out of the bag every twenty yards, drove it about six inches into the sand, and punched some buttons on a touchscreen on the side of the box atop the pole. When they reached the northern extent of the beach adjoining the anchorage, Simmons sat down on a larger log and pulled two Gatorades out of a cooler in the bag. "Have a seat for a few minutes." He handed a bottle to Ben.

"Really?" Ben was grateful for the cold drink. Even in the relatively mild mid-morning temperatures, the sun and long trudge through the soft sand had left him rather hot and thirsty.

"Yup, take a load off. I need it quiet while we take the measurement."

Ben sat down while Simmons clicked some buttons on the laptop. Within a few minutes, he heard the dreaded buzzing heralding the inevitable mosquito swarm and began brushing at his ears quietly. After a few more minutes, Simmons clicked some more keys, then said, "OK, that's it."

"What's the purpose of that?"

"The poles have audio sensors, laser seismometers, and GPS. We added pingers to our nukes so we could find them quickly in a Broken Arrow scenario. There's no reason to believe the Russians wouldn't do that too. If anything, they're more accident-prone than we are, as the current scenario proves. We record a few minutes of data stream pairs from the sensors in each place. I'll upload those to the cloud now, and Victoria can pull them when she gets back. If she finds any uncorrelated tremors, particularly rhythmic ones, they may be from a nearby homing signal. The difference in time between arriving surface vibrations and audio can tell us the source's distance to each sensor pole. We then use True Range Multilateration of multiple sensors to discover the source's estimated location."

"Oh, I see." Ben had learned about True Range Multilateration—using distance to multiple fixed points to fix a position—in his coastal navigation classes at the academy. "I'm glad you're not just dragging me around kicking crabs."

"Oh, come on, friend. I told you we would not see anything the Puma's can't. Let's get going. We've got three more beaches to visit. Oh, and there's a can of DEET spray in the bag."

Ben gratefully pulled it out and started spraying. "You guys carry bug spray with you?"

"Don't leave home without it. You can't be slapping and scratching when you're staking out bad guys." He continued typing, packaging, and uploading the data to the unseen high-altitude UAV, which passed it at a reduced rate into the DIA "cloud" via SATCOM. Finally, he closed his laptop and stood up. The two men retraced their steps, picking up the sensor probes on the way. By the time they returned to the car, more than an hour had passed since they arrived.

Edward M. Hochsmann

Reconnaissance—Land

USCG Cutter *Kauai*, Gulf of Mexico, twenty nautical miles northeast of Key West, Florida
07:28 EST, 18 January

Sam

With *Kauai* down one of her OODs, Sam took the 0400–0800 Morning Watch to give the other duty standers a break. Although it meant rousting up about a quarter past three in the morning, the 'Four-to-Eight' was Sam's favorite. He never tired of seeing the sunrise at sea. He couldn't put his finger on exactly why, but the gradual lightening of the eastern horizon and the first stab of bright fire were rejuvenating, regardless of how tired he was. It also provided the opportunity to practice the ancient art of celestial navigation in the pre-dawn twilight. He loved the challenge of measuring the altitude of several stars using his treasured Cooke Kingston sextant Bobby Moore had given him as an OCS graduation gift. After his relief, he planned to break out the nautical almanac and trig tables to "reduce" the star sights he recorded to a celestial "fix" he could compare to the GPS readings. Although unneeded in the GPS age, the activity provided Sam with a stimulating connection to the past.

Around 07:30, Deffler appeared on the Bridge and walked over to Sam. After saluting, he said, "You wanted to see me, Captain?"

Sam returned the salute. "Yes, Fritz. I heard from Mr. Wyporek that he and Dr. Simmons, and another team of agents, will do land surveys in the Keys today. Can both birds be in the air with Dr. Simmons ashore?"

"Yes, sir." Deffler nodded. "I can bring Mike Morgan up here to help monitor after the second launch. We'll need to stagger the launches by at least thirty minutes for setup and to avoid a crunch at the end."

"That would work out well. The teams' work start times are about three hours apart, and it'll be standard overwatch flights for both."

"Good to go, sir. When do you want us airborne?"

"Plan on a 08:30 launch for the first bird. Work out a sortie plan with Hopkins—she has the survey schedule—but get up with comms with the land teams to confirm around 08:00 that it's still a go."

"Yes, sir." The airman smiled.

Sam noted the spring in the tall airman's step and voice. "You're pretty chipper for someone on his fourth day of patrol boat austerity."

"Like I said, sir." Deffler held up both hands and, looking at one, said, "Back home, I have snow and cold." Holding up the other, he continued, "Here, I've got sun, warmth, excellent food, and great company. I can hack sea showers for that any day of the week."

"Marvelous company? Anyone in particular?"

"Um…" The petty officer looked down at his feet.

"Ah, I see. Disregard the question," Sam said, thinking *I need to keep an eye on my OS1—good for her!* "OK, let me know if you run into any problems."

"Will do, sir." Deffler saluted.

Watching him go, Sam noted the arrival of Lee, going through her preps to relieve him as OOD at 07:45. After a few minutes of very diligent preparation, she offered relief to Sam, who accepted with a smile and returned her salute. He had to admit he was starving and knew Hebert stood by to toss on a Western Omelet for him. His thoughts moved inward as he stepped off the sunlit Bridge to head below for his meal.

Although he only decided last night, Sam grew increasingly uncertain about the mission on which he had signed up his crew. He then chided himself for his irrationality. The discovery of the smuggling enterprise had drawn in a host of agents, and that was a vast pool of resources available for surveillance and backup. Yet, this advantage could be lost by the reckless approaches the DIA agent seemed inclined to take. Bobby Moore had told him many sanitized accounts of being dropped in the middle of a shit storm by an eager-beaver intel weenie back in his days on the teams. Simmons fit the general description, except he seemed to drop *himself* into a shit storm rather than send others to get chewed up. Sam didn't care that much about the man's safety. He did, after all, pick Sam's sorest spot to hit. What worried him was his influence on Ben.

He had no doubts about Ben's courage or tactical skills. What troubled him was the young man's lack of experience with this sort of operation. Hoppy had nailed it, as usual, *"you aren't trained for this."* Anyway, not in the soft skills of situational awareness or, more importantly, recognizing when matters were getting out of hand and taking a stand. Particularly with Simmons. Sam shook his head to clear these evil thoughts. The comforting routine of the cutter underway helped, but did not vanquish the lingering undercurrent of worry he felt for his young friend and protégé. *A couple more days, then we'll be done*, he thought. By then, someone in authority would wake up to this nonsense, and they could return to their regular job.

U.S. Route 1, near Resolution Key, Florida
14:28 EST, 18 January

Frankle

Frankle and Bell had seen the analyst team safely to Homestead Air Reserve Base south of Miami and onboard an agency plane for the flight back to Maryland. After watching the plane take off and climb out, the two agents grabbed a quick bite at a local Burger King and then headed down toward their first survey point of

Resolution Key. Their casual clothes and National Marine Fishery Service badges and hats would offer cover for their activities in the survey areas. These would come in handy if they ran into tourists or the elderly beachcomber Simmons encountered during his earlier visit.

Frankle loved being in the field, especially when the assignment was within the United States. Here, he did not have to worry constantly about running afoul of foreign law enforcement or counterintelligence. In his late fifties, he was pushing on the edge of retirement, at least from field ops. Even he had to agree it might be time to size up a less "kinetic" assignment. Not today, though. He was in the field with a partner he liked and trusted.

Bell was fifteen years younger than his partner, an able performer, and a very cool customer. He was not a college graduate, unusual for a DIA man. Bell was a good athlete but didn't have enough talent to draw a sports scholarship and wasn't interested enough in academics to compete there. He found his stride in three enlistments in the Marines, the last ending as a Team Leader in the 2nd Recon. After several successful joint missions during Southwest Asia deployments, his tactics and intel talents were well-known enough to draw agency recruiters. Bell took the jump to the better-paying but more hazardous career as a DIA field agent.

Bell was an enigma to his contemporaries. He was more comfortable listening than jumping in on office discussions on sports and entertainment and rarely indulged in the usual banter when in the field. Although valued for his professional skills, he ran through several partners unable to get on with such a reticent wingman. When Frankle's name came up for a partner, the word around the team was "an afternoon with Lashon Bell is like an afternoon alone."

Frankle enjoyed having younger partners because he liked their relatively unjaded outlook compared to his contemporaries, and he relished the mentor role. Several junior agents, including Simmons, had matured under his tutelage and went on to success in the agency. Frankle had a knack for finding common ground with his charges, and Bell was no exception. A former Marine himself, Frankle had a ready lexicon and "carousing protocol." He used these to fix a bond with the younger man, and they soon formed a solid and enduring partnership founded on mutual respect and complementary skill sets.

As suited both men, Bell drove while Frankle navigated and kept the conversation going. Both felt relief the analysis team had departed, if only because it allowed them to shift from defense to offense. They each had affection for Victoria, but neither thought it a good idea to bring her into the field. It was another point of dispute between Frankle and Simmons on this op.

The fact was, Frankle thought his former mentee had lost a step with this idea of recovering a lost nuke. The veteran agent wondered how Simmons convinced their superiors to go in as deep as they had. He saw nothing conclusive in any of the evidence the junior agent presented. *Well, it's above my paygrade*, Frankle thought. *But at least it's drawn out the bad guys.* If nothing else, this mission had uncovered a major U.S. smuggling axis for the association known as the 252s. They weren't the only TCO, but its nameless, ruthless pervasiveness in Europe and South America put it in a class by itself. *We should be running down leads and kicking in doors, rather than pounding stakes into a beach hoping to hear Russian beepers,* he concluded to himself.

He looked at his partner. He suspected Bell thought the same, but twelve years as a Marine Recon Specialist does not leave one questioning or bitching about lawful orders. Frankle had learned before you couldn't wind Bell up—he'd just draw up in silence like a stolid turtle and await the storm's passing. Finally, he broke the silence. "About two miles to go. Keep an eye out on the right. It's not well-marked, apparently."

"Roger that."

"What did you think about our new Coast Guard friend?"

"Young and green, but I get a good vibe from him. I think he'll be one of the better ones if Pete doesn't get him killed."

"Better one what?" Frankle was glad this line of questioning had connected.

"Officer. Most of them aren't worth a shit before they make O-3, some even then. This guy thinks, and he listens. He also has balls—you saw his file, right? But he doesn't let them overrule his head. I'd work with him once he got over being green."

"Yeah, kids today, whattaya gonna do, eh?"

Bell glanced over and gave a rare hint of a smile. "He'd make an excellent candidate for your next partner."

"Two things wrong with that, partner." Frankle smiled back. "First, I'm not searching for a new wingman. Second, it will be a few more years before he works through his obligated service and gets into the itchy feet stage. By then, I'll be sitting in my cabin down on the Santee, drinkin' beer, shootin' ducks, and waiting for that pension check from Uncle each and every month."

"That'll be the day. OK, here's the turnoff."

He slowed for the turnoff, and Frankle turned away with a slight smile and radioed, "X-ray One Delta, Foxtrot Six Echo. Over."

"Foxtrot Six Echo, X-ray One Delta, go ahead. Over," Morgan's voice replied. He had relieved Deffler of communications.

"One Delta, Six Echo, arriving on-scene area one, request status. Over."

"Six Echo, One Delta, roger, overflight complete. One low-risk contact in sight, stationary on the island's northern tip. No other activity. Over."

"One Delta, Six Echo, roger, maintain overwatch. Over."

"Six Echo, roger out."

Frankle secured the radio in his pocket and turned to Bell. "Sounds like the old geezer Pete ran into is still hanging around. Just for grins, let's keep the pistols in the sensor bag."

"Roger that."

"OK, let's follow the trail. It leads through the middle to a spit on the northern tip. That's where we'll take the readings."

"Copy." Bell concentrated on keeping the car on the trail and clear of the trees. "Maybe you and the old geezer can swap Viagra tips while we're waiting."

"Hey, that's hilarious, junior. You're getting mighty smartassy to the guy who signs your evaluation!"

"I like to live dangerously."

Bell pulled the car over a quarter-mile south of the shack. The old gentleman sat in his chair, fishing, and turned when the agents stepped out of the car. Shading his eyes, he watched until they planted the first sensor stake, after which he got up and went inside the shack.

"What's got into him?" Bell asked while they paced out the distance for the next sensor insert.

"Probably hiding his catch. We are NMFS agents, you know."

"Oh, right, like we're on the lookout for beach poachers." Bell shook his head.

Frankle smiled. "Hey, he's Canadian. He doesn't know any better. Maybe he thinks he'll have to pay us off. Suits me. I'm not interested in a conversation." He glanced at his partner. "Even if it means I miss some Viagra tips."

Bell grinned as he drove in another sensor stake and flipped on the switch. The process continued until all twelve sensors were in place. While the two agents waited for enough time to pass, Frankle's cell phone buzzed with an incoming text message. He put on his reading glasses to read the message, and as he read, his eyebrows raised appreciatively.

"Well?" Bell said somewhat impatiently after several seconds. Frankle didn't reply; he just handed him the phone with a smile.

"Hot Damn!" the younger agent continued in a whisper, handing Frankle back his phone.

"Yep, something to look forward to." He glanced at his watch. "OK, that's long enough. Let's go." After uploading the sensor data collected, he turned and glanced toward the shack while Bell moved forward on the sensor line. Frankle wondered if he shouldn't walk over and ask a question or two as a genuine NMFS agent might. It was a passing thought. He turned to follow the other agent as he gathered the sensors and moved to the car.

Lantern Key, Florida
15:27 EST, 18 January

Ben

Ben had just parked the car, and they were both stepping out on their final survey run when Simmons's phone gave an incoming

IM tone. He read the message and smiled at Ben. "Good news! It seems they have a strong lead on our evil lady villain." He paused and glanced up at Ben. "I'm allowed to use such terms for *her*, right?" Receiving a "Give me a break!" look in return, he continued. "It seems 'other technical means'—you can read that as the NSA—have localized her on Little Pine Key. I imagine one of her flying monkeys forgot to turn off his cell phone. Our third team is on the way to set up surveillance. Frankle and Bell will head over as soon as they wrap up their last beach. When Team Three gets eyes on, they'll call the Justice folks in to keep it legit and disengage once they are relieved."

"What about us?" Ben asked hopefully. The fact was, their activities that day had left him very bored.

"Sorry, young padawan. It's heads down on data and charts for the likes of us tonight. Someone has to stay on the mission. Besides, as my friend Matt Kemper would say, 'you couldn't swing a dead cat down there without hitting a Fed.' Soon they'd be asking who you are and why you're there."

"Oh, I guess you're right," Ben said with obvious disappointment.

"Buck up, friend! While they're tangling with Eurothugs, we could save the world! 'And gentlemen in England, now a-bed, shall think themselves accurs'd, they were not here, and hold their manhoods cheap, whiles any speaks, that fought with us upon Saint Crispin's day!'"

"Now, that's from Shakespeare's *Henry V*. I know that much," Ben said with resignation.

"I should hope so. Once more unto the beach, dear friend, and then we can go for a beer."

USCG Cutter *Kauai*, Gulf of Mexico, twenty-one nautical miles northeast of Key West, Florida
19:56 EST, 18 January

Hopkins

Hopkins came off the 16:00–20:00 OOD watch and swung by the mess deck for soda and chips from the community snack storage. She was pleasantly surprised to see Deffler with a tub of parts she presumed were UAV components. He stood and smiled on seeing her, and she decided to sit with him. Hopkins had grown to like the tall flier over the few days they had worked together. She admired his quiet professionalism and intelligence and enjoyed his sense of humor. And he was damned good-looking.

"Mind if I join you?" she asked, pouring a cup of coffee instead of soda.

"Please do," He gestured at the seat across the table.

"I won't interfere?"

"No, no. Routine checks for water intrusion. I take from Pile A," He selected a small part. "Inspect for any signs of water, plug it in the tester, all green, good to go, and deposit in Pile B."

"I thought you said they're water-sealed."

"I did indeed, but water always finds a way, particularly when it's especially salty and going after airplanes produced by the low bidder, we're deliberately crashing into the water. No worries here, just preventive maintenance."

"Hmm."

"Can I ask you a question?" Deffler inquired after a minute of silence and two more completed components.

"Sure."

"Can I help you with something? It seems like you've got the burden, as my old grandpa used to say."

"Yeah, I do, actually. It's this mission. Is it me, or is the world coming unglued?"

Deffler replaced the part he had just picked up on the "to do" pile and sat back. "What do you mean?"

Hopkins took a sip of coffee, then set down the cup. She started small, carefully weighing what she could say in the openness of the mess deck. "What's your read on Simmons?"

"He's a force of nature." Deffler smiled. "I only know him from a brief meeting and working alongside him here. It's like working with the eggheads from the R and D Center, but the secret agent shit brings in a whole 'nother dimension. He seems to know his stuff, but he's deep and dark. What of it?"

"Do you trust him? I mean, would you trust him with your life?"

"You mean, would I be worried he'd have my back if the shit hit the fan? Honestly, I'd be OK with him. I talked with one of his tech buddies while we were waiting around at Homestead, and he implied the guy is a James Bond-type legend. He's really put a twist on the other side's ops. And he's all about putting as wicked bad a twist on them as humanly possible. He doesn't worry about getting promoted or anything like that."

Hopkins relaxed a little. "So, you feel safe with him?"

"Oh, hell no, I didn't say that." He shook his head. "He *is* the go-to guy when the shit hits the fan. The problem is, if he can't find a handy shit-fan collision, he'll do his best to create one." When Hopkins's eyes widened, he quickly added, "Whoa, what's with this? He's gone, right?"

"Yes, but he's got the XO with him."

"It seems to me the XO's got a good head on his shoulders. He'll be OK. I don't know what's going on here, but I don't think the bad guys are interested in Doc's science project. They're trying to get their boat back. Hey, I can see the CO and XO are pretty good guys, but they're still officers. What's worth getting so worked up about?"

Hopkins's eyes narrowed, and she sat back. "Fritz, you wouldn't be asking that question if you'd been here a year ago when they came in to replace the old command."

Deffler could tell from the body language and tone he had stepped into it, but he pushed forward. "I've heard a few people mention problems with the last CO, but nothing specific. Feel like telling me about it?"

Hopkins felt the anger that had cropped up subsiding. *How could he know? Looking at us today, you could not believe it.* "Okay, you found a sore spot. Sorry about that. No need to unload this on you." Deffler reached across the table and touched her hand. Oddly enough, she didn't flinch or pull away.

"No shit. I'd like to hear the story if you don't mind telling me."

"There's a short but very exciting story behind it. Have you ever had a bad CO, a really bad one?"

"I've had some I didn't care for, but I wouldn't consider them as 'bad.' Seen a few bad officers in my time, but they usually get sorted out or shit-canned by the end of their first tour. I can't imagine one of them making it to Commander, much less CO of an air station."

Hopkins nodded. "Yeah, I couldn't imagine it either. Like you, I've seen good and bad officers, but the COs are a cut above. When I got here eighteen months ago, the CO had been for here six. Fritz, I've never seen a boat as messed up as this one. People were just plain *scared.* The CO had two settings—uptight and detonate. If he was around, you would get screamed at or talked down to."

"What about the XO or the chief? I can't figure Drake putting up with that."

"Chief Drake wasn't here yet. The chief that was here was 'retired on active duty.' He just did what he needed to avoid getting chewed up. The XO? He was broken by then. He was OK before, not a hard-charger, but he did the job. He was as scared as the rest of us, trying to get by until he completed his tour. The CO was even harder on him."

Deffler rolled his eyes. "I don't get guys like that. I heard they relieved him. What did him in?"

Hopkins closed her eyes briefly as she remembered the day. "It was right after Chief Drake got here. We were working on that last big Alien Migrant Interdiction Operation from Cuba. Ever done an AMIO patrol?" Deffler shook his head, and she continued. "They're heartbreakers at the best of times, but this one was terrible. We were headed to Bahia de Cabañas with a couple dozen migrants for repatriation when something stirred them up. The ICE guy and translator were handling it, but the CO decided to rip them a new one in front of the prisoners. That kicked off a no-shit riot. When we finally got things under control, we had to MEDEVAC the XO and BM1, and two of the Cubans were dead."

Deffler gaped in astonishment. "My God, 'we got things under control'? What did you do?"

"Let's just say some creative, complex rudder maneuvers on my part, combined with a fire hose team led by Chief Drake, did the trick and leave it there. After that, we couldn't continue the mission, so the Command-and-Control cutter took off the migrants, and we headed back to Miami. The Sector Commander and the Coast Guard Investigative Service were waiting at the dock for us, and they took the CO off as soon as we moored. They brought in a squad of agents who put everyone on board through a hard-core interrogation. At least the CO was gone. So was the XO. I'm sorry he got hurt, but his leaving was for the best.

"So, there we were, low as you get, wondering what's next. I was in the deepest funk I can ever remember, but Chief held us together. Lieutenant Powell showed up the next day, took command, and started turning things around. A couple of weeks later, Mr. Wyporek arrived and dropped right in like an old hand. I've never seen anything like it. I don't know how they did it, but they got rid of the loafers and whiners. They brought in John, Shelley, and Lope, and we're back in the game and far better than before, even considering the CO."

"That's quite a story." Deffler smiled. "I see why you like them. You have an impressive team here, and they deserve a lot of credit if they made it happen. But I'm still not getting why you're so wound up about Wyporek. Surely, he can handle a simple shore detail."

"Look, you said yourself that Simmons is a loose cannon. He says he has backup, but I wouldn't trust him as far as I can throw him. I see him running straight into a buzzsaw without a care in the world, and guess what? I couldn't give a damn. My problem is that my XO, who I happen to think is one of the best men I've ever known, has a big blind spot when he thinks duty calls. Did you know Simmons almost dragged him into a shootout in Key West?"

"What?"

"Yep, the first hint the XO had that trouble was brewing was when Simmons asked him out-of-the-blue if he could do stunt driving. Next thing he knows, they're speeding through Key West with a carload of armed psychos on their tail. Simmons did have backup. His guys staged a car wreck—no shit, a car wreck, I'm not making this up—to take out the bad guys, but our guy was a sitting duck the whole time. If he'd been chewed up, I'm sure Simmons would have just said '*C'est le Guerre*' and moved on. And yet, when that creep says, 'I need a PB expert,' off he goes, with the CO's blessing. Dammit!" She paused when she saw the concerned look on Deffler's face. "Sorry, I'm a little loony when it comes to stuff like this."

"Don't worry about it. I'm glad to take the heat for you. I would be a little careful about going on full afterburner in front of Chief or one of the O's, though." Deffler tilted his head.

"Too late." Hopkins shook her head sadly. "I sort of lit them up during the brief. *Respectfully*, of course."

"Of course." Deffler smiled, relieved the tension in the conversation was subsiding. "I take it from the fact you're here and not locked in the brig means the Old Man has a soft spot for you."

"No. Well, maybe a little, but not like you think. He knows this is déjà vu for me."

"How so?"

"Um, you know I lost my husband, right?"

"Yes, I heard that. I'm very sorry."

"Thanks. the XO reminds me of him, is all."

"Really?" Deffler asked with a sly smile, and his left eyebrow raised.

Hopkins chuckled. "Not like that, you idiot!" Her smile disappeared when she continued. "He charged off on a SAR case he shouldn't have taken and didn't come back."

"He was in the Guard?"

"Yeah, a BM2 coxswain. We were stationed together in Oregon. My younger son Jamie was just a year old. I was thinking hard about getting out, and we were trying to figure out how to swing it financially when it happened. The surf was up, too high, but he went anyway. It took out him and his crew."

"Geez, I'm sorry. It must have been hard."

"It was hell. But the station really helped. We worked around it until my mom got there, and she, the boys, and I have been together since. I'm still mad at him for taking that mission." She brushed away a tear. "And I miss him every day."

"I wish there's something I could say, but I know there isn't." He gave her hand a brief, soft squeeze.

"Thanks. Enough wailing by me. What's your story? I hope I'm not crying on a married man's shoulder here." She had noticed he didn't wear a ring, but operational people seldom did in the field because of the risk of injury.

"Nope. Tried it, but it didn't work out."

"Oh, now I'm sorry. Her fault or yours?"

"I think it's shared between us and the detailer," Deffler replied, referring to the chief petty officer in charge of enlisted assignments at the Coast Guard Personnel Command. "My first tour was at Barbers Point, and I fell for and married a local Hawaiian gal. Any place after Hawaii would have been a step-down, but they sent us to Elizabeth City."

"Ouch," Hopkins imagined the culture shock of moving from Oahu's western shore to rural North Carolina.

"Yeah, we had two little girls by then, and she was missing her family, but at least it wasn't *too* cold in the winter. The next tour did us in, though. I asked for Barbers Point, St. Petersburg, or Sacramento, and I got, wait for it, Kodiak."

"You're kidding!"

"Nope. I was paying back for that tour in paradise in the detailer's mind. The CO and XO tried to help, but that just made the detailer dig in harder. I get it; everybody's got a sad story. The system would blow up if they got down in the weeds all the time, yadda, yadda. So, we went. She did her best, but she just couldn't take it anymore after a year, and neither could I. So, we broke up, and she moved back home to Oahu with the girls, and I stayed on."

"Wow, it's hard enough to be away from my boys for patrols. I can't even think about *living* apart from them."

"Could be worse. I'm still friends with the ex, and she makes sure I get Skype time with the girls every day I'm not deployed. Plus, every visit I have with them is a treasure. Would you like to see them?"

"Heck, ya," Hopkins replied with a smile.

As she looked through his smartphone pictures of the two young girls, clearly Hawaiian, but with some of the angular features of Deffler's face and large blue eyes, Hopkins gushed, "My God, they're beautiful! Oh, I'm so sorry you're apart, Fritz."

"Yeah, hopefully, I can build enough brownie points and get back there. If I work it out right, I can get there on my twilight tour and see them through high school."

"Sometimes, hope is the only strategy you have." Hopkins nodded.

"Don't I know it. So, what's your hopeful strategy?"

Hopkins looked up. "I'm above the cut for chief. I'll have to rotate off the boat to pin it on. My hope is to get a nice quiet sector job in someplace that's not crazy expensive to live in. I love my mom, and she's my hero for taking care of the boys when I'm out, but I need a house with some space, if you know what I mean."

"Yeah, I get it. Sounds like you're not so happy about moving on."

"Believe it or not, I considered turning it down. I really like the crew, and the captain has practically made me an operations officer. Wouldn't happen anywhere else, even as a chief." She looked down and shook her head. "But we need the money, and the captain said staying's not an option."

"I thought he liked you."

"He does. A lot, and that's why he said no way."

Deffler nodded. "Powell is something special. He knows losing you will hurt, no matter who they get in behind you."

"Thanks." She glanced awkwardly at her watch. "It's been real, but I need to do some XO stuff and hit the rack. Anything I can do to help?"

"You already have." He smiled, then looked down. "Nah, just doing a little extra to pass the time. I'll be checking out soon."

"OK, I'll see you in the morning." She gave his hand a quick squeeze back as she got up.

Preliminaries

4601 Bryant Ave, Little Pine Key, Florida
20:18 EST, 18 January

Frankle

Frankle and Bell approached the surveillance position occupied by the two agents from Team Three, Gerard and Kelly. The last of the twilight faded an hour ago, and the first quarter moon would soon follow. The Team Two men had parked their vehicle about a quarter-mile away to avoid revealing their presence. They walked carefully through the brush using low-light field goggles, the receding moon and stars providing plenty of illumination for the latest night vision devices. Both teams were equipped with Blue Force Trackers feeding position information for "friendlies" into a heads-up display integrated into their goggle lenses. These made elaborate verbal challenges and countersigns unnecessary. The incoming agents were silent until Frankle kneeled beside the seated Gerard and took off his goggles.

"Long time, no see, Billy," Frankle whispered. "How come you guys are staking out the rear? Didn't you get here first?"

"True, old man," Gerard replied, drawing a good-natured cuff on the back of his head. "Turns out the Feebs are bringing in their primo breach team from Miami and didn't want us in the way. I can't argue with that, honestly. Those guys trained up together. We stand an excellent chance of crossing wires during the big push if we're mixed in with them. They'll be here in a couple of hours, and then we go live. Plan is to wear 'em down for a few hours to get them punchy, then breach at 05:15."

Frankle gave a non-committal grunt. His experiences working with the FBI had been unsatisfactory. He did not like the rigidity of their tactics. Also, he had never met a situation lead that was not a first-class asshat. The house was a large ranch-style, with a screened porch. A path led from the house to a dock hosting a large speedboat. Like many on the Keys, the house was raised as a hedge against the storm surge accompanying hurricanes. Two sets of stairs led down off the front and back porches. The underside of the house was open except for two bathroom-sized enclosures. "Hmmm. Defensible, but it kinda commits you to a last stand." Frankle returned his view to the house proper and noted some lights, but no sign of movement. "They on to the stakeout, you think?" he asked.

"No question. Haven't seen a sliver of a silhouette since sunset."

Frankle turned his view to the dock and fixed on the RHIB. "That's plenty of boat. What do you think, thirty knots?"

"Forty at least would be my guess."

"The big chief didn't think that is a good egress option?"

"Nope. She's got that covered with a CBP Blackhawk. One door, easy to pick them off coming down. Figures they'll see they're sitting ducks on the run, even if they make it to the boat and either give up or shoot it out."

"Won't work," Bell interjected as he took off his goggles.

"I don't know, partner," Frankle responded. "I'm not the biggest fan of the Bureau, but it sounds reasonable to me."

"They can't cover the back with a helo when there's fog."

Both senior agents turned toward Bell. After a few seconds of astonished silence, Frankle said, "Fog? You've got to be kidding, son. This is the Florida Keys, not Monterey, California."

Bell shook his head in the dark. "Don't you guys check the weather before an op? Stable air mass, warm water, and a weak cold front is moving through around 01:00—no wind, just enough to cool down to the dewpoint. Twenty bucks says that we'll be socked-in by 03:00," he said. "If I were them, I'd wait until I could barely see that dock, then I'd kick off a firefight in front. Or wait until we try to breach and throw us off-stride. Once the rearguard has the DOJ occupied, I think we'll see Valentina squirt out the back with cover fire and haul ass in that boat. She can scoot across Florida Bay and be on the mainland in an hour. With nothing in the air, our chances of running her down or even tracking her to a landing onshore are on the 'none' side of slim-to-none."

"Kind of a long shot, don't you think?" Gerard asked.

"Better than no shot, which is what she'll have trying to plow through the front. Just sayin', we might want to scope out a blocking position on that path from the house."

Frankle considered the possibilities. He knew that, although very rare, fog was not unknown in the Florida Keys, particularly in the winter. He also knew Bell was an old hand at planning ops on unfamiliar ground, and including weather in the planning could be the difference between success and failure. The deciding factor was the man's certainty. He wouldn't have brought it up, much less pushed hard, if he wasn't confident in his prediction. Frankle turned to Gerard. "If he thinks we'll have fog, we'd better plan for it. That's the worst case. It couldn't hurt to set up for it." He handed his partner the low-light camera. "OK, mister science guy, find us a good setup to cover that dock and a covert route."

"On it." Bell took the camera and crept off.

Frankle turned back to Gerard. "Are you sure she's in there? It doesn't figure her going to ground here when she probably could have made it to the mainland in the initial breakout."

"No doubt. We got an excellent shot of her looking out the window, and facial rec kicked back a ninety-seven percent match. But I'm with you. Something's wrong. She's making a lot of mistakes for someone who's supposed to be a shit-hot operator."

Frankle frowned. "Maybe that jolt the Coasties gave her tumbled her gyros a bit. I'll take 'em any way I can get 'em, but we'd better stay sharp and assume they're up to something."

"Like?"

"Like everybody with a federal badge is gathering here. It's the kiddie soccer scenario—everybody runs to the ball. Meanwhile..."

"Yeah, I get what you mean. You want to check with the boss?"

"Can't hurt. At least we see it gets passed to Pete that he's on his own until morning." After a pause, Frankle looked around and continued, "We'll set up a defense in depth. You guys take it close and cover the stairs, and we Marines will dig in by the boat."

"Roger that." Gerard nodded. "What do I tell the Head Fed if she wants to talk to you?"

Frankle snorted. "Tell her I'm out taking a piss or a nap or something. Remind her of my 'advanced age.' Should be enough to convince her to go elsewhere for castle stormers."

Gerard grinned. "Roger that."

Conch Inn, Room 118, Marathon, Florida
20:47 EST, 18 January

Ben

They had ordered dinner via GrubHub to avoid the open exposure in a restaurant. Simmons used a new credit card under one of his aliases, and Ben had the only contact with the delivery driver. The food was decent, Ben was glad not to deal with fast food again, and the beer was excellent. The conversation was light, with Ben sharing details of his upbringing in Northern Illinois, his academy experience, and his first tour on *Dependable*. His efforts to elicit similar information from his DIA companion were politely rebuffed, which did not come as a surprise. He got Simmons to admit the "pretty grad student," for whom he had gained his literary knowledge, and his late fiancée was the same person. However, he cut off further inquiry along that line, and even Ben could see through the agent's carefully preserved bonhomie that her death was still very painful for him.

Simmons wiped his hands after a long pull on his beer and said, "You know, that cooking on *Kauai* spoiled me. You can keep the close quarters and sea showers, but man, take out just won't measure up anymore."

"You can always head to a swanky restaurant and live it up." Ben smiled in return.

"Um, yeah, let me run down the 'list of swankies' in Marathon. Putting aside that we need to reduce public presence to a minimum when we're in the field, any notions you have of DIA agents running around high-class venues in tuxes are in error." He noticed Ben grinning at him. "What?"

"Sorry, trying to picture you stepping out of an Aston Martin in black tie, and someone hands you a martini. Yup, you're right. Does not compute."

Simmons feigned a severely insulted expression. "I take deep umbrage at your implication, sir! I'll have you know that I've masqueraded as some of the finest people in the social register on many occasions!"

"You have my most sincere apologies, your lordship." Ben joined in the game. "I hope this will circumvent the need to demand satisfaction or other regrettable social rituals."

"Very well." The agent nodded with mock solemnity. "The lack of ready cape-holders compels me to accept your apology, but do not think for a minute you can expect treats like this in the future!" Both shared a hearty laugh, cut short by an incoming call on Simmons's encrypted cell phone. He smiled when he saw the originating number and hit the speaker button before laying it on the table between them. "Hello, Victoria! You're on speaker with Benjamin and me. How was your trip?"

"Hello, Peter and Benjamin. My flight was three hours, twenty-seven minutes…, um, I mean, my trip was fine, thank you, Peter." Her voice dipped slightly at the end. "I have finished processing your surface sensor data. Would you like me to tell you the results?"

"Yes, very much, thank you, Victoria. Can you give us a summary, please?" the agent replied carefully, winking at Ben.

"All sensor arrays showed many transients congruent with natural background vibrations in the area. Three sets showed unusual readings not consistent with the natural phenomena of the area, but none of these were persistent or rhythmic."

"It's OK if you can't answer this, Victoria, but can you speculate on what could've made the transient vibrations?"

"I have put the signatures through a comparative database we have assembled. Some are consistent with metal-on-metal collisions, and others are plastic rubbing on plastic. A few are classified as 'relay closing.' However, our comparative database is sparse because the technology is new. Those classifications, particularly the last one, are low probability matches compared to the others."

"That is very useful information, Victoria. Can you tell me which locations' data included those unusual readings? Also, were the readings stronger in any location compared to others?"

"Yes," the analyst replied with more animation. "Lantern Key, Johnston Key, and Resolution Key all had the unusual readings. Resolution Key was significantly stronger than the others, almost an order of magnitude stronger."

Ben perked up. "Do you think..." He stopped when Simmons raised his hand.

"Victoria, could the presence of the old beachcomber on Resolution account for the high transients you noted?" Simmons asked.

"Yes, Peter. It would suggest a problem with the sensor array had it not read an increase when a human is active in the vicinity."

Simmons nodded. "Yes, I thought as much. I was hoping the stronger signal was not on Resolution—that would have been a 'man bites dog' story."

"Peter, I do not understand why a man would bite a dog or how that is relevant."

"Sorry, Victoria." The agent smiled. "I was using a journalistic aphorism. The point is that a man biting a dog would be a significant news story."

"Oh, yes, I see now. That is clever."

"OK, if there's nothing else to report, I'll let Benjamin say hello."

"No, Peter, nothing else."

Simmons took the phone off the speaker and handed it to Ben. He then retired to another room.

Grateful for the privacy, Ben said, "Hello, Victoria. We are off speaker, and I'm alone here."

"Hello, Benjamin. It is good to hear your voice. I hope you had a pleasant day."

"Far better if I could have spent it with you, but I would say that it's been an enjoyable day." He imagined her smile at the other end. "Peter provided your email address, and I'd like to send you a letter occasionally if that would be OK."

"Yes, I would like that, thank you. I know it will have to wait until you return to your ship, perhaps longer if you have communication restrictions."

It encouraged Ben she knew and understood operational security. One of his earlier relationships had foundered on that very issue. "Yes, or even after we return home when I can access my personal email. I just wanted you to know that I was thinking about you and looking forward to seeing you again."

"Oh, that's very sweet of you. I am also looking forward to your visit. There is much to do and see."

"Yes, I'm sure there is. Victoria, I really like the sound of your voice. I appreciate that Peter had to short-stop you, but would you mind telling me more about your trip and whatever else you would like to share?"

"No, I don't mind at all!" Ben was content to let the conversational roles of the previous night reverse. He enjoyed listening to the plummy sound of her voice and the intricate detail in her language. Ben regretted ending the session when Simmons returned to the room about ten minutes later and pointed at his watch.

"I'm sorry, Victoria. Peter is reminding me we have more work to do."

"I understand. I enjoyed our conversation and hope we can have another one soon, Benjamin. Goodbye."

"Me too, Victoria. Goodbye." Ben disconnected and handed the phone back to Simmons. "Not complaining here, but I'm surprised you allowed that on a government phone."

"Ah, young padawan, we buy burner phones and use adapters to put the sim cards in our encrypted gear. Now that you're done sweet-talking my little sister, I can switch out the sim." He winked. "It's a practice bordering on paranoid, perhaps over the border.

"I admit to being more than a little disappointed at the results today," he continued. "I was hoping the ground sensors would tell us something more than they did."

"So, what do we do now? *Kauai* heads out for refueling at the end of the day after tomorrow at the latest." He hoped Simmons would tell him of a deadline for ending the hunt.

"We hit the imagery tonight for a couple of hours, then head back to Lantern, Johnston, and Resolution tomorrow. We plant and leave the sensors in place for hours instead of minutes this time." He rubbed his temples absentmindedly. "Something will break tomorrow. I can feel it." He moved to hook the laptop up to the room's TV with an HDMI cable. "Ready for some genuine intel work?"

Ben groaned. "Can I have my job application back, please? The IC is not for me."

Simmons chuckled and pulled up the Park Service and UAV composite image files. "Alas, once you have strayed into the Dark Side, forever will it dominate your destiny!"

4601 Bryant Ave, Little Pine Key, Florida
05:12 EST, 19 January

Frankle

Bell was off by half an hour, but the rest of his weather forecast was spot-on. A light mist had crept in about half past midnight and blanketed the entire area within an hour. Frankle could barely make out the few lights showing at the house from his position near the dock. The FBI had formally announced their presence at midnight, with negotiations ongoing since. Government agents closed off any egress but lacked any alternative for a clean takedown other than an exposed assault "uphill" on the stairs. Fog prevented any use of helicopters, as Bell predicted. The plan was for a simultaneous push from the front and underside of the house. After breaching through the floor and tossing in flash-bangs, the main assault would push through the front, with sharpshooters clearing the windows and explosive charges on the door. With no hostages to worry about, anybody not lying prone with arms outstretched after entry would draw kill shots. Except for Valentina Petrova. She was a High-Value Target or HVT. Everyone wanted her alive, if practicable.

Although Frankle couldn't see him through the fog and concealment, Bell hunkered down on the left side of the path, deadly still. The Blue Force tracker in his goggles showed Gerard and Kelly closer to the house. Their position covered the back door and stairs. The assault teams were getting into position. Negotiations, if you could call them that, cut off at 05:00. The deal offered was, essentially, surrender or die. Their reply was an Eastern European version of "Screw you!" *So much the better.* Frankle had seen and read enough about the 252s that he had no issue with snuffing out them all.

Frankle shivered. It wasn't cold, but the light chill and the dampness of fog, combined with lying still for an extended period, cut right through him. *Cold in the goddamn Florida Keys—you are getting on, old man!*

"Two minutes, team leads call ready," the Scene Lead called on the tactical net. "Alpha Ready,"; "Bravo Ready,"; "Charlie Ready," replies followed, the last from Gerard up near the house.

"Delta ready," Frankle sent. He shifted in his position and thumbed the selector of his M4 from "safe" to "burst," then gave his Glock a touch check. While the seconds counted down and he stared into the fog, he could see in his mind's eye a dozen other agents tensely shifting, grasping weapons and equipment, coiled to spring.

His headset came alive. "Standby, ten seconds, five seconds, three, two, BRAVO GO." At the last word, a loud boom sounded from the house, and almost simultaneously, his headset shrieked briefly and went silent, and his goggles flashed a blinding light and immediately darkened.

"What the hell?" Frankle said to himself, then keyed the radio. "Any station, Delta, over." No reply—the headset and goggles were dead. He tore them off and tried to blink away the afterimage of the flash. After a few seconds, the sounds of flash-bangs arrived from the direction of the house, followed at once by a continuous overlapping staccato of automatic gunfire. Whatever shit the targets just pulled, the assault teams had recovered quickly and pressed the attack, he thought. His night vision was slowly returning when he heard Bell shout the fallback verbal challenge and receive two streams of shots in return. Frankle aimed in the general direction of the gunfire and fired bursts with his M4, hearing a cry suggesting at least one round had struck home. He stood up and swept his sights, ready to fire again, when a figure flashed past.

He spun around and raised the carbine for another burst when Bell shouted, "Check fire!" The thuds of running feet followed shortly afterward. A second later, a loud crash on the dock, with the yells from Bell and a woman, set Frankle into a run. A few steps later, he could make out two figures struggling on the dock. The larger figure grasped the smaller by the leg with one arm, the other dragging behind while the smaller figure reached forward. Frankle immediately stepped on the smaller figure's hand, drawing a female cry of pain, and kicked away the object he presumed was a handgun. He pressed the muzzle of the M4 into the prone figure's temple and shouted, "Enough!" When she stopped struggling, he continued, "Right hand back!"

"Fuck you!" was the muffled reply.

"Go ahead, give me a reason, bitch!" Frankle spat. "Right hand back! Do it now!"

As her right hand came back, Frankle grabbed her thumb, laid down the M4, and snapped and tightened a handcuff on the woman's right wrist to another yelp of pain. He then seized her left arm, took his foot off her hand, drew the other wrist back, and applied the other handcuff. He reached into his pocket, drew out a syrette, popped the cap, and jammed it into his prisoner's thigh. Within about ten seconds, the woman's body went limp. Frankle checked her pulse and then turned to Bell, gently helping him over onto his back. "Talk to me, partner!" he said, noticing the gunfire from the house had ceased.

"Shit." Bell groaned, gasping for breath while trying feebly to raise his head. "Took one…in the arm…the other in…the vest. Tasting blood…busted rib, lung."

"Okay, Okay. Lay back; I've got you." Frankle grabbed another syrette holding a morphine dose and jammed it into the younger man's unwounded arm. "Just gave you a dose of the good stuff. Hang in there." He pulled out a handkerchief, found and applied direct pressure to the arm wound, feeling Bell tighten in pain at first and then go slack as the morphine took effect. "Billy! You there?"

"Yo!"

"Lashon's hit! Get the medics back here; my comms are down!"

"Shit, Art! Everybody's comms are down! Kelly's running to get someone! I'm coming back. Hold your fire!"

"Come ahead, hurry, I need a hand. Follow the path!" Frankle drew his Glock with his free hand. In the dark and fog, he was taking no risks.

"On the way!" After a few seconds, a figure appeared in the fog.

"Beagle!" Frankle challenged, his Glock at the ready.

"Baron!" came Gerard's reply. Both agents, who had scoffed at spoken passwords in the digital age, gave silent thanks for the resilience of the old habits. Gerard approached and kneeled beside Bell. "How is he?" he asked with deep concern.

"Not good. Besides this, he took one in the chest. Looks like he cracked a rib and punctured a lung. I gave him a shot, so at least he's out of it. I don't want to move him without a stretcher." Frankle nodded toward the woman. "Help me watch that piece of shit. I gave her a thirty-minute amp, but you can never tell with them."

"Damn, you still got it, old man."

"Not hardly. Bell tackled her after getting shot to hell. I just cuffed and scuffed her."

"Okay. Man, this was one shit sandwich. I heard at least two 'Agent Downs' from up front." Gerard continued staring at the woman. "I don't get it. We nailed the only one coming out the rear door, and there's no way in hell anyone else got by us."

"When it gets light, I'll bet we'll find a bolt hole between here and your position. Gotta give 'em credit—that might have worked. If it wasn't for this hardhead." Frankle gazed hard at his stricken partner. "Where the hell is that medic? Billy, run over there and tell them we have an agent down, critical. I don't want to hear that they're up there patching up bad guys. Bring back a litter by yourself if you have to. And tell her nibs we have the HVT. That should produce some attention.”

“On it,” Gerard jumped up and trotted forward.

After the junior agent disappeared into the dark and fog, Frankle turned back to his friend. “It will be OK. Hang in there, partner.” *Goddammit! I AM getting too damn old for this crap!*

Contact

Conch Inn, Room 118, Marathon, Florida
06:18 EST, 19 January

Ben

"Holy shit!" Ben bolted awake. Simmons rolled out of his bed with a thud and grabbed for his gun. "Wait, wait, it's OK," Ben blurted.

"Dammit, friend, you'd better find a more peaceful way of rousing yourself!" Simmons exclaimed. "What the hell is going on?"

"I think I may know where it is." Ben opened the laptop on the table. After a brief boot period and logon, he opened two files they were looking at last night. "Something was bothering me, like I was missing something, but I couldn't put my finger on what. I guess I was too tired to think straight. OK, here—Resolution Key, the Park Service comparison set from three months ago." He turned the screen to Simmons.

"OK. Same thing I looked at a dozen times. I don't see anything," Simmons said with irritation.

"Exactly! The dog that didn't bark! Where's the shack?"

Simmons leaned down, and after a second, a broad smile opened on his face. "Where indeed! Well done, Sir! That crafty little bastard was the lookout. I'll bet they found the impact point right off the island. He's keeping watch until things cool down and they can get some heavy recovery stuff in there. Nothing to see here—move along, folks!" He clapped Ben on the back and then turned and grabbed his cell phone.

Ben had folded up the laptop and finished dressing when he noted a concerned expression on Simmons's face. "What's wrong?"

"I can't get Frankle or Bell or anyone on Team Three," Simmons replied with concern. He turned back to his phone. "Hello, Gypsy-1 here. I need Gypsy-2 and Gypsy-3's status now." He covered the microphone and glanced at Ben. "They're pinging them now. Get ready to go—we may have to bolt." Turning back to the phone, he answered, "For how long? OK, OK, pull your heads out of your asses and get everything else moving! Target is Resolution Key—north end of the island. We're on our way, ETA in thirty-five. Right." He punched off the phone and turned back to Ben. "Leave it! They've been down for at least sixty-five minutes, and they can't raise or even ping them. At last comms, they were moving in to assault, and then everything went dark. They've sent a unit down to investigate, but somehow it didn't occur to them to tell the guy the two teams were covering! If they're down, the odds are good the opposition has eyes on us, and they're calling in the heavies. Move!"

Both men darted to the car, grabbing the weapons bags and leaving the rest. With Simmons driving, they sped out of the parking lot onto U.S. 1 westbound, heading for Resolution Key.

****

A second car pulled out from across the highway a minute later and started following Ben and Simmons. The driver and his companion had taken heed of their predecessors' mistake—they would not show themselves. A tiny tracking transmitter they had attached to the rear bumper earlier that morning allowed them to track the Americans' vehicle while following out of sight in the foggy twilight.

The car's passenger called in to alert the assault team the targets were moving. With luck, they were following the lures to the prepared ambush point. The two men would call in the new position if their destination were elsewhere and keep watch until the assault team arrived.

The coordinated operation to the west had worked perfectly. Dozens of federal agents who could have provided support were now out of play. Simmons was on his own except for his military companion, who was not even special forces, given his grooming. The Organization had a positive lock on the nettlesome agent's position and an overwhelming advantage in force for the first time. Simmons was the prize, perhaps even worth the cost of the shipment lost through his interference.

U.S. Route 1, two miles west of Marathon, Florida
06:26 EST, 19 January

Ben

It was misty on the U.S. 1 bridge with fog in either direction. Ben worried about the impact on air surveillance and surface support if they ran into trouble before it burned off. He pulled out the handheld radio to make contact, hoping the fog was a localized issue today.

"*Kauai*, Shore-One, radio check in the green, over." Ben released the press-to-talk switch. After a brief pause with no response, he tried again. "*Kauai*, Shore-One, radio check in the green, over."

"Shore-One, *Kauai*, read you lima charlie in the green, how me, over?" Bondurant's voice replied.

Ben was relieved their high-altitude UAV still provided a communications relay. "*Kauai*, Shore-One, have you the same. Need to talk to Charlie Oscar in private, please, over."

"Standby One," Bondurant replied. Within a minute, Sam's voice came on the radio.

"Shore-One, *Kauai* Actual, on the headphones with speaker off."

"*Kauai*, Shore-One, we believe we have a lead. We are on U.S. 1, en route to Resolution Key. The target is the shack we saw on the spit on the island's northern tip; estimate possible contact in twenty-five minutes."

"Shore-One, we are about fifteen west right now in moderate fog. We'll make the best low-vis speed toward you, but it will be an hour and a half before we can get to you. Can you hold on making contact until then? Over."

Ben looked over at Simmons, who shook his head. "We can't wait. By now, the other guys may be en route, and we can't allow them to get to that warhead. This is a no-shit national security priority. Tell them to hurry because we're committed."

Ben nodded. "Negative, sir. It's a race between us and the other side. We've lost comms with Simmons's teams about an hour and a half ago, and he's sure the opposition is on to us. We must beat them to it, over."

After about half a minute, Sam replied, "Shore-One, *Kauai*, roger, proceed at discretion. National Defense ROE now active, acknowledge, over."

Ben noted the stress in Sam's voice, understandable, given he had just approved Ben to use deadly force at discretion. "*Kauai*, Shore-One, acknowledge National Defense ROE, over."

"Shore-One, *Kauai*, maintain contact, if practicable. We will transmit situation reports in the blind every fifteen minutes, starting on the hour. Godspeed Ben, over."

"*Kauai*, Shore-One, roger, thank you, sir, out."

"Just to be clear," Simmons began. "We'll go in with weapons drawn and rounds in the chamber. We don't want to shoot, but we take him out if it looks like him or us, OK?"

"Yes, Doc," Ben tried to keep his voice even. "That's what National Defense Rules of Engagement means. You'd better be right about this. My CO's and my asses are really hanging out right now."

"Same as all the rest of us, friend."

Ben pressed the point. "Doc, are you sure there's a nuke there?"

"What?" Simmons replied in astonishment.

"Look, the evidence is all circumstantial. There are some fearsome assumptions behind the conclusion there's a loose nuke. What if you're wrong?"

Simmons continued staring ahead and took a deep breath before answering. "OK. Am I one hundred percent sure this is a

Broken Arrow? No, obviously not. But it's the best theory I have to explain everything. You need to approach this from a risk management perspective rather than a criminal justice, 'beyond a reasonable doubt' view."

"I don't follow."

"If there's no nuke and we waste our time, what's the harm? Negligible. If there is, and we let the 252s get to it, it'll be a catastrophe."

"And if we get bottled up by the 252s before *Kauai* or your guys show up to support us?"

After a slight pause, Simmons replied, "OK, I guess 'negligible' wasn't the best word to use, but the risk calculus is still the same."

The excitement of his discovery disappeared. Between Sam's response and Simmons's cold reasoning, Ben felt like he was being carried along by events he was powerless to control. It was the car chase all over again, and he hated it. But after a few more seconds, the rational part of his brain won out, and Ben conceded. "OK, I guess I can see the logic of that point."

"See, good news! Hey, I get this is scary—remember what I told you about fear? This is one of those times when you hang it out there, trust your colleagues, and hope the breaks come your way."

"Right," Ben concluded, staring forward as they drove through the fog.

****

Twenty minutes later, they reached the turnoff of the highway on Resolution Key. Ben's head had been on a swivel throughout the trip, scanning for trailers while Simmons drove. Nothing. He hoped that was a good sign, and they weren't waiting to pounce when they arrived at the shack. Time for one last check-in. "*Kauai*, Shore-One, over."

"Shore-One, *Kauai*, go ahead, over," Sam's voice answered almost immediately.

"*Kauai*, Shore-One, turning on to Resolution now. Estimate contact in one-zero minutes, over."

"Copy. We're still in fog here. Our ETA is one hour, fifteen minutes, over."

"Roger that, sir. We'll look forward to seeing you then, over."

"Take care, Ben. Out."

Simmons nodded and said, "Now, what we will do is pull up next to the shed and step out with our guns drawn and held behind us. If he's outside, we'll try to get close enough to keep him from getting inside before we make our move, but if he goes for the door, we jump him. Clear?"

"Clear."

"If he's not outside, we'll just play it on the fly. It will be hard, but don't shoot if you have a choice."

"Thanks, Dad."

"OK, that *was* a little condescending, sorry." Simmons smiled sadly. "Just stay cool and keep your head in the present."

After about six minutes, the car rounded a dense patch of bush and coconut palms. Once clear of the vegetation, the ground formed a natural causeway leading to the spit on the island's northern tip. The fishing shack lay near a copse of palm trees, invisible in the light fog. A minute later, Ben could see the shack a quarter-mile away, the view becoming clearer as they approached. When the car pulled up to the structure, no one was in sight, and the two men quietly got out, drawn pistols held behind them.

"Should we split up and flank him?" Ben whispered as he walked carefully through the soft sand.

Simmons shook his head, whispering back, "Too much chance of getting into each other's line of fire. Let's move about five feet apart and advance in line abreast." Simmons glanced at Ben and received a thumbs-up in return.

As the two rounded the shack, they suddenly faced the old Newfoundlander. All three men stopped in their tracks about twenty feet apart, and Simmons said, "Hello again, friend. We have more questions for you."

After a brief instant, the man dropped the pail and fishing rod he held and bolted toward the door. Ben reacted on instinct, holstering his weapon as he ran in pursuit. "Stop, Federal Officer!" Simmons followed just a step behind.

The squatter was stepping through the door when Ben leaped for a flying tackle and crashed into the man. The two rolled several times past the shack, and Ben's attempt to get his arms around the man drew a blow to his solar plexus that knocked the wind out of him. As he rolled clear and lay gasping for breath, Simmons jumped on the man. Ben watched in complete astonishment as the two men traded blows in rapid succession in a martial arts display that would have put Donnie Yen to shame.

Finally, Simmons got the upper hand and shouted, "Tase him, dammit!"

Ben snapped out of his awed paralysis, quickly drew and activated his taser, and fired it into the squatter's chest. As the man began convulsing, Simmons disengaged and shouted breathlessly, "Cuffs! Cuff him!"

Ben dropped the taser, grabbed a pair of flex cuffs out of his belt pouch, pulled the stunned man's arms behind him, and cinched the loops over both wrists.

"Legs too, then search him carefully," Simmons said, bent over and panting.

Ben took out another pair and attached them below the man's ankles. Then he carried out a laborious search that netted a box cutter, combat knife, and what looked like a penknife. He turned to Simmons and said, "That's it."

Simmons had finished panting and stood upright, glaring at the bound man. "Stand off to my left, pull and charge your sidearm. If he breaks loose, shoot him. Try for a leg if you can."

Ben nodded, eyes wide, took a couple of steps to the side, and drew and charged his Sig pistol. The man on the ground rolled onto his back and then sat upright, his legs to the front. He shook his head briefly, then glanced back and forth between Ben and Simmons, finally settling on the latter.

"CIA?" the man asked.

"*Please.*" Simmons shook his head in disgust. "My compliments, friend. For a minute there, I thought you would get the better of both of us. I don't suppose you'd care to tell us who and what you are."

"As you said—*please.*" The man smiled slightly.

"While you and I trade unenlightening pleasantries, my colleague here will have a look in your little hovel over there. Before that, we need to reach a mutual understanding to behave in a civilized fashion from here on out. I have absolutely no problem ending you, nor doing so in an excruciating and gruesome way. Given that, are there any booby traps waiting for him in there?"

The man smiled. "No, you managed to get the drop on me."

Simmons smiled back, drew and charged his pistol, pointed it at the man, then turned to Ben. "Peek in the door, do not enter. If you see a phone or any other hand-helds within reach, check them for tripwires before picking them up."

"Roger that," Ben said, holstering his pistol. As he walked toward the shack, his fear grew, with his heart pounding, and he started looking down to make sure he wasn't stepping on anything that could maim or kill him. Ben reached the doorway, drew and turned on his flashlight, and began a close examination around the perimeter of the opening. He could hear Simmons and the squatter talking, but couldn't make anything out as he concentrated on his check.

Once the doorway examination was complete, Ben shined the flashlight in the doorway in a systematic search of the floor and walls of the shack. Nothing was visible inside besides a low, bamboo-framed bunk and a small table with a wallet, cell phone, and an opened pack of cigarettes. Ben drew and extended his 16-inch expandable baton and poked the cell phone and wallet. No tripwires. He reached in and carefully lifted the phone and then the wallet, then turned and walked back to Simmons and the squatter.

"Lieutenant, I think we have found our target, or at least the caretaker. My money is on there being a nuclear warhead somewhere in the water just north of here, and we can do a grid search once my people show up."

Ben opened his mouth to reply, but remained silent when the cell phone emitted two beeps, three seconds apart.

"Looks like your backup has arrived," the squatter said with a rueful smile.

Ben glanced at Simmons, who shook his head at the squatter and said, "Not us. Are you expecting anyone?"

The man stopped smiling and replied, "No."

Simmons looked over at Ben, who asked, "The 252s?"

Simmons nodded and looked back at the squatter. "You heard of the 252 Syndicate?" After the man nodded grimly, Simmons added, "Well, they are headed straight for us. I presume you'll suffer the same fate as us if they grab you."

"Worse, probably. The signal indicates two vehicles, just clearing the highway," the man replied.

"That gives us about ten minutes. Ben, check on *Kauai*. This group won't be rookies—they'll be combat-ready, probably with armored vehicles."

Ben donned his headset and keyed the radio. "*Kauai*, Shore-One, over."

After about five seconds, Sam's relieved voice replied over the channel, "Shore-One, *Kauai*, read you loud and clear."

Ben moved the selector to the voice-activated position. "*Kauai*, Shore-One, you need to go off-speaker again."

After a few seconds, Sam replied, "Shore-One, *Kauai*, the speaker is off. I'm on the headset."

"*Kauai*, Shore-One, we've made contact and confirmed. We have one in custody; believe he is with the Russians. The bad news is the TCO is headed this way. Two confirmed vehicles, expect hostile action in ten minutes, and Doc tells me this will be their A-Team. They'll have plenty of firepower and armored vehicles."

"Roger Ben, is there any way you guys can dodge them?"

"Negative, sir. The only clear route is a narrow path in the center of the island and just a causeway in the north, leading to the spit. If we left now, we would run right into them and be sitting ducks."

"What about Simmons's people? Over."

Simmons shook his head. "They're at least thirty minutes out."

"Negative, sir. They're at least thirty minutes out," Ben repeated.

"Roger." Sam's voice was low and even, but Ben could still hear the concern, even over the radio. "We are seven miles away. I'm ordering emergency speed; fog be damned. Do whatever you need to do to stay alive, clear?"

"Roger that, sir. See you soon, out." Ben took the transmit switch back to off.

"How long before they get to us?" Simmons asked, slamming a magazine into his Uzi.

Ben paused. *Seven nautical miles, twenty-eight knots.* "Fifteen minutes, give or take, but they will need a visual target to engage." He glanced offshore at the fog with concern. "I doubt this will clear by then."

"I don't suppose he can fire high to scare them off."

"No way. A stray shot could reach down to U.S. 1. He won't take that risk, even for me."

"Right." Simmons finished the readying of his firearms. "I guess we'll just have to hold until they can get in the fight."

"Pretty much."

"OK, go grab the guns."

Ben trotted to the back of the car, opened the trunk, and took out his and Simmons's weapon bags. When he came back around the shack, he almost dropped both when he saw the squatter uncuffed and helping Simmons drag a log over to the shack. "What the hell, Pete?"

"We have reached an understanding," Simmons replied. "Don't just stand there! We're screwed without cover!"

Ben dropped the bags by the shack and got to work, dragging logs and driftwood to the shack. The frantic effort of building up the makeshift barrier out of driftwood and hand-shoveling sand to fill in the gaps kept Ben's mind off the fact that they had been in a fight to the death with the man working next to him just minutes ago.

✶✶✶✶✶✶✶✶✶✶✶✶✶✶✶✶✶✶✶✶✶✶

It surprised the 252 scouts that Simmons and his companion had not taken the bait but departed the highway on Resolution instead. It was a pleasant surprise: they considered using Resolution for the trap, but its geography was so ripe for an ambush that no one believed the American agent would fall for it.

And yet, here he was. According to the tracking instrument, he was stopped on the island's northern tip, and it was the least defensible spot on the least defensible island in the group. Amazing.

When the assault team arrived, the scout lead passed on orders that the two Americans were to be taken alive at all costs and no explosives were to be used in the capture. Something brought Simmons to Resolution—they decided to find out what it was. After the assault team passed, the scouts repositioned off the highway within the scrub beyond the tree line. They would watch the escape route until the assault team completed their work and departed.

Engagement

USCG Cutter *Kauai*, Gulf of Mexico, seven nautical miles west of Resolution Key, Florida
07:13 EST, 19 January

Sam

"Green Deck! I need eyes on scene—get that bird airborne and screw the regulations!" Sam shouted across the Bridge. "OOD, what's the bearing from here to the north tip of Resolution?"

"A moment, Captain. OK, zero-eight-three magnetic at six-point-eight," Hopkins replied.

"Deffler, initial heading zero-eight-three, set altitude at five hundred, fast as she'll go!"

"Right, Captain. Airborne at 12:14 Zulu, heading zero-eight-three, passing seventy-five for five hundred." After a minute, he continued, "Level at five hundred feet, max thrust selected, operations normal, checking the optical package now. OK, eyes working, speed of advance forty-seven knots."

Despite Deffler's objection about unmanned aircraft operating regulations in restricted visibility, Sam was kicking himself for not launching earlier. "Very well, when you are a quarter-mile from the scene, throttle back, and activate Ghost. And get that second bird up in case they splash number one—green deck. Keep it a half-mile dead in front of us for now with wide-angle on the camera. If you see ANYTHING, shout it out. You're our advanced lookout."

"Yes, sir!"

Sam stared at the display screen. He could barely make out the waves on the water passing below as the Puma sped through the mist at fifty-five mph. "OOD, get us there. I want everything the old girl has."

"Yes, sir!" Hopkins contacted Main Control on the Ship's Service Telephone. "Chief, OOD, we need every knot you can give us. It's what we were afraid of. Roger, take the engines. We're heading into shoal water, so you can expect a crash back order as soon as we get a target lock. Yeah, thanks, Chief." She turned to Sam as she hung up the phone. "Chief's got engine control now and is pulling out the stops, Captain."

"Thank you." Sam turned and grabbed the microphone for the PA system. "All hands, Captain speaking, we're heading for Resolution Key at full speed to back up Mr. Wyporek. He and Dr. Simmons are pinned down by a heavily armed criminal force. Set General Quarters Condition One. This is not a drill." He hung up the microphone and pulled the switch on the GQ alarm box, starting the twenty-second alarm gong.

Sam grabbed one of the spare handheld radios, stepped outside, turned up to the Flying Bridge, and shouted, "Lookout!"

Seaman Pickins appeared at the rail. "Yes, sir!"

"Get down here!"

Pickins grabbed the ladder and slid down, hands and feet on the outside, landing with a thud. He pulled up to attention in front of Sam. "Yes, Captain!"

"Pickins, take this radio...." Sam handed it to the young seaman. "And get down on the bow. We're hauling ass in fog, and you're our last line of defense against a collision. You see or hear anything that we can hit, you call it in on the radio and then run like hell, got it?"

"Yes, sir!"

"You might hear shooting off in the distance. Ignore it. Keep your sweep thirty degrees on either side of the bow, understand?"

"Yes, sir! Sweep from three-three-zero to zero-three-zero!"

"Right on! I'll call you if I can, but don't wait for any orders when you feel us doing a crash stop. Just beat feet back to the boat deck and report to Bondurant, clear?"

"Yes, sir!"

"Well done, son." Sam clapped the young man on the arm. "Good luck. Off you go!"

"Yes, sir!" Pickins saluted, then ran off to his post on *Kauai*'s bow.

Sam turned to glance forward. Repositioning the lookout to the bow would only buy them a few extra seconds of warning at twenty-eight knots, but Sam was banking every second he could.

Drake

Machinery Technician Third Class Brown was assisting Drake in running his routine morning checks in Main Control when the phone rang. Drake lifted the phone with concern—if the Bridge was calling, it couldn't be good. "Main Control, Drake."

"Chief, OOD, we need every knot you can give us. It's what we were afraid of."

"He's jammed up, isn't he? Okay, Hoppy, if you can pass me engine control, I'll pull the topping stops. I think I can squeeze a few extra knots from the old lady."

"Roger, take the engines. We're heading into shoal water, so you can expect a crash back order as soon as we get a target lock."

"Right then, I need you to give me a heads up about a minute before so I can replace the stops and slam in back full without blowing us up. On it now."

"Yeah, thanks, Chief."

He slammed down the phone, grabbed a set of pliers out of the box, and turned to Brown. "Dave, take the throttles and hold at ninety-eight percent until I give you the signal and then edge it up. We'll start with Number One!"

Drake laid down between the engines, carefully reached the pliers in, and gripped the topping button on the fuel control, extracting it and putting it into his pocket. He glanced at Brown and held up one finger, and the junior petty officer put his hand on the right-hand throttle. Drake gave an exaggerated nod and then fixed his gaze on the fuel control, providing a repeating pinching signal with his fingers for Brown to advance the throttle. When the control arm reached the point Drake couldn't risk anymore, he held up a fist and looked at Brown, who held both hands. They then repeated the process on the number two engine. He got up, moved to the control station, glanced at the digital reading for the cutter's speed through the water—thirty knots—and let loose with a "Hot damn! Payback time—hold together, baby!" The engine instrument readings were a nightmare scenario for any engineer, but Drake knew the engines could take it for a brief time.

Brown, wide-eyed after the procedure and aghast at the readings, turned and shouted over the noise of the engines, "How long will they take this Chief?!"

"As long as they need to!" Drake shouted back.

"What should I do if one lets go?!"

"If parts start flying, we hit the fuel shutoff and get out!"

"What do I do then?!"

"You damn well better catch up to me, son!"

Sam

After a minute, the engines were running at maximum, and Sam felt they were running faster than any full-power run they had before. "OOD, ETA, please."

Hopkins was not freaked-out, exactly, but a full-power run in low visibility was very high-risk, bordering on reckless. A collision was likely if another vessel appeared directly ahead of them out of the fog, ending this mission, if not the patrol boat herself. Hopkins had dropped the scale on the search radar to two miles when Sam ordered full speed to achieve the highest resolution and probability of detection. And she stayed bolted to the screen. She glanced at the SeaWatch panel and replied, "Captain, speed of advance is twenty-nine. I make it... twelve minutes now, maybe eleven and a half."

Sam was impressed. *Twenty-nine knots and thirty through the water. Well done, Chief!* "Very well. Any shoaling to worry about?"

"Captain, if it was low tide right now, I'd be pissing my pants, but we'll be OK all the way. It will be close at the end. And, by the way, we're violating the wake limits in the Great White Heron National Wildlife Refuge," she added with a slight grin.

Sam returned a sad smile. "Book me. When this is over, the Department of Interior guys will be the least of my worries." According to the book, Sam should connect with the District Command and seek a Statement of No Objection for use of force. Of course, there wasn't a hope of getting an SNO in time to help Ben. He shared a look with Hopkins. Sam would do whatever it took to save his friend and shipmate, even if that violated standing orders. Calling now would only risk the more severe charge of disobeying a direct order. The look they shared made clear both knew this truth, and neither would say it. After a few seconds, Hopkins looked down at the radar screen, and Sam turned back to the fire control station.

The crew scrambled to their GQ stations, donning vests and helmets. Sam fastened his vest and stepped over to the Fire Control Station, where Williams had activated his console and worked through the warm-up of the main gun. "Williams, load with armor-piercing when you get online. How will the infrared sight do in this fog?"

Williams pressed a few buttons and moved the joystick to check the infrared gun sight's operation. "Better than visual with the long-wave camera, maybe seven hundred yards, sir." He made another selection, and with a series of "clanks," the chain mechanism loaded the first Armor Piercing Discarding Sabot-Tracer round into the twenty-five-millimeter main gun. "APDS-T loaded; gun ready."

Sam turned back to Deffler, who was just putting on his helmet. "Deffler, reposition over here at fire control, please. I may need your eyes for shot spotting."

"Yes, sir." He activated the internal antenna of his laptop and then pulled it out of the docking port to cross the Bridge. "Hi, sailor!" He winked and kneeled next to Williams.

"Don't start," Williams growled back.

Sam grabbed his binoculars and went out onto the starboard Bridge wing. He need not have bothered with binoculars—visibility was a quarter-mile in the fog—but he needed something to steady his hands. Hebert was already in battle gear and was preparing his machine gun for action. "Whattaya say, Chef?" Sam said with a forced grin.

"Same as always, sir," Hebert replied with a tight smile. "You catch 'em, and I'll cook 'em."

Sam patted him on the back and continued to the end of the walkway. He gazed astern and briefly watched the "rooster tail" produced by thrust from the propellers. *Kauai*'s creamy white wake stretched straight back and spread out behind on the smooth water until fading from sight in the fog. He then turned his gaze inward and took in the sounds: the muffled roar of the diesel engines; the bumping and clanging as the crew prepared for battle; the snapping of the U.S. flag and Coast Guard ensign in the stiff wind high on the mast; the rush of the water passing at thirty knots and the intermittent thumping from the hull hitting the small waves. Through all this, the captain of the Coast Guard Cutter *Kauai* bowed his head and prayed. "Please, God, keep him and us safe for just ten more minutes."

Resolution Key, Florida
07:25 EST, 19 January

Ben

"I can see them," Ben said when he could make out the black shape of the large SUV coming through the mist. His "barricade," if it could be called that, was barely two-and-a-half feet high. "They don't seem too worried about us."

"Not much to fear from small arms. You don't happen to have an anti-tank rocket on you, by any chance? No? No." Simmons's face was expressionless as he stared at the approaching SUVs.

Their new companion, who still held to his assumed name of Bill, crouched to Simmons's left, staring at the approaching SUVs with Simmons's Glock in his hand. The two men had agreed on a temporary alliance against the impending threat, with the understanding that Simmons and Ben would look the other way afterward when the man fled, assuming they were still alive. Ben was not at all happy about this, trying not to think about how easy it would be for Bill to shoot both of them in the back.

Ben couldn't remember ever being so scared and swallowed hard as he watched the vehicles' slow approach. "Shouldn't we spread out? I mean, one shot with an RPG can take out all of us."

Simmons shook his head. "No, we need to keep close to the shack. They won't risk an explosive shot this close to the target, at least, until they figure out what it is. We move off, and they'll blow us away for sure."

"OK. Just a reminder. It's my first firefight."

Simmons shot Ben a glance and smiled. "Yeah, I remember. Don't worry, Ben, you'll be fine. Keep your head down, and other than that, it's just like the gun range."

Ben selected the voice-activated position on his radio. "*Kauai*, Shore-One, hostiles in sight and approaching, over."

"Roger One, we're almost there, and we have eyes on scene. Where are you? Over," Sam's voice replied.

The sound of Sam's voice and the knowledge a Puma was providing him situational awareness provided some relief from the gnawing fear. "We are all barricaded by the shed, sir, within fifteen feet. Everything moving is hostile, over."

"Roger that. Hang in there! Out."

"Hell is empty, and all the devils are here," Simmons quipped.

"Shakespeare, *The Tempest*," Ben responded.

"Well played, sir. We'll set you up with a pretty Lit major yet." Simmons smiled grimly with his eyes fixed on the approaching vehicles.

The line brought the thought of the lovely young analyst he had met a mere day and a half ago to mind. "If I don't make it back, would you tell Victoria… Well, you know what to tell her."

"You will make it back," Simmons snapped. "Just keep your head in the game!"

"Perhaps you should have considered a more experienced wingman," Bill said snidely.

"He'll do. Why don't you give us a break and shut up!" Simmons replied.

The two SUVs split apart and continued their slow approach. Simmons noticed the rear window of the left one coming down and put two Uzi bursts toward it. The window quickly raised. "Stand by for dismounts. They'll be using the vehicles for cover. You take the one on the right. Shoot at anything you see outside the vehicle, but don't take a lot of time aiming. We need a steady fire on them, or they'll rush us. Remember, stay low!"

Ben's vehicle slowed, and a head appeared around the back. Ben raised his carbine, firing a three-round burst, and the head disappeared. The SUV stopped, and two more heads popped up over the hood and fired automatic weapons. Rounds slammed into the wood barrier and ground, throwing up sand and wood splinters. Ben returned quick bursts in the general direction, noting Simmons and Bill were doing the same toward their vehicle. "*Kauai*, Shore-One, we are taking fire; repeat, we are taking fire. Request immediate assistance!" Ben discarded the radio and laid down a quick set of bursts, and one black-clad figure tumbled from behind his vehicle. *Steady fire, stay low, steady fire, stay low.* Ben drilled his mind to the task at hand.

USCG Cutter *Kauai*, one nautical mile west of Resolution Key, Florida
07:27 EST, 19 January

Sam

"Conn, Mount 51, sound of gunshots zero-four-zero relative, no visual target!" Hebert shouted through the Bridge door from his position on the starboard machine gun.

"Conn, aye!" Hopkins replied.

Sam watched the scene ashore unfold in real-time in the video feed from the orbiting Puma. His heart pounded, and he felt rising nausea as he watched the SUVs split apart and then stop. Figures emerged from both vehicles.

"*Kauai*, Shore-One, we are taking fire; repeat, we are taking fire. Request immediate assistance!" Ben's voice burst from the radio.

"Conn, Mount 51, sound of continuous gunfire zero-five-zero relative, no visual target!" came the redundant report.

"Conn, aye! Captain, one point seven miles to shoal water."

Hopkins had called down to Drake at the two-mile point, and Sam saw the engine speed back down slightly to "normal" emergency ahead in response.

"Very well, prepare for crash back. Williams?"

"Nothing yet, Captain, sorry," Williams said, shifting in his seat.

Hopkins announced, "Captain, one and a half miles to shoal water." Into the telephone, she said, "Chief, stand by for crash back."

"Very well, stand by," Sam responded.

On the Puma's video display, Sam saw Bill take the fatal hit and fall back dead. His heart was in his throat until he leaned forward to peer at the screen, then a wave of relief when he saw the long hair and beach clothing, apparent even in the low-resolution image. It must be the prisoner. He noted a pause in the action and saw the figures behind the westernmost vehicle aim a mortar-like device and fire it. The camera picked up a flash of a small object, then a burst overhead Ben and Simmons's redoubt. Either Ben or Simmons—from the camera aspect and mist, he couldn't tell which—fast-crawled to the other briefly, then returned to his position. Sam was unconsciously pounding his right fist on his thigh as the scene played out before him.

"Getting something," Williams said. "Yes! Two targets on long-wave IR."

Sam leaned in. "Surface action starboard, train on the target on the far left and standby. Deffler, illuminate the hostile vehicle farthest west." Standing up, he shouted, "OOD, Crash Back Now!" He keyed his handheld radio. "Pickins, haul ass back to the boat deck now!"

Hopkins shouted into the telephone, "Main Control, Conn, Crash Back, all back full!"

"Unmasked," Deffler piped up. "Target illuminated."

Sam held on to the safety rail as the patrol boat pitched down and violently shuddered while shedding speed quickly in the emergency stop. He watched the firing resume on the screen, and the figures started moving from behind the vehicles and closing on Ben and Simmons's position.

"Main Control, Conn, All Stop!" Hopkins shouted into the phone when the speed dropped to zero. The roar of the engines immediately died away.

"Conn, Mount 51, more continuous gunfire bearing zero-six-zero relative, no visual target!"

"Conn, aye!"

"Target identified, target confirmed, on target and tracking!"

"Batteries release. Commence fire!"

Drake

Drake held the phone to one ear and his finger in the other to hear Hopkins's orders over the engine noise. Sweat poured down his face as he stared at the instruments—the engine room was sweltering during normal cruise conditions. After ten minutes at extreme speed, it was like an oven.

Hopkins held the line open. When Drake heard Sam shout the initial crash back order, he did not wait for Hopkins to repeat it—he just dropped the phone and smoothly but quickly closed the engine throttles. When the RPMs had died down enough, he declutched the engines from the propeller shafts, shifted to reverse drive, and reclutched. After a short spine-tingling shriek from the clutches, the propellers showed reverse turns, and Drake advanced the throttles. The propellers bit against the cutter's forward speed and sent a fearsome vibration through the hull. The engine room was a cacophony of roaring engines, rattling tools, and the sharp pings of propeller cavitations. Holding the phone to his ear again while gripping a stanchion to stay upright, Drake watched the ship's speed readout drop to zero. He retarded the throttles to idle and declutched when Hopkins's "all stop" order came. He switched the engine control selector back to the

Bridge, picked up the phone, and reported, "Conn, Main Control, engines at all stop. Returning engine control to Conn."

Main Control seemed almost quiet compared to the last few minutes with the engines at idle. Brown had just started to relax when a series of loud thuds and sharp vibrations startled him. He looked frantically between the engines and instrument panel and shouted, "Shit, Chief! What now?"

"Relax, son." Drake wiped the sweat from his forehead while staring forward with a worried expression. "It's the main gun."

Resolution Key, Florida
07:20 EST, 19 January

Ben

Ben had already spent one magazine and slammed another into the carbine, resuming fire. His pistol was also charged and ready. Suddenly, there was a pause in the firing, and all the targets were out of sight. Ben glanced left along the barrier and froze in shock. Bill was sprawled out face up behind Simmons, eyes open and blood leaking from a hole in his forehead.
"Eyes front!" Simmons whispered urgently.
Ben whirled back to peer at the SUVs and whispered, "What are they doing?"

"Retasking," Simmons said, pulling a small package out of one of his pockets. "They'll try to take us now for interrogation."
"What do we do?"
"Don't get taken."
"Thanks."
"No, I mean, whatever you have to do, DO NOT get taken by these guys." He looked Ben in the eyes. "Nothing would be worse, believe me."
"Right."
Some activity behind his SUV attracted Ben's attention. There was a "whump" sound, and a grapefruit-sized object sailed overhead their position.
"FACE DOWN!" Simmons shouted.

Ben turned and buried his face in the sand when a loud "pop" sounded overhead, followed by a "whir" and a stabbing pain in the back of his right leg. A severe muscle cramp-like pain spread over his body within seconds, and he could not move. He tried to shout in terror, but all he heard was, "Ahhhhhh!" He felt another prick in his neck, and the pain subsided, although he still could not seem to get his muscles to work.

"It was a micro-flechette with a tetrodotoxin derivative. I've given you the antidote, but it'll be about thirty seconds before it's fully effective," Simmons whispered as he pulled the now empty syrette out of Ben's neck. "Fight it! They'll be rushing us in a few seconds—you need to be shooting."

The pain subsided, but the world moved in slow motion. Ben sensed time was passing, perhaps while the enemy waited for their chemical attack to take effect. Finally, he saw movement again near the vehicles. Ben's hand closed on the grip of his pistol, and it felt like it weighed a hundred pounds as he raised it off the ground. He squeezed off first one and then several rounds in quick-fire. Simmons fired his Uzi in full automatic, and two of the approaching figures fell to the ground. Another burst of automatic fire from the SUVs threw up more sand, and Simmons grunted and crumpled with a hit.

Suddenly, the SUV on the right lurched and leaned to the left, its tires flattened. The windows of the stricken vehicle shattered, and the fuel tank exploded, engulfing it in flames as a series of loud thump sounds arrived from offshore. The two dismounts still standing darted toward the remaining SUV.

Holding his wounded left arm, Simmons grimaced. "What the hell?"

Ben recognized the sound of a twenty-five-millimeter gun and croaked, "It's *Kauai*!" He laboriously brought his pistol to bear on the other SUV.

A black-clad gunman next to the SUV blind-fired a rocket-propelled grenade to seaward in the general direction of the incoming tracer fire. He then piled with the other survivors into the vehicle, its rear tires spinning and throwing up sand and dust.

USCG Cutter Kauai, six hundred yards off Resolution Key, Florida
07:30 EST, 19 January

Sam

"Check fire, check fire, shift target right. Deffler, illuminate the other vehicle." Sam struggled to keep his voice low and even.

"Check fire, aye, shifting right," said Williams, punching "Lock/Unlock" and moving the console's trackball to the right until the reticle sited on the other glowing object and flashed green. The Puma's illumination dot now appeared on the image.

"Target illuminated," Deffler said.

"Target identified, target confirmed, on target and tracking," Williams punched the "Lock/Unlock" button again. The artificial intelligence in the gun sight fixed on the signature of the selected "hot" object. It noted the need to realign and signaled the main gun's traversing system, slewing it a few degrees to the right.

"Incoming rocket!" Deffler shouted. The warhead flashed just clear of the cutter's stern with a hiss and self-detonated a second later.

"Commence fire!"

Another series of loud bangs with the rattle of spent cartridges hitting the deck meant more quarter-pound twenty-five-millimeter rounds were on the way. The penetrators shed their sabot jackets on leaving the barrel, and their tracer tails made them look like glowing streaks as they vanished into the mist at almost four times the speed of sound. At slightly under six hundred meters to target, flight time for each round was a little under half a second. The SUV driver started turning to return to the causeway immediately instead of building up speed first. It was his last mistake. The aspect change increased the image size, and the low speed allowed Williams to target it expertly. The brief flight time meant lead and windage were not a factor. He came on target at once. The first hit severed the right front wheel, and the second punched through the door armor, spewing lethal fragments in the cabin. The last hit shattered the fuel tank, igniting the scattering gasoline with its tracer tail. Soon, the infrared picture on Williams's gun sight was again washed out with heat from another wrecked and burning SUV.

"Check fire. Standby." Sam gazed at the UAV display. Two SUVs were burning, with three motionless human figures strewn between them, and it appeared several more lay near the second vehicle. He waited impatiently while the Puma continued its orbit in slow flight, finally clearing the drifting smoke. "Zoom in on that." Sam pointed at a figure crouching beside another near the hut and jammed the transmit button on his radio, "Shore-One, this is *Kauai*." No response. "Shore-One, this is *Kauai*, respond!" Turning, he said, "Deffler, can you get his attention?"

"Yes, sir," While he slewed and zoomed the image, Deffler goosed the engine to full and switched off the Ghost system. The kneeling figure looked up and around. He fixed on the aircraft, exaggeratedly touched his ear, and gave a thumbs-down. He then held his right arm straight up with his left pointing horizontally into it, giving the "Send Litter" signal—a general call for medical aid. Deffler zoomed in on the scene, and it became clear Ben was the one signaling. Simmons was prone and not moving, and both were very bloody.

"Ceasefire. Secure the twenty-five." Sam grabbed the PA microphone. "Stand Easy General Quarters, Away Rescue and Assistance Detail, Health Services Technician, contact the Bridge." Sam leaned down, gripped Williams's and Deffler's shoulders with each hand, and gave them a soft shake. "Thank you, guys." Williams and Deffler shook hands firmly as Sam crossed the Bridge. "OOD, in this calm, any course works for the boat launch. Let's try minimum steerageway to the northwest, please."

"Very good, sir," Hopkins replied, blinking away tears. She looked across at Deffler, nodding when he looked up at her and received a nod in return. The ship's telephone buzzed, and she picked it up. "Bridge, OOD. Right, standby. Captain, it's Doc."

Sam nodded and took the phone. "Doc, Captain."

"Yes, sir," Bryant replied.

"The UAV has eyes-on. The suspects are down, but the XO and Simmons both appear wounded. XO is ambulatory and hand-signaling for a litter. Comms are down, so I can't tell the severity."

"Understood, sir. I've got the full kit with me, and we'll bring the litter in case we need it."

"Good. Now listen carefully, Simmons's people are on the way, and they'll probably have EMTs along. However, unless *you* are convinced he really needs a hospital, you get the XO away from those people and back to the boat. I'll back whatever decision you make."

"Understood, Captain," Bryant replied.

"Right, good luck." Sam hung up the phone and keyed his radio. "Boat Deck, Captain."

"Captain, Boat Deck, go ahead, sir," Bondurant replied.

"Boat Deck, how soon before you can launch?"

"The boat's at the rail and ready, sir. They'll be off thirty seconds after Doc boards. Lee and the boat seaman have sidearms, and I put Jenkins in with a shotgun. Hold, sir. Doc's here and onboard. Request permission to launch the boat."

Sam was going to order the boat crew to be armed. *I should have known Bondurant would cover that.* "Standby," Sam said and turned to Hopkins. "OOD, the boat is ready. How's our course?"

"Steady on two-nine-zero, bare steerageway, sir," she replied.

"Very well, hold that." He keyed the radio again. "Boats, you're cleared to launch. Good call on the weapons. Tell Lee to head zero-eight-zero until she sees the shoreline, then continue to land as close to the scene as possible."

"Yes, sir!"

Sam touched Hopkins gently on the shoulder and quietly said, "Thank you, Hoppy." Then he stepped outside to wipe his own eyes. He tried to work a painful cramp out of his right hand while watching the RHIB drop into the water for launch. When the RHIB was away, he stepped back inside. "Williams, start a secure chat with OPC, please."

"Yes, sir," Williams replied, shifting to the SeaWatch station.

"Sir?" Hopkins asked Sam when he stepped behind Williams.

"OOD, I'm about to put what my H-65-flying brother-in-law Eddie calls the 'Aviator Approach' to the test." Sam smiled sadly.

"What's that, sir?"

"It's easier to obtain forgiveness than permission."

Aftermath

Resolution Key, Florida
08:01 EST, 19 January

Ben

Bryant had just finished initial treatment on Simmons's arm wound when several agency SUVs arrived, and three well-equipped EMTs stepped out and ran over. "Through and through in the upper left arm, bone seems OK, no bleeds," Bryant said to his counterpart.

"Right, we've got it."

"OK, XO, that was a four-point-oh job with the first aid. Let's have a look at you now." Bryant pulled on fresh gloves.

"I'm fine, Doc." With an expressionless face, Bryant reached up, touched the right side of Ben's head, and showed him the blood on his glove. "OK, except for the hole in my head."

"You'll live, XO. Just let me get this patch on to keep the rest of your brains from leaking out, and I'll sew you up when we get back to the boat." After cleaning and applying a bandage to the wound, Bryant took Ben's arm. "OK, sir, let's move along."

"Give me a few minutes, Doc."

Bryant started to protest, then pointed at his wristwatch. "I'll give you one hundred twenty seconds, sir."

"For sure, thanks." Ben glanced over at Bill's body—his head and torso were covered by a blanket he had retrieved from the shack. He kneeled beside Simmons. "It seems we're shipmates no more."

Simmons smiled as the EMT worked to prepare him for the stretcher. "I'm sorry about that. You did real good today, and I'd like to keep you around."

"Bull. I was scared shitless and damn near blew the whole deal by getting myself speared."

Simmons frowned and grabbed Ben's arm gently with his right hand. "Don't kid yourself. Everybody's scared shitless in a gunfight, present company included. Do you think you 'blew it' by getting hit? Guess what? I took one too. I juiced up before the shooting started just in case, but I was hoping to spare you the hangover—it's a bug we're still working on with the antidote.

"Think what would have happened had those goons gotten to our 'friends' before they could jump. No, you and your crew were really something today." He smiled warmly. He noticed Ben staring at the two covered bodies. "You bothered by that?"

"I don't know. It was righteous then, but I haven't killed anyone before."

"That's the downside. You might have issues later because you're a good man. If it comes to that, remember that those animals would have blown up *Kauai* and murdered any survivors if it weren't for the fog. If you need something to keep you going beyond the fact that you saved your family out there, call me. We have people who're good at that sort of thing."

"Thanks." He turned again to look at Bill's body. "I was afraid he was going to cap us both."

"He might have, but I doubt it. There is a certain threshold of honor in this business, and we'll treat him right."

"You think the Russians will claim him?"

"If they don't, we'll give him a good burial under the tricolor."

"Sir, we need to get him to a hospital," the EMT interjected.

"Sorry, carry on, please." Ben shook Simmons's hand and then stood up. "Seeya, spook."

"Sooner than you think." He then looked past Ben and cried, "Art!"

Ben turned to see Frankle trotting up to them. Upon arriving, he kneeled with a look of concern and took Simmons's right hand. "Pete! Damn glad to see you're still with us."

"Yea, verily, brother. What the hell happened? Where's Bell?"

"They pulled another of their surprises. Suckered us into an assault and then activated some kind of EMP generator. Radios, cell phones, and vehicles were all knocked out. Hell, they even brought down the overwatch UAV. It was back to 'charge up the hill,' but we got them. Bell took one in the arm and one in the vest that broke a couple of ribs. He'll be OK, but he'll be out of action for a while. He took down the Dragon Lady with an open-field tackle, though. That was *after* they had shot him, the tough bastard!"

"She dead?"

"Nope. She's knocked out in the back of a CPB Blackhawk, flying to Homestead."

"Nice one. They decide what they will do with her?"

"The Frankle Plan would be either tell us everything you know and live out your life in the safety of a Supermax or don't, and we'll announce that you did and leave you to your fate in the system. Those making the call are unlikely to seek my keen insights." The agent chuckled.

"Gentlemen," a clearly annoyed EMT said. "We need to move this man now!"

"Sorry." Frankle smiled. "Please go ahead. Pete, I'll see you at the hospital." While two EMTs carried off the litter, he turned to Ben and offered his hand. "Thanks for bringing him through this, Coast Guard."

Ben shook it readily. "It was more the other way around, but you're welcome."

"No, we really owe you on this one. I hope we'll have a chance to work with you guys again—I love folks who bring cannons to a gunfight!"

They all turned when the other EMT standing by cleared his throat. "Your officer has been exposed to a classified nerve agent," he said to Bryant. "He's had the counteragent, and no further treatment is required. He needs to be kept under close observation for forty-eight hours, and," he glanced at *Kauai* offshore, glistening white in the emerging sun. "No operating motor vehicles." He turned to Ben. "You'll have a hell of a headache in about three hours. I recommend acetaminophen—no aspirin—and plenty of water." He turned to Bryant again. "You know, it wouldn't hurt to let us take him to the hospital, just in case."

Bryant shook his head, remembering the direct order from his CO before he boarded the RHIB. "Thanks, but I've got this."

"That OK with you, Lieutenant?" the EMT asked somewhat rudely.

"Petty Officer Bryant's medical judgment will always do for me," Ben replied coldly.

"Suit yourself." The EMT walked off to catch up with his comrades and Simmons.

Frankle flashed Ben a mock salute. "Be seein' ya, Coast Guard!" He then turned and followed the others.

As Ben turned to Bryant, the latter's face spread into an evil Grinch-like grin. "Looks like we'll be roomies for the next couple of days, sir."

"Yeah. You're enjoying this, aren't you, Doc?"

Bryant took Ben's arm to steady him, and they walked through the soft sand toward the RHIB. "XO, you have NO idea."

****

Simmons's compatriots had taken over the battle scene for cleanup. No evidence of the encounter, not even the ersatz beachcomber shack, would remain in a few hours. However, there was still a Russian warhead, probably nuclear, in the vicinity. That meant *Kauai* had to stay on security watch while other federal forces closed off access to the island on the land side. A flotilla of recovery vessels was en route for extensive surveys of the area.

Lee threaded the needle between the need for speed and a smooth ride in the RHIB as she transported Ben and Bryant back to *Kauai.* She maintained a calm, professional exterior despite the shock of seeing her XO with his head bandaged and covered with blood. Lee smoothly slewed the boat alongside the cutter, grabbed the fall, and slammed it in place on the lift frame in a single swift maneuver. Looking up, she gave a thumbs-up to Bondurant. "Ready for pickup!"

Seeing Ben was still a little shaky climbing out of the RHIB, Sam came down from the Bridge to meet him. He was concerned at the sight of all the blood, but relieved at his young friend's smile and mock salute. He gripped Ben's right hand and shoulder and feigned his best "angry dad" expression. "Mister, you scared the shit out of me back there!"

Ben replied with mock solemnity, "No excuse, sir. Shall I retire to the captain's cabin for the requisite flogging?"

"No, too much paperwork. Say fifteen 'Hail Marys' and contemplate your many inadequacies."

"About that, sir. I'm ready to give you a hand on the reports...."

"Like hell," Sam interrupted. "Doc gave me the picture on you, and your rack is your duty station until further notice."

"Sir, I can still...."

"Enough. That's an order, discussion over."

"Yes, sir. What are our orders, sir?"

Sam smiled. "When the fireworks ended, I started a SIPRNET chat to report in. I got as far as reporting we had taken out two vehicles and a mess of bad guys when I got a 'Shut the Hell Up!' order. We're holding on here for now. They're establishing a maritime security zone and aviation Prohibited Area over the island and out to two miles offshore until further notice. They've diverted *Mohawk* from her Yucatan patrol, and she should be here to relieve us in about twenty-four hours. It'll be close on the fuel, but we'll head straight back to Miami when relieved."

"How do they expect to keep this under wraps, sir? You can see that smoke plume down in Key West, and all the feds crawling over this place are bound to cause questions."

"Ah." Sam smiled. "Haven't you heard? It's already on commercial radio that an F-22 out of Tyndall Air Force Base crashed on Resolution during a training flight. Happily, the pilot ejected and is safe. But the island is closed to the public until the mishap investigation and cleanup is complete."

Ben nodded and turned to see Drake approaching. The big chief petty officer said nothing, just stepped up, gripped the young man's shoulders firmly, and gazed into his eyes, beaming. After a few seconds, he released Ben and turned to Sam. "Captain, I respectfully request that you put this young man in hack until we get back to Miami. I've got plenty of shit on my hands without any more emergency power runs and crash stops."

"Already done, Chief. How do things look?" Sam smiled.

"We'll get home all right. I will need a butt-load of parts when we get there, though. We overstressed, over-torqued, over-temped, and over-sped almost every damn thing in the hull. I would be obliged if we could limit her to twenty knots on the trip back. Also, for planning purposes, we'll be hard down when the mooring lines go over."

"I hear ya, Chief. I need to hold down the fuel consumption, anyway. Should I worry about you finding the parts?"

"Naw, I know some guys." Drake saluted, then sauntered off.

Sam pointed at Ben. "Rack, mister, now!"

"Aye, aye, sir." He glanced up at the Bridge to see Hopkins looking down with a slight smile. They exchanged nods, and Ben turned and retired to his room.

The prognosis from the agency medic was accurate—the headache that came on three hours later was blinding and debilitating. The Tylenol Bryant administered was only just enough to keep Ben from wanting to blow his brains out. Fortunately, after about four hours, the pain passed as quickly as it started, and he fell into a deep and sound sleep under Bryant's watchful eye.

Six hours later, rested but still slightly wobbly, Ben submitted to a going over by Bryant, who refused to sign him off for duty. He reluctantly consented to Ben walking accompanied up to talk to Sam. Seeing Ben walking unsteadily across the darkened Bridge, Sam stood up from his seat and motioned for him to sit down. "No, I'll be all right, sir," Ben said.

"Do as you're told, sir." Ben sat down, and Sam leaned over and continued softly. "We got a follow-up SIPRNET message while you were out. We are officially quarantined until further notice—no one leaves the ship and no comms of any kind. When *Mohawk* arrives on station and assumes the watch, they will flash us their callsign, and we are to reply 'Tango' by signal light only and depart. We are to send the RHIB over to the island in about ten minutes to pick up a special medical crew. They'll check all of us for radiation exposure on the way. When we arrive in Miami, the crew will be confined to the boat incommunicado. You and I are to report to the District Office at 02:30."

"Zero-Two-Thirty? What's happening at 02:30 on a Wednesday, sir?"

"Our interrogation, apparently. The orders are to secure all logs and present ourselves in a conference room over there."

"Shit, Skipper!" Ben felt an icy ball forming in his stomach. "What can we do?"

"Shave, put on a fresh tropical blue uniform, and hope for the best. Same as always. OK, you've put in an appearance. Why not head below? I'll be down in an hour or so, and we can chat about your little adventure." Seeing Ben hesitate, Sam continued with a warm smile, "Number One, you're in my seat. Kindly retire below to your own, please."

"Very good, sir." Ben stood unsteadily. Bryant moved quickly from the opposite side of the Bridge to help and, taking Ben's arm, helped him down the ladder to his room. About an hour and a half later, Sam appeared at Ben's door, holding a chair.

"Doc, I need the room," Sam said as Bryant stood. "I want you to stake out the forward end of the passageway. No one, and I mean no one, is to pass until I come out and tell you otherwise, clear?"

"Yes, sir," Bryant replied crisply, taking the chair from Sam and moving forward. As Bryant sat down, he saw Lopez at the other end, and they nodded at each other and sat in watchful silence as Sam shut the door.

****

Ben sat on his bunk, and Sam sat on Ben's chair, putting a box of tissues on his desk. Noting Ben looking at the box, Sam said, "Just in case." When Ben looked back at him, Sam continued. "Ok, it's not a SCIF, but it's as close as possible. Ben, I need you to take me through your experience, the full monty, from the moment you got into the car with Simmons in Key West until you stepped back aboard. We're completely off the record here, absolutely between you and me, no rank, friend to friend, so don't hold back. Be as detailed as possible in describing how you felt during the events. I understand that's hard because it's unnatural for us, so I'll prompt you if that's needed." Seeing Ben staring at him in astonishment with his mouth half-open, Sam continued. "I want you to trust me on this. You need to talk about everything now. It will make an enormous difference to you later."

At Sam's prompting, Ben went through the chronology of his off-cutter actions, beginning with the arrival at the hotel and meeting with Simmons's team. Ben saw the slight twinkle in Sam's eye at his description of his conversation with Victoria, despite the latter's silence and diligent effort to keep his face expressionless. Ben described the relative boredom of the next day, the excitement of discovering that Resolution was the target site, and the encounter with the Russian agent that followed.

When he revisited the battle with the TCO gunmen, the fear inside returned to the surface, and he trimmed down the detail in his description. Sam leaned forward and insisted Ben dig in and describe his feelings completely and accurately, prompting him when he hesitated. The full range of emotions returned while he completed the story. Ben again felt the gnawing, escalating fear of watching as the vehicles moved in slowly. Then, the stark terror of the chemical attack and Simmons's wounding. Last was the intense elation and relief when *Kauai* could finally engage. At that point, Sam handed him the box of tissues, and Ben was astounded to realize he was crying.

What seemed like minutes passed, and Sam reached across and gently gripped his shoulder. With the worst over, Ben steadied down. He looked up at Sam, who smiled back, released his hold, and sat back. Eventually, Ben could ask, "How did you know?"

Sam shook his head. "I didn't. But *I* damn near lost it on the Bridge just watching you go through that ordeal. I thought you had to be carrying a lot more inside, and knowing you, you'd just let it sit and fester. I figured I would drag it out of you now. It's better than risking it popping up tomorrow when we're not among friends."

Ben nodded. It embarrassed him to break down before his CO and friend, and doing so in an interrogation would be infinitely worse. He looked across at a grinning Sam. "What?"

"You know, lad," his friend said as he stood. "They should use you for a template for the next Jack Bauer. Let's see, you find a lost Russian nuke and capture one of their spies. Check. You step from there into a firefight outnumbered five-to-one by a bunch of murdering sociopaths and win. Check. And, naturally, hook up with a beautiful girl. Check." He stepped out the door and told Bryant and Lopez, "That's all, guys, thanks." He looked back in and finished with a slight smile. "Please hold off on doing anything like that again until after I'm tour complete! Will you be OK, or do I need to call Doc back?"

"I'm awesome, sir," Ben replied, drawing a broad smile from his friend. "Isn't there anything I can do to help, sir? Doc has me pinned down, and I'm going bat-shit crazy here."

Sam nodded. "If you feel up to it, can you draft a memo from me to the CO of Air Station Cape Cod? I want to give Fritz and Mike cover on the flights yesterday. Keep it unclassified. Just say Fritz called out the regs against flying in fog. I overruled him because of national security and safety-of-life and now take full responsibility for the decision. You know what I need. That would take a big rock out of my backpack."

"Consider it done, sir, and thank you. I already thanked him for saving my life, and it feels good to pitch in something tangible."

Sam didn't reply, just gave a thumbs-up.

****

USCG Cutter *Mohawk* arrived the following morning and anchored a comfortable distance offshore of Resolution Key. Sam had ordered the main engines restarted when the large cutter appeared on the horizon, and *Kauai* weighed anchor as *Mohawk* set hers. After about ten minutes, during which her underway routine was secured and anchor watch set, *Mohawk* signaled "NRUF" by flashing light, to which Hopkins replied simply "T" using the hand-held signal lamp. Within a minute, *Kauai* was cruising for home at the stately speed of twenty knots.

Ben found himself at loose ends after the warhead discovery, firefight, and cathartic debriefing session. He was desperate to get his mind off what he assumed would be a thorough grilling on their return to Miami. He completed and polished the memo Sam had requested. Ben tried to resume OOD duties, but Bryant put that to rest after running a weird procedure he called a "Mini-BES-Test." An appeal to Sam was equally futile, and Ben resigned himself to catching up on the paperwork that had languished in his absence and convalescence. He was surprised to find the stack of paperwork he had left in his inbox completed and filed. In its place was a handwritten note: "You're Welcome. Never do it again! With Respect, J. Drake, MKC; E. Hopkins, OS1." Reflecting on the similarity to Sam's enjoinder earlier, Ben placed the note in a document protector and stiff folder and put it carefully with the other personal items in his bag.

He thought about composing a draft of his first email to Victoria for when they came off lockdown and even laid out a few sheets of paper before deciding he was in the wrong mood. He was putting them away when he spotted Hopkins walking by in the passageway. "Hoppy?"

"Yes, sir," she replied, stopping in the doorway.

"Thanks for taking care of, well, everything."

"That's my job, sir."

"I think it went well above and beyond your normal job. You were right back in the session in Key West, and I don't want to think about what could have happened if you guys hadn't got there when you did."

She looked back at him coolly, stepped into his room, and dropped her voice so what she said next would be private. "*Do* think about that, sir. You guys walked straight into a blind alley without backup. Why do a damned fool thing like that? You know the captain had to throw away the book to save your ass, and he stands a good chance of getting relieved of his command over his decisions yesterday. You could have avoided putting him in that position by saying 'enough' at any stage of the game to that crazy spook. Remember *that* when you two are standing tall downtown tonight, *sir*."

Ben hung his head. "Yes, I definitely will."

After a moment, her expression softened. "XO?"

"Yes?" He looked up dejectedly.

"On and off the record, I'm really glad you've come back to us, sir." She gave him a warm smile.

"Thank you," Ben replied with a slightly quavering voice. Hopkins nodded and turned to leave him to digest this latest lesson in leadership.

A few hours later, Ben was on the Bridge with Sam, overseeing Hopkins as she brought *Kauai* back into port in Miami. After an uneventful transit and quick maneuver dockside, Hopkins turned to Sam. "Ship is moored, Captain. Request secure main engines and set Charlie status."

"Very well. Outstanding job, as usual. We will miss you, Chief-select."

"Thank you, sir," she replied, then turned to issue the orders to snug the vessel down for a dockside stay.

Sam turned, and Ben noticed he looked exhausted and old, with the lines around his eyes and mouth visible even in the low lighting on the Bridge. "I guess we might as well get squared away for tonight's festivities, XO."

"Yes, sir," Ben replied with concern. "Is there anything else I can do for you, sir?"

"Nope," his friend replied, and, seeing Ben's expression, he smiled and patted him on the shoulder. "Don't worry, Ben, we'll be OK." He then turned and headed off to his cabin.

Verdict

Brickell Plaza Federal Building, Miami, Florida
02:25 EST, 21 January

Ben

Ben hated the Federal Building. A lot. Nothing good happened when you visited the Federal Building—the best you could hope for was to break even. That was true for visits during a typical working day. And when they summon you and your CO here to explain yourselves at two o'clock in the morning with your crew locked-down incommunicado awaiting the results? Well, my friend, you can be sure you're facing one *hell* of a climb to "break even."

The fun started the moment they arrived. The guards at the entrance took advantage of the absence of a lengthy queue of irate federal employees at this hour to give Ben and Sam a thorough examination. Then, the two men passed through a similar screening by two cold-as-ice defense counterintelligence special agents outside the secure conference space on the eighth floor. After checking their IDs, scanning their fingerprints, and confiscating their cell phones and anything else electronic, the agents ushered the two officers into an anteroom. Before leaving and locking the door, the lead special agent said a curt, "Wait here until they call you."

Ben was desperately worried. Nothing in his training or experience prepared him for the events he faced over the last week. Hell, before a week ago, he couldn't even *conceive* of them. Sam's expression did not help. Also deep in thought, he was apprehensive, and rightfully so: Sam bore the entire responsibility for everything within his command. After a brief time, Sam glanced over, and, seeing Ben's worried look, his face softened into a sad smile. He put his hand on Ben's shoulder and gave it a soft shake. "Take it easy, Ben. We'll come through this OK."

Ben and Sam's decisions and actions seemed right in the heat of action, but many violated Coast Guard regulations, perhaps even the law. In the cold light of day, the achievements of bringing their crew through the ordeal alive and succeeding in their mission may not be enough. It was time to pay the piper. That potential payment ranged from a "slap on the wrist" in his next fitness report to dismissal from the service and imprisonment. Ben was anxious about what they faced, both for himself and his best friend.

A muffled conversation outside the entry door made him turn. The door opened, and Simmons came in, unusually dressed in a suit and tie, with his left arm in a sling. When the door closed, Ben stepped forward with his right hand outstretched. "Hi, Doc. Guess I'm glad to see you here. How's the arm?"

"Still hurts like hell. How's your head?" Simmons replied, eyeing the small bandage on Ben's head while he shook the young officer's hand.

"Been better, but OK now."

Sam watched the exchange with open hostility. Ben knew that in Sam's view, Simmons was a reckless fool who nearly got his best friend killed and forced Sam to risk his crew and ship to save him. Thanks to the agent's appalling judgment, Sam and Ben's professional life might come to an ignominious end in the next few minutes. Simmons's smug expression obviously infuriated him under the circumstances, and Sam's folded arms and icy glare squashed any notion the agent had about a cordial handshake.

Simmons turned to continue his chatter with Ben when the inside door opened, and Captain Mercier entered. The two junior officers snapped to attention, and Mercier quickly said, "Carry on. Mr. Powell, Mr. Wyporek, and Dr. Simmons. We are ready for you now. Please come with me."

The men filed past Mercier into the conference room, and she closed the door behind them. Three men and two women, by appearance and dress, senior government people, already sat on the far side of a large table across the room, and Mercier sat down with them. A third, much younger woman sat at the end. An elderly man in the center spoke. "Please be seated, gentlemen." He motioned to three empty chairs in the center of the room, about five feet away from and facing the table.

The sight severely rattled Ben. The setup of the three chairs in a brightly lit area of what was otherwise a moderately darkened room screamed "inquisition" to him. *Shit, they will rip us to shreds,* Ben thought as he approached the chair on the far left. He was grateful he wasn't going through this alone.

After the three men sat down, the elderly man nodded to the young woman seated at the end of the table, and she activated what Ben assumed was a recording device in front of her. The man continued. "For the record, this interview is conducted under Executive Order 10273, and all material discussed here is classified top secret, under codeword JUBILEE. Gentlemen, I need you to state your name and position and that you understand the security level of this discussion."

"And gents, that means if you talk about anything said here, you go away forever," Simmons intoned. "Oh, yes, Dr. Peter Simmons, SA2, DIA-5B." He turned to Sam and nodded.

"Samuel Powell, Lieutenant, United States Coast Guard, Commanding Officer, Coast Guard Cutter *Kauai*. I understand the classification and penalties for disclosure."

Ben's mind raced as he stared at the people sitting at the table, noting that none were providing their names for the record. After a few seconds, Sam nudged him with his elbow. "Um, Benjamin Wyporek, Lieutenant Junior Grade, United States Coast Guard, Executive Officer, Coast Guard Cutter *Kauai*. I acknowledge the classification of this discussion and the penalty for disclosure."

Frowning at Simmons, the elderly man resumed. "Thank you, gentlemen. We are inquiring into the events occurring in the Gulf of Mexico, Florida Straits, and the Florida Keys from the 13th through the 19th of this month. Let the record show the U.S. Coast Guard is represented in these proceedings with an observer." Turning to Mercier, he added, "Please state your name, rank, present station, and acknowledgment of classification, madam."

"Jane C. Mercier, Captain, United States Coast Guard, Chief, Office of Response, Seventh Coast Guard District. I acknowledge the classification of this discussion."

"Thank you, Captain." Turning to the three interviewees, the elderly man said, "Now, gentlemen, this is a fact-finding session, not an interrogation. We need the full picture of this operation as quickly as possible. Dr. Simmons's flippant remarks aside, we depend on your honesty and forthrightness here and discretion afterward. Now we've dispensed with the formalities, gentlemen. What the hell happened out there? Please start at the beginning of your involvement, Lieutenant Powell."

****

"Lieutenant Powell, do you have any other comments on the engagement?" the elderly man asked.

"Sir, I regret there was no alternative to the force I used, given the circumstances."

"I think we agree the decision was completely justified." He looked at his colleagues, who all nodded in agreement. "About the warhead recovery. How secure is this information within your crew?"

"Mr. Wyporek, Chief Petty Officer Drake, Petty Officer Hopkins, and I are the only ones who know anything about that. For the rest of the crew, the XO engaged a group of murderous drug smugglers, and we had to take part."

"I am glad to hear that, but please keep alert." The elderly man nodded, turning to Mercier. "Captain Mercier, your officers' actions in this incident were fully justified and consistent with the finest traditions of the military service. We will certainly convey this at the highest levels, and I encourage you to take care of them to the best of your ability, within the need for utmost discretion."

"I certainly will, sir," Mercier replied.

The weight on Ben's chest lifted. *OK, not fired or going to prison. Going to make lieutenant. Well, maybe.*

"Dr. Simmons, do we have any information on the man known as 'Bill' or how he could locate the missing warhead so quickly?" the elderly man asked.

"No to both, I'm afraid, sir," Simmons replied. "He was obviously one of their Canadian sleepers, but his cover was rock-solid, and so far, the Russians haven't owned up to him. As far as his ability to find the crash site, he was not forthcoming about this or anything else. I would speculate that the Kinzhal has a default flight profile that activated automatically after launch. Tracing that from the launch location would get them in the ballpark. I don't know what he could have used for the final search—we found nothing among his effects. He might have ditched it when he set up his watch in the area. We just don't know."

"I see. Do we have anything more on the men you engaged?" the elderly man asked.

"No, sir. Fake passports, IDs, etc. The tactics and weapons suggest it's the usual opposition. The only survivor of the firefight on Resolution suicided before any of us could reach him. We weren't able to recover anything new from the vehicles or personal effects. Our people are running through the port of entry records and videos, but we don't expect to find anything. We have the woman in custody, and she might offer some insights."

"It seems odd we could track her down so quickly," the third man commented. "Someone like her should have been able to slip away completely or, at least, evade capture for a longer period than eighteen hours."

Simmons replied with a slight smile, "I'd like to say that it resulted from a dazzling combination of our excellent forensic and cyber skills. However, I think—and this is more speculation—that we weren't as sharp as we believe. I think they caught on to JUBILEE right after they took a crack at us in Key West. They probably didn't know what it was about, but if it had a connection with their lost product, they wanted to find out. They helped her escape and then plugged her into a safe house, not so much so she could fight another day, but so they could use her as bait. When the word got out that she was there and it was confirmed, everybody we had in the area closed in on her, even my two teams. Lieutenant Wyporek and I were on our own when we went for that warhead, which is what I believe they were hoping to achieve. They came damn close to pulling off quite a neat trick by grabbing us. I would suggest the interrogators lead with the concept her comrades sold her out when they question Ms. Petrova. Not sure she'll break even with that wedge, but it's worth trying.

"The unpleasant news is this EMP weapon they cooked up to cover her escape. The possibilities are frightening. We have a hard enough time keeping the infrastructure safe and stopping the spread of man-portable, surface-to-air missiles and other nightmares. Imagine creating devices from ordinary electrical components that are small enough to hide in the back of an SUV. Park it under a departure corridor in Canarsie, flip a switch, and bring down an Airbus with three hundred people and a full load of fuel right in the middle of Queens again. They blew that one up during the breakout attempt. We need to lean hard on the FBI to give the remains to our tech guys.

"That issue aside, the good news is the radar masker we secured on Ms. Petrova's sailboat. It pulled into MacDill a few hours ago. We ran preliminary tests en route, and it seemed to be effective. Our people took a harder look at the hull of the original wreck once we discovered the device on the *Sunrise Surprise*. We found the remains of the self-destruct bomb and a pile of electronic scrap that could have been another masker. This suggests the device is in general service. Anyway, the DARPA folks and our engineers are hot to get their hands on it for reverse engineering and countermeasure development.

The elderly man nodded. "Yes, it's nice to have gotten more on them, at least. Now, I suppose that is it. Does anyone else have anything?" He scanned his associates again. "No? Very well, this inquiry is concluded. Gentlemen, I remind you this discussion and all information associated with this incident are classified at the highest level. Any disclosure will have the gravest impact on your country, not to mention yourselves. That's all. Thank you." He nodded to the door, and Ben and Sam stood up to leave. Ben turned to see Simmons still sitting.

"So long, friend," the agent said.

"Yeah, please tell Victoria I'm thinking of her, and I'll email her as soon as I get my head straight."

"Will do," Simmons whispered, offering his right hand as he smiled. "Good luck, Ben."

Ben shook his hand warmly. "You too, Pete."

Ben rejoined Sam, and they were making their way out of the room when Mercier pulled them aside. "Listen, I know you guys are tired, but let's chat down in my office," she said.

"Very good, ma'am," Sam replied.

"I'll meet you down there in about ten minutes."

"Yes, ma'am," Sam and Ben said together.

****

"I'll start by saying I'm sorry we had to keep you guys on edge for so long—it can't have been easy after the grommet you've been pulled through," Mercier said.

"We understand, ma'am," Sam led off. "Honestly, I'm feeling pretty lucky right now, still having a job after shooting up two civilian vehicles on U.S. soil without an SNO."

"The circumstances were what they were, and nobody will second guess you on that call. Changing focus, how did your crew do with all this?"

Sam leaned forward. "They could not have been better. Ben, in particular, deserves the highest praise and reward, and I'll be putting him and the Bridge crew in for personal awards."

Ben was deeply moved by the recommendation from the man he admired so highly. "Ah..." was all that he could say before Mercier interrupted.

"No, we can't have documentation referencing this mission." Seeing Sam's face darken, she added quickly, "We have that covered. You two will each be getting the Coast Guard Medal. I'm afraid all that will show up in the official record and your fitness reports are you received it for a 'Classified Action.' I presume you want individual awards for some of your crew as well?"

"Yes, for Chief Drake and Petty Officer Hopkins. Commendation Medal, at least. Deffler deserves one too, but he doesn't work for me."

"He's covered. Consider all those awards done. It's a pity no one will be able to brag about them. Hopefully, there will be more opportunities soon."

"Thank you, ma'am. They won't mind. If you don't mind, ma'am, what do you mean 'more opportunities'?"

"Yes, it goes with why you haven't chopped back to Sector Miami yet. We will hold on to you guys for a while, indefinitely, actually, and we'll be making a few changes."

"I don't understand."

"Did you think you acquired all that talent by accident or good luck? *Kauai* was on our radar long before the mishap, with the negative personnel actions and equipment casualties well above the norm. We sent Drake in to relieve the previous chief to find out what was happening. I'm sure you realize by now that Drake is a 'fixer' in general rather than just the technical sense."

Sam nodded. "Yes, he has shown a scary ability to get around things to keep us operating, and Ben has leaned on him for the XO uglies."

"That's for sure," Ben agreed, realizing for the first time how timely and correct Drake's "If I were you, XO, I would..." suggestions had been.

Mercier nodded. "He let us know right away the old command had to go. We were working on doing that quietly when the mishap forced our hand. The challenge was finding people we could send in on short notice who could pull things together. Sam, you were already here, working up as an Ops Center supervisor, and had come off a very successful PB command in Hawaii. For XO, we took a hard look at the Prospective XO list and plucked Ben off *Dependable* a few months early, at Drake's suggestion."

"I hadn't met Drake before," Ben said.

"True, but he 'knew a guy' on the ships of several of the candidates, and you came up on top. As usual, he was spot-on.

"After *Kauai*'s mishap, we decided to rebuild her crew wholesale. This provided an opportunity to try out a proof of concept of an elite Seventh District patrol boat that we can send into sticky situations like this one. We quietly made a few 'corrections' in the complement around your arrival. Then it was just a question of waiting for the proper test. This was it. It was pure luck you guys found that wreck; otherwise, we would have gotten you underway to take over."

"Okay, Captain, so we have a dream team, thanks to you and Chief Drake. I'm still happy but humbler." Sam half-smiled.

"Don't sell yourselves short. It took good leadership to save that boat. If we hadn't found a solid command cadre like you two, we would probably have just written her off and moved up the decommissioning. As it stands, you're a very useful asset, particularly now."

"Why now, ma'am?"

"You've been introduced to the challenge and understand our need to respond quickly, competently, and discreetly. Our experiment to set up a 'dream team,' as you say, has grown out of our hands. The National Command Authority needs an option to use quick, surgical actions in the maritime environment that don't gin up the chaos of diverting Navy destroyers or subs. The ability to act in home waters without stirring up issues with the DoD doing law enforcement is also a big plus. You and your crew proved yourselves able to provide that capability. We had a lengthy discussion before you guys showed up, and your pal Simmons had put in a really stellar assessment of you in his official report. You made a highly favorable impression on him."

"Ma'am, I can promise you he won't be as happy if I ever cross paths with him again."

Mercier frowned. "Oh, I see. Anyway, you impressed that committee with how you pulled off this one. Despite what you might have thought when you came in, the 'interrogation' was a genuine fact-finding and a chance to gauge you in person. They had already decided to move you along to 'better things,' provided you didn't blow yourselves up in there. Now, exercising that capability comes at a big jump in personal risk, as you have also seen. So much so, I can't order you to take it on."

"Ma'am, let me get this straight: doing this job is a voluntary assignment?" Ben asked.

"No, you can ask to be relieved, and we will approve it, regretfully. But consider carefully before you do that. Remember, the request and relief will be on the record."

After a thoughtful pause, Ben broke the silence. "What's to think about? I'm in, ma'am. But if we expect to take on any more murderous TCOs, I'd like more firepower and training than a P229 pistol and boarding officer school."

"Yes, we already put together a scratch tactical course for you in Quantico. You, Bondurant, Guerrero, and Lee, that is." Mercier smiled. "We'll be sending Lopez to Charleston for the next Maritime Law Enforcement Specialist class in a couple of weeks, and he'll get, um, 'extra attention' there. We'll add an ME3 billet to *Kauai* to hold him when he graduates."

"How did you know I would ask for... Oh, Chief Drake." Ben grinned.

"Yep, he's already felt them out about it. They're in if you are. Also, we're pulling *Kauai* out of action for an upgrade of the armory and combat systems. We'll see you'll have something to use when you return. For once, we have both official backing and enough funding. The shipyard availability will be an excellent cover for your absence at training."

She turned back to Sam. "I get this was a rough one, and you are too knocked out to give a considered answer. It's also a tough job for a man with a young family. Consult on the home front and call me as soon as you can."

"Thank you, Captain. Given everything you've told us, it's tough to ask to be relieved," Sam responded. "I think Jo will swallow hard and bless this, but it's a new ballgame, and she gets a vote."

Mercier sat back and smiled. "Thank you. I don't see how we can pull this off without you, and so I'd personally be very grateful if she could be persuaded. Let's see, what else? Oh yes, one last thing. We'll be moving you up to Canaveral. On the record, you will be the permanent Range Safety Cutter for the Space Center. There should be fewer questions about the Seventh hanging on to a one-ten that way."

"Um, ma'am, changing homeport generates a lot of paperwork for both the skipper and XO. How can I take care of that while I'm eating snakes up in Quantico?" Ben asked.

"We'll put a team together to cover you. It won't go into effect until after the shipyard work is complete. Anything else? With your stock so high, now's the time to ask."

"Ma'am, I'd sure like to hang on to Hopkins," Sam began. "We'll be rewriting the book to make the best use of our new stuff, and I need what she brings to the table. But I don't want to keep her if that means she gives up pinning on chief. Is there any way we can bump her billet up to E7 since we will take this boat 'off the books' anyway?"

Mercier nodded with satisfaction. "You continue to impress. Get a thumbs up from her that she wants to stay, and I'll make it happen. Anything else?"

"Yes, ma'am, one last thing. We'd have been dead ducks without our UAV support, and Deffler went out on a limb to fly them in that fog. Since he was technically the pilot-in-command, he'll be in a real jam if any pearl-clutchers start second-guessing. I'm sending a memo to Deffler's CO explaining and taking responsibility for the flights and recommending him for a decoration. It would carry a lot more weight if you pitched in."

"Man, you want *everything*, don't you?" Mercier grinned. "Don't give it another thought. Send me a copy of the memo, and I'll ring him up for a chat. We're academy and flight school classmates, which should provide some heft for you. Now, last call, anything else?"

"No, ma'am," both men replied.

"Great. One last order for both of you. Go home, get some rest and blow off steam. You need it. *Kauai* is offline until further notice. And don't even try sneaking back aboard to work for at least seventy-two hours—you know I have eyes there now," she said, shaking their hands.

"That we do, ma'am," Sam said as he led Ben out. They passed wordlessly through the outer office and down the hall before pausing at the elevator. Sam broke first, doubling over in laughter, and Ben was startled but quick to follow.

"Holy shit, Skipper! What the hell just happened in there?"

"You heard the captain. We saved the world, changed homeports, and became the Coast Guard's first Special Operations team." Sam chuckled as the elevator door opened. "Hooyah!"

After they entered and the doors closed, Ben asked, "Honestly, you think Jo will be OK?"

"She won't like it," Sam replied. "It will be a hard sell, given what she knows about Hoppy's personal history. I may have to lean on Hoppy to help close the deal, and it'll be a stretch, even with her help."

"Yes, sir," Ben said soberly, his thoughts returning to the infuriation Hopkins had expressed over his decisions on this operation. He was suddenly very concerned that this deal might be DOA.

"You OK?"

"Yes, sir," Ben replied. "It's just all settling in for me. I'll be fine."

Coda

Hopkins

When *Kauai*'s GV turned onto the dock around 05:30, Hopkins had been waiting anxiously on the Bridge with Deffler for over an hour. She looked over at him, and he smiled and reached out to take her hand. He really was a fine man—smart, funny, good-looking, and sensitive. He seemed to know she was terrified for the two officers and just stayed with her until they returned. They went down together to join Drake, already on the dock.

Hopkins's heart was in her throat until Ben flashed them a grin and thumbs-up when he stepped out of the GV. After returning their salutes, Sam and Ben each shook their hands. "Welcome home, Captain, XO," Drake said.

"Thanks, Chief," Sam replied. "Let's cut the crew loose for normal post-patrol liberty as soon as possible. You can hold off tearing down the mains for now. We're offline indefinitely, and we have an unscheduled shipyard period. No sense doing a lot of work that may just be undone."

"Very good, sir. Can you elaborate a bit?"

"I think you know the score already, Chief, based on Captain Mercier's very complete intel on *my* crew." Sam ended the answer with a raised eyebrow.

"What can I say, Captain? I know a gal downtown."

"Right. Remind me to discuss that with you later." He turned to Hopkins. "Hoppy, can we move on to the cabin in a minute, please? There's something I need to talk to you about." Seeing the sudden look of concern on her face, he added, "Don't worry, I'm pretty sure you'll think it is excellent news."

"Yes, sir."

He then turned to Deffler and shook his hand. "Fritz, unfortunately, this is the end of our time together. I can't find the words to tell you how grateful I am for what you and Mike have done for us on this op. I'm sending a memo to your CO singing your praises and stating that any violations of Federal Air Regulations were because I held a gun to your head. It's not much, but I'm sure it will cover you."

"I appreciate that, Captain." Deffler smiled in return. "I don't suppose you can find some ISR work for us around here until, I don't know, maybe April?"

Sam chuckled. "Sorry, Airedale, there are things even a PB skipper can't do. Good luck, stay warm, and be safe up there." He returned Deffler's salute and then turned to go inside.

Hopkins smiled at Deffler and said, "See you in a minute?"

"I'll be on the messdeck," he replied.

Hopkins ducked into the ship, and when she reached the cabin, Sam pointed at the spare chair. "Take a seat, please." He continued after she sat. "Hoppy, a bunch of people in high places are satisfied with how we carried off the last operation. So much so that they will invest in equipment upgrades and specialized training. We will be the go-to folks for special operations. As part of that, I asked for, and they agreed I can keep you—with a bump up to chief."

Sam paused as her eyes widened and her mouth hung open in shock.

"It's your decision, and if you decide to move on, you'll get complete support from me. I want you to stay, and we need your insight and skills, but you need to understand what this means. We will probably be committed to operations like the last one, some of which will involve serious hazards. I can promise you we'll be better-trained and smarter in the future, but the risks will still be high. I appreciate your candor on the last op, which was on the nose in the end. But I need to know you can take it when the kids have to launch out because it will happen, and we won't have the luxury of time for soul-searching when it does."

She could not believe her ears. Just a few minutes ago, she had been afraid of getting caught up in the relief for cause of the finest men she had ever known. Now, not only was that horror vanquished, but the most significant conflict she ever faced, leaving *Kauai* or turning down a promotion, had also been removed. She grinned and said, "Sir, I'm in if you and Mr. Wyporek are. I hope I can still point out when I have concerns, *respectfully*, of course."

"You damn well better call us out when we screw up. It's your ass too," Sam said as they both stood.

She was so delighted that she couldn't hold back and gave him a quick, warm hug.

"Dammit, Hoppy, dismissed!"

"Sorry, sir, won't happen again, sir. Thank you, sir!" she said, rushing out of the cabin. She bounded to the messdeck, Deffler standing just in time to be enveloped in another, more passionate hug.

"Things went well, I take it," he said dryly.

"You could say that," she replied with a warm smile. "I get to stay on board AND make chief!"

"Oh, Emilia, I'm so happy for you!"

"Yes, yes. Enough about that. Want to take a pre-chief out for some breakfast?"

"Let me get changed," he said with a smile.

Ben

After Sam, Hopkins, and Deffler left the dock, Drake turned to Ben. "What's going on with Hoppy, sir?"

Ben grinned. "The skipper worked his spooky magic and found a way to keep Hoppy aboard *and* let her pin on chief." His smile faded. "If she wants to hang around."

"Seriously, sir? Why wouldn't she?"

"She ripped me a new one yesterday for my little adventure. I had it coming, too. Put a new spin on the dangers of glory-hunting for me. I'm unsure she still wants to work for me."

Drake looked at Ben in surprise and shook his head. "XO, you sure have some dense patches for a smart fella. She *loves* you, sir, you and the CO. Yes, she's mad as hell at you two for putting yourselves on the spot like that, but that doesn't mean she would want to be anywhere else." When Ben looked down and shifted nervously, he added, "Don't let it get inside your head, sir. Just keep doing what you're doing, and everything will be fine."

"Thanks, Chief."

Drake nodded, and they both crossed over onto *Kauai*, Drake aft toward the messdeck and Ben to his stateroom. After hearing Hopkins depart, Ben got up and stood in Sam's doorway, watching him type out something on his workstation, probably an email to Mercier.

Finally, Sam looked up, and Ben said, "I'm your ride this morning, Captain."

"Thanks, man, but I can make it OK."

Ben shook his head firmly. "No, sir. Remember a few days back, around the last time *you* slept, when you pointed out the fatigue in our passenger? I'm seeing the same thing in you right now. Look, you just saved my life at the risk of your job. Let me give back a little."

"OK, you win. Let's get going before I decide to crash here."

They strolled down to Ben's white Camaro, an academy graduation present from his parents, and climbed in. Sam nodded off before they even reached the base security gate. Observing his friend fast asleep, Ben activated his phone and used the voice feature to dial Sam's home number.

"Um, hello?" Jo answered groggily after four rings.

"Hi, Jo. Ben here."

"Ben?" He could hear the alarm rising in her voice. "What...?"

"It's OK. Everybody's fine," he interjected. "We're on the way there. Sam is pretty knocked out, and I think he's been up for about three days solid. He dropped off right after he got in the car."

"OK." Her relief was palpable. "I guess you had an interesting trip?"

"It was rough. I'll let Sam tell you about it. I just wanted to let you know he might not be the usual super-attentive hubby when he gets home."

"Thanks, I'll shunt him straight to bed," she replied. "What about you? Do you need to flop here? I can make up the couch for you."

"No, I'm fine. I'm a lot younger than you two, remember?"

"I'll pass on calling you a jerkwad just this once because I love you for taking care of my man."

"All part of my usual awesomeness." Ben smiled. "I'll see you soon."

"Goodbye Ben, and thank you *very much*," she said, hanging up.

The trip home was slow, but typical for Miami. Ben pulled into the driveway a little after 06:30, climbed out, and opened the passenger door. "Skipper." He shook Sam's shoulder gently. "Sam?"

Sam startled awake. "Wha… Oh, right." He climbed out of the Camaro and grabbed his bag. He turned to Ben and hugged him. "Thanks, man."

"You too, Boss. See you in a few days." Ben watched Sam walk tiredly to the front door before climbing into the Camaro. As he drove off, his thoughts returned to the beautiful analyst in Bethesda. Ben knew he shouldn't get his hopes up, as there were so many ways things could go off the rails. Yet, for some reason, he was sure things were about to get as interesting in his personal life as they were in his professional one.

Sam

The relief and surprise of going from the edge of career death to being lauded and decorated had passed, and Sam was dead on his feet. If anything, the brief nap in Ben's car had rendered him dizzier than he was before. Sam fumbled with his key briefly, then unlocked and opened the door and entered the quiet house. He wondered if he might be the only one up when Jo emerged from the kitchen barefoot in her red nightshirt. *God, she's so beautiful,* was the single thought his fatigue-addled brain could form when Sam looked at her long raven hair and lovely dark eyes. "Jo, I…" He stopped when she put a finger to her lips. She stepped forward, cupped his face in her hands, gazing into his eyes for what seemed like minutes, and then tightly hugged him, all without a single word.

She released him, took his arm, led him toward the bedroom, and whispered, "It's rack time for you, my dear captain. Ben called me with a head's up while you were on the way. You can tell me all about it after you've had some sleep."

Sam nodded. "Aye, aye, my love." He paused at Robby and Danni's bedroom, as he did every morning when he was home, and peeked in to ensure they were sleeping comfortably and covered. Sam then let himself be led to the bed and undressed, practically falling onto the bed afterward. He felt a soft kiss on his lips as he drifted off to sleep.

Notes from the Author

None of the characters in this book represent any particular person (you got that, all you lawyers out there?). However, some of the best qualities of the fictional crew members of *Kauai* were inspired by many of the fine people with whom I had the honor and pleasure to serve while I was a part of the Coast Guard.

USCGC *Kauai* is fictional. There is no "D Class" of the 110-foot patrol boat series, and the last of those built was USCGC *Galveston Island* (WPB-1349). I created a fictitious D-Class to buy some extra margin of verisimilitude and get the nitpickers off my back. The cutters *Poplar* and *Skua* are also fictional instantiations of the *Juniper*-class buoy tender and Marine Protector class coastal patrol boats. The medium endurance cutters *Dependable* and *Mohawk* are real and currently in service as of this writing.

The mishap in the story that led to Sam's assumption of command of *Kauai* is another fictitious plot device. That said, I think I am in agreement with most other Coast Guard veterans in asserting that, while necessary, Alien Migrant Interdiction Operations were the most heartbreaking duty I ever performed.

The dialog between the Coast Guard people and in radio transmissions depicted in this story has much more "plain language" than what you would hear during actual operations. Including all the acronyms, jargon, and formal protocols vital for clarity and brevity in real life would have been more authentic. However, it would also be a great deal more tedious or confusing for the average reader. I ask all veterans and any other purists' forgiveness for this compromise for the sake of readability.

Now that all the lawyer crap is out of the way, time for the interesting stuff. I wrote the plot for *Dagger Quest* over a year ago, well before the crisis in Ukraine erupted into full-scale war. At the time, I thought the crisis that precipitated the incident serving as the trigger event for the story, an aggressive Russian move to seize and annex a corridor to Kaliningrad, to be somewhat fanciful. Today we talk of that very thing as Lithuania imposes a partial blockade of railroad traffic between Russia and Kaliningrad from sanctions imposed due to the war in Ukraine. A fascinating case of life imitating art, and very, VERY frightening.

Dagger Quest was my first novel, and with it, I learned a lot about the objectives of fiction writing and the publishing process. One of the most challenging things to achieve in a fictional military thriller is the balance between realism and readability in the characters' dialog. Military people use a lot of technical terms and jargon (as well as very "salty" language) in their everyday speech. Replicating this would be very realistic, but people who haven't lived in this environment would have difficulty understanding what is being said and what is going on. The language today is a good deal less "salty" (in the Coast Guard, at least) than it was when I came up, but it is still more than you would typically experience outside of a locker room, which also has the potential to turn off readers.

On the other hand, having a character refer to the "bow" as "the pointy end up at the front of the boat" and never using a four-letter word is eye-rolling unrealistic. So, I compromised, toned down some of the jargon and most foul language, and put a glossary in the front for some of the less self-evident technical terms. Hopefully, I hit close to the center of the target and ask for the patience of both veterans and people with no experience in this world.

The *esprit de corps* of the crew of *Kauai* is somewhat atypical, but not unknown, particularly for a purpose-built elite unit (as *Kauai* is revealed to be at the end of the story). The team/family feel of a small unit like this is not unusual. These people depend on each other for their lives, which yields a closeness not generally found among co-workers outside the military. The closest analog in civilian life would be police officer partners. The relationship between the officers and crew is also more intimate than you would typically see, but not beyond the realm of the possible, particularly for command cadre handpicked to clean up the wreckage left by an incompetent tyrant relieved for cause. Bad commanding officers are fortunately scarce, but not unknown—

the man portrayed as Sam's predecessor was based on a true story of a Navy cruiser captain relieved for cause for abuse of the crew.

I originally envisioned Victoria Carpenter as a "brush-by" character to provide some quirky color to the DIA ground team. As things developed, I realized she had tremendous potential as a romantic interest for Ben, if not a main character in her own right. Giving her a more significant role in Dagger Quest was not feasible, but she features prominently in the subsequent stories. She was another difficult element for balance, giving her an unusual challenge (her mild autism) without making her into a caricature. I thank Helen Hoang for this—her novel *The Kissing Quotient* presented an excellent reference for a point of view from someone "on the spectrum."

This story is a sea adventure, plain and simple, designed to help you escape the madness that pervades the real world (for a while, at least). It does not feature superheroes or super-soldiers—just ordinary but dedicated people rising to the challenge. A reader of an earlier edition said that when the story ended, she felt sad at having to leave the crew. I hope you feel that same level of closeness.

Caribbean Counterstrike

Main Characters

<u>Benjamin "Ben" Wyporek, Lieutenant Junior Grade, U. S. Coast Guard</u>. Ben is the Second-in-Command or "Executive Officer" of the Coast Guard Cutter *Kauai*. He is young for an officer, but his demeanor and experience have earned the respect of the professionals around him, and although he is firm in his job, he never lets his position go to his head. Ben is currently in a long-distance relationship with Victoria Carpenter, the beautiful Defense Intelligence Agency analyst he met during a mission a few months ago.

<u>Victoria Carpenter</u> is a mathematical genius employed by the Defense Intelligence Agency as a Data Scientist. Her talents for "connecting the dots" in large databases and Internet searches have proven invaluable to the organization. She suffers from a mild form of autism that makes relationships and some life activities challenging for her. Her relationship with Ben is warm and durable.

<u>Dr. Peter Simmons</u> is a field agent with the Defense Intelligence Agency. He has a talent for deception, which has led to his success as a DIA field agent but is the antithesis of Ben's ethos. Simmons also has a risk-seeking bent that borders on pathology. He shares a cordial relationship with Ben and is supportive of his relationship with Victoria, his protégé and sister of his beloved late fiancée.

<u>Samuel "Sam" Powell, Lieutenant, U. S. Coast Guard</u>. Sam is Ben's boss and Commanding Officer of the Coast Guard Cutter *Kauai*. Sam is one of those people who is the total package - knowledge, judgment, experience, and "people sense." He was raised in a wealthy family and was being groomed to become another Wall Street "Master of the Universe" when a clash with his father led him to abandon that path and enlist in the Coast

Guard. He is over ten years older than Ben, but despite this and their different backgrounds, they are best friends.

Emilia "Hoppy" Hopkins, Chief Operations Specialist, U. S. Coast Guard. She is close in age and a lot like Sam in terms of competence and professionalism, and they have as strong a friendship as people in their respective positions can. She has enormous respect and an exasperated affection for Ben, who reminds her of her late husband. Although a straight arrow, she is not afraid to forego convention in highly unusual circumstances.

Shelley Lee, Boatswain's Mate Second Class, U.S. Coast Guard. The premier small boat driver of the crew is more rough-and-ready than Hopkins and a solid, courageous performer. She and Ben are close in age, similar in personality, and share a strong mutual respect and trust bond.

James "COB" Drake, Chief Machinery Technician, U. S. Coast Guard. The senior enlisted member of the crew and the classic father figure among the enlisted and, to some extent, Ben. He is the quintessential "operator" and has what amounts to an underground network of fellow CPOs from whom he can acquire technical assistance, materiel, and "intel." His background is somewhat mysterious, but he is "connected" up to the senior officer level of the Coast Guard.

Horatio "Harry" Pennington, Rear Admiral, U. S. Coast Guard. Pennington is the Director of the Joint Interagency Task Force South, responsible for coordinating all law enforcement activity within the United States Southern Command. *Kauai* and her crew are under his command for the operation depicted in the story.

Joana Mendez Powell. Wife of Sam and unofficial "First Lady" of *Kauai*. She is a former navy petty officer and work-from-home computer graphics artist who looks after the crew's families while they are at sea. She is close friends with Ben and Emilia.

Military Ranks

Commissioned Officers		
Coast Guard/Navy	**Army/Air Force**	**Characters**
Admiral	General	Miller (USA)
Vice Admiral	Lieutenant General	Irving (USN)
Rear Admiral	Major General Brigadier General	Pennington, Brown (USCG)
Captain	Colonel	Mercier (USCG)
Commander	Lieutenant Colonel	Keener (USCG)
Lieutenant Commander	Major	Becker (USCG) Roberts (USA)
Lieutenant	Captain	Powell, Holmgren (USCG) Davis (USN) Landry, Fergus (USAF)
Lieutenant Junior Grade	1st Lieutenant	Wyporek (USCG)
Enlisted		
Coast Guard/Navy	**Air Force**	**Characters**
Master Chief Petty Officer	Chief Master Sergeant	Shipley (USAF)
Senior Chief Petty Officer	Senior Master Sergeant	D'Agostino (USN)
Chief Petty Officer	Master Sergeant	Drake, Hopkins (USCG)
Petty Officer First Class	Technical Sergeant	Bondurant, Williams (USCG) Parker (USN)
Petty Officer Second Class	Staff Sergeant	Lee, Guerrero, Brown, Hebert (USCG)
Petty Officer Third Class	Senior Airman	Bunting, Jenkins, Lopez, Zuccaro (USCG)

Select Technical Terms

1MC	Ship's internal announcement system
252s	Transnational Criminal Organization
AUTEC	Atlantic Undersea Test and Evaluation Center
Bridge	Control center for the ship
CO	Commanding Officer
COB	Chief of the Boat
Conn	Position controlling operation of the ship
Coxswain	Position controlling the operation of a small boat
DIA	Defense Intelligence Agency
EO/IR	Electro-Optical/Infrared
ETA	Estimated Time of Arrival
FC3	Fire Control/Command and Control system
GPS	Global Positioning System
Helm	Position or station controlling the ship's rudder
Knots	Nautical Miles per Hour
"Light Off"	Start or activate an engine or device
Main Control	Control station for the ship's main engines
NVG	Night Vision Goggles
OOD	Officer of the Deck
PB	Patrol Boat
Port (side)	To the left, when facing the bow aboard a ship
RHIB	Rigid Hull Inflatable Boat
RJ	Rivet Joint Electronics Warfare Aircraft
Salinas Cartel	Honduran drug gang
SEAL	SEa-Air-Land – U.S. Navy Special Warfare Operators
Starboard (side)	To the right, when facing the bow aboard a ship
UAV	Unmanned Aerial Vehicle
WILCO	Brevity code for "Will Comply."
XO	Executive Officer—second-in-command of a ship

"There are no great men; there are only great challenges, which ordinary men like you and me are forced by circumstances to meet."

Attributed to Fleet Admiral William F. Halsey, Jr., U.S. Navy

Part I—Pre-Mission

Atlantic Ocean
Port Canaveral
Clearwater
PCA 403
Freeport
Northwest Providence Channel
Miami
Northeast Providence Channel
Bimini
Gulf of Mexico
Nassau
AUTEC
Key West
Florida Straits
Old Bahama Channel
Caribbean Sea

The Crack of Doom

USCG Cutter *Kauai*, Atlantic Ocean, ten nautical miles east-southeast of Hollywood, Florida
02:27 EDT, 11 March

Sam

Lieutenant Samuel "Sam" Powell watched the image of the "go-fast" boat on the right-hand multi-function display of the Bridge's Fire Control/Command and Control or FC3 station. The ghostly green image was transmitted from a Customs and Border Patrol DHC-8 maritime patrol aircraft, flying at a minimum speed at two thousand feet, zigzagging back and forth to avoid overrunning the target. The aspect of the speeding boat's image gradually changed as the plane traced a broad S-shaped pattern behind it while the data display overlaying the bottom of the screen showed its latitude, longitude, heading, and speed. An open forty-footer with three large outboard engines and eight people on board, the boat was on a course leading slightly ahead of *Kauai's* current position on this heading. Still, the latter's slow motion would bring the two vessels to the same point in the ocean in about five minutes.

It was the darkest of nights, a solid overcast blocking out both moon and stars. The only light was the glow of the Miami-Ft. Lauderdale metroplex stretched across a broad arc of *Kauai's* starboard beam. Sam would have preferred meeting the target boat further offshore, where the city light would not silhouette his patrol boat, but this was the only place the intercept geometry worked. Both seas and winds were very light, making for a comfortable ride. The only sound was the low and steady hum of the three diesel engines. All things considered, they had a pretty good chance of catching the incoming smuggler by surprise.

It was *Kauai's* first operational mission after completing an extensive rebuild and a few weeks of shakedown training. They should be heading for the Atlantic Undersea Test and Evaluation Center, better known as AUTEC, at Andros Island in the Bahamas to complete testing and evaluate the new gear added to the cutter. However, the Coast Guard had hard intelligence; the boat racing toward them carried a high-ranking member of an Eastern European human-trafficking gang, whose notoriety prevented travel to the U.S. by conventional means. He was a high-value target, or HVT, armed and dangerous, and had to be stopped. But the boat also held other people, illegal immigrants, yes, but people undeserving of being caught in a lethal crossfire between a dangerous sociopath and law enforcement. Sorting out this dilemma was the type of mission for which *Kauai* was rebuilt, and her crew retrained.

"Target still constant bearing, decreasing range. Range now two-point-four, ETA four minutes fifty," said Electronics Technician First Class Joe Williams. He sat in the center position at the FC3 console, the tactical station controlling the cutter's 25-mm main gun, the automated searchlight, and the new "entangling weapon" mounted just forward of the main gun they had spent the previous week testing. Operations Specialist Third Class Natalia Zuccaro sat to his right, monitoring navigation and radar, and Electronics Technician Third Class Darryl Bunting sat on his left, tending to systems and communications.

"Very well," Sam replied. "Warm up the Squid and start the targeting feed." "Squid" was the nickname for the entangling weapon, essentially a three-barreled recoilless cannon shooting encapsulated nets that popped open at the end of their flight and landed in a pre-set pattern. The launcher took target and environmental data from Williams's console and adjusted the firing bearing and elevation to deploy the nets in a pattern a speeding boat could not avoid. The boat would overrun a net, foul the propellers, and be stopped without using lethal gunfire. Hopefully.

The sad fact was a lot had to go just right for this device to work. The target needed to be within two hundred meters of *Kauai*, with both vessels on parallel courses in calm seas. It was a calm night, and Sam had absolute confidence that his Officer of the Deck, or OOD, Chief Operations Specialist Emilia Hopkins, would bring *Kauai* into position in the minimum time possible. The rub was their opponent—success depended on him turning to the left to avoid *Kauai*. If he turned right, he would scoot past their tail and be out of range before they got the heavier patrol boat turned around. Sam had positioned the cutter's Rigid Hull Inflatable Boat, referred to as "the rib" for its acronym RHIB, two hundred yards to seaward and slightly behind to counter this possibility. The RHIB's crew would unmask their floodlight as soon as *Kauai* illuminated the target with her searchlight, which should persuade the incoming boat to turn left to escape. Of course, he could also turn back to Bimini—not as good as a seizure, but it was still a win.

Using the RHIB was a calculated risk—the target could try to force past it using ramming or gunfire, but the odds against that were long. The HVT might be armed and dangerous, but the smuggling crew's priority was to stay alive. They knew if they assaulted law enforcement, the response would be both lethal and instantaneous. Far better to turn tail and outrun the plodding cutter, which they could easily do with their five-knot speed advantage.

"Captain, I have target lock and tracking now on EO," Williams announced, referring to the cutter's electro-optical camera. Although his nominal rank was lieutenant, Sam was addressed as "Captain" aboard *Kauai* by service tradition as her commanding officer. "Laser rangefinder is active, feeding data directly to searchlight, fire control, and the Squid. Range now one-point-nine, ETA three minutes fifty-two seconds." As he spoke, the unlit searchlight swung out onto the bearing of the incoming target.

"Roger that," Sam replied, then keyed the radio transmit button for his headset. "*Kauai* One, *Kauai* Actual, target in sight, ETA three forty-five."

"Roger, sir, standing by," replied the RHIB's coxswain, Boatswain's Mate Second Class Shelley Lee. Lee commanded the RHIB as the coxswain, even though her passengers included her immediate boss, Boatswain's Mate First Class John Bondurant, and *Kauai*'s Executive Officer, Lieutenant Junior Grade Ben Wyporek, who would lead the target's boarding once it had been disabled.

Hopkins keyed the intercom connecting the Bridge to the engine control station deep in the cutter's hull. "Main Control, Conn, take engine control, expect Emergency Full Ahead in three minutes."

"Conn, Main Control," Drake's baritone voice replied. "I have engine control, maintaining three knots, standing by for Emergency Full Ahead in three minutes." "Emergency Full" was a command to route power from the battery bank and three diesel generators for rapid acceleration of the cutter's two electric motors from a full stop or their current slow speed to maximum thrust, either ahead or astern. It required transferring engine control to Drake's station, where he could watch the generator and motor instruments and achieve the highest acceleration with the safeties bypassed.

Sam watched the two screens on the FC3 station, one now showing the approaching boat from the view of the EO camera alongside the full-motion video feed from the plane. Williams had selected the boat's range in yards, bearing, and ETA for the data display. Even at full zoom, no boat details were visible in the darkness, just the spreading white "mustache" of the bow wave. "Chief, we are at two thousand yards now. I'm going to light him up at two hundred yards. You are cleared to maneuver as required."

"Very good, sir," Hopkins replied. Emilia "Hoppy" Hopkins was a fast-tracker in the Operations Specialist rating and a twelve-year veteran of the Coast Guard. Thanks to Sam's request to his superiors after their last mission, they upgraded her billet to E7 so she could stay on board *Kauai* while advancing to the coveted rank of chief petty officer. The tall and fit thirty-three-year-old widowed mother of twelve- and nine-year-old sons, Hopkins shared a house with her mother, who looked after the boys when she was at sea. Both Ben and Sam shared considerable respect, affection, and trust for their new chief, and she felt the same for them.

Sam watched the range readout tick down and, at three hundred yards, announced, "Stand by searchlight."

"Searchlight ready, sir," Williams responded. Then he leaned slightly to the right and nudged Zuccaro, then whispered, "Watch the EO screen when I light off the searchlight."

"OK." She nodded vigorously. Zuccaro had only been aboard a few weeks, an addition that came with the added functionality of the new FC3 console. She looked up to Williams as a mentor and with a bit of awe over his role in *Kauai*'s dustup last January—he had controlled the main gun in that engagement, and his shooting had saved the XO's life.

Hopkins smiled at the interplay between the two petty officers and then keyed the intercom. "Stand by, Main Control."

"Main Control ready."

At 210 yards, Sam leaned over and put a hand on Williams's shoulder. "Illuminate target."

"Illuminate target, sir," Williams responded as he pressed the light on/off button. In the same motion, he punched on the floodlight illuminating the Coast Guard "Racing Stripe" painted on *Kauai*'s hull and the cutter's running lights.

"Main Control, Conn, Emergency Full Ahead," Hopkins ordered.

"Emergency Full Ahead, aye!" Drake replied as *Kauai*'s engines roared, and she jumped forward into the darkness.

The searchlight flickered on and directed a fifteen million candela beam directly into the approaching boat's cockpit. Williams smiled with satisfaction, watching the driver's eyes widen and jaw drop in shock on the EO display, then turned to Zuccaro. "Ah, the 'Oh, shit!' moment. Now THAT never gets old!"

As Williams chuckled, the RHIB's floodlight came on to the target driver's right. He glanced in that direction for half a second and then spun his steering wheel to the left, nearly capsizing the speeding vessel during the turn. The boat steadied on a southerly course and picked up speed rapidly, slowly drawing ahead about sixty yards away off *Kauai*'s port bow.

"Conn, Main Control, that's all I can give you right now," Drake's voice came up from the intercom.

"Conn, aye, hold that." Turning to the helmsman, Hopkins ordered, "Left five degrees rudder."

"Left five degrees rudder, Chief," the helmsman replied. "Chief, my rudder is left five degrees."

When Hopkins was satisfied the vessels were running parallel, she turned to the helmsman. "Rudder amidships."

"Rudder amidships, aye. Chief, my rudder is amidships, heading one eight three."

"Very well," Hopkins responded, then turned to Sam. "Target aspect and relative motion stable, Captain."

"Very well. Williams, prepare to fire Squid."

Williams noted the yellow "Solution" light on his panel, showing that the projector's control system had locked onto the fleeing target boat. Its internal artificial intelligence had calculated the required azimuth and elevation to lay down an optimal pattern of the three nets. "Targeting solution achieved."

"Match generated bearings and shoot."

Williams hit the activation switch. The projector pivoted to match the generated azimuth and elevation angles, resulting in a green "Ready to Fire" light on the panel. Williams announced, "Firing Squid." Then he pressed the trigger.

Ben

Ben sat on the RHIB's left side and glanced across the water at *Kauai*, visible in the city glow two hundred yards off the boat's starboard side. He looked back into the boat. Lee was sitting at the helm, making minor adjustments to keep station on the larger cutter as they moved slowly through the water. Lee was single, twenty-five years old, and on the short side for boatswain's mate, barely five-foot-three, but very athletic. Ben liked Lee; besides their being close in age, she was competent and dependable. She was also the finest coxswain he had ever known—she *lived* for driving the RHIB.

Ben's gaze moved to Bondurant, sitting on the opposite side of the boat, holding the floodlight. He was a full foot taller than Lee and powerfully built. The thirty-four-year-old father of two high school-aged boys, Bondurant was Ben's choice for known hostile boardings. Not that Lee couldn't handle herself, quite the contrary, but violent idiots were discouraged from trying anything physical by the size of the hulking Bondurant. Better to avoid the fight to begin with, a philosophy with which Lee heartily agreed—she couldn't drive the RHIB if she were in the boarding party.

"*Kauai* One, *Kauai* Actual, target in sight, ETA three forty-five," came over Ben's headset, followed by Lee's acknowledgment. Ben smiled as he pictured Sam calmly walking around the Bridge two hundred yards away. To Ben, Sam had the total package: knowledge, judgment, experience, and "people sense." He considered him a model officer and his closest friend. He was about an inch taller than Ben and similarly slim and athletic.

Ben himself was a little over average height at five-foot-ten. At twenty-four, he was also among the younger members of *Kauai*'s complement. Although somewhat awed by his fight with the drug gang a few months previously, the crew appreciated his cheery demeanor and the respect he showed them as valued professionals. His close brush with death dispelled whatever boyishness he had, but he kept his bright wit and approachability.

Ben gazed out to seaward. Not long now. They would hear the incoming boat long before they saw it and act when *Kauai*'s searchlight activated. In the meantime, they were to hold station on the cutter. Ben's thoughts returned to the worst case, the boat turning right. If they tried to ram and Lee couldn't evade.... He glanced at Lee and noted her rapid visual scan and cool look in the soft light of the RHIB's instrument panel. Ben smiled to himself and looked out to sea again. *Yeah, as if!*

Across the boat, Bondurant stirred. "I hear them!" He brought the floodlight to the ready and unlocked the shutter. The light was already turned on, so it would be instantly available. Both men kneeled and braced themselves for a quick start. Ben could hear the roar of the target boat's engines now, coming from left to right across RHIB's bow. Almost simultaneously, *Kauai*'s engines roared to full power, and the cutter's searchlight settled on the incoming boat.

"Light him up!" Ben shouted.

Bondurant dropped the shutter and trained the floodlight on the boat. The driver glanced their way momentarily, then swung the speeding boat into a hard left turn.

Yes! "Go, Shelley!" Ben shouted.

Lee slammed the throttle forward, and the RHIB seemed to leap ahead after the speeding target. Bondurant struggled to keep the floodlight on target as the RHIB thumped across the target boat's wake. Lee pulled the RHIB into a parallel track about fifty yards away on the target's port quarter as briefed. The RHIB had the speed to overtake the target, but Lee knew her job tonight was herding.

A minute into the pursuit, Ben heard three bangs in quick succession from *Kauai*. The three Squid canisters arced invisibly over the speeding target vessel in the darkness, with small fins spinning them at fifteen revolutions per second to provide stability and help spread out the nets when their internal charges detonated at the end of their flight. Sam's voice came over Ben's headset. "*Kauai* One, Squid fired, break left in three, two, one, NOW!" Twenty-five feet above the water, all three capsules fired within a second, dropping an unavoidable Kevlar trap forty yards ahead of the target boat as the RHIB and *Kauai* sheared off to the left and right.

The boat narrowly missed the right-hand net but ran straight through the center one. When its propellers contacted the netting, two engines sheared their driveshafts and oversped, triggering the automatic shutoff. The third engine ground to a stop with its propeller wrapped up in the net. The boat lurched to a quick halt, throwing all occupants but the driver onto the deck. As the RHIB swung around through the turn, Ben watched the driver hang his head and beat on the steering wheel with his fist in frustration as his crew and passengers began standing up in dazed confusion.

"All right, Shelley, let's heave to until *Kauai* gets into position," Ben said. He didn't want the RHIB to overrun a net in the dark—it had a propeller too, and was just as vulnerable as the target boat. As Lee closed the throttle and brought the RHIB to a halt, Bondurant shut off and secured the floodlight.

Kauai took five minutes to complete her turn and edge into position—she also had propellers plus stabilizing fins on her bilge turns, which could suffer severe damage if fouled on a net. Sam's voice came over the headset again as the cutter stopped about fifty yards west of the disabled boat with her searchlight locked on. "*Kauai* One, *Kauai* Actual, commence a slow approach. Nets one and three are behind us. Net two is fouled on the target."

"*Kauai, Kauai* One, roger, sir, commencing approach," Lee replied as she moved the throttle off idle.

"LE-One, *Kauai* Actual, believe the HVT is the individual conversing with the helmsman. No weapons are visible, but the threat level is still red. Overwatch is in position and ready. We will make initial contact now." Ben had his own callsign, LE-One, on the comms net since he would act independently of the RHIB during the boarding.

"Roger, sir. Continuing," Ben replied. This was the hard part. Somehow, Ben had to talk down a dangerously excited murderer and convince him to surrender. He saw two men arguing in the boat's cockpit, one black and the other white. The black man had to be the boat's Bahamian master, and the other, the HVT, undoubtedly pushing for a more satisfactory outcome than his arrest. At least no guns were out. *Overwatch is in position.* Overwatch was Gunner's Mate Second Class Deke Guerrero, positioned with a fifty-caliber sniper rifle on the Flying Bridge above *Kauai*'s main Bridge. Guerrero could deliver a kill shot reliably from a mile away—fifty yards on a calm night was point-blank for him. If Sam, Ben, or Bondurant uttered the word "Yankee" on the radio, Guerrero would fire that kill shot as soon as he had a clear target.

As the RHIB edged toward the target boat, Williams's voice came from the loudhailer on *Kauai*, "Master of the disabled vessel, this is the United States Coast Guard. Your vessel is forfeit under Title Eight of the United States Code, Section 1324. All persons on board will be placed under arrest. You will muster all persons on board aft of the cockpit, where they will be seated with their hands on top of their heads. All persons on board are to discard any weapons in their possession. Any person on board observed holding a weapon after this announcement will be subject to lethal force. To repeat..." The announcement was repeated and ended with: "You will comply at once. Start mustering all persons now."

The master lowered his head, then gave an order. As the other six people started moving aft, the HVT began an argument. When the RHIB pulled within earshot, Ben could hear the final statement of the master, "It's broken, man! We are done."

The HVT started looking back and forth, then reached for something in the cockpit. He rose, placed a pistol against the master's head, and pulled the man between himself and *Kauai.*

Shit! "Gun!" Ben shouted as he and Bondurant crouched and pulled their pistols. Lee brought the RHIB to a halt and crouched behind the helm console. One woman screamed on the disabled boat, and all but the HVT and his human shield immediately laid down. "*Kauai*, LE-One," Ben said into his headset. "HVT has a handgun and has taken the master hostage. We are stopped with sidearms ready. Recommend I try to negotiate surrender from our present position, over."

After a brief pause, Sam's voice came over the headset. "LE-One, *Kauai* Actual, approved. Do not continue the approach without confirmed surrender and disarming of the suspect. Go on hot mike, and keep it open during negotiations."

"*Kauai*, LE-One, WILCO." Ben moved the transmit switch to Hot Mic. Both he and Bondurant brought up and aimed their pistols. "On the disabled boat, this is the Coast Guard! Put your weapon down immediately!"

The HVT turned his head in surprise and adjusted to make himself a smaller target for Ben and Bondurant while still shielding himself from *Kauai.* "Screw you! You are going to let me go, or this man dies!"

Ben lowered his voice to be inaudible on the target. "Overwatch, LE-One, do you have a shot? Over."

Guerrero's voice responded at once. "Negative, LE-One, no clear shot."

"Roger." Ben resumed his interchange with the HVT. "Sir, that is not an option! Your vessel is disabled and cannot be repaired! It's over! Please, no one has to die today!"

"Fine! Then I take your boat!"

"Sorry, sir, we can't do that! Even if we could, you wouldn't have enough fuel to get anywhere!"

"Then get me a boat that can! I'm not fucking around! I will kill this man!"

The master's eyes, flitting back and forth in terror, fixed on Ben. Ben took his support hand off the pistol and made a slow, down-waving motion until the master nodded slowly, then placed his hand back on the gun. He whispered into his microphone, "Yankee." Then more loudly. "That is not going to happen! There are only two possible outcomes here—you drop that gun, and we arrest you, or you get killed!"

"Then I'll see you in Hell!"

What followed happened in under one second. The HVT took the pistol's muzzle off the master's temple and started to draw on Ben. The master immediately twisted and bent over, disrupting the HVT's aim. There was the loud "Crack" of a large-caliber rifle shot. Then the pistol dropped to the deck, followed by the HVT, who crumpled like a marionette with the strings cut. The former hostage knelt and put his hands on top of his head.

"Suspect down, repeat suspect is down," Ben said. "Hostage is safe and signaling surrender." Then, he remembered to take his transmit switch off Hot Mic. And to breathe.

"LE-One, *Kauai* Actual, roger, approach with discretion, over."

"WILCO, sir." Holstering his pistol with a trembling hand, he turned to Lee. "Shelley, move in dead slow, please. If anyone else pops up with a gun, duck and haul ass."

She flashed him a relieved smile as she moved the throttle out of idle. "Sir, I'm the *quintessence* of discretion."

Ben smiled warmly in return, then turned to Bondurant. "Boats, how about I go on first with you covering, then I'll cover you when you board?"

"Sounds right, sir. You want me to do the hook-ups?"

"Yes, let's start with the skipper and move aft from there. Stay alert, although I'm pretty sure they've had enough excitement for tonight."

"Let's hope so."

Ben called out as they approached the boat, "On the boat, this is the U.S. Coast Guard. Remain seated with your hands on top of your head. Do not stand or make any sudden movements. Comply with the boarding officer's instructions completely and immediately." Ben stepped aboard and drew his pistol as the RHIB contacted the boat with a soft nudge. *Kauai*'s searchlight lit the scene, and the only sounds were the low growl of the RHIB's engine, the gentle lapping of small waves on the hull, and the soft sobs of a woman, presumably the one who screamed at the incident's outset. After a quick visual sweep and count of seven people seated with hands visible, he felt for a pulse on the downed suspect. Nothing. The man was dead before he hit the deck, his spine severed just below his skull. Ben stood and nodded to Bondurant. "Now, Boats." The big boatswain nodded, holstered his pistol, and stepped on board. Ben motioned him over and whispered, "Leave the woman for last. We'll need to swap Shelley in for that pat-down."

"Yes, sir." Bondurant turned and went straight to the kneeling master and spoke quietly. "Are you the captain?" After getting a nod in return, he continued, "Please stand up, keeping your hands on top of your head, sir." The man complied, and Ben was startled to see he was as tall as Bondurant, although much thinner.

Bondurant completed a pat-down for weapons and said, "Right hand, please." He attached a zip cuff. "Left hand, please." After securing the other cuff, he said, "Please, sit down." After helping the man to a sitting position, Bondurant moved on, and the man turned to Ben and mouthed, "thank you." Ben returned a nod.

After servicing the remaining six male prisoners, Bondurant re-boarded the RHIB to relieve Lee, who completed the female prisoner's pat-down and handcuffing. When she rejoined Ben near the cockpit, he called over to the cutter, "*Kauai*, LE-One, vessel and prisoners secure. Just the one fatality, over."

"LE-One, *Kauai*, roger, well done. I'll need you to send back the RHIB so we can retrieve those nets. Do any prisoners need immediate evacuation?"

"Negative, sir. They're all OK for now."

Lee looked up at Ben. "OK, sir. I'll just be going then...."

"Sorry, Shelley." Ben shook his head. "A female prisoner means you get to stick around."

"Yeah, I figured as much." She looked sadly on as Bondurant steered the RHIB back to *Kauai*.

Reap the Whirlwind

Los Robles La Paz, Departamento del Cesar, Colombia
06:27 COT, 17 March

González

This would be a textbook annihilation operation—swift and complete. *Teniente Coronel* Óscar González, *Ejército Nacional de Colombia*, bent over a map table, making notes in various locations as the updates came in via encrypted radio. His short battalion of *Brigada Especial Contra el Narcotráfico*, or BRCNA, was deploying into launch position for a full-on armed assault on a large supply depot for the cocaine cartel known as La Cantaña. He had every enemy strong point zeroed in for mortar fire and every route in and out covered by anti-tank and heavy machine guns. Half a dozen snipers occupied elevated positions in the area. González was confident of success. His troops were the elite of one of the finest armies in South America and, at least in counterinsurgency operations like this one, among the world's best.

This operation and the circumstances were very unusual these days. Large, heavily armed quasi-armies that characterized the cartels running the Colombian drug trade had mostly disappeared. The army pivoted and broke up the larger gangs after defeating the *Fuerzas Armadas Revolucionarias de Colombia,* or FARC rebels. What remained usually followed such a low profile they were known as "the Invisibles." Not that the trade itself subsided, quite the contrary. But these organizations had abandoned trafficking cocaine to the United States in favor of the more lucrative and less risky and violent markets of Europe, China, and Australia. *Plata no Plomo*: Silver, not Lead, was the new business model. As long as these groups kept the violence among themselves and at a low level, the government was content to leave them alone.

La Cantaña was an exception. They had established a tightly coupled relationship with one of the European syndicates, whose increasing demand for product pushed the organization into a larger logistical frame. More massive stockpiles, shipments, and accompanying security escalated violence that moved beyond their competitors. After the ambush and murder of two police patrols that stumbled onto active operations, La Cantaña was no longer an "Invisible." They broke the rules and would now pay the price.

Man-for-man, there was no comparison between his troops' quality and their opposition this morning, but González took nothing for granted. These were his boys, and he wouldn't waste one of them because of miserly allocation of force or shoddy preparation. His troops knew this and reciprocated confidence in the man whose martial skill and coolness under fire garnered the nickname *Coronel Relajado*. Most of the gunmen in these cartels were former FARC members, at liberty because of the Colombian government's peace deal. González understood, in principle, the need to break the cycle of violence after fifty years of civil war. Still, he hated the idea that some of the most sadistic murderers in history had escaped justice. He smiled to himself. At least these three dozen La Cantaña murderers would meet God for judgment in about fifteen minutes, and his men would conduct the introductions.

González looked over at the American intelligence agent following the operation. Usually, he would not have had any *Nord Americano* anywhere near his headquarters. The duplicity and arrogance of the American Drug Enforcement Agency and Central Intelligence Agency men displayed in joint operations with the Colombian Army during the 1990s and 2000s cemented his resentment and contempt for those organizations.

This Defense Intelligence Agency man was different. He brought the first intelligence that contributed to the localization of this drug cache and much more about La Cantaña's activities. Despite himself, González had become personally fond of the younger man in their two weeks together. Besides his "How can I help?" attitude, his Castilian Spanish was impeccable, and his knowledge of Cervantes and Unamuno, González's favorite authors, led to several spirited and enjoyable discussions. The American would return to Washington this evening—González would be sorry to see him go.

"Any thoughts, professor?" González asked.

Peter Simmons smiled at the Colonel's use of the nickname. It was not far off—Simmons held a Ph.D. in Astrophysics from Princeton—but he had done nothing professorial in the six years he had been with the DIA. "Ah, *señor*, this is one area I would not dare to offer critique. I just create messes—it's up to you professionals to clean them up."

González chuckled. "Very well, my friend. Watch and learn."

The last reports came in two minutes later: all units were in position and ready. González took one last, long look at the map and dispositions, then turned and picked up his rifle and helmet. "OK, let's go," he said as he climbed into his command vehicle with his radioman and Simmons. A short, five-minute drive later, they pulled up on one of the follow-on units. González wanted to personally lead the first assault troops into the compound, but accepted that it was no longer his place as a senior officer and commander. His men understood.

He stepped out of the vehicle and walked up to his second in command, Major Enrique Moreno, who turned and said, "All ready and awaiting your order, *Coronel*." There were no salutes, standing at attention, or any other parade ground crap in the field. Not that BRCNA was an egalitarian unit, it was that such displays just made it easier for enemy snipers to pick who to shoot first.

"Thank you, *Mayor*," González replied. He looked up at the clear, early morning sky. In a few minutes, the sun would clear the Serranía del Perijá mountains to the east, and soon after, it would become a typical, scorching hot lowland Colombia day. "Let's get on with it. Wake up the bastards."

"*Si, señor.*" Moreno held the handset to his ear and pressed the transmit button. "Mortar teams, on designated target, five rounds high explosive, commence, commence, commence!"

Six soldiers each dropped a twenty-seven-pound, 4.2-inch round down the barrel of an M30 mortar at virtually the same time. In the twenty seconds it took this first salvo to reach their targets, a second had been fired, and a third was in mid-launch. After the fifth distinct set of "crumpf" sounds from mortar explosions, Moreno turned to González and, after receiving a nod, pressed the transmit switch again. "Mortar teams, check, check, check! Assault teams, advance!"

Within half a minute, the sounds of distant automatic gunfire filled the air. After about two minutes, this tapered off to sporadic single shots. Moreno's handset buzzed, and he put it to his ear, "*Commandante. Si*, stand by." He looked up at González. "All objectives secure, *señor.*"

"Excellent! Pass on to all commanders well done and to remind their rookies to watch out for booby traps." Turning to Simmons and the radioman, he continued, "Let's roll." The three mounted the Colonel's vehicle and headed for the La Cantaña facility half a kilometer distant.

By the time the vehicle arrived at the target, the shooting had stopped, and soldiers were collecting the bodies at a central location. After the three had dismounted, a junior captain ran up and, in his excitement, barely stopped himself from saluting. "*Coronel!* We've just assessed the amount of product in storage, and it's three thousand, not one thousand tons!"

"*Maravilloso!*" González smiled. "This might break the back of La Cantaña—they'll have the devil's own time trying to recover. Well done, *Capitán!*" The smile then disappeared. "What are our casualties?"

"Three wounded, *señor*, none seriously. Our mortars really pasted them. The survivors were still stumbling around in shock, looking for their weapons, when our assault troops hit them. Only a few got shots off before being cut down."

"Thank God for that!" The smile returned as he turned to Simmons. "An outcome far better than even I had hoped, my friend!"

"Indeed. Congratulations, *señor!*" Simmons nodded. "What will you do with all this product?"

"We were going to burn it in situ. Capturing three times the amount in the intelligence brief was not a situation I expected. I must arrange for transport and disposal now, dammit!"

"I'm sure your men will figure it out. There seems to be nothing they can't do. With your permission, *señor*, I would like to go over and collect biometrics from the corpses."

"Granted, with pleasure, but I caution you like my rookies—don't go poking around the camp and take extreme care rifling the pockets of the dead. These bastards love leaving behind surprises."

"I'll be on my guard. *Gracias, Coronel.*"

As the American turned and walked toward the lengthening row of bodies, González motioned over Moreno and the young captain. "Gentlemen, let's get the wounded evacuated and bring up the trucks for the dead. I want the *Sargento Mayor* and one officer supervising the contraband until we can get it transported away. In the meantime, set up a perimeter; I don't want any survivors of La Cantaña or their competitors getting any bright ideas."

"Si, *señor*," both men replied, then turned to their duties.

González removed his cap and wiped his forehead. It was already getting uncomfortably hot, and, with the sun almost directly overhead this time of year, it would be miserable by noon. He watched as Simmons moved from corpse to corpse, taking electronic fingerprints and cell phone photos of faces, for those that still had hands and faces, that is. He envied that the young man would be on his way back home to the United States by nightfall while he would be here, guarding this poison. Still, the unexpected need to safeguard and transport the cocaine was a minor annoyance compared to their brilliant victory. González was looking forward to getting home and telling his wife and children that the world was safer today than yesterday thanks to his men.

He could not have been more wrong.

OSUV *Carlos Rojas*, Moored, Berth 142, Port of Maracaibo, Venezuela
11:32 VET, 18 March

Holtz

Anton Holtz was a very unhappy man, but not as unhappy as the man sitting before him. It was bad enough to be cooped up in this stinking tub with lousy food, cramped quarters, and no entertainment of any kind. Dealing with this sniveling brown wretch was just too much. Holtz slammed a fist on the table. "I don't want to hear excuses. You promised us this product today! Where the hell is it?"

"It, it's still in Colombia." The man looked down and shifted in his seat. "The BRCNA raided our depot."

"That's unfortunate for you. When can you reroute the replacement product?"

The man shifted again and looked at Holtz with a pained expression. "There is no replacement. They got everything."

Holtz could not believe his ears. "Everything? Did they raid your entire export network? How did they track all your locations? Your security must be shit!"

"We had it gathered in a single depot just over the border. It was too difficult to disperse and secure that much product. We didn't have enough men. We had a secure place—it was one of our bases during the war. No one knew about it."

"Stop!" Holtz interrupted. "I told you I wasn't interested in excuses. What is your plan to fix this?"

"Um. We know most of the product is still there. With your help, we can launch a raid...."

"WHAT? You want us to invade Colombia and attack the best combat unit they have to fix your fuck-up? Are you insane? What else do you have?"

The man looked down and shook his head.

"Alright, here's the deal. The only reason you are still alive is that I need you to convey a message to your bosses. They will return every euro of our down payment within two weeks, plus twenty percent. Fifteen days from now, if we don't have every bit of that sum, we will issue irrevocable hit contracts on every member of La Cantaña and their families. Questions?"

The man looked up in horror. "I don't know if we can gather that amount. We have obligations...."

"I'm not interested in excuses. If you don't have the cash handy, get it. Hit your competitors, rob banks, whatever. This is not negotiable. Pay us or die, you and your families."

The man said nothing, just blinked and nodded.

Holtz turned to one of his men. "Show this piece of shit out." After they had left, Holtz turned to his assistant, Fedor Dorshak, who was knowledgeable in the local drug trade. "Start a sweep. We need to get what we can together for the next rendezvous. Then I need options for future deliveries. We'll be paying through the nose for this one, which will lessen our negotiating power in Venezuela, at least for now. Is there anything we can work on in the north?"

"There are the Mexicans. They have the product and complete control of the supply chain."

"No, not the damn Mexicans! We can't go cap-in-hand to them—they're too powerful already. What about Guatemala or Honduras, anyone young and hungry there?"

"I'm not sure. I've heard of a few, but they're not the sort of people we normally deal with."

"These are not normal times. Look into it."

"Yes, Boss." Dorshak got up and left.

Holtz was the head of the first large-scale operation in South America by the 252 Syndicate, a diverse criminal enterprise spread across much of the former Warsaw Pact countries of Central and Eastern Europe. The syndicate was founded by the worst of not only the Soviet KGB, but the East German Stasi, Romanian Securitate, and Bulgarian State Security. Named for the Warsaw Pact's disbanding date, 25 February 1991, the 252s built a criminal empire of drugs, prostitution, extortion, and murder for hire throughout Eastern Europe in the decades following the collapse. Ironically, these former communist henchmen became some of the most aggressive entrepreneurs the continent had ever seen, recruiting former spies, counterintelligence agents, and mercenaries to increase their reach and power.

The 252s were the leading broker in the illegal opiate trade east of the former Iron Curtain—no one operated in the trade anywhere in the region who was not either a client or had reached some manner of reciprocity agreement with the syndicate. Their supply chains through Afghanistan were productive and resilient, secured by alliances with local chieftains and bribery of what passed for government in the country. The cocaine trade was considerably more challenging, with the supply points laying over twelve thousand kilometers to the nearest seaport servicing 252-controlled territory. Just as critical, unlike Afghanistan, Colombia was not a geographic free-for-all with no effective government—the 252s could not just walk in and set up a supply depot.

Fortunately, Colombia's neighbor Venezuela was an economic basket case approaching Afghan anarchy levels. Holtz had led the setup of a mobile headquarters aboard the *Carlos Rojas*, secure from the crime-ridden streets and focusing the overhead of bribery on a relatively limited set of port and customs officials. The ship herself was not used for smuggling—she was too small and slow for economic shipments. But, being a converted offshore construction vessel, she had plenty of space for staff and abundant internal electrical generation capability that made her ideal for coordinating the transfer of illicit cargo to larger ocean-going vessels.

The 252s had a preferred contractor for cocaine within Colombia, the La Cantaña organization, who could arrange for the short cross-border shipments required. Quantities needed were higher than any set before, but the organization was confident they could meet the demand. The first shipment went as planned, but even with heightened security precautions, the movement of so much product drew the Colombian government's attention, with the inevitable result.

Holtz was worried—the syndicate had made enormous investments in infrastructure and bribery to prepare for the large influx of cocaine. That La Cantaña was his boss's choice, not his, would not count for much if the 252s fell behind in deliveries to their downstream suppliers and dealers. He had to find another source and get things up and running again before the boss found out. He grimly shook his head again when he considered the alternative: it would be a quick and relatively painless bullet in the back of his head if he were lucky.

Then there was his other problem: the mad scientist downstairs. The *Carlos Rojas*, in addition to providing a mobile command and control hub for the 252s, also contained a laboratory to conduct their research into exotic poisons supporting their murder-for-hire business. The security provided by having a tightly accessed, mobile platform with self-contained power and the ability to dispose of highly toxic waste without documentation outweighed the inconvenience of shipboard life. And the organization needed to keep this work a closely guarded secret.

Since their founding, the 252s operated a lucrative murder-for-hire business around Europe and Western Asia, eliminating anyone, men, women, even children, if the price was right. The organization's reputation for brutality was supported by the remorseless pursuit of targets, regardless of the opposition or collateral damage. Gradually, civilization returned to former soviet bloc countries. The randomness of drive-by shootings and car and airliner bombings became too difficult for even the most corrupt officials and politicians to tolerate.

Like all successful organizations, the 252s adapted to the new reality. Impressed by the effectiveness and selectivity of the poisons developed by the former Soviet Union's Foliant program, the syndicate hired several chemical researchers associated with the Russian intelligence services' weapons development programs. Before long, 252 killers were equipped with the latest nerve agents of the Novichok family, and their targets started dropping dead without the headline-generating acts of explosive mayhem and gunfire.

The Russians were not amused. Their intelligence services used the Novichok variants sparingly since the West had obtained samples and knew what to look for when someone opposed to Russian interests suddenly and mysteriously died. They were reserved for the highest-value targets only. The application of 252 knockoffs for mere "thuggery" that left evidence pointing to Russia was an alarming development requiring corrective action. When ten 252 operatives met a violent demise at the hands of the Russian GRU within days every time a knock-off was used, the 252 senior management got the message and stopped their Novichok program. But the attractiveness of this assassination mode generated a new research and development effort for similar quick and clean weapons, so they built the lab aboard the *Carlos Rojas*.

The man running the lab, Dr. Piotr Gronkowsky, was probably among the top five biochemists globally. He was a genius in organophosphates and other nerve agents and was well along in developing a new line to replace the Novichok knock-offs. His history was mysterious—Holtz suspected the Russian GRU had recruited him as a student. Given that, it was somewhat surprising he was working for the 252s. Holtz suspected money was probably a factor, but he could see why the GRU was glad to see him go after meeting the man.

Gronkowsky was creepiest man Holtz had ever met. He was utterly unemotional, dead-eyed, and laser-focused on whatever research occupied his attention at the time. Holtz's charter was to keep him and his lab secret at all costs and provide him with whatever he needed, be it power, chemicals, or test subjects, including humans. Gronkowsky was not a sadist—he derived no pleasure from the suffering and death of his human victims; he simply did not care about them. He was, by definition, a psychopath. Even Holtz, who had known some of the most ruthless killers in history, was chilled by his presence.

Holtz gathered himself together, then stood and headed down to the lab on the lower decks. He found Gronkowsky seated at his desk in the lab, typing furiously on his computer workstation with several machines humming nearby. He stopped and looked over when Holtz knocked on the bulkhead.

"Yes, Holtz?" he asked.

Holtz shivered as the cold, dead eyes fixed on him. "We will need to move the ship to another location. Our source of supply for cocaine has been disrupted."

"How unfortunate for you. When do you plan on moving?"

"I don't know. Probably between one and two weeks from now."

"Make it twelve days."

"Why twelve days?"

"Because I will complete testing and be ready for production by then. The testing requires a stable platform, whereas the production of the binaries does not."

"You are ready for production?" Holtz asked in surprise.

"No, I am still testing. I expect to be ready for production in twelve days."

Holtz blinked and smiled at the possibility of good news to help offset the setback with La Cantaña. "Well, this is great! How will it compare to Novichok?"

Gronkowsky tilted his head without changing his expression, as if he was confronting a stubborn problem. "Testing is required, but I expect it to be between three and five times more effective, with an environmental half-life an order of magnitude less."

Holtz asked, "I don't understand what half-life means. Is this a significant improvement?"

"Definitely. The biggest drawback of chemical weapons is their persistence in the environment and the difficulty of completely cleaning up. For all practical purposes, an area subjected to a chemical attack is uninhabitable indefinitely without an enormous effort to remove every trace of the agent from all surfaces. If this agent performs as expected, it would be self-cleaning to a safe level within days." After a few seconds of silence, he continued. "This agent could revolutionize chemical warfare, making it a practicable alternative to other means of eradicating enemy forces that leave behind widespread destruction or contamination of infrastructure. The profits from marketing it could be immense."

Holtz struggled to keep the horror from his face. He had grown up in what was then East Germany and was an apprentice with the Stasi when the Warsaw Pact broke up. Everyone in the Stasi knew the use of chemical weapons was assumed in a conflict with NATO and what that would mean for the population of East Germany. The costs of this outcome, like that of nuclear war, had kept the peace for decades. The idea that weapons of this lethality could be used without lasting consequences by anyone.... *Not even the syndicate would market something like that, would they?* Holtz honestly didn't know. "I see. Well, the boss will be pleased."

"I should hope so. Now, I need to return to my work. I have emailed you a list of my requirements for the testing and setup of production." He turned back to his screen and began typing again.

Holtz turned and walked slowly back to his office. His sense of dread had returned, greatly magnified now as he contemplated what *supplies* would be required for testing. He was sure these would include a variety of human test subjects. It would not be easy, but he had contacts within the local law enforcement and criminal gangs he had used before for this sort of thing. *Hopefully, this will be the last time,* he thought as he stepped into his office and closed the door.

Dead Stick

Pan-Commonwealth Airways Flight 403, Airborne over the North Atlantic Ocean, two hundred eight nautical miles northeast of Nassau, Bahamas
14:57 EDT, 26 March

Taylor

Captain Emma Taylor worked through the stretching exercises she always performed before an approach to landing. This day was long for her and her crew, a flight from London Heathrow to the Lynden Pindling International Airport in Nassau, Bahamas, with an intermediate stop just past the midpoint at the L. F. Wade International Airport in Bermuda. The first leg to Bermuda had taken just over three hours, and after an hour-and-a-half to refuel and swap out a few passengers, they took off for the remaining two-and-a-half hours to Nassau.

Taylor loved flying in general and the Airbus 321 LR in particular. The plane was the latest in the narrowbody family of Airbus airliners, with increased fuel capacity for overwater flights—"LR" meant Long Range. She was delighted working for the relatively new airline Pan-Commonwealth, built to compete with the UK state airline British Airways using more economical, smaller cabin planes for routes between the UK and Commonwealth Nations in Africa and the Western Hemisphere. This particular route was her favorite this time of year—nine hours of work, then two days off in a lovely beach hotel in Nassau before another two legs back to London's dreary cold and wet.

Her co-pilot, First Officer Samesh Patel, handled the flying on this leg, although he was doing little more than monitoring the plane's performance with the autopilot engaged. She liked Patel and the four flight attendants servicing the cabin, and they regularly flew together. PCA was founded by an eccentric billionaire, but run by some old-time Royal Air Force and Fleet Air Arm fliers. They firmly believed in crew integrity and teamwork and kept crews together for scheduling whenever practicable.

Taylor was a statuesque five foot eight, and at forty-two, her shoulder-length blonde hair was just starting to show hints of gray. She was ex-RAF, a squadron leader tanker pilot who opted to leave the service for the higher pay and politics-free world of commercial aviation. Her application to British Airways was met with marginally polite disdain, which led her to PCA—a far better deal in her mind. She was still recovering from the breakup of a childless marriage to another RAF officer—she was happily single with nothing in the works but her current job.

Patel came through the commercial pilot route, working several jobs to pay for the training and qualifications to get an airline transport pilot license. Then he slogged through the grueling pace of working up through the commuter lines after moving to the UK from Australia, finally landing a coveted major airline job with PCA. Patel was devoted to his wife and two children. Although he was not particularly outgoing, Taylor liked him personally and admired his diligence and dedication to the craft. Unlike some of the other pilots she had worked with in the RAF and PCA, she had complete confidence in Patel.

Chief Steward Richard Burgess led the crew in the cabin. He was a seasoned flight attendant with twenty-two years at British Airways before coming to PCA. He was consistently cheerful and patient and had a fantastic sense of humor. His safety briefs were more like standup comedy routines that never failed to engage the passengers. He was celebrating his fifteenth wedding anniversary tomorrow, and his husband Gerry was among the passengers on this flight.

The only rub on this trip was the weather. A rare early-Spring depression was moving through the northern Bahamas, generating an unusual amount of thunderstorm activity at the tail end of their route today. Taylor could see build-ups in the distance, which boded for a bumpy ride ahead. It was time to check in with approach control. With Patel on the flight controls, Taylor's job was communications, and she handled the radio call to the oceanic air traffic control center.

"Miami Center, Peregrine Four-Zero-Three, two hundred to Nassau, ready for approach, over." PCA's company callsign Peregrine was another subtle jab at their rival British Airways, whose callsign for international flights was "Speedbird."

"Peregrine Four-Zero-Three, Miami Center, roger. Information India current, runway one-four in use at Lynden Pindling, expect visual approach, altimeter two niner eight three. Descend and maintain flight level two four zero."

"Miami Center, Four-Zero-Three, roger, two niner eight three, leaving three eight zero for two four zero. Are you showing any convective weather? Over."

"Four-Zero-Three, Miami Center, affirmative. Satellites and PIREPs show medium to heavy convective activity, from three-three-zero to zero-two-zero out to one hundred fifty miles from Nassau. Airfield and approach are clear within sixty miles. Over."

"Miami Center, Four-Zero-Three, roger, we may need to maneuver. Over."

"Four-Zero-Three, Miami Center, no traffic in your area, maneuver at discretion, over."

"Miami Center, Four-Zero-Three, roger, out." She turned to Patel and added, "Let's cruise down to twenty-four thousand, Sami."

"Roger, Boss," Patel dialed in the new altitude and selected a constant speed descent.

Taylor picked up the intercom phone and pressed the call button. After a minute, Burgess picked up and said, "Cabin here."

"Chief, we are starting down now. Looks like some rough stuff ahead, so get everything tied down, please."

"Oh, Skipper. You always have to make things interesting, don't you?"

"It's what I live for," she said with a smile as she pressed the "Fasten Seat Belts" announcement button. She hung up the handset and selected the weather radar on her main cockpit panel screen. The multicolor display was ominous, almost a continuous line of heavy rain cells stretching across the sixty-degree scan ahead. As they got closer, she saw a gap opening slightly to the right of their current course. "Sami, looks like a hole to the right. I make it around two three zero. Let's slow to two-seventy."

"Roger, coming right to two three zero and two-seventy." As Patel dialed in the new settings, the aircraft responded with a slight bank to the new heading while the thrust levers pulled back to slow the plane. Taylor wanted to stabilize the altitude before they got near the weather ahead, and two hundred seventy knots was the recommended airspeed when dealing with turbulence.

As they approached the weather line at a little over seven miles per minute, Taylor was distinctly displeased to see the "gap" she had picked out was closing. It was still the best route in sight, but they were going to take a beating. "Better go on manual, Sami."

Patel grasped the sidestick control with his right hand, laid his left on the thrust levers, and punched the autopilot release button. "Autopilot off."

"Right," Taylor said, scanning back and forth between the dark gray mounds of cloud approaching fast and the increasingly red trace of the weather radar. Her stomach flipped, as it always did when they first punched into the solid-looking cloud wall. Almost immediately, the eighty-seven-ton aircraft began bouncing as it passed through the alternating up- and down-drafts in the center of the cloud. After a few seconds, the plane broke into clear air and steadied down.

"So far, so good," Patel said.

"Hold on. We're not through yet," Taylor replied. "Come about fifteen degrees to port," she ordered, selecting the least red-looking path ahead. They punched into another boiling gray cloud a few seconds later, and the change was immediate. The A321 entered a period of violent bucking that only worsened with time. When she began having difficulty reading the instruments, Taylor had had enough. "Start a climb, Sami!" As Patel pushed the thrust levers forward, she pushed the radio button and said,

"Miami Center, Peregrine Four-Zero-Three, we are in severe turbulence at flight level two four zero and need to climb. Over."

"Four-Zero-Three, Miami Center, approved. Climb at discretion. Are you declaring an emergency? Over."

Taylor was about to reply when the sound of rapid-fire hammering nearly made her jump from her seat. *Hail!* She did not have time to press the transmit switch before a series of sharp gunshot-like sounds came from behind. Her eyes immediately went to the center screen of the cockpit panel, flashing emergency and displaying turbine temperatures in the red. "Bloody Hell! Compressor stalls—reduce power!"

It was too late. Large hailstones and rain flooded both engines, blocking airflow and allowing the burning combustion gases to backfire into the compressors, spiking the temperature and damaging the rotating and stationary vanes. Taylor watched in horror as the engine speed and torque plunged, first on the right engine, then the left. "Flameout number two, flameout number one! I have the controls!"

Instinct and training immediately kicked in for both pilots. As Taylor grabbed her sidestick and pulled the thrust levers back to idle, Patel reached up and punched the button to deploy the Ram Air Turbine. A small pod holding an emergency generator locked into a position where the aircraft's slipstream could spin its propeller, providing electrical and hydraulic power lost when the engines shut down. "Your controls, RAT deployed!" Patel announced. He reached down to the pocket beside his seat, drew out the emergency procedures book, and ran through the checklist.

They were punching out of the storm, at least, as the clouds fell away and bright sunlight illuminated the cockpit. Taylor set the optimum glide airspeed using the pitch attitude, then keyed the radio transmitter. "Mayday, Mayday, Mayday, Peregrine Four-Zero-Three has dual engine flameout, total power loss, over."

"Peregrine Four-Zero-Three, Miami Center, roger. Say number of souls and fuel on board and position."

"Center, Four-Zero-Three, one two six souls, twenty-four thousand pounds, zero two four and one hundred fifty-three from Nassau, over."

"Peregrine Four-Zero-Three, Miami Center, copy one two six souls, twenty-four thousand pounds, zero two four, one hundred fifty-three from Nassau. Nassau has you radar contact but stay with me. We are standing by this frequency, out." The air traffic controller knew the crew would have their hands full and cleared off to let them get to work.

They were dropping fast toward the bright blue Atlantic. Patel was running through the main engine restart procedure, having already started the auxiliary power unit to supplement the RAT. They would have time for one restart attempt on each engine. If they could get one relit, it would provide enough thrust to keep them in the air. While there was always hope, Taylor geared herself for the most likely outcome: neither engine was salvageable. With eight miles of travel possible before they ran out of altitude and over fifty to the nearest land, they were going to end up in the water, a nightmare scenario for a fully loaded airliner.

Taylor grabbed the intercom handset and pressed the call button. Burgess answered immediately, "Cabin, here."

"We're going in, Chief. Get them ready for it. We'll try for the Hudson River scenario, so keep the aft doors closed."

"Understood, Captain. I have two burly beauties from the RN on guard in the last row. You worry about bringing us in safe. We'll be alright back here."

Taylor smiled slightly. *I might have known. God bless you, Richard!* "Well done! I'll ring the bell five seconds before contact. Get them moving as we come to a stop."

"WILCO. Godspeed, Captain. Out."

The scenario Taylor referred to involved the ditching of a similar Airbus in New York's Hudson River when bird ingestion knocked out both its engines shortly after takeoff from La Guardia airport. The flight crew executed a masterpiece of judgment and skill, saving everyone on board. *Not so easy this time. They landed in the sheltered water of a river—we'll have waves and swells to deal with.*

"Peregrine Four-Zero-Three, Miami Center, Nassau is losing radar contact. Observe you heading two one five magnetic, over." Surveillance radar was limited to line of sight, and at this distance, the aircraft dropped below the radar's horizon at around thirteen thousand feet. The controller would use the aircraft's last heading, descent rate, and speed to estimate the impact point to be passed to rescue forces.

"Center, Four-Zero-Three, roger, estimate six miles to contact, over."

Four-Zero-Three, Center, copy. Best of luck, Captain. Out."

"No joy, Captain," Patel said as he took his hand off the starter.

"Right, leave it. Give me flaps four at one thousand." Taylor had held off the flaps until the last possible moment. They would reduce the aircraft's touchdown speed dramatically, but also added significant drag. "Ring the cabin bell once you position the handle."

"Will do, Captain."

They were passing through two thousand feet now, and Taylor could see the swells clearly. Stirred by the prevailing east-northeasterly trade winds over thousands of miles of ocean, the waves ran roughly in a direction aligned to their present heading. She began a ninety-degree turn to bring the aircraft heading parallel to the swells, rolling level as they passed through one thousand feet, and Patel dropped the flaps and rang the bell. She knew Burgess and the other flight attendants were shouting at the passengers to brace for landing, gripping the seat or bulkhead in front of them and bending over at the waist.

As the water rushed upward toward them, Taylor pulled back on the sidestick, trading airspeed to arrest their descent in a flare maneuver. The tail section contacted the water first with a growing tugging sensation. *Stay level, you beauty!* The wings quickly lost lift, and the aircraft settled into the water. Taylor held her breath as an on-coming swell caught the left wingtip and engine nacelle, yawing them abruptly to the left and her eyes grew wide as the nose plunged into the water with a loud thud. She released her breath when the cockpit windows emerged from the water. *Thank you, God!* She pressed the transmit switch on the radio one last time, "This is Peregrine Four-Zero-Three in the blind. We are down in the water, commencing evacuation." She took off her headset and turned to Patel with a sad smile.

"That one was a bloody beauty, Captain," Patel said with a nod.

"Thanks, Sami. Let's get moving.

The evacuation of the passengers was orderly, with less hysterics than one would typically expect in a situation as dire as they all faced. Filing out the forward cabin doors and four overwing exits, the passengers made their way to the large life rafts inflated alongside. Taylor and Patel watched from the cockpit door, and Burgess, the last person in the cabin, gave them a thumbs-up before going out one of the wing exits.

It was understood in these situations that the captain would make one last check for stragglers, if practicable. There was already flooding visible at the opposite end of the aircraft, but Taylor had to concede that a final tour was feasible, as frightening as it was to go deep within a sinking plane. *Lovely.*

Patel sensed her anxiety and said, "I can go walkabout, skipper."

Taylor shook her head and said, "Skipper's job. Off you go, Sami. Get a count. I'll be along straight away."

"Very good, Captain. Be careful," Patel said, then stepped through the door.

Taylor walked aft down the passageway between the seats, checking each row. As she passed the middle rows with the overwing exits, she was already knee-deep in water and anxiously looked out onto the wings. The plane was pitching up and down slowly with the passing of the sea swells, as the last-second pivot had turned the aircraft's nose into them. *Four flight attendants have already checked. Do I really need to do this?* Taylor swallowed hard and continued down the aisle.

She was almost waist-deep in the rapidly flooding cabin when she reached the rear and, after peeking in both lavatories, turned and hurried forward. She climbed through one of the wing exits, walked to the nearest raft, and jumped in as the passengers cheered. Taylor looked around and spotted Patel in another raft. "Report, Number One!"

"All present and correct, Captain! No deaths, thirteen injuries, none serious!"

"Good! Let's cast off, but we need to tether the rafts together!"

"Very good, Captain!"

Progressive flooding claimed the Airbus five minutes later, which sank upright, her white tail painted with the PCA falcon logo finally disappearing into the blue Atlantic. Burgess, his arm around Gerry's shoulder, said softly, "Alfa-Delta was a good ship, Captain," Burgess said softly, referring to the aircraft's tail number G-PCAD. "And a proper lady—never once showed her knickers."

"She was that," Taylor replied, brushing away a tear. *So much for my airline career. Still, thank God I didn't kill a hundred-odd people in the process.*

She caught Patel's eye in the adjacent raft and gave him a rueful smile. His face was grim, and he silently mouthed, "Check your six," then nodded past her. Taylor turned and saw clouds building to the west, as ominous as those they had come through in the northeast.

I spoke too soon.

**USCG Cutter *Kauai*, Northeast Providence Channel, twenty-one nautical miles north-northwest of Nassau, Bahamas
15:23 EDT, 26 March**

Ben

They had just turned into the Northeast Providence Channel for the last leg in their journey to AUTEC for a few weeks of testing on the squid and other new equipment. Ben was wrapping up some paperwork in his stateroom when Bondurant's voice boomed from the 1MC, "Captain to the Bridge!"

Ben grabbed his cap, bounded to the ladder, and was on the Bridge within twenty seconds, with Sam behind him. "Captain on the Bridge!" Bondurant said.

"Carry on. What's happening?" Sam asked.

"Big-time SAR case, Captain. Commercial airliner down one hundred and ten miles northeast of here. Our orders are to proceed there at max speed. I have changed course toward the approximate position, and Main Control is bringing the third main online," Bondurant said.

"Well done! Carry on." Sam replied.

As Ben stepped over to the communications position, he could hear the whine of a diesel engine starter as the remaining two increased speed. The message on the chat from the Rescue Coordination Center in Miami was terse:

CGC KAUAI proceed at max speed for mayday-downed aircraft in position 27.0N 77.4W. PCA flight 403 reported total power failure, radar and radio contact lost. Position correlated with EPIRB signal on 406 MHz. Casualties UNK, reported 126 POB. CGNR 6017 ENR from Nassau, ETA 1.5 hrs. CGNR 1718 ENR from Clearwater, ETA 1.3 Hrs. KAUAI assume OSC on arrival.

An icy ball formed in Ben's stomach. His father was an airline pilot with United Airlines and a former Naval Aviator. Ben had once brought up the possibility of being involved in a rescue effort for a downed airliner, and his father just shook his head and said, "Bring a lot of body bags."

The message indicated that a Coast Guard MH-60T "Jayhawk" helicopter was launching in response from the forward base in Nassau, and an HC-130H "Hercules" Long-Range Maritime Patrol Airplane was underway from Air Station Clearwater. Neither would be of much help in recovering one hundred twenty-six people, but they would hopefully eliminate the need for *Kauai* to search for the survivors. The fact that the rescue system was picking up an Emergency Position-Indicating Radio Beacon, or EPIRB, suggested they got at least one raft launched.

Ben looked at the electronic navigation page—even at their best speed, it would be almost four hours before *Kauai* could reach the crash site. Ben checked the astronomical display on the adjoining screen—sunset at 19:23, right about when they got on the scene. *With luck, we can get them on board before we lose all the light.* He stepped over to where Sam was on the intercom to Main Control.

"Captain, I'm pulling every trick I know that won't melt down the rotors. I think I can get you thirty-two knots, at least for a while," Drake's baritone voice intoned from the speaker.

"Do what you can, COB," Sam responded. "Every minute counts."

"On it, sir."

Sam turned to Ben and Bondurant. "Guys, the upside of our ETA is we have some time to prepare. Best case, everyone is in rafts, and we can come alongside for a direct pickup. Even then, though, a fair number of them won't be in any shape to climb a Jacob's ladder. We need some way to hoist them up to the main deck. Thoughts?"

"We can rig a davit with a block and tackle, sir," Bondurant said. "We'll have to jury rig some sort of Bosun's chair."

"I like the davit, sir," Ben piped up, "But I'm not a fan of any jury-rigged chair. Maybe we can get the helo to leave their rescue basket for us.

Sam nodded and said, "That would be great. I'll certainly ask, but I wouldn't count on it. XO, let's get Chief Hopkins up here to take over OOD so you guys can get to work. Besides finding them and getting them on board, we have to find a way to get them all inside the hull."

Ben was flabbergasted. "You're kidding, Captain! A hundred twenty-six people? No one could even sit down."

"You're probably right, but consider that that storm brought down a commercial airliner. Between the wind and the lightning, we can't leave anyone on the weather decks while we get clear. Get with COB and Chef and come up with a plan to maximize interior floor space and get the people inside fast. We won't have time to stand there scratching our heads."

Ben nodded. "Understood, Captain."

Salvation

**Atlantic Ocean, one hundred twenty-eight nautical miles
north-northeast of Nassau, Bahamas
16:51 EDT, 26 March**

Taylor

The Coast Guard Hercules aircraft had arrived overhead twenty minutes previously. The initial excitement among the passengers quickly subsided when they realized the plane could not land in the water to pick them up. Still, it was good news that they had been found, and the aircraft would linger to vector in the ships and other aircraft that could rescue them.

The appearance of the Coast Guard helicopter brought similar optimism, also quickly dashed when everyone realized it could pick up only a few of them at a time. Taylor could imagine that the conversation within the aircraft as it circled their position was some variation of "Holy Shit!" After two circles, it came to a hover about fifty yards away from Taylor's raft and lowered a crewman into the water with its hoist cable. Even from this distance, the downdraft was noticeable—it would be a difficult situation if it had to hover directly over the rafts.

The crewman swam quickly to Taylor's raft, took off and tossed his fins in, then climbed in using the ladder and pulled up his swim mask and snorkel. He was not a large man, but his short wetsuit made no secret of a highly athletic physique. He scanned the raft and, seeing the four stripes on Taylor's uniform shirt, said, "Petty Officer Sean Moran, U.S. Coast Guard. Are you the pilot, ma'am?"

"Yes, Captain Emma Taylor."

"Glad to meet you, ma'am," the young petty officer said. "Can you tell me how many people you have here?"

"Yes, one hundred twenty-six."

The young man grinned. "You got everyone off safe? That's fantastic! Hell of a job, ma'am."

"Thank you, petty officer." She glanced at the helicopter circling the rafts. "Somehow, I don't think we'll all fit on your bird."

"No, ma'am, we might get six or seven, depending on how large they are. But the good news is a cutter is headed this way balls-to-the-walls and should be here in about two hours." He looked around in surprise when most of the people in the rafts started clapping and cheering. He struggled to make himself heard. "Ma'am, ma'am!" The crowd quieted down when he whistled. "As I was saying, ma'am, we can take a few earlier if we need to get them urgent medical attention. But it will be pretty rough on everybody if that H-60 has to do any hoists, so I wouldn't recommend it unless we really have to."

Taylor shook her head. There were two physicians and one registered nurse among the passengers who had checked the injured. The two with broken bones had those splinted, and the other eleven had only minor complaints. "We have thirteen injured, but none seriously. I think we can all wait two hours, petty officer. But several might have problems scrambling up ladders."

"Got it covered, ma'am," Moran said. "My crew will transfer the rescue basket to the cutter just before it gets here. They're rigging a davit to hoist up anyone who can't climb."

Taylor smiled with relief. "I am glad to hear that."

Moran nodded. "If you'll excuse me, ma'am, I have to report in." He drew a handheld radio, pressed the button, and said, "Six-Zero-One-Seven, swimmer."

"Swimmer, One-Seven, go ahead," said a voice from the radio.

"One-Seven, swimmer, all POB accounted for. Repeat, one-two-six survivors. Pilot says thirteen, that's one-three injured, but none require medevac, sir."

"Swimmer, One-Seven, roger. We'll go with Plan A, then. Keep us posted if anything changes.

"WILCO, sir." Moran tucked the radio back into his vest.

"Plan A?" Taylor asked.

"I wait here with you all, ma'am, and help with the on-loading. The helo will maintain contact for as long as possible."

"Is he running short of fuel?"

"No, ma'am," Moran answered and nodded to his left toward the weather building in the west. Lightning flashes were now clearly visible among the clouds.

"I see," Taylor said. "Well, I'm sure you have plenty of interesting stories from your line of work. We would certainly be grateful if you could regale us with a few while we wait."

"Really?"

"Yes, indeed. What do you say, folks?"

After a chorus of "yes," "give it up, mate," and the like, Moran nodded and said, "OK." Then he adopted a fierce expression and said with a mock dramatic tone, "There I was...."

USCG Cutter *Kauai*, Atlantic Ocean, one hundred twenty-three nautical miles north-northeast of Nassau, Bahamas 19:02 EDT, 26 March

Ben

It had already started raining, cutting visibility in half and making deck activity more hazardous and unpleasant. Ben could see many heavy rain cells marching west to east across the screen displaying *Kauai's* weather radar, each of which held the potential for heavy rain and lightning. *It just couldn't be easy*, he thought ruefully.

The HC-130 already had to pull back because of severe turbulence at the flight levels it operated and was orbiting out of the storm's reach to the southeast. The MH-60T helicopter was doggedly hanging on over the rafts—it worked at far lower levels not prone to turbulence—but it could not risk lingering much longer with the threat of lightning and wind shears building. The helicopter had ducked out briefly to rendezvous with *Kauai* to drop off the rescue basket before returning to the scene. The basket was necessary as it was the only safe way to hoist untrained people. The risks were too high to use a bosun's chair or horse collar to lift people out of the rafts, particularly if they were injured.

Every crewmember that could be spared would be on deck, helping to get the survivors on board and safely tucked inside the shell of *Kauai's* hull and superstructure. Only four would be on the Bridge: Sam, Hopkins as OOD, Williams handling the entire FC3 console, and Pickins on the helm. Ben would head down as soon as they had visual contact with the rafts to supervise the operation and provide an extra set of hands. Lee and Fireman Connally would be underway in the RHIB, stationed outside of the rafts, in a position to respond to anyone falling overboard. The remaining eight crew, including Ben, would work the operation on the main deck.

Speed was of the essence, given the thunderstorms in the area. The cutter was an inviting target for lightning, being the tallest object within 50 miles, but her hull would act as a Faraday cage and protect anything inside. The rub was that it was a deadly risk to anyone caught outside during a strike, and both the crew and survivors were highly vulnerable during the recovery operation.

"I'm picking up the scene on IR, sir," Williams said, pointing at one of the display panels showing the output of the Infrared camera on *Kauai's* mast. Something that looked like a tiny comet blazed horizontally across the screen. "See? There's the H-60's exhaust."

"I got that. Still don't see the rafts," Ben said.

"Wait a sec for the helo to clear," Williams said, then pointed at some hazy glows below the helicopter's path. "See? There and there."

"Roger that." Ben plugged his headset into the radio console and selected the helicopter's frequency. "Six Zero One Seven, *Kauai*, over."

"*Kauai*, One Seven, go ahead."

"Can we talk directly to your swimmer?"

"Affirmative. He's on channel eighty-three."

"Roger, out." Ben switched his selector and dialed up channel 83 on the cutter's VHF-FM radio. "Swimmer, *Kauai*, on channel 83."

After a brief delay, Moran's voice answered, "*Kauai*, Swimmer, got you Lima-Charlie."

"Roger. We have you on infrared about three miles out. We should be alongside in about five minutes or so. We have two ladders and a davit rigged out on the starboard side with the basket. Do you feel comfortable working all three at once? Over."

"Affirmative. I've briefed everyone on what to expect, and I have the flight crew plus two Royal Navy guys who will be assisting. We are in four rafts, all lashed together. I recommend we do one at a time and take people directly from their current raft rather than having them cross over. I'll transfer to whichever raft we are working to supervise."

"Sounds like a plan. Our RHIB will stand by to pick up any leakers. Explain to the survivors that we have to get everybody inside out of the weather, and it will be a tight fit. They must follow our crew's instructions and be patient with the cramped quarters. Also, if there's anyone with a serious claustrophobia problem, we'll take them last." Ben had a touch of claustrophobia and knew the cramped quarters they planned to pack everyone into could be a trigger. The last thing they needed was someone having a meltdown inside the ship. The nervous folks would go on the messdeck, a larger space with windows.

"WILCO."

"Right. We'll be standing by on this channel. Out." Ben unplugged and turned to Sam. "Captain, request permission to lay below."

Sam clapped him on the shoulder. "Go. Please be quick and careful, XO."

"Will do, sir." Ben turned and hurried to the port-side door in the rear of the Bridge, then down the ladders to the main deck. The rain had already soaked him to the skin by the time he arrived. The RHIB was at the port rail, ready for Lee and

Connally to jump in and launch—they would do so when Hopkins slowed down to approach the rafts. It was only a six-foot climb from the water level up to the main deck, which all but the infirm should be able to manage. Bondurant already had the two Jacob's ladders attached to cleats on the deck and a small davit rigged with a block and tackle and the rescue basket. He and Machinery Technician Brown would work the davit while Ben oversaw the ladders during the onload. The other five crew were standing by, ready to lead people to the interior spaces where they would wait out the storm.

Although it was still twenty minutes to sunset, the clouds and rain made it seem more like twilight. "Conn, Main Deck, could we get the deck lights on, please?" Ben asked over the intra-ship radio. Within seconds, the white deck lighting along the ship's sides and the large red floodlight on the mast came on, compensating for the fading daylight.

"*Kauai*, Swimmer, we have you in sight. You're getting a big applause over here, sir!"

Yeah? We'll see how much they love us after they're stuffed inside like sardines in a can! "Roger. Just a couple of minutes now," Ben replied on the radio. The diesel engines slowed a few seconds afterward, and *Kauai* settled into the water from planing to displacement mode. "Boats, let's get the RHIB ready," Ben said.

As Lee and Connally jumped into the boat, Ben transmitted, "Conn, Main Deck, RHIB ready for launch."

"Main Deck, Conn, cleared to launch," Williams's voice replied.

Ben leaned over to Lee and said, "OK, keep it tight, Shelley. Any questions?"

"No, sir!"

"Right. Good luck!" Ben turned and gave Boatswain's Mate Third Class Jenkins on the crane a thumbs-up, and the RHIB was motoring twenty yards off the starboard quarter ten seconds later. Ben could barely make out rafts now through the fading light and rain about a quarter-mile distant. Hopkins was maneuvering to put the rafts alongside to starboard in *Kauai*'s lee, a challenging task given the visibility and variable winds. Ben could make out people on the rafts now and see an individual standing in one of them. *That must be Moran.* Ben keyed his radio microphone and said, "Swimmer, *Kauai*, is that you standing?"

"Affirmative, sir," Moran replied.

"OK, we will take your raft first. Stand by for a heaving line. We'll be passing a sea painter, but I want you to pull to us and hold the raft to our side—don't tie off the line. That way, we cut the risks of dragging the raft, and you can just carry it to the next one. Got it?"

"WILCO, sir."

Ben turned to the other crewmembers on deck. "OK, put over the ladders. Jenkins, come over here and bring the heaving line," he said.

The young boatswain stepped forward as the crew hung the ladders off the side. "Yes, sir."

"OK, you see that raft with the guy standing?"

"Yes, sir. I've got him."

"Good. When you're confident you can reach him, let fly with the line."

"Yes, sir!"

The rafts slid closer as Hopkins used rudder and asymmetric thrust from the engines to walk *Kauai* sideways. Jenkins was staring intently at Moran's raft, unconsciously bouncing up and down on the balls of his feet. Finally, he nodded and cast the line with a sidearm throw. The line stretched out and draped across the raft just to Moran's left, and he grabbed it and started pulling in.

"That was a beauty of a throw, Brian. Nice job," Ben said.

"Thanks, sir," Jenkins replied as he fed out the line.

The end was tied to a thicker line better for handling and supporting the raft's weight. Soon Moran had the line, and he and two large men Ben presumed were Royal Navy sailors pulled it until the raft was snug against *Kauai*'s side with the ladders dangling inside. A woman wearing a white shirt, tie, and epaulets with four stripes was first up the ladder, and Ben took her hand to help her on deck.

"Captain Emma Taylor," she said with a smile.

"Lieutenant J.G. Ben Wyporek, ma'am," Ben replied. "Would you care to stay and observe?" he added as more survivors followed up the ladder, helped by other crewmembers.

"Yes, indeed. Thank you for coming so quickly."

"Our pleasure."

The unloading of the rafts proceeded quickly. A line of wet and bedraggled people rapidly formed into the door leading inside as *Kauai*'s crew tucked them wherever there was space. They were about one-third of the way through the on-load when lightning struck off the starboard beam with a bright flash, followed by a loud boom a second later. Almost everyone instinctively ducked, and several people in the rafts started screaming and scrambling toward the ladders. It was what Ben feared—a contagious panic that would kill dozens while they were helpless to stop it.

"KNOCK IT OFF!" Bondurant bellowed from his position at the davit, shocking everyone into motionless silence. He then nodded to Ben. "All yours, sir."

"Thanks, Boats," Ben whispered and then shouted, "We're OK! One spot's as good as another out here! Just stay calm, wait your turn, and we'll wrap this up quicker!"

The procession up the ladders from the rafts resumed, and Taylor whispered to Ben, "This spot includes a rather tall object, *Leftenant.*"

"You'll be safer inside, ma'am, if you'd like," Ben whispered back.

"No, I'll stay and grin like an idiot. 'Keep calm and carry on,' as they say."

"That's why they pay us the big bucks," Ben said with a smile.

An older woman stepped up and embraced Ben. "Thank you, sir!"

"Our pleasure," Ben repeated, patting her on the back. "Please move along, ma'am."

The woman rejoined the line leading into the ship. It took around thirty minutes before the last passenger climbed the ladder to the main deck, followed by Patel, Burgess, and Moran. There were several more lightning strikes, but none were as close as the first nor caused any pause in the operation.

Ben gripped Moran's hand as he came up and said, "Nice job, Petty Officer Moran."

"Thanks, sir."

"Head inside. If you need anything, just grab one of the guys."

"Roger that. See you at the other end, sir."

As Moran walked off toward the door, Ben turned to Taylor. "Would you follow me to the Bridge, ma'am?"

"Of course." They had climbed the ladder and nearly reached the Bridge door when a second close lightning strike shook the ship. "Bloody Hell!"

Ben smiled as he held the door for her. "I couldn't have said it better, ma'am!"

Bondurant's voice came over Ben's headset on the intraship radio as they stepped into the Bridge. "Conn, Main Deck, RHIB cradled and secure, ready for maneuvers."

"Conn, aye," Hopkins replied. "Left full rudder," she said as she pushed the thrust levers forward. "Steady on two-one-three."

"My rudder is left full, coming to two-one-three, Chief," Pickens repeated.

As Ben and Taylor stepped up to the command chair, Ben said, "Captain, this is the pilot, Captain Emma Taylor."

Sam climbed from his chair and shook Taylor's hand. "I'm sorry about your bad luck, Captain."

"Thank you. It turned out to the good in the end, I'm happy to say, thanks to you and your crew."

"Part of the job. Is there anything we can get for you?"

"A large Tanqueray gimlet would go well about now."

"I'd keep you company. Unfortunately, we're as dry as the Navy here, and water or some bitter coffee is the best I can do."

"A coffee is second in the heavenly queue, Captain. May I ask where we are heading?"

"Nassau. It's the closest port."

"Well, that's convenient for everyone. Do you have an ETA?"

"We are figuring that out right now. Our maximum sustainable speed is twenty-eight knots, but I need to make sure I don't have over a hundred people throwing up on each other down below."

"I'm grateful for that, Captain. I'm no stranger to *mal de mer* myself."

"Same can be said for anyone assigned to a patrol boat. Chief Hopkins will find a sweet spot for us, and we'll make as quick a trip as possible."

"Thank you, Captain. Now, if practicable, I need to rejoin my crew and passengers."

"Sure. XO, can you handle that, please?"

"Absolutely, Captain," Ben replied. "Would you follow me, ma'am?"

"Certainly." As they stepped to the rear of the Bridge and headed down, Taylor said quietly, "I'm afraid we are likely to have some motion sickness issues, based on my experience with air travelers."

"I know, ma'am," Ben replied. "We have trash cans in every room, and our Health Services Technician can administer Dramamine in severe cases."

Taylor sighed. "It's going to be a long night, *Leftenant.*"

"Yea verily, ma'am."

USCG Cutter *Kauai*, moored, Prince George Wharf, Nassau, Bahamas
02:29 EDT, 27 March

Ben

Ben was exhausted, his eyes burning and legs aching with fatigue as he scanned the dock. It was crowded with news crews and other people striding purposefully among the milling passengers. *Probably scum-sucking ambulance-chasers looking for a payday,* Ben thought with disgust. *Kauai* was almost surrounded by towering cruise ships in the busy port, and a port authority official had already paid a call to inquire when they would be sailing so he could clear the dock for more arrivals. The last survivors were moving ashore to the waiting buses the airline had chartered to take them to hotels. Soon after they departed, *Kauai* would resume her journey to AUTEC.

The trip had been mercifully uneventful, with no serious illness or injuries. Ben had spent six hours moving among the survivors, consciously suppressing his claustrophobia while inquiring about their health and jotting down their names for the report. Taylor accompanied him and proved to be a very calming influence on the crowd throughout the journey. Their joy at being pulled from the water and delivered to their original destination certainly helped. The conversation snippets with the pilot were also interesting and reminded Ben of his many aviation discussions with his father growing up.

Ben had tremendous sympathy for Taylor, whose ordeal was only beginning. A one-hundred-thirty-million-dollar aircraft entrusted to her care now lay at the bottom of the Atlantic. The reckoning for that was likely to be severe, regardless of the circumstances. When the last passenger departed, Taylor turned to Ben and said, "I guess this is goodbye, Ben."

"You have a hotel room, ma'am?"

"Yes, indeed, checking in a bit later than planned. Later still, if I can find an open pub to get legless in."

"I'd love to join you," Ben said. Then, sadly added, "Captain, I wish you the best of luck. Please contact me if there is anything I can do to help."

Taylor stepped forward and hugged him warmly. Then she stepped back and said, "That's from all of us. Please take care." She turned, walked off the ship, and disappeared into a swarm of media people.

Ben had turned to walk to the Bridge when Bondurant called out, "XO, there's a gentleman from the embassy here to see you."

Ben sighed, turned, and followed the big boatswain to a man wearing a suit and tie standing on the quarterdeck. "Lieutenant Junior Grade Wyporek, Executive Officer, how can I help you, sir?"

"Hello, Lieutenant Junior Grade. I'm Frederick Gianni, the ambassador's deputy for public affairs. I would like to speak to the captain."

"I'm sorry, he's not available. Perhaps I can be of assistance."

"When will he be available?"

"Not today. The Port Authority has requested we vacate this berth as soon as practicable, and he is engaged in sailing preps."

"Oh, well, I guess you'll do," he said, oblivious to Ben's icy stare. "Several camera crews from the major networks are here and would like to do some interviews."

"No."

"I beg your pardon?"

"I said no. As I told you, we have been asked to depart, and all of us will be heavily engaged in making that happen."

"Well, perhaps one or two of the crews could ride with you...."

"Are you serious? Absolutely not."

"Well, what's your next port? They can meet you there."

"Ship movements are classified, Mr. Gianni. I'm sorry, I can't help you."

"You are being most uncooperative, Lieutenant Junior Grade. That will not reflect well on you in my report."

"I am doing my job, sir. Speaking of which, all of us are pretty busy right now, and I am sure the news networks can get all the information they need from the Seventh District Public Affairs Office. So, if you don't mind, please leave the ship."

"And what am I supposed to tell the news crews?"

"Tell them to go to Hell."

After Gianni turned and stormed off the ship, Bondurant said, "Missed opportunity, XO. Wouldn't your folks like to see you on TV?"

"My mom would be pretty upset hearing me using the kind of language I would direct at those bastards, Boats."

As they turned and headed for the Bridge, Bondurant chuckled and said, "Your stock just keeps going up, sir!"

Rogues Amongst Themselves

Suite 224, La Paloma del Mar Hotel, 43 Ave. Dionisio de Herrera, La Ceiba, Honduras
08:53 CDT, 1 April

Holtz

Holtz knew the news was bad when the satellite phone buzzed this early in the morning, but he had no idea how bad it could be. The first words out of Dorshak's mouth once the phone connected were, "Boss, they are killing our men!" After half a minute of shouting and shooting in the background, Holtz heard a banging sound, a crash, then muffled voices.

"Holtz?" a fresh voice said.

"Yes?"

"We have your boat, your crew, and your lab workers. Pay us twenty million euros, or we kill them all." Holtz knew the voice. It was the cartel's lead man, whose face was a mask of tattoos. The one Holtz believed was thoroughly intimidated by the power and reach of the 252 Syndicate.

"Do you know who you're talking to, asshole?"

"*Tráelo!*" Holtz heard a scuffle and then two shots, followed by a shriek of pain. "I just blew the balls off one of your guards, *bendejo!* Maybe I should do that with one of your pretty boys next!"

"No, no, wait!" Holtz temporized. These sub-humans had him cold. The guards were one thing—losing them was the cost of doing business. The same went for *Carlos Rojas*'s crew. But

Gronkowsky? If he let anything happen to him…. "OK, I don't have that much with me. It will take time."

"How much time?"

"Two weeks."

"One week."

"I can't get that much in seven days!"

"Then call someone who can! *Comprende*? In one week, I cut pieces off your pretty boys here." The line went dead. Holtz stared at the phone for about half a minute before putting it aside.

It was not supposed to be this way. He had landed this contract and arranged all the logistics. The possibilities for future purchases of cocaine were unlimited, and Holtz's star would rise high in the organization. Even with the misfortune of their original cocaine source in Venezuela drying up, he found a satisfactory solution at a lower cost. Or so he thought.

The first meeting carried a warning. Holtz flew into Barbello, an island about ninety miles off Honduras's coast, in his chartered seaplane. Barbello was nominally part of Honduras but was effectively ruled by the Salinas Cartel, an ultraviolent death cult financing themselves through drug trafficking. Holtz was not concerned—the reputation of his organization was such that he expected to roll over the negotiations quickly and easily. And so it seemed, with the head man, a rather frightening figure with his tattoos, piercings, and twin forty-four-caliber Auto Mag pistols, nodding in sullen acceptance to Holtz's terms.

Holtz activated one of his burner phones and dialed his control number in Bucharest. After several rings, Holtz was greeted with the deep baritone of his superior's voice. "Yes?"

"Boss, this is Holtz."

"Yes, Holtz, what is it?"

"We have a problem with the cocaine delivery."

There was an audible sigh. "What sort of problem?"

"The suppliers have seized the vessel and everyone on board. They've shot several of our men and are threatening our researcher if they aren't paid twenty million euros within one week."

"I don't believe it. La Cantaña wouldn't dare fuck with us like that."

"It's not La Cantaña, boss. They got rolled up by the BRCNA a couple of weeks ago. I went with a new supplier in Honduras, the Salinas Cartel."

"You *what?*" came the incredulous reply.

"I set up with the Salinas Cartel. They had the product, the transshipment point, and the cost was right." Holtz said defensively.

"You did a deal with those animals? Idiot! Did it occur to you that there might be a reason we *haven't* dealt with them? Alright, where is the ship?"

"It's in the harbor at Barbello. I thought moving to the source was prudent...."

"Stop! Let me get this straight. You took it on yourself to set up a new supply chain without clearing it through us. Then you set up a deal with the worst, most insane gang in the Western Hemisphere, bringing their shitstorm into our business. Finally, you sail our ship, with our scientist and his equipment, into the middle of their stronghold. Am I missing anything?"

"Um...."

"Never mind, that question was rhetorical. Where are you now?"

"L-La Ceiba. The La Paloma del Mar."

"Good. At least you weren't stupid enough to put yourself in their hands."

"What should I tell them? When can we get them the money?"

"Are you insane? We aren't paying them to screw with us! We're going to cure this cancer before it gets out of hand. One week, you said?"

"Y-Yes."

"Fine, if we bring everything else to a halt, we should be able to concentrate there in time." The voice softened. "I need you to stay where you are and brief the team when they arrive. We'll need your insights if we are going to unscrew this thing. Clear?"

"Yes, boss."

"Fine. Out." The phone call disconnected.

Anton, you are a dead man. His brain reeled briefly over the realization, and then his survival instinct awakened. Holtz was a despicable human working for one of the world's most evil organizations, but he was a survivor. He quickly stuffed his cash, passports, and gun into the shoulder bag he carried for just such an occasion, leaving the satellite phone and his still turned-on cell phone behind under his underwear in the drawer. His only hope at this point was to convince his former associates that he was still lounging in the room while making his escape. Holtz didn't know of any other 252 men in La Ceiba. Regardless, they had connections and would use them to close his case quickly.

He glanced at the closed bedroom door and paused for a second. Rosita was still asleep in the bed they had shared. She would suffer a very unpleasant death if they caught her. Ordinarily, he wouldn't have wasted a single thought on another human being, but Rosey was something special. He slammed open the door, shouting, "Get up!" The woman groaned and rolled over. "Get up if you want to live!"

Rosita's eyes opened wide. "What?"

"Here are your wages," He dropped a hundred euro note on the nightstand. "Grab your stuff and get out. Don't follow me or try to contact me. Get out of this place and run!" He turned and ran out the door, tuning out her cries of "Anton!" Well, he had given her a chance. Hopefully, she had enough brains to use it. He eschewed the elevator and flew down the stairs to the exit.

He left the hotel and merged into the sizeable crowds heading for the beach. Traffic was far heavier than usual in the Semana Santa, as the Holy Week was known here. Holtz worked his way through and picked up a cab. Once well clear of the hotel, he pulled out one of his burner phones and dialed his pilot.

"Yeah?"

"I need you at the plane now."

"Are you fucking kidding me? There's nothing scheduled today."

"We need to leave now. I'll tell you where we are going once we're in the air."

"Man, I can't fly! I'm too hungover. Call me in six hours."

"Look, asshole, if I don't get out of here, they'll kill me. While they're at it, they will wring out of me the names of everyone I've associated with here, so they can run them down and clean up any loose ends. Get down here now if you want to live!"

"Shit! Alright, alright, I'll be there in half an hour. Stay out of sight until I get there."

"I'll be watching." Holtz hung up the phone and tossed it out the cab window. While he believed it would be almost impossible for his associates to trace him this soon, he took no chances. Holtz had the cab driver drop him at the bus station, where he picked up a second cab to the marina. While considering his situation, he strode to the seaplane slip and hid behind a storage building.

Fleeing La Ceiba provided temporary safety at best. Holtz knew his former employers would relentlessly track him down to eliminate any potential threat he posed. He had to find someone who could help fix this mess or give him the means to fade out of sight. If he could reach the Americans.... Holtz knew they were becoming troublesome—his boss had complained enough about them. Maybe he could work a deal with them, trading knowledge of the organization and the threat posed by Grankowsky's gas for immunity, or at least a new identity and safety. The Americans were well known for that.

He tensed when a local police officer arrived and stood about fifty yards from his hiding place behind the building. Holtz flattened himself against the wall and drew the 9-mm pistol out of his shoulder bag before placing it aside. The officer was standing still and talking into his hand—Holtz couldn't tell if it was into a radio or a mobile phone. *Move along, son. Nothing to see here!* He didn't want to shoot a police officer. Not because he had any affection for the police or any other person. He just knew shooting a cop would only bring all hell down upon him and likely prevent his escape. He almost cried out with relief when the man pocketed his phone and walked off in the other direction. There were no other encounters before the pilot arrived.

"You better be right about this," the bleary-eyed pilot grumbled. "If we run into any trouble, I'll probably get us both killed."

"If we don't leave now, we're both dead for sure. So, let's go."

"Okay, take in the aft mooring line and get in." Holtz complied and climbed into the cockpit of the seaplane, a trim Lake Buccaneer. The pilot unhitched and stowed the forward line, then staved off the dock with an oar. The engine fired at once, and within three minutes, they were airborne, heading east.

"OK, now where the hell are we going?" the pilot asked.

"Can you make it to Grand Cayman and back without refueling?"

"Barely, but I won't be flying into any airport without a flight plan."

"Not a problem. You'll be dropping me off at a secluded beach I know and return to La Ceiba with no one the wiser."

"Fine. You realize there will be a significant surcharge for this premium service."

Holtz smiled. "If we live through this flight, you'll go back with double the usual rate."

The pilot nodded. "That works for me."

The three-hour flight was uneventful, almost boring, and the pilot made a reasonably smooth landing, given his condition, in the cove Holtz had directed. They pulled within fifty feet of the waterline, and Holtz grabbed his bags and hopped out to wade ashore. He did not look back as the plane turned around and made a hasty departure.

Holtz made his way to a nearby road, then over to one of the less-frequented public beaches, where he turned on another burner phone and called a cab. While waiting, he called American Airlines and booked a round-trip flight from George Town to Miami under an alias he had kept secret from the syndicate for just this sort of emergency. Not that Holtz intended ever to return here, but he knew a one-way booking would arouse suspicion. He had fabricated an entry stamp on the passport bearing his alias that would hopefully escape scrutiny at George Town. Once the plane had taken off, Holtz would carefully remove the adhesive patch bearing the exit stamp and paste it into his genuine passport. He could not take a chance on using an alias coming through American customs, and even if the syndicate learned of his arrival through some leak, he would be long gone before they arrived at the airport.

After the cab dropped him off at the Owen Roberts International Airport terminal, Holtz went in and picked up the ticket, paying in cash. Then he hurried to a nearby pub to nurse a drink until he saw a crowd building up at the customs exit. Taking advantage of the hurried state of the agent, he breezed through with only a cursory glance at the entry stamp on his passport. So far, so good. An hour later, he was in the air, heading to Miami.

Holtz had no illusions that the entry into the United States would be as easy as his exit from Grand Cayman. He bought several mini bottles of gin during the drink service. They weren't for fortification during the flight—he intended to rinse his mouth with it and sprinkle a bit on his clothing to complete the effect of the boozy tourist when he arrived. Holtz did not draw any added attention on his arrival; they just captured an entry photo while stamping his passport and moved him along.

Leaving the terminal, Holtz grabbed a cab for the cut-rate hotel he had booked using the flight's Internet access, arriving just after nine p.m. local time. Only when he reached his room did Holtz relax. He had escaped to the temporary safety of the United States. He would present himself at the local FBI field office and work out a deal the following day.

****

Holtz was jarred awake by the crash of the chair and wastebasket he placed in front of the door. He could do nothing to stop the three hooded men wearing the night-vision goggles from entering the room, and he was seized immediately and shoved face-down into the bed.

As he felt the needle prick into his neck, his final thought was, *Almost, almost!* Then his vision and consciousness closed down.

5 Intrarea Florilor, Snagov, Romania
16:13 EET, 1 April

Crețu

Dragoș Crețu jammed the disconnect button on his desk phone, then swept the phone and most of the items on his large wooden desk off to the floor with a primal growl. His secretary came into the room at once. "Yes, sir?" she asked fearfully.

"Get out!" The secretary quickly fled and shut the door, leaving Crețu to his rage. "Damned paper-pushing imbecile!" He stood, walked over to the bar, poured himself two fingers of Stolichnaya Vodka, and gulped it down. *The damned Salinas Cartel! If that fool Holtz had done scientific research, he could not have found a worse business partnering option!* The syndicate had an unbelievably profitable opportunity with Gronkowsky's product, now and in the future, and Holtz had pissed it away in one stroke.

He looked out the large windows of his office across Snagov Lake to the trees on the other side. As he felt the rage subsiding, he poured himself another portion of vodka and took a measured sip this time, pulling out a cell phone and selecting a saved number.

"Yes?"

"This is Crețu. I have a job for you."

"Yes, boss?"

"Liquidate Holtz. He's staying at the La Paloma del Mar Hotel in La Ceiba, Honduras."

"Um, we don't have anybody there, boss."

"GET somebody there on the next flight! Or hire a local! I want him dealt with before he gets any bright ideas about cutting a deal with the police."

"Yes, Boss!" The call hung up, and Crețu pocketed the phone.

"Angelika!" he bellowed.

Within three seconds, his secretary was back in the room, trying not to shake badly enough for it to be seen. "Yes, sir!"

Crețu's face softened when he saw her fear. "I'm sorry for yelling. It's been one of those days. Find Stefan and Grigore and get them up here at once."

"Yes, sir," the woman said with palpable relief.

He liked Angelika. She was an efficient secretary and as pleasing to look at as she was in bed. He tried to keep his temper when she was around—it made things more comfortable after work. Ten minutes after summoning them, Crețu's business and military operations chiefs were sitting with him at the table in his office.

"Where in the hell is Barbello?" Grigore asked.

"Off of Honduras in the Western Caribbean," Crețu answered. "We obviously can't let this go unanswered, and we need to know everything we can before we hit them. Get your people on it."

"Putting together a rescue will take time."

"We have seven days. Whatever it takes, we have to get that ship and Gronkowsky back. And when our men are done, I don't want a single Salinas left alive on that island. Clear?"

"Clear."

"What's our personnel status?"

"Still recovering after the Florida deal and that cock-up in Cyprus. If you want to go within a week, we must strip men off other jobs."

"I feared as much. Do it. As soon as you figure out your personnel needs, see Stefan here to arrange it." He turned to the other man. "Before you say anything, we must recover that boat before the Salinas animals learn what they have. And they will learn it, believe me, as soon as they start working on those eggheads. We have less than a week. Get moving."

"Yes, boss," they both said as they got up from the table and left the room.

Crețu stood and walked back to the bar for another vodka. He was drinking too much these days, he knew. It was not only bad for business; it was personally dangerous. If word got out that he was a drunk, the other senior council members would green-light his elimination, and then who would sit in this office? Probably Grigore. Stefan was the better manager and more profitable. But Grigore had an edge in terms of cold ruthlessness.

Crețu was a former junior thug in the Internal Security Directorate of the Securitate, as the Romanian secret police were known in the days of the Communist Dictator Nicolae Ceaușescu. Before they were disbanded a few days after Ceaușescu's death, the Securitate was one of the most brutal secret police forces in the world, and the Internal Security agents were the most vicious of the lot. After the collapse of the Soviet Union and its communist satellites in Eastern Europe, many secret police murderers had to flee for their lives. Some less widely known ones were able to carve a niche in the underworld that sprang into place as soon as the totalitarian governments collapsed. A select few joined into crime syndicates that soon exerted influence over broad geographic areas and segments of individual economies.

The 252s had a central committee of the founders, of which Crețu was one, each holding an underworld fiefdom controlling the syndicate's activities in a particular geographic area. In Crețu's case, this was Romania, Moldova, Bulgaria, North Macedonia, and Albania. With profits shared centrally, each fief holder was free to work outside his territory, even within another's territory, using an "Eat What You Kill" business model. They were almost invulnerable within their domains, working mostly below the local government radar when possible and readily applying bribery, intimidation, and murder to stay free to operate otherwise.

The deal with La Cantaña was a remarkably profitable enterprise—very high income, at almost no risk. That it was run efficiently by a former low-level Stasi clerk like Holtz was amazing. Holtz was a plodder who thought he was James Bond, almost laughable among the organization people who knew him. Crețu chided himself. *You were complacent. He was operating out of his depth, and you should have put one of our more intelligent people with him. Too late now.* He shook his head and took another drink.

The Recollected Choice

USCG Cutter *Kauai*, Moored, AUTEC, Andros Island, Bahamas
18:53 EDT, 1 April

Ben

Ben finally finished securing classified publications, zeroing out the codes on various pieces of cryptological and other gear, filing paperwork, and planning and preparing the next day's activities that went along with a vessel availability at a test range. Executive Officer, or XO for short, on a Coast Guard patrol boat as small as *Kauai* also meant Operations Officer, Engineer Officer, and [Fill in the blank with anything other than Commanding] Officer. Hence, his days were long and full at even the quietest times, and workups and test and evaluation periods were the opposite of the quietest times.

He looked across at Hopkins, sharing the final wrap-up activities. *Thank God! I'd be working straight through until the damn thing began tomorrow if it weren't for her.* "Come on, Chief," Ben said. "Let me stand you to the best three-course meal that fits in a microwave."

"XO, you sure know how to treat a girl," Hopkins said and followed as Ben led the way to the messdeck.

After their successful mission in January, it had excited Ben when he learned of the upgrades and the new purpose for their ship. He rued that day when he learned of the added security burdens these would entail. They had gained another Operations

Specialist petty officer in Zuccaro and Electronics Technician in Bunting, which helped but did not eliminate the extra load Ben and Hopkins had to bear.

When they reached the messdeck, it surprised Ben to find Sam, Chief Drake, and Culinary Specialist Second Class Thomas "Chef" Hebert standing near the stove. He was even more surprised to smell what had to be Chicken Crepes and Cilantro Lime Rice, one of Chef's specialties. "Captain, COB, have you held up your dinner and Chef's liberty just for us?" Ben asked.

"Not at all. COB and I just got back from our nightly harangue at Harbor Ops Office, and Chef was just making sure we didn't screw up the new chafing dish he's breaking in."

"Now, Captain, you know that's not true," Hebert said. "I know y'all were working late, and besides, it's not like there's anywhere to go on this sand heap." Hebert was one of Sam's aces in the hole in terms of morale. Born and raised in New Orleans, Hebert apprenticed in a small family-owned and run restaurant in the Vieux Carré before enlisting in the Coast Guard. Besides the service's regular commissary support, Sam and Drake contributed funds and scavenging to provide for his more "exotic" condiment and equipment needs. The result was superb meals for the crew when underway, a significant plus in a patrol boat's otherwise spartan existence. As for Hebert, he loved the work, relished the appreciation he received, and, best of all, got to shoot a fifty-caliber machine gun in his general quarters billet.

"You'll go to Heaven, Chef," Ben said as he and Hopkins took the proffered plates of food and walked to the mess table to sit with Sam and Drake. "Captain, what's going on with this harangue stuff? Did I mess up something?" Ben asked after he sat.

"Seems we missed our dockside time by thirty-eight minutes, which apparently poses a significant threat to the republic. I pointed out things happen on shakedown, in this case, that phasing problem we had to fix while underway, but the dockmaster wasn't having it. Said a navy ship would have sent a proper notification, and he would have to consider reporting whoever was responsible in a letter to our chain of command."

"What did you say to that, sir?" Ben asked with concern.

Sam smiled. "Nothing. I took out my notebook, wrote 'LT Samuel Powell, CO (i.e., Officer Responsible), USCGC *Kauai* and Captain Mercier's name and address, tore out the page, handed it to him, and then walked out."

"Oh, Captain, My Captain, you're such an evil influence on us." Ben shook his head in mock disapproval. "What am I to do with you?"

"Mmmm, yeah. As I think about it, I guess I should have been more circumspect, but I was too tired and fed up. I hope it doesn't come back to bite us."

"Captain, I'm sorry," Hopkins interrupted. "I'll get Joe Williams onto a go-no-go alarm on the FC3 panel. It won't happen again."

"Don't worry about the navy, sir," Drake said. "I'll tell the kids to stay on their toes when they're ashore." Drake was the senior enlisted member and the oldest man on the boat at forty-four. Since Hopkins's advancement to the same rank, the crew informally called Drake "COB" for "Chief of the Boat" on *Kauai*, a tradition borrowed from navy submarines. He was the best chief petty officer Ben had ever known because of the mastery of his trade and his leadership among the crew. Six-foot-four and physically imposing, he needed just to lean in to get someone's attention or administer a well-deserved dressing-down. Still, he quickly found an opportunity to work with the individual and give quiet encouragement.

Drake was also a master "wheeler-dealer" who worked an extensive network of connections among fellow chiefs and officers up to Captain's rank to keep *Kauai* well-supplied and running. Somewhat concerned about his "Don't worry, sir, I know a guy…" activities earlier in their tenure, Sam and Ben had learned not to ask too many questions, just sit back and enjoy what happened next.

"Anyway, I was just telling the skipper we're pretty much there with the new plant," Drake said to Hopkins and Ben. "One more day, maybe two, and we'll have the data those geeks need." The "geeks" Drake referred to were the scientists from the Defense Advanced Research Projects Agency, or DARPA, on board to observe and record the post-shakedown tests of *Kauai*'s new diesel-electric drive and stealth features.

Drake himself was learning plenty. His love/hate relationship with the original aging engines on *Kauai* was over. He now was getting to know the ins and outs of high-efficiency generators, electric motors for propulsion instead of direct-drive diesel, and a high-capacity battery bank for near-silent operations. Drake considered retirement after twenty-four years, going out with *Kauai* when she decommissioned. Her new lease on life changed everything. Despite her engineering make-over being more aligned with Chief Electrician's Mate than Drake's rating, he had pressed hard to stay on board to see things through. Sam was relieved and delighted to make that happen.

Sam's face brightened. "And the good news is our shooting case is officially and favorably closed."

"That's a relief," Ben said. "Although he doesn't show it, I know Deke was worried since he's the one who pulled the trigger." It had been a sticky situation. The FBI wanted that suspect alive for interrogation and was after a pound of flesh. With senior Coast Guard backing, Sam arranged for one of his father's high-powered lawyer friends to represent anyone from *Kauai* called in for an FBI interview. Given that and the fact the full-motion video from *Kauai*'s and the Customs plane cameras and the body cameras on the boarding party made it one of the most documented justified shootings in human history discouraged further interest. Besides, even the FBI had no stomach to go after a Coast Guardsman who put down a murderous sex slaver and child rapist.

The technical discussion continued as Ben ravenously attacked the chicken—he had had nothing but coffee and water since his breakfast at 05:00. He ached with fatigue, having stood on the Bridge on OOD watch continuously since that time except for bathroom breaks. It had been his lot on this trip, with Sam and all other qualified OODs tied up with test events. He wanted to savor Hebert's cooking and then grab some sleep, but he had a date of sorts. When Ben finished, he would call Victoria, a moment he anticipated all day and would not miss for anything.

****

Victoria Carpenter was the greatest surprise of Ben's life. A twenty-three-year-old Data Scientist and Mathematical Analyst for the DIA and protégé of his erstwhile shipmate, Peter Simmons, they had met during the search for the lost nuke. The two men left *Kauai* to focus on the hunt ashore with Simmons's DIA associates. En route from Key West to a hotel in Marathon, where the team had set up shop, Simmons described Victoria as a mathematical genius with a "neurodiverse" streak. It was a warning for Ben not to be surprised by eccentric behavior. The image that formed in Ben's mind as they drove through the night was a plainer, geekier, neurotic version of Velma from the Scooby-Doo cartoons. This image shattered the instant the door to the hotel room opened.

Victoria, who led the greetings, was the most beautiful young woman Ben had ever seen—petite, with long auburn hair pulled back to reveal large aquamarine eyes, high cheekbones, and full lips in a heart-shaped face. Rather than the frumpy dress that Ben expected, she wore a loose-fitting top and jeans that hinted at a smashing figure. She hugged Simmons and said in a husky voice with a midwestern accent, "Hello, Peter! I am pleased to see you." She turned to Ben with a smile that made him melt. "You are Lieutenant Junior Grade Wyporek?"

Holy crap! Even her voice is incredible. Breathe, boy! Ben took a breath and played it as cool as he could. "Yes, I am. I am very pleased to meet you. You can call me Ben if you like."

"Why would I like to do that when your name is Benjamin?" Her smile faded.

Oops. "Well, some people prefer to call me Ben because it's shorter to say, but I like how you say 'Benjamin,' so I would be happy if you called me that." That lovely smile returned.

"Good. We have been working all day and ordered pizza. Mine is a thin crust with pepperoni and green peppers. Would you like some as well?"

"Victoria, I can't think of anything I would rather do more right now."

"That's good." She then pivoted, walked behind the table holding a large computer monitor and keyboard, sat, and began typing, gazing at the screen. *OK, there it is.* Ben was thankful for Simmons's heads-up, as otherwise, he would have been shocked by the apparent rudeness of the gesture. After the introductions, the team settled into a planning session, with Victoria engrossed in her computer work and Ben munching pizza and stealing looks at her whenever he could. As the team conversation ended with a decision to send Victoria and her programmer partner, Steve, back to Maryland the next day, the analyst opened another door to Ben.

"I wish we had more time to work together, Benjamin."

Ben's heart leaped. "Well, Victoria, we have a few hours, don't we? Can I pitch in?"

"No." Victoria glanced back at the computer work area. "Everything is batch processing right now. However, I read your paper on the SAROPS project that provided the basis of your search strategy. There were several flaws and shortcomings. Would you like me to tell you about them?"

Ka-thunk! Ben blinked and opened his mouth in surprise, then noticed over her shoulder that Simmons was watching him with a slight smile. He consciously dialed down his ego. "Of course, Victoria. I'm always looking for ways to make progress." He then rolled through the most thorough intellectual beating of his life as she listed every flaw in the paper, from basic principles to punctuation errors. She was entirely correct—when he completed that project, he was sick of school and just shooting for "good enough." He found it ironic that his intellectual laziness would come back to haunt him with the most attractive woman he had ever met. "I hope you aren't disappointed in me, considering I'm not the mathematician you are. Also, there were many demands on my time when I wrote that."

"I'm not disappointed." She nodded. "Very few people are as intelligent as I am. I hope you are not sad; sometimes, it is hard for me to tell."

Hope sprung anew, and he smiled. "On the contrary, you can never go wrong being honest with me."

"Oh, good. In that case, I like you. Very much."

Ben's heart skipped a beat. *OK, careful now.* "Despite my inferior scholarship compared to you?" he teased with a smile.

"I am not bothered by that. You are very handsome and a hero." She smiled at him.

The knowledge that was a frank statement threw Ben for a moment. He blushed and said, "Oh, ah, thank you, I'm not a hero."

"I do not understand." The smile disappeared again. "You received the Coast Guard Commendation Medal for saving three lives last year, and you just arrested a dangerous criminal."

Ben had started stammering, then saw Simmons over Victoria's shoulder, giving a thumbs-up and mouthing, "Take the Win."

Suddenly, a couple of things were obvious. First, Victoria must have researched his background—he wasn't wearing his uniform, so there was no other way she could know about his medal. Second, she was utterly honest and literal without nuance. Her critique of his report was not an expression of disappointment; it was a statement of fact, like identifying the color of paper on which it was printed. Likewise, the "aw shucks" modesty normally expected had no place here. There was no need to downplay actions or achievements; just lay out the facts. It was unique and the most delightful situation he had ever found himself in with a woman.

At her request, he described his life in the Coast Guard for almost two hours. Despite the concentration required to ensure everything he said was logically consistent and idiom-free, he enjoyed this first conversation with the beautiful and attentive woman. They parted that night with a warm hug, and it delighted Ben to find Victoria even more beautiful the following day.

"Will you come and visit me in Bethesda?" she said to Ben after he placed her case in the car.

"Yes, I'd like that very much. But it might be some time. I can't leave the area while *Kauai* is operational or in readiness, you understand."

"Yes, I know," she said and then kissed him on the cheek before driving off. The encounter left Ben reeling—even Simmons could see the young woman's effect on him. As they continued the search, he had a frank discussion with the young officer, pointing out the issues associated with carrying on a relationship with someone with even a mild form of autism, like Victoria's. Not that he had any question of Ben's integrity or other personal qualities. It was just the challenges that went with her condition. He had seen Victoria in other relationships, which had failed when what her partners initially regarded as eccentricities morphed in their minds into annoying tics. He was highly protective of her—she was the younger sister of his beloved late fiancée, and he didn't want to see either of them hurt.

Ben took Simmons's caution to heart. He had never known, much less been in a relationship with someone on the spectrum, and did not know how he would feel over time. He also appreciated that relationships with Coast Guard junior officers like himself brought plenty of their own challenges, even for someone without special needs. Then there was the distance—her duties with the DIA and challenges with public transportation limited her to the DC area. Finally, he was slammed with the demands of *Kauai's* rebuild and the special training their new role required. As interesting as she was, Ben set out carefully. The last thing he wanted was to hurt her.

They settled into a comfortable friendship supported by phone whenever he had the time and connectivity. He loved listening to Victoria's voice's deep and plummy timbre and the precision in her language as she excitedly described what details she could of her work. He wasn't sharp enough to follow along with all the big-brain math she talked about, but he could hang in there enough to be a valuable sounding board.

On the other hand, he could talk about anything with her, and she listened intently, fascinated by his experiences with his job and coworkers. Whenever he called, she was there and thrilled to talk to him. She also understood the demands of his position. She did not resent that sometimes there would be several days between phone calls and things he couldn't discuss with her for operational security reasons. More than one of Ben's earlier relationships had foundered on that very issue.

Over the two-and-a-half months since their meeting, their conversations became more and more precious for him. He missed them terribly whenever he was underway or otherwise tied up with an operational demand. He had never felt this way about anyone else and began thinking he might be falling in love with her.

****

The conversation was winding down as Ben finished the last of his supper. Sam concluded the impromptu dinner meeting with a positive thought: "A couple more days, guys, and then we're off for home. No more speed runs, sound runs, turning around, and heading back to start because some egghead had the green-with-white wire patched into the white-with-green plug. Just good ol' drug and migrant blockade for us, with the occasional rocket launch from the Cape."

"Amen to that," Hopkins said as she wiped her mouth. "I shudder, thinking what my boys have put over on their grandmother since we left."

"Aw, MOM!" Ben said, getting hearty, tired laughs from the others, with Hopkins good-naturedly shaking a finger in his direction. He turned to Sam. "By your leave, Captain?"

"Off for the nightly call, Number One?" Sam asked.

"You know it."

"Good on you. See you in the morning, everyone."

They pushed away from the table, and Ben patted Hebert on the shoulder as he left the messdeck. "*Merci beaucoups, Maître Cuisinier!*"

"*De rien, mon lieutenant!*"

Ben shuffled up to his stateroom, closed the door, and sat at his mini desk. He looked longingly at the two pictures fastened securely to the ship's bulkhead above his desk. Ben had taken the first one with his cell phone after he and Victoria dined at a pleasant restaurant on their first date. He was in a jacket and tie that night, while she wore a gorgeous green cocktail dress with her hair up. The second picture was a candid shot of Ben and Victoria strolling on the Washington DC Mall, taken by an aspiring photographer about a month ago. She held Ben's arm and looked up at him with a bright smile as he looked at her, both in light jackets and jeans. In those everyday clothes, so different from the green dress, she conveyed a wholesome beauty every bit as alluring.

The pictures were artifacts of the only visits he had been allowed with her. He was going through an intense combat training course in Quantico, Virginia, preparing for *Kauai*'s new special operations role. It exasperated Ben to be so close to Victoria, a mere hour-and-a-half drive away, yet unable to pry out time to be with her.

Finally, Ben had wrangled an evening off. It was the first time he had seen her since the Florida Keys operation, and as lovely as he had remembered her then, Ben was unprepared for what awaited him in Bethesda. Ben had always thought the expression "Breathtakingly beautiful" was hyperbole until experiencing it himself at his first sight of Victoria that night. She had to call his attention to the flowers he had bought for her, which snapped him out of his paralyzed state, starting the babbling phase, leading finally to a simple, "You look wonderful" after he pulled his head out of his ass. Not his smoothest moment, but she didn't seem to mind—quite the contrary. After the awkward beginning, they recovered to their usual banter as the evening wore on over dinner. As pleasant as it was just hearing her voice, it was magic when combined with that gorgeous face and lovely eyes as emerald green as the dress. When they returned to the apartment at the end of the evening, Ben asked if he could take her picture. Victoria was terrifically self-conscious, and it took all the persuasion he could muster to get her to agree to pose. It was worth it, this and every time he could look at the picture and remember that first night.

The second visit occurred a couple of weeks later, an entire Sunday off, and Ben was determined to make the most of it. He drove up early in the morning, and they went out for breakfast and then spent the day at the museums around the Washington, DC Mall. Ben remembered little about the exhibits. He just enjoyed being with Victoria and seeing her fascination with them. He was surprised at the breadth of her knowledge and tastes— his previous experience with mathematical masters was confined to his professors at the academy, most of whom were one-dimensional people barely able to converse with someone outside their specialty. Unlike them, Victoria never held her encyclopedic knowledge over him. She didn't seem to care a wit about how much he *knew*; she was just intensely interested in what he *thought*. It was a marvelous experience. The second picture happened afterward when they strolled in the beautiful sunshine on the Mall.

The day had a hiccup as they were leaving. They had taken the Metro subway system down to avoid wasting time on driving and parking. Metro traffic was light in the morning, and although Victoria was silent during the trip, Ben did not give it any thought. The trip back was a different story. The crowds were heavy and loud, and Victoria was clearly affected. It was the first time her condition had become an issue, and Ben was in a terrible plight. He had mild claustrophobia himself, and the noise and pressing in of the crowd was getting to him—it had to be far worse for her. He wanted to suggest they get off and take a cab, but was afraid of embarrassing her. Finally, her severe reaction to a child's scream jolted Ben out of his indecision, and he immediately asked her if they could get off at the next stop. He was kicking himself on the way out of the station for letting her distress go on for so long and was terrified he had destroyed their wonderful day with his indecision. He was almost giddy with relief when Victoria hugged him gratefully after they got outside.

After a wonderful dinner at an Italian restaurant across the street from the station, they completed the rest of the journey to the original Metro station by cab, with Victoria snuggled under his arm, her head on his shoulder. Then back to her apartment in his car. Unlike their earlier outing, Ben did not have to report back for training in Quantico until the following day. He desperately wanted to stay with her, but got hung up on how to ask. After the Metro near-miss, Ben was unsure how she would react and rationalized that he shouldn't be pushing in just to take off in a few hours. After a very awkward goodbye, he was almost halfway to his car when he realized he could not just leave it like that and went back. Her joy when she opened the door was apparent, and their night together was warm and tender.

It was the most beautiful day of his life, and when they parted with a passionate kiss early the following day, he realized he was in love with her. Yet, he couldn't find it in himself to tell her. Victoria was so honest with him about everything; he felt sure she would have shown some sign if the feeling was mutual—but she had not. Ben had decided it wasn't fair to lay that on her on the way out the door. He had already pressed his luck and was afraid to risk driving her away and ending what they had.

He had accepted the satisfying but static relationship since, but having a gun pointed at him by a murderous criminal a week ago had changed the calculus. Ben had resolved to press his case to her directly, admit his love for her and see where it led. But he needed to do it in person rather than by phone. Fortunately, Sam had agreed to cut him loose on several days of leave once they returned home from AUTEC—provided they received the promised operational stand-down.

He retrieved his cell phone from his desk and dialed Victoria's number after turning it on and syncing to the patrol boat's off-network Wi-Fi connection. As usual, she answered after two rings.

"Hello, Benjamin."

Ben smiled, as he always did at her use of his full name and the quiet cheeriness of her greeting. "Hello, Victoria. How was your day?" It was the standard exchange at the beginning of their phone calls. Ben knew Victoria liked things a certain way and enjoyed obliging her.

"Oh, it was an exciting day. First…"

****

"… and so, seems we may wrap things up and head home in a couple of days," Ben said.

"That is excellent news. I am concerned about your workload while you have been there. Do you think you and your crew will be granted relief when you return to Port Canaveral?" Victoria asked.

"Hopefully. That's another thing I wanted to talk to you about. Sam has agreed to give me a few days of leave if we stand down.

I would like to fly up there and spend it with you. Would you be agreeable to that and able to take leave yourself?"

"Oh, yes, that would be wonderful! I have an abundance of leave accumulated, and I am sure my supervisor would not object when I tell him it is for you."

I *am known around there? That's an interesting revelation.* "I'm glad to hear that. I'll let you know when I can nail down the dates."

"Oh, good. I am very excited to be able to see you again. I hope it will be soon."

"Me too. Well, I'm pretty tired, Victoria, and I have another long day tomorrow. Would it upset you if I asked to make this one of our shorter phone calls?"

"Of course not, Benjamin. I am very concerned you are not getting enough rest. Will you be able to call me tomorrow night?"

"If we are not on our way home, then definitely. Otherwise, I'll call you as soon as I can."

"I am looking forward to that. Goodnight, Benjamin."

"Goodnight, Victoria," Ben said, hanging up the phone.

He looked at the pictures again, managed a wistful smile as he remembered the details, then turned off the phone. "Goodnight, my love. I'll hold you again soon."

The Blue Swan

USCG Cutter *Kauai*, Moored, AUTEC, Andros Island, Bahamas
08:13 EDT, 2 April

Ben

"Take in Line Three!" Ben shouted, giving a thumbs up to Bunting as soon as the dockworkers cast the line into the water.

Bunting picked up the 1MC public address system microphone, blew a short "tweet" on the whistle he was holding, and announced, "Shift Colors."

Ben watched with satisfaction as Lee snatched the U.S. Flag from the flagstaff on the stern, Fireman Sean Connally did the same with the Union Jack on the bow's jackstaff, and Zuccaro ran up the U.S. Flag on the mast halyard, all within one second. As he moved the thrust levers ahead to an eight-knot setting, he said, "Helm, right ten degrees rudder, steer zero eight five. Bunting, sound one long blast."

"Right ten degrees rudder, steer zero eight five, sir," Seaman Pickins, the helmsman, replied.

"Sound one long blast, sir," Bunting said, pushing and holding the button for *Kauai*'s horn for five seconds. The long blast was an aural signal indicating a vessel getting underway. It was of little utility in the bright sun and clear visibility of the harbor that morning, but by the book. And after Sam's run-in with the Harbor Master yesterday, Ben and Hopkins were determined that *Kauai*'s sailing this morning would be an exemplar for everyone present in the harbor. As the patrol boat hurried out to the test area, Bondurant relieved Ben of the OOD to allow him to supervise the morning series of tests from the boat deck.

The morning activities were a series of test runs for the Squid. *Kauai* had been very fortunate to surprise the villains off Miami, and more so that they turned in the right direction and held a straight course. A few days before, Ben had sat down with Hopkins, Bondurant, and Lee to "war-game" workable tactics for targets that were not so accommodating. They had devised a series of live testing scenarios, with the RHIB standing in for the target. Rather than shoot off actual net canisters, which were expensive and hazardous to the boats, the contractor had developed color-coded "paint rounds" with identical ballistics to those containing nets. They had internal charges that would fire at the end of the flight, but instead of a net, a harmless paint pattern would deploy into the water to allow observation of the tactic's effectiveness.

Of course, Lee was the coxswain and very excited to "go tactical" with the RHIB. Although Hopkins was the most skilled OOD on board, Sam wanted a more "average" person at the conn to provide a realistic assessment, so Bondurant got the nod. Hopkins was still present on the Bridge, directing the test. The contractor who developed the Squid insisted on having an observer in the RHIB, a youthful engineer named Paul DeChamps, whose thick round glasses had earned him the nickname "The Owl" among *Kauai's* crew. Connally was the last member of the RHIB's crew, added as a safety crewman to watch over the contractor.

Ben gathered the crew of the RHIB and delivered a safety briefing. With ballistic projectiles being fired over the boat, even benign ones like the paint rounds, the crew was equipped with battle helmets and standard life jackets. At the end, he drew Lee and Connally aside for a private chat. "OK, Shelley, where is it?"

"What's that, sir?" She asked innocently.

"The coffee can with dish soap you intend to tell The Owl is 'prop wash' so he can furnish some hilarious cell camera footage moving back and forth in the boat."

"Why, sir, I'm *shocked* you think me capable of such tomfoolery!" There was a scraping sound as she tried to move the can out of sight with her foot.

Ben reached down, picked up the can, and sniffed it. "Ahem. Well, at least you used biodegradable soap." He put the can aside and continued. "OK, I appreciate that you'd like a little payback for having a civilian perched on your shoulder on this ride, but with ballistic rounds flying around, we need everybody's head in the game. So, besides no prop wash, I don't want to see him manning the mail buoy lookout or rummaging through the toolbox for a left-handed screwdriver or any more boot camp tricks. Consider that an order. Clear?" he said with a grin.

"Yes, sir. Very good, sir," Lee replied with a mock sad look. "You know, I bet you were a lot more fun at the academy!"

"Nope. I was hanging on by my *fingernails* there, and I couldn't afford to get caught screwing around," he said with a wink. "Look, it's DeChamps's first time in the RHIB. Show him a good time rather than hazing."

Lee smiled in return. "You've got it, XO."

"Thanks, Shelley. Off you go. Good luck!"

Lee

The RHIB launched shortly afterward with its crew of three, and it and *Kauai* went into the test range. Each test involved the RHIB moving to a half-mile distance, barreling in at thirty knots, and executing evasive maneuvers. Bondurant, guided by Hopkins, maneuvered *Kauai* in response. Williams activated and fired the projectors on Sam's command if the Squid got a firing solution. The projectiles fired paint charges into the water, resulting in either a "Hit with Net X" or "Clean Miss All Nets" report from Lee. Wash, rinse, repeat.

They had repeated the cycle enough times to get a reasonably rich dataset when something went awry. A defect in one canister's fins created a "wobble" in flight that caused it to fall behind its companions. When the dispersing charge fired, it was just forward of the speeding RHIB and doused it and its occupants with two-and-a-half gallons of bright blue paint. Lee closed the throttle slowly to bring the rib to a smooth stop, took off her paint-coated sunglasses, and said, "Everybody OK? Give me a thumbs up!"

After getting a thumbs-up from both passengers, Lee shook off her hands, put them on her hips, and glared at DeChamps.

"I think some of our projectiles might need adjustment," the engineer said, squinting up at Lee while holding his paint-fouled glasses.

"Ya think?" Lee replied.

"*Kauai*-One, *Kauai*, report!" her radio barked.

"*Kauai*, *Kauai*-One, direct hit by blue paint, no damage or casualties," Lee replied.

"*Kauai*-One, *Kauai*, roger, cancel operation and return to ship."

"*Kauai*, *Kauai*-One, WILCO, out." Lee took a deep breath and turned to Connally. "Sean, *carefully* help Mr. DeChamps with his glasses." She swished her sunglasses clean in the water beside the RHIB, then sat back down at the helm. Once Connally had helped DeChamps with his glasses and both were seated again, Lee opened the throttle and headed back to the patrol boat. *I'll bet the cameras got an awesome shot of this. I'm SO looking forward to seeing it again, and again, and AGAIN!*

While operating the boat crane, Jenkins left the RHIB at the deck rail after the crew climbed out so the paint could be hosed off before returning to its cradle. The XO met them there with an armful of sodas—he knew they would be dried out after a couple of hours in the sun. He was always doing thoughtful things like this, unlike any other officer she had ever served with, and it was the thing she liked most about him.

"So, Petty Officer Lee," he said with a perfectly straight face as he handed her a can of Coke. "I think we need to get you some vacation time. You're looking mighty blue."

Ha, ha, ha! So, it starts already! Lee paused after taking a swig of Coke and replied, "Thanks, sir. You know, XO, you're wasting your talents here on the bounding main. You should run a comedy podcast!"

"OK, OK, but I have to get a selfie with you guys," he said, holding up his cell phone.

"Alright, sir, but it will cost you," Lee replied with a smirk. *This is going to be good!*

"Name it."

"You have a blue pirate mustache in the selfie."

"Done!" The XO swiped some blue paint off her helmet with his finger and painted on a curly-cue mustache. "Sean, come on. You get in this too!" With the XO grinning, they crowded together, Connally in a "smirky" shrug and Lee with her best "Oh, no!" pose, and the XO snapped the picture. "Thanks, guys. Now you hit the shower and then see Doc. We'll handle the cleanup."

"Aw, come on, XO. It's just paint," Lee sighed.

"It's a chemical, Shelley. No discussion."

"Yes, sir," she said, taking a swig of Coke as she started forward. As she walked, she grumbled, "If I hear a word that even sounds like 'Smurf,' somebody's gonna get their ass thrown overboard!"

Interrogation Room B, Security Division, U.S. Army Garrison-Miami, Doral, Florida
11:47 EDT, 2 April

Holtz

Holtz opened his eyes, then quickly shut them again, almost crying out from the pain in his forehead. It was deathly quiet, brightly lit, and white wherever he was. Holtz was sitting in a hard chair, head resting on his folded arms on a table. He slowly opened his eyes, allowing them time to get used to the bright light. Once his eyes were fully open, Holtz sat up slowly in the chair. His left hand was manacled to a rail stretched across the empty table, with an empty chair sitting on the other side. He looked around the room, which was painted white and featureless other than a single door and a mirror across the room. Someone had dressed him in orange, one-piece coveralls, and laceless, slip-on cloth shoes—*a prisoner's uniform.*

Through the fading headache, Holtz experienced a glimmer of hope. He had not been taken by the 252s from his hotel room last night. *Was it last night?* His watch had been removed, and there was no clock in the room. The 252s would not have bothered with torture or interrogation; they would simply have shot him and left his body in the hotel room. This was a government facility, probably American, he reasoned. The Russians could not have tracked him down so quickly, even if they were interested in him. "Hello?" he asked, gazing at the mirror. "Is anyone there? I have information you'll be interested in."

Silence. Wherever this room was, it was isolated from anything else going on in the building. After what seemed like hours but was probably only minutes, the door opened, and a slender thirtyish man of medium height entered, walked to the table, set down the leather case he was carrying on the far side, and sat in the chair across from Holtz. He was dressed in a plain blue suit, white shirt, and red tie, dark brown hair cut medium-short above a plain face with a close-cropped anchor beard and brown eyes. The man said nothing, just stared expressionlessly at Holtz without moving.

After an uncomfortable period of silence, Holtz could not take it any longer and asked, "Do you have questions of me?" No response. "You must want something. Why am I here?"

After a few more seconds of silence, the man finally spoke. "You are Anton Holtz, correct?"

Whoever had taken him had obviously grabbed his passport. "Yes."

"Late of the 252 Syndicate?"

Holtz was shocked by the question. Nothing he was carrying had any reference to the syndicate. "I'm unfamiliar with that term."

The man leaned back with a slight smile. "Oh, come now, Holtz. You have been a member of that organization for at least twenty years. I'm not sure why you decided to come to the United States, but I am sure you must be in a hell of a jam with your employers to do so. What you do not want to do is lie to me. Doing that would prove you are of no value whatsoever. If that is the case, I'll have you turned over to the FBI for a very public tour of our criminal justice system."

The thought of what the man was threatening chilled Holtz to the bone. He knew that any public tour would be a very short one—his erstwhile comrades would make sure of that. "Alright, yes, I have been a member of the 252 organization."

"Good answer. So, Holtz, what brings you to Miami? It can't be the sun and mojitos. The evident lack of preparation leads me to believe you are fleeing something. What did you foul up that convinced you to run to us?"

Frightened as Holtz was, he knew better than to offer what he had for nothing. "I need a guarantee of my safety first. You don't really expect me to give you everything so you can then cast me aside, do you?"

The man leaned forward. "I'll give you one guarantee, Holtz. If you don't tell me the whole truth and nothing but the truth when I ask you a question, you get dumped into the system immediately. On the other hand, if you cooperate fully and without hesitation, I *may* find your information interesting enough that I'll want to keep you alive. Now, what's it going to be?"

Holtz was familiar with interrogation tactics from his apprenticeship in the Stasi and his years rising in the 252 organization. This man was not bluffing. If Holtz didn't offer something up now, he would not get another chance. "The organization is on the verge of marketing a weapon of mass destruction." Holtz knew he had scored a hit when the man suddenly leaned forward.

"What kind of WMD are we talking about, Holtz?"

"Chemical weapons, a carbamate-based nerve agent."

The man sat back disgustingly and scoffed, "Oh, come on, Holtz. There's nothing new there. VX? Novichok? It's all been done."

"Not like this one."

"What, you're going to tell me this one is *deadlier* than the others? We are well beyond the threshold of that making any difference."

"Yes, it's much more lethal, but that is not the important thing. It is also self-cleaning." The man's expression changed, as

Holtz knew it would. He had experienced the same shock when Gronkowsky revealed this to him on the *Carlos Rojas*.

"What do you mean, self-cleaning?"

"It breaks down on exposure to moisture and oxygen into innocuous inert compounds. The half-life is such that applications at a level that ensures death to everyone not in full chemical gear will be down to a safe level within a few days, with no clean-up effort. It is also a binary, with indefinite shelf life and safe handling characteristics. You can set it up to self-mix in an artillery shell or bomb and eradicate everyone in a village or small town, leaving nothing to clean up but the bodies."

The man's expression returned to its previous nonchalance. "I don't believe you. Our intelligence would have picked up on something like that. They couldn't hide it, even in Eastern Europe."

"It's not in Europe. It was developed aboard a repurposed petroleum support ship."

"Alright, let's say I believe you. What difference would it make? If the 252s are producing and getting ready to market it, there's not much we could do to stop it."

"You're wrong. The lab, materials, production facility, data, and even the developer are all still aboard that ship. And the 252s don't have it anymore."

"What do you mean they don't have it anymore?"

"A drug gang from Honduras seized it."

"A Honduran drug gang seized a 252 ship? You don't expect me to believe that." He paused, tilted his head, and smiled. "Ah, now I think I see. You were working a drug deal that went south. Whether it was bad faith by you or them is not important. You are the one that will hang for it. Am I correct?" After Holtz looked down without speaking, the man continued. "I'll take that as a yes. Did the cartel offer terms?"

"They want twenty million euros within a week, but the organization won't pay. It would set a bad precedent."

"I can't say I blame them. So, I presume they will mount a retrieval and punitive operation?"

"Yes, within five days."

"Five days? Rather longer than I would expect."

"The ship is in Barbello. It takes time to gather and position a sufficient force to overcome the resistance without wrecking the ship."

The man nodded. "Holtz, you have just bought yourself some consideration. I'm done with you, but I'll send in some experts to debrief you on the ship, the 252s, and their opposition. Keep talking, and you might just live through this." The man stood, put the leather case under his arm, and left the room.

Holtz released the breath he was holding. *Well, the die is cast.*

USCG Cutter *Kauai*, AUTEC Weapons Range, off Andros Island, Bahamas
13:17 EDT, 2 April

Ben

The rest of the day involved a trip to the gunnery range to test and exercise the new targeting system for the 25-mm gun that aimed at specific Global Positioning System coordinates. Williams's reaction in the briefing was the same as Sam's and Ben's when they first heard of it. "Why do we need something like this? We're not shooting over the horizon with this thing, and it's less accurate than visual or infrared targeting."

The contractor's response mainly was unintelligible gibberish and the fact that they had been hired to do it by the people paying for *Kauai*'s upgrades.

"So, in other words, 'cause," Williams finished with a smirk.

"Joe...," Ben said warningly.

"Sir, I'm sorry, but I'm worried it might mess up the electro-optical or infrared systems. We need those, unlike this thing. Could we put a few rounds through the tube at the end to make sure the others still work?"

Ben looked at Sam and nodded. Sam said, "That's a good idea. We'll hold on to a couple of targets, and you can tear them up at the end."

"Thank you, Captain," Williams replied, directing a scowl toward the hapless contractor.

The gun exercise proceeded as planned, and the new system performed as advertised, with rounds landing within thirty feet of the target, a steel buoy with a shielded GPS receiver attached to the top. *Kauai* engaged the target at various speeds and bearings with the same results.

"Well, it's reliable anyway," Williams grudgingly acknowledged after the last test run.

They continued on the range for about half an hour to run the other targeting systems through their paces and then turned back toward the harbor. Ben looked at the Bridge clock—16:47—and nodded to himself. *An early day. With any luck, we'll be in by 17:30, buttoned-up by 18:30, and I can have a nice, leisurely talk with Victoria and get some decent sleep tonight.* He couldn't wait to share the selfie and story of the Great Paint Deluge with her. As interested as she was in the significant events that made up his day, she always seemed delighted to hear about the little ones, particularly if humor was attached.

****

"XO, we're headed for the Thousand Fathoms Club for beers. Want to come along?" Williams asked as he poked his head into Ben's room. "It's Karaoke Night!" Ben could see Lee, Bunting, and Jenkins waiting in the hallway.

"Alas, Joe, I have tons of paperwork and a phone call to make. I'm sure sorry I won't get to hear Shelley's version of 'Song Sung Blue,' though."

Lee gave him a scowl while the others laughed. "You're not going to let that go, are you, sir?"

"Sorry, Shelley, this one's got legs like Eliud Kipchoge. You guys have fun but drink responsibly, don't drink and drive, practice safe sex, stay in school, um, and all that other dad stuff."

"You're an inspiration to us, sir," Lee smirked. She looked at the pictures on Ben's bulkhead with a slight smile. "Tell her we said 'Hi.'"

"Will do. Have fun, guys." Ben smiled as he listed to their conversation fade as they walked down the passageway.

"Who the hell is Eliud Kipchoge?" Bunting asked.
"He's a marathon runner, you idiot," Lee replied.

Only the Important Words

4527 Sangamore Road, Apt. B23, Bethesda, Maryland
18:47 EDT, 2 April

Victoria

Victoria had just completed her nightly dinner routine that involved cooking the main course, then the vegetable, and eating them on separate plates with separate dinnerware. It entailed extra effort in the cleanup phase, but it was well worth it to avoid the stress of keeping the food items separate on a single plate. She washed, dried, and put away everything before settling with a glass of wine and, hopefully, a phone call from Benjamin. They agreed such calls would happen between seven and nine p.m. to preserve her dinner and sleep routines. Benjamin had accepted that rule with his usual good-natured acquiescence—his understanding of her peculiar needs was one of the many things she loved about him. Of course, if the phone rang at 6:45 pm or 9:30 pm with his callback number displayed, she would pounce on it like a cat on a helpless mouse.

Victoria's apartment was a small but fashionable one-bedroom, practically across the street from her workplace, the DIA's Data Analysis Division within the National Intelligence University. It was pricey but affordable on her GS-12 pay since she did not travel, had no family, and had few interests outside of work. It was great to be home after a ten-minute walk without the stress of Maryland driving or the horror of the DC Metro subway system with its crowds, confined spaces, and the noise and all those people *touching* you. She had a car, useful on weekend shopping for foodstuffs or, on rare occasions, drives on one of the parkways in the area when the leaves were changing or the cherry blossoms bloomed. The apartment was not spartan but sparsely decorated with books, no knickknacks on the shelves, and just a few impressionist landscapes decorating the off-white painted walls.

Victoria sat at her computer desk to pull up Scholar Google and check for any new data science papers while waiting to see if Benjamin would call tonight. Although work-related, she preferred to do her academic research at home—her system was far faster for Internet searches than her work computer behind the government firewalls and other security protocols. She looked at the two framed pictures on her desk as her computer booted. One was the picture of her and Benjamin on the Mall. The second was Benjamin, alone in the same setting, and he was beautiful. Victoria knew that was the wrong word to use for a man, but it was the most accurate in his case, with his short sandy brown hair mussed by the breeze, the deep azure color of his eyes matching that of the sky, and the delightfully warm smile on his lightly tanned face. It was a treasured artifact from the full day they had together a month ago, the second of their two dates, and as perfect a day as she had ever experienced.

Benjamin was as surprising to Victoria as she was to him. After receiving their first report of the derelict drug vessel last January, Peter had asked her to pull data for a quick brief on *Kauai*'s command. Samuel Powell's record was very unusual: the elder child of a wealthy family dropped out of the prestigious Wharton Graduate School to enlist in the Coast Guard? She dug deeper and found an arrest for felony assault with charges dropped a couple of months before he enlisted, the victim now a fugitive from justice believed to be living in Serbia. Interesting. Digging deeper into that man, she found a contemporaneous guilty plea for reckless driving with injury, victim Gabrielle Powell—aha! Samuel's younger sister. That explained the anomaly of the arrest in an otherwise flawless personal record. Still, the decision to enlist was strange. Quick advancement to chief petty officer, selected for officer candidate school, followed by tours of duty on Coast Guard cutters in Boston, Honolulu, and now Miami, several personal and unit awards.

Benjamin's record was lean by comparison. He was a mediocre performer at the Coast Guard Academy, had an uneventful tour of duty aboard USCG Cutter *Dependable* in Little Creek, Virginia, then was assigned to *Kauai* as second in command. There was something unusual—he had been awarded the Coast Guard Commendation Medal for heroism in saving three lives after a traffic accident. She had noted this with approval and pulled the men's official photos. They looked like they could be brothers. All official military photos looked the same to her, like instead of "say cheese," the photographers said, "Now, give us your most menacing scowl!"

Victoria was very excited the next day when Peter included her in the scratch team of agents and technicians deployed to the Florida Keys to process Unmanned Aerial Vehicle data. She enjoyed the challenge of the austere information technology environment, and the Florida Keys were not the worst place to be in the middle of January! After a few days on-site, Peter left *Kauai* to join the search team ashore, bringing Benjamin. Victoria expected little from the association. She had downloaded a report of Benjamin's academy project that served as their search strategy and was not impressed, even considering it was undergraduate work. She hoped to avoid engaging in deep technical conversations with him while they were together. Still, there was that medal for bravery, and the day before, he had arrested a dangerous criminal on a boat rigged to explode. She wondered what a hero might be like in person.

The young man who arrived with Peter for the team meeting that first night was nothing like she expected. Some height, but not overly tall, with a slim, athletic build and the most captivating blue eyes she had ever seen. He was not the militaristic buffoon she took him for after reading his personnel file, but a modest, almost shy, intelligent young man who provided fascinating conversation. She suspected he was attracted to her as well—she had caught glimpses of him looking at her while she worked at her computer during the discussions.

She would have welcomed such attention at one time, but then her self-doubt kicked in again. *I like Benjamin and must not drive him away by being too clingy.* Too clingy. That was what her last love interest had said to end their relationship. She knew she had difficulty reading people's feelings—it was a fact of life for someone on the autism spectrum. But the thought she could make herself repellent to someone she loved had been emotionally devastating, and she resolved never to make that mistake again. Hence, as attractive as Benjamin was, Victoria was very cautious in revealing her interest in him.

Victoria opened the door to Benjamin at the end of the team meeting, offering some helpful critique on his report he took in stride. She then expressed admiration for his heroism, which he tried to brush off. Victoria supposed there was a military code of modesty that expected such things. It was strange, but she accepted they must have a reason for it. She finally connected with him by asking about his life in the Coast Guard. Among the other exciting elements, she persuaded him to tell how he got his medal—crawling inside a car about to fall off a cliff to pull out an unconscious woman and her two young children! *And he was shy talking about that? Why?*

After two hours of conversation, mainly Benjamin answering questions and telling anecdotes about his job and himself, Victoria could see the fatigue taking its toll. His descriptions of operations on patrol boats conveyed a general state of sleep deprivation, along with the more exciting aspects. She also noted he had quickly adapted his conversation style to remove the jargon and idioms. Victoria appreciated his thoughtfulness, but realized it required him to put particular effort into almost every sentence. She was sure he was struggling but soldiering on in deference to her, so she offered him a graceful exit.

"You look exhausted, Benjamin. I am tired too. I think it is time we went to bed."

"What?" Benjamin sputtered, eyes wide.

Oh no! No, no, no! He thinks I am inviting him to have sex with me right now! How could I be so stupid? So clingy!

Fortunately, Peter was still present and came to the rescue. "You're right, Victoria. Why don't we all head to our rooms, and we'll pick it up again in the morning?"

The shock on Benjamin's face retreated, and the warm and tired smile he had before her blunder returned. Victoria stood and, after going through the motions of checking her computer for progress on the automatic computations, took a chance and gave Benjamin a warm hug. For the first time in a long while, her last thoughts before falling asleep did not focus on mathematical algorithms. As they were saying goodbye the following day, she to return to Maryland, Benjamin to continue the search with Peter, she took another chance and kissed him on the cheek. The smile he returned made her tingle and gave her hope.

She spoke to him that evening after she had returned to Bethesda, and he had completed the search activity for the day. This time Benjamin was the receiver, and she was talking. It thrilled her he was interested in what she did, and although she suspected he did not quite understand it all, he still seemed to hang on to every word. It was several days before they spoke on the phone again after Benjamin returned home. Something had happened during the mission, but he could not discuss it. Working in the world of classified information and secrets, she understood. However, whatever happened must have been extraordinary, for both he and Samuel received the Coast Guard Medal, a top award for heroism.

They settled into a routine of nightly phone calls whenever Benjamin had the connectivity. They were a welcome distraction at first, becoming an increasingly important part of her day as she got to know him. He was interesting, charming, and funny all at once, and unlike anyone she had ever met, she could discuss anything on her mind with him. Given this, she was puzzled that he was not married or had a steady girlfriend. When she finally asked why that was, he went silent, and she quickly tried to withdraw the question.

"No, it's OK, Victoria. I've asked myself that a few times. The only answer I can come up with is I haven't met anyone who needed what I could provide." Then he quickly changed the subject, and she was careful not to raise it again. Benjamin's answer created a paradox for her. She often could not connect with people she liked and felt much closer to him, knowing he shared this experience of loneliness. On the other hand, it made her even warier of making any "clingy" blunders. It was a specter hanging over their early conversations, fading over time as she became more comfortable with him.

Between the distance and the relentless demands of Benjamin's job, the conversations were all they had. Benjamin had hoped they could get together when he was close by in Quantico while completing his combat training in February and March, but the short time and large volume of training requirements extended through the weekends. During his course, the only free time allowed was just one evening that served as a somewhat awkward first date and one other full day together, and they seized on those opportunities.

Their first date had been a maelstrom of emotion for Victoria. They had arranged it a week in advance, and Benjamin could only get off for the evening, so they planned for him to pick her up for dinner and return her to her apartment before he had to report back to Quantico. Victoria was terrifically anxious about making a good impression, so much so that she let it slip to Debbie, the office administrative assistant, the next day. Debbie was one of the few people who could see past Victoria's idiosyncrasies and was the closest thing she had to a good friend. When Victoria confessed her anxiety, the middle-aged woman's maternal instincts kicked in at once, and she took Victoria shopping for a suitable dress that afternoon.

"I am not sure I like this one. It is not the style I normally wear," Victoria said as she checked herself in the mirror. The green dress fit snugly and left little to the imagination.

"Trust me, dear." Debbie smiled admiringly. "The color is perfect with your eyes and hair, and the fit is perfect for everything else. This one will knock him for a loop. And before you ask, yes, that is what you want to do."

When the big day came, Debbie stopped in to help her get ready. She knew Victoria found the subtleties of makeup particularly challenging. "Dear, you are beautiful without makeup, but this is one of those times when you need to have makeup, but not look like you're wearing makeup," Debbie explained. Victoria's head spun at the contradictions, but decided it was not prudent to overthink the process. The last rub was her hair. She always wore it pulled back, but Debbie insisted it needed to be up.

"Why?" Victoria asked.

"Sweetie, I don't know how to tell you other than this is a hair-up dress," Debbie explained.

Victoria deferred to the expert on the subject, which proved to be a sound decision. When she answered the door an hour later to Benjamin's knock, he stood transfixed with his mouth hanging open. The uncomfortable moment lasted until she asked about the flowers he was holding. "Those flowers are lovely, Benjamin. Are they for me?"

He broke into an embarrassed smile at the question and said, "Yes, they are. Excuse me, please, but you are just so much more beautiful than I expected. I mean, I expected you to be beautiful, but not...." He stopped, took a breath, and said, "You look wonderful, Victoria!"

"Oh, what a nice thing to say!" Victoria replied. *This brave, intelligent man reduced to babbling by a dress? OK, now I know what "being knocked for a loop" means. And I like it!* "Shall we go?" she said as she took her coat off the hook.

"Yes, indeed," Benjamin had replied as he helped her put on her coat.

The dinner began a little awkwardly, with Victoria asking the server many questions and giving detailed instructions on how the meal should be cooked. Benjamin simply ordered a steak, cooked medium, which worried her. *Does he think I am too obsessive with all these specifications?* She was sure he must have noticed after their food arrived when she tried as subtly as possible to separate the various food items on her plate so they would not touch each other. Benjamin did not display any reaction she could observe, but she did not trust her ability to tell. Before long, they were just eating, wrapped up in their usual banter, and her worries faded. It was the same comfortable conversation as their phone calls, with the bonus that he was gazing at her with those lovely blue eyes.

The one tricky part of the evening came at the end when Benjamin asked if he could take her picture. Victoria <u>hated</u> getting photographed. She was always conscious of everything that was not just right with how she looked, and a picture would preserve those flaws in vivid detail forever. However, when he prevailed upon her and explained how much it would mean to him to have this memento, she could not deny it to him. In the end, even she admitted to being pleased with her appearance on seeing the picture on his phone.

Overall, it was a satisfactory first date.

****

For the second date, Benjamin had driven up from Quantico early on a Sunday morning and picked her up at her apartment. After a lovely brunch at a Bethesda café, they took the Metro to the Smithsonian. The Metro system was lightly traveled on Sunday mornings, not as terrifying as usual. They had strolled through the National Museum of American History and the West Building of the National Gallery of Art. As they walked along the Mall afterward, Victoria noticed and pointed out a middle-aged man taking their picture. Benjamin took her hand gently off his arm, patted it, and said, "Wait here." The man looked concerned as Benjamin approached and began the conversation with, "Hello, friend. What are you doing?" After a few moments of quiet discussion, the man began showing his pictures, stopping on one when Benjamin smiled and beckoned to her. "I like this one, and he has agreed to sell me a digital copy. What do you think?" he said, showing her the image that became the picture on her desk.

"I like it, too," she said.

"Twenty bucks, and I have full rights?" Ben asked the man.

"Certainly. I'll IM it to you now. Would you like more?"

"Yes," Victoria interrupted. "I would like one just of him, please." She recognized the man had an excellent sense of lighting and pose.

"Done. Could you stand over here, please?" he asked Benjamin, who awkwardly complied. The comical expression on

Benjamin's face led her to suppress a laugh—the situation discomforted him for some reason she could not fathom. Finally, the frustrated photographer said, "Relax, man, think of how much pleasure your girl will get from this." Benjamin looked at her, she smiled at him, and his face thawed. Click! She nodded her approval when the photographer showed her the result. "OK, now how about one of you?"

"No! No, no, no." She shook her head firmly. What would he do with her image after he had it? The thought of it spreading over the Internet filled her with horror. *No wonder Benjamin had been so nervous. I should never have asked him for that. What a clingy thing to do!*

"These two will do, thank you," Benjamin said as he stepped over and gave her a brief hug across her shoulders. He paid the man $40, and they resumed their walk.

After a couple of minutes, she worked up the nerve to tell him. "I dislike strangers taking my picture. That is why I was so upset."

"You don't need to explain it to me. I don't like having my picture taken at all. That's why I behaved like a doofus when he was lining up mine. He won me over by reminding me it was for you." Benjamin squeezed her hand, and with palpable relief, she leaned into him and rested her head on his upper arm as they walked. She had never felt this way with anyone and had difficulty identifying the emotion. Safe, that was it. She felt safe when he was with her, despite being in this frighteningly public place with its crowds and noise and disorder. None of the terrors could touch her while he was with her.

They continued their walk for another hour, ending at the Smithsonian Metro station. The ride back was far less peaceful than the ride down. Weekend sightseers crowded both the stations and the trains at this time of day. Their car seemed filled with screaming, unruly children by the second stop, and Victoria could do nothing but face downward with her eyes closed, trying at least to reduce the visual stimulation. She felt the oxygen being depleted in the car, her chest tightening and heart-pounding, despite Benjamin's presence. Victoria desperately wanted to flee, but was afraid Benjamin would be disappointed in her lack of fortitude. Then there was a spine-tingling child's shriek, during which her grip on his arm reflexively tightened so much she feared she had caused a bruise. He leaned over at once and whispered, "Look, I'm embarrassed to admit this, but my claustrophobia is getting to me. Do you mind if we jump at the next station and take a cab the rest of the way?"

"No, not at all," she replied. They rose at the next stop, and Benjamin positioned himself between her and the little demons as they left. A short walk through the station returned them to the sunshine and air one could breathe in safety. They stopped outside the station entrance, and she hugged him and buried her face in his chest.

He stroked her back and said, "Thank you for being so understanding. I can usually keep it together better than that. I don't know what came over me."

You are lying, Benjamin. You noticed I was nervous at the station, but you did not want to embarrass me by asking if we should leave. You held out as long as you could without intervening until you saw I was about to break down, and you saved me from that. Now you are worried I will be humiliated, so you are trying to save me from that too. Are you doing this because you feel something for me? Or is it because you are a good and kind man and feel sorry for me? She looked up at him and forced a smile. "That is alright, Benjamin. I am nervous in confined spaces too and was relieved you suggested we step out."

"No harm done then," he said with a wink. "It's been hours since brunch. Would you like to grab dinner here before we get that cab?" He motioned toward an Italian café across the street.

"Yes, I would like that very much."

"*D'accordo, andiamo, la mia bella signora!*"

"Do you speak Italian, Benjamin?"

"Only the important words, Victoria."

The dinner was delicious, and Victoria regained her feeling of complete safety as they rode in the cab back up to Bethesda station, her head resting on Benjamin's shoulder as he held her close. After the short ride in his car, they were back at her apartment door, and he looked into her eyes tenderly as he held her hands in his. *Ask me if you can stay. Please, Benjamin! I do not want this day to end!*

"Victoria, I, um...." He gazed longingly at her for a few seconds, then looked down. After another moment, he held her eyes again. "I had a great time today. Thank you."

"Yes, I did too." She willed herself not to cry. "I hope I can see you again soon."

"Yes. Definitely. As soon as possible. Goodnight, Victoria."

"Goodnight, Benjamin." She reached up and kissed him fully on the lips. After a few seconds, Victoria pulled back, then stepped inside the apartment, and closed the door. She sat on the floor, oblivious to the fact that you are not supposed to sit on the floor, pulled up her legs, and put her chin on her knees. *OK, he* was *just being kind because he felt sorry for me. I will not cry!* And then, of course, she cried. About half a minute later, a knock on the door startled her. She stood slowly, walked shakily to the door, and looked out the peephole. She gasped and fumbled with the lock and wrenched the door open. "Benjamin!"

He stood in the doorway with a serious expression on his face. "Victoria, I'm sorry, but I can't leave it like this. I want to be with you. I know it's unfair to lay this on you so late at night and then run out at oh-dark-thirty tomorrow. But after today, I want to have every moment I can with you. If you don't feel the same, I'll understand, and I'll go, but I had to tell you."

She stepped up to him, put her arms around his neck, and pressed her head onto his chest, listening to his deep breaths and pounding heart while blinking away her tears. After a minute, she hugged him tightly, then took his hand, led him inside, and closed the door.

It was the most perfect of days.

✲✲✲✲✲✲✲✲✲✲✲✲✲✲✲✲✲✲✲✲✲✲

She almost jumped out of her seat when the phone buzzed on her desk. She checked and made sure it was Benjamin's number, then waited. It would appear clingy if it seemed like she was waiting by the phone. After the second ring, she waited three seconds, took a deep breath to steady her voice, and punched the "Answer" button. "Hello, Benjamin," she said calmly.

"Hello, Victoria. How was your day?"

Part II—The Mission

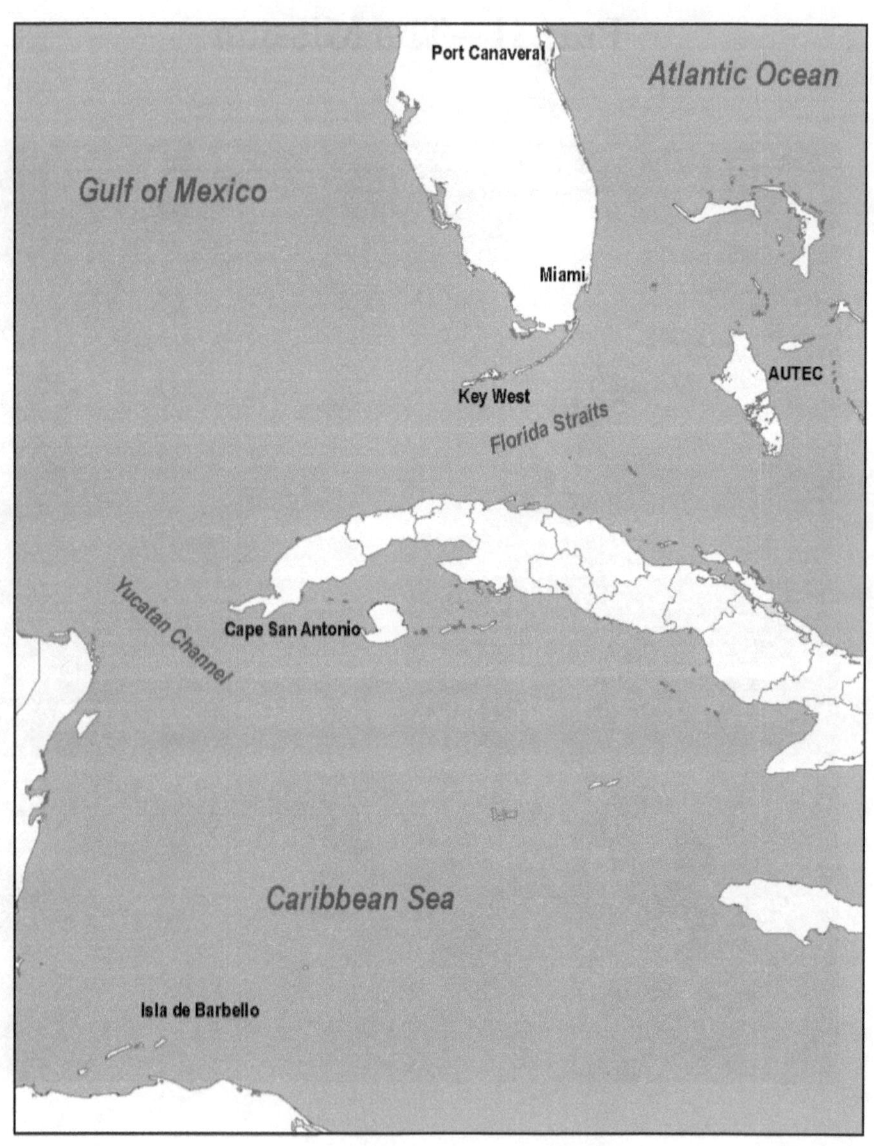

Port Canaveral
Atlantic Ocean
Gulf of Mexico
Miami
Key West
Florida Straits
AUTEC
Yucatan Channel
Cape San Antonio
Caribbean Sea
Isla de Barbello

The Offspring of Necessity

Office of the Commander, U.S. Southern Command, Doral, Florida
08:17 EDT, 3 April

Pennington

Rear Admiral Horatio "Harry" Pennington, USCG, Director, Joint Interagency Task Force South, had just arrived in the office with his Executive Assistant, Commander Daniel Keener, USCG, after the three-and-a-half-hour drive from Key West. Air Force Chief Master Sergeant Charles Shipley, who served as SOUTHCOM's administrative assistant, stood and saluted smartly, with Pennington nodding in return. "Good morning, Admiral," he said. "The general requests you go right in, please." Turning to Keener, he continued, "I'm sorry, Commander, but it's principals only for this meeting."

"Sorry, Dan," Pennington said. "I'll back-brief you when we're done."

"Yes, sir," the officer replied.

"Please come with me, sir," Shipley said. He walked over to a set of heavy wooden double doors, knocked, opened the door, and stuck in his head. "Admiral Pennington is here, sir."

"Bring him in, please."

Shipley held open the door as Pennington entered the room and closed it behind him as he departed. Pennington snapped to attention at the sight of his superior and said, "Good morning, General!"

"Good morning, Harry! Relax, please," General Lamont Miller said as he came around the table with his right hand outstretched. The army four-star general leading Southern Command was six-foot-five and 245 pounds of solid muscle. The only difference between his appearance today and thirty-six years before as a middle linebacker on the University of Tennessee Volunteers was his shaven head and the wrinkles gained from years of standing in the sun in the commander's cupolas of M2 Bradley Fighting Vehicles and M1A1 Main Battle Tanks. "I'm real sorry to drag your ass all the way up here on no notice. How was the drive?" he continued with a noticeable Tennessee accent as he warmly shook the admiral's hand.

"No problem, sir," Pennington replied. "It was long but productive. Although I'll need a wrist brace—I haven't signed that many papers since the last time I bought a house!" The physical contrast between the two men was notable. At five-foot-ten and 175 pounds, Pennington was not a small man but seemed so next to the big general. His full head of short-cropped graying brown hair and round metal-rimmed glasses provided more of a professor look than an athlete.

"I hear ya, bubba," Miller chuckled. "Come on over here, so we can read you in on JUBILEE," he said as he put an arm around Pennington and guided him to the large table where four people were standing. "You know Fred, of course." Pennington recognized the Coast Guard Seventh District Commander, fellow Rear Admiral Fred Brown, but was unfamiliar with the female Captain at his side or the two other people, one female and one male, both in civilian clothes. The female was older, about his age, and her face seemed familiar, but he could not put the finger on where he had seen her. The younger man was unfamiliar to him.

"Hello, Fred," Pennington said, shaking the man's hand. "It's good to see you."

"Likewise, Harry," Brown said. "This is Jane Mercier, my Response Chief."

"Captain, I'm glad to meet you." Pennington shook her hand. "I've heard lots of good things."

"Thank you, sir," Mercier replied.

"OK, on to the new folks," Miller said, steering him down the table. "I don't believe you know Vice Admiral Jennifer Irving, Director of the DIA?"

"How do you do, ma'am," Pennington said, shaking her hand. *Aha! That's where I've seen her.*

"Pleased to meet you, Admiral," Irving replied. "May I introduce one of my DCS officers, Dr. Peter Simmons? He'll be providing the Flag Brief this morning."

"Doctor," Pennington said, shaking Simmons's hand. *DIA? Holy shit, what the hell is going on here?*

"OK, let's get started," Miller said as he and everyone but Simmons moved to sit down. "Harry, you're both the last one to the table on this and the guy carrying the ball. Sorry about that." As Pennington nodded, Miller turned to Simmons and said, "Take it away, Doc."

"Thank you, sir," Simmons said. "Admiral, we have a situation involving a WMD falling into the hands of a Central American drug cartel."

Pennington's eyes widened, and his mouth opened in shock and then closed. He looked at Irving and Miller, receiving a nod from each. "Well, Doctor Simmons, it looks like nobody will accuse you of burying the lede. Is this speculation or known?"

"It's known, sir," Simmons replied. "Admiral, we're pressed for time. May I proceed, please?"

"Yes."

"Thank you, sir. Are you familiar with the 252 Syndicate?"

"Unfortunately, yes." Pennington nodded. "They are coming up more and more these days."

"Yes, sir." Simmons nodded in sympathy. "The night before last, one of their mid-level bosses suddenly appeared at Miami International after flying in from Grand Cayman. He was immediately tagged when passing through customs, and we put a tail on him until we could get a snatch team together. We bagged him in his hotel room just before dawn yesterday and interrogated him here."

"Why you? Why not the FBI?" Pennington asked.

"The 252s are a TCO operating outside the U.S.—that puts them in our lane. We didn't want him to get away while the

Bureau and we were locked in a jurisdictional turf war, so we went ahead and grabbed him. Anyway, he was the lead 252 man for their South America operations, working out of a converted Offshore Petroleum Support Vessel in Venezuela. This ship doubled as a mobile laboratory for the 252s' chemical weapons development program.

"The 252s have been in the contract-killing business since they were formed. They recently started using a line of Novichok knock-offs to support that. The Russians persuaded them to abandon that particular horror and develop their own line since we naturally associate any Novichok deaths with Moscow. The 252s hired a biochemical genius with a psychopathic streak and located the lab outside Europe to avoid tangling with the Bear. Things got interesting when the Colombian Army clobbered the 252s' cocaine vendor in Colombia, and they went looking for a new one. According to the 252 man, he struck a deal with the Salinas Cartel for a significant load," he paused as Pennington rolled his eyes. "I see you have heard of them, sir."

"Yes, they're the new kids on the block in the Western Caribbean. What they lack in brains and organization, they make up for in arms and sadistic violence. It's surprising the 252s would have anything to do with them."

"This 252 guy we picked up did not strike me as one of their rocket scientists, and, true to form, the Salinas mob double-crossed them as soon as their ship pulled into Barbello. At last report, they had killed the security guys and were holding the crew and the biochemist heading the lab for ransom."

Pennington looked around the table. "I don't know about you folks, but I'm having a hard time seeing a downside here. The 252s got a black eye, and the Salinas crowd is about to get an education in choosing your enemies."

"Well, sir," Simmons said. "I would agree with you that it's hard to get worked up about 252s and Salinas killing each other. However, the problem is that the resident genius has cooked up a new super-lethal nerve agent in the lab and the prototype rig for mass production. It has the lethality, safe handling, and self-cleaning characteristics that make it highly marketable as a large-scale battlefield munition rather than just an assassination weapon."

"Wait a minute," Pennington said. "The 252s already have this thing, right? I can see the worry, but what can we do at this point?"

"No, sir." Simmons shook his head. "The 252s were seriously afraid of the Russians, so they isolated everything on the boat. Even the lab's computers are air-gapped. Apparently, our 252 guy thought the cocaine pipeline was his primary mission and moved the boat closer to the source of supply. That would be a sound business approach with sane vendors, but it was a big mistake with the Salinas crowd. He knows this now and is singing like a canary to us, trying to stay alive. The bottom line is all the 252 eggs are in that basket, and they need it back. Within a few days, they'll have enough force gathered to go in and get it, and they won't give a damn about hostage casualties or collateral damage."

As Simmons paused, Pennington looked over at Miller. "It sounds like we need to blow that ship to Hell, sir," he said. "That's more your lane than mine."

Miller shook his head. "No, Harry. Besides the foreign relations disaster of our pounding a nominally friendly country with an airstrike, we can't take a chance on releasing that agent. Imagine a mass casualty event involving both chemical weapons and our bombs. Even if they are all cartel scumbags, we'd be international pariahs. There must be another way."

Pennington's face quickly shifted to disbelief. "Sir, it sounds like you are talking about a cutting-out operation." He looked around the table. "What do you think this is, the War of 1812? Have any of you seen the charts on Barbello? I read through everything we have on the way here. It's impossible! Nothing we have bigger than a PB could get within half a mile of that rock, and the Salinas's weapons' coverage of the only entrance into the harbor is solid. They'd pick up on anything we send in before it got within a mile. Even if we could get an assault team in there without getting detected, they would get swarmed as soon as they lit off the diesels on that ship. Success would require a high-firepower assault that would be no different from an airstrike, except a lot of our guys would probably get killed."

"And if you had an asset with stealth capability?" Miller pressed.

Pennington scoffed, "Sir, if I had something with a low radar cross-section that was silent and could tow that ship out of RPG range before the need to start its engines, it might be possible. But I know of nothing like that anywhere, much less in theater."

Miller turned to Brown. "Fred?"

"Harry," Brown began. "We have an asset available that might meet your requirements."

"You're not serious!"

"I am. I'll let Jane explain. It's her baby."

"Do tell, Captain," Pennington said warily.

"Yes, sir," Mercier began. "You might recall about a year and a half ago when *Kauai* had that mishap during the last Cuban migrant surge?"

"Yes, her CO and XO were relieved for cause."

"The CO was, sir. The XO went out on a medical because of injuries during the mishap. We took a long look at the unit to see if it was better to salvage it or just bump up her scheduled decommissioning a couple of years. The hull was in good shape, and she had the gun the new patrol boats are getting, so we hung on to her. We identified some solid command cadre and rushed them on board. Things were turning around nicely, so we went all-in on an experimental Special Ops capability. If it didn't work out, no harm, no foul. So, we stacked the deck with the crew and ended up with a very smart unit.

"So, fast forward to January. You remember that sailboat drug seizure that happened north of the Keys?"

"Yes, I remember that." Pennington acknowledged the information. "It was almost a record seizure. Wrecked in a storm was the story."

"Yes, sir. That was the cover story. It was actually a 252 smuggling boat, wrecked when a nuclear-tipped Russian Kinzhal hypersonic missile impacted right next to it."

"*What?* The Russians launched on us?"

Mercier nodded to Simmons, who said, "It was an accident, sir. Do you recall how tense things were over Kaliningrad back then? They were saber-rattling with a Backfire off Miami when it got bumped by an F-16, triggering an uncommanded launch. We lost track of the missile almost immediately. We knew it hadn't detonated and did not know where it ended up other than it did not impact on land. Needless to say, it was in everyone's best interest to pretend nothing happened, but also to keep an eye out for anything unusual along the missile's track. The 252 boat got creamed by the kinetic energy of the impact, but the product it was carrying in sealed containers kept the wreck afloat. It drifted for about three days before being spotted by an HC-144 flying out of Miami and then boarded by *Kauai*'s crew.

"*Kauai* provided a very detailed description of the wreck's condition that immediately drew our attention. Within a day, I confirmed that this was an artifact of the impact. Admiral Brown had already detached *Kauai* from her drug patrol to help search for the warhead. Thanks to a clever off-label application of the SAROPS search planning tool suggested by the boat's XO, we narrowed down the search target list. After a focused, hard-target search for a few more days, we located the impact site just off Resolution Key. Unfortunately, the 252s picked up our trail, and we had to shoot it out with them."

"Let me guess," Pennington began. "That 'F-22 Crash' on Resolution was another cover story?"

"Yes, sir." Simmons nodded. "It provided an excellent account for the fire and smoke and subsequent restricted area. We picked up the warhead and any missile fragments we could find offshore, sanitized any trace of the fight with the 252 men, and salted the site with a few banged-up and scorched F-22 parts 'missed by the search' in case someone was curious enough to dig around. As far as we know, it worked. There is nothing in the news, and we have seen nothing online other than the usual 'tinfoil hat brigade' ravings that go with any plane crash."

"Impressive duplicity. You were obviously the right people for the job," Pennington said, then turned to Mercier. "So, how does that incident play into this discussion, Captain?"

"It was pure luck, *Kauai* being the one to find that wreck, sir. If it hadn't been her, we would have gotten her underway to take over. Anyway, there were about a dozen ways that the crew could have fouled up on that mission, but they performed perfectly. The officers, in particular, carried off some brilliant and gutsy moves."

"I'll second that, Admiral, if you'll excuse the interruption, Captain," Simmons said. "I was there throughout the mission, and I wouldn't be here now if it weren't for them. No one could've done that one better."

"Thank you, Doctor." Mercier nodded again. "The Director of National Intelligence agreed and invested about fifty million dollars on upgrades to move *Kauai* from a proof of concept to a standing special operations capability. We rushed her through a yard period that replaced her main plant with electric motors, high-capacity generators, and battery bank using the new Lithium-ion batteries the Japanese are using in their latest *Soryu*-class subs. She can do up to twenty knots with no sound other than the props for two hours. We also upgraded the Bridge and sensors, added composite armor resistant up to fifty-caliber, and cut her radar cross-section to about what you'd see on a Response Boat, Small."

Pennington was incredulous. "How did you manage that?"

"Mainly coatings, sir. But we also replaced the mast with a composite design."

"And this capability is available now?"

"Yes, sir." Mercier nodded. "She's just finishing workups and fine-tuning at AUTEC. I can get her moving this morning, and she can be off Barbello in as little as two-and-a-half days."

"What about the crew? This shindig will not be a day at the regatta. We're talking about close combat, even if everything goes right."

"We'll get a SEAL team to handle the assault," Miller interjected. "*Kauai* will need to tow the boat out of range."

"Yes, sir," Mercier continued. "Plus, we put the XO, two boatswain mates, and the gunner's mate through the boat assault team course at Quantico and Little Creek while *Kauai* was in the shipyard. Whoever we send over can look after themselves and do the ship-handling on the target vessel while the SEALs do the heavy lift neutralizing the opposition."

"Sounds like you have this all figured out," Pennington said with resignation. "What do you need me for?"

"They'll be under your command, Harry," Miller said. "Barbello is a law enforcement concern, and, as far as everyone outside this room is concerned, it stays that way. DoD has practically nothing on the Salinas Cartel and nothing at all on the ground on Barbello. We need you to work your Drug Enforcement and Customs people to provide the Intel prep."

"What about our Honduran liaison? Do I bring him in on this?" Pennington asked.

Miller shook his head firmly. "Absolutely not. No foreign nationals are to have even a hint that this op is going on, and keep it to the absolute minimum among our guys. Do whatever you need to do to make sure of that. If you feel the need to move the op out of your HQ because of all the foreign presence, Fred assures me Sector Key West can fix you up."

Pennington said, "OK, sir. Now, other than this wonder boat, what can you give me?"

Miller nodded, "We'll have twenty-four-hour Global Hawk coverage and one Rivet Joint sortie monitoring emissions each night until the assault to generate a pattern of life. For the op itself, we'll have the RJ for Command and Control, an MQ-9 for EO/IR, and a SEAL team for the actual assault—they'll be flying into Key West this afternoon to meet with your staff to work out the plan. If they go in with *Kauai*, they can board when she's topping off in Key West. Otherwise, they can launch from there."

"Any chance of naval support, sir?" Pennington asked. "I lost my last destroyer about a week ago."

"Nothing I can get down there in time," Miller replied. "What's your situation with the Coast Guard cutters?"

"Three two-seventies and one two-ten are in theater. One of the two-seventies has one of the armed helicopters, so I'll move her in to support. Not much help in this situation compared to a destroyer, but better than nothing." Pennington smiled ruefully. "While we are on the subject, sir, where are we supposed to sail this thing, assuming we can cut her out?"

"An interesting question," Miller replied. "Over to you, Jenn." He looked at Irving.

"Admiral, your orders are to sail her north until you cross the five-hundred-fathom line of the Cayman Trench and then scuttle her," Irving said.

"What?" Pennington said in astonishment.

"This comes straight from the president. With everything else going on, he doesn't want that boat turned into a cause célèbre. That location's deep enough so that no one can get at her or what's onboard without a major, obvious effort. Our intel is that the precursors of the agent are harmless and water-soluble. Even if they get mixed somehow on the way down, they'll hydrolyze quickly. Dr. Simmons will accompany the assault team to ensure any documents and computer data are destroyed. If the creator is still alive, he'll take him into custody. Hopefully, we can drop the boat at night before anyone gets any pictures."

"But what about the data on the agent? Are we just going to let that go?" Pennington sputtered.

Irving nodded. "Admiral, this is something we wouldn't dare use or even study. The costs of keeping it secret are immense, and if it got loose, the consequences would be catastrophic. Far better to be rid of it."

"Hmm. Did I miss something? What happens with casualties? Barbello is eight hundred miles from any of our bases, and there's nothing more than a battle dressing station and a single health services petty officer on our ships. We need combat medical support standing by."

"That's an unnecessary security risk. We don't expect anything that can't be handled locally." Irving waved a hand dismissively. "These are SEALs we are sending in, after all."

"Oh, for God's sake, Admiral!" Pennington responded with open irritation. "The Salinas crowd are nuts. If they once pick up on that operation, they'll unload everything they have on it with a religious fury. If that happens, there will be wounded, regardless of how awesome the SEALs are." He turned to Miller. "I won't throw away lives, sir!"

"What do you suggest, Harry?" Miller tilted his head. "We don't have any carriers available, and the air force Jollies can't reach that far, even with tanking. This is one of those times we may have to roll the dice."

"I don't accept that, sir." Pennington shook his head. "What about the Special Ops Ospreys up at Hurlburt Field?"

Miller shook his head. "Sorry, Harry, no time to get them lined up and down there through the usual channels, and we can't fast-track anything without blowing the cover on this op. Even if we could, it would be a miracle to pull it off in two days."

Pennington turned to Brown. "Give me two of the Jayhawks out of Clearwater, Fred, and I can lily-pad them down and back on the two-seventies. It's risky, but a helluva lot better than just writing off the casualties."

"Consider it done." Brown nodded.

"I'll call up to Fort Benning after we adjourn and get a combat surgeon and a couple of surgical medics on a plane to Key West, and they can ride down on *Kauai*," Miller added.

"Good." Pennington looked at his folder. "Good." After a few seconds, he looked up again at Miller. "Is that all, sir?"

"Yes, Harry. I'm putting my J3 staff at your disposal. They'll coordinate the DoD stuff and iron out any wrinkles. Can I offer you my Blackhawk for the trip back? An hour flight is better than three more hours on the road."

Pennington thought briefly, then replied, "Thank you, General. Mind if I use it to get to AUTEC instead?"

Miller sat back. "OK, if that's what you want." He gave Pennington a stern look. "Are you sure that's a good idea?"

Pennington nodded. "If I'm going to send those kids into a buzzsaw, I will give it to them face-to-face. The staffs can handle any planning without my kibbitzing, and my EA can hang around here to provide a direct liaison with your J3." He smiled sadly and turned to Mercier. "Besides, I'm curious about this wonder boat and would like to see what it can do firsthand. They'll have to stage out of Key West—I'll just ride over with them."

"OK, Harry," Miller said. "I don't suppose it would take if I gave you any advice about getting too personal."

"No, sir."

"Didn't think so." He looked around the table. "Well, let's get'r done then." As Miller rose, the rest of them followed and stood at attention. "Carry on, thank you."

The group filed out after handshakes all around, with Pennington bringing up the rear. He stopped at the desk, motioned Keener over, and turned to the standing administrative assistant. "Chief, any chance of getting a private office with a secure phone?"

"Yes, sir," Shipley replied. "The general thought you might need one. Specialist Folsom here will escort you and get it set up. When would the admiral like the helicopter to be ready to depart?"

"An hour from now?" Pennington responded with a raised eyebrow.

"Very good, sir. Is there anything else I can do for the admiral?"

"No, thank you, Chief." He turned to the saluting specialist. "Thank you. Lead on, please."

As the specialist led them out, Keener turned to Pennington. "Helicopter, sir?"

"Yes, I'll be heading to AUTEC. The bad news is you still have a three-hour car ride back to the office. The good news is I'm sparing you a fifteen-hour boat ride," Pennington said, his gaze fixed ahead as they walked.

"Yes, sir."

Return on Investment

USCG Cutter *Kauai*, AUTEC Weapons Range, off Andros Island, Bahamas
10:04 EDT, 3 April

Ben

When the message arrived, *Kauai* was nearing the turning point at the end of the radar sensor range. Ben had the OOD watch with Zuccaro monitoring navigation and sensors and, by default, the message center on the FC3 console. "XO, incoming operational immediate message."

"Right, standby." Ben waited another minute to clear the southernmost buoy, then turned to the helmsman. "Left ten degrees rudder, steady on three-five-three, belay passing headings."

"Left ten degrees rudder, steady on three-five-three, belay passing headings, aye, sir."

Kauai listed slightly to the right in the gentle left turn, and Ben took one last scan to port as a final safety check, then strode to the FC3 console to read the message. Sent by the Seventh District Commander in Miami, it immediately ended the testing operation and transferred *Kauai's* operational control to JIATF-South. If that were not surprising enough, they were to return to port at AUTEC at once, meet Admiral Pennington himself at the AUTEC Command Building, and transport him to Key West. With raised eyebrows, he lifted the telephone and called Sam.

"Captain, we received incoming immediate tasking you will not believe. Could you come to the Bridge, please, sir?"

"On the way," Sam replied. He arrived on the Bridge a minute later and walked straight over to the console.

"Captain on the Bridge," Ben announced.

"Thank you, carry on, please." Sam sat at the console to read the message as Ben resumed his OOD duties. When Sam finished, he walked over to Ben for a quiet conversation. "The DARPA guys won't like this one bit."

"From the tone of that message, I don't think we'll be high-fiving either, sir."

"Well, it is what it is. Let's set the Special Sea Detail and return to port. Now that we're suspending testing, who's in the rotation for the mooring?"

"Bondurant, sir. He was planning to let Lee try with him over-the-shoulder."

"Sorry, but not today," Sam said as he glanced back at the console. "Get things rolling while I break the news to the head geek." As he strode aft, he stopped and turned with a smile. "And when you contact Harbor Control, be sure to say *please*."

Ben smiled back as he picked up the microphone for the 1MC public address system. "It's what I live for, Captain!" He keyed the microphone. "Now, discontinue all testing and secure test gear. Set the Special Sea Detail for entering port."

****

An hour-and-a-half later, Sam, Ben, and Hopkins were hurrying toward the Command Building in fresh tropical blue uniforms. If it hadn't left them disheveled and sweaty, they would have been running—junior officers and chiefs do not keep admirals waiting longer than necessary.

There was no question Pennington had arrived. An army helicopter made several orbits of *Kauai* on her way in, and there was a two-star admiral's flag flying on the flagpole near the building. Hopkins had left Lee and Zuccaro rummaging through *Kauai's* flag locker to rig a similar display once the admiral came aboard. The three quickly passed through the reception desk to the center's secure compartmented information facility and were ushered in by a navy sailor. They stood at attention as Pennington came around the table to greet them.

"Carry on, please. Hoppy, is that you?" Pennington asked with a smile. "My God, what a terrific surprise. How are you?" He stepped up and shook her hand.

"I'm fine, thank you, Admiral."

Pennington turned to Sam and held out his hand. "I hope you'll forgive the breach of protocol, Lieutenant. But Hoppy and I were shipmates on the *Escanaba*. Do you go by Sam or Samuel?"

Sam shook Pennington's hand. "Sam, sir. May I present my XO, Ben Wyporek?"

Pennington shook Ben's hand, "Pleased to meet you, Ben. I've heard some pretty amazing things about both of you guys."

"Likewise, sir," Ben said.

"Come over here and sit down, please." Pennington beckoned to the table. "Before we start, I will be talking at the Top Secret level." He directed a glance toward Hopkins.

"We are all cleared and read in, sir," Sam said.

"Outstanding. Well, your old friends, the 252 Syndicate, have been very naughty. They have been employing a converted offshore petroleum supply vessel as a lab to create chemical weapons. They were doing a good job keeping a low profile until a couple of days ago. Then they got themselves in a jam—landed in the middle of a drug war, and now the boat and their lead chemist are hostages. The boat is being held in Barbello, just north of Roatan." He pulled a high-resolution chart from a leather case on the table, and they all stood to look at it. "The island is an ancient volcanic caldera, with the remaining topography roughly crescent-shaped. It has an almost enclosed lagoon, with the buildings and quay here." He pointed at the center of the interior shoreline. "It's all shoal water except for a channel leading into the lagoon, passing a quarter-mile south of this point."

Sam looked at the chart in deep thought. "Yes, sir, I remember. We staked it out for a few days when I was assigned to Spencer. Good harbor, not much else. We thought it was a drug transshipment point, but nothing came of it." He looked at Pennington again. "Who grabbed them, sir?"

"An outfit called the Salinas Cartel."

"Are they new, sir? I don't remember hearing that name."

"Yes, they're oozing up to the top in Honduras and Guatemala. They're really bad news. Think of a gang of a hundred guys too sadistic for MS-13 standing up a drug-funded death cult. Anyway, they are about to get some genuine experience in total war. The 252s don't take insults or prisoners."

"Sir, why us?" Sam asked. "I mean, Delta Force or the SEALs would be the right choice for a rescue mission."

"It's not a rescue, Sam. I wouldn't lift a finger to save those bastards, much less risk your lives. The problem is they have come up with a particularly nasty nerve agent, and we can't let that loose. We are sending you in there to tow it to deep water and scuttle it. What happens to any 252 scientists is incidental."

"I don't understand, sir. Surely, the 252s have everything now. What would it accomplish if we succeeded?"

"Great question." Pennington nodded. "They don't have it, according to the defector that brought us the news. They had run afoul of the Russians earlier, using knockoffs of their Novichok agents for assassinations. To keep the development a secret from them, they confined everything to the boat, even air-gapping the computers."

"Excuse me, Admiral," Sam interrupted. "Why not bomb the boat?"

"No, Sam, it's in Honduras territory. We can't launch an airstrike against a Central American country without provocation. Neither can we run a search-and-destroy commando raid that leaves a sunken ship at the dockside. And if that agent got loose and slimed the island, we would really be in trouble, even if we could prove we didn't create it."

"Sir, stealing a ship violates sovereignty too."

"Only if we're caught, Sam. The Hondurans ceded that island to the cartel—they have no presence there. We go in at night, steal the ship from a criminal organization that stole it from another criminal organization and dispose of it. If called on it, we'll claim it held a classified weapon of mass destruction, which is perfectly true. Even if the Hondurans figure out it was us, a nasty problem is solved, and they still have plausible deniability. The 252s will hit that place and leave no one alive, anyway."

"Admiral, I suppose we could get in there undetected if we waited until moonset and used the batteries. But as soon as we hit that ship, all hell will break loose. We'll have a running fight from the moment we board until we clear the harbor. Assuming we aren't sunk before then."

"Sam, you think I would send you in alone?" Pennington shook his head. "There's a SEAL team en route to Key West as we speak. As you guys glide in there, they'll have taken the ship and discreetly knocked out any lighting on the quay. A Rivet Joint plane is heading in tonight and tomorrow night to read the pattern of life, patrols, and radio comms. During your penetration, they'll be there to control the ground force and keep you advised of any hostile activity. Your biggest challenge will be running the gauntlet of this point of land here." He pointed at the chart. "It's fortified and has an armed watch. But if you clear it before first light, there's a good chance you can slip by unseen and unheard." Pennington paused and scanned the faces across the table. They all focused on the chart before them and were long with worry. "Anything else?"

After a second, Sam looked up with a stony expression. "Yes, sir. What about casualties? It will be a miracle if no one is wounded. Given what you've told us, we can hardly cruise into a nearby port to put them in the hospital, and it's seven hundred miles easy to a U.S. facility."

"You'll be taking an army combat surgeon and two medics on *Kauai*. I'm pre-positioning *Thetis* with a Clearwater H-60 twenty miles away and *Northland* off Cozumel as a lily pad. It's five hours of flying from Barbello to the nearest trauma center in Miami, but the surgeon will stabilize any casualties before they're lifted."

"Yes, sir." Sam nodded, then continued. "Admiral, suppose the worst case happens, and they pop open our hull with a couple of RPGs. What's the contingency plan? I need to know my crew won't be sacrificed for nothing."

Pennington gave a solemn look. "In Key West, you will also take on board a pair of DIA agents who will destroy the agent precursors with thermite charges."

Sam scowled. "One of those DIA agents wouldn't be Peter Simmons, would it, sir?"

"Yes, I understand he was with you on the Resolution mission."

"That he was, sir," Sam continued. "He damn near got Ben killed twice. The second time I had to drive *Kauai* at flank speed through fog and shoal water to save Ben's and his asses and shoot up two civilian SUVs on U.S. soil to do it! He's not my number one favorite guy, sir."

Pennington nodded. "I understand, Sam. I assume I can rely on your professionalism to overcome your personal feelings regarding Dr. Simmons. Am I in error?"

"No, sir, I can do the job. I just need you to be aware of the nature of our relationship." He glanced at the others and then continued. "Admiral, can we take these charts out of the SCIF? We'll need them to devise approach and departure strategies."

"Yes, they're unclassified. But you need to keep them out of sight until you leave Key West."

"Yes, sir. Admiral, I would like a chance to discuss the op with Ben and Chief Hopkins, so they can begin planning. Could we keep the SCIF for half an hour?"

A sad smile spread across Pennington's face. Sam's question was a politely coded request to get the hell out so they could talk openly about the load of crap just dumped on them. "Not a problem, Sam. It's mine for as long as I need it. I'll just have a chat with the CO while you're working. When you're done, send someone to fetch me."

"Yes, sir. You still want to ride with us to Key West?"

"Definitely." Pennington nodded. "I'm interested in a hands-on tour of your new setup."

"Sir," Sam said as he, Ben, and Hopkins stood at attention.

"Carry on, please. Thank you," Pennington said as he walked out and closed the door.

Sam turned to the others, who gazed back in silence. "Folks, things just got very, very real. Comments before we start?" Ben and Hopkins both shook their heads. "OK. We need to develop an approach doable in complete darkness using GPS and night-vision goggles only. Then we need an egress plan with a one-hundred-fifty-ton vessel in tow. Chief, that's yours."

"Yes, Captain."

"It handicaps us not knowing exactly where the ship is moored or its orientation, so have alternatives for both north and south."

"Yes, sir."

Sam turned to Ben. "Number One, your job will be planning the actual assault. We'll put that combat training to use now. I want you to pick your boarding team with the assumption that your guys will have to handle getting the tow rigged and casting off all mooring lines and shore ties. You might get help from the SEALs, but I wouldn't plan on it."

"Yes, sir. Should I bring an engineer to try lighting off the mains?" Ben asked.

"You can, as long as it's Brown. You'll need a lot of muscle to pull up the towing hawser. The engines can't be started anyway until we clear the harbor—can't take a chance on them being heard. They probably won't be available even then. If I were one of the cartel guys, I would sabotage the mains or remove a critical part so the crew couldn't try anything.

"Yes, sir. It will be hard to plan anything before getting a sense of the boat's size, layout, and orientation on the quay. Maybe the admiral can help?"

"Definitely. I'll tell him we can't plan without it. Now, here's the deal as far as the rest of the crew goes. I'll pull COB aside and give him the bones of the plan so he can help us squelch any rumors. I know it's not our usual way, but I don't want any discussion of our destination or mission until after we leave Key West. We need to determine what everyone else will do before we finalize our role, and I don't want the crew to work themselves up on speculation. I expect a full mission briefing at JIATF-South, and it will be at least a day to Barbello, so we have plenty of time to fill everyone in en route. One benefit of hauling a flag officer around is everyone will focus on that rather than why we are hauling ass to Key West." He smiled as he looked at them. "Questions?"

"No, sir," both Ben and Hopkins said in reply.

"OK. I'll grab the admiral and meet you guys by the flagpole." He then turned and left.

Ben looked at Hopkins with a smile. "You continue to surprise, *Escanaba* shipmate!"

"Hey, I know people too, XO." She smiled back as she stuffed the charts into the leather case on the table.

Pennington

The Coast Guard party left the Command Building in a brisk walk toward the piers, with Sam and Pennington side-by-side in the lead and Ben and Hopkins behind them. When they reached *Kauai*, Pennington was piped aboard with proper ceremony by Drake and Bondurant. After a brief tour of the new engineering plant, he settled into the captain's chair on the Bridge. After an uneventful departure, the cutter set a north-northeast track toward the New Providence Channel. It was a lengthy roundabout route, but the only way available because of the vast shoals of the Great Bahama Bank west of Andros Island.

As soon as they cleared the harbor and set the regular watch, Sam took Pennington around the Bridge to point out the recent overhaul upgrades. He left the FC3 station's presentation to Williams, who provided a proud, hands-on demonstration of its capabilities. Finally, Sam ordered the diesel engines to shut down to show the electric motors using only battery power. As *Kauai* glided along at twelve knots, the only sound being a very slight hiss of the passing water, Pennington shook his head and turned to Sam.

"Amazing. It gives me the shivers scooting along like this without a sound or any vibration."

Sam chuckled. "Yes, sir. That was the common feeling for us the first couple of times." He then ordered up the full battery speed of twenty knots. *Kauai* was no longer silent as the intensity of the propeller thrumming sound and vibration increased.

"Full speed is definitely audible, but still pretty quiet. How far away can it be heard, Captain?" Pennington asked.

"On the surface, it's audible to the unaided ear at a maximum of one-hundred-fifty yards, sir," Sam said. "With an enhanced audio sensor, about five times that. Underwater, the blade beat carries much further, but we're still about as stealthy as you can be for a powered vessel."

"Remarkable. Can we adjourn to the cabin for a private chat? I'm interested in hearing a firsthand account of your adventure at Resolution."

"Yes, sir. Can you excuse me for a moment, please?"

"Of course."

Sam stepped over to Bondurant, who had the OOD watch, gave some last instructions, and returned. "Could you follow me, please, sir?"

"Right behind you."

After reaching the cabin, Sam shut the door, and they sat down facing each other. Sam led the discussion. "Sorry, sir. I'm sure we're more cramped than what you are used to."

"Nonsense. My first command was a PB."

"Really, sir? Which boat?"

"The good ship *Kauai*. I was the old girl's first CO." He paused as Sam's jaw dropped in silence. "No way I was passing up the chance for another ride."

"That's incredible, sir. I did not know. Is it bringing back memories?"

"Some. Mostly good ones, although a pre-commissioning detail has plenty of headaches."

"Yes, sir." Sam paused in thought. "Is there anything, in particular, you wanted to discuss, sir?"

"Yes. I wanted to avoid putting you on the spot in front of Ben and Hoppy, but I'm interested in your assessment of the mission and chances of success."

"Um, is this one of those 'tell truth to power' moments, sir, or would you prefer the rainbows and unicorns version?"

Pennington rocked his head back in a hearty laugh. "I guess I had that coming, Captain. I hope you can trust me enough to give me the former."

"Very good, sir." Sam nodded. "A lot depends on where that ship is, exactly, and the defense measures the cartel guys are using. My sense is that they aren't military geniuses, so they probably just have armed guards and a roving watch. If I were them, I'd put down an anchor. That would be game over for what we're planning—we wouldn't have time to weigh it or cut the chain before they swarmed us. But they're not seamen, and they're expecting either a payoff or a gunfight from the 252s, not a smash and grab. We'll need up-to-date intel with visuals ASAP, sir."

"We're working that as we speak. Please continue."

"Yes, sir. Then it depends on the SEALs. They must take out any cartel guys in the immediate area without raising the alarm. I don't know how in hell they'll do that, but I'll take it on faith they'll find a way. My guys can't help. They'll have their hands full for the first fifteen minutes, rigging the tow and unmooring the ship. A lot can happen in fifteen minutes, sir.

"So, assuming everything goes right, it will be about ninety minutes from ingress to egress. That is cutting it close on my battery charge life at full power, sir. Just saying."

"I hear you, Captain. Do you think it might be prudent to light off at least one of your diesels after clearing the quay?"

"No, sir. I think I'll push my luck. Anyone awake in that harbor would hear our starters, given the topography. I can light them all off quickly enough if things go south. We have drilled this pretty hard to knock down the time needed, and our last trial had it down to thirty-three seconds."

"I see. So, what's the bottom line here?"

"Sir, if we can work up to full speed on the tow without detection, we should get through, even if we have to shoot it out with that sentry post."

"And if you're detected before that?"

"In that case, I think the Servicemembers Group Life Insurance will make a pretty big payout this month, sir," Sam replied with a crooked smile. "But we'll buy enough time to torch that lab."

Pennington looked down for a moment. Then he looked up, leaned forward, and rested his right hand lightly on Sam's shoulder. "Thank you, Captain."

Assemble and Sortie

USCG Cutter *Kauai*, Moored, Truman Annex, Naval Air Station, Key West, Florida
08:33 EDT, 4 April

Ben

Berthing at the Truman Annex was a novel experience for *Kauai*—they usually moored half a mile to the northeast at the Coast Guard Sector at Trumbo Point. However, they carried the Director of JIATF-South himself, and his office was here, so the accommodation was made. At least, that was the story. One of the most secret pre-mission briefings in history was about to occur, involving various *Kauai* crew members and the JIATF-South staff, among others. Proper operations security argued against a lot of traveling back and forth.

Once Pennington was piped ashore, *Kauai* started the regular activities for a mid-patrol in-port period. Ben cleared paperwork and personnel issues and met and settled the first of their guests, army Major Shane Roberts, the combat surgeon, and his team of two surgical nurses and their equipment. They showed no concern about *Kauai*'s messdeck's close quarters as the operating room's venue. Ben correctly suspected that they had seen much worse in Southwest Asia. He left them in the capable hands of Bryant, who was a former army combat medic himself.

Drake supervised the topping off of the cutter's diesel fuel and water supplies, then moved on to the special mission preparations Sam had ordered. The Squid launcher unit, useless for the task to come, was detached and stored ashore for their return in a few days. The gasoline for the RHIB, stored on deck in a jettisonable fifty-five-gallon drum to reduce the risk of an internal fire, was also put ashore. Sam did not expect any small boat operations, and the gasoline was a dangerous source of fire and illumination if hit by hostile gunfire. Guerrero supervised the replacement of the twenty-five-millimeter ammunition they had expended at AUTEC and the rest of their solid rounds with high-explosive shells. These were more suitable for suppressing the small arms and rocket-firing opposition they expected to encounter. Along with the *Kauai*'s two junior seamen, Bondurant and Lee managed the special towing hawser's on-load and layout for the mission.

By 11:30, the preparations were complete, and the crew took a breather. This was accompanied by a surprise as a taxi pulled up to *Kauai*'s berth and deposited Seaman Juan Lopez, freshly graduated from the Maritime Law Enforcement Specialist School in Charleston, South Carolina. Lopez was a solid hand before he left, and Sam and Ben were delighted to have him back aboard for the challenging mission. Ben led the greetings. "Glad to see you back, Lope, but I think you might regret not hanging around for the graduation blowout."

"Sir, you don't think I'm going to be OK sitting around drinking beer while you guys are headed into action?"

Sam's face froze in a half-smile. "What makes you think that?"

"Captain, I've seen the towing hawser. You've also offloaded that net cannon and the gasoline—no reason to do that before a normal patrol. Finally, you've pulled in here instead of Trumbo Point, where we always stage. Something very unusual is going on here."

Sam looked at Ben. "I guess we should have pulled in and out in the dark. I'll keep that in mind for the next one." He looked back at Lopez and smiled. "I can't confirm or deny anything, but do me a favor and keep it to yourself for now. We'll give everybody the full story once we're underway."

Lopez smiled and saluted. "Aye, aye, sir!" After the officers returned the salute, he picked up his bags and headed inside the boat.

Sam looked at Ben and shook his head. "Operations Security. It's not the leaks; it's the signs that get you. Well, can't be helped now."

"Yes, sir," Ben replied. "I just got a call from the JIATF office. Final planning conference in the secure conference room at 13:00, sir."

"So much for beers over at Sloppy Joe's," Sam said with a smile. "I can't wait to hear what you and Hoppy have in store for us."

Briefing Room, JIATF-South Headquarters, Key West, Florida
12:58 EDT, 4 April

Ben

The Briefing Room at JIATF-South was not large—even a planning session as restricted as this one created quite a crowd. Sam, Ben, and Hopkins sat together on one side of the room. Also present were the navy lieutenant leading the SEAL team effort, a DEA representative, and two air force captains, one an electronic warfare specialist and the other a meteorologist. Simmons arrived to take his seat with one minute to go, receiving a friendly nod from Ben, icy glares from Sam and Hopkins, and studied indifference from the remaining attendees.

Ben understood why Sam, Hopkins, and Drake disliked Simmons. In their minds, he was a reckless fool who put himself and Ben in a situation that required Sam to break all the rules and risk his command to save their lives. But this was one of the very few issues on which Ben and his shipmates parted company. He didn't know if it was the one-on-one time he had had with the DIA officer, that they had stood, or rather, kneeled shoulder-to-shoulder through that shootout, or the genuine possibility the man could end up being a quasi-brother-in-law. Ben liked Peter Simmons and enjoyed talking with him, even if they didn't see eye-to-eye on what the agent casually referred to as "Risk Management."

The door opened, and the navy lieutenant called out, "Attention on deck!" as Pennington entered the room. Everyone came to their feet, and the military attendees stood at attention as Pennington took the podium.

"Carry on. Be seated, please," Pennington said. After they all sat down, he continued, "Ladies and gentlemen, we are here to set up a mission of extreme importance. I will express my regrets that some details are so sensitive they will need to be withheld, and I ask for your patience. There is to be no outside discussion of what we say here, and I remind you all that you signed a non-disclosure memo.

"Bottom line up front: a weapon of mass destruction is mounted on the commercial vessel *Carlos Rojas* moored in the harbor of Barbello, Honduras, and under control of the Salinas drug cartel. To our knowledge, they are unaware of what they have. A second criminal organization is moving to seize the *Carlos Rojas* and its cargo within three days. We will prevent that, and because the vessel is within the sovereign territory of a foreign nation, we will go in covertly, with a dangerously light footprint. These are top-level decisions and are not open to discussion. Your purpose here is to complete a plan of action to execute those decisions. Now, before I yield the floor, does anyone have questions?"

"Sir." Sam stood.

"Yes, Lieutenant Powell?"

"I respectfully request an explicit statement of our rules of engagement, Admiral."

Pennington smiled. "Yes, I thought you would." His smile disappeared as he looked around the room. "This is a national defense mission, and you will employ whatever deadly force is needed without warning to overcome any resistance."

"Thank you, sir," Sam said and then sat.

"Any other questions? Very well. Dr. Simmons, you have the floor." He left the podium and took a seat in the front row beside one of the air force captains.

Simmons stood, took the podium, and said, "Thank you, Admiral. Ladies and gentlemen, as the admiral has said, there is a WMD capability on the *Carlos Rojas* that, if copied and distributed, could result in mass casualties, if not global nuclear war. Our primary goal will be to board and seize the *Carlos Rojas*, remove her from the harbor, and sink her in deep water. Once aboard, I and another operative will rig everything we can find related to the weapons for destruction with thermite charges. We will wait to activate those charges until just before the *Carlos Rojas*'s scuttling if our vessel extraction is successful. In the event of a successful counterattack, we will activate the charges at once. Does anyone have questions?" Many of the participants exchanged looks, but none had questions. "Thank you. I believe you are next, Lieutenant Powell." He sat down.

Sam stood and took the podium while Ben and Hopkins stood alongside. "Admiral, ladies and gentlemen, I'm CO of the Coast Guard Cutter *Kauai*, for those who don't know me. We have modified her from the original Island Class design to diesel-electric-battery propulsion, allowing near-silent operations for brief periods. We will use this capability to enter the harbor undetected, lay alongside the *Carlos Rojas*, and put over a boarding party who will unmoor and rig her for towing. My XO, Lieutenant Junior Grade Wyporek, will lead the boarding party and command *Carlos Rojas* during the egress. *Kauai* will tow her clear of the harbor using battery power to avoid detection. We will switch to diesel power when clear and continue the tow, or escort, if the *Carlos Rojas*'s engines prove serviceable, to the five hundred-fathom line of the Cayman Trench. There, we will evacuate all aboard using our RHIB, then sink her using explosive charges. If they detect us, we will light off our diesels and use twenty-five-millimeter and fifty-caliber machine gun fire to enable our escape, if possible. If not, we will delay the counterattack long enough for Dr. Simmons to destroy the weapons and associated materials.

"Our intelligence from the DEA agent on scene is that the Salinas gang has a large stockpile of small arms and RPGs. We can assume that these will be available at the fortified position on the point of land defining the entrance and on small boats. My chief concern in terms of a firefight is the KPV our overflights observed on that promontory. They'd be pretty lucky to tag us in a vulnerable spot with an RPG from five hundred yards, but they have a good chance of roughing us up with the KPV. Therefore, we'll be throwing everything we have at it if it comes to a fight." The presence of the Russian KPV heavy machine gun had been terrible news. It fired 14.5mm armor-piercing rounds that could punch through *Kauai*'s light plating even from a quarter-mile away. There were worried looks and murmurs around the room before Sam continued. "I'll pause for questions before yielding to Chief Petty Officer Hopkins, who will brief the approach and egress."

There were no questions, and Hopkins replaced Sam at the podium and activated a projection showing Barbello harbor beside an overhead diagram of a ship. "Admiral, everyone, there is a single, narrow channel leading into the harbor just beyond this point of land to the north and shoals and islets to the south," she said, pointing at the display. "Moonset is at 00:56 local time, and we plan to pass through 'the gate,' as we call it, at 01:10. Once inside, as you can see, we have a large area of good water we can use to set up the approach. The *Carlos Rojas* is moored heading north along the quay as shown here, and we will approach from the southeast. As soon as we touch, Mr. Wyporek's boarding party and the DIA men will cross over. We will stay alongside until the towing hawser is passed and rigged to the vessel's anchor windlass here on the bow." She pointed at a co-projected diagram of the *Carlos Rojas*. "When Mr. Wyporek signals the vessel is unmoored, we will tow her eastward through the gate and turn north once we are out of weapons range of this point." She pointed at the small point of land making up the northern side of the gate. "We estimate twenty minutes in the ingress, fifteen to rig the tow and unmoor the vessel, and forty-five to fifty-five minutes to clear the gate. We will keep a short tow inside the harbor for better navigational control and keep us in range to provide suppressive fire on that point if needed." She looked at Pennington. "Any questions, Admiral?"

"None, thank you, Chief."

As Hopkins stepped aside and Ben took the podium. "Admiral, ladies and gentlemen, I will board the *Carlos Rojas* with three other men. We will be occupied with the towing hawser until we rig it. It weighs over ten pounds per linear foot and will need all of us to lift it to and through the bullnose in the bow. As soon as we rig the tow, I will lead a seaman along the ship's port side and throw off any mooring line or shore tie we encounter, leaving a man on the bow to stand by the hawser. Once the moorings are clear, we will move to the Bridge and stay there throughout the exfil. We will be armed with carbines and suppressed pistols for self-defense, but we will be occupied and unable to aid in *Carlos Rojas*'s seizure. Once the tow is stabilized, we can contribute to the vessel's defense, but I must stay on the Bridge. Do you have questions, Admiral?"

"No, thank you, Lieutenant."

"Sir. Anyone else? OK, Lieutenant Davis?" *Kauai*'s personnel sat as Davis, the navy SEAL officer, stood and took the podium.

"Admiral, ladies, gentlemen, I have a nine-man detachment loading up at Virginia Beach as we speak. They will fly to Barbello and execute a jump into the water west of the island at 01:45 tomorrow morning. They will rendezvous with the DEA man on the scene and execute a covert reconnaissance of the harbor facilities and opposing forces over the day and evening. At or around 00:45 on the 6th, they will take the *Carlos Rojas* by force, secure the vessel and the adjoining quay, and await *Kauai*'s arrival. My men will signal the Rivet Joint aircraft when the target has been secured. If practicable, they will sabotage the power to the lighting on the quay in the ship's vicinity. That one they must play by ear—if they can't make it look like an ordinary failure, it may tip off the enemy to the assault later. After departing the quay, they will rig explosive charges at key points in the hull to ensure the ship's rapid scuttling. They will then prepare fortified positions along the port side in case there is a firefight on the way out. Do you have questions, Admiral?"

"No questions, thank you, Lieutenant."

"Sir," he said, sitting down.

"Captain Landry?" Pennington said.

The air force electronics specialist got to her feet and took the podium. "Yes, sir. Admiral, Chief, and gentlemen, the Rivet Joint aircraft has been conducting electronic surveillance in international airspace just east of Barbello for the past two nights. We collected enough data to identify every emitter on the island and establish a pattern of life. We will revisit tonight to look for any changes. During the assault, the aircraft will carry Lieutenant Davis, who will oversee the ground forces until *Kauai*'s arrival. We can jam every communications device on that island. Still, I recommend holding off on that capability until the SEAL assault is underway to avoid premature disclosure. We will transmit updates on request starting at midnight on the 6th and stay thirty minutes after *Kauai*'s departure to watch for any pursuit.

"The downside is we have forecasted weather in the area that will negate the MQ-9—it can't handle the wind shears at low level and won't be of much use up high. So, no EO/IR or close support will be available. Do you have questions of me, Admiral?"

"No. Thank you, Captain."

"You are welcome, sir. I will hand off to Captain Fergus for the weather brief." The other air force captain stood, made his way to the podium, and switched the display to a meteorological map as Landry returned to her seat.

"Admiral, ladies, and gentlemen, as Captain Landry pointed out, we have a low-pressure area moving over the Northwestern Caribbean that will generate unstable air across the region. This pattern is very unusual for the season—it's usually dry there. I am forecasting persistent scattered cumulonimbus cells throughout the area, moving east to west for the operational period's duration, with lightning and locally heavy rain and wind. The storms' scattered nature and general lack of prevailing winds should result in calm to light seas in the area. Are there questions?"

Sam stood. "Admiral, I have a question." At Pennington's nod, he continued. "Can we predict when a cell might come over the island, Captain?"

"Perhaps thirty to forty-five minutes beforehand, no earlier," Fergus replied.

"What are you thinking, Lieutenant?" Pennington asked.

"Sir, these storms could help or hurt us. If I can ride in and out during one of them, that would be an immense advantage remaining covert, assuming we aren't struck by lightning." He paused as the attendees chuckled. "On the other hand, they might see us coming in with no rain and lightning strobing. I recommend we keep a little flexibility in the timetable in case we have an opportunity or hazard to deal with. Can you support that, Mr. Davis?"

"While I am in contact with the ground force, there should not be a problem."

"Good," Sam said and turned to Pennington. "Sir, with your permission, we'll keep flexible in terms of the timetable."

"Granted. That's good thinking." After Sam and Fergus sat, Pennington turned to Bartlett, the DEA man. "Agent Bartlett?"

Bartlett stood in place and said, "Thank you, Admiral. Folks, we have a man undercover on Barbello named Dominguez. He's not deep in the gang, just posing as a mechanic among the day workers they employ. I expect to hear from him in a few hours for a regular check-in, during which I'll brief him to expect the SEALs and prepare for their arrival. I want him to come off with your guys, Lieutenant," he said to Davis. "Once you snatch that ship, there's no way to predict the gang's reaction, and I don't want him around then."

"We'll get him off with us, sir," Davis replied.

"Good. Now let me tell you about the Salinas gang. It's more of a cult, with its own death-worship features that make MS-13, Al Qaeda, and ISIS look like a church choir by comparison. They recruit young boys from the barrios of Honduras and Guatemala and brainwash them with some truly vile initiation rituals or kill them in the process. Lieutenant Powell asked earlier about rules of engagement. If you encounter someone carrying a gun on Barbello, that is a Salinas soldier. He may be as young as fourteen, but rest assured, that meeting will end with one of you being killed. Make sure it's him." He paused to let that grim thought sink in before continuing. "Questions?" After waiting to scan all the participants, he said, "Thank you, Admiral," then sat.

Pennington scanned the room. "Does anyone have anything to add?" After pausing briefly, he continued. "Folks, I think we have the best plan available under the circumstances. I want to emphasize that once on the scene, I expect you to evaluate the situation and adjust, if needed, according to your best judgment. Do what you think is necessary to carry out the primary mission and get your people home. You have my full trust and support, come what may. I will be in my office if any of you need me. I wish you good luck and a safe return." As he rose, the other attendees came to their feet, with the military people coming to attention. "Carry on, thank you, everybody." He then turned and left the room.

After Pennington departed, Sam turned to Ben and said, "Number One, I'll leave you to link up with our DIA friend. Find out about this other guy he's bringing along and what sort of handling arrangements they need for the thermite. The only thing I know about it is that I don't want it anywhere inside the ship."

"Yes, sir," Ben responded. After Sam and Hopkins left, Ben walked over to Simmons. "Good to see you again, Pete." He shook Simmons's hand.

"Same here, Ben." He glanced toward the door. "I perceive I'm still *persona non grata* among your shipmates?"

"I'm afraid so. Don't worry; they won't let it impede the mission." When Simmons looked back in his direction, he continued. "I need to ask you who you are bringing along. We don't have any bona fides on him."

"You will shortly. His name is Billy, William Gerard. He was around during the Resolution op, but you guys didn't meet up. He's solid as they come."

"Good to hear. So how did you get mixed up in this particular mess?"

"After Resolution, I went back to my actual job—poking the 252s in the eye. I found they were stirring up trouble in Colombia, grabbing up such large amounts of cocaine that their vendor was getting out of the box the government likes those people to stay inside. So, I called in Victoria the Data Jedi, re-tasked some satellite surveillance effort, and *voila*! I have a nice, tight target package I can bring to the Colombians. They run a raid and end up clobbering the 252's vendor. Good news, right?

"Well, because the Law of Unintended Consequences must be obeyed, this sent the local 252 knothead scurrying for another vendor. His choice of the Salinas mob would have been serendipitous had it not been for the fact the boat he lost to them was carrying a particularly nasty WMD. Said knothead legged it when he realized he was holding the bag for a colossal foul-up and came to Miami to turn himself in to the FBI. We spotted him at the airport, tailed him to his hotel, and grabbed him before he could get tangled up with Hoover's boys."

"Not exactly good form."

"Perhaps not, but if he had turned himself into them, they'd still be processing the paperwork just to talk to him. Besides, TCOs like the 252s are in our lane, not FBI or CIA's."

"OK. One other question. I was a little surprised there was no discussion of protective equipment, you know, suits and respirators. Won't we need that if this thing gets loose?"

Simmons frowned as he looked back. "You don't want to be wearing that when we assault. You'd get tagged by even the dumbest Salinas goon because you'd never be able to see him or hear him. Besides, with this thing, all the MOPP gear and atropine in the world won't help you. The good news is it will be quick—one whiff will stop your heart within five seconds."

Ben swallowed hard. He had been worried about getting shot, but the possibility of dying from a chemical agent filled him with horror. He had a taste of being on the receiving end of a chemical attack at Resolution when he was hit with a paralytic agent employed by the 252s. Simmons had saved him with the antidote, but Ben still had nightmares from the experience. It was an effort to keep his voice steady.

"Right. We shove off at 18:00. I need you guys on board and settled in by 17:30, but don't show up before 17:00. It will take time to prepare the ground with Sam."

"Understood. See you at 17:00!"

"Can't wait," Ben said, turning to the door for the short walk back to *Kauai*. On the way, he came to terms with his fear. *Dead is dead, whether it's from a bullet or a gas. At least this one kills quickly.*

Once in his room, he stared longingly at Victoria's picture and considered calling her for one last chat before the mission, but it was too early in the day. She could not bring her cell phone into the office because of security concerns, and he didn't want to put her on the spot by calling on her office line. Besides, the timing would trigger a lot of questions from her. He did not want to get her on the phone, upsetting her routine, and then dump a load of "sorry, can't tell you" answers on her. Ben knew it was the right thing to do, but he was still down that it would be at least two, perhaps three, days before he could hear her voice again. He compromised and sent her a text message. "V, going offline for a few days, but thinking of U as always. Pls set aside Apr 12–16 for me. Can't wait to see U again. B." He then shut off the phone, locked it in his desk, and left for pre-sail preparations on the Bridge.

Gaze Long into the Abyss

Isla de Barbello, Honduras
16:03 EDT, 4 April

Dominguez

Jorge Dominguez walked carefully through the heavily forested hills above the harbor. The trail he had set up was a compromise between something he could remember and follow in most daylight conditions and one that his "associates" would be unlikely to stumble across or be able to follow to his storage place. The man knew what would happen then: they would kill him. In that case, the only question would be whether it would be a merciful bullet in the back of his head or a matter of him joining the ranks of the *No Consagrado*, the poor wretches crucified and left to die of thirst outside the main hacienda. He was sure it would be the latter—as an undercover agent of the U.S. Drug Enforcement Agency, he would be considered among the most unholy by the Salinas leaders.

The trail led to a hidden cache of weapons, ammunition, MREs, satellite phones, and spare batteries. This store was his last line of defense if things went wrong. Hide out, call in the cavalry, survive. It was also a link to the real world. Once per week, if practicable, his orders were to call in and report his status. It was not the usual procedure for a UC, but the Salinas Cartel was new, deep, and dark, and his bosses needed as much current information as possible about them and their new stronghold on Barbello. In his earlier days, he would have been infuriated by this "management" level and its risks. Now Dominguez was nonchalant about the dangers, almost bordering on indifference. He had been in the field too long and had seen too many horrors in his UC assignments. So much so that this pack of animals' depredations could not make much of an impression.

Dominguez should have rotated out of the field more than a year ago. Still, he had remarkable skills with language and was a genius as an engine mechanic—always a marketable skill to drug gangs in need of reliable transport. These factors meant he could always work his way into the targeted gang, and he was just too valuable to spare. Now, however, even his controls at the agency could see that he was pushing over the edge. Dominguez had the DEA equivalent of combat fatigue, and, like the military version, it could only lead to mistakes that endangered his life. Or worse. His supervisors had decided. Although he didn't know it yet, Barbello would be Dominguez's last field assignment, and it would end soon.

Dominguez stopped suddenly and turned. He could have sworn he heard something, a rustle of the grass. Although he was probably hearing things, he opted for safety. He turned right off the trail on the next viable path and picked up the pace. When he was sure he was out of sight of anyone who could follow, he broke into a trot, veered left into a cul-de-sac in the jungle, and concealed himself, looking and listening.

After about twenty minutes of sitting in silence, Dominguez shook his head. *OK, I guess you've been paranoid enough this day.* He stood up and started retracing his path to the trail. After a few minutes trek, he regained the main trail and turned to follow it to the end. After another ten minutes, he reached the cache and booted up one of the satellite phones. He made a satellite link and, after a brief delay, established a connection with his boss and executed the usual security kabuki.

"Dom! I'm relieved to hear your voice. How are things there?"

"Mostly same-old/same-old, but we had some excitement a few days ago when my masters went Barbary Pirates on one of their customers."

"That was one thing I wanted to talk to you about. Tell me what you know."

"Well, this offshore oil service boat pulled in, there was some shooting, a few bodies dropped, and a couple of fresh faces showed up on the crucifix field. My masters sent me on board to disable the main engines so that no one would get any ideas. That night, the local *jefe* announced that the boat owners had disrespected the Salinas's holy order and been assessed for tribute. It serves the damn fools right, sailing into a bottle like this. You need me back on board to get eyes on the inside?"

"No. We can't risk you right now. Dom, we're pulling you off this one."

"What? Do you know what it took me to get in here? What the hell, man?"

"I know, I know. The thing is, the Salinas cartel just poked the bear and is about to be crushed. When it's done, we don't expect to see anyone left alive on Barbello. So, you are coming off. You said you disabled the engines on that boat. Is that permanently disabled, or can you fix them?"

"I just took out the control cabling for the starters. I can have them up and running again in twenty minutes."

"Good, good. We are sending in some sailors to take that boat out of the harbor, and they'll need your help to get it running. They'll also need the latest on forces and dispositions. Do you have a suitable spot picked out where you can hole up and observe?"

SEALs? Shit, what the hell is on that boat? "Naturally. When should I expect company?"

"About 02:00 tomorrow morning. They'll drop in the drink and come ashore on the island's west side. I need you to set up a rendezvous point and safe approach to the harbor. Call me when you have that. You'll remain with them once they arrive and give them whatever help they need. Questions?"

"No," Dominguez replied, his bitterness plain.

"Don't take this wrong, Dom. This operation comes right from the top, and you're a critical part. We need you to stay clear and stay safe from here on out. No contact or reconnoitering on your own, clear?"

"Got it." Dominguez shook his head. What the hell was the matter with him? This was good news—he was to be pulled out of hell on earth, and he wasn't leaving a job undone. "I'll call you in two or three hours once I scout the west beach."

"Roger that. Stay out of trouble until then."

"Will do. Talk to you soon. Out." He had just turned off the phone when he froze at the sound of a soft crack behind him. Someone had stepped on a fallen palm branch and snapped it. Pretending not to hear, he put the phone back into the storage bin, extracted a silenced Glock, quietly inserted a magazine, and chambered a round. Keeping the gun out of sight, he locked the container, then walked a short distance away from the sound's direction and crouched where he could monitor the cache site unseen. After about five minutes, a figure emerged from the brush and walked over to the site, moving slowly with his head swiveling, looking for the owner. Satisfied, he kneeled to examine and try the lock.

Dominguez recognized the visitor. He was one of the adolescents recruited, or sometimes snatched, from the barrios of Honduras and Guatemala as small boys and brought up within the Salinas gang's brutal faith. Basically, it was a twenty-first-century version of the Hitler Youth, only much worse. Those of average intelligence furnished the muscle and fodder for gang operations, while the smart ones were refined and groomed to enter the gang's leadership. This was not one of the smart ones.

Moving quietly, Dominguez stole behind the youth undetected, bringing the gun up and sighting it on the back of his head. *Do it! One less monster in the world. It's not like you have a choice!* His hands began shaking, and he realized he couldn't just shoot the young man, not like this. He lowered the gun and said, "*Hola, amigo.* What are you doing here?" The youth startled and stood, drawing a large bowie knife from his belt. Dominguez fought the urge to laugh when the thought of "bringing a knife to a gunfight" flashed across his mind.

"I saw you! I heard you, *traidor*! *Espía*! I'll see you dead today!"

"Alright, let's pause and think a bit. I have a pistol; you have a knife. If I die today, you won't live to see it." He paused, seeing the youth's jaw working, his eyes darting, looking for some advantage. "Come on. Put the knife down. I give you my word, short incarceration. Then I'll let you go unharmed." He pressed

that point. "Come on, son. There is nothing here worth dying for."
The youth's eyes widened, and a snarl curled his mouth. *Oh, shit!*

"I AM NOT YOUR SON!" He charged Dominguez and took two
shots in the center of his chest before falling on his face well short
of his quarry.

Dominguez stepped forward carefully, his gun sighted on the
fallen young man while checking his pulse. Nothing. Dominguez
sat down heavily and stared at the body for a full five minutes. It
wasn't the first time he had killed an opponent, but the futility of
the youth's attack troubled him more than any earlier time. *Why?
Why did you do that, kid? What did you think you would
accomplish?* He finally shook himself out of his stupor and
reopened the storage case. He retrieved a couple of phones,
batteries, water bottles, and a few magazines for the pistol and
placed them in a shoulder bag. After locking up the case, he
walked over, picked up the body, and slung it over his shoulder—
he would drop it off in the jungle en route to the western beach.
*I'm sorry, kid, you got a shit deal and deserve a decent burial, but
this thing is bigger than either of us.* He moved off down a trail
he had scouted leading west.

Two hours later, Dominguez reached the island's western side
and found a stretch of beach reasonably free of rocks suitable for
the SEALs to come ashore. He scouted out a good hideout and
made notes of the trail leading down so they could make their way
back in darkness early the next morning. Once he had set
everything up, he called in again on the satellite phone.

"Dom, good to hear from you. What have you got?"

"I have a nice, isolated beach, a solid trail leading east, and a
suitable spot to lie up for the day tomorrow. I have the lat-long
when you're ready to copy."

"Sweet. Send it, please." After Dominguez had provided the
coordinates, his boss continued. "OK, the master plan is still
coalescing right now, but the basic gist is that you will help the
SEALs get on board and then fix the engines."

"Um, you know, as soon as we start an engine, they'll be on us
like flies on shit. It'll be Little Bighorn II."

"I'm told that will be taken care of. I'm sorry to be so cryptic, but you need to take it on faith that we will get you guys out of there."

"OK. Still on for oh-two-hundred?"

"Yep. Just lie low until 01:45, then turn on your beacon. The visitors will have Blue Force Trackers and will contact you. Authentication combo is Stake-Tent."

"Got it. Anything else?"

"No. Stay safe, and I'll see you when you get back. Out."

"Roger that." He switched off the phone. *God willing.*

USCG Cutter *Kauai*, Florida Straits, twenty nautical miles southwest of Key West, Florida
18:58 EDT, 4 April

Ben

Kauai cleared the harbor of Key West and passed the sea buoy about thirty minutes previously. Sam had called for a meeting of the dozen crew not on watch and the embarked army personnel on the open afterdeck at 19:00. He usually held meetings on the messdeck, where people could sit comfortably, but there were far too many attendees today.

Rumors were flying through since they started heading southwest after clearing the sea buoy instead of the expected easterly course back to the homeport of Port Canaveral, Florida. Sam chafed under the need to keep their mission a secret and was eager to brief the crew on those aspects he could share. As the appointed hour approached, Drake gathered the crew into ranks and settled the army personnel to the side. When Sam stepped out onto the afterdeck with Ben a step behind, Drake shouted, "Attention on Deck!" The crew came to attention, and when Sam halted before them, Drake saluted and said, "Crew present or accounted for, sir."

After he and Ben returned the salute, Sam said, "Thank you, Chief. Fall out and gather 'round everybody!" Sam continued as the crew formed a semicircle in front of the officers. "I'm sure most of you have heard that we will take the scenic route back to Port Canaveral. I wanted to get you the good news that the Coast Guard is providing this special Caribbean holiday completely free!" He waited for the laughing to subside and then continued. "More on that later. Right now, we have some important business to attend to. Seaman Juan Lopez, front and center!" Lopez stepped forward and came to attention. "Carry on, please. Everybody, I'm pleased to announce that we have a brand-new Maritime Law Enforcement Specialist School graduate in our midst. Congratulations, Seaman Lopez!" Sam led the crew in applause and held up his hand after a few seconds. "As the TV commercial says: But wait! There's more! Normally, when someone goes to A-school from a patrol boat, they move on to another unit on graduation. We are lucky enough to get Lope back with us, but he seems to be out of uniform!" Sam smiled at Lopez's concerned look and said, "Chief Drake, would you assist me, please?"

"With pleasure, Captain," Drake said as Ben handed him and Sam each a third-class petty officer's collar insignia.

After the two men had pinned them on Lopez's collar, they stepped back, and Sam announced. "Crew of *Kauai*, I have the pleasure of presenting Maritime Law Enforcement Specialist Third Class Juan Lopez!" He stepped forward and shook Lopez's hand as the crew cheered and pounded his back. After allowing a few minutes for congratulations, Sam raised his hand, and the crew went silent and stepped forward.

"OK, folks, that was the fun part. Now, I'm going to fill you in on what we will be doing for the next few days. I know some of you wondered why our trip to AUTEC was cut short and what the hell a two-star admiral was doing riding with us to Key West. I'm sure you also recognized our old friend Dr. Simmons when he came aboard, and those of you who surmised that meant we are going into action are correct." He paused for a few murmurs, then raised his hand again.

"We are heading down through the Yucatan Channel to an island off the coast of Honduras called Barbello. Now that place is the stronghold for a drug gang called the Salinas Cartel. They have seized an offshore supply vessel from another criminal organization and are holding it for ransom. I know your first reaction is the same as mine: 'who cares?' Unfortunately, that OSV is also carrying a weapon of mass destruction, and we cannot let that go. So, tomorrow night we'll sneak in under battery power, hook up a towing hawser, and tow that boat out of there. Once we clear the harbor, we'll either tow or escort the boat up to the deep water north of the island and scuttle her." Once more, there were murmurs, and Sam paused briefly before raising his hand.

"Now, obviously, the Salinas gang might have some objections to our planned activities, but you'll be happy to know that we have a team of Navy SEALs on their way down there right now. They will take the boat and enough pier space for us to do our job without raising the alarm. The tricky part will come on the way out, as the only usable channel comes within five hundred yards of a promontory the Salinas gang has fortified. If we're lucky, we'll slip past them in the dark. But even if we're not lucky and they spot us, we have enough firepower between our twenty-five-millimeter and fifty-caliber and the SEAL's weapons to muscle our way through. While I'm confident we'll get through without casualties, we are shipping an army combat medical unit with us, just in case." He looked over to the army personnel and said, "Everyone, this is Major Roberts, combat surgeon and specialists Langley and Rabin, who will live on our messdeck for the trip. Please do your best to welcome them aboard and help them as needed. Now, does anyone have questions?" There were more indistinct murmurs, but no one stepped up.

"OK, thank you all. If I were a gambler, Petty Officer Lopez, I'd bet you wish you were back in Charleston sucking down beers at your graduation party right now!"

"You'd lose that bet, sir!" Lopez replied with a smile, generating a fresh round of laughter.

"Happy to hear that!" Sam nodded with a smile. "OK, one last thing. Dr. Simmons brought a specialist with him to help find and deal with that WMD aboard the boat. Much of what they do is super-secret, so any conversation with them is likely to be uncomfortable for everyone. By mutual agreement, we will suspend our normally friendly and hospitable behavior in their case. Just don't talk with them and keep your distance. Any other questions? OK, since this will be a night job and in honor of our new petty officer, *Kauai* will be on holiday routine until tomorrow at midnight. Get all the sleep you can when you're not on watch." He turned to Drake. "That's all, Chief."

Drake said, "Yes, sir. Attention on Deck!" Then rendered a salute as the crew came to attention.

Sam and Ben returned the salute, and then Sam said, "Thank you, Chief. Carry on, please." He and Ben then turned and left as the crew drifted over to talk with Lopez and the army personnel. As they walked forward, Sam said, "The same goes for you, Number One. I want you well-rested for tomorrow night. Lay off whenever you can."

"Yes, sir." They stopped before the entry door, and Sam looked back at the afterdeck in grim silence. After a moment, Ben said, "It will be all right, Captain. We all knew what we were signing on for."

"Yes." Sam nodded. "Yes." Then he turned and went inside, Ben a step behind.

4527 Sangamore Road, Apt. B23, Bethesda, Maryland 21:06 EDT, 4 April

Victoria

Victoria shut down her PC and then looked at Benjamin's text again. "Can't wait to see U again." She was disappointed when she read it after picking up her phone outside the office on the way home. He had only sent the message half an hour before, and she called back at once, hoping to catch him before he left. The call rolled over to voice mail, and she hung up immediately—she could not risk leaving a foolish-sounding message she could not erase. It worried her all the way home that Benjamin would see the missed call without a voice mail and wonder what was wrong with her. She sat down as soon as she got home and laboriously composed a reply. This was important, and she had to be sure not to make any mistakes. "Benjamin, I will request leave for 12-16 April. I tried to call you back without success. I will miss talking to you. Please call me as soon as it is convenient. Victoria." She had initially put "as soon as you can," then "as soon as you return," before settling on the needy-neutral version she sent.

Regardless of the message, she observed the nightly ritual at her desk. There was always a chance of a change allowing Benjamin to call, and she needed to be able to answer. Regardless, the pictures and her eidetic replay of the events of their two dates were comforting for her.

Isla de Barbello, Honduras
02:16 EDT, 5 April

Dominguez

Dominguez was startled when he heard the click of a weapon safety coming from the water's direction. "Stake!"

"Tent!" came the reply, and nine figures rose from the surf and waded ashore carrying equipment.

Dominguez walked to meet them. "Howdy, boys. The name's Dominguez, but you can call me Dom."

The leader shook his hand. "Glad to meet you. Senior Chief D'Agostino, plus eight. Give us a minute to get into traveling gear. How far to the observation point?"

"Two-and-a-half, three hours, tops. But it's a little tricky in total darkness."

"Not an issue for us. Have you ever used the ANVS-9 night vision goggles?"

"Nope."

"Parker here will hook you up."

The junior petty officer extracted a spare set of goggles and harness and fitted the device to Dominguez's head. The capability was startling to the agent, who had only used hand-held scopes before. "This is amazing!" he whispered.

"Take it easy, small steps, and let one of us lead. You call the trail. The resolution is pretty good, but your depth perception will stink, so be careful," D'Agostino said. "OK, we're ready to move.

Parker will lead; you keep your hand on his shoulder and tell him where to go."

The party of ten set off quietly, with Dominguez calling the turns in a whisper. It was almost dawn when they pulled up on Dominguez's cache hideout. After shedding their goggles, the team made their way through the jungle to the ridge overlooking the harbor and took cover. D'Agostino sent two groups of three men each to the opposite ends of the ridge to hunker down and observe. He turned to Dominguez. "Tell me about the boat."

"Pulled in four days ago, looking for an on-load. As soon as she was tied up with the engines shut down, the Salinas hitters boarded and capped all the guards and about half the crew. The other half they strung up on crucifixes outside the main hacienda."

"Dead?"

"Unfortunately for them, no. They will be soon, though."

"Shit!"

"Yeah, that's the word. There are two left onboard still alive, and I think they're passengers or sponsors or some damn thing the *Jefe* thinks can bring in some money. You guys here to rescue them?"

"Nope. Couldn't give a rat's ass if they live or die. There's something on the boat that means we have to sink it and sink it in deep water."

"Wow. What is it, some sort of weapon of mass destruction? I didn't see anything unusual when I was on there."

"Brother, all I know is that we take that boat, wait for one of ours to tow it out of here, and then sink it into the Cayman Trench."

"They're crazy! They bring a tugboat there, and it will wake up every Salinas hood on the island. I've seen their armory—they have enough RPGs to blow a damn Aegis Cruiser out of the water. A tugboat won't get to first base!"

"It won't be a conventional tugboat. All I know is it will be quiet, almost invisible at night, and it will tow us out. They catch on to us, and we'll light off the engine and fight our way out. That boat and whatever's on it needs to be destroyed. I understand you disabled the engines. How long to get them running?"

"Fifteen minutes, twenty tops."

D'Agostino nodded. "That should do. Now tell me about the lights on the pier and where they get their power."

The Gift of the Magi

**USCG Cutter *Kauai*, Yucatan Channel, thirty nautical miles southwest of Cape San Antonio, Cuba
11:48 EDT, 5 April**

Ben

"I relieve you, sir," Lee said as she rendered a crisp salute.

"I stand relieved," Ben replied. "On the Bridge, Petty Officer Lee has the Deck and Conn!"

"Aye!" replied everyone on the Bridge.

Ben turned back to Lee, now taking a visual sweep of the horizon with the OOD binoculars. Something was off that he could not quite put his finger on. "Are you OK, Shelley?" he whispered.

Lee, startled, turned to look at him and hesitated briefly before whispering back. "Um, I'm a little worried about tonight, XO."

"Just a little? I envy you. What are you worried about?"

She looked down again. "I've never been a towmaster before, sir. I mean, I've done a few tows of sailboats or pleasure craft, but nothing this big or important. If I screw it up, that's the ballgame." She looked up at Ben with an anxious expression.

Ben smiled back. "I have some worries too, and your role in this is definitely not among those. In fact, knowing you'll be the one setting up and tending to the towline that will save my ass is a considerable comfort to me."

"No shit?"

"No shit. You'll do fine. We'll all get through this." He leaned in with a broad grin. "I have too many 'blue' jokes left for anything bad to happen."

Lee rolled her eyes and smiled. "Well, when you put it that way...." She nodded again. "Thanks, XO."

"You're welcome. Have a nice watch, and I'll see you later."

Ben stepped over to stand beside Sam, saluted, and said, "Captain, I've been relieved by Petty Officer Lee. Request permission to lay below for lunch."

Sam stood and returned the salute. "Very well, thank you. Can I keep you company?"

"My pleasure, sir."

"Right." He turned and headed down, with Ben following. Once they were off the Bridge, he said over his shoulder, "Everything OK with Lee?"

"No worries, Captain."

"Good. No sign of a reprieve, I'm afraid. How's it going with your team?"

"As well as it can be, sir. We've studied the latest pictures, what-if-ed, and talked everything pretty much to death. I finally think I've pried the smile off Lopez's face with the reality of it."

"You're not bringing him along to talk down any Salinas guys, I hope. If so, I'll be happy to re-clarify the rules of engagement for you."

"No, sir, but some crew might be left alive, and my Spanish just isn't up to it."

"OK, good thinking." Sam nodded as they stepped onto the messdeck. Regular cooking was out of the question with the crowd of visitors aboard *Kauai*, so Sam and Ben raided the freezer for microwave meals. Ben looked around as they waited. The two army specialists were working on setting up an autoclave in the corner. Jenkins was sitting at one table chatting with Bondurant over a meal, and Gerard and Simmons were sitting in silence at the other. Sam and Ben moved over to the table with the boatswain's mates when their meals were cooked, Sam waving his hand as the two petty officers moved to stand. "Relax, guys."

"Thank you, sir," Bondurant replied. "Anything new?"

"Nope. Still heading south, no change in plans," Sam said as he opened his meal. "The SEALs are on the island now. At least we know that much."

"That puts things in perspective," Bondurant said. "Don't know if I could jump into a nest of armed psychos hoping someone would sneak in and pick me up."

After that preamble, the conversation was mainly light with a discussion of kids, the latest basketball news, and the new baseball season's start. By unspoken agreement, anything but what awaited them that night. After working through the meal, Ben excused himself and headed for his stateroom. In the passageway, he saw Hopkins and called out, "Hey, Chief, got time for a question?"

"Yes, sir."

After they stepped into his stateroom, he asked, "I noticed Williams, Zuccaro, and Bunting seem to be on an odd schedule with the FC3 watch. Anything I should know about?"

"No, sir, nothing you need to know about officially."

"OK, I'm officially not listening. Now, what's up?"

"I'm trying to keep Natalia and Shelley from standing watch together."

Ben frowned and said, "Um...."

"Relax, XO, it's nothing like that. Shelley found out Natalia was getting ogly-eyed with Joe while she was up north, and they had words. There are still hard feelings, and I'm trying to keep them undistracted while on watch, which translates to they shouldn't be on watch together. I put a stop to ogly-eyeing after Natalia tried it on you when you got back. Fortunately, you were impervious to her attempt."

"More like oblivious. What the hell does ogly-eyed mean? I'll bet there's no such word."

"Is so! It's been about ten years for me, but allow me to demonstrate." Hopkins took off her glasses, opened her eyes wide, looked at him from the side, tilted her head, and said in a throaty voice, "Oh, sir! You just *slayed* those drug guys. I would have been *soooo* scared." She batted her eyelashes at the last sentence, then put her glasses back on and resumed her expressionless look. "Ogly-eyed. Got it?"

"Got it. Wow, I must have been wicked tired. I don't remember anything like that."

"She was more subtle. I was exaggerating for demonstration purposes. Anyway, Shelley's still mad, though no longer homicidal, and I'm just trying to keep the temperature down. Welcome to chief stuff, sir."

"Actually, it's a relief to know that normal life is still happening. Joe and Shelley? How long has that been going on?"

"Sir, you are just adorable, you know that? Try about a year. And again, no need for you to worry. Nothing physical is happening on the boat. COB and I made it clear to both of them that we would kill them if they crossed that line."

"Does the captain know about this?"

"Nope. You need to tell him?"

"Not as long as it stays like this. Any change and I need to get the word, please."

"Naturally, sir. The chiefs of *Kauai* will always ensure the officers know everything they need to know." She winked.

Doing his best imitation of Hopkins's ogly-eyed shtick, Ben said, "Oh *Chief,* you and COB are just *soooo* Mom and Dad!"

Hopkins smiled and shook a finger at him. "Now, careful, sir. You know I can straighten out commissioned officers just as thoroughly as third-class petty officers!"

Ben laughed. "That I do. Thanks, Chief." As she turned and walked away, Ben recalled the respectful but scathing dressing down she had given him for not putting a stop to Simmons's recklessness during their last encounter. Although Sam never spoke to him about it, Hopkins had made it clear that Ben had put their lives and careers in danger. It was a turning point for Ben in his view of personal responsibility.

Simmons appeared at the end of the passageway, and as they passed, Hopkins delivered a cold nod. "Doctor."

"Chief," Simmons replied with a smile.

When he reached Ben's door, he said, "Can we have a private chat, please?"

"Come in," Ben replied. Simmons shut the door, and they sat in the cramped room.

"Brrrrr. I guess I have a way to go before I get on her good side."

"A man's reach should exceed his grasp, or what's a heaven for?"

"Browning, no less. Well played, sir!" Simmons smiled, then leaned forward. "You looked worried yesterday. We're pretty well supported on the ground this time."

"Shit, ya! If that KPV gets into the game, it will cut us to pieces. Where in the hell did a bunch of looney dopers lay their hands on ordnance like that?"

"Bought it in Nicaragua, probably. A nice leftover from the Sandinista days. Everyone's a capitalist now." He looked at the pictures on the bulkhead over Ben's shoulder. "I'd like to continue on a more personal note, if you don't mind."

"Personal? I wonder what that could be about," Ben said with a raised eyebrow.

"I think you know."

"Well, I think your worries about Victoria were unfounded. I'm a goner for her, but it's not mutual. We have built a strong friendship, but that's it, as far as she's concerned."

"Is that what she told you?"

"No, I didn't ask her straight out, but she's an open book. If she felt something beyond that, she'd tell me. She doesn't hold back on anything. I was going to take leave to pitch my case with her when we got back from AUTEC, but then we got assigned to this op, and I'm having second thoughts."

"Why? You love her, right? That's what you mean by goner, isn't it?"

"Yes, but it's complicated."

"Complicated? With Victoria? She's the most straightforward person I've ever known. You've told me yourself you could talk to her about anything. Explain, please."

"It's because of this," Ben said, sweeping around with his right arm. "I don't mind telling you, I'm damned scared about what we're going into tonight, but I wouldn't even think about being anywhere else when my family here is heading for a fight. And this won't be our last one. Captain Mercier made that clear when she put the question to us—we're the go-to guys for 'dangerously light footprint,' as the admiral put it. You told me Victoria doesn't take loss well. How can I lay something like that on her and then run off whenever there's a call?"

"I think you misinterpreted what I said. Victoria's bad experiences were because of being discarded, not from a loss. Let me explain: her last emotional attachment was one of the analysts in another office up in Bethesda who thought he was God's gift to women. He wanted to have his cake and eat it with her—when she told him she was in love with him, he told her she was 'too clingy' and dumped her. Can you imagine what that did to her?"

"Bastard!"

"Indeed. It gets worse. He had the nerve to hit on her again after she recovered, intimating that 'word might get around' about her if she didn't consent."

"Is he still alive?" Ben asked in complete seriousness.

"Yes, but after I learned of it, well, let's just say Lashon and I paid him a visit at his apartment. He became convinced that he would end up doing a federal prison term in a wheelchair if he continued to pursue anything like that course of action. Being hung upside-down by your ankles off your sixth-floor balcony by Lashon Bell can really focus your attention."

Ben nodded. Bell was a former U.S. Marine Recon Sergeant and one of the DIA team present when Ben had first met Victoria. The day after that meeting, he single-handedly tackled and captured a 252 fugitive after being shot twice. You did not want to get on the wrong side of Lashon Bell.

"So, you can see the difference between the risks associated with your job and what that scumbag did. Let me ask you this. If the roles were reversed and Victoria had a dangerous job, would you want to be with her?"

"Yes."

"Even if it meant she might not come back one day? You could accept that loss?"

"It would kill me, but yes. I would take that risk to be with her, even if it was only for a while."

"Then how can you justify taking that choice away from her?"

Ben looked at Simmons intently. "That's not the choice. The choice is whether I want to win her over. To make her need me and then not be there when she does."

Simmons put on an icy scowl. "Wow, you really are a *noble* son of a bitch, aren't you? You could flip on your charm and have her fall at your feet anytime, but you want to spare her poor little broken heart when you strap on that body armor and sail away. What an *awesome* guy you are!"

"Screw you!"

"You need to get over yourself, boy. Do you think you can manipulate her like that? Why? Because she is not 'neurotypical?' Do you think so little of her?"

Ben was shocked into silence. Simmons had just held up a mirror, and Ben was ashamed of what he saw. "No, I don't think that. The fact is that I've gone from being worried about hurting her to worrying that she might have passed me by because I didn't reach out."

Simmons's face softened into a smile. "Now there's the Ben I remember. Sorry, friend, but I needed to show you that you are overthinking things. She needs to know how you feel, and she needs to hear it from you. And you don't need to worry about her passing you by."

"Thank you for saying that, but I have a tough road ahead. Victoria would have told me if she felt that way, and she hasn't."

"I wouldn't be so sure of that if I were you."

"What are you telling me?"

"That you should not conclude she is not in love with you. She's not a robot, you know. There are some things even she would hold back." He glanced at the picture on the bulkhead. "That picture of you two together on the Mall in DC—how did you feel about her when it was taken?"

"That was the day that removed any doubts for me."

"I see the same thing in her face. It's not wishful thinking. Look at the picture!"

"But if that were true, why doesn't she tell me? She shares everything else, good and bad."

"Think of what happened the last time she told someone she loved him."

"She can't think I would do *that!*"

"No, no, I'm sure she knows you would let her down kindly if you didn't feel the same. But you must see her dilemma: she would be afraid of driving you away if she led the disclosure. And she *does* feel something for you." He pointed at the DC Mall picture. "I have it on good authority that she had that picture on her desk at work for a time, and then she took it home because it was too distracting for her to work." He shook his head, still smiling. "I think we have two people in love with each other but afraid they'll drive the other away if they admit it. Remarkable."

"I am glad you're so amused, Obi-Wan," Ben said with a frown. "Can you find a point somewhere among the laughs?"

"My point, young padawan, is that you need to pick up my satellite phone this evening after I accidentally dial her number and tell her how you feel. Don't worry about the mission; you're going to come back. I was right when I told you that on Resolution, and we were in much deeper shit there than we will be tonight. And in the tiny chance that you stub your toe or something over there, she will remember that you told her you loved her. Not somebody else. I had only one regret with Julie about this topic: I didn't tell her sooner."

"I'll bet you picked an extraordinary place, just the right time, and took a lot of prep with the setup, didn't you? Would you care to explain how to do that on a satellite phone, please?"

"No, actually, I didn't. The moment came when we were waiting outside of a seminar. Do you know what Julie said after I blurted it out? 'Took you long enough! I love you too.' Now, the marriage proposal, you need to put some effort and prep into that baby.

"This is one of those situations where Victoria's condition will work for you. She couldn't give a rat's ass about music, bluebirds, or fancy restaurants. She will assess value in every additional second she knows your genuine feelings."

Ben knew this was all correct. He was thinking of flowers and another trip to the Mall to get the mood just right when all that would only be a distraction. Ben would at least have liked to hold her hand and look in her eyes when he said it, but he knew Simmons was right. He had to take what he could get. "Alright, you win. But it will need to wait until 19:00. We have an arrangement to call between 19:00 and 21:00, and I want to stick to that."

"Good call. I'll see you then," Simmons said, standing up and walking out of the room.

4527 Sangamore Road, Apt. B23, Bethesda, Maryland
19:06 EDT, 5 April

Victoria

Victoria's phone rang, but it wasn't Benjamin's callback number. Instead, the caller ID said, "INMARSAT Unk." She was annoyed. What if Benjamin were to call while she was tied up with this person? She willed herself to settle down. *I will keep the call short, and if Benjamin calls, I will switch over to him or call him back.* Now it was past the third ring and approaching the fourth! *No, no, no!* She picked up the phone and said, "Hello?"

"Hello, Victoria, it's me."

Benjamin! What is he doing? Why isn't he using his cell phone?

"Hello, Benjamin. I am astonished it is you. I almost did not answer the phone."

"Yes, I'm sorry about that, Victoria, but we are at sea, and I can't use my mobile. One of the people we are working with has a satellite phone and was gracious enough to offer it up so I could call you."

"Oh, how wonderful!"

"Yes, so, let's return to normal. Hello, Victoria. How was your day?"

After about ten minutes of chatting about the details of the day, she turned the call over to him as usual. "So, Benjamin, you are at sea. Can you tell me about your mission?"

"No, I'm sorry. It's one of those that I can't discuss. I would like to talk about something very important, though.

"Of course, whatever you like."

"Are you at your desk where you can see the pictures of our day together?"

"Yes. I always sit here when I am talking to you."

"Good. I'm outside of my room. The satellite phone must be in the open air to work, but I'm holding the picture of the two of us on the Mall that day. I would like to be there with you right now to hold your hand and look into your eyes, but this picture will have to serve as a proxy for me. Could you please pick one of your pictures and do the same?"

What is happening? Why is he saying this? Is he breaking up with me?

"Victoria, are you still there?"

"Yes, Benjamin." She looked at the single picture of him, the beautiful blue eyes and the smile. "I am looking at your picture now."

"Good. I love you, Victoria Carpenter."

She gasped. "What did you say?"

"I said, I love you, Victoria. I know it's wrong to tell someone the first time over the phone instead of in person. But I couldn't wait any longer. I hope you will forgive me for that."

"Forgive you? Oh, Benjamin! I have been in love with you since that day we spent together." Her eyes welled up. *Oh, no, no, no! I cannot choke up, not now!* "I was so afraid to tell you because I thought it might drive you away."

"Well, it was earlier for me than that day, but I had the same fear. It's just incredible. I thought we could talk about anything, yet an entire month went by because I was afraid to say it. I feel like the biggest fool on Earth."

"No, no, no. Please do not say that." She wiped away her tears and went on. "I wanted to tell you too, but it is so hard for me to tell how people feel, even you, and it was too important for me to get it wrong. Can you forgive *me*?

"Every day Monday through Saturday and twice on Sundays!"

Victoria laughed. "That is funny. I did not expect you to say that."

His voice became more subdued. "I love the way you laugh. It's beautiful, like everything else about you."

"Oh, Benjamin!"

"Victoria, I'm sorry, but these satellite calls are obscenely expensive, and I have to go. We have a lot to talk about when I get up there. I can't wait to see you and hold you and, well, you know."

"Benjamin, I love you. It feels so good to say that to you, and I cannot wait until you get here."

"Goodnight, my love. I used to say that after every phone call since our wonderful day. I'm glad I can say it to you now. Goodnight, my love."

"Goodnight, my dearest Benjamin!"

The line disconnected, and Victoria sat in the chair, gazing at Benjamin's picture, replaying the conversation in her mind like a video clip on loop playback. After an hour, she got up, brushed her teeth, changed into her nightshirt of the day, and went to bed. Victoria would not fall asleep thinking of mathematical algorithms tonight. She would not fall asleep thinking of mathematical algorithms ever again.

USCG Cutter *Kauai*, Caribbean Sea, ninety nautical miles north of Isla de Barbello, Honduras
19:33 EDT, 5 April

Ben

Ben ambled up to Simmons on the messdeck and handed him the satellite phone. His expression was inscrutable; eventually, Simmons couldn't take it any longer.

"Well?"

"You called it. She's been in love with me since that day on the Mall. We're all set; God help us."

"Good for you, both of you!" He clapped Ben on the arm. "Now you can relax and get on with the job. I know it's tough, but try to get some sleep. Every bit will help."

"Right. I'll see you in a few." He turned and headed for his stateroom. The most important issue of his life had been resolved. Now on to the most urgent.

What the Day Demands

Isla de Barbello, Honduras
23:08 EDT, 5 April

D'Agostino

Shortly after sunset, the SEALs rallied at Dominguez's base camp to share intelligence and finalize the attack plan. The weather had deteriorated throughout the day, ending in rain showers that passed over and around the island. The rain made for a miserable existence in the already hot and humid jungle environment. Operationally, it was a significant boon as the Salinas men were disinclined to spend time out in the rain. Dozens of individual decisions opting to limit discomfort had a significant overall cumulative effect of gutting security. D'Agostino wished he had access to whatever the Honduran equivalent of the Weather Channel was called so that he could plan his marches to occur in the middle of a rain shower. As it was, they were frequent enough for his men to return in about half the time expected.

After consulting with his men, D'Agostino checked in with his command via satellite communications. The operation was still on. Not only that, but the patrol boat CO had seen the potential in the weather forecast to leverage the rain showers and was adjusting accordingly. Although they'd never met, D'Agostino was beginning to like this guy. If they could execute the takedown and exit when most of the dopers were hunkering down in the rain, that would significantly reduce mission risk. He hoped that boat jockey wouldn't wait for the perfect rainstorm and launch too late.

The other thing on D'Agostino's mind was the four speedboats the Salinas gang had tied up at the dock. It could be dreadful news if they got those babies spun up during the retreat. There was some question about whether low-trained thugs could hit moving vessels with RPGs fired from the promontory five hundred yards away. But they couldn't miss from a speedboat a few dozen yards away.

D'Agostino looked across at Parker. "P, we need those boats disabled. How many dopers were on guard at the marina?"

"Just one, Boss. And that was before the rain. There may be nobody there now."

"OK. Take your squad down there and cut the fuel lines. Tap anyone you see and hide the bodies. And by cut, I don't mean just slice it and leave an easy splice; take a big section out of it. When you're done, head for the IP; we'll meet you there."

"Aye, aye, Senior Chief!" Parker replied as he stood and motioned his men to follow.

****

D'Agostino's forces had completed the infiltration and sabotage, raising no alarm, and were now positioned at opposite ends of the quay, ready to converge on the *Carlos Rojas*. The rain showers in the area had provided a mixed blessing: almost perfect cover for movement when a storm was overhead, but playing hell with their NVGs otherwise. His force was equally split. Parker, his three men, and Dominguez were with D'Agostino, while Banks and his three men were poised on the other side. It had been forty-five minutes since the last storm's passing, and the Salinas men were at their posts. One was about fifty yards ahead of the ship on the quay, another about fifty yards behind, with one walking around on the ship's large well deck. Those three men were about to die. D'Agostino took no pleasure in it. Neither did he have any qualms after looking at the corpses and soon-to-be corpses strung up on the crosses before the hacienda. It was just another mission.

Another rain shower was arriving, and D'Agostino decided this was the one. "Cadillac Two Three, this is Greenman One, over."

"Greenman One from Cadillac Two Three, go ahead." replied the Rivet Joint, or "RJ" aircraft, an air force electronic warfare version of the venerable Boeing 707 passenger jet orbiting twenty-five thousand feet overhead.

"Cadillac Two Three, Greenman One, is Orchid on station? We are about to step off, over."

"Greenman One, Cadillac Two Three, affirmative. Orchid is holding at the IP now."

"Cadillac Two Three, Greenman One, roger, we are going dark, initiating assault in two minutes. Over."

"Greenman One, Cadillac Two Three, roger, out."

D'Agostino switched his radio over to the team net. "All Greenmen, launch in two mikes. I expect the watch to duck under cover in the same spots as before. Take them first. Drop anyone else you see moving."

"Roger One," Banks acknowledged on the radio, while Parker just patted his shoulder twice.

As the rain's intensity increased, the guard on the quay stepped under an overhang of a building. D'Agostino keyed his radio. "Greenmen, GO!" Two pops sounded behind him as Parker's marksman fired his noise-suppressed SR-25 rifle, dropping both the man by the building and the man on the ship within three seconds. The five men stood as one and trotted on the boat, linking up with Banks's group by the boarding port and stepping aboard. Parker's group split in two, each of two men moving along the outside of the ship to take out any other guards. D'Agostino led Banks's group inside the main entry. This group also split in two, with D'Agostino leading two men along the main deck in the ship's interior and Parker with two men and Dominguez headed for the engineering spaces.

The first pass resulted in five Salinas dead, all taken by surprise, either sitting or lying down. D'Agostino's men then began a thorough sweep of all compartments. The senior SEAL himself burst into the room holding the two hostages, who immediately went to their knees with their hands raised.

D'Agostino bound both men and left one of his men as a sentry. He met up with Parker in the passageway.

"Mainspace secured, boss. Dominguez is working on the engines, now," Parker said.

"Right," D'Agostino replied. He switched his radio back to the tactical frequency. "Cadillac Two Three, Greenman One, objective secured, no casualties."

"Greenman One, Cadillac Two Three, roger that. Well done, guys. Orchid is through the gate, ETA three mikes, over."

"Roger, out." He looked at Parker. "Let's go up and welcome the cavalry."

USCG Cutter *Kauai*, Caribbean Sea, four nautical miles east of Isla de Barbello, Honduras
01:58 EDT, 6 April

Ben

Kauai had gone to General Quarters Condition One when they reached the final departure point around ten nautical miles east of "the Gate" at Barbello at one a.m. The patrol boat was buttoned up and at darken ship—doors were closed and dogged down to prevent the spread of flooding and fire in case of damage. Before reporting to the Bridge, Ben had made an inspection tour to ensure no light sources were exposed. The crew had been briefed and took the warnings to heart, but sometimes fasteners or covers worked themselves loose, and even a sliver of light could alert and draw fire from their opponents.

The fact was that despite these precautions and the selective armor enhancements on the Bridge and engineering spaces, *Kauai* was extraordinarily vulnerable to any weapons larger than small arms simply because, unlike larger warships, she didn't have the space to absorb punishment. Sam was quite correct in his warning to Pennington about RPGs—she would be lucky to survive one hit along or below the waterline, and two would do her in for sure.

Everyone on the Bridge and working on the weather decks, as the ship's exterior was known, was in full battle gear: body armor, anti-flash garments, and Enhanced Combat Helmets. The Bridge was crowded, with the FC3 console fully manned by Williams, Zuccaro, and Bunting. Pickins was on the helm, Hopkins OOD, and, of course, Sam was there in his role as commanding officer. During the initial approach through the Gate, Ben would also be on the Bridge as a supernumerary, ready to take over if Hopkins or Sam were hit and disabled. He dutifully stood his position, although the idea amused him that any weapon capable of penetrating the Bridge's light armor would be selective enough to disable Sam or Hopkins and leave him standing. Once they cleared the Gate and were maneuvering within the harbor, Ben would join his team below to be ready for the assault.

The plan remained as briefed in Key West. Hopkins would conn *Kauai* into contact with *Carlos Rojas*. Ben and his team of Bondurant, Lopez, and Machinery Technician Third Class Dave Brown would jump on board, along with Simmons and Gerard. Ben, Bondurant, and Lopez would carry suppressed pistols besides carbines in case they encountered any Salinas soldiers missed by the SEALs on the way to *Carlos Rojas*'s bow, while Brown carried the messenger line. The messenger line was an ordinary rope attached to the heavy hawser *Kauai* would use to tow the other ship. The hawser weighed ten pounds per linear foot, and it would take all four of Ben's team to pull it up the thirty feet from *Kauai*'s afterdeck to *Carlos Rojas*'s bow and manhandle it into position for the tow. On *Kauai*, Lee would supervise the deck party of the junior boatswain's mate Jenkins and the three medical technicians to handle the hawser on her end.

As predicted, the weather was stormy, and Sam hoped one of the transient rain showers would give him a ticket in, unseen by whoever might be watching on the promontory. *Kauai*'s refit had included installing a new multi-mode radar capable of both surface search for navigation and tracking targets and weather mapping for tracking precipitation. It was in the latter mode now, and Sam stood behind Zuccaro, watching the blobs representing rain showers come and go. There had been two promising candidates in the last hour that fizzled, but a strong one was forming now that offered some promise. Regardless of how this one turned out, Sam was determined to head in—they simply couldn't wait any longer.

Under standard navigation rules, you waited for storms or anything else restricting visibility to pass before entering harbor. The Global Positioning System-enabled navigation management system was accurate to within fifteen feet and agnostic to environmental conditions. Still, it was prudent to use visual and radar fallbacks to improve the margin of safety. However, on this occasion, the benefits of being obscured on the journey outweighed the risks. Sam nodded in satisfaction at the screen as their storm firmed up and moved toward the island. He turned to Hopkins. "This looks like the one, Chief. Start your approach."

"Very good, sir. Helm, come left, steer two-six-five," Hopkins ordered as she moved the engine thrust setting up to ten knots. At this rate, they would enter the rear of the storm about half a mile outside the Gate and penetrate about halfway through by the time they reached the quay.

"Chief, my heading is two-six-five."

"Very, well. Zuccaro, shift to surface search range four on the radar and bring up navigation mode on screen three."

"Aye, Chief, switching to surface four on radar and nav mode on screen three," the petty officer repeated.

Hopkins pressed the transmit button on the intercom. "Main Control, conn, shift to battery and shut down diesels. Prepare for emergency restart."

"Conn, Main Control, shift to battery complete, placing all engines in Bravo-Zero."

"Conn, aye," Hopkins said, then stood back as the low growl of the diesel engines went silent.

Sam put on his headset and switched to the common tactical frequency on the encrypted radio. "Cadillac Two-Three, this is Orchid, over."

"Go ahead, Orchid from Cadillac Two Three."

"Cadillac Two Three, we are starting our approach into the harbor, ETA eighteen minutes. Request update on OpFor, please."

"Orchid, Cadillac Two Three. Roger, no radar emitters are currently operating. Reading a normal pattern of life on all communications. Greenman is beginning assault now, will report when the objective is achieved. Buzzer is coming on, over."

"Cadillac Two Three, Orchid, roger, out." Sam took off his headset and switched to the speaker on the tactical radio. He was relieved to hear that the Salinas mob was not operating any radars, although it would be nearly impossible for them to pick up *Kauai* through the rain with her stealth coatings. Greenman was the SEALs, now beginning their effort to seize control of the ship and its immediate vicinity along the quay. Buzzer referred to the radio jammer the RJ would employ to disable the gang's communications. The RJ had mapped out every transmitter on the island during the previous nights' flights and would render them all useless with the flip of a switch. The trick was to do this early enough to disrupt any counterattack, but not so early as to warn the opposition an attack was imminent. Since the attack was underway, now was the time.

They were catching up to the storm now. The patter of the large raindrops quickly sped up to a low roar. Sam keyed his tactical radio again, "Overwatch, Actual, might as well come in out of the rain. You won't be able to see anything out there, anyway. You too, Mount 51."

"Roger, sir, coming down," Guerrero's voice replied. Half a minute later, there was a thud from aft, then Guerrero came in the Bridge door with his sniper rifle slung on his shoulder and Hebert right on his heels. "Thanks, Captain. Whew! It's really coming down out there."

"Captain, I'm losing both EO and infrared on the Gate," Williams announced.

"Very well. Shift forward and report when you have the quay," Sam said.

The loss was expected, since the rain would work both ways. Sam stepped aside to allow Hopkins to reposition behind the console, using the navigation screen to conn the patrol boat since she no longer had visual references. Sam's stomach tightened as he watched the electronic map representation of Barbello's entrance channel close in from both sides of the pipper in the center that stood for *Kauai*. He jumped when a sudden flash of light illuminated the Bridge, followed almost at once by a clap of thunder. *Shit! I never thought I would ever say, Thank God, it's only lightning.* He was glad he had issued orders for hands to stay inside during the approach, as the lightning moved the concern from simple discomfort to the safety of life. He glanced over at Hopkins and noted the intense expression on her face in the glow of the screens as she issued helm commands to keep *Kauai* in the center of the channel.

As they cleared the Gate and the area of good water broadened around them, Ben stepped up to Sam and said, "By your leave to lay below, Captain?"

Sam turned and gazed into his eyes, then shook his hand firmly and said quietly, "Very well. Godspeed, Ben."

"Thank you, Captain."

The tension of the passage through the channel over, Hopkins turned and gave him a hug, whispering, "Take care, sir."

"I'll be back directly, Chief," Ben said as he returned the hug.

Williams turned from his screen and bumped fists with Ben. "Give 'em hell, XO."

"Thanks, Joe. Keep them off my back, will ya?"

"Same as always, sir."

Ben nodded to everyone, then turned and went below.

****

The messdeck was far more crowded than the Bridge between the three-man army medical team, plus Bryant, Lee, and Jenkins, Ben and his three teammates, and, finally, Simmons and Gerard. Standard white lighting was turned off in favor of the red illumination that preserved night vision. The conversation was subdued as everyone contemplated the upcoming mission, with only the near-silent electric motors and drumming of the rain on the decks providing background noise.

Ben slung his carbine and touched the three spare magazines in his vest by habit. He then clipped the night vision goggles onto his helmet, plugged in the battery, and checked them for focus and operation, flipping them up to the off position when he finished. Finally, Ben picked up the suppressed nine-millimeter pistol, checked the magazine and chamber, and slipped it into his holster. His checklist complete, he turned to his teammates, already rigged for action. "Any last-minute issues or questions, guys?"

"No, sir," Bondurant said. "Let's get it done."

"Roger that." He pressed the transmit button on his radio. "Orchid, Alpha-One, Alpha Team ready."

"Alpha-One, Orchid," Bunting's voice said. "Roger, that. Break, break. All teams, Orchid. Man positions, ETA five minutes, over."

"Alpha-One, roger, out," Ben said.

"Towmaster, roger, out," Lee said.

"Alright, let's do it, everybody!" Ben announced. "Dr. Simmons, you and your man stick with me until we get on board."

"Yes, sir," Simmons said, picking up and slinging his Uzi. He turned to Gerard and said, "Ready, Billy?"

Gerard nodded and stood. "Let's do it."

Ben turned to Lee and put out his hand. "Be careful, Shelley."

She shook his hand, looked up at him, and nodded grimly. "You too, sir."

After Simmons and Gerard joined him, Ben led the way out of the messdeck and into the rain, flipping down his NVGs to turn them on. He immediately realized they were useless in the rain and flipped them back up. Ben was sodden within a few steps and could barely see the details of the afterdeck as he led his group to the rail and crouched. Nothing was visible off the patrol boat's side, just the large fenders hanging alongside and a curtain of rain.

As *Kauai*'s silent approach continued, Ben continued to sweep his view from side to side. The knowledge that they were moving at five knots in zero visibility near land and other vessels was unnerving to a trained mariner like Ben.

"Alpha-One, Orchid, fifty yards. Cleared to board at discretion."

"Orchid, Alpha-One, roger, out," Ben said.

Finally, Ben could make out details off the port side. First, the quay and its buildings and then, the *Carlos Rojas* herself, looming forward of the beam. He could hear the soft starting and stopping of the electric motors as Hopkins "walked" *Kauai* sideways into the other vessel. Two figures appeared on the *Carlos Rojas*'s afterdeck, and Ben was reaching for his pistol when one gave the "safe" hand signal. *Kauai* finally made contact, and the fenders compressed with a loud squeak that made Ben's hair stand up.

"Alright, let's go!" Ben whispered and jumped over to the other vessel, followed by Simmons, Gerard, and the rest of his team. He stopped briefly to talk to the two men whose appearance left no doubt they were SEALs. "Lieutenant J.G. Wyporek, Cutter *Kauai*."

"Welcome aboard, Lieutenant. Senior Chief D'Agostino, Petty Officer Parker," D'Agostino said. "Please put these clips on your left shoulder. They're keyed to our NVGs. We're still doing a sweep and don't want to tap you guys by mistake." He handed each team member one clip, which they attached to their vests. "There's a DEA guy in plain clothes down below trying to get the engines working. Please don't shoot him."

"Thanks, Senior Chief. This is Simmons of DIA. He and his man here will deal with the device."

"Roger that, gents, follow me," D'Agostino said, then turned and walked off, followed by Simmons, Gerard, and Parker.

"OK, let's go," Ben said, drawing his pistol and moving forward. The four men stepped carefully forward—the decks were running with water in the rain, and a slip and fall was a particular hazard for men carrying loaded weapons. They quickly reached and climbed the ladder leading to the foredeck. Brown then continued to the bow, carrying the messenger line. After threading it through the bullnose in the bow, the four men started pulling on the line, taking in the slack. After they had boarded, *Kauai* crept forward to put her afterdeck directly alongside *Carlos Rojas*'s bow to shorten their distance to lift the hawser. Finally, the messenger line was paid out, and Alpha Team started pulling up the hawser. More and more of the heavy line came off *Kauai*'s deck, and the grunts and panting among the four men reached a peak just as the hawser's eye went through the bullnose. As the other men continued to pull in the hawser, Ben took the end and dragged it to the capstan. "Lope!" he whispered.

Lopez broke off from the group and helped Ben wrap the heavy line around the capstan with three loops, then secure the end to a mooring bitt.

"OK, guys, we're done," Ben panted. "Boats, you stay here. Lope and Brown follow me." They went first to the mooring line leading from the bow, removed it from its bitt, and dropped it overboard. They moved aft, repeating the process with every line and cable connection they encountered. When he was satisfied they had cleared everything, Ben turned and said, "Brown, get down to the engine room and see if you can help that DEA guy. Remember, do not start any engines, or do anything else noisy without an order from me. Clear?"

"Yes, sir," the engineer replied.

"Lope, we're heading to the Bridge."

"Right behind you, sir."

As they made their way to the Bridge, Ben caught a last glimpse of *Kauai* as she disappeared into the rain, and *Carlos Rojas* drifted off the dock. Ben stopped and kneeled as he saw a shadow move in the Bridge door window, and Lopez crouched behind him. *SEAL or Salinas?* Ben thought as he sighted his pistol on the figure. Finally, the figure turned, and Ben could see he was not in military gear and was carrying an AK-47. "Pop-pop" went his pistol with a tinkle of glass from the broken window, and the figure dropped to the deck. Ben and Lopez quietly opened the door and crept inside, sweeping the interior through their pistol sights. Nothing. Lopez leaned over and checked for a pulse. "He's dead, XO."

"Right. Help me figure out the helm," Ben said as he pulled out the NVG flashlight. He could see the rudder indicator, and it was rudder amidships, thank God. Ben had feared the crew had left the rudder hard over to port or starboard, a condition which would have made the *Carlos Rojas* impossible to tow without being corrected. He keyed his radio. "Orchid, Alpha-One, hawser secured, all moorings cast off, ship ready for towing."

"Alpha-One, Orchid, roger. We've lost sight of you in the rain. Advise us when heading is right of zero-seven-five."

"Orchid, Alpha-One, WILCO, out."

Within seconds, they felt more movement as the towline alternated between tightening and loosening. Somewhere out of sight in the rain, *Kauai* was applying small bursts of thrust to pull *Carlos Rojas* off the quay and get her lined up and moving. They had to start slowly, pivoting the ship to alignment with the towline before applying full thrust or risk parting the hawser or destroying the tow points on the bow. It was essential, but it took time, and Ben knew that the time available for hiding under this squall was running out. He checked the compass—it read zero-two-zero, basically north-northeast, and was inching slowly to the right. The bow had to swing past zero-seven-five, roughly east-northeast, before the side loading on the towline was low enough for *Kauai* to pull in earnest.

After two minutes, which seemed to stretch to two hours, the compass finally swung past zero-seven-five. "Orchid, Alpha-One, passing zero-seven-five, still swinging right."

"Alpha-One, Orchid Actual, roger, hang on back there," Sam's voice said. "We are coming out of the squall now, out."

Ben grimly accepted that last bit of news. The storm that allowed them to slip in unseen and begin the tow had been a godsend, and it was too much to hope that it would also cover them on the way out. Now things could get interesting. He keyed his transmit button again. "Alpha-Two, Alpha-One, Orchid's taking a strain on the tow now. Leave it and report to the SEAL commander. Over."

"Alpha-One, Alpha-Two, WILCO, out," Bondurant said.

There was no sense having Bondurant stay on the bow, as the tow line's tension would prevent any slippage from the windlass or bitt. He needed to be back where he could help or be helped as required if shooting were to start. Ben looked forward through the Bridge windows and saw the formerly solid curtain of rain was wavering. They were coming out of the storm. And safety.

Simmons

As Ben and the rest of Alpha Team made their way toward the foredeck, D'Agostino and Parker led Simmons and Gerard below to the living quarters. The ship's interior was dark—Dominguez had shut down the generator to prepare for their silent departure. D'Agostino used his red-lensed flashlight to lead the way, and Simmons took out his for immediate use.

"You guys both DIA?" D'Agostino asked.

"Yup," Simmons said.

"Right," D'Agostino said with a scowl, turned, and continued down the passageway. As they rounded a corner, Simmons could see three bodies dressed in civilian clothes spread along the corridor floor and a SEAL standing casually beside a door. "OK, we've got it. Head back to the well deck," D'Agostino said.

"Roger, Boss," the man said and moved past them toward the vessel's rear.

D'Agostino opened the door and shined in the light, and the two occupants startled and sat up.

"They say anything to you, Senior Chief?" Simmons asked.

"Negative, not a peep."

"OK, we'll take it from here, thanks."

D'Agostino gave them another sour look. "You sure?"

"Yes, thank you. It's all on me."

"Suit yourself. P, let's get going." The two men turned and moved briskly back down the corridor as Simmons turned on his flashlight, led Gerard into the room, and shut the door.

Simmons shined the flashlight back and forth between the two men and asked, "Which one of you is Gronkowsky?"

The man on the right looked at the other man, who stood. "I am Gronkowsky."

Simmons stepped forward, cocked his Uzi with purposeful menace, and turned slightly toward Gerard, keeping his eyes on the two men. "Take a good look, Billy. Behold a genuine mad scientist." He turned to face the two men. "There are only two possible outcomes from this encounter, gentlemen. One is that you comply with our orders instantly and completely and live to take your chances in an American court. The other is that I kill you without hesitation or remorse. What is it going to be?"

"I want to live, of course," Gronkowsky replied.

"I agree," Dorshak answered sullenly.

"Good choice. Now for some ground rules. Know that the assault force has killed everyone on this ship except you two. Calling for help will only get you a broken jaw, and running will get you shot in the back. Let's move out to the lab."

Dorshak nodded and stood. Simmons led the way out the door, with Dorshak and Gronkowsky following and Gerard bringing up the rear. As their procession wound down the ladder and into the production lab, Simmons noted the vessel was moving. Ben and his team had gotten it underway and clear of the quay.

The lab was dark, and the lack of any sound other than the distant creaks of the slowly moving vessel lent an ominous gloom to the compartment. Simmons gestured to two chairs at one of the tables. "Pull those chairs into that corner and sit down," Simmons said to the two prisoners. Simmons continued to Gerard as they complied. "OK, Billy, get to work."

Gerard nodded and started exploring. The computer set was relatively compact and concentrated on the desks on one side of the room. He started tracing network cables to ensure every external storage device was identified for destruction. Simmons noted two large tanks, positioned on either side of the room, with control devices mounted at the top and piping leading to large, complicated apparatuses sitting atop two of the tables.

"This is it? All the equipment?" Simmons asked Gerard.

"If the info we got from Holtz is legit, yes," Gerard replied.

"OK, rig the computers with thermite first, then the gizmos on the tables and the tanks." As Simmons continued to guard the prisoners, Gerard went to work. He had just finished laying out the thermite charges on the second table-mounted apparatus when a loud whirring sound erupted from behind them, followed by the familiar grumble of a diesel engine start. It worked up to speed within a few seconds, and the lights came on.

"Thank God! We're through!" Gerard said with relief.

Simmons shook his head. "No. It's too soon. We're in trouble." His words were followed by more whirring and an abbreviated grumble, indicating a second diesel engine had failed to start. A few seconds elapsed, then a second failed start try, and Simmons could now hear gunfire from topside. "Right, rig the tanks!" he said.

The Nearest Run Thing

USCG Cutter *Kauai*, Underway, Departing Harbor, Isla de Barbello, Honduras
02:18 EDT, 6 April

Sam

"Orchid, Towmaster, Alpha Team away, messenger line passed, recommend slow ahead," Lee passed to the Bridge.

"Towmaster, Orchid, roger," Bunting said.

"Rudder amidships," Hopkins said as she pushed both thrust levers just forward of the "Stop" detent. After five seconds, she moved both thrust levers back to stop, as *Kauai's* momentum allowed her to continue to creep slowly forward.

"Orchid, Towmaster, twenty feet to go…ten feet to go… Recommend stop."

Hopkins pulled the thrust levers back to provide a small burst of reverse thrust and then moved them to stop. The silent kabuki between *Kauai* and *Carlos Rojas* continued for about five minutes. Lee issued guidance from the afterdeck, and Hopkins used engines and rudder to hold the patrol boat in position while the tow was rigged.

"Position is good. Hold," Lee transmitted, then provided a running report of the operation. "Messenger line paying out. Hold position. Messenger line is out. Hawser is going up. Hold position. Hawser is on board. Hold position. Alpha Team signaling hawser is rigged. Standing by."

"Towmaster, Orchid, payout six hundred feet and then hold."

"Helm, right ten degrees rudder, steer zero-four-five," Hopkins ordered.

"Chief, my rudder is right ten degrees, coming to zero-four-five," Pickins responded.

Hopkins moved both thrust levers just forward of stop, and *Kauai* crept forward, turning slowly to the right. Within one minute, *Carlos Rojas* was lost from sight in the rain. After two more minutes, Ben's voice burst from the radio speaker.

"Orchid, Alpha-One, hawser secured, all moorings cast off, ship ready for towing."

As Bunting responded, Hopkins moved the thrust levers forward to a slightly higher power setting. "Bunting, I need an update on the towline," Hopkins said.

The petty officer nodded, "Towmaster, Orchid, say status."

"Orchid, Towmaster, six hundred feet paid out, hawser secured to towing bitt. Hawser is taking the load. Hawser lifting."

Hopkins pulled the thrust levers back to stop.

"Hawser steady, hawser settling," Lee reported.

And so it went for the next five minutes. Hopkins applied bursts of thrust to pull the *Carlos Rojas* into alignment on a due east course out of the harbor. The deluge of rain was tapering off, and visibility was improving ahead when Ben's voice finally reported again.

"Orchid, Alpha-One, passing zero-seven-five, still swinging right."

Sam stepped forward and put his hand on Bunting's shoulder. "I'll take this." He pressed his radio transmit button.

"Alpha-One, Orchid Actual, roger, hang on back there. We are coming out of the squall now, out."

As quickly as it had come, the storm passed on, and *Kauai* was in clear air, with *Carlos Rojas* just coming into view behind. Sam's heart sank as the visibility increased to virtually unlimited, and flashes of lightning from other storms to the south and east were strobing at a rate of several strikes per minute. *OK, not ideal, but we've been lucky so far.* He looked over in the promontory's direction. *Stay asleep, you bastards, and we'll all live through this.* "Williams, Surface Action Port. Load high explosive incendiary. Find that KPV emplacement and put the gunsight on it. Weapons tight.”

“Aye, Captain, searching,” Williams said as he cued the EO/IR camera in the general direction they had recorded. He selected another control, and the main gun issued a series of clanks as the autoloader chambered a round. “Gun loaded with H.E., still searching for the target.”

“Very well,” Sam said and turned to Guerrero. “Up you go, Gunner.”

“Yes, sir. On the way,” Guerrero said, then turned and left the Bridge.

“You want me on Mount 52, Captain?” Hebert asked.

“No, you hang out here. That promontory is too far for effective fifty-caliber fire, and you’ll be too exposed on the mount. If we tangle with small boats, I’ll cut you loose.”

“Yes, sir,” Hebert said with some relief.

“Captain, I have movement on the promontory with the infrared camera,” Williams said. “Looks like two individuals.”

“Stay on them,” Sam said. *Come on, don’t look this way.* He winced as more lightning flashed off their starboard side. “Zuccaro, what’s our battery status and speed of advance?”

“Forty-one percent and four knots, sir,” the young petty officer replied after checking the figures.

It’s going to be close. From their testing, Sam knew the battery figure was deceptive. Power output from the battery bank dropped precipitously at levels below five percent. They had another fifteen minutes before he had to start the diesels. A series of lightning flashes erupted from the south as if on cue.

“Orchid, Cadillac Two Three, I’m getting calls from the peninsula. They may have seen you. Over.”

Sam grabbed the handset. “Cadillac Two Three, Orchid. Can you confirm they have us?”

“Orchid, Two Three, negative. They are just trying to get through to the primary base. We are still jamming. This behavior is unusual—they do not have a regular call schedule.”

“Two Three, Orchid, roger out.” Sam replaced the headset and keyed his tactical radio. “Overwatch, Actual, you are weapons-free. Any searchlights swinging our way or gunfire, and you're cleared to fire."

"Understood, sir. Out," Guerrero responded.

They were a little under a quarter-mile from the Gate; they would be abeam in three minutes at this speed. Another series of lightning flashes strobed off to starboard, and suddenly the bright beam of a searchlight stabbed into the darkness and hastened toward them.

"Crack!" went Guerrero's rifle.

The searchlight went out at once, and gunfire erupted from the promontory. A rocket launched two seconds later and sped far overhead, sparks spewing from its tail. There was a loud pop, and both ships were silhouetted in the blinding white light of a parachute flare. Hopkins keyed the intercom, "Main Control, Conn, Emergency Engine Start Sequence, now!"

"Williams, target on last known GPS coordinates for the KPV. Lay down a pattern. Suppressive fire, Batteries Release, Commence Firing!"

As the first diesel engine whirred to life, the main gun barked three targeting shots, then started automatic fire on the hidden gun emplacement at two rounds per second, each shell a mini grenade exploding on contact. A series of pops distinct from the intensifying gunfire sounded from the nearby land. Within half a minute, all three diesel engines were operating and supplying power to the motors. Hopkins pushed the thrust levers ahead to two-thirds speed—now was the time to push the towline to the limit. She keyed her radio. "Towmaster, Conn, how's the towline?"

"Conn, Towmaster, towline is taught. Almost no catenary, but it's holding. I don't think there's much left!" Lee replied.

"Roger, stay under cover until further notice!" Hopkins regretted speaking the order as soon as she said it. Lee knew her job and had been briefed on what to expect.

"WILCO, out!" Lee said.

Sam's primary worry, the KPV, had so far failed to materialize. The automatic fire from small arms was mainly falling short, with the occasional thump of a strike on the hull. He looked back at *Carlos Rojas*—the SEALs were returning fire with their squad automatic weapons. He unconsciously winced as he heard two objects hiss past the Bridge in the darkness. RPGs! There wasn't anything more he could do about that threat except hope the long odds against a hit held. "Zuccaro, speed and position."

"Six knots, sir. We are through the gate. *Carlos Rojas* is coming abeam now."

Sam was about to reply when an enormous crash sounded just behind the Bridge, shattering the port Bridge door window and almost throwing Sam and Hopkins off their feet. Standing back up, Sam shook his head to clear it. *Shit, so much for the odds!* "Everyone OK?" After receiving a thumbs up from the Bridge crew, he keyed his radio. "All stations, RPG hit aft of the Bridge, report status. Williams, keep firing!"

"Yes, sir!" He had released the trigger in the shock of the hit. A moment later, the gun was banging away again.

"Conn, Towmaster, one casualty," Lee's voice said. "Jenkins is wounded and being moved inside now. Towline is holding. Hit appears to have been on the boat deck. No fire, over."

Jenkins! Sam's jaw clenched at the thought, but he had to put the young boatswain out of his mind for now. "Roger. Overwatch, report."

"My ears are ringing. Otherwise, OK, sir. Over," Guerrero reported.

"Conn, Main Control, systems normal, no damage, no casualties," Drake reported over the intercom.

"Conn, aye," Hopkins said.

"Hebert, Lee's on her own. Get down to the afterdeck and help her!" Sam said.

"Aye, aye, sir!" Hebert said, then turned and ran back off the Bridge.

Sam winced again as a second flare burst over the scene just as the first burned out. *Dammit, that guy knows his job!* The flare was far behind them but was almost overhead the *Carlos Rojas*, and the gunfire was shifting to follow. Almost immediately, two explosions in close succession sounded from the towed vessel, followed a couple of seconds later by a sound like a cannon shot, and *Kauai* lurched forward.

"Conn, Towmaster, the towline has parted!" Lee reported.

As Hopkins brought the thrust levers to stop, Sam hung his head and unconsciously pounded his right fist on his thigh. "Towmaster, Captain, cut the line!"

"Aye, aye, sir!"

Williams's jaw tightened as he tried to concentrate on laying down fire. They had to cut the hawser—it was useless now and, dragging over the stern, was an extreme risk to *Kauai* during maneuvering. Unfortunately, "cut the line" meant Lee had to take the sharpened ax and chop through ten inches of strengthened fiber out in the open air of the afterdeck in an environment alive with gunfire and rockets. Hopkins glanced down, saw Williams's expression, and reached down to give his shoulder a light squeeze.

"Alpha-One, Orchid Actual, prepare to abandon ship. We'll be dropping back to pick you up."

"Orchid, Alpha-One, roger, sir. We may have engines shortly, will advise."

After a minute, which seemed like an eternity to Sam, Lee came on the radio again. "Captain, Towmaster," she panted. "Towline cut and clear!"

Thank God! "Well done, Lee! Get inside now!"

"Chef and I <pant> are already <pant> there, sir!"

Williams let out his breath, and Hopkins released her hold on his shoulder with a soft pat.

OSUV *Carlos Rojas*, under Tow, Isla de Barbello Harbor, Honduras
02:53 EDT, 6 April

Ben

Like Sam over on *Kauai*, Ben had to suppress the urge to jump every time lightning flashed out on the starboard side. The rain had passed entirely, and visibility was nearly perfect. Ben and Lopez had nothing to occupy their attention as the ships slowly moved out of the harbor, unlike their shipmates on the other vessel. He was thoroughly frightened and deduced Lopez was in the same state.

"So, Lope, when we were debriefing after the last one, Captain Mercier told us you would get some 'special' attention over at Law Enforcement School. Did that come to pass?"

"Oh, yeah, sir. While everyone else in my class was living the good life in Charleston every weekend, I was getting advanced small arms and personal defense training shoved up my ass!"

"I hear ya. I got the same thing up in Quantico. Like to freeze my ass off on that small arms range all day." He winced again in the darkness as a long series of lightning flashes strobed across the starboard side. It was actually quite beautiful, the bolts weaving up from the surface of the Caribbean and then winding through and lighting up the clouds from within. He wished he could enjoy the view. "Quite a show."

"No shit, sir," Lopez said in a measured voice. "I'd prefer to see this movie in the next showing, though."

Ben laughed, then looked forward in alarm as a searchlight lanced into the darkness from the promontory, followed by the sound of gunfire. "Shit!" He keyed his radio. "Alpha-Four, One, light off now!"

"Alpha-One, Four, roger, lighting off!" Brown replied.

As the first flare burst off to starboard, a muffled whirring sounded deep in the hull, followed by the rattling rumble from the smokestacks as the ship's generator fired. The main engines needed a lot more power to turn over than the batteries could provide, so step one was getting a generator running. As the generator's noise topped out, a second, louder whirring came up from the engine spaces. Ben's heart sank when the initial rumble of the large engine died away. A second main engine start sequence sounded a few seconds later, with the same result. Ben was about to key his radio, then thought better of it. An inquiry at this point would just distract Brown from his work. The sound of automatic gunfire came up from the well deck—the SEALs joined the fight with their heavy machine guns.

The fight between *Kauai* and the promontory was heating up, and Ben could hear the 'thumps' every half-second from the main gun and see the tracers streak across the water. Williams was doing a good job keeping the pressure on. So far, nothing more than small arms fire was being thrown their way. Suddenly, a flash followed by an enormous boom came from *Kauai*, and the main gun ceased firing. "Shit, shit, shit!" Ben exclaimed, pounding his fist on the helm console. After a few seconds, the rapid thumping and twenty-five-millimeter tracer streaks returned, and Ben let out an enormous sigh of relief.

Ben was about to comment on a second flare that had appeared almost overhead when an enormous blast threw him onto the deck. One moment he was standing there; the next, he was flat on his face, covered in broken glass. "Lope!"

"Here, sir! I'm OK!" the young petty officer said as he got to his knees.

Ben looked behind the Bridge. The rocket had apparently hit the port smokestack, which was now shredded. He had just gotten to his feet and pulled Lopez up when the second rocket hit the foredeck. This time, the forward windows shattered, and the two men were thrown down again. Worse, shrapnel from the explosion sliced through some outer strands of the towing hawser. Given the enormous strain the line was under, there could be only one result: the cascade of individual strand failures in milliseconds merged into one loud "Bang." The two new ends shot away from the breakpoint, one slamming into *Carlos Rojas*'s superstructure with a loud "clang" and the other falling into the water just short of *Kauai*.

Ben looked forward in shock as they got to their feet again, then keyed his tactical radio. "Alpha-Four, Alpha-One, we just lost the towline. We need main engines now, or we're dead!"

"Almost there, sir! We've fixed the problem and are closing up now!"

"For God's sake, hurry!"

"Yes, sir!"

Ben's command radio came alive. "Alpha-One, Orchid Actual, prepare to abandon ship. We'll be dropping back to pick you up."

"Orchid, Alpha-One, roger, sir. We may have engines shortly, will advise." He turned to Lopez. "Lope, get down to the well deck and tell the SEALs to evacuate as soon as *Kauai* comes alongside, then find Simmons and tell him to light the torch."

"Yes, sir!" the young man said, then made for the door with his feet crunching on the shattered glass covering the deck.

"Alpha-Four, One, we'll be abandoning in about two minutes!"

"Yes, sir. Attempting start on starboard engine now!"

The whirring of the start sequence sounded again, but this time, the rattling grumbles continued and built up volume and tempo. *Yes! Go, baby!*

"Alpha-One, Alpha-Four, starboard engine on the line and ready to answer all bells!"

"Well done, Dave!" He moved the right thrust lever forward, watching with satisfaction as the propeller pitch and r.p.m. increased. "Orchid, Alpha-One, starboard engine online, and we're making way!"

"Well done, Alpha Team! Follow us." Sam's voice responded.

Ben reminded himself that they were not out of the woods as a few stray rounds from shore pinged off a windowsill. "Alpha-Three, One, we're sticking with it for now. Get back to the Bridge."

"One from Three, on the way, sir," Lopez said.

Ben looked at the panel. At two-thirds speed on the starboard engine, they were making eight knots. They would have to follow *Kauai* to navigate as the rockets' explosions had knocked out the compass. The whirring sound returned, signaling a start attempt on the port engine. This one was successful.

"Alpha-One, Alpha-Four, port engine ready to answer all bells."

"Four, One, roger, out." He was advancing the left thrust lever to match the right when Lopez came through the Bridge door. The firing was tapering off as the pit log steadied at twelve knots. "Feel like taking the helm? You need to stay on *Kauai*'s tail—the compass is shot to hell."

"I've got it, sir," Lopez said, stepping over to the helm.

"Thanks. I'm heading down to see what's going on."

"Right, sir."

Ben crunched over to the door and headed to the well deck. When he arrived, he noted two men were down and being tended by a medic and froze in his tracks. "John!"

"Over here, sir," came a voice from his right.

Ben almost cried out with relief. "Glad to see you in one piece."

"Yes, sir, you too. It was pretty hot down here, but I about shit myself when those rockets hit forward. How are things back at home?"

"*Kauai* took a rocket hit behind the Bridge. I heard on the command net that Jenkins went down. Shelley was on her own for a while. She's the one who axed the towline after it broke."

"Shit! Any word on the kid?" Bondurant's face was a mask of concern.

"Hang on a minute. Senior Chief D'Agostino?"

"Here, Lieutenant."

"How are your men?"

"I've got two with minor wounds, but they're both ambulatory."

"That's good news. We're making twelve knots, but the dopers could still catch up with us in the boats we saw."

"Not happening, sir. We cut all their fuel lines before we took the ship, and we also have their only mechanic below us now. This one's over."

"It's a distinct pleasure dealing with professionals, Senior Chief," he said as he offered his hand.

"Likewise, sir," D'Agostino said as he shook it. "If you'll excuse me, sir, I need to get back to my guys."

"Certainly." He keyed his command radio. "Orchid, Alpha-One, Alpha Team is all OK. Greenman has two casualties, both minor wounds. Do you have any report on Jenkins? Over."

"Alpha-One, Orchid Actual, roger. He took some shrapnel in the arm and thigh. He's out for this round, but should recover."

"That's a relief, sir. We have both engines online, but the Bridge is beaten up. We'll need to follow you to the dump site."

"Roger that. Two hours at present speed."

"Thank you, sir." He turned to Bondurant. "Jenkins took some shrapnel from the rocket hit, but he'll be OK."

"OK. Thank you, sir," Bondurant said with his head down.

"Hey, we're not done yet. Could you head up to the Bridge and keep Lope on the straight and narrow for me?"

"On the way, sir." The big boatswain shouldered his carbine as he headed forward.

Ben turned and went inside to find Simmons and Gerard. According to the briefing, the lab was just forward of the engineering spaces in a medium-sized compartment. As Ben neared the room, he could hear a muffled conversation. When he reached the door, he knocked and called, "Wyporek!"

The door opened. Gerard stepped out and nodded for Ben to enter. As Ben walked into the room, he noted Simmons guarding two men in the corner. Gerard stepped in behind him and started gathering up some loose gear in the center of the compartment.

"I presume we survive to fight another day," Simmons quipped.

"It was close, but yes, we're clear," Ben said. He glanced at the two tanks. "Is that it?" he asked as a chill ran through him.

"Yes. It's a binary compound, and each component is safe on its own," Simmons answered. "We have the computers and hard drives rigged with thermite and just finished un-rigging the product generators and tanks. Don't want to take any chances."

"Right. Well, I have to get back to it. We've got a couple of hours to go before we get to the dump point," Ben said.

"I'm afraid to ask, but what was the final bill?" Simmons asked.

"*Kauai* took an RPG just aft of the Bridge, and Jenkins was hit by shrapnel, but he'll pull through. Two of the SEALs are down, but D'Agostino says they'll be OK. It could have been a hell of a lot worse."

"Jenkins? Dammit! I really like that kid. I hope he bounces back."

"Time will tell. OK, you need any help down here?"

"No, we've got it. Please give me a heads-up when we're ready to leave. We don't want to activate the thermite until we are ready to step off. It will burn through the tables and go right on through the deck. We don't want to be around if there's anything flammable below here."

"Got it. I'll see you soon."

Ben left the men in the room and walked back to the well deck. It felt good to get back into the open night air, and he indulged himself for about a quarter of an hour, watching the lightning arcing through the distant rain clouds. Then he headed back to the Bridge for the rest of the transit.

The Last Gasp

**OSUV *Carlos Rojas*, Underway, Caribbean Sea, four nautical miles east of Isla de Barbello, Honduras
05:17 EDT, 6 April**

Ben

"Alpha-One, Orchid, we've reached the location. Heave to and shut down. Over."

"Orchid, Alpha-One, WILCO, out." Ben pulled both thrust levers back to stop, and the noise of the main engines drew back to idle. He keyed the transmit button on his team radio and said, "Alpha-Four, One, that's it for this one. Secure all engines and come up."

"Roger, sir," Brown said.

"OK, guys, I'll meet you on the well deck," Ben said to Bondurant and Lopez. After they had crunched away, Ben stood briefly looking around the Bridge. "You did good, old girl," he said, patting the helm. Then he turned and left the Bridge for the ladder.

When he reached the well deck, the SEALs were gathering in one corner, and his team, plus one man in civilian clothes, were chatting in the other. As Ben walked over, Brown spoke up, "XO, this is Mr. Dominguez, DEA. He's the one who got the engines running."

Ben grabbed his outstretched hand and shook it warmly. "I don't know how to thank you, sir. You saved all our asses for sure back there."

"Believe me, Lieutenant, it was my pleasure. Couldn't have done it without Dave here." Dominguez nodded toward Brown.

"Noted. Thank you," Ben said. He turned to Bondurant. "Boats, how about you guys check with the SEALs and see if they need any help with their wounded guys or gear?"

"On it, sir. C'mon, guys," Bondurant said, leading the other two petty officers to the SEAL group.

Ben watched as *Kauai* swung around *Carlos Rojas*'s stern in the pre-dawn twilight. Since the rocket hit on the boat deck had wrecked the RHIB, *Kauai* would have to come alongside to take them off. *The paperwork on that one is going to be a nightmare.* Ben smiled to himself. *How do you know you're safe? When the paperwork is your chief worry.*

Dominguez stepped up beside him. "I heard she took an RPG hit. It looks like she came out OK."

"Yes, it definitely could have been worse. Changed our plans for getting off using the small boat. It's a little riskier for her to come alongside, but at least the seas are calm. Should be pretty quick."

"Right," Dominguez said. "This will be my first time on a Coast Guard cutter."

Ben was about to reply when his vision exploded in stars and then went black.

Sam

"All hands, prepare for a direct approach to the vessel, rig fenders on the port side," Hopkins announced over the PA and replaced the microphone. She set the patrol boat up for a shallow approach to *Carlos Rojas*'s starboard side, pressing the vessels together just long enough to disembark everyone. The sense of relief on the Bridge was pervasive. They had all come through, and now only one last detail to carry out.

She glanced over to ask Zuccaro for a position report when the sound of gunfire, first one, then several guns, erupted from the other vessel. In shock, Hopkins froze for a moment, then pulled the thrust levers back to stop. "Captain!"

Sam keyed his radio. "Alpha-One, Orchid Actual." He paused as the gunfire came to a stop. "Alpha-One, Orchid Actual, report!"

"Orchid, Alpha-Two, XO is down, repeat, XO is down," Bondurant's voice came from the speaker.

Sam's mouth opened in silence. A gigantic icy ball had formed in his stomach. *No! That can't be right.* He blinked and looked around the Bridge—everyone was looking at him. He keyed the radio again. "Alpha-Two, Orchid Actual, roger, report, over."

"Orchid, Alpha-Two, one of the gang bangers must have been hiding out somewhere. He just opened up with an AK, and the SEALs shredded him. I'm going to the XO now. The DEA man is down, too."

"Alpha-Two, Orchid, roger, see to them and report when able."

"Roger, sir, standby."

Ben

"XO, XO!" Bondurant's voice echoed from a distant place.

Ben could feel hands on him, and he was being shaken gently. He slowly opened his eyes and had a brief bout of panic as he saw only a faint light. *What's wrong? Why is it dark?* He relaxed as he remembered. *Because it's night, dumbass!* His head felt like it was exploding. "Wha…What happened?"

"Lie still, sir. The medic's coming," Bondurant said.

Ben started to turn toward the voice when his head exploded in pain again. "Shit!"

There was some movement, and another voice said, "Freeze, Lieutenant, let me check you out." Gradually, his head and vision cleared, and the voice continued. "OK, sir. It looks like you took an AK round off your helmet. I don't see any wounds. Can you tell me how you feel?"

"Bad headache. It's fading, though. No other pain, and I can feel everything." Ben wiggled his toes to make sure.

"Orchid, Alpha-Two, XO is OK, just got his bell rung," Bondurant reported. "Yes, sir. Yes, sir, I will."

He's talking to the captain. *Why can't I hear it? Oh, my helmet is off.*

The medic leaned over. "Right, I want to see if you can sit up. Don't push it. We'll stop if something doesn't work or there's too much pain."

"OK," Ben said. He felt hands under his shoulders lift him, and he sat up. Another wave of pain passed over him, and then he said, "So far, so good."

"Alright, we're going to help you to your feet now. No heroics, sir. If you can't make it or the pain gets too much, say so."

"WILCO," Ben said. Then hands helped pull him up. "I'm a little dizzy, but I think I can stand OK."

"That's enough for now, sir. You lean on your shipmate for a while."

"OK," Ben said. His head was still clearing, and he would not argue. "Boats?"

"Yes, sir," Bondurant said.

"What happened?"

"One doper just popped up. He must have been holed up in a hidden compartment. No one saw him until he opened up with an AK. Then the SEALs took him out."

"Anyone besides me get hit?" At Bondurant's silence, he continued. "Tell me."

"Sir, the DEA man, Dominguez. He's dead. Took one right through the head. The rest of us are OK."

"Son of a bitch!" Ben hung his head, his headache returning. "He saved our lives, and I don't want him left behind. That's an order."

"Yes, sir, I've seen to that. We are putting him in a litter we took from the ship's sickbay."

I should have known. "Sorry, Boats. I'm not at the top of my game right now."

"No worries, sir. *Kauai*'s coming alongside now. We'll get you on board and have the doc look you over."

"Don't fuss over me, Boats. See to the rendezvous. Get a headcount and make sure everyone gets off OK."

"Yes, sir. Dr. Simmons, could you look after him, please?"

"Yes, John, I've got him," Simmons said, taking Bondurant's place at Ben's side. Whispering to Ben, he said, "You scared the shit out of me, friend! I thought I would have to make 'that call' to Victoria."

"How the hell did a cartel guy get by the sweep?" Ben asked.

"It was one of their 'Hitler Youth.' He couldn't have been over thirteen. He was probably hiding in a cabinet somewhere. Unbelievable."

"I had time. I should have searched. Dominguez..." he shook his head.

"Don't go there. This is not on you. It's not on anybody. These things happen, particularly on wild-ass ops like this." He looked over as *Kauai* snugged up against the side. "Let's go, partner. We've got a fire going on the computers downstairs that will light up this barge in a minute."

Ben nodded, started to bend over to pick up his helmet, then stopped and stood up as another wave of pain washed over him. "Ahhh," he said, putting his hand to his head. "Can one of you guys bring that helmet, please? The NVGs alone are worth nine grand."

"I've got it, Lieutenant," Gerard said as he picked up the helmet.

Ben was still a little dizzy and had an intense headache, but with Simmons's help, he made it to the side and over the rail onto *Kauai*'s afterdeck, with additional support from Bondurant and Lopez.

"Everyone accounted for, sir," Bondurant reported.

"Thank you, Boats. Carry on, please."

"Yes, sir."

Bondurant stepped aside as Lee trotted up. She took a deep breath as she looked into Ben's eyes, then snapped a crisp salute. "Welcome home, sir."

Ben returned it. "Glad to see you in one piece, Shelley."

"Same here, sir. The bastards broke my boat, sir!" she blurted out.

Ben glanced up at the mess on the boat deck, smiled, and turned back to her. "Don't worry. The taxpayers will buy you a new one."

"I suppose. But I had this one all tuned up!" She grinned back.

Ben put his hand on her shoulder, gave it a soft squeeze, and watched as *Kauai* pulled away from the other vessel. D'Agostino walked up and got his attention.

"We're ready to blow her, sir."

"How is she rigged, Senior Chief?"

"I've got charges right above the bilges in each compartment. Give the word, and I'll blow her bottom out."

"Boats? Call the Bridge and tell them we are ready to scuttle on their order."

"Yes, sir," Bondurant said, then keyed his radio. "Conn, afterdeck, seized vessel ready to scuttle. Very good, sir." He looked at Ben. "Let'r rip, sir."

After getting a nod from Ben, D'Agostino announced, "Fire in the hole!" Then he pressed a button on a hand-held controller.

Seven quick thuds sounded from the *Carlos Rojas*, and the ship settled, slowly at first. As the bow sank level to the sea, the vessel rolled left and quickly plunged out of sight, leaving a spreading patch of white foam and debris.

"Now, I think you should head in to see the doc," Simmons said.

"I'll let him finish with men who are actually bleeding before I go to him for a headache," Ben said. He turned back and looked at *Carlos Rojas*'s grave as his head started pounding again. "You should be elated. Another win for the good guys."

Simmons shook his head. "They'll just be another one when I get back. 'Tomorrow, and tomorrow, and tomorrow, creeps in this petty pace from day to day.'"

Ben closed his eyes to another wave of pain and struggled to think. "Man, you're not pulling a Mac...Mac...." He tried to move to the rail but ended up falling to his knees and throwing up on the deck. The pain was blinding, all-consuming. He couldn't see, just heard shouting.

"John! Help me get him inside!"

Strong arms lifted him off the deck and carried him like a baby. It had to be Bondurant, but he couldn't see. He struggled to think. Pain! He felt himself being put down gently on the mess table.

"What were his symptoms?" *A new voice. That army doctor. What is his name?*

"He's had a headache, and he collapsed and threw up."

"Was he unconscious after the injury?"

"Yes, for a couple of minutes."

"Shit! Where's his helmet? Find it!"

"Why do you need that?"

"Don't argue with me, goddammit! Get me his helmet! Rabin, I need an IV stat and pump in forty milligrams of propofol as soon as it's running. Langley, get the craniotome bit into the autoclave and wipe down the ultrasound wand."

Ben felt a hand on his face, then a blinding light and what felt like a knife in his eye. "AHHH!"

"I know it hurts. I'm sorry, Ben. Right pupil, normal and reactive, left, fixed and dilated."

"Here it is, sir!" *John's voice again.*

"Yes, yes. OK, there it is."

"Propofol going in, Doctor."

"Thank you." The voice became louder. "Ben, you have a type of brain injury that is causing a bleed inside your skull, and I have to knock you out so I can treat it." The voice became distant. "Is he married?"

"No, but his girl's name is Victoria." *Pete's voice.*

Louder again. "Ben, you'll be going to sleep now. I want you to think about Victoria. You'll see her soon."

The pain was subsiding, and he was back in Bethesda. The apartment door opened, and she was standing there looking so beautiful, more beautiful than he ever imagined—*Victoria!* Then the vision narrowed to blackness.

Sam

Sam had just finished watching *Carlos Rojas*'s last moments. He had expected to feel happy, or at least satisfied at this point, but he just felt drained. *Is that all I have, the absence of despair? I guess it beats the alternative.* He had been quite close to complete despair twice in the last few hours. First, when the towline parted, then when the report came that Ben had been gunned down. Each moment had been resolved with a seeming miracle, and Sam wondered how much longer his luck would hold. He shook himself. *Take the win. Let's go home.* "Chief, Port Canaveral via Key West, twenty-four knots, if you please."

"Very good, Captain," Hopkins responded, advancing the thrust levers to the required power setting.

Sam lifted the microphone to contact the Coast Guard Cutter *Thetis* and tell her to stand down the helicopter on alert for MEDEVAC when the phone rang.

"Bridge, Bunting," the young technician said. "Standby. Captain, it's Doc, urgent."

Sam took the phone. "Captain."

"Captain, Bryant here. The XO has collapsed. It looks like some sort of TBI. We've just moved him onto the table. I recommend you get the MEDEVAC helo spun up."

"I'm coming down." He hung up the phone without waiting for a response. "Bunting, contact *Thetis* and get that MEDEVAC bird in the air ASAP. Chief, the XO just went down with a head injury. I'm heading down, but I'll be on the headset if you need me. Stay on your present course, but call flight quarters as soon as the helo calls airborne and get on a good course and speed for hoisting when they are inbound."

"Yes, sir," Hopkins said.

Sam ran to the rear of the Bridge and slid down the ladder railing without his feet touching a rung, the dad's voice in the back of his mind hoping none of the junior enlisted members saw him. He pulled up to the messdeck door, crowded with crew members gazing in with worry. "Gangway," he said, and they stepped aside.

Ben was stretched out on the mess table, unmoving, an IV in his arm and an oxygen mask over his face. The surgeon moved a small held-held device over Ben's head, watching a monitor and making an occasional mark with a sharpie pen. Sam stood silently, watching as the surgeon finished his exploration with the device.

"Rabin, Betadine everything within two inches of the X." He turned, saw Sam, and stepped over. "Captain, the lieutenant was shot in the head. His helmet kept the bullet out, but the impact was akin to a hammer blow to the side of his head. He has a severe bleed inside his skull. I'm going to do a stopgap procedure to keep him alive, but he needs to be medevac·ed to one of the Miami trauma centers as soon as possible."

"I've got a helo spooling up on a cutter about twenty miles away."

"Good. I'll need about twenty minutes to get it done. Then it's a race against time to get him to surgery."

"What are you going to do?"

Roberts looked at him for a second, then pulled him away from the other crew. When they were out of earshot, he continued. "I'm going to drill a hole in his skull and drain out the excess blood, Captain," he whispered.

Sam's mouth hung open briefly. "My God!"

"I know how that sounds, but if I don't do it, he'll be dead before he gets halfway to Miami."

"I understand. Is there anything I can do, anything you need?"

"Yes. As you can imagine, this is about as delicate a procedure as it gets. Anything you can do to dampen down the deck motion would help."

"Of course," Sam replied and keyed his microphone. "Conn, Captain."

"Conn aye, sir," Hopkins replied immediately.

"Chief, Major Roberts needs to perform…a surgical procedure on the XO. Get the speed down and maneuver as required to get the lowest pitch and roll possible. Do you copy?"

"Affirmative, sir. Throttling back now."

The engine noise reduced, and Sam felt *Kauai* come down from the semi·planing mode as her speed slackened. "Good, keep her as steady as possible from now through the helo hoist. Maneuver at discretion."

"Understood, Captain."

Sam shut off his microphone. "Doctor, it will probably take Chief Hopkins a minute or two to find a sweet spot."

"That's fine, thank you, Captain."

"Doctor, we're ready," Langley said.

"Right. Captain, I need you and everyone else out of here. I know he's a buddy, but you can't help and won't be able to unsee this."

"Yes, yes." Sam turned and said, "Everyone out, now!" As he followed them out the door, he looked back and said, "Good luck, Doctor."

The Golden Hour

USCG Cutter *Thetis*, Underway, Caribbean Sea, twenty nautical miles northeast of Isla de Barbello, Honduras 06:15 EDT, 6 April

Becker

The ship had been at Flight Quarters Condition Three (Modified) since 02:00 to prepare for rapid turn-up and launch of the embarked MH-60T helicopter. Firefighting and rescue equipment were readied and laid out. The flight deck crew were attired in their color-coded flash-protection gear, and the Helicopter Control Station was manned. The helicopter crew had "cocked" the aircraft on the flight deck, pre-flighted the airframe, removed all engine and sensor covers, and taken off all tie-downs other than the primary chocks and chains.

The aircraft commander, Lieutenant Commander Stephanie Becker, was in *Thetis*'s Combat Information Center, following the latest information on the mission and keeping a keen eye on the weather. Lieutenant Douglas Holmgren, her copilot, was lounging by the aircraft, along with the Flight Mechanic, Mikita Harris, and Rescue Swimmer Greg Daniels. All were ready to jump in the helicopter and start the auxiliary power unit, or APU, a tiny jet engine turning a generator providing electrical power for the various electronic systems and main engine start.

The rainstorms providing a welcome sanctuary for *Kauai* during her approach had proven quite a challenge for *Thetis*. Her flight deck was barely broad and long enough to support the landing of the MH-60, and her hangar was far too small to house the large helicopter. With a vulnerable aircraft parked on the open air of her flight deck, *Thetis* had to be kept clear of thunderstorms, with their powerful shearing winds and lightning. Occasionally, an anxious OOD had to pour on full speed to dodge a rapidly building storm.

Becker was about ready to call it a day. Reports from the cutter involved in the mission, callsign Orchid, indicated a few minor wounds in action, nothing justifying the risks of a helicopter hoist and long flight back to the States. She was gathering up her charts and kneeboard when an urgent call came over the command net: "*Thetis*, this is Orchid. Request immediate assistance. Require MEDEVAC for one patient with traumatic brain injury and one medical attendant, over."

So much for calling it a day. Becker quickly jotted down the cutter's latitude, longitude, course, and speed and headed back to the flight deck as the announcement to set Flight Quarters Condition One reverberated through the ship. On the flight deck, Holmgren donned his survival vest and flight helmet, jumped into the cockpit's left seat, and began the initial checks while Harris grabbed a small fire extinguisher and headed for the APU intake. The flight crew had reached an agreement with the ship's captain that they could start the APU independently without waiting for the ship's fire parties to man up fully during an emergency launch like this. By the time Becker reached the aircraft, the APU was running, and Holmgren was well into firing up and checking the electronic systems.

When *Thetis* reached full readiness at all flight quarters stations, the yellow-shirted Landing Signal Officer, or LSO, gave the pilots a thumbs up. Holmgren keyed his radio. "*Thetis*, Six-Zero-Two-Three, request permission to start engines and engage rotors."

"Six-Zero-Two-Three, *Thetis*, permission granted to start engines and engage rotors. Amber deck."

"Six-Zero-Two-Three, roger."

After starting the two main engines and getting the rotors up to full speed, Becker and Holmgren completed the last cockpit checks, called for a takeoff, and received a reply. "Six-Zero-Two-

Three, *Thetis*, cleared for takeoff to port, take signals from the LSO. Green deck."

Holmgren gave the "remove tie-downs" hand signal to the LSO, who dispatched the aircraft's tiedown crew. They removed the wheel chocks and tiedown chains from the helicopter and scurried forward clear of the flight deck. The LSO kneeled for one last visual check, then stood, waved his hand in a circle, and pointed off to the ship's port side. Becker lifted the helicopter into a brief hover over the flight deck, then slid left clear of the ship and began an acceleration and climb. Once clear and climbing, Holmgren keyed the radio again. "*Thetis*, Six-Zero-Two-Three, flight operations normal, over."

"Six-Zero-Two-Three, *Thetis*, roger, maintain guard with me for now. Good luck. Out." Becker glanced at the aircraft's clock: 06:30, thirteen minutes from callout to airborne, very respectable, especially considering the shipboard launch.

The flight from *Thetis* to *Kauai*'s position was a short nine minutes. In the last five, the cutter's officer of the deck discussed the operation with Holmgren to complete plans and decrease the helicopter's time overhead. There would be two hoists: the first of the cutter's health services technician, the medical attendant for the flight, then the litter containing the patient. On arrival, Becker slowed the helicopter and said, "Complete rescue checklist part one for direct delivery of the rescue strop." Harris slid the cabin door open and attached the strop to the hoist hook.

"Rescue check part one complete," Harris announced. She keyed the intercom again as the helicopter pulled into a hover alongside *Kauai*. "Holy Shit! Look at the boat!" A large black smudge stretched across most of the rear of *Kauai*'s superstructure, the boat crane's arm was severed, and the tubes on the RHIB were shredded and deflated.

"OK, let's stick to business. Complete rescue check part two," Becker responded.

Harris snapped out of her awe and completed the check. "Rescue check part two complete."

"Orchid, Six-Zero-Two-Three, ready for hoist."

"Two-Three, Orchid, cleared to hoist."

The medical technician and his go-bag came up first. Once he and it were safely aboard, Harris and Daniels hauled out the litter and sent it down. After a minute, the patient was positioned in the litter and hoisted aboard. Harris shut the cabin door, and as the helicopter climbed and accelerated away, Daniels handed the medical technician a flight helmet and plugged it into an intercom cord.

"Can you hear me?" Daniels asked after the technician had put on the helmet.

"Loud and clear," the technician responded.

"I'm Greg, and this is Mikita," Daniels said, gesturing to Harris, who waved. "Anything we can do to help?"

"Not right now, thanks. The name's Mike Bryant."

"OK. What's in the bag?"

"Two IV bags, two units of O-negative, medical disposal bags, and a lot of towels."

"Towels? You expecting rain?" Daniels quipped.

"No, blood. A lot."

"What the hell?"

"The patient has a brain bleed. The surgeon made a burr hole and installed a drain. I have to keep it clear until they get him to surgery, or he'll die. So, we're going to have bleeding."

"Shit, what happened down there?"

"Sorry, that's classified."

"Did he get it when the boat was hit?"

"Again, sorry. Can't discuss it."

"OK." Bryant's reticence would have probably put off the average person, but Daniels was not to be denied. "Who is he, anyway?"

"He's our XO."

"Oh, well, you guys won't have to worry about shoeshines and haircuts for a while."

Becker cringed and was about to put a stop to the conversation when Daniels hurriedly said, apparently to a reaction from Bryant, "Hey, I'm kidding!"

"Kid about something else, asshole!" Bryant shouted.

"Daniels, how about you stick to business and give everyone a break?" Becker said. "We've got a long trip ahead of us."

"Yes, ma'am," Daniels said contritely. "Sorry, man."

"Forget about it. Can you give me a hand with the towels here?" Bryant asked.

"You've got it."

Office of the Director, Joint Interagency Task Force South, Key West, Florida
06:45 EDT, 6 April

Pennington

"We have a report from Orchid, sir," Commander Keener called on the intercom.

"Bring it in, please," Pennington responded. After realizing that he was thoroughly demoralizing his staff by hovering in the situation room, Pennington had confined himself to his office. His relief on hearing that both *Kauai* and *Carlos Rojas* had cleared Barbello harbor and were en route to the dump point with only three casualties was immense. None of the wounded required medevac, even better. He was happy to be proven wrong, even if it was by that callous DIA asshat.

There was a knock on the door, and then Keener came in holding a clipboard with a **TOP SECRET** cover, closing the door behind him. "Here it is, sir."

"Read it." Pennington took off his glasses and rubbed his eyes. He had gotten about five hours of sleep in the last three days and could barely see his desk, much less read message text.

"*Carlos Rojas* sunk at 10:12 Zulu and gives a position." He paused with his mouth open.

Pennington looked up with concern. "What is it?"

"Revised casualty list, sir. There was a Salinas stowaway on the *Carlos Rojas*, and he opened fire as the boarding party was gathering to disembark." He paused again.

"Well?"

"One killed, Dominguez, DEA agent. One serious injury, Lieutenant J.G. Wyporek. He's just been hoisted from *Kauai*. His condition is listed as an epidural hematoma. It's some kind of traumatic brain injury."

Pennington pressed his palms against his eyes. *They punched through that gauntlet of machine guns and RPGs and then got blindsided by a nut job with an AK? How does that make sense?* "Where is the helo going?"

"Miami. He'll need a neurosurgeon and a trauma center, sir."

"We know which one?"

"Um. No, sir."

Pennington took his hands from his eyes and put on his glasses. "What do you mean, no? Do you expect them to make arrangements via INMARSAT? For God's sake, Dan, give them some help. I don't care which one it is, but I want a top-flight neurosurgeon scrubbed and ready to cut when that helo touches down. Get on it! If I need to bust Fred Brown's or General Miller's balls to make that happen, you tell me! Move!"

"Yes, sir!" Keener said, then fled the room.

Pennington stared at the door after it closed. *Ben, we'll get you right if I have to chew up every commander, captain, admiral, or general from here to DC. We owe you and your crew that much!*

National Intelligence University, Bethesda, Maryland
07:32 EDT, 6 April

Victoria

Victoria was walking on air as she made her way to the office. She only had a few hours of sleep, excited as she was after her phone call with Benjamin the previous evening. This would have left her tired, grumpy, and unproductive on a typical day. Not today. She felt like she could solve P versus NP if she put her mind to it. After locking up her bag and cell phone, she cheerfully presented her badge and almost skipped through the metal detector at the security checkpoint. It was just a short walk to the Data Analysis Division and her cubicle.

Debbie was away from her desk, which was typical, as she usually had administrative housekeeping tasks piled up at the start of each day. Victoria sat in her cubicle, booted her computer, and started the login process. A knock on the wall behind her startled her. She turned and smiled when she saw it was Debbie—she couldn't wait to tell her about the phone call. The smile quickly faded. Something was wrong. Mr. Fletcher, the office director, was standing behind Debbie, and they both looked.... What? Her brain searched for the correct term. Grim. Yes, that was it. She must have done something very wrong.

"Dear, could you come with us, please? There's something we need to talk to you about," Debbie said.

"Yes," Victoria said, standing up. The situation was alarming. So much so that she almost left her Common Access Card plugged into her computer, which would have been a serious security violation on top of whatever faux pas she had committed. She followed them silently into Mr. Fletcher's office and sat at the table next to Debbie while Mr. Fletcher sat on the edge of his desk.

"Victoria, this is about that young Coast Guard officer you've been seeing. His name is Ben Wyporek, is that right?" Mr. Fletcher asked.

I cannot be in trouble for that, can I? Benjamin is a commissioned officer with the highest security clearance, not a foreigner. "Yes, Mr. Fletcher. Is there a report I should have submitted for that?"

"No, it's nothing like that. I..., I just...."

"Sir, may I, please," Debbie interrupted on seeing his distress. At his nod, she continued. "Dear, I got a call from Peter Simmons this morning right after I got to work."

"Yes?" Victoria was confused. *What did Peter have to do with this?*

Debbie reached over and took her hand. "He was with Ben last night. I don't know how to say this, but Ben was badly hurt."

Her vision seemed to close into a tunnel centered on Debbie's face, and the sound echoed in her head. She felt like she couldn't breathe and squeezed Debbie's hand. All that came out was, "No, No, no, no. He's not...not...."

"He's not dead, Victoria, but he was badly hurt. They have taken him off his ship by helicopter, and he is on the way to a hospital in Miami. He should arrive there around one o'clock."

"Miami?" Her brain was spinning, but math quickly took hold. Over six hours by helicopter, average speed one-hundred-fifty miles per hour, eight hundred miles. They would bring him to the closest hospital trauma center in the US, so eight hundred miles from Miami. "What was he doing in the Caribbean?"

Debbie and Mr. Fletcher looked at each other in surprise. "I'm sorry, dear, we don't have that information," she said.

"How was he hurt?"

"Peter said it was a head injury. Something called an epidural hematoma."

"Oh, no!" An eidetic memory like Victoria's could be a gift or a curse. Just now, it was the latter. She had read about epidural hematomas and knew that if Benjamin did not receive immediate neurosurgery, he could die or be permanently disabled. Five hours did not equal "immediate" in her mind. "I must go to him. Mr. Fletcher, I need to take leave. I am sorry. I know I am supposed to submit a request for leave two weeks in advance."

Mr. Fletcher shook his head. "Victoria, that is not a problem. But are you sure you want to go right now? I'm told he could be unconscious...indefinitely with these things."

"Mr. Fletcher, he will either wake up in one to two days, or he will die." She nodded firmly. "I need to be there when he wakes up." Victoria knew Mr. Fletcher was right. She did not bring any knowledge or skills to bear that could influence the outcome in the slightest. However, as irrational as it seemed, while Benjamin's life hung in the balance, she was determined to be with him. She turned to Debbie. "Can you help me find a flight to Miami? I do not have time to learn how."

"Yes, I'd be happy to, dear," Debbie replied with tears in her eyes.

"I'll see if we have anyone headed down that way who can escort you," Mr. Fletcher added.

"Thank you, Mr. Fletcher. I will go in any case, but having someone I can trust along would be very helpful."

"Good. I'll let you two move along to make arrangements while I make some phone calls. Victoria, I'm very sorry about Ben, and I pray he will be OK. If there is anything we can do, I hope you will call us."

"I certainly will. Thank you, Mr. Fletcher."

USCG Cutter *Kauai*, Underway, Caribbean Sea, eighty-five nautical miles north of Isla de Barbello, Honduras
08:52 EDT, 6 April

Sam

Sam looked across the messdeck at Simmons as he sat, head down, staring at his hands resting on the table. Sam's attitude toward the DIA man had fluctuated considerably since their first meeting almost three months ago. What started as a wary acceptance and understanding of a man with an enormous challenge had ended in white-hot anger when Simmons had carelessly blundered into an ambush and dragged Ben with him. At the end of the last mission, he had told Captain Mercier in no uncertain terms that there would be a reckoning if he and Simmons ever crossed paths again.

That moment had come. The anger had faded in the interval, but the distrust and dislike remained. That Ben had a cordial, almost friendly attitude toward the man who had so flippantly risked his life was a great mystery to Sam and one of the few issues on which he and Ben disagreed. He supposed you could not stand under fire with another man without developing some attachment. There was also Simmons's young protégé, admittedly quite beautiful, and with whom Ben was utterly smitten.

Sam had to admit that the current crisis was not a result of anything Simmons had done. They had all performed their duty, took appropriate actions, and did their best to minimize the risks. Ben's injury was a matter of bad luck, not recklessness this time. Sam swallowed hard and walked over to the table. "Doctor, are you alright?"

Simmons looked up at Sam, who was surprised to see actual pain in the man's face. "No, Captain, I'm really not. For the second time in three months, I've set events in motion that may finish, if not kill, the finest man I've ever known. I just made a call up to Bethesda so Victoria's boss can share with her the wonderful news that the man she loves may die today. How can I possibly be alright?"

"Doctor, you know I'm not your biggest fan. So, you can believe me completely when I say that this situation is not your fault. Even I am good enough at math to know the butterfly effect theory is bullshit. No act of yours long ago and thousands of miles away had any influence on events here. And, by the way, Ben is not finished yet. Roberts says all the factors line up on his side."

"Yes, sir. I hear what you're saying, but I'd like to continue to wallow in self-contempt for a time if you don't mind. At least until we get some good news."

"Suit yourself. I'm not here to console you, but I need to use your satellite phone to arrange for my wife to see to things back in Miami. I will, of course, pay for any charges incurred."

"Don't be ridiculous, Captain. I will not bill you for that."

"Yes, you will. I want no favors from you, and I won't have any pencil-necks hanging an ethics charge on me down the road."

"OK," Simmons said, pulling the phone out of his bag. "Do you know how to use one of these?"

2035 SW 14th Terrace, Miami, Florida
09:17 EDT, 6 April

Joana

Joana Mendez Powell was juggling three balls this morning. Her two children, Robbie and Danni, were, naturally, her most important and demanding ball. Fortunately, new birthday toys from Robbie's namesake, Sam's mentor, Bobby Moore, held their attention for a while. The second demand on her time was working up the chain to find *someone* who knew *something* about the household goods move coming up in a couple of weeks. It drove her crazy that a move of two hundred miles from Miami to Patrick Air Force Base proved more difficult than one of *five thousand miles* from Honolulu to Miami! How her parents managed eight of these during her father's navy career and kept their sanity was a wonder to her. The final and least urgent was the book cover she had contracted to design for a self-published author. She still had a couple of weeks to finish that, but he was nice, and she wanted to deliver early, if possible.

Joana hit save on her computer when the phone rang, grabbed it, and moved to a position where she could monitor the kids while she talked. She had learned that at least one sensor had to be trained on the children continuously, or mayhem would shortly ensue. The caller ID simply said INMARSAT Unk—it was probably from Sam. Who else would call using the International Maritime Satellite service? "Hello?"

"Hi, sailor."

"Well, my beloved captain, to what do I owe the surprise of an INMARSAT call? Did you forget my birthday or something?"

"Jo, I…"

Joana's blood went cold. This was going to be bad. "OK, darling, let's have it."

"It's Ben. We just medevac-ed him. He's on the way to Miami now and should get there about one o'clock."

"Oh, My God! How bad is it?"

"Very. He has a head injury, a kind of brain bleed."

Tears welled up, and her hands shook. Ben was not just another shipmate for Sam, but his closest friend and the brother he never had. And it didn't end with Sam. Joana was closer to Ben than her brother Eddie in many respects. She took a deep breath and tried to steady her voice. "Is he going to make it?"

"Jo, I want to tell you yes in the worst way. I don't know. The doc we have with us says he has the best shot we can give him, but there's just no way to tell with this sort of thing.

She wiped her eyes and took a deep breath. "OK, what do I need to do? Do you want me to call his parents?"

"No. Ben and I discussed this situation as a possibility when we took the new job. He didn't want them freaked out when there was nothing they could do. The service has to do the notifications anyway—protocol.

"I need you to be at the hospital when Ben gets there. The JIATF guys are working on it and will call you when they get one locked in. Mike Bryant is attending him on the flight and could use some help. Also, Ben's girl has been contacted by her people and is probably on the way down."

Oh, God! The math geek? What can I say to her? "OK, I'll do my best. Is anyone else hurt? You damn well better not be holding out on me that you're bleeding somewhere!"

"No, my love, I'm fine except for an acute case of the guilts. We had one other guy catch a hit, Brian Jenkins, but he'll be OK."

As hard as it was for her, she knew the responsibility factor would crush Sam. He would normally lean on Ben for help with that, but now Ben was the one in danger. "I wish I was there to hold you. Promise me you'll get Emilia to help you. And don't worry about anything here; I've got it covered."

"Jo, I… I don't have the words."

"Don't worry, my captain, I'm an artist; I know all the words."

"I love you, *querida*. I'll see you in a couple of days."

"Come home safe, *mi amor*."

The call disconnected, and she put the phone down. Robbie had come over and was looking up at her with the most profound concern a three-year-old could conjure.

"You're crying, Mommy. Do you have an owey?"

She picked him up and hugged him tightly as she blinked away the tears. "I'll be OK. Thank you, my little man!"

USCG Cutter *Kauai*, Underway, Caribbean Sea, 107 nautical miles north of Isla de Barbello, Honduras
09:47 EDT, 6 April

Lee

Drake stepped onto the Bridge and walked over to Lee. "You got the OOD?"

"Yes, COB."

"How's he doing?" Drake said, nodding toward Sam, sitting in his captain's chair.

"Don't know. He hasn't said a word since I reported the relief." *If he's anything like me, he's a wreck.* Lee had been frightened when the towline had broken, but the urgency of cutting away that loose end had pushed back the fear. But that had been nothing compared to the horror she felt when Mr. W suddenly just collapsed in front of her, writhing in pain on the deck.

The relief Lee experienced on hearing that he was OK after being shot was overpowering. She had almost hugged him when he stumbled back aboard, getting hold of herself at the last second and firing off a salute instead. Mere minutes later, John carried him into the medical station while she did all she could not scream.

"OK." Drake nodded. Then walked behind Sam's chair and said, "Captain?"

Sam turned slowly to him. "Yes, COB?"

"Sir, we have set up a makeshift ward for the wounded in the forward port berthing area. We've cleaned up the messdeck and cleared it out sufficiently for Chef to maneuver. He would like permission to resume normal meal preparation."

"Yes, that's a good idea." Sam nodded. "We have almost twice the compliment on board. Can he prepare enough food for everyone?"

"I think he's got gumbo and primavera planned for the next two meals. They should stretch OK."

"That's fine. Make it so."

"Yes, sir." He turned to leave, then hesitated. "You know, the XO will be OK, sir."

Sam turned to him and said, "Yes, he will."

Drake nodded, turned, and departed. A minute later, Roberts came through the door. "Permission to enter the Bridge?"

"Permission granted, sir," Lee said.

Roberts walked over to Sam, who stood up to greet him. As Sam extended his hand, he said, "Doctor, I can't thank you enough for your work today."

"All part of the job. Heard anything from the helo?"

"Not from them, which I'm hoping is good or, at least, not bad news. The guys at JIATF South lined up a surgeon at Dadeland Hospital in Miami. Ben should go straight in."

Roberts nodded. "That's good. I'm pretty sure he'll make it to Miami. After that, it's up to them. And Dadeland's one of the best."

"Good to hear. And how are your other patients? Do I need to arrange another airlift?"

"No, they're stable where they are. Getting knocked around in a helo hoist would do more harm than good at this point. They can hold out fine until we pull into Key West."

"OK. May I ask what you were doing with that wand when I came into the surgery this morning?"

"That 'wand,' as you call it, is an ultrasound transducer. I was mapping the hematoma to find the best location for the burr hole."

"I thought you needed MRIs or CAT scans to treat these things."

"You do, and he'll get one first thing in Miami. Understand, Captain, I wasn't fixing anything this morning. I was applying the neurosurgical equivalent of a tourniquet."

"Yes. I'm impressed you'd have tools available for this sort of thing."

"It's a different environment in combat medicine now. Twenty years ago, we didn't have a lot of injuries like that. That bullet would have gone straight through the helmet and killed him on the spot. The good news with the new materials is fewer immediate deaths; the bad news is more traumatic injuries. We learned quickly that head bangs can be as deadly as bullet wounds, so I added a craniotome to the kit."

"I see. What are Ben's chances?"

"You can never tell with the brain; everyone's different. I wish he'd come to me as soon as he got on board. He had a huge bleed, which is why his symptoms progressed so quickly. That said, all the risk factors and medical resources coming in are on his side. If I had to make a bet, I'd say he'll be fine if there are no other issues on the way."

"Well, I'm certainly glad you were with us on this trip. If you or your guys need anything, let me know."

"Will do. Thanks, Captain."

"Thank you, doctor."

After Roberts had departed, Sam walked over to Lee. "Lee, I'm heading below. Before I go, I just wanted to say what you did last night was one for the books. We probably wouldn't be here right now if it weren't for you."

Lee blushed and looked down. "Just doing my job, Captain." After a second, she looked up at Sam almost pleadingly. "Mr. Wyporek will be alright, won't he, sir?"

Sam smiled and lightly patted her shoulder. "Like the doctor just said, I'd bet on it. Have a good watch."

"Thank you, sir." Lee watched Sam leave, then turned to the radar for a check. *I don't know if we can rely on what that army guy said, but it picked the captain up a bit, Thank God.*

Hopkins

Hopkins was sitting in her stateroom, just completing a good fifteen-minute cry. She was utterly drained by the intense cycling of emotions since yesterday evening, starting with the fear of the extreme danger facing the crew. The battle itself was a fog except for that moment of sheer terror when the towline parted, and it seemed they were all lost. Then the relief of getting through, followed by the devastating report the XO had been shot, then he was OK, then at death's door again.

Hopkins thought the world of Ben Wyporek. He and the captain had come in together and turned what was a complete shitstorm into not just the best unit she had ever been assigned, but the best she'd ever *heard of.* They were both good, kind, and professional men she admired. Thank God she hugged the XO before he departed. It was the second time she had done that; the first was the mission back in January when that bastard Simmons almost got him killed. It was a serious breach of protocol for an enlisted member to hug an officer, but screw it. She never forgave herself for failing to hug her husband Brad before he left on the day he was killed on a search and rescue case. They had had a ridiculous snit that morning over something she couldn't even remember. She would not make that mistake again with someone special to her.

She looked at the picture on the wall of her two sons, with her and Fritz standing behind them. It was a Soccer Saturday from a couple of months ago, and Fritz was down from Cape Cod on a two-week leave. Fritz was a wonderful addition to her life. A tall Aviation Electronics Technician First Class stationed at Coast

Guard Air Station Cape Cod, Massachusetts, Erich "Fritz" Deffler was a master Unmanned Aerial Vehicle pilot who had deployed with them briefly last January.

Hopkins had vowed never to get involved with another Coast Guardsman after her husband's tragic death. Yet, she found herself drawn to Fritz during their time together on the deployment, and they arranged to see each other afterward. He was a divorced father of two young girls living with their mother in Hawaii and had immediately clicked with her two pre-teen sons. She loved his quiet confidence and sense of humor; he was one of the few people she knew who could regularly make her laugh aloud. Her smile faded, and the pain returned when she remembered that Ben Wyporek was another of those very few people. *God, I wish I could talk to Fritz right now, just to hear his voice.*

The knock on the door startled her. She wiped her eyes and took a deep breath. "Yes?"

"Emilia, it's me," came Drake's deep baritone voice. "Got a minute?"

"Sure, come in, Jim."

The door opened, and Drake stuck in his head. "I was just passing by and thought I'd ask how you are holding up."

"Maintaining an even strain, thank you. Just needed to pop in here for a minute to re-cage the gyros."

"I get it. This getting banged-up shit is becoming a regular thing with the XO. You and I ought to sit him down and straighten him out when he gets back," he said with a sad smile.

"Yeah, junior officers. What are we going to do with them?"

"Don't know. This is one of the few times I don't know a guy to see about the problem. Look, if you're up to it, I was hoping you could join me on a walkabout. I sense the kids are reeling after everything that's happened. We should help take some of the load off the skipper."

"I'm with you." She stood. "You know, it's ironic. The XO was just joking with me yesterday that me and you were soooo mom and dad."

Her tears welled up again, and Drake stepped in, shut the door, and hugged her. "He's going to be alright. Believe that."

After a few moments, she nodded and said, "I'm OK. Let's go."

USCG MH-60T 6023, Airborne, eighty nautical miles southwest of Key West, Florida
10:48 EDT, 6 April

Becker

Becker loosened her restraint harness and lifted herself slightly out of her seat. The slight pain in her upper thighs shifted to a much sharper pain in her coccyx. Being a pilot of a helicopter held several advantages over being a crewmember. As a commissioned officer, you were much better paid, of course. Then there was the matter of control—you drove in front and rode in the back. One significant disadvantage was that you were planted in a seat built for survival rather than comfort for hours at a time. The crewmen could get up and move around during the flight, but not so the pilots. Becker had what she called a "four-hour ass," meaning things really started to ache about four hours into a sortie. She was four and a half into this one, with two hours to go. *Ouch.*

The refueling operation aboard the Cutter *Northland* had gone without a hitch. *Northland* was a sister ship of the *Thetis*, and the similar configurations and procedures made the approach and landing easier. They employed "hot refueling" on this visit, accepting a slightly higher risk to save time and avoid the chance of problems during shutdown and start. The fuel hose was laid out along the deck edge before the helicopter arrived. After the landing and applying chocks and tie-downs, a refueling crew appeared and hooked up the single-point fueling nozzle to the aircraft. The process was reversed after pumping in enough fuel to top off all tanks. The crew disconnected the fuel hose, removed the chocks and tie-downs, and the helicopter was once more on its way to Miami, a mere twenty-two minutes after landing. They now had ample fuel to reach Dadeland Memorial Hospital in Miami, perhaps even enough to continue all the way home to Clearwater without refueling again after dropping off the patient. They would decide on that later.

There were no repeats of Bryant and Daniels's earlier hostility; the latter had learned his lesson for this trip. Neither was there much conversation, which was fine as far as Becker was concerned. Even in the relatively quiet, long en route segments like this one, the crew should have their heads in the game and eyes outside looking for trouble. This was doubly true of Daniels—he was a good man and an excellent rescue swimmer. Still, he was also one of the most empathically dyslexic individuals she had ever known. It wasn't the first time she had to intervene to prevent an actual fight in the cabin because of his mouth. She made a mental note to talk with his chief about it when they returned to Clearwater.

United Air Lines Flight 1990, Airborne over Myrtle Beach, South Carolina, en route Miami International Airport 11:53 EDT, 6 April

Victoria

Victoria appreciated the minor miracle that Debbie and Mr. Fletcher had achieved this morning. She was sitting in Seat A of the last row of the Airbus A319, her sometimes teammate Lashon Bell was seated in Seat C, and Seat B was empty. No one was sitting behind her, kicking or jostling her seat, and no stranger was sitting next to her, *touching* her throughout the flight. There were two exit doors directly behind her, and Lashon was steady enough to handle any emergency. It was a direct, non-stop flight, so there were only two horror-filled airport terminals to deal with instead of three, and they would arrive only fifteen minutes after Benjamin was scheduled to land at the hospital. It would take them at least an hour to deplane, get the rental car and drive over, but at least she would be nearby. Anyway, she was sure Benjamin would be rushed in for an MRI and from there into surgery—it would be several hours before she could see him, even if she were at the hospital when he arrived.

Bell focused on reading a book he had brought, his eyes coming up and scanning the cabin at regular intervals. Victoria knew

Lashon was very reticent and would be content to go the entire flight without speaking. She respected that and tried to keep herself occupied by reading the latest data science literature on her tablet, but she could not get her mind to focus. Victoria was still reeling from this morning's emotional upheaval of going from as happy as she could ever recall to this terrible fear of losing everything. She finally gave up, pulled up the two pictures of Benjamin from their day together, along with the others he had sent of his shipboard friends, and looped through them on her tablet. Each one told a wonderful story in her mind that pushed back some fear, at least a little.

Victoria never had a family or close friends in the conventional sense. Her parents were killed in an automobile accident when she was eight years old. Her sister Julie had raised her through high school and the beginnings of college. When her genius and autism revealed themselves after her parents' deaths, it became too difficult for her to interact with other children. So, she turned inward, focusing on her studies, which sped her through school but left her lonely. When Julie died, she thought her world had ended, but Julie's fiancé Peter came to the rescue. She completed her schooling with his help and was soon a vital part of the DIA team, but still without family or anyone she could call a friend, except Debbie. When Victoria saw the faces in Ben's pictures, even she could read the affection and trust they had for each other. His stories connecting those images were warm and funny, and she vicariously lived her dreams of a family through them. They were a great comfort to her just now.

About an hour later, they began their approach to Miami and Victoria raised the window's shade. Usually, she kept the shade open since seeing the outside helped her deal with the aircraft cabin's confined space. But with the sun on that side of the aircraft, she needed to reduce the glare on her tablet. Victoria was fascinated by the processes that went into flight and watched intently through the window as the wing's high-lift devices deployed, and they wallowed in for a soft touchdown on the runway. She could easily do the math of airfoils in her head. Still, it was a wonder to her that mere changes in the air's momentum could support the weight of a sixty-three-ton plane. She was curious why the pilot retracted the flaps and slats after landing when they would be used again for the next takeoff. *Benjamin's father is an airline pilot; I can ask him when we meet.* Then reality retook hold, and she fought back the urge to cry. *If we meet.*

As they were waiting for the other passengers to deplane, Victoria turned on her phone and checked her voicemail and text messages. There was no news of Benjamin's condition, but Debbie had sent a text message that he would go to Dadeland Memorial Hospital and provided an address. She showed it to Bell, who nodded and typed it into his phone to use for navigation after they rented the car. The trip through the terminal was loud and terrifying, and Victoria hung tightly onto Lashon's arm throughout the long walk and the wait in the car rental line. She did not mind being thought of as "clingy" today.

Finally, they were through the line, driving to the hospital. The weather was pleasant, sunny, and warm. The traffic was moderately heavy for mid-day. Benjamin had mentioned that traffic here was among the worst he had seen, although he admitted he had never driven around DC during rush hour. It took the better part of an hour to drive the ten miles from the airport to the hospital in University Park. As Victoria walked to the door with the stoic Bell, her apprehension increased with every step. She had never been in a hospital waiting room before but was sure it would be frightening and very lonely.

A Confluence of Souls

Dadeland Memorial Hospital, Miami Florida
14:21 EDT, 6 April

Victoria

After signing the visitors' log at the trauma center, Victoria and Bell headed for the waiting room. She was almost praying that seats were available away from other people, where she could hear her thoughts without distraction. When they came to the door and started looking around, an attractive, dark-haired woman noticed them and came over.

"Excuse me, are you Victoria Carpenter?"

"Yes, I am," Victoria answered, wondering how this strange woman could know her name.

"I'm pleased to meet you," she said with a smile. "I'm Joana Powell. My husband is Ben's commanding officer."

Victoria almost fainted with relief. Benjamin had described Joana Powell as one of the finest women he had ever met and considered her a close friend. He shared many stories of her warmth and kindness, and Victoria had been looking forward to meeting her. "Oh, Mrs. Powell, I am so happy to meet you! Benjamin speaks of you so often." She smiled as she looked her up and down. "He was correct; you are very beautiful." Joana gasped, and her eyes filled with tears. *Oh, no! I made her cry! Why can I never say the right thing at times like this?* "Mrs. Powell, I am very sorry. I did not mean to upset you," Victoria said hastily.

"No, please don't think that!" Joana said, then took a breath and wiped her eyes. "You could not have said anything more right just now. I know we've just met, but I want very much to hug you. Do you mind?"

"Oh, not at all!" Victoria answered and then gave her a warm hug. When they separated, she continued. "This is Lashon Bell. He escorted me down from Bethesda."

Joana held out her hand and said, "I'm pleased to meet you, Mr. Bell."

"Likewise, Ma'am," Bell said, shaking her hand.

"If you'll follow me, I have staked out seats for us over here. And I wish you two would call me Joana."

As they approached the empty seats, a young man with short hair in surgical scrubs and wire-rimmed glasses stood up.

"Victoria Carpenter, Lashon Bell, this is Mike Bryant. He's the Health Technician on *Kauai* and attended Ben on the flight," Joana said.

"Oh, yes. Benjamin has told me about you as well. How are you, Michael?" Victoria asked, holding out her hand.

"I'm well, thank you, Miss," Bryant replied, awkwardly shaking her hand.

"Oh, good. You are wearing surgical garments. Are you going to assist with the procedure?"

"No, Miss, they loaned me these after we got here. My uniform was...dirty."

"Oh, I see. Can you tell me what is happening?"

"Yes, Miss. It would be better if we sat down, I think." After they were seated, he continued. "What have you been told?"

"Benjamin suffered a head injury that resulted in an epidural hematoma. He was evacuated by helicopter from his ship and flown directly here."

Bryant relaxed a little. "That's right, Miss. Do you know what an epidural hematoma is?"

"I have read about it." She recited the definitions and details she had read on the MedlinePlus site.

Bryant was clearly impressed. "Wow. OK, after the lieutenant collapsed, the army surgeon we were carrying had a look and called the condition. He, um, did an initial treatment to remove the excess blood and relieve the pressure. Then we were hoisted by the helicopter and taken here. They took the lieutenant straight in for an MRI while I briefed Dr. Chaudhri, the surgeon, on how he got hurt and the steps we'd taken so far. He went into surgery about half an hour ago."

"Oh, I see. I am sorry to ask all these questions, but I am very nervous. Benjamin told me you were a heroic medic in the Army before you came into the Coast Guard. Can you tell me from your experience what we can expect?"

Bryant's mouth hung open briefly, then he said, "He told you *that*? Um, well, it's like this, Miss...." He then engaged in a serious discussion with the young woman for over thirty minutes.

The exchange astounded Joana. She and Sam had had Bryant over for dinner, along with a couple of other crew members. Despite their considerable talents at putting people at ease, they had barely gotten five words in a row out of him. This young woman had him excitedly telling his life's story minutes into their first meeting. Joana's turn came next.

"Joana, I hope you do not mind answering questions, but I am still very nervous and am hoping for a distraction while we await news of Benjamin's operation. He told me you do computer graphic design. I am comfortable working with computers, and I enjoy art, but I struggle with the concept of how they can be put together. Would you mind explaining how you do that, please?"

"My pleasure, Victoria," Joana answered. They went into a lively back and forth about raster graphics and bitmaps, 3D modeling, rendering, and the various other tools and techniques she used. Victoria's voracious interest in her work was so captivating that Joana could gratefully lose herself in the conversation and put aside, for a time, the crushing worry that brought them here.

A few minutes into the conversation, Bell realized what was happening, got up, and walked to Bryant. "Come on, kid. Let me buy you a cup of coffee," he said. Bryant nodded and followed him out of the waiting room. Once in the hallway, Bell said, "Don't take it personally. She has a one-person lock-on function."

An hour-and-a-half later, they were all together again when a staff member came into the room and announced, "Michael Bryant."

Bryant looked at the others and said, "This is it. I listed myself on the check-in form." They all stood and walked over to the woman calling his name. "I'm Bryant."

The woman looked at the others and said, "Are all these people family?"

"The women are cleared," Bryant said. He turned toward Bell. "I'm sorry, Lashon, you're not on the list."

"Not a problem. I'll hang out here."

"Thanks." He turned back to the woman. "After you."

The woman led them to a small room with a table and four chairs. "Wait here, please. The doctor will be here shortly."

After they all sat down, Victoria's mind was racing. *Why did they move us in here? Is it because it is bad news? Are they afraid we are going to make a scene?*

Joana looked at her and must have realized she was upset. She reached over and took her hand. "Don't go crazy, Victoria. The privacy laws prevent them from saying anything about Ben's condition in public, and that's why they moved us here."

"Thank you, Joana. I was worried about that."

There was a knock, and a tall, dark-skinned man with eyeglasses pushed up on his forehead stepped in and closed the door as Victoria, Joana, and Bryant stood. "Hello, I'm Rajesh Chaudhri. I have already met Mike. You are?"

"Doctor, this is Victoria Carpenter and Joana Powell. The patient has cleared both on his releases."

"Oh, good, please sit down."

When they had settled, Victoria's hands were shaking. Joana put her right arm around Victoria's shoulder and put out her left hand for Victoria to hold.

"I have good news. The procedure went very well." Chaudhri paused when Victoria exhaled. "I closed up the damaged artery with a very small craniotomy. He will be in recovery for another hour, and then we will move him to the ICU."

"So, when will he wake up?" Victoria blurted out. *Why did you say that? Give the man a chance!* "I am sorry, Doctor. I am very nervous."

"That's perfectly understandable." Chaudhri reached out and patted her hand. "I would not expect him to come out of the coma for at least twenty-four hours, possibly as much as seventy-two."

Victoria took a deep breath. "He will be alright then, correct?"

"There is every chance of that. I didn't see any damage to the brain structures, either on the MRI or when we had him open, but it was a huge bleed. We won't know for sure until he awakens, and we can do some tests."

Victoria closed her eyes. "I need to be with him."

"We can certainly arrange that once he is settled in the ICU, but honestly, he won't be conscious again for at least a day."

"I need to be with him, Doctor. I can talk to him. Would that help?"

"I don't know. I'm sure it wouldn't hurt."

"That is it, then. I am staying."

Chaudhri smiled and patted her hands again. "Very well, I'll see to it. If you'll excuse me, I need to look after another patient." They all stood and shook hands, then Chaudhri left the room.

"I need to get down to Key West to meet the ship if I can," Bryant said. "Lashon is heading down there, and I thought I could bum a ride off of him."

"I can stay here with you if you like, Victoria," Joana said.

"No, you need to attend to your children. I would be very grateful if you could wait with me until Benjamin is in his room."

"Absolutely. Mike, do you need anything before you go?"

"No, thanks, Mrs. P. I'll be fine."

"Well, I guess we can go rejoin the world then."

They moved back into the waiting area and met up with Bell.

"Victoria, I need to get on to Key West to meet Pete. I think they will be in a little after dawn, so I need to head down tonight. Will you be OK here?" Bell asked.

"Lashon, I'll take care of her," Joana said. "You and Mike hit the road before it gets too crazy."

"OK, if you're sure," Bell said.

"I am sure, Lashon. Thank you very much for taking care of me!" Victoria said as she hugged the agent.

"OK, let me bring up your bag, and then we'll roll."

The two men left after retrieving her bag, and Victoria and Joana sat down again. "Joana, may I ask you a personal question?"

"Naturally. What's on your mind?"

"I do not know if I am right for Benjamin. I was so frightened, and I am still so frightened about what happened to him. Does it go away?"

"No, it doesn't. You can learn to live with it, but it's always there. When Sam is out and the phone rings, my heart is in my throat until I find out it's not bad news. It might be a little easier for me than for some other spouses. My dad was a Navy submariner, and we never knew where he was or what he was doing. We learned how to live with the fear."

"Have you thought about asking Samuel to stop and do something else?"

"I have. And he could, too. He turned his back on a lucrative Wall Street career to join the service long before we met. If I were to push hard and make it a choice between the Coast Guard or me, I know he would resign his commission. To provide for us, he would go cap-in-hand to his father and, after a suitable period in scut jobs to atone for his previous career mistake, be welcomed back into the fold, start making big money and be home every night. Cool, right? The problem is he wouldn't be Sam anymore, just another soulless suit commuting in every day and doing anything, everything to make more money because that's all they live for.

"So, I hold my breath when the phone rings and treasure every day he's home with us. He's worth it."

"Do you think Benjamin is worth it?"

Joana looked at Victoria and raised her eyebrow. "That's a question only you can answer. I can tell you that Ben is certainly a close second to the finest man I've ever known. I am friends with Emilia Hopkins, and she swears there isn't anyone in the crew who wouldn't take a bullet for him. But I can't tell you he's worth being a Coast Guard spouse. I can only assure you that there's no one else who would be more worth it."

"I see," Victoria said with a furrowed brow. "Do you think I would be good for him?"

"Victoria, I've only known you for a couple of hours, but I think you're wonderful. I know Ben is crazy about you. But, besides the sudden death thing, which is admittedly quite big, there's the career thing. I work from home and am very happy with that. Sam could be assigned to Kodiak, Alaska, and I'd be OK with living there, as long as they have the Internet. Would you? If you want a top-flight career, moving up the corporate ladder, you need to find someone else because there will eventually be a collision. Then it's either a breakup or someone compromises big time, which probably still ends in a breakup. Just saying, better now than later."

"Oh, I have no aspirations toward a career. I am not good with people at all. There is a...a *problem* that hinders my understanding of affect, so I could never cope with being a manager. I like to do mathematical analysis, and I am very good at it. I think I can find that work anywhere. Perhaps I could even do that online, like you. But I am worried about the fear and if I can handle it."

"So, here's your test, girl. This is almost as bad as it gets. You'll have your answer when it's over."

Victoria turned to face her. "It could be worse than this?"

Joana nodded, thinking of Hopkins's experience. "Yes. You can get the final news without the wait." She put her arm around Victoria's shoulder. "But you'll always have your Coast Guard family to help you."

Victoria was contemplating that last point when the hospital staffer appeared again and came over to their location. "Miss Carpenter? Mr. Wyporek has been moved to his room in the ICU, and you can see him now."

"Yes. Thank you. Please go ahead." Victoria grabbed the handle of her rollaboard, and she and Joana followed the woman through several hospital corridors before arriving at the door. Victoria froze at the door, locked in an internal conflict of desperately wanting to be with Benjamin and a mind-numbing fear of what she would see when she walked into the room.

After a few seconds, the staffer remarked with some annoyance, "You can go in now, Miss Carpenter."

"Thank you, that will be all. We can handle it from here," Joana responded with even more annoyance. After the staffer wheeled and strode off, Joana took Victoria's free hand and whispered, "There's no hurry at all. We can go in whenever you are ready."

Victoria took a deep breath, nodded, and said, "Thank you, Joana. We can go in now." They walked through the door together. Victoria went slightly weak in the knees at her first sight of Benjamin, then recovered when Joana put her arm around her and steadied her. Victoria carried out the process she had planned while they were waiting. She positioned her rollaboard against the wall, pulled up a small chair, sat, and took Benjamin's left hand in both of hers. His hand was warm but limp, and she briefly held it to her cheek as she looked at his face. His eyes were closed like he was asleep, and his head had a small bandage on the right side. He breathed silently and steadily through a nasal cannula, connected by a clear tube to a bubble humidifier. Several tubes and wires led from under his blanket to a monitor station displaying pulse, blood pressure, respiration, temperature, and O2 saturation. Victoria observed with relief that all these readings appeared to be within the normal range from what she had read.

Joana kneeled beside the chair and asked. "Are you OK? Is there anything I can do for you?"

Victoria put her arm around Joana's shoulders and said, "No. You have done so much for me already. I was really frightened when I arrived, and I was relieved that I could meet and talk to you while waiting. Benjamin is fortunate to have friends like you."

Joana brushed away a fresh tear and said, "Thank you." She handed Victoria a note. "This is my cell phone number. I'll be in tomorrow, but if you need anything or just want to talk, it doesn't matter what time you call me. OK?"

"Thank you, Joana. I will see you tomorrow," Victoria said and turned back to Ben.

Joana stood, leaned over, kissed Ben lightly on the forehead, then turned and did the same to Victoria before leaving the room.

"Benjamin," Victoria began. "I do not know if you can hear me. But if you can, I want you to know I am here and waiting for you to return." She held his hand to her cheek again. "I love you so much, Benjamin. Please come back to me."

USCG Cutter *Kauai*, Underway, Yucatan Channel, fifty-seven nautical miles south-southwest of Cape San Antonio, Cuba
16:48 EDT, 6 April

Hopkins

The smell of the primavera was very inviting. Hopkins knew Chef was putting his heart into this meal, appreciating the opportunity it furnished to restore some balance after the mayhem. Sam had requested everyone not on watch muster on the afterdeck as they had the day they left Key West. The mood was subdued—everyone was thinking of the wounded men, especially the XO.

"Attention on Deck!" Drake shouted as Sam appeared. He stopped in front of the assembled group and returned Drake's salute. "All present or accounted for, sir."

"Thank you, COB. Fall out and gather round, please!"

Hopkins made her way to stand behind Sam as the crew moved forward. All looked concerned, as they knew some important news had arrived. Hopkins noticed that even Lee, usually solid as a rock, seemed almost fearful and held Williams's arm with both hands as they moved forward.

"Folks, I have some good news. We just got word from JIATF South: Mr. Wyporek's surgery was successful, and he has been moved into recovery."

There were a few gasps, then a chorus of cheers and clapping. Hopkins, holding her breath, exhaled and shared a look with Drake, who nodded and mouthed, "Told ya."

Sam held his hand up, and the celebration subsided. "Definitely cause to celebrate, but he may be out for a while. The next couple of days will tell the tale. I want to call out Major Roberts and Specialists Rabin and Langley, who no shit saved the XO's life and did some fine work to make Brian Jenkins and our other wounded guests as comfortable as possible. Let's hear it for our army guests." There was more clapping and nods to Roberts and his aides. "Sadly, we are carrying back the remains of Jorge Dominguez, the DEA agent. He saved the mission and most of our lives by getting *Carlos Rojas'*s engines operating at that most critical time and fell alongside the XO in that last firefight. Let's remember him always as one of our shipmates." There was more subdued clapping and a few nods.

"I want to finish with a personal thank you from me for the terrific job you have done on this mission. I can't give you much in the way of details, but I can assure you it was of supreme importance to the country. Alright, I don't want to keep you from Chef's culinary masterpiece any longer. We will pull into Key West for a fuel stop tomorrow at 09:00, and I'll pass along anything I hear about the XO. Questions?" After a brief pause, he continued. "Chiefs, hang around for a bit. Everyone else, dig into that primavera!"

"Attention on Deck!" Drake shouted, and everyone came to attention.

"Carry on, thank you!" Sam said.

Hopkins moved over to Drake, and together they went to see Sam. He was talking with one of the SEALs and turned as they stepped over.

"Chief Drake, Chief Hopkins, have you met Senior Chief D'Agostino?"

After greetings and handshakes, Sam continued. "We will obviously be tight for space. Fortunately, it will be a quick trip. COB, get Major Roberts set up in the XO's stateroom, then you and Chief Hopkins work with the senior chief to find a spot for his guys." He turned to D'Agostino. "I'm sorry, Senior Chief, but the best we can offer until Key West is some deck space for each man."

"We've had worse, Captain."

"Yes, I'm sure you have. Anyway, please see COB here if there's anything you need. Thank you, Senior Chief, and I'll see you later." After returning D'Agostino's salute, he turned to Drake and Hopkins. "Chiefs, we need to keep a lid on this mission. I need you to do a personal sit down with every crew member and emphasize what classified means and what can happen to them if they spill to anyone. Read me?"

"Yes, sir," Drake and Hopkins said in unison.

"OK, let's head in before Chef runs out of chow."

Sam

The arrival at Truman Annex was a solemn event. As soon as *Kauai* moored, the wounded were taken off and placed in ambulances for the local hospital trip. Admiral Pennington and his command staff were standing in ranks on the mole and came to attention and saluted when Dominguez's body was brought ashore. The seven unwounded SEALs carried the body as an impromptu honor guard as Bondurant blew the salute on his Boatswain's Pipe, and *Kauai's* crew rendered honors in tropical blue uniforms. Everyone stood at attention until the body had been turned over to Agent Bartlett and placed in the hearse standing by on the mole.

When the hearse had driven off, Sam came ashore, walked over to Pennington, came to attention, and saluted. Pennington returned the salute and shook Sam's hand. "Congratulations on a magnificent job and bringing your crew back safely, Sam."

"Most of them, sir. But thank you."

"Yes, I can't tell you how sorry I am about Ben. I inquired over there before I came down—no change. But it's still early, and I think we can count on him being back with us soon."

"Yes, sir," Sam nodded. "Beyond the personal stuff, he's left quite a hole Hopkins and I are struggling to fill."

"I know, I know," Pennington said, then turned and looked at *Kauai's* crane and boat damage. "Our beautiful Orchid got a bit roughed up. I'm relieved you had as few casualties as you did. Listen, I know you're beat, but can you take me around and give me a personal report?"

"Of course, sir. Do you want me to hold off on refueling until after you leave?"

"No, no. Please have the crew carry on with the work. We need to get you all home ASAP."

"Yes, sir," Sam said tiredly. "If you could follow me, please."

Dadeland Memorial Hospital, Miami, Florida
14:38 EDT, 7 April

Victoria

It had been a long, mostly sleepless night for Victoria. The nursing staff had provided her with sheets and pillows she could use in the room's recliner, and she made the best of it. However, besides the new surroundings and general discomfort of the chair, the monitor station beeped loudly after recording Ben's blood pressure at fifteen-minute intervals. Her brain's rational part acknowledged the beeping was a normal part of the hospital environment, and there was no reason for alarm. Yet, that tiny, less rational part saying, "Yes, but what if this time there is?" always won out, waking her up and forcing her to check for herself.

For most of the day, Victoria talked to Benjamin and read to him from a Patrick O'Brian adventure novel she had downloaded to her tablet. She knew he enjoyed the sound of her voice and had expressed his enjoyment of the historical fiction genre in one of their talks. Victoria hoped she was reading it correctly—the authenticity of the language O'Brian employed was very challenging for her. By mid-afternoon, fatigue won out, and Victoria put her head down on the bed next to Benjamin's hand and slept.

It was that wonderful day again, back on the DC Mall. The weather was perfect, and she was walking close to Benjamin, feeling his warmth, feeling totally safe in his presence. They stopped outside the Metro station, and she looked up into those beautiful eyes, blue as the sky, while he pushed her hair back and stroked her temple. She loved the feeling as his fingers gently caressed her hair. Then the wonderful dream faded away.

But not the gentle stroking of her temple.

Victoria's eyes flew open, and she bolted upright. Benjamin's hand fell away as she sat up, so she reached out and grasped it with both of hers. He looked at her with those beautiful eyes and a slight smile on his stubble-covered face. *I am not still dreaming, please; I am not still dreaming!* "Benjamin!"

He was trying to say something, but was too hoarse to speak. Finally, he mouthed, "Water, please." Victoria put his hand down carefully and poured a cup of ice water. Her hands were shaking as she moved the cup to his lips until his hands closed over and gently steadied them. After a few sips, he nodded, and she placed the cup back on the table, then returned and took both his hands in hers. He smiled more broadly at her and squeezed her hands softly.

"Hello, Victoria," he said in a creaky voice. "How was your day?"

She couldn't find the words to speak, couldn't even find the thoughts to think. She just leaned over, gripped Benjamin's shoulders, buried her face in his chest, and quietly sobbed as he gently stroked her hair.

The Reckoning

USCG Cutter *Kauai*, Moored, Truman Annex, Naval Air Station Key West, Florida
15:49 EDT, 7 April

Hopkins

They were just completing sailing preparations, and Sam was discussing some last-minute details in his cabin with Hopkins. "I just saw Major Roberts and his crew off an hour ago. Has Dr. Simmons left yet, Chief?"

"Yes, sir. He and his pal slithered off while you were tied up with the admiral. Good riddance."

Sam sat back and rubbed his eyes. "I know how you feel and would like to pile on, but the man was just doing his job this time around. He can't be blamed for what happened. I also talked to him afterward, and he's pretty twisted up about the XO. You might want to cut him some slack."

"With respect, sir, not going to happen."

"OK, just a thought," Sam said and stood up when his cell phone rang. Hopkins recognized the ringtone as belonging to Joana and said, "I can step out, Captain."

"No, please stay." He picked up the phone and pressed the talk button. "Hello, sailor. I'm here with Emilia, and I hope you have some good news."

"Better than that, hang on," Joana said, followed by a ruffling sound.

"Hello, skipper." It was Ben's voice, a little raspy sounding but clear.

"Ben!"

"Yes, sir, back from the dead. Sorry to give you such a rough time."

Sam tried to say something but couldn't get the words to come out. Hopkins, blinking back tears herself, noted his struggle and gently took the phone from his shaking hand. "XO, is that really you?" she said.

"Chief? Yes, it's me. Is the captain alright?"

"He's... temporarily indisposed. How are you, sir?"

"Still a little loopy from the drugs and all, but everything seems to work."

"I'm so glad to hear that! Hang on, the captain's back." She handed the phone back to Sam, who had just finished wiping his eyes.

"Ben, words fail me. We didn't expect you awake for another day or so."

"Oh, Captain, you know Wyporeks are too ornery to follow the rules."

"So it would seem. Truthfully, you can't imagine how relieved I am to hear your voice. Is there anything you need?"

"Captain, Victoria is here holding my hand and smiling at me. I can't think of a single thing I could add to that, but thank you. Before I hand the phone back to the captain's spouse, do you have any orders for me, sir?"

"Yes. I order you to take it easy, mend, and enjoy your time with your lady. Clear?"

"Aye, aye, sir! Here's Jo."

More shuffling, then Joana's voice returned. "OK, my captain, I've stepped out of the room. How are you?"

"Absolutely exhausted and deliriously relieved. How did this come about?"

"I was on my way and almost at the hospital when I got the call from Victoria. When I got to the room, the scene was one for the ages."

"Wow, I wish I could have seen that. What do you think of her?"

"Victoria? She had me crying like a baby within a minute of meeting her. She's amazing! If Ben doesn't marry her, I'll ditch you and marry her myself."

"I'm crushed!"

"It's not personal. Men are just soooo overrated," she teased. "Seriously, I can see why Ben is so bowled over by her and hope they can make it work."

"OK. Emilia is pointing at her watch, and I need to get us underway for home. I'll call you when we are snugged down at PC."

"Do it safely, please, and get some rest. I'll see you soon, my captain."

"Goodbye, my love." After hanging up, Sam turned off the phone and dropped it in his desk drawer. "Chief, it looks like we have a pre-sailing announcement that should put some spring in everybody's step."

"That we do, Captain!"

"Well, let's get it done. Set the Special Sea Detail, and I'll see you on the Bridge.

"Very good, sir."

Isla de Barbello, Honduras
04:23 EDT, 8 April

The attack began with a twelve-man assault team landing just north of the fortified position of the Gate and pushing south. They used silenced pistols to kill anyone they met and were guided by observations of a small, infrared camera-equipped UAV hovering overhead. Resistance was surprisingly light, but even had it been heavy, it would have made no difference—former Spetsnaz soldiers trained and led the team while their opponents barely knew how to aim and pull the trigger. They had pushed to the water's edge within fifteen minutes, leaving no survivors. After setting remote-controlled and booby-trapped demolition charges on the heavy machine gun and in the ammunition magazine, they reembarked on their rubber boats to rejoin the main force.

The assault on the quay was carried out by a twenty-man party split into equal groups and landing at opposite ends. The operation proceeded much like the landing at the Gate: the two groups swept inward from each end, silently dispatching any person they encountered until finally converging in the center. It was here that the men discovered that their target, OSV *Rojas*, was missing. The only evidence of her presence was the discarded mooring lines still hanging in the water from the quay. The assault team leader quickly changed the rules of engagement to kill only armed persons on sight—he needed prisoners to interrogate. Now augmented by the twelve-man team, the primary force spread out to assault the hacienda and dormitories.

The main assault was almost anticlimactic. Two ten-man teams each took a dormitory while the twelve-man team attacked the hacienda. The guards' dispatch was the last silent operation of the day—the teams used grenades and automatic rifles for the buildings' forced entry, since there was no further need for stealth. True to form, the Salinas members resisted to the last, futilely, as their opponents hopelessly over-matched them. At the end of the assault, only a couple dozen day workers remained alive. These were interrogated and then penned up while the team leader called in for instructions.

"Boss, this is Piotr," the leader said, once his satellite phone achieved a connection.

"Yes, Piotr. Give me some good news," Crețu responded.

"Sir, the good news is the assault on the port was completely successful. We have liquidated all Salinas members on Barbello."

"I am awaiting the news of the boat."

"There is no news, sir. The boat is gone."

"*What?*"

"It apparently sailed two nights ago. The day workers we took said there was a big firefight off the point. The mooring lines we found dangling off the dock suggest that someone came in and took the boat out from under the Salinas's noses."

"Who in the hell would have the resources to do something like that? What did those workers see?"

"Practically nothing, sir. The fighting occurred off the point at the entrance to the harbor. None of these people could see anything in detail in the dark or with the storms at that distance. We found that heavy machine gun emplacement beat to hell and picked up a couple of dud M792 rounds lying around it."

"What is an M792?"

"Sir, the M792 is a high-explosive round fired by the American Bushmaster cannon. The Americans and Canadians are the only ones in this hemisphere who use them. My conclusion is the American navy came in under cover of darkness and extracted the vessel."

"Shit!"

"What do you want me to do, sir?"

"Alright. We can at least complete the punitive aim of this raid. Search the warehouses for product. If you find a worthwhile amount, use the day workers to load it on the command vessel. Then blow up any magazines and arms or munitions and burn every building to the ground."

"Shall I dispose of the day workers when we are done?"

"No. Kill any who resist or refuse to work, but leave the rest alive with any food and water you find. Make sure they know you are with the 252 Syndicate. We want this object lesson to be shared far and wide. Report back when you are done. Questions?"

"No, sir."

"Get on with it. I want all our men off that island by sunset. Out." The call disconnected.

USCG Cutter *Kauai*, Moored, USCG Station, Port Canaveral, Florida
08:03 EDT, 8 April

Sam

"Captain, quarterdeck here. There's a captain headed this way with another lady officer, sir."

Sam cringed, then said, "Right, I'm on my way. And Connally, there are no 'lady officers,' just 'officers.' OK?"

"Yes, sir," the young fireman replied.

Sam hung up the phone and grabbed his cap. "Another lady officer" implied the captain was female, and a female captain was almost certainly his boss, Captain Mercier. That was quick— they'd only secured from mooring stations about half an hour ago. With her crane and boat destroyed and possible structural damage from the rocket hit, *Kauai* was in no shape to go out again, thank God. So, he wondered what mischief would put the Seventh District's Chief of Response on a three-hour car trip up from Miami instead of just picking up the phone. Fortunately, Sam was well rested for the encounter after six good hours of sleep—exhaustion, relief, and a thorough but respectful browbeating from Hopkins and Drake had seen to that.

Sam made his way to the quarterdeck and stepped over onto the pier. He saw it was Captain Mercier and a female lieutenant he did not recognize, and Sam rendered a crisp salute as they approached. "Good morning, Captain."

"Good morning, Sam," Mercier said as she and the lieutenant returned the salute. She shook hands, saying, "I'm delighted to see you back in one piece." She turned to her companion. "This is Lena Huang from SFLC Norfolk, and she's here to have a look at your damage and get the ball rolling on repairs."

"Lena, Sam. Pleased to meet you," Sam said, shaking her hand.

"Same here."

"Ma'am, if you'll follow me, please." Sam led the other two officers past *Kauai*'s bow, stopping when they were alongside and could see the damage clearly.

"Holy shit!" Huang said. "What happened?"

Sam looked at Mercier, who said, "The action is classified. Sam will share whatever aspects are needed to complete repairs, but the location and nature of the mission are 'need to know' only."

"I understand, Captain," Huang said. "Sam?"

"We were hit by a rocket in the crane's arm. As you can see, it's severed. My chief engineer says the boat has had it—the console is smashed, and the hull tubes are shredded. We have minor shock damage on the rear superstructure and, I suspect, the deck below the crane and boat, and the windows of the port

Bridge wing door are blown in. We haven't done a thorough assessment yet."

"Right," Huang looked at him in wonder. "Did you have casualties?"

"Just one from this hit. Shrapnel wound. He'll recover."

"Wow. I'm glad to hear that," Huang said.

"Sam, could Chief Drake take Lena around for the inspection? There are some things I need to discuss with you in private."

"Yes, ma'am. Excuse me, please." Sam stepped over to the quarterdeck and picked up the phone. Within a minute, Drake had come ashore and rendered the proper greeting. "COB, Lieutenant Huang is from the Surface Force Logistics Center, and she's here to do an assessment for repairs."

"Glad to have you, Lieutenant," Drake said. "I hope you brought something to crawl around in besides tropical blue."

"What engineer would leave home without coveralls, Chief?" Huang smiled, patting her gym bag.

"Ma'am, I think this is the beginning of a beautiful friendship. Will you follow me, please?" Drake said.

As they walked off in deep discussion, Sam said, "Well, I guess 'he knows a guy' up at SFLC now."

****

Sam had finished providing his action report, recorded on an encrypted audio recorder Mercier had brought. They had moved on to award recommendations. "I want the Silver Star for Ben and Lee."

"That's a pretty tall order. It will be hard to push that through without going public on a lot of stuff," Mercier said.

"That's my recommendation, ma'am. I understand I'm not the last word, but there it is."

"OK, I'll do my best. But Lee? Are you sure?"

"Ma'am, do I need to remind you she went out into the open, under rocket and automatic gunfire, and single-handedly cut away the towline wreckage with an ax, saving the ship and

491

mission? They should name a Fast Response Cutter after her, for God's sake."

"Touché. Next?"

"Bronze Stars for Hopkins, Bondurant, and Williams. Also, for Roberts, if you can push it through the army."

"Those should be doable. Anyone else?"

"Yes, Commendation Medals for Drake, Bryant, Brown, and Lopez. Achievement Medals for Hebert and Jenkins. Oh, yes, Purple Hearts for Jenkins and Ben if we can swing it."

"I'll do what I can."

"I appreciate that, ma'am."

"That was fun. Now on to the hard stuff. I've combed the lists for a good J.O. to send up here, and I'll need your opinion on some candidates."

Sam's face darkened, and he said coldly, "Why, ma'am?"

"I think you know why."

"It will be at least a month before we're repaired and operational again. Ben will be back in a couple of weeks."

"You don't know that, Sam. The initial report looks promising, yes. But I read up on this type of injury. We must come to terms with the fact that he might be finished. In that case, we need to have a replacement in the pipeline."

"It's only been one day, ma'am. I'm not ready to just write him off like that!"

"We haven't written him off, Sam. Believe me, if he can come back, he will. But you need to face reality here. If he can't return, you need to have an XO who can do the job. If nothing else, you'll have help to put things back together while Ben is healing up." She paused as Sam's head sank. "C'mon, you know I'm right about this."

Sam squeezed his eyes closed for a few seconds. He was so relieved and happy Ben was awake that he had not considered the long-term implications. Now, that realization had come home with a vengeance. "Yes, I understand, ma'am. I'll look at whoever you decide to send up."

"Thank you, Sam. Do you want me to swing by the hospital and tell him when I get back?"

Sam looked up and shook his head. "No, ma'am. That's my responsibility. I'll head down there as soon as I have things squared away here."

"I'm sorry about this, Sam. Is there anything I can do for you? Anything you need?"

"I guess I'll know better when Lena is done with her inspection. I'll let you know, ma'am."

Secure Conference Room 6A, National Security Agency Headquarters, Fort Meade, Maryland
15:35 EDT, 8 April

Simmons

Simmons looked around the table at the select committee's assembled members, and his thoughts returned to the last mission debriefing he had attended, sitting in the hot seat with Sam Powell and Ben Wyporek. Those poor men thought they would be hanged as they went into that meeting—keeping the secret that they were already acquitted was very distasteful to him. *At least I'm on my own this time, right where I belong.* Kevin Welles, the Director of National Intelligence, led the committee. It included the Chairman of the Joint Chiefs of Staff, the Directors of the CIA and NSA, and Vice Admiral Irving, the DIA Director.

"Dr. Simmons, we have your report," Welles said. "And we would like to ask a few follow-up questions. Do you have questions before we start?"

"No, sir."

"Good. Admiral Irving?"

"Thank you, sir. Dr. Simmons, did you have difficulty understanding your orders before this mission?"

"No, ma'am."

"In that case, why didn't you follow them?"

"I am not aware of any breach of my orders, Admiral."

"You were ordered to secure Dr. Gronkowsky and his research materials. Yet, you destroyed the latter."

"My orders, Admiral, were to secure Dr. Gronkowsky and all his research materials, *if practicable,* and ensure their destruction otherwise. It was practicable to secure and extract Gronkowsky, but his research and data were all stored on air-gapped computers without removable hard drives. I could not ascertain a practicable means of extracting the data, so I ensured its destruction." *Which I would have done, anyway. My God! Don't we have enough of this crap already?*

"I find it difficult to believe that a man of your intelligence, learning, and skills could not find a means in the time available."

"I am neither a computer scientist nor an IT engineer, Admiral. I do not have the learning and skills to crack into a well-secured computer."

"You had plenty of manpower available between the SEAL team and Coast Guard personnel. You could easily have physically extracted the computers to the Coast Guard cutter."

"And when they asked me, 'What's this?', what was I to tell them? That they risked their lives and violated Honduran sovereignty to be accessories in a violation of the Chemical Weapons Convention? I remind you that you gave your word to General Miller and Admiral Pennington that this horror would be destroyed, and I doubt they would have agreed to this mission otherwise."

"Don't pretend you're an idiot, Doctor. You tell them what you need to in order to complete your mission. You serve the nation best by seizing opportunities, not catering to the sensibilities of people outside the community."

So that's how it is. You were trying to build brownie points with the President with a fait accompli *over-delivery on the mission. You knew Miller and Pennington would raise a stink over something like this, so you lied to them.*

"I think the nation is best served by adhering to core principles that separate us from rogue nations and criminal syndicates. If you wanted someone without scruples on this mission, Admiral, you should have sent one of your toadies, not me."

"You insolent bastard! I'll...."

"Enough!" Welles said as he slammed the table with his fist. Then he looked back and forth between them. "What the hell is the matter with you two?"

Simmons took a breath, then said, "I apologize for my outburst, sir."

Irving glared at Simmons and said, "If I can continue...."

"No!" Welles said. "I move we rule that Dr. Simmons complied with his orders and table further discussion of that point. In favor?" All committee members except Irving raised their hands. "Carried." Welles looked around the table. "Does anyone else have questions? No? Then I guess we can adjourn this one. Thank you, everyone." As everyone at the table rose, he continued. "Dr. Simmons, can I have a moment with you, please?"

"Yes, sir," Simmons replied. Irving glared at him as she picked up her notebook and walked out.

When only the two of them remained, Welles said, "Have a seat, please." After they sat down, he continued. "I take it Admiral Irving did not discuss her issues with you beforehand."

"No, sir."

"How do you assess your present situation?"

"I not only failed to rid the king of the turbulent priest, but I also flipped him off for good measure. I don't think I'm much of a contender for employee of the month over at DIA."

The older man chuckled. "You really are a wiseass. What do you plan to do?"

"I think I'll be looking for something else. This last one did it for me. Going down there with one hand tied behind our back sucked, sir! It ended up with one good man dead, four wounded, and the numbers would have been the other way around if Irving had had her way. She would have sent us in without medical support if Pennington hadn't stood up to her. Did you know that?"

"No, I didn't."

"After tonight, I can't work for her. She'll be looking for payback, and I don't need to be worrying about that, along with everything else. I guess I can fall back on the original career, maybe teach. I don't know."

"I understand, but I have to ask you for a favor. We really can't spare you from the committee work. Let me set up a detail position for you to work directly for me. That way, you can stay in DIA but be out of her reach. The DIA Director is a temporary appointment, and you can think about moving back once she moves on. You won't have the reachback into the organization you're used to, but it will keep you in the game."

Simmons was silent for a moment. "Give me a couple of days to think about it, but I'm inclined to accept. Thank you, sir."

"I'm glad to hear it. I'll get the ball rolling on my end. Let me know as soon as you can."

"Yes, sir."

They both stood, and the older man offered his hand. "Take it easy, Pete. Hope to hear from you soon."

Simmons shook his hand firmly. "Thank you, sir. You will."

Coda

Ben

Ben remained in the ICU for a day after recovering consciousness and had just completed a move to a standard room for three more days of observation before his eventual release. He and Joana worked on Victoria all day to get her to go somewhere where she could get some good sleep. She elected to take a room at the hotel across the street from the hospital while Ben was still an inpatient. She also insisted on being with him at his apartment for the two weeks he was "Sick in Quarters," what the Coast Guard called sick leave, to complete whatever rehab he needed. Fortunately, Ben still had his Miami apartment—between the shipyard, his training up in Virginia, and *Kauai's* relentless shakedown and operational schedule, there wasn't time to close out his lease and clear out the place.

Ben was delighted but visibly nervous about learning of Victoria's decision to stick around after his discharge. When she left the room to call her office to give them an update, Ben turned to Joana with a worried look. "Jo, can I use your cell, please?"

"Sure, here you go," she said as she handed it to him.

Ben hurriedly dialed the number of his apartment management office. "Janie, Ben Wyporek. Well, been better, but OK. Yes, do you have a cleaning service that can do a quick turnaround on my place? Yes, everything from bottom to top. As soon as possible. Tomorrow? Yes! That will be fine. Could you let them in, pleeeeease? Thank you, Ma'am!" After hanging up, he looked at the ceiling and said, "Thank God!"

Joana took her phone back and said, "Are you freaking kidding me? You're out of a coma one day, and your biggest worry is a dirty apartment?"

"Jo, it may just be because I got my bell rung, but I can't remember whether I left dirty skivvies on the floor in the bathroom." He peered hard at the door. "This situation was not on the list of possibilities the last time I left! What? Did you think I was some kind of neatnik?"

Joana shook her head sadly and said, "No, just dreading what I can expect when Robbie hits puberty!"

Victoria returned with a smile a couple of minutes later with the news that they had approved her leave. Sam and Hopkins, both in civilian clothing, came in almost on Victoria's heels, with Sam drawing a tender hug and passionate kiss from Joana before moving to Ben's warm handshake. Then Hopkins received a hug and handshake.

"Victoria, this is my CO, Lieutenant Sam Powell," Ben said as Sam stepped forward to take Victoria's hand.

"Oh, Lieutenant Powell, Benjamin has told me so much about you!" She turned to Hopkins. "And you are Chief Petty Officer Emilia Hopkins! Benjamin has also told me much about you. I am so glad to meet you!"

"Victoria, we are all on first names off the ship. You can call me Sam if you like."

"I think she would prefer Samuel, dear," Joana corrected him.

"Yes, and please call me Emilia," Hopkins said with a smile. "What a treat to meet you at last." She turned to Ben. "Here's your keys and phone, XO," she said as she handed them to him.

"So, what do you think of driving the Camaro?" Ben asked.

"A bit too much horsepower for a mom like me. And I don't want one anywhere near Chris when he gets his license in a few years!"

"Aw, MOM!" Ben quipped to a smile from Victoria and laughs from everyone else.

After more laughs and conversation, Sam turned to Joana. "Dear, would you mind giving Emilia a ride over to her place, please? I need to discuss something with Ben."

"On it, my captain. I'll see you when you get home." She turned to Ben, shook her head with a smile, and walked out of the room.

Hopkins walked over and shook his hand again. "I'm thrilled you're OK, sir. I can't wait for you to get back and take over the inbox again! Victoria, it was wonderful to meet you, and I hope to see you again soon."

"Thank you, Emilia!" After Hopkins left, Victoria turned to Sam. "Do you need me to leave, Samuel?"

Sam gave Ben a sadder look, and Ben said, "No, Victoria, please stay. Sam is about to explain that my injury may keep me from coming back to *Kauai.*"

Victoria's smile disappeared, and she sat next to Ben and took his hand in hers.

"Well, so much for breaking it to you gently," Sam began. "I want to emphasize that we will do everything we can to get you back, but the boat is off-limits for you for two weeks, at least. That's why I had Hoppy bring your stuff. After that, you'll need a full physical with a special neurological workup. Don't ask me what that means; it was just what they told me. If that clears you, you're in."

"Then I guess I had better study!" Ben said lightheartedly. On the inside, he was quite worried. It was a wait-and-see situation, and there was little he could do to affect the outcome. Victoria turned to him with a tragic expression, and he gently squeezed her hand and said, "It will be alright." He turned back to Sam. "Will you be able to get someone in there to help, sir? I can't stand the thought of all my work being dumped on Hoppy and COB."

"Captain Mercier has put together a slate of candidates for a temp slot, and I'll be giving her feedback first thing tomorrow."

"OK, sir. Whoever gets picked, please have them see me before they head over. I'd like to set them up as best I can."

Sam nodded and said, "I knew you would say something like that. You're a class act, Ben."

"I've been the understudy for the best, sir." Ben offered his hand, and Sam shook it briefly, then pulled him into a hug.

He rose again and blinked a few times before continuing. "I need to get back home and administer some hugs. I'll swing by tomorrow before Hoppy and I head back to the boat. Is there anything I can bring you?"

"I'm good, sir. Please give R & D a hug from Uncle Ben!"

"Will do. Goodbye, Victoria. I wish we could have met on a happier occasion."

"Thank you, Samuel."

After he left, Victoria turned to Ben with tears in her eyes. "Oh, Benjamin! I am so sorry! I do not know what to do!"

He caressed her face, wiping away one of her tears. "Hey, I'm not out of the game yet. And what you have done, what you are doing…. When I came to yesterday and saw you sleeping next to me, I thought I was hallucinating. I didn't want to wake you, but I had to touch you to make sure you were real. When I brushed your hair back, you smiled in your sleep. Then when you woke up, it was finally real; you were really here. Can you even imagine what that meant to me?

"But I'm worried about you. Victoria, I love you so very much, but maybe you need to consider your interests now."

"What are you saying, Benjamin? I love you."

"Yes, but look at where we are. I will either be out of a job soon or return to the job that put me here. No matter which way this turns out, what do I have to offer you?" Victoria looked at him, and her face slowly changed into a soft smile. "What?" Ben asked.

"You provide exactly what I need, Benjamin."

Ben looked back in befuddlement. *She is saying this like it has some profound meaning. It is from something…. What?* Then he remembered. *Oh, THAT!* He smiled back and held his arms open. Once she had snuggled in, he said, "Victoria Carpenter, you are a very foolish woman." She hugged him tightly, and he kissed the top of her head. "We'll figure this out somehow."

****

Ben was a few days out of the hospital, but still reporting daily for testing and physical therapy. Victoria was doing what she could to help, driving him to and from the clinic, cooking and cleaning up, standing firm against Ben's resistance to the doctor's orders prohibiting such activities until they were sure his balance and depth perception were up to it. She had never been so assertive with another person, which both found surprising and pleasing.

This night, they were headed to Sam and Joana's for what Joana called a "House Cooling Party"—a celebration of her finally besting the bureaucratic dragon and securing the household goods move to Canaveral. The only other guests were Emilia Hopkins and Fritz Deffler, who was down on leave from Massachusetts. Ben was nervous, despite the small gathering, as this was the first social occasion he had attended with Victoria, and he wasn't sure how she or they would react.

He needn't have worried. Joana met them at the door, gave each a warm hug, and then led Victoria to the kitchen, where Emilia was already waiting with wine. As Ben started to follow, Joana turned and said, "Whoa, sailor. We're going in for girl talk. You can join your mates in the den."

Ben forced a smile and dutifully joined Sam and Fritz in the friendly technical discussion they were having in the den. After a few minutes, several bursts of raucous laughter, including Victoria's, were drifting in. Sam and Ben paused, directing puzzled looks at the kitchen. Looking back and forth at the two men, Fritz smiled and said, "Gentlemen, you're being dished up in there. Em and I haven't been together long enough for her to have any stories that funny about me."

The dinner and the rest of the evening went swimmingly. Emilia and Fritz announced that he had been given orders to the new UAV unit standing up at the Coast Guard aviation deployment center in Jacksonville with a promotion to chief petty officer. They all celebrated that Fritz and Emilia's separation distance had shrunk from a two-and-a-half-day drive to one of two-and-a-half hours. Not cohabitation, but an improvement. The evening came to a pleasant end, with Victoria sharing warm, tearful hugs with Joana and Emilia as she and Ben left. The drive home was quiet—Ben did not want to distract Victoria as she drove home at night in a strange place and car. However, even back at the apartment, she was pensive, and Ben finally had to say something. "Are you alright, Victoria? Did someone say something to upset you?"

"No, Benjamin. On the contrary, I am very sad I will have to leave. Joana and Emilia are so wonderful and welcoming. I know I am very different from everyone else in how I think and talk, but they made me feel like I belong. I have never felt that way before tonight. Between them, the pictures you sent me, and stories you told about your shipmates and their families, I long to be a part of this world."

"Why don't you then?"

She gave Ben a puzzled look. "I do not understand."

Ben swallowed hard. "Why don't you become part of this world? Assuming I pass the physical and get back in the game, why don't you move down here?"

"Benjamin, are you suggesting we live together?" Victoria replied in astonishment.

"Yes, I am. I love you, Victoria. I'm probably not the easiest guy to live with, but I want to be with you."

"Benjamin, I..." She looked down. "I have issues that would be difficult for you to deal with, things you do not know about that do not come out in phone conversations or sporadic dates. It is not as easy as you think."

"Victoria, with respect, I think you are selling me short. Do you love me?"

She looked up into his eyes. "You know I do."

"I probably have quirks you haven't seen or thought of. Would you discard me without at least trying to accommodate them?"

"No, certainly not."

He took her hands. "I can't imagine anything about you that would make me not want to be with you. On my honor, I promise you I would not give up on us without the fight of my life. I know this is a big decision, and I don't expect you to answer right now, not until this medical thing sorts itself out, but please consider living with me."

Victoria blinked away tears, put her arms around Ben's neck, and pulled him into the most passionate kiss either had experienced. When she pulled back, she cupped his face in her hands, looked into his eyes, and said, "I will live with you, medical issues notwithstanding." She broke into a playful smile. "You are a very foolish man, Benjamin Wyporek." Then she hugged him tightly. "We will figure this out somehow."

Victoria

Victoria sat anxiously in the waiting room of the Patrick Air Force Base Medical Center. In the two weeks since his discharge from Dadeland, Benjamin had completed his week of physical therapy and several consults, culminating in a cranial MRI. This final consult with the neurologist was the last step in determining whether Benjamin would return to duty on *Kauai* or begin processing out of the Coast Guard with a medical discharge.

They had spent the last week at a local hotel with Benjamin, meeting with medical professionals, Victoria interviewing with local scientific consulting firms, and looking at apartments together. Victoria was confident that Benjamin would be cleared for duty, but increasingly discouraged by what she felt was a series of failed interviews. Benjamin had the opposite view. While he was worried about his medical issue, he confidently expected Victoria would connect with a company that could see past her abbreviated people skills and leverage her genius with data science.

Every time Victoria had left Benjamin to go inside for an interview, he had given her a passionate kiss "for luck." When his name had been called in the waiting area, she stood with him and gave him an equally passionate kiss. "For luck," she said.

"Hopefully, you are better at passing it on than I seem to be," he said with a rueful smile.

That had been almost an hour ago. Victoria was flipping through apartment photos on the Internet to get her mind off the current situation, trying to find one that optimized their combined travel time to Port Canaveral for Ben and Melbourne, where the firms she interviewed with were located. Her decision to leave the DIA was not an easy one—it was the only job she had ever held, and she knew she would miss Debbie and Peter. She was surprised when Peter encouraged her decision to leave, given how he had always been so protective of her, and wondered if it had something to do with his new special assignment to the Director of National Intelligence's staff. In any case, he expressed his delight that she was getting together with Benjamin and giving living together a test before they took things further.

Victoria was still pondering this and the many things she had to take care of starting her new life when the door opened, and Benjamin emerged. She almost jumped out of her chair to go to him. He was smiling, an excellent sign. "Benjamin, please tell me!" she pleaded.

"Fit for Duty!" he exclaimed happily. "They will keep an eye on me for a while, and I am to avoid…." He opened the folder and read, "'Elective activities associated with a high risk of head injury.' So, no skydiving, boxing, or other contact sports for me."

"Oh, Benjamin, I am so happy for you!"

"Thank you, Victoria, for being here. I don't know how I could have gotten through it without you. Now let's get lunch, and then we'll get you to that next interview. I'm feeling very lucky right now, and I'm sure some will rub off on you!"

Ben

They had just returned to the hotel room from the last interview. Like the others, Victoria was convinced that she had bombed, based on the interviewers' questions and her perceived reactions, and she was inconsolable. Ben was frustrated with himself for not finding something to say or do that could help her. He was about to suggest they go out, perhaps to the Space Center Visitor's Complex, anything to get her mind off it, when her cell phone rang.

"It is them! It is them!" Victoria said after checking the caller ID.

"OK. Do you want me to leave while you talk to them?"

"No! No, no, no. Please stay and hold my hand."

"Alright, I'm here for you." He took her left hand with his right and held up crossed fingers on his left as she answered the phone.

Victoria took a deep breath to control her voice, then answered the phone. "Hello? Yes, it is. Yes, I have time to talk now." The conversation lasted about ten minutes, but Ben could tell it was excellent news after two. "Yes, that would be acceptable. That is correct. Very good. I look forward to receiving them. Goodbye." She hung up the phone and squealed, which stunned Ben, given her voice's typically low pitch. "I have the job!" They both jumped up, hugged, and then kissed.

"Congratulations, my love!" Ben gushed. "I knew it was just a matter of finding the company that had brains. When do you start?"

"It will be in the package they are sending me, but I have so much to do!"

"I'll be there to help. I guess we really do need to pick out an apartment," Ben finished with a smile.

"Not yet! I have something else in mind right now!" Victoria said with a mischievous grin that surprised Ben.

"By all means, lead on, My Lady!"

"Heroic Airline Crew Awarded Queen's Commendation for Valuable Service in the Air," *The Times*, 7 June.

The Queen's Birthday Honors list published yesterday included the award of the Queen's Commendation for Valuable Service in the Air to each of the six crewmembers of the Pan-Commonwealth Airways flight downed by adverse weather over the North Atlantic Ocean last March.

PCA Flight 403, originating from London Heathrow to Nassau Lynden Pindling International via Bermuda on March 26th, encountered unforecast severe thunderstorms with hail on approach to Nassau, resulting in complete loss of power. Unable to reach land, the Airbus A321LR was forced down in the open Atlantic Ocean over 100 miles (169 km) from Nassau. The crew managed what was described in official reports as "an extraordinarily difficult power-off open sea landing of the crippled jet and subsequent evacuation of the 120 passengers on board without loss of life or serious injury." A U.S. Coast Guard Cutter rescued the passengers and crew within hours.

The flight crew, Captain Emma Taylor, 42, Pilot; First Officer Samesh Patel, 36, Co-pilot; Chief Steward Richard Burgess, 53,

Senior Flight Attendant; Ms. Nancy Hamilton, 43, Flight Attendant; Ms. Bryony Weaver, 33, Flight Attendant; Mr. Naveen Ashkani, 24, Flight Attendant, were cited for exceptional skill, judgement, and perseverance in the award. The crew's noteworthy performance had been previously mentioned in the official Department of Transport, Air Accidents Investigation Branch report on the incident released on May 13th.

Asked for comment, PCA Chief Executive Officer Ralph Desmond (Gp Capt RAF, Ret., DSO, MC, DFC) said, "We are, of course, proud, pleased, and extremely grateful to Her Majesty for her recognition of this magnificent crew. A 'dead stick' landing of a large airliner at sea and evacuation of its passengers afterward is one of the worst situations a crew can face. Captain Taylor and her crew provided a shining example of how skill, professionalism, and teamwork can overcome this most daunting challenge. It is a great privilege to include people of this calibre among the PCA family."

Captain Taylor was characteristically modest, commenting simply, "I was serving with the best crew in the world and did what PCA trained me to do. We were lucky in the end, with both a benign sea and rescue close at hand. I want to extend my most sincere gratitude to the crew of the U.S. Coast Guard Cutter *Kauai*, who plucked us from the sea and storm at substantial risk to themselves and carried us safely to Nassau."

Notes from the Author

USCGC *Kauai* is fictional. There is no "D Class" of the 110-foot patrol boat series, and the last of those built was USCGC *Galveston Island* (WPB-1349). I created a fictitious D-Class to buy some extra margin of verisimilitude and get the nitpickers off my back. The medium endurance cutters *Dependable*, *Northland*, and *Thetis* are real and currently in service as of this writing. The "Fast Response Cutters" referred to by Sam Powell in Chapter 18 are a real class of patrol vessels and a-building of this work's writing. They are each named for a Coast Guard enlisted member of historical note.

Pan-Commonwealth Airways is fictional. However, the incident depicted is a fictional composite of two real-life incidents:

- USAir Flight 1549, an Airbus A320 with 150 passengers and five crew, on January 15, 2009: the aircraft collided with a flock of geese and lost power on both engines shortly after takeoff from La Guardia Airport. Unable to reach La Guardia or any other airport, Captain Chesley Sullenberger made a forced landing in the Hudson River west of New York City and successfully evacuated all passengers and crew.

- Garuda Indonesia Flight 421, a Boeing 737-300 with fifty-four passengers and six crew, on January 16, 2002: the aircraft entered a severe thunderstorm and lost power on both engines due to rain and hail ingestion. Unable to reach an airport, Captain Abdul Rozaq made a forced landing in the Bengawan Solo River in Central Java, Indonesia. One flight attendant died of injuries received in the crash, but the remaining crew and all passengers survived.

✱✱✱✱✱✱✱✱✱✱✱✱✱✱✱✱✱✱✱✱✱✱

Caribbean Counterstrike is the second novel in the Cutter *Kauai* series and my second novel. It benefits from the experience I acquired in its predecessor and the fact that the crew and their life aboard have been established, allowing more focus on the plot.

It has the same feeling of team and family among *Kauai*'s crew—this is one persistent element throughout the series. The most significant change from the earlier novel is the "special mission" status the boat and crew have obtained.

During *Dagger Quest*, the shadowy "JUBILEE Committee" of senior U.S. government intelligence community officials has discovered the handiness of having a seaborne platform that can respond almost immediately to a crisis, more or less stay in the background while doing so, and perform well independently. It is also instrumental in having a crew that is free to act across the lines between law enforcement and combat operations (the Department of Defense is expressly prohibited from conducting law enforcement by the Posse Comitatus Act). The downside, of course, is that an aging Coast Guard patrol boat brings far less combat capability than a Navy vessel. The storyline includes the fact that the Director of National Intelligence has invested heavily to modernize and harden her. The crew knows the investment implies a special status and steps up to the increased demands with pride.

If *Kauai* existed in the real world, she would be worked just as hard in her "day job" as other Coast Guard cutters, and the first two vignettes in the novel reflect this. The smuggler intervention in the first to stop and arrest a dangerous criminal trying to enter the U.S. secretly reflects a very unusual level of "intel" involvement and coordination relative to the real-world context. However, having an asset with *Kauai*'s capability opens the door to many things not done today. The second involving the airliner's forced landing at sea is a more conventional mission, but still quite outside the norm regarding the number of survivors the boat must deal with and the need to move them inside (due to the storm).

For those inclined to say "Oh, come on!" to a modern airliner brought down by hail and rain ingestion, I invite you to read about the USAIR Flight 1549 Hudson River ditching in 2009 and the Garuda Indonesia Flight 421 mishap in 2002. If anything represents a leap of faith for this vignette, it is a successful ditching of a large aircraft in the open ocean. This is an immensely difficult task that must work on the first try—there are no do-overs for a "dead stick" landing. Believe it or not, the pervasive calm amongst the survivors is not uncommon. Large groups can get out of hand if panic takes hold (as almost happens with the lightning strike during the rescue), but people tend to rise to the occasion if they have confidence in folks trying to help them. Both the flight crew and the coastguardsmen know this and maintain a calm demeanor, despite their natural anxiety over the situation.

This story explores personal and emotional command challenges at the senior and junior levels. Admiral Pennington must send this elite crew in on a mission that is not only difficult to pull off, but, if it goes wrong, they will likely be wiped out in a horrifying manner. In the story, he was *Kauai*'s first commanding officer, and so he understands at a deeply personal level what he is asking of Sam on this mission. It is even more personal and stressful for Sam, as every decision he makes could result in the deaths of some or all of the people he has come to love over the past year. Sam does not have the luxury of standing down when his best friend and second in command, Ben, is gravely injured, and he must carry on with the command burden alone while awaiting news of his fate.

The relationship between Victoria and Ben took careful effort because of the need to wrap in so many extraordinary elements. Their ability to build a strong relationship, despite the physical distance between them, is another leap of faith. But, when you consider each was bowled over by the other in their first meeting, and they were able to talk openly and frequently from the outset, the quick transition to a loving physical relationship makes sense. The fact neither could admit their love, given their openness about everything else, might seem odd until you consider both had been burned badly by such a revelation in previous relationships. Each thinks, "this is too good to be true," until events finally force their hands.

Bravely and Faithfully

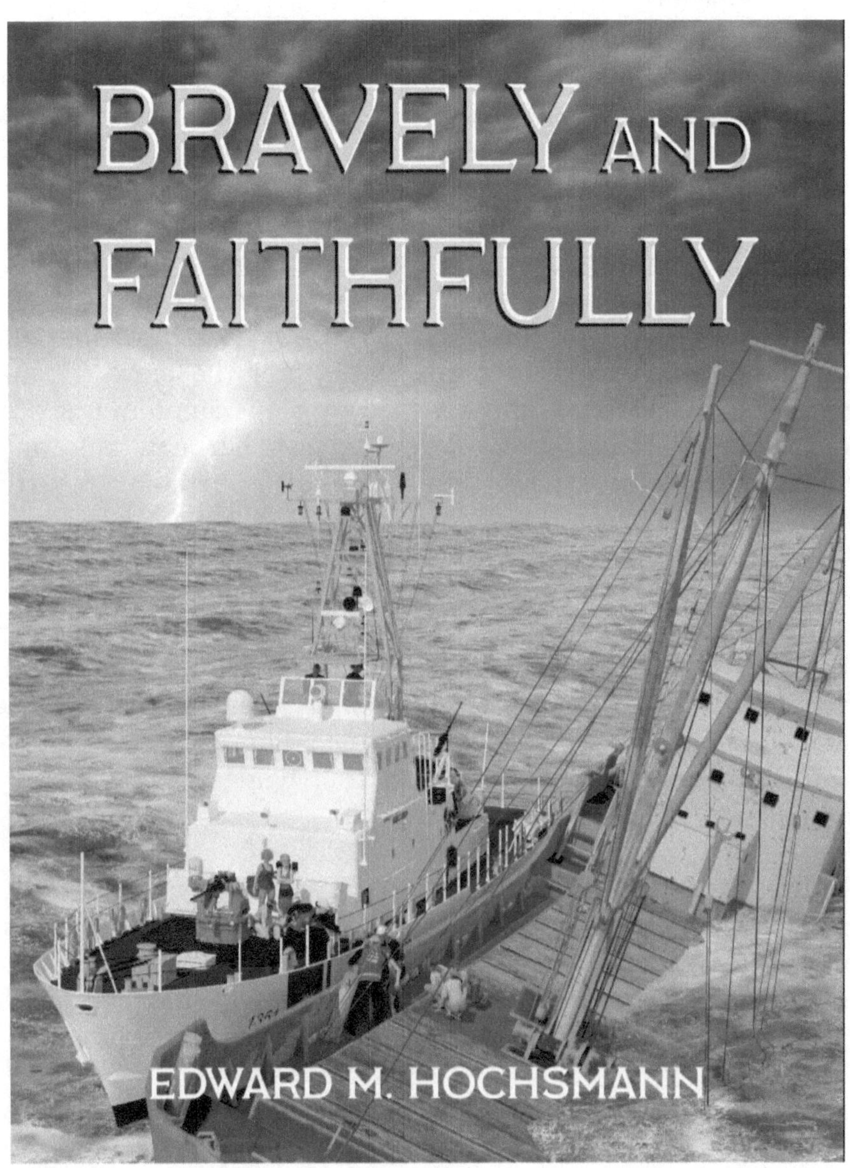

Main Characters

<u>Haley Reardon, Lieutenant, U.S. Coast Guard</u>. Haley is a superbly competent, hard-charging young officer offered her dream job—command of a patrol boat on the front lines of Coast Guard operations. Easier said than done. Haley must find a way to win over the elite crew of the Coast Guard cutter *Kauai*, replacing a beloved commanding officer promoted out of the job.

<u>Benjamin "Ben" Wyporek, Lieutenant Junior Grade, U.S. Coast Guard</u>. Ben is the executive officer or second-in-command of the Coast Guard cutter *Kauai*. He is a young officer, but experienced and heroic, holding the complete trust of the crew. He must overcome the challenge of the departure of his commanding officer and best friend and help Haley fit into her new role as his commanding officer while managing his courtship of Victoria Carpenter, the love of his life.

<u>Victoria Carpenter</u>. Victoria is a neuro-diverse mathematical genius, formerly an analyst with the Defense Intelligence Agency, who met Ben during a joint operation almost a year ago. Her condition makes some ordinary life activities challenging. She is deeply in love with Ben, who helped her leave her safe but unfulfilling sheltered existence. She struggles with her fear for Ben's safety when he is out on missions.

<u>Arthur "Art" Frankle, Senior Case Officer, Defense Clandestine Service, Defense Intelligence Agency</u>. Frankle is a veteran field officer, instructor, and mentor to many younger agents. He is approaching retirement age and considering moving from the field to a less "kinetic" post as an instructor or administrator.

<u>Emilia "Hoppy" Hopkins, Chief Operations Specialist, U. S. Coast Guard</u>. One of the "old salts" among the crew, she is a vital source of counsel for the officers and leadership for the enlisted. She has enormous respect and an exasperated affection for Ben, who reminds her of her late husband. Although a straight arrow, she is not afraid to forego convention in highly unusual circumstances.

<u>Shelley Lee, Boatswain's Mate Second Class, U.S. Coast Guard</u>. The premier small boat driver of the crew is more rough-and-ready than Hopkins and a solid, courageous performer. She and Ben are close in age, similar in personality, and share a strong mutual respect and trust bond.

<u>James "COB" Drake, Chief Machinery Technician, U. S. Coast Guard</u>. The senior enlisted member of the crew and the classic father figure among the enlisted and, to some extent, Ben. He is the quintessential "operator" and has what amounts to an underground network of fellow CPOs from whom he can acquire technical assistance, materiel, and "intel." His background is somewhat mysterious, but he is "connected" up to the senior officer level of the Coast Guard.

Select Technical Terms

1MC	Ship's internal announcement system
252 Syndicate	Transnational Criminal Organization
BRI	Belt and Road Initiative—a global infrastructure development strategy adopted by the Chinese government
CAC	Common Access Control [card]
CO	Commanding Officer
COB	Chief of the Boat
Conn	Position controlling operation of the ship
DIA	Defense Intelligence Agency
EO	Electro-Optical
EPIRB	Emergency Position-Indicating Radio Beacon
FC3	Fire Control/Command and Control system
FRC	Fast Response Cutter—replacement for the Island Class patrol boats
Gitmo	Nickname for Naval Base Guantanamo Bay, Cuba
GPS	Global Positioning System
Helm	Position or station controlling the ship's rudder
Knots	Nautical Miles per Hour
"Light Off"	Start or activate an engine or device
Main Control	Control station for the ship's main engines
NHC	National Hurricane Center
NVG	Night Vision Goggles
OOD	Officer of the Deck
PB	Patrol Boat
Port (side)	To the left, when facing the bow aboard a ship
RHIB	Rigid Hull Inflatable Boat
SAMC	Sino-American Mining Corporation
SFB	Space Force Base
Starboard (side)	To the right, when facing the bow aboard a ship
UAV	Unmanned Aerial Vehicle
WILCO	Brevity code for "Will Comply"
XO	Executive Officer—second-in-command of a ship

515

Dear God, be good to me;

The sea is so wide,

And my boat is so small.

Breton Fisherman's Prayer

Part I—Foundations

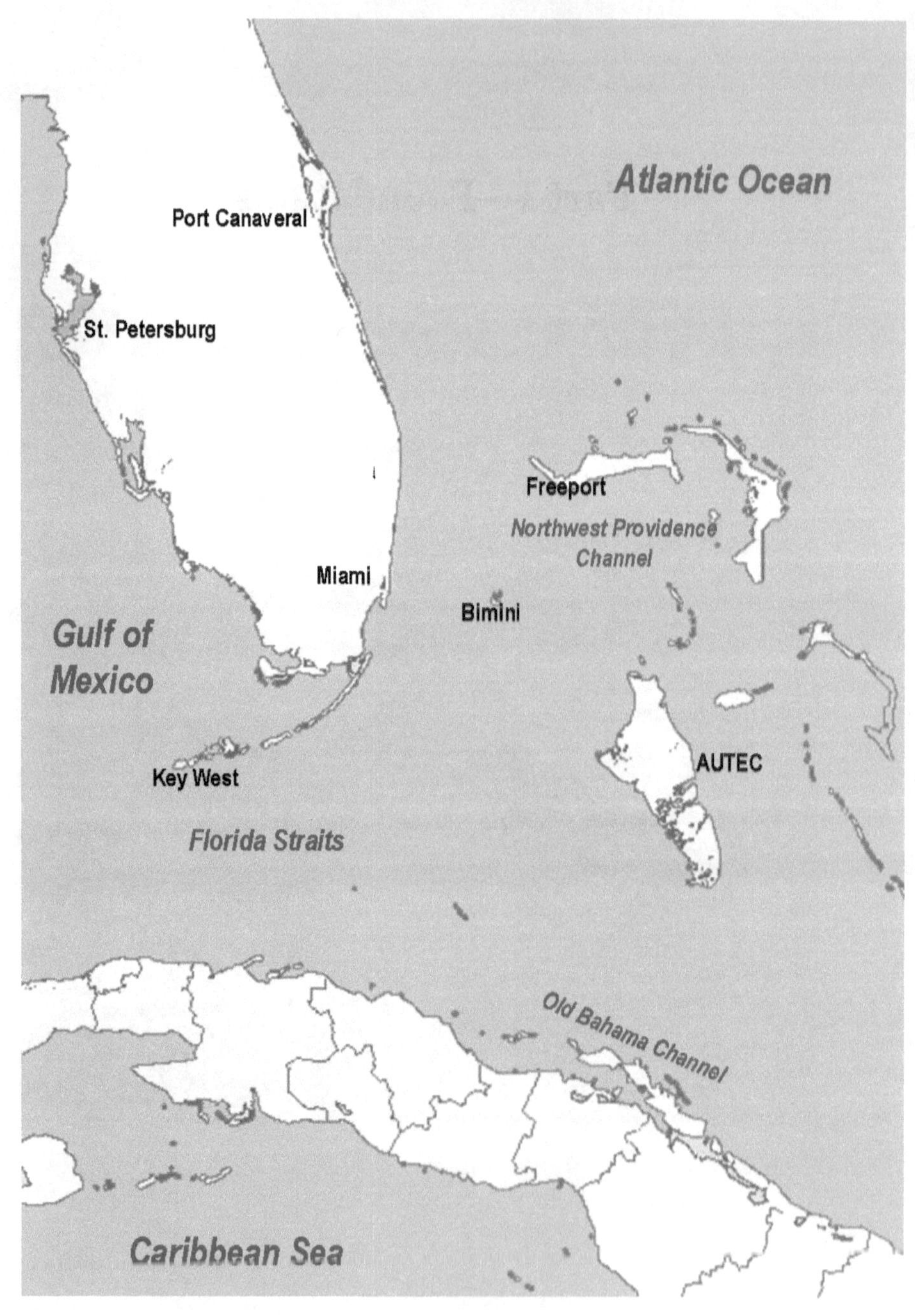

Atlantic Ocean
Port Canaveral
St. Petersburg
Freeport
Northwest Providence Channel
Miami
Bimini
Gulf of Mexico
Key West
AUTEC
Florida Straits
Old Bahama Channel
Caribbean Sea

From the Jaws of Death

It started as a wobble in the African Easterly Jet, a river of air flowing across the continent of Africa from east to west just north of the equator between the scorching Sahara Desert and the relatively cooler rainforests adjoining it. The disturbance created an area of unstable air, which allowed the formation of thunderstorms as the disturbance drifted westward across Cameroon and southern Nigeria. The persistence of the thunderstorms, fed by enormous amounts of evaporated water from the forests, eventually created a narrow trough of low pressure drifting off the coast into the Gulf of Guinea. A tropical wave was born.

Tropical waves often dissipate as they move over the slightly cooler environment of the Atlantic Ocean. Still, it was just past the autumnal equinox, with the sun almost directly overhead at noon, and the water was warm enough to sustain the thunderstorms within the system. It was being tracked and observed by this time, with computer models churning through terabytes of weather observational and simulation data, trying to forecast the risk of development. As the wave drifted west-northwest and away from the equator, it started drawing in air from its surroundings. But the system was large enough that Coriolis force began pulling the inflowing air to the right. Eventually, an equilibrium between the inward draw of the low pressure and the outward pull of the Coriolis force created a circular spin of the atmosphere. The weather satellites noted this change, and the wave was officially labeled Tropical Depression number 16, or TD16 for short.

The meteorologists at the National Hurricane Center, or NHC, in Miami, Florida, were very interested in the system by this time. They hoped that the moderate wind shear suppressing the deeper convective thunderstorms in TD16's center would persist long enough for the system to hook on to a low-pressure trough crossing just north of its track and be pulled safely northward into the open Atlantic. It was not to be. The trough passed without connecting, and TD16 moved slowly out of the area of wind shear. The thunderstorms in its center were now free to build to great heights, the condensation of water vapor releasing vast amounts of heat trapped by the spinning air around the storm. A convergence and lifting of warm, moist air releasing energy into the closed circulation created a positive feedback loop, steadily decreasing the air pressure in the center and pushing the spinning winds above the threshold of thirty-nine miles per hour. When the satellite data revealed that the sustained winds had reached this next stage of cyclogenesis, system TD16 acquired a name; the tenth issued that season. Tropical Storm Jacob had arrived.

Jacob plodded steadily westward, carried along by the easterly trade winds like many Cape Verde storms. Unfortunately, this kept it above some of the warmest water in the world, and the storm hungrily fed on the energy released as the converging winds lifted the moist air aloft in its center. After two days over the warm water, with little wind shear or other environmental impediments, Jacob charged past the seventy-four miles per hour sustained wind threshold and became the season's sixth hurricane.

The meteorologists at the NHC issued hurricane warnings for the Lesser Antilles Islands, Puerto Rico, and Hispaniola. The consensus of the myriad storm models was firm on this point: these islands would take a hit. From Hispaniola on, things got crazy—several forecast weather effects in play could send Jacob anywhere from straight west over Cuba, the Yucatan Peninsula, and the Gulf of Mexico to curving north into the Atlantic east of the Bahamas. Jacob continued to build, surging through Category 2 to reach Major Hurricane, Category 3 status a few hours before its first landfall on the island of Antigua. After battering that unfortunate land and the neighboring islands of Monserrat, Nevis, and St. Kitts, Jacob roared onward toward the Virgin Islands and Puerto Rico.

As Jacob penetrated the Caribbean basin, the meteorological picture became less uncertain. A turn to the north was now forecast—the average of the models predicted a path somewhere between Florida's gulf coast and the Atlantic just east of the Bahamas. The cities in the dead center of the prediction cone, from Miami to Jacksonville, began emergency preparations with the evacuation of people, aircraft, and ships. In the meantime, recovery vessels and personnel converged on the areas damaged in the storm's wake.

The amount of energy powering a Category 3 hurricane almost defies belief. The largest explosion ever triggered by man released the energy equivalent to the detonation of fifty million tons of TNT—the condensation of water vapor rocketing upward in Jacob's core released an equivalent amount of heat energy into the storm *every hour.* Jacob delivered the worst pummeling Puerto Rico had experienced since its direct hit by Hurricane Maria and then began skirting the northern coast of Hispaniola. Here, finally, Jacob faltered.

Free of the trade winds, Jacob slowed, allowing the mountains of the Dominican Republic and Haiti to disrupt the airflow into Jacob's core. The storm lost some of its intensity and enough forward speed to "sense" a low-pressure trough coming off the Carolinas and begin a northward turn. Jacob's eye passed between the Turks and Caicos and Great Inagua, then skirted the eastern islands of the Bahamas before curving north and east into the center of the Atlantic after another close brush with North Carolina's Outer Banks. As it passed over the cooler waters north of the Bahamas, Jacob's energy supply was cut off, and the storm rapidly de-intensified into an extratropical cyclone headed for Europe.

With dozens of deaths and billions of dollars in property damage, Jacob was a tragic disaster for the areas it touched in the Caribbean and the Bahamas. Yet, it could have been worse if the storm had ranged up Florida's east coast as a strong Category 3 storm. The citizens of Florida and the meteorologists of the NHC breathed a sigh of relief as people, aircraft, and ships returned from their exile. On the other hand, there was little sense of comfort for those caught in the storm's path—only a fight for survival.

Sailing Vessel *Aurora Mist*, Northwest Providence Channel, thirteen nautical miles south-southwest of Freeport, Bahamas
15:42 EDT, 29 September

Murray

Phillip Murray had just murdered his family.

Well, perhaps not murdered. They were still alive at the moment. But tied down in the sealed cabin of the rolling, pitching, and heaving remnants of the once beautiful sailing yawl *Aurora Mist*, they were as good as dead. His lawyer's logic also objected technically—there had been no Malice Aforethought, not even the reckless negligence that would have qualified as Depraved Indifference Homicide back in New York. *Is that a thing in the Bahamas? What is the correct crime for a series of decisions that puts your wife and two little girls in the path of an intense hurricane with no hope of escape?*

A particularly violent combination of pitching and the roller-coaster heaving of the *Aurora Mist* wrenched his mind from these feeble professional distractions, and his stomach roiled again. Murray was breathing through his mouth now, in a desperate but vain attempt to remove one sense contributing to his nausea in the sealed, vomit-soaked cabin. He desperately wanted to open the cabin hatch or a window to at least get some fresh air in, but doing so would admit the angry sea and sink them in a heartbeat. Leaving the cabin for any reason would be certain death, as the loud thuds of wave impacts and the shrieking of the wind through the remaining deck fittings reminded him.

He directed his bleary gaze at the clock across the cabin—3:43 pm—seven and a half hours since the masts went by the board. He turned to Gemma, his wife of fourteen years strapped down four feet away. Dull, red-rimmed eyes gazed back, her face set in a gray mask of despair. Gemma was a sailor too, and she knew quite well the desperation of their situation. Her arms held their daughters tightly, faces buried in her chest. The girls had passed out from the exhaustion of vomiting and holding on against the boat's chaotic motion. It was a small blessing that he did not have to look them in the eyes anymore as they pleaded, in words unspoken,

Do something, Daddy!

It was not supposed to be this way. Murray had been an avid sailor since he was a child and had crewed for a contender for the America's Cup a decade and a half ago. He was not one of the lubberly imbeciles who thought reading Richard Henry Dana or watching a season of *Below Deck* made them expert seamen. He knew boats and respected the sea.

He could have continued sailing. But he had met, fallen hard for, and soon married Gemma Langton, a beautiful college classmate who shared his passion for the law and, to a lesser extent, sailing. The demands of school, the bar exam, and building a law practice in one of the most litigiously competitive locations in the world reduced their sailing time to summer day trips in rentals on the Long Island Sound. Then the kids came. When he held his newborn daughter Jamie in his arms, he knew he had too little time as it was to spend with his family. He would sacrifice none of it to indulge himself, regardless of how much he missed the challenge and exhilaration of bending the wind and sea to his will. Gemma appreciated this and promised that when the girls were old enough and he had a big case under his belt, he would take them all on a sailing sabbatical.

That day had come last March. He was the attorney of record for a class action that netted a nine-figure settlement. Now forty-five million dollars richer, Murray decided this was the time to live his and Gemma's dream of a sailing cruise around the Caribbean. Taking a few months to close out his remaining cases while Gemma put together a home school curriculum, the family traveled to Miami at the end of June. Everyone fell in love with the *Aurora Mist*, a beautiful fifty-three-foot yawl with a fully decked-out cabin and two bedrooms. Murray bought the boat, and the family set sail for the Yucatan Channel and Cozumel the next day.

The following three months were idyllic, with exotic ports, gorgeous beaches, lush tropical islands, and the wonders of the sea. The girls' excitement at seeing their first flying fish brought Murray the greatest joy he had experienced since Lydia was born.

Like their parents, the girls took to the sea and were soon standing their own helm watches as Murray pretended to doze on the long sails between destinations.

Hurricanes were a genuine threat in the area throughout the trip. Murray was no fool—he knew what would happen if the *Aurora Mist* was caught at sea by one of those monsters. Thus, he gathered the National Hurricane Center's updates twice daily and tracked any systems that popped up with an almost religious fervor. He had even altered their voyage plan twice as a precaution when systems appeared to have a chance of reaching them.

Jacob had vexed Murray as much as it had the NHC forecasters. The *Aurora Mist* was in the Northern Bahamas, ready to run to the East or West as needed to stay clear, but Jacob stubbornly refused to commit, and the track uncertainty "cone" remained broad. Finally, the track guidance firmed away from the Florida coast and through the Eastern Bahamas. Murray set the course to the southwest around Great Abaco Island, through the Northwest Providence Channel just south of Grand Bahama Island. They would have to use Jacob's winds to help run clear, but Murray expected no problems.

But Jacob had other ideas.

The track unexpectedly jogged back to the west and picked up speed as a low-pressure trough moving off the East Coast had reached down farther than expected and tugged at the storm. It was now a race between the powerful hurricane barreling northward and the sailboat carrying progressively more reefs in the mainsail as the wind velocity increased. The Murrays and the *Aurora Mist* were winning. With Grand Bahama Island limiting the fetch, the term for the distance over which the wind could push on and build up the waves, the seas were moderate, allowing the winds to sweep them along at close to eighteen knots. Then it happened.

The boat had been running and riding well with a thrice reefed mainsail in a steady wind of twenty-five knots when a sudden gust of twice that speed took down the mizzen mast. Absent the balancing force of the mizzen sail, the boat immediately fell off from close haul, exposing the full breadth of the mainsail. The resulting strain was too high: the windward mainstays and the mast snapped in quick succession. In seconds, the *Aurora Mist* transformed from a racing thing of beauty to a wallowing wreck. The only good news was that no one was hurt—Gemma and the girls were in the cabin, and the flailing booms and stay wires somehow missed Murray at the helm.

Murray was a careful man and had prepared for this, the worst eventuality. It took a few seconds to overcome the shock of the quick sequence of events, but then he launched into action. The first step was to cut away the wreckage of the masts held alongside by the leeward stays. Then to the bow to cast the sea anchor—essentially a parachute attached to three hundred feet of reinforced line. The drag would keep *Aurora Mist*'s bow to the wind and seas and hopefully keep her from capsizing or pitch polling in the ever-building seas. As the gyrating boat swung into the wind, Murray crawled aft to the cabin, fastened the hatch cover, manually activated the Emergency Position Indicating Radio Beacon or EPIRB, and then turned to help Gemma secure herself and the children in the cabin. The girls were already seasick before the mishap. Now that there was no alternative to continuous pitching and heaving, shut tight in the airless cabin, things would get much worse for all of them.

"Phil?" Gemma asked pleadingly over Jamie's and Lydia's quiet sobs.

"The EPIRB's on, honey. It will just be a matter of time before they come for us." He was lying, of course. The rescue capabilities of the Royal Bahamian Defense Force were rudimentary at best, and they were over sixty miles from any U.S. Coast Guard station. The chance that a ship large enough to attempt a rescue would be in these narrow waters with a hurricane bearing down was vanishingly slight. *But not zero.* Despite the dread he felt inside, he smiled to encourage his wife.

The following seven and a half hours were a descent into Hell. The boat was riding well to the sea anchor, all things considered. But the wave heights were progressively increasing along with the fetch as they were pulled toward Jacob's center and away from the shelter of Grand Bahama Island. The constant strain of holding on against the motion and the throwing up from the seasickness exhausted everyone. Murray was becoming increasingly listless, no longer caring about what could be causing the lurches and what bumps and thuds could be heard over the howling wind.

There was a lurch, somehow different from what Murray had been feeling in the boat's motion, followed almost immediately by a loud thud from overhead. He wondered what could have broken loose or collided with the *Aurora Mist* when the hatch suddenly opened with a roar of wind. Murray turned in panic and reached for the release on his strap—the hatch had somehow broken loose, and if not secured immediately, waves breaking over the boat would soon swamp the cabin. He had grabbed a secure handhold when a man wearing a white helmet, goggles, and an orange life vest appeared in the opening.

Shouting to be heard over the wind screeching, the man said, "Howdy, folks! Petty Officer Juan Lopez, U.S. Coast Guard! Would anybody like a ride in my boat?!"

Murray blinked at the apparition and, unable to reply, nodded vigorously.

"OK!" the young man said, ducking as a wave broke over the boat. "This is going to take careful timing! We have to take you off one at a time! Our boat can only hang alongside for a few seconds, so I will hand you off to my shipmate in the boat, understand?!"

Murray nodded again.

"Sweet! OK, sir and ma'am, this is important! When I push you off, the only thing you grab is the man in the boat! You grab at anything else, and it won't go well, clear?! I need a thumbs up from each of you!"

Murray gave a thumbs up with his free hand and turned to see Gemma wearily doing the same.

"Alright! Ma'am, can you pass the first child to the gentleman here while I call over the boat?!"

Gemma nodded and unhooked Jamie's strap, then released her once Murray had a firm grip and pulled her over. The child was listless with fatigue, mumbling something Murray couldn't hear over the wind. He leaned over to speak in her ear. "I know it's hard, honey, but it will be over soon. Go with the Coast Guard man now."

Jamie looked fearful and then nodded, turning to Lopez and reaching out. Lopez quickly pulled the child into the crook of his arm, and then they disappeared from the hatch. After what seemed an eternity to Murray but couldn't have been more than half a minute, there was another perceptible lurch in the boat and several thuds on the deck. After a few more seconds, Lopez reappeared in the hatch opening.

"OK, folks! She's safe on board the boat!" Murray stifled a cry of relief while Lopez continued, "Let's take the second child, please!"

Murray and Gemma repeated the transfer process, but Lydia was frantic. "No, Daddy! No!"

Murray held her close and spoke in her ear. "I know it's scary, sweet pea, but you have to go with the Coast Guard man to be with Jamie. Mommy and I will be there with you before you know it."

Lydia was still sobbing, but released her grip on Murray as Lopez took her under his arm. As the two disappeared through the hatch, Murray reached over and drew Gemma over to him, hugging her tightly. Lopez soon reappeared at the hatch.

"Both girls are safe and secure in the boat! Let's take you now, ma'am!"

Gemma looked into Murray's eyes and gave him a quick kiss and hug, then followed the young petty officer out of the hatch. After they were clear, Murray grasped the handhold, released his strap, and then squatted in the hatchway. Before long, Lopez reappeared.

"OK, sir, just you and me now! We'll be going over together! What we're going to do is hang out right outside the hatch! You'll see the boat coming, but don't move until I pull your arm! When I do, you jump for the boat with everything you've got, copy?!"

Murray nodded exaggeratedly and shouted, "Yes! Let's do it!"

Lopez nodded and then pulled Murray through the hatch. He could barely hold on as the roaring wind gripped him, immensely strong even in the partial lee of the cockpit. The scene on deck was surreal. In all directions, from what he could see in the limited visibility, was a gray sea and waves at least twelve feet high with spray blowing from the tops. A solid overcast of clouds whipped overhead at unbelievable speed. A white vessel with a Coast Guard red racing stripe gyrated a hundred yards off the starboard side, dipping and slamming into the on-coming waves each ten to twelve seconds. He turned aft to see a small orange boat approaching, disappearing from sight as the *Aurora Mist* crested a wave and dipped, reappearing a couple of seconds later. The boat approached slowly, briefly held about ten yards away while another wave passed, then shot forward. Lopez leaned over, shouted, "Let's go!" and yanked his arm.

Murray leaped with every ounce of strength he had. As soon as he cleared the lee of the cockpit, the wind seemed to slap him in midair. He was falling and turning as he collided with a soft object, the crewman in the boat, then slammed onto the hard deck. A large hand gripped and dragged him to the side, where Gemma and the girls were already lashed in.

The big crewman placed his hand on a grab handle and shouted, "Hold this, stay down, and keep your arms inside the boat!" Once Murray had a firm grip, the crewman pulled a strap across his lap, fastened it to a ring fitting on the deck, and cinched it. The small orange boat pitched up as it climbed another high wave, and the strap across Murray's lap bit into him as they seemed to come near to vertical. Then the bow abruptly pitched down for yet another sickening drop to a tremendous splash.

"That's it! We're done for!" Murray thought as wind and water tugged at his body. But the boat came up again, the deck cleared, and from what he could see with his spray-fogged eyes, everyone was still there. He looked toward Gemma, sitting beside him with her free arm stretched across Jamie's and Lydia's chests, and placed his free hand over hers on the grab handle. They rode out two more monstrous wave events before reaching the cutter, which provided little shelter from the gale for the tossing boat.

Murray had turned to look at the nearby cutter when a gunshot rang out, followed by the thump of a line on the bow. Murray surmised the winds were too high for a standard heaving line, so the Coast Guardsman used a rifle to pass a line to the boat. The big boat crewman was hauling in a thin line that Murray knew was attached to the hook used to crane the boat aboard. This was the time of maximum risk—with the cutter and boat writhing in the wind and seas, attaching the hook would be a nightmare. He leaned over to cover Gemma's head with his body and closed his eyes.

And then he prayed.

The boat suddenly jolted upward after two clangs, audible even over the shrieking wind. Murray opened his eyes to see the big crewman kneeling on the deck, gripping handles on either side of a metal block attached to the boat frame. He looked over his shoulder to see they were even with the cutter's deck, which receded as they rolled to the left, then came on with a bone-jarring crash.

"Heave in, goddammit!" the big crewman shouted at several men on the cutter's deck. The small boat drifted out again with another roll, but far less than before. The boat stayed snug on the cutter's side on the next roll. The big crewman shouted, "Get ready!" The crewmen on the deck moved to the side of the boat, squatted, and seized grab handles. The cutter pitched upward, then down with a tremendous splash that inundated the scene with rushing water. It had not yet cleared when the big crewman yelled, "Take them!" Four pairs of hands released the Murray family's straps and hauled them onto the deck, moving briskly to and through an open door in the superstructure.

The room they entered seemed to be some sort of dining area. There were two tables with chairs bolted to the floor in the center and what appeared to be a stove with two large refrigerators in the corner. The oven and refrigerator doors were secured with straps, and perforated mats covered the entire deck. The crewmen who had escorted them inside were busily seating Gemma and the children against the wall and connecting them with new safety straps, while Murray's crewmen did the same for him. Even inside, the wind's howling was very loud, but conversation was possible, at least. The motion of the cutter was still quite violent— the crewmen were essentially climbing from one location to the next. Finally, one of the crew pulled off his goggles and spoke into what looked like a thin headset, "Conn, Deck Party secure and ready for maneuvers."

Murray looked up as a voice came over the loudspeakers in the room. "Attention, everybody. The good news is the ride is about to get a lot smoother; the bad news is we will have to turn beam-on. Stand by."

The crewmen all kneeled and seized railings on the wall with both hands, and the one with the headset looked at Murray and said, "Hang on tight, folks. We will run with the wind and seas to tamp down this motion, but we have to turn broadside to get there."

Murray nodded, then turned to gaze at his family across the room and locked eyes with Gemma. The cutter pitched down, plunging into the wave trough with a thundering crash, followed by the muffled roar of running water. Then, after a few seconds, the cutter began another rapid pitch up and climb up the next wave. At the crest, instead of plunging downward, the cutter rapidly yawed to the right, accompanied by a brief roll to the left so deep he felt like he was hanging off the side in his harness. The cutter then rolled back to vertical and plunged forward, the engines below the deck on which he sat roaring above the sound of the wind. He could feel the difference in the motion as the cutter picked up speed—instead of colliding with the water in the next wave, she rode through the trough, then pitched more slowly as the wave slid by. Murray released the breath he was holding. The danger was not past by any means, but running with the wind and seas now, they were hurrying away from the storm's center.

In minutes, the motion steadied to a slow roll of twenty degrees to each side, with a pitch of about ten degrees. The voice came over the loudspeakers again. "Alright, guys, the worst is behind us, and we are making thirty knots over the ground in the best direction. Normal movement is OK, but a big one can come along at any time, so remember, one hand for the boat at all times. All weather decks remain secured until further notice. Well done, everybody!"

The crewmen kneeling around the messdeck stood and removed their helmets. Crewmembers, Murray corrected himself—the shortest among them was an African American woman. Murray was astonished as they started chatting and laughing, as if this heart-stopping experience was just another day at the office. A tall, youthful crewman with the single silver bar on his uniform that marked him as an officer came over and released his harness. Murray took his proffered hand and stood unsteadily.

"Sir, were you the Master of the *Aurora Mist*?" he asked.

Murray had never thought of himself in those terms, but supposed that was the correct formal usage. "Yes, I am, or was, I guess. I'm Phillip Murray."

"How do you do, Mr. Murray? I'm Lieutenant Junior Grade Ben Wyporek, Executive Officer. Welcome to the Coast Guard Cutter *Kauai*. Are these people your family?"

"Yes, sir. My wife, Gemma, and daughters Jamie and Lydia. Thank you for coming for us."

"We're glad to have you aboard. Right now, we are going to move you to one of our berthing areas where you can rest, and our Health Services Technician can check you out."

"Thank you, sir." It was entirely inadequate for the emotion he felt for the deliverance of his family from what he believed was certain death, but it was all his exhausted mind could muster. He smiled at Gemma as she and the girls were released from their harnesses and helped to their feet. The young officer led them forward through a passageway to a tiny room almost filled with two pairs of bunk beds and four narrow lockers. A corridor barely two feet wide between the bunk pairs provided the only floor space in the room. "I'm sorry it's so cramped in here, but it's the best we can offer you right now," the officer said.

"Lieutenant, considering where we just came from, this is heaven."

"Good. I think putting the children in the top bunks is best, and there is no risk of their falling out—as you can see, we have retention rails installed."

"Yes, I agree," Murray said as he looked closely at the bunks.

"Right then," Wyporek said and kneeled to speak to Jamie. "Miss Jamie, my name is Ben, and I'm going to help you into the top bunk. Is that OK?"

"Yes. Ben, I feel sick."

"I know, honey. My friend Mike will be here in a minute to get something to help you with that."

"Thanks," Jamie said as Wyporek lifted her so she could climb into the bunk.

He then turned and kneeled by the other child. "Miss Lydia, I'm Ben. I'm going to help you into the other top bunk, OK?"

"Yes, Ben," Lydia said as she put her arms around Wyporek's neck. He lifted her to the bunk and then turned to Murray after the child climbed in.

"OK, sir. Do you or your wife need help?"

Murray turned to Gemma and got an exhausted smile and a head shake. He turned to Wyporek. "No, Lieutenant, we'll be fine."

"Right. This is our Health Services Technician, Petty Officer Mike Bryant," Wyporek said, gesturing to a shorter crewman with close-cropped blond hair and wire-rimmed glasses. "He needs to do a health check on you and the children."

"We'd be grateful," Murray said. "I'm glad to meet you, Mr. Bryant."

"Likewise, sir," Bryant replied. "XO, I've got this."

"Roger that," the officer said. Then he left the room.

Bryant closed the door and said, "I'd like to start with the children. Could you and your wife get into the lower bunks, please? I need room to work here."

"Yes, certainly," Murray said. After helping Gemma into her bunk, he climbed into his own. Under normal circumstances, he would have been mildly claustrophobic in the tight space, but he was too tired and worried at present. After a few minutes, Bryant kneeled.

"Folks, both your children are OK. They have mild dehydration and are still experiencing motion sickness. With your permission, I would like to give them an oral solution. It is Pedialyte with a small dose of ondansetron to knock out nausea and help them rest."

Murray nodded to Gemma, and she said, "Yes, please. Go ahead."

"Thank you."

Bryant finished with the children within a few minutes and kneeled again for the adults. "Ma'am, your turn." Five minutes later, Bryant had completed his examination on both adults. "Folks, same diagnosis for you two. I want you each to drink a bottle of Pedialyte, and I have a dimenhydrinate pill for you if you're still nauseous, but it might make you sleepy."

"Dimenhydrinate?" Murray asked.

"The trade name is Dramamine."

"That sounds like an excellent prescription to me," Murray said.

When Bryant turned to Gemma, she said, "Yes, I would like both, please."

"Coming right up."

The drink was not as unpleasant as Murray expected, and the pill soon eliminated his remaining nausea. Gemma was also returning from the dead, and she gave a grateful smile to the young medic. Bryant excused himself, saying he would be just a shout away if they needed anything. After he had left, Murray got up from his bunk to check on Jamie and Lydia—both were sleeping peacefully and securely in their bunks. He then kneeled beside Gemma's bunk, cupped her cheek gently with his right hand, and kissed her warmly. He then pulled back and smiled. "My dearest, I think we'll stick with daysailers on the Sound from here on out."

Gemma smiled in return. "An eminently sound legal strategy, counselor."

Murray returned to his bunk, then reached across the space between the bunks to lay his hand on Gemma's arm. Between the cutter's gradually moderating motion, the ordeal's exhaustion, and the Dramamine's narcotic effects, both were asleep within fifteen minutes.

Part of the Job

**USCG Cutter *Kauai*, Straits of Florida, twenty-one nautical miles southwest of Freeport, Bahamas
16:29 EDT, 29 September**

Ben

Lieutenant Junior Grade Benjamin "Ben" Wyporek wearily climbed the ladder leading to *Kauai*'s Bridge. Every muscle ached from fatigue after the hours-long fight through wind and seas to reach the stricken sailboat, followed by the harrowing ordeal on the main deck during the recovery of the survivors. Ben and the two others in the deck crew had nearly gone overboard in that last wave when the cascading water had swept their legs from under them. All three men would be dead now if it had not been for the safety belts connecting them to the deck railing. He looked aft through the port bridge door window—the cutter's Rigid Hull Inflatable Boat, known as "the rib," for its acronym RHIB, was still there, snugged into the side with tie-downs on every available fitting. His internal mariner objected to the situation, but the risks of injury while cradling the RHIB were too high with a thirty-knot tailwind and these seas. The RHIB was replaceable, the crewmembers were not, and they had already pressed their luck too far on this trip.

They had sortied three days ago from their Port Canaveral homeport when it looked like Jacob might impact Florida's east coast. While the last place on Earth you wanted to be in a patrol boat when a major hurricane hit was in the open sea, being moored to a pier subject to storm surge was a close second. Better to get some sea room and scurry out of the way. When the storm had finally settled on a northerly course through the Bahamas, they turned back for home in relief. Then came the call from the Rescue Coordination Center in Miami.

One satellite in the Copas-Sarsat constellation had picked up an emergency signal from an EPIRB registered to the sailing vessel *Aurora Mist*. The signal was localized to a spot about eleven nautical miles south of Freeport in the Bahamas, thirty miles from their position. The owner-operator had filed a sail plan listing four people on board, two of them children. The risks of responding to the distress call were considerable for *Kauai* and her crew. If they lost control in those seas and narrow waters, whether from the storm's effects or some mechanical problem, their only achievement would be adding the names of sixteen Coast Guard men and women to Jacob's death toll. Even if they could get to the scene and find the boat, odds were long against the successful launch and recovery of the RHIB. But when you knew there were lives at stake, particularly children, you went if there was any chance of rescue. This time, luck was on their side.

Ben was the Executive Officer, referred to as XO, the second in command of *Kauai*. A lean five-foot-ten, with close-cropped sandy brown hair surrounding a lightly tanned, chiseled face and startlingly blue eyes, he was among the younger members of the crew at twenty-five years of age. *Kauai* was his second tour of duty after graduating from the Coast Guard Academy in Connecticut three years previously.

Ben made his way to the captain's chair in the Bridge's center, moving from handhold to handhold as the deck rolled and pitched beneath him. He stopped beside the chair, fired off a crisp salute, and said, "Survivors are secured in the Port Non-rate Berthing Area, Captain. Doc says they're OK, and he's treating them for dehydration and seasickness."

Lieutenant Samuel "Sam" Powell, commanding officer of *Kauai*, returned Ben's salute. By tradition, he was addressed as "Captain" on board his ship, despite his nominal rank. About an inch taller than Ben but equally lean and tanned, Sam had dark hair, a friendly round face, and soft brown eyes. At thirty-six, he was the second-oldest member of the crew. Unlike Ben, he had been commissioned from the enlisted ranks after attending officer candidate school as a chief petty officer. Despite the differences in background and age and their positions, the two men had become best friends since their arrival on board *Kauai* nearly two years previously. "Thanks, XO. That was a hell of a job on the main deck in that mess. If I had known it would be this bad, I think I might have turned it down."

Ben smiled in return. "I don't think you would, sir. And if you have any lingering doubts about whether it was worth it, I suggest you peek in on that family we picked up when you get a chance."

"I'll do that once things calm down. Now, for real: how are *you*? I about had a heart attack when I saw you guys go down in that wave."

"No worries, Captain. Just another bruise or two."

"Just the same; I want you to have Doc give you a head check as soon as we're done here."

Ben's smile vanished, and his stomach flipped at the reminder that he was still under scrutiny for his injury during a secret mission six months previously. Ben had been shot in the head by a crazed drug cartel assailant, and though his helmet kept the bullet out, the impact caused a hematoma that nearly killed him. His continued service in the Coast Guard was contingent on special neurological evaluations in each annual physical and checkups after any mishaps that could have caused head trauma. "Captain, I didn't hit my head, so there's no...."

"Uh-uh," Sam interrupted, shaking his head. "You know the deal. You go down, you get checked. End of story." He reached over and gave Ben's shoulder a friendly shake. "Don't worry. It will be strictly routine if you haven't cracked your bean again. Now, how's everything else holding up?"

"I went from stem to stern on the inside, sir: no leaks or engineering issues. I'm sure the lifelines are trashed, and I don't want to even think about the gun right now," Ben replied. Seawater weighs nearly sixty-three pounds per cubic foot and is almost incompressible. Waves impacting at over thirty miles per hour would wreak havoc on anything exposed topside. Lifelines, the wires strung along stanchions on the periphery of the deck to prevent personnel from falling overboard, and the main gun on the foredeck were the usual casualties when any cutter, particularly a small one like a patrol boat, encountered heavy seas.

Sam said, "Yes, I suppose I'll have some 'splaining to do when we get back. They can't ding me too hard with four lives saved."

"God, I would hope not, sir. I'll start the RHIB's crew's writeups if you don't object. Can't let a good rescue go to waste."

"Thank you, XO. That will be *after* your head exam, of course."

"Yes, sir," Ben replied.

"Buck up, son! Remember, we could all be dead now."

"Yes, sir, there is *that*. By your leave, sir?"

"Carry on, XO."

Ben turned and stepped over to Chief Operations Specialist Emilia Hopkins, scanning the horizon with binoculars in her role as the officer of the deck. Hopkins was the best shiphandler on board and was the go-to person for OOD in a sticky situation like the recent rescue. The tall and fit thirty-four-year-old widowed mother of twelve- and ten-year-old sons, Hopkins shared a house with her mother, who looked after the boys when she was at sea. While not friends in the strictest sense, as the Coast Guard did not permit such relationships between officers and enlisted members, Ben respected and admired her professionally and as an individual. He knew Sam felt the same. Hopkins was one of those most trusted voices who would give it to you straight in private, but had your back at all times. "How goes it, Chief? Do you need some relief here?"

Hopkins, who overheard Ben and Sam's conversation, returned a grin. "Sorry, XO, I can't help you. Now that I'm not puking my guts out every five minutes, I've found my second wind."

"Right. You know *I* am always here for *you*," Ben said with a mock huff, drawing a chuckle from the chief petty officer. Ben's bonhomie concealed a genuine worry that nagged at him as he departed the Bridge to find Bryant. He *had* hit the deck hard after that wave—he was sure he would have a substantial bruise on his right hip from the impact. An event like that, even one not involving a direct blow to the head, could bring the career he loved to a close.

He found Bryant in the ship's dispensary, monitoring the Murray family as they slept in the adjacent compartment. Health Services Technician Michael Bryant, known as "Doc" among the crew, cut an unimposing figure at a thin five-foot-seven with round wire-rimmed glasses. Ben knew this concealed a calm dedication to his shipmates' well-being, his courage proven with the Silver Star and Purple Heart medals he earned as an army combat medic before his transfer to the Coast Guard and his service aboard *Kauai*. He had received special training and equipment to conduct neurological assessments in the field to monitor Ben's recovery. "I need a quick check under the hood, Doc," Ben said in greeting.

"On it, XO," Bryant replied.

The assessment comprised inspections of his ear canals, pupillary responses, and general balance, not a simple task on a pitching and rolling patrol boat. He followed up with a check of Ben's right side. Ben exhaled in relief when Bryant finished and said, "Neurologics are normal, sir. You'll have a helluva bruise by tomorrow, but nothing's broken."

"Good to hear. How are our passengers doing?"

"Fine, sir. They'll sleep for a while between the exhaustion and anti-nausea drugs I gave them. I was a little concerned about the kids at first—they were both close to passing out from dehydration. But they took the Pedialyte well."

"Good. Let me know when they wake up, please."

"Will do, sir."

Ben nodded and then went to the messdeck, where Chief Machinery Technician James Drake shared coffee with two of *Kauai*'s boatswain's mates. Drake was the senior enlisted and oldest member of the crew at forty-three. He was also the tallest at six-foot-four and had a muscular build and graying hair, cut short like all the other males on board. Drake was the senior engineer aboard *Kauai* when Ben and Sam arrived. He remained with the unit even after her conversion to a diesel-electric powerplant called for a change in the senior enlisted to the Electrician's Mate rating. Drake was an old-time chief in the sense of resolving problems before they came to the officers' attention. He operated a network of "connections" from fellow chiefs to senior officers for scrounging and "intel." Ben and Sam had learned quickly not to dig too deeply into how some seemingly intractable problems were being handled; they just had to sit back and enjoy the results.

Boatswain's Mate First Class John Bondurant sat across the table from Drake. Bondurant was almost as tall as Drake at six-foot-three, but even more powerfully built. His great strength came in handy, particularly today—he was the large crewman in the RHIB who manhandled the passengers aboard and seized and hooked up the chaotically whirling hoist block. He was a quiet and even-tempered man, with a wife and two sons in high school.

Bondurant's subordinate, Boatswain's Mate Second Class Shelley Lee, sat to his right. Lee was a full foot shorter than Bondurant, but had the athletic build of a gymnast. She was the most skillful small boat operator Ben had ever known and was the coxswain of the RHIB during today's rescue. Lee and Ben were close in age, temperament, and interests, and they shared the same mutual admiration and respect Ben had with Hopkins. Lee was the most courageous individual Ben had ever known, as evidenced by her jumping on today's rescue sortie and the mission in which Ben was injured six months ago. In that action, a towline was hit and broken, and she ventured into the open in an environment alive with automatic weapons and rocket fire to single-handedly cut away the wreckage and save the boat.

Drake turned on Ben's arrival and said, "Pull up a seat, XO." After Ben was seated, he added, "So, I presume the head exam went OK?"

Ben's mouth dropped open, then he replied, "Shit, Chief, is there anything you don't know about?"

"Oh, sir. There are so many things. For instance, how much longer will we be buttoned up?"

"The center has already passed us to the east, and things should calm down in a couple of hours. Not sure if we will open up before we hit PC, though, if the lifelines are as chewed up as I expect them to be."

Lee piped up immediately. "Hey, sir, I don't like leaving my boat hanging off the side like that. It was bad enough to leave her there to begin with."

Ben smiled. *My boat.* "Well, Shelley, if nothing has happened to her yet, I don't think anything will. However, I will present your protests to the skipper—I'm sure he wouldn't want to let anything happen to *your* boat."

"Damn straight. What's the point of being the Boatswain Diva if you can't get your way!" Even the taciturn Bondurant joined in the chuckles on that one.

Ben excused himself after some more light banter, but as he stood, a sharp pain from his injured hip made him pause with a grimace. A look of genuine concern instantly replaced Lee's smile. "Are you OK, sir?"

Ben waved in dismissal. "Just a reminder of the need to set your feet properly when in swift water. I may not be sleeping on my right side for a few days, that's all. Please, don't worry about it."

"OK, sir. Take it easy, will ya?"

"Roger that," Ben replied as he made his way forward. He was surprised and embarrassed by Lee's reaction. *Have to be a little more poker-faced from now on.* Ben's stateroom was a short walk from the messdeck. The officers and chiefs each had their own room aboard *Kauai,* but they were tiny, and Ben's was just big enough for his bunk, desk, locker, and file cabinet. The other crew shared rooms like the one currently occupied by the Murray family. As Ben sat down and opened his laptop to jot down his notes of today's action while they were fresh in his mind, he glanced up and then fixed on the pictures of Victoria mounted on the wall above his desk.

Victoria Carpenter was the love of Ben's life. They had met in January when *Kauai* had been pulled off her regular duties to support a Defense Intelligence Agency team on an operation in the Florida Keys. The mission was so secret that only a handful of people in the world were aware of it. Ben had come ashore to serve as liaison, while *Kauai* remained offshore in support. Victoria was the protégé of Ben's DIA teammate, Peter Simmons, who warned him before their meeting that Victoria was mildly autistic and that he should expect some unusual behavior. Expecting to meet some geeky neurotic, Ben was surprised to find a beautiful, extraordinarily charming young woman who made him feel like the most exceptional person in the world during their first conversation. The interest was mutual, and although separated by their duties, Ben's in South Florida with *Kauai* and Victoria's in Washington, DC with the DIA, they shared the details of their lives on the phone each night when Ben was not out on patrol. With each passing day, these conversations became more precious to Ben, and he chafed at the operational pace that kept them apart.

Finally, *Kauai* was taken offline for a major upgrade, and Ben was assigned to an intense course of special operations training in Quantico, Virginia. During his training, they had the chance to meet for two short dates, resulting in the pictures. The first picture was of Victoria in an elegant pose from their first date, with her auburn hair up rather than pulled back into her usual ponytail. She was wearing a stunning jade green cocktail dress, a perfect match for her large aquamarine-colored eyes. Ben was so stunned at the sight of her that evening that he was speechless at first, then could only stumble through some inanities before she came to his rescue.

The second picture was a candid shot of them in jeans and jackets walking arm-in-arm on the Washington DC Mall, looking at each other happily. Ben followed the man who'd taken the picture and purchased an electronic copy. This one remained his favorite. Ben thought Victoria looked every bit as alluring in these casual clothes as she did in the green dress, and it reminded him of the night they spent together afterward. The night he knew he was in love with her.

Ben kept his feelings to himself for about a month afterward. While he knew Victoria was physically attracted to him and enjoyed their conversations, she had given no sign she was interested in anything beyond friendship. She was a mathematical genius and polymath, and Ben knew her intellect was on an entirely different level from his—although he could keep up to a certain degree on the math thanks to his studies at the Academy. Ben finally shared his feelings via satellite phone on the eve of the mission on which he was wounded and was astounded to find that Victoria felt the same about him.

It was ironic that hours after sharing their feelings, Ben was hit in the battle with the drug cartel. As he fell unconscious in the makeshift surgery on *Kauai*'s messdeck afterward, his last thoughts were of his first sight of Victoria in her beautiful green dress. A couple of days later, as Ben revived in the intensive care unit of a Miami hospital, he saw what he took to be a hallucination: Victoria asleep, sitting next to him with her head on the bed next to his hand. He reached out tentatively and brushed her lovely auburn hair back—she was real. He continued to stroke her forehead lightly, and she smiled in her sleep at his touch, then suddenly bolted awake.

His mouth was so dry that he could not talk until Victoria got him a drink of ice water from the table by the bed. He wanted to say something clever or romantic under the circumstances. But, still fuzzy-headed from the anesthesia, the only thing he could think of was the greeting he always used at the beginning of their phone calls:

"Hello, Victoria. How was your day?"

From Victoria's reaction, he could not have made a better choice.

She remained with him through his recovery, driving him to his physical therapy and checkup sessions while he recovered his balance and mobility. As she neared the end of her stay, she expressed regret at leaving behind what she referred to as "Ben's world" of welcoming and supportive friends, having never experienced such a thing. Ben saw an opening and took it, inviting Victoria to move in with him. She was uncertain—her condition had proven to be a relationship-killer in the past when her eccentricities evolved into annoying tics in the perception of her would-be partners. Ben was undeterred and pressed his case. Victoria was persuaded to try living together and quickly secured a position with a government contractor in Melbourne. They picked out an apartment together and moved in.

Like all couples, they had some collisions that they worked through, easier than most since neither was particularly ego-bound. The quirks associated with Victoria's condition, which she was convinced would drive Ben away, endeared her even more to him. He was in awe of Victoria's vast knowledge and intelligence, and the fact she needed help with some fundamental things in life made her more human to him. He loved listening to her talk. She had a surprisingly deep voice for someone so petite. Her precise elocution, even in casual conversations, was an appealing contrast to his previous girlfriends, who all seemed compelled to say "like" at least once in every sentence. Victoria never used contractions or diminutives; even at the most intimate times, he was "Benjamin" to her.

Victoria genuinely and openly appreciated his company and affection and understood the demands and separations that went with his job from her experience with the DIA. Several of Ben's earlier relationships had foundered on that issue, and her cheerful acceptance provided him with considerable relief. His worry that Victoria might have difficulty fitting into the insular community of the ship's crew and their families dissipated quickly. Although she knew her intelligence and eidetic memory were well outside the norm, to her, it was not a mark of superiority, just another personal characteristic like the color of her eyes or hair. Victoria was careful not to use her intellect to show up someone she was talking with, and her natural curiosity and openness were quite disarming. His coworkers and their families took to her at once.

Ben shook off his reverie and bent to the task on his laptop. As *Kauai*'s motion had calmed from the violence they had experienced when driving straight into the wind and seas to a still disconcerting but much more slow and tolerable pitch and roll, his seasickness had passed, and he was starving. He was due on the Bridge to relieve Hopkins for the second dog watch at 17:45 and needed to wolf down a microwave meal before that. He glanced at his laptop's system clock—17:04—and began typing furiously. After ten minutes, he was satisfied he had captured the basic details of the action and saved and closed the file. As he stood, he pulled and pocketed his Common Access Card, commonly known as a "CAC," from the computer's card reader, grabbed his cap, and headed back to the messdeck.

As Ben walked, his thoughts went back to Victoria and how he would describe today's activities to her when he returned. He knew she worried about him when he was underway, and events like today's rescue did not help. Ben did not want to add to those worries but could not gloss things over, much less lie to her—she would see right through it. He had sought advice from Sam's wife Joana on this subject shortly after he and Victoria had moved in together. Joana was a close friend of his in her own right and did not pull any punches.

"Sailor, you're on your own with that one. You and Victoria have to work out your own system. Sam gives me the details, I ask questions, and we deal with it. She *is* going to worry about you, that's the way it is, and nothing you can do short of quitting will change that. But she's smart enough to know that this is part of the package, and she's willing to pay the price to have you as you are. All I can say is never bullshit her—if she loses trust in what you're telling her, it's all over."

Ben had found that framing his descriptions in terms of calculated risk helped—Victoria enjoyed quantitative thinking and was comforted by the knowledge that something as amorphous as danger could be rationally bounded. Joana was right: Victoria never stopped worrying, but she seemed to come to terms with it. Ben smiled as he walked. Echoing his captain, Ben would have some 'splaining to do, particularly with the large bruise forming on his right hip. But the safe outcome and the rescue of a young family would help.

And Ben always looked forward to the aftermath of these "debriefings."

USCG Cutter *Kauai*, North Atlantic Ocean, twenty-two nautical miles east of Vero Beach, Florida
07:09 EDT, 30 September

Murray

Murray thought these were the tastiest omelet and home fries he had ever eaten, and it wasn't just that he had not had a bit of food since their nightmare began over a day ago. Gemma and the girls were also digging in heartily, without conversation. A crewman working the stove in an apron and *toque blanche* had met and seated them when they arrived on the messdeck and prepared omelets for him and Gemma and banana pancakes for the girls. Ben showed up a couple of minutes later and sat with them to consume some oatmeal and coffee.

"Will we be pulling in soon, Lieutenant?" Gemma asked.

"Yes, ma'am, and you can call me Ben if you like."

"Thank you. Please call me Gemma. 'Ma'am' makes me feel old."

Ben smiled. "Well, we can't have that. We will pull into Port Canaveral about nine o'clock, Gemma. I'm sorry, it's a little off the usual beaten path, but it's our homeport, and we'll be nailed to the first dock we tie up to until our lifelines get fixed."

"Completely understandable. You've done so much for us already, and we're grateful for wherever you put us ashore," Gemma said.

"Yes, there's no way I can repay you all for what you've done, but I'd like to try," Murray added.

Ben shook his head firmly. "You can't do that, sir. For starters, it's illegal for us to accept any gifts or gratuities, and if you tried, we'd just have to turn it over to the Treasury." Then he smiled,

"Besides, this is the sort of op we all signed up for, and the CO and I will make sure everyone gets recognized."

Ben was about to add to that when he stood and said, "Attention on deck!"

"As you were, please!" was the reply from another officer entering the room, who smiled and walked over as soon as he saw Ben. This officer was older; Murray guessed the new arrival was around his age and wearing two silver bars. *What is the naval rank? Oh yes, lieutenant.*

Murray and Gemma both stood as the officer reached the table, and Ben introduced him. "Folks, this is our commanding officer, Lieutenant Powell. Captain, this is Phillip Murray, Gemma Murray, and their daughters Jamie and Lydia."

"I'm pleased to meet you. Please sit, everybody." He turned to the cook and said, "Mornin', Chef. What are the chances of a Western and Homies this day?"

"Pretty near one-hundred percent, Captain."

"Sweet!" He turned and said, "You folks have everything you need?"

"Captain, your crew is killing us with kindness," Murray replied. He recognized the voice as the one on the loudspeaker immediately after they were brought aboard. "Not least of which is this meal. Did I hear you say Chef?"

The officer's face brightened. "That's our nickname for him. More properly, he is Culinary Specialist Second Class Thomas Hebert, although he *was* working up to Chef back in Naw'lins when he signed on with us instead."

"A good deal for you and us today," Murray said.

"Every day for us."

"Agreed." Murray nodded. "Is there a possibility of getting a tour of the ship? We would all be fascinated by a look around."

The officer shook his head sadly. "I'm sorry, but I can't permit that while we are underway. Space is tight, and there's a lot going on everywhere; we can't risk you being hurt. I'm afraid I have to ask you to remain here on the messdeck until we are moored. It will only be a couple of hours. After we are secure, one of us can take you on a tour if you care to hang around."

"That would be wonderful, thank you," Murray said. The light conversation continued until the captain completed his meal.

"Folks, you'll have to excuse us," Ben said as he stood. "The captain and I have to complete preparations for entering port. Chef can help you out if you need anything."

"Thank you, Ben, Captain, for everything," Gemma said.

"Our pleasure," the captain said.

****

The rest of their stay was uneventful, although rather dull. The girls watched children's shows on the messdeck television that Hebert had switched to local broadcasting while Murray and Gemma looked out the windows at the passing port sights. Murray longed to be on the Bridge, or at least on deck, to watch the activity as *Kauai* entered port. Still, as an attorney, he understood completely the liability considerations that kept them quasi-confined.

A few minutes after Murray felt *Kauai* bump into the pier, the engines below them ceased their rumbling hum, and a voice on the loudspeaker announced, "Secure the Special Sea Detail, set the in-port watch, section three on deck."

Murray looked over at Hebert, who said. "Give them a couple of minutes to square away all the classified gear, folks. Then we can sashay on up to the Bridge—you can see most everything from there. After that, we can get you a ride off base."

"A ride off base? I thought we pulled into the port," Murray said.

"No, sir. We have a berth and warehouse in the East Basin. It's on the Cape Canaveral Space Force Station, so you can't exactly get a cab. We'll have someone drive you to Melbourne, where you can rent a car, or fly out, or whatever."

"I see, thank you."

The phone rang, and Hebert answered. "Messdeck, Hebert. Right. Thanks, Chief." He hung up the phone and said, "Follow me, please, folks!"

The tour was fascinating. The Bridge was far more modern than he expected, with a three-seat console in the middle equipped with keyboards and joysticks at each station in front of large, single-panel screens, now dark. A single seat was positioned behind and above the console seats. Hebert explained that this was the captain's chair, placed to have a clear view of all the screens and the rest of the Bridge. Typically, three people were on the Bridge monitoring the operations when the craft was underway, but every station was manned during special evolutions. Murray shook his head. It was no wonder the captain didn't want him on the Bridge—there would not have been room for them to turn around.

As they were nearing the end of the tour, Gemma nudged him and pointed out the window at the area ashore between the pier and a parking lot. Ben and a pretty, petite young woman with her long red hair pulled back into a ponytail were trotting toward each other. The woman threw her arms around Ben's neck, and he picked her up off the ground in one of the most passionate kisses Murray had ever seen. He felt Gemma's arm around his waist and pulled her close while they watched.

Kauai was home from the sea.

The Journey of Four Billion Miles

§ 165.T07-0450 Temporary Security Zone; Atlantic Ocean, Cape Canaveral, FL.

(a) Location. The following area is a safety zone: All waters of the Atlantic Ocean, from surface to bottom, encompassed by a line connecting the following points beginning at Point 1: 28° 36' 51.88" N 80° 35' 57.33" W, thence to Point 2: 28° 34' 0.00" 80° 25' 0.00" W, thence to Point 3: 28° 14' 0.00" 80° 13' 0.00" W, thence to Point 4: 28° 12' 0.00" N 80° 23' 0.00" W, thence to Point 5: 28° 16' 0.00" N, 80° 26' 00.00" W, thence to point 6: 28° 26' 31.81" N, 80° 33' 8.02" W.

(b) Definitions. As used in this section, designated representative means a Coast Guard Patrol Commander, including a Coast Guard coxswain, petty officer, or other officer operating a Coast Guard vessel, and U.S. Air Force range safety personnel, and a Federal, State, and local officer designated by or assisting the Captain of the Port Jacksonville (COTP) in the enforcement of the safety zone.

(c) Regulations.

(1) Under the general safety zone regulations in subpart C of this part, you may not enter the safety zone described in paragraph (a) of this section unless authorized by the COTP or the COTP's designated representative.

(2) To seek permission to enter, transit through, anchor in, or remain within the safety zone, contact the COTP Jacksonville by telephone or the COTP's representative via VHF-FM radio on channel 16. Those in the safety zone must comply with all lawful orders or directions given to them by the COTP or the COTP's designated representative.

(d) Enforcement period. This section will be enforced from 13 October through 15 October, during times when a Broadcast Notice to Mariners informs mariners that space vehicles are being launched in a direction resulting in a southerly trajectory.

Signed: D. L. Hemmings, Captain, U.S. Coast Guard, Captain of the Port.

USCG Cutter *Kauai,* North Atlantic Ocean, four nautical miles south-southeast of Cape Canaveral, Florida 11:18 EDT, 14 October

Ben

The situation was tense on the Bridge while *Kauai* kept pace seventy-five yards from the eighty-two-foot motor yacht *Bon Temps,* heading north at eighteen knots. The cutter was at Law Enforcement Stations with the Bridge's command console fully manned and operating. Hopkins was conning the ship while keeping a close watch on the *Bon Temps*'s movements—at this speed and close range, a collision was a definite risk. Ben was fully outfitted in law enforcement gear and would head to the boat deck to lead the boarding when the vessel had stopped. Sam was overseeing everything from the command chair.

Kauai was doing her "day job" on this sortie—enforcing range safety for large payload research mission launches from the Cape. It was a perfect day for a launch, with a high-pressure area over the Cape bringing clear skies, a comfortable temperature of eighty-two, and light winds out of the east. The two boats rolled gently in the three-foot seas coming out of the east as they sped northward.

Launches at Cape Canaveral occurred at a rate of one every month and a half, on average, a mixture of commercial and government research payloads. The military payloads and reconnaissance satellites were usually launched from Vandenberg in California or Wallops in Virginia, which eased the security burden at Cape Canaveral. The launches here drew excited spectators looking for the anticipation and thrill of a giant rocket liftoff rather than geopolitical activists.

Not today.

The Galle-Adams-Le Verrier spacecraft, known as GALV, was scheduled for liftoff at 13:27 local time atop a Delta IV Heavy launch vehicle on the first dedicated mission to explore the planet Neptune and its satellites. GALV would be the heaviest interplanetary probe ever launched, weighing slightly over three-and-a-half metric tons. Like the earlier *Voyager 2* mission, GALV would make close approaches to Jupiter and Saturn and use their massive gravity to slingshot to the vicinity of the Solar System's outermost planet, approximately 4.6 billion kilometers from the sun.

To complete a journey of over a decade and still have the power to conduct scientific observations and reliably transmit data the four and a half billion kilometers back to Earth, the spacecraft needed the most long-lived and durable power source available. Solar power was not an option with the dim sunlight available in Neptune's orbit. The ship would require solar panels larger than those of the International Space Station to meet the 2.5-kilowatt system demand. This left nuclear power, provided by eight Radioisotope Thermoelectric Generators, using the heat released in the radioactive decay of their plutonium-238 fuel to generate electricity. It was an elegant balance of space, weight, power, and longevity.

And like anything else incorporating the words "nuclear" and "plutonium," it drove some people batshit crazy.

An amorphous collective of environmentalists, with anti-big government activists and religious fanatics thrown in, had banded together to oppose the launch for various reasons. The issue for the environmentalists was fear of the release of the vehicle's highly radioactive and chemically toxic plutonium into the atmosphere. The few who believed that GALV was actually a world government-enabling weapons platform or that it was an offense to God made excellent copy for Internet journalists but were hardly representative of the majority. After failing in Congress and the courts, several thousand people converged on the area in an effort of civil disobedience self-titled Occupy Cape Canaveral. But Florida was not New York City—protesters who tried to disrupt traffic outside Space Force Station Cape Canaveral were immediately arrested and removed by state police and national guard troops deployed to assist. Those who scaled the station's perimeter fence were instantly scooped up and incarcerated by federal law enforcement personnel.

The seaborne element of OCC fared no better against the Coast Guard and Florida Marine Patrol, deployed in force in the near-shore area. After a few arrests and the threat of Asset Forfeiture against any boats involved in security zone violations, both sides lapsed into an uneasy stalemate. The *Bon Temps* was the last gasp. A leased yacht contributed anonymously and staffed with fifteen activist grandmothers, aging nonconformists, and radical college students excited for the cause. The FBI had infiltrated the group and relayed intelligence of their intention to dash into the security zone and tie up the Coast Guard long enough to abort the launch.

The vessel was tracked from the moment it sailed from West Palm Beach, both by the federal authorities and the public, via an embedded Internet journalist named Austin Childress. He published regular podcast updates to his employers at the Global Multicast Network, GMN, which were breathlessly relayed to the public. As the *Bon Temps* approached Canaveral Bight, *Kauai* moved to be able to intercept if it crossed the boundary line into the security zone.

The *Bon Temps* had penetrated the perimeter of the security zone five minutes ago, heading for the inner prohibited area. This was the no-go area directly downrange of the launch complex along the flight path, into which fragments of the launch vehicle were likely to fall in the event of a mishap or post-liftoff abort. If this area were not clear, the launch would have to be scrubbed for safety. A two-billion-dollar mission was at stake—the launch had been delayed three times already because of weather and technical issues. The launch window, constrained by the movement of three giant planets and the Earth, was rapidly closing.

The yacht occupants knew this and that they would risk substantial penalties, including prison terms, for this act. They were gambling their lives that the U.S. Government would not use deadly force just to enable the launch of a peaceful scientific mission. They were right—the Coast Guard would not use gunfire to stop them, and the yacht was too large to risk a shouldering maneuver by the patrol boat. What they did not know was *Kauai* had a non-lethal ace up her sleeve: a projector firing nets that entangled a boat's propellers and disabled it.

The action was recorded in real-time, both by *Kauai*'s powerful electro-optical camera on her mast and a smaller camera mounted in an RQ-20 Puma drone orbiting the two vessels. The full-motion video feed captured by the cameras was displayed on screens in the command console and relayed digitally by radio to the Seventh District Command Center in Miami. Sam was awaiting a "Statement of No Objection," essentially a permission slip from the District Commander to employ non-lethal force to stop this target. *They had better pull their thumbs out of their asses and decide,* Ben thought as he looked at the navigation screen. *This sucker will be in the prohibited area in about fifteen minutes!*

"Williams, switch to targeting on EO and warm up the Squid," Sam said. "Squid" was the nickname for the entangling weapon, essentially a three-barreled recoilless cannon shooting encapsulated nets that popped open at the end of their flight and landed in a pre-set pattern. The launcher, mounted on the foredeck forward of the main gun, took target and environmental data from Williams's console and adjusted the firing bearing and elevation to deploy the nets in a pattern a speeding boat could not avoid. The boat would overrun a net, foul the propellers, and be stopped without using lethal gunfire.

Electronics Technician First Class Joseph "Joe" Williams, sitting at the Fire Control Station in the center of the command console, pressed two buttons and said, "EO in targeting mode and locked on. All systems are feeding the Squid, sir." The Electro-optical camera was now tracking the yacht automatically and pinging it with a laser rangefinder to deliver precise bearing and range information to the Squid. The system's artificial intelligence combined the bearing and range information with GPS and environmental data to generate and update an optimal firing solution for the launcher. As long as they were within two hundred meters and the relative motion was stable, a launch would almost certainly result in the *Bon Temps* running afoul of at least one net.

Chief Avionics Electrical Technician Erich "Fritz" Deffler sat to Williams's left at the console, controlling the Puma's flight and camera operations. Deffler was not part of *Kauai*'s standing crew, but was assigned to the Coast Guard's aviation deployment center in Jacksonville. When *Kauai* needed UAV support, Deffler usually led the aviation team, allowing him to be together with Hopkins. They had met in his first deployment on *Kauai* last January and had built a romantic relationship since. When onboard the boat, they were consummate professionals—when they were off duty, well....

Operations Specialist Third Class Natalya Zuccaro, sitting to Williams's right at the console, completed the command-and-control crew. She monitored navigation and communications and kept the ship's electronic logbook. She was a relative newcomer to the crew, assigned last March after *Kauai* had completed her bridge systems upgrade. Zuccaro suddenly sat upright and turned. "Captain, incoming SIPR chat message from D7. D7 Commander has no objection to the use of non-lethal force to stop motor vessel *Bon Temps* if the subject is still within security zone 165.T07-0450."

Sam nodded. "Thank you, Zuccaro." He turned to Ben. "XO, give him a final warning."

"Aye, aye, sir," Ben said, grabbing the microphone and switching to the VHF-FM radio. "Motor Vessel *Bon Temps*, this is the U.S. Coast Guard on Channel 16. Stop your engines immediately for boarding, or we will use force to compel compliance. Repeat, stop, or we will use force. This is your final warning." He then switched the microphone over to the loudhailer and repeated the message through the powerful speakers on the mast. Ben hung up the microphone and looked at the EO camera display. There was no question that the dozen people visible on the Bon Temps's deck heard and understood the message. The reaction was a mixture of bewildered looks, laughing, waving, and middle fingers up. After a moment, Ben turned to Sam. "No joy, Captain."

Sam nodded back. "OK, they had their chance. Petty Officer Zuccaro, log the time, our position course and speed, and the *Bon Temps*'s position, course, and speed. I am employing non-lethal force to stop this vessel for violation of security zone 165.T07-0450, as authorized by D7 Commander's SNO."

After sounds of furious typing in the electronic log, Zuccaro said, "Log entry complete, sir."

Sam said, "Very well. Williams, surface action port, target Squid on the *Bon Temps*."

With the targeting data continuously updating, Williams had only to push a single button on his console. Within a second, the amber "Target Solution" light came on. "Targeting solution achieved, Captain."

"Match generated bearings and shoot."

"Aye, aye, sir," Williams replied, then pressed the "Set" button. On the foredeck, the projector came alive, pivoting to a bearing pointing slightly forward of the speeding yacht and then trained upward around fifteen degrees. The Target Solution light turned green, and Williams said, "Firing." Then he pressed the "Fire" button.

Three loud "bangs" erupted from the foredeck. The canisters sped over the yacht, tiny fins spinning them at fifteen revolutions per second to stabilize them in flight and disperse the nets on detonation. Immediately after the third bang, Hopkins brought the thrust levers back to a ten-knot setting as she ordered, "Right full rudder!"

Seaman Pickins, standing in front of the helm console, replied, "Right full rudder, Chief!" After putting his helm lever fully to the right and noting the rudder position showing a swing over to the "30" mark on the right side, he added, "Chief, my rudder is right full."

"Very well."

The reaction on board the *Bon Temps* to the Squid firing was a universal shock. Some people on deck instinctively ducked or cried out, and others caught sight of the canisters and stared in fascination as they arced overhead. The twenty-year-old college student manning the helm watched in confusion as *Kauai* suddenly swung away to the right in its clearing maneuver after the bangs and did not attempt any course change. Even if he had, it would not have made any difference.

As the canisters reached the end of their three-second flight, explosive charges popped them open. Small weights on the periphery instantly spread the nets to their full fifteen-meter diameter, and they dropped into the water in an overlapping pattern thirty meters in front of the *Bon Temps*. The yacht ran over the left-hand and center nets, drawing them into both its spinning propellers, wrapping them in a fatal embrace. The engine safeties noted the dramatic spike in torque and instantly tripped, declutching the propeller shafts and rolling the diesel engines back to idle. The *Bon Temps* coasted to a stop within half a minute, adrift a good three and a half nautical miles short of the prohibited area boundary.

As *Kauai* came through and completed her right-hand circle, Hopkins brought the thrust levers to stop and ordered, "Rudder amidships."

"Rudder amidships," Pickins repeated. As the rudder angle approached zero, he said, "Chief, my rudder is amidships."

"Very well. At all stop, Captain."

"Thank you, Chief," Sam said. "Petty Officer Williams, report on the target and nets, please."

"Captain, the target is stopped bearing three-four-nine true at two hundred ninety yards. Nets one and two are fouled on the target, and net three is at three-five-two true and one hundred forty yards." A small buoy with a radar reflector in the center of each net allowed *Kauai* to track it. Now that its primary function had been served, the third net was just a hazard to navigation that *Kauai* needed to recover. For now, they needed to keep track of it while they completed the boarding on the *Bon Temps.*

"Very well. Petty Officer Zuccaro, log our position and that of the *Bon Temps.* Record vessel successfully stopped using non-lethal entanglement system, initiating boarding. Pass that to the command center using SIPR chat when you're done."

"Aye, aye, sir," Zuccaro replied.

"Chief Hopkins, maneuver to clear net three and put the *Bon Temps* fifty yards off our starboard beam."

"Very good, sir," Hopkins said as she pushed the thrust levers out of the stop detent to a slow forward setting.

"Chief Deffler, keep the UAV over the *Bon Temps.* I need continuous overhead EO coverage through the boarding."

"Very good, Captain," Deffler said, then made some adjustments using the console controls.

Sam reached over and gave Ben's arm a soft squeeze. "You're on, XO. Any questions?"

"No, sir," Ben replied. They had briefed thoroughly before the *Bon Temps*'s arrival. This would be one of the most complex boardings Ben had ever conducted—these were ordinary citizens, not drug or human smugglers, and emotions were running high. With his boarding team outnumbered three to one and use of force options pretty limited, it would take a lot of luck and patience to prevent a disaster. *Piece of cake*, he thought ruefully.

"Right. Good luck," Sam said with a nod.

As Ben turned and departed down the bridge ladder, he heard Williams begin the broadcast over the loudspeakers. "On the Motor Vessel *Bon Temps*, this is the U.S. Coast Guard. You have been stopped for violation of the United States Code of Federal Regulations, Title thirty-three, Section one-thirty-five. Standby for boarding by federal officers. If you are carrying any weapons, place them on the deck and stand away from them. For your own and our officers' safety, do not approach the officers unless told by them to do so...."

Ben reached the main deck and approached his boarding team, grouped beside the RHIB positioned for launch at the rail. Bondurant would be his assistant boarding officer on this one. Besides being a cool customer, his great size might give any hotheads on the *Bon Temps* pause. Lee was included instead of driving her beloved RHIB because of the presence of females on the target. Maritime Enforcement Specialist Third Class Lopez and Seaman Mitchell Harris completed the boarding team, and Boatswain's Mate Third Class Brian Jenkins would be the RHIB coxswain. With the entire deck force absorbed by the boarding, Chief Drake would work the boat crane for the operation. Ben decided to get a jab in as he approached. "Good to see you in the sunshine, COB. Are you sure you can operate this thing?"

"I think I can muddle through, *sir*," Drake replied with a mock scowl.

"Well, my insurance is paid up anyway," Ben quipped. He turned to the rest of the crew. "OK, folks. Things are going pretty much as we expected so far, so no change in what we briefed. Anyone have questions?" Seeing nothing but head shakes, Ben continued. "Right, the watchword is to play it cool and courteous. Let me do the talking. Remember there's an Internet *journalist* on board, so don't say or do anything you don't want the entire world to see." Ben turned to Bondurant and said, "Boats, if it looks like I'm going to throw him overboard, please do an intervention."

Bondurant grinned and said, "If you say so, XO. Personally, I'd pay real money to see that."

The rest of the gathering chuckled. It was not an entirely facetious comment. While Ben understood the need for journalism in principle, he had a spectrum of dislike for journalists in practice. He thought the print and local news reporters were alright—a little loose with facts, but they tried. Ben regarded the national network news as just a bunch of clowns starring in another TV show. But he despised the cable and Internet news for their lack of integrity and thought their employment of information warfare techniques to boost ratings and "clicks" to be borderline treason. He had to concentrate on maintaining his objectivity today.

They remained on deck during *Kauai's* slow approach. As they pulled abeam from the *Bon Temps*, Ben could feel and hear Hopkins slowing *Kauai* and then goosing the engines to maintain position and orientation. Finally, Ben's headset crackled. "LE One, *Kauai*, cleared for launch."

"Alright, let's do it," Ben said, leading his crew into the boat. They launched from the port side, opposite from the *Bon Temps*, and after releasing the crane hook, Jenkins took the heavily loaded RHIB in a wide left-hand turn off *Kauai's* stern. The *Bon Temps* had a boarding port and ladder on her transom, and Jenkins headed for that point. As they approached, Ben could see that a half-dozen people had gathered on the yacht's upper deck, and three men stood near the boarding ladder. Ben turned to Jenkins and said, "Coxswain, park us ten feet off the stern until I clear those people back."

"Aye, aye, sir," Jenkins replied, his face a mask of concentration.

Ben scanned the three men standing near the ladder as they pulled to a stop behind the *Bon Temps*. One was a white, forty-ish man with long hair, wearing a stern expression with his arms folded. One was another white man, more youthful, in his twenties maybe, pointing what looked like a small camera in their direction. Ben recognized the third man as the Internet journalist, Childress, giving directions to the cameraman. Ben looked at the older man and said, "Fellas, you need to go on the upper deck so we can come on board."

"Why do I need to do that? This is my boat, and I'll stand where I want," the older man responded.

"You need to comply with our instructions, sir," Ben said coldly.

"Or what, you'll arrest me? You're going to do that, anyway."

"True, but there's an easy way and hard way. Let's assess the situation. Whatever you intended with this stunt, it's over, and that rocket will launch regardless of what happens with your folks and my folks. So, the decision before you now is: do you want to be charged with trespassing in a security zone, or do you want to add interfering with a federal officer and resisting arrest to that charge?"

The man stared without replying for about ten seconds, then turned and climbed the ladder to the upper deck. The cameraman and Childress watched him leave, then turned to look at Ben.

Ben stared back coldly. "Was I unclear about something, gentlemen?"

"I don't think you know who we are, officer," Childress replied.

"No, I know exactly who you are, sir. You are two men suspected of trespassing in a security zone, about to become two men in custody on that big white boat over there for trespassing in a security zone, interfering with a federal officer, and resisting arrest. This is your last warning. Rejoin the others, NOW."

The cameraman stopped filming and immediately turned to climb the ladder to the upper deck. Childress watched with a disgusted look and, after one last glare at Ben, turned and followed. Ben turned to his crew and said, "Well, that was fun. OK, Coxswain, let's move in."

Jenkins brought the RHIB close, and Ben grabbed on the ladder rail and boarded, followed by Bondurant and the rest of the team. When they were all on board, Ben turned to Jenkins and said, "Stay close. We might need a quick getaway."

"Understood, sir," Jenkins replied, then backed the RHIB away about ten feet.

Ben led the way up the ladder, followed by his team. Word had apparently been passed around—the people on board were gathered on the forward part of the deck, leaving plenty of space around the ladder. Once his team had followed and positioned themselves behind him, Ben addressed the crowd. "Ladies and Gentlemen, I and these people behind me are United States Coast Guard officers. The Coast Guard is impounding this vessel for trespass within security zone 165.T07-0450, and will tow it into Port Canaveral for disposition. You will be detained on board for questioning until otherwise advised. Please remain here unless you are directed otherwise by one of us."

A young man, barely out of his teens by the look of him, stepped forward and said, "We don't recognize your authority to detain us without charge!" There were murmurs and looks of alarm in the crowd, particularly among the older people.

Great, the undergraduate law expert makes his appearance. Ben was careful not to show any emotion. "That would be a mistake, sir. As things stand right now, depending on your level of participation in the chartering and operation of this vessel, you *may* be cited for trespassing—a misdemeanor." He paused and looked meaningfully over the crowd. "Or not.

"On the other hand, if you fail to comply with our directions or attempt to interfere with us in any way, you *will* immediately be placed under arrest and charged with a violation of title eighteen, section one-eleven, United States Code. *That* charge could result in a felony conviction. Do you have any questions about this?"

The young man shut his mouth and sullenly stepped back into the crowd.

"Does anyone else have questions?" There was more murmuring and head shakes, but no one in the crowd spoke out. Ben nodded and continued, "Thank you. Now, is there anyone who needs medical help or any special accommodations?" There was visible relief among the crowd at Ben's solicitude, particularly among the older members, but no one called out. Keeping his eyes toward them, Ben whispered, "Lope, take Harris and do a security sweep for any holdouts. Call me when it's complete."

"On it, sir," Lopez replied, and then Ben heard their steps on the ladder behind him. After three minutes, which seemed like three hours, Ben's headset crackled again to Lopez's voice. "Sweep complete, XO. Nothing found."

"Very well, head to the bow."

"WILCO, sir."

Ben then switched his headset from intercom to radio and keyed his microphone. "*Kauai*, LE-One."

"LE-One, *Kauai*. Go ahead."

"*Kauai*, we have completed a sweep and detained all POB without incident. Standing by."

"LE-One, roger. *Tarpon* is in sight now and should be alongside in twenty mikes."

"*Kauai*, LE-One, roger, out." Ben let out a sigh of relief and whispered, "Stand easy, guys, but keep your head and eyes in the game."

"Roger that, sir," Lee muttered from behind him.

Just as the tension seemed to wane, Childress and his cameraman stepped from the crowd and walked toward Ben.

Great, Ben thought. *Here we go.*

"Officer, I'm Austin Childress, Global Multicast Network. Now that things have calmed down, I wonder if I can ask a few questions," he said with a smarmy smile.

"I don't have any information I can provide you, Mr. Childress," Ben said. "I suggest you contact the Seventh Coast Guard District public affairs office when you reach port. They are best equipped to handle these..." he gave Childress a contemptuous scan from head to foot. "*Things.*"

"Can I get your names for my report?" Childress asked. The boarding team's nametags were concealed by their survival vests.

"No."

"Well, fine. My viewers would like to hear your comment about the Coast Guard's firing on an unarmed civilian vessel."

OK, there it is. "Now, Mr. Childress, you know that is a lie. The *Bon Temps* was not fired upon, and no Coast Guard member has employed any firearm in this operation. The operators of the *Bon Temps* knowingly violated a lawfully established security zone. After they ignored repeated warnings to stop, the Coast Guard deployed a non-lethal device that safely brought the *Bon Temps* to a stop with no harm to the vessel or anyone on board."

"And what was the nature of that device?"

"No comment."

"I can find out, you know."

"Knock yourself out."

Childress turned to Bondurant and asked, "Would you care to comment, officer?"

"You must be joking," Bondurant replied.

Childress said, "I see." He turned to Lee. "And you? Any comment?"

Lee returned a scowl. "I'd like to say screw you and your viewers, but that would be unprofessional. So, I'll settle for no comment."

Childress turned to Ben and said, "It's a shame you and your people won't cooperate. It would be in your personal best interests to get ahead of this story."

For the first time, Ben smiled. "In our *personal* best interests? Really? Someone might take that as a threat." Ben leaned forward, and his expression grew intense. "Are you *threatening* federal officers in the course of their duties, sir?"

Childress reflexively took a step back. "No, of course not."

"Very well. Neither my crew nor I have any answers for you. So, you and your assistant need to rejoin the group." When Childress seemed to hesitate, Ben said firmly, "Now!"

After Childress and his cameraman turned and returned to the crowd, Bondurant whispered, "Real money, XO."

Ben turned and gave him a warm smile. "Knock it off, Boats. I'm having a hard enough time holding back as it is."

The remaining wait was tense, but uneventful. Ben and the two boatswain's mates maintained a steady, friendly demeanor while the crowd relaxed and chatted amongst themselves. The Coast Guard Cutter *Tarpon* arrived fifteen minutes later. It conveyed over two FBI agents and four more Coast Guard Maritime Enforcement Specialists to whom Ben was glad to turn over custody of the *Bon Temps* and her passengers.

After picking up Ben's team, the RHIB retrieved the last net used in the operation and returned to *Kauai*. Ben had just stepped aboard when a roar from the northwest caught his attention. He turned and watched as the two-hundred-fifty-ton rocket carrying GALV lifted into the azure blue sky atop three pillars of flame. After a minute, it had faded from sight, leaving a dissipating white contrail behind. Ben smiled—he always enjoyed the view of those beautiful and powerful machines as they launched, and this one was particularly meaningful to him. *Godspeed, GALV!*

Bittersweet

USCG Cutter *Kauai*, North Atlantic Ocean, six nautical miles east of Cape Canaveral, Florida
18:07 EDT, 14 October

Ben

Kauai was marking time offshore to return to her homeport in darkness. With the rocket launch complete, there was little chance the Occupy Cape Canaveral crowd would be determined or even interested in exacting any retribution. However, the District Commander was hard against crowds grabbing pictures of the victorious cutter returning to port.

FBI agents in *Tarpon*'s boarding party seized the cell phones and the GMN video camera onboard the *Bon Temps* and scrubbed any footage of the encounter with *Kauai*. Here, the media ululations that usually followed such perceived government high-handedness were conspicuously absent. This curious lack of reaction led Ben to speculate later that the FBI had uncovered some interesting media involvement in the *Bon Temps*'s fruitless sortie. The Squid projector was dismounted once the *Bon Temps* was out of sight, and it was stored in an innocuous case on the boat deck to be removed to the warehouse after they moored. It was not a classified piece of gear, but the Coast Guard still had an interest in not revealing it to casual onlookers and people inclined to develop countermeasures.

Ben completed supper and stretched out in his stateroom for rest before the port entry evolution when his desk phone rang. He sighed, reached over, and grabbed the receiver. "XO."

It was Hopkins. "XO, could you come to the Bridge, please? There's something you need to see."

Ben straightened. "I'm on the way, Chief. You want me to grab the skipper?"

"No, sir. Just you."

"Right." He grabbed his ball cap, hastened to the ladder, and climbed to the Bridge. Bondurant, who had the watch, smiled as he entered the Bridge and nodded to Hopkins sitting at the console. Ben said, "What's up, Chief?"

Hopkins patted the seat on her right and said, "Have a seat and get a load of this, sir."

Ben sat and looked at the screen in front, which displayed an official Coast Guard message. He skipped past the message header and began reading:

ALCGPSC 093
SUBJ: ADPL LIEUTENANT COMMANDER SELECTION BOARD RESULTS
A. Officer Accessions, Evaluations, and Promotions, COMDTINST M1000.3(series)
1. The Secretary, acting for the President, has approved the report of the Selection Board convened on 2 August, which recommended the following officers on the active-duty promotion list (ADPL) for promotion to the grade of lieutenant commander. Officers selected are listed below in ADPL precedence order:

Ben scrolled down through the names, and one jumped off the screen.

16. POWELL, SAMUEL J.   CGC KAUAI

Ben blinked, looked again, and a smile spread across his face. "Holy shit! The skipper wasn't in the zone! I didn't know he was even eligible!" Officers in the Coast Guard were selected by annual promotion boards who considered officers within a window that moved down the list of officers ordered by precedence. The board could also choose an officer eligible for a promotion by virtue of time holding their rank but not yet within the window, but these selections are extremely rare. That the board reached past so many eligible below-zone officers to pick Sam was an immense compliment to his performance.

Ben was delighted for this man, who had become his closest friend. *Deep selected, as deep as you can get! Not only that, but advanced to the top of the list!* Each event was rare in the Coast Guard; it was unheard of for both to coincide. It meant that Sam would get promoted several years ahead of what was usually expected. He turned to grin at Hopkins and saw the sad look on her face. At that point, reality hit home, and his face fell.

Sam was Ben's CO, but although there was a very formal Superior-Subordinate relationship between them set forth by the Coast Guard, they were more like partners in the practical sense. Ben regarded Sam as his closest friend and the finest officer he ever knew. He was definitely not looking forward to parting company with him on top of getting a new boss. But there was no getting around the basic fact.

"Yes, we really will lose him now. They can't keep him on board as a lieutenant commander." He turned to look at the screen again, and his smile returned. He sent the message to the bridge printer and grabbed an envelope from the cabinet below the console. "C'mon, Chief, let's grab COB."

A couple of minutes later, Ben knocked on Sam's cabin door.

"Come in."

Ben opened the door and entered, followed by the two chiefs. Sam looked at the three and then put on his best Anthony Hopkins as Captain Bligh impression. "What's this, Mister Christian? A mutiny?"

Ben waved his hand dismissively and replied, "No, no, Captain. I put down today's mutiny hours ago."

After the laughter subsided, Ben continued, holding out the envelope. "We have something for you, sir."

Sam took the envelope with a puzzled glance at his guests, opened it, and started reading. His eyes opened wide, and he looked at Ben. "Is this a joke?"

Ben beamed back. "Not a chance, sir."

Sam rechecked the page and said, "Wow!"

"We wanted to be the ones to tell you, sir, and the first to congratulate you," Ben said.

Sam stood, shook Ben's hand, then pulled him into a hug. After doing the same with Hopkins and Drake, he said, "Thanks, guys. As awesome as this is, it's much more amazing coming from you."

"Thank you, sir," Ben said. "By your leave, Captain? We need to start preps."

Sam looked into his eyes again and said, "Yes, thank you."

After pulling the door closed, Ben turned to the other two and said, "Well, I guess we'd better get on it."

Drake smiled, patted him on the shoulder, then turned and walked down the hallway. Hopkins reached over and gently squeezed his upper arm, then turned to the bridge ladder and climbed. Ben paused for a minute, glanced at Sam's door, and then turned to follow Hopkins to the Bridge.

3532 Slidergate Drive, Rockledge, Florida
20:52 EDT, 14 October

Victoria

Victoria Carpenter put the phone down and breathed a sigh of relief. Benjamin was safe—*Kauai* had moored, and he called to say he was leaving for home and ask if she needed him to pick anything up on the way. She knew she shouldn't have been worried. This was a low-risk sortie, or so Benjamin told her. But, given the increasing tensions and violence associated with the anti-launch demonstrations, Victoria feared the *Kauai* would land in some sort of conflict. She knew of the *Bon Temps*'s voyage from the news feeds and dreaded the confrontation they seemed determined to force on the Coast Guard.

Victoria watched NASA's live stream of the launch from her office that afternoon, anxiously awaiting the final moment when the rocket cleared the pad. She usually enjoyed watching the rocket launches. Like Ben, Victoria appreciated the aesthetic beauty of the machine and the precision required for a successful mission across vast distances. Today, she felt only a brief sense of relief. The launch occurred on time, so Benjamin and his crew must have prevented the *Bon Temps* from interfering. She knew that the lack of any other news was probably a good sign, but she could not help worrying about it until Benjamin's call.

Victoria sat at her desk and picked up the picture of Benjamin from their day on the DC Mall back in March, taken by the same photographer of the photograph on Benjamin's wall on *Kauai*.

Victoria persuaded him to take this solo shot of Benjamin after agreeing to sell them the other picture and was delighted with the result. The photo was comprehensively perfect in her mind: the lighting, venue, composition, and the ideal subject. It was also a tangible mark of what she regarded as her most perfect day, followed by the perfect night when she and Benjamin made love for the first time in her apartment.

Benjamin had been as much a surprise to Victoria as she was to him. They met by chance on the only occasion Victoria had gone into the field from her office job with the DIA in the Washington, DC, suburb of Bethesda. She'd appreciated the challenge of processing UAV imagery data in the austere environment of a hotel room. The location of the Florida Keys was also agreeable, particularly in January. Even the journey was tolerable—because of their sensitive and highly classified equipment, they traveled on a government plane, avoiding the horror of the commercial airport terminals with their crowds, confined spaces, noise, and all those people *touching* you.

Later in the week, her mentor, Peter, notified her he was coming ashore and bringing one officer, Benjamin, with him as a liaison. Victoria had pulled Benjamin's record for Peter's review before the operation, and she was decidedly unimpressed. Benjamin was a mediocre performer at the Coast Guard Academy, had an uneventful tour of duty aboard USCG Cutter *Dependable* in Little Creek, Virginia, then was assigned to *Kauai* as second in command. There was something unusual—he had been awarded the Coast Guard Commendation Medal for heroism in saving three lives after a traffic accident. She noted this with approval as she pulled his official photo, which was also unimpressive. All official military photos looked the same to her, like instead of "say cheese," the photographers said, "Now, give us your most menacing scowl!"

The young man who arrived with Peter for the team meeting that first night was nothing Victoria expected. Some height, but not overly tall, with a slim, athletic build and the most captivating blue eyes she had ever seen. Benjamin was not the militaristic buffoon Victoria took him for after reading his personnel file, but a modest, almost shy, intelligent young man who provided fascinating conversation. She suspected he was also attracted to her—she caught glimpses of him looking at her while she worked at her computer during the team discussions.

After the team meeting, they had a long conversation, mainly with Benjamin describing and answering her questions about his life aboard ship. The next morning Victoria had to return to Bethesda, but she spoke to him that evening after he completed the search activity for the day. This time Benjamin was the receiver, and Victoria was talking. It thrilled her he was interested in what she did, and although she suspected he did not quite understand it all, he still seemed to hang on to every word. Several days passed before they spoke on the phone again after Benjamin returned home. Something had happened during the mission, but he could not discuss it. Working in the world of classified information and secrets, she understood. Whatever happened must have been extraordinary, for he and Samuel received the Coast Guard Medal, a top award for heroism.

They settled into a routine of nightly phone calls whenever Benjamin had the connectivity. They were a welcome distraction at first, becoming an increasingly important part of her day as she got to know him. He was interesting, charming, and funny all at once, and unlike anyone she had ever met, she could discuss anything on her mind with him. Given this, she was puzzled that he was not married or had a steady girlfriend. When she finally asked why that was, he went silent, and she quickly tried to withdraw the question.

"No, it's OK, Victoria. I've asked myself that a few times. The only answer I can come up with is I haven't met anyone who needed what I could provide." Then he quickly changed the subject, and she was careful not to raise it again. Benjamin's answer created a paradox for her. She often could not connect with people she liked and felt much closer to him, knowing he shared this experience of loneliness. On the other hand, it made her even warier of making any blunders. It was a specter hanging over their early conversations, fading over time as she became more comfortable with him.

Between the distance and the relentless demands of Benjamin's job, the conversations were all they had. Benjamin had hoped they could get together when he was close by in Quantico while completing his combat training in February and March, but the short time and large volume of training requirements extended through the weekends. During his course, the only free time allowed was just one evening that served as a somewhat awkward first date and one other full day together, and they seized on those opportunities.

Their first date had been a maelstrom of emotion for Victoria. Fortunately, her coworker friend Debbie, knowledgeable about such things, helped her select a suitable dress and put on the appropriate makeup. Benjamin's stunned reaction to her appearance made things awkward initially, but they quickly recovered their usual banter over an excellent meal at a lovely restaurant. It ended up an excellent first date.

For the second, Benjamin had driven up from Quantico early on a Sunday morning and picked her up at her apartment. Although they had a lovely day touring the Mall and Smithsonian, the outing was marred when Victoria suffered a panic attack on the crowded Metro train on their return trip. Benjamin escorted her off the train to safety once he realized what was happening, but she was sure this stark presentation of her affliction would drive him away. Her fears seemed well-founded when they returned to her apartment, and he made to leave. It was one of the most emotional moments of her life, and she often replayed the memory of it like one replayed a favorite song:

He took her hands and said, "Victoria, I, um…." He gazed longingly at her, then looked down. After another moment, he held her eyes again. "I had a great time today. Thank you."

"Yes, I did too." She had willed herself not to cry. "I hope I can see you again soon."

"Yes. Definitely. As soon as possible. Goodnight, Victoria."

"Goodnight, Benjamin." She kissed him fully on the lips. After a few seconds, Victoria pulled back, then stepped inside the apartment, and closed the door. She sat on the floor, oblivious to the fact that you are not supposed to sit on the floor, pulled up her legs, and put her chin on her knees. *OK, this is how it ends. He was just being kind to me today because he feels sorry for me. I will not cry!* And then, of course, she cried. About half a minute later, a knock on the door startled her. She stood slowly, reeled to the door, and looked out the peephole. She gasped and fumbled with the lock and wrenched the door open. "Benjamin!"

He stood in the doorway with a serious expression on his face. "Victoria, I'm sorry, but I can't leave it like this. I want to be with you. I know it's unfair to lay this on you so late at night and then run out at oh-dark-thirty tomorrow. But after today, I want to have every moment I can with you. If you don't feel the same, I'll understand, and I'll go, but I had to tell you."

She stepped up to him, put her arms around his neck, and pressed her head onto his chest, listening to his deep breaths and pounding heart while blinking away her tears. After a minute, she hugged him tightly, then took his hand, led him inside, and closed the door. They did not talk again until the morning, but neither did they sleep. When they embraced the last time before Benjamin left to return to Quantico, Victoria wanted to tell him she loved him, but the old fear returned, and she could not say the words. Instead, she smiled warmly at him, gave him one last kiss, and said simply, "Goodbye, Benjamin."

Benjamin had no other opportunity to visit during his training and had to return immediately to Florida once it concluded. They resumed their routine of the nightly phone calls whenever Benjamin had the connectivity. Victoria longed for these calls all day, hoping he would say something or give her some sign that it was safe to reveal her love for him.

Victoria caressed Benjamin's picture—she remembered how she had been holding and looking at this picture when he told her he loved her for the first time—a surprise call on a satellite phone before he went into action at Barbello. The call was like a dam bursting, each admitting they had been in love with the other since the night of Benjamin's last visit and lamenting the lost month they kept the truth to themselves. She went to bed that night with the most joyous feeling in her life.

Victoria woke up the following morning with the same excited joy, only to have it crushed when she arrived at work to learn Benjamin had been grievously wounded and evacuated by helicopter. His survival was in doubt, and Victoria knew nothing she could bring to bear would affect that outcome, but she was determined to be with Benjamin through whatever was to come. Fortunately, she had plenty of help.

Her coworkers helped her arrange a flight to Miami, where Benjamin was transported for emergency surgery. One of the original January team agents went along to help her cope with the airports and transport to the hospital. She arrived just after Benjamin went into surgery and was greeted in the waiting room by Joana Powell, Samuel's wife and a close friend of Benjamin. Joana stayed with Victoria and comforted her through the operation.

Although the operation was a success, the nature and severity of Benjamin's injury left doubts about whether he would recover consciousness or even survive. Victoria stayed with him, speaking and reading to him during his coma and sleeping fitfully in a recliner the hospital staff set up for her. She had dozed off from exhaustion late the following day with her head on Benjamin's bed and dreamed about their day on the Mall when his light touch awakened her. The intensity of her relief at finding him awake and able to talk rivaled her joy at finding out he loved her.

Victoria stayed with Benjamin for the two days during his post-op recovery at the hospital and then at his apartment during his two-week convalescence, helping him while he recovered his coordination and balance. Victoria cherished the time they had together and the chance to meet and talk with Benjamin's shipmates and their families. As the time approached for her to return home, Victoria's sadness at the thought of leaving grew, culminating at a small dinner party Joana put on for her and Benjamin with Emilia Hopkins and her beau, Erich Deffler. Victoria had a grand time, particularly in what Joana called the "girl talk" session involving the three women. She discovered she fit right in with the discussion and laughter and felt a sense of belonging she had never before experienced. Benjamin sensed her sadness on the way home—he was wonderfully good at that—and asked her about it when they got to his apartment. To Victoria's shock, after she explained her pensiveness, Benjamin asked her to consider moving in together.

The surge of emotions created by that request was overwhelming. Victoria had settled into a steady existence of home-work-home in a government position with the DIA and known no other reality. She feared leaving this safety for the uncertainty of a private-sector job with different people and working in a whole new place. On the other hand, she could be with Benjamin every day, going to sleep and waking in his arms, enjoying meals, outings, and the other pleasures of life in his company. Victoria had also grown to love Joana and wanted to spend time with her. She was warming to the idea when the reality of her condition reasserted itself. Victoria was realistic—

she knew her many behavioral anomalies concealed at work or on short dates would show themselves when living with someone. The thought of these coming between her and Benjamin filled her with dread, and she told him as much. Benjamin was undeterred, pointing out that he was sure he had quirks she would find abnormal, suggesting that they could work through them.

In the end, Benjamin prevailed, but only after Victoria extracted a promise from him not to propose marriage until they completed a six-month trial co-habitation period. She was not convinced they could work through the bugs and did not want the pressure to commit to what might be the disaster of a failed marriage. They were approaching the six-month point, and looking over it now, her demand seemed rather silly. She could never return to her earlier "safe" existence—despite her recurring worries about Benjamin's safety, she had never felt happier or more alive.

The sound of a key in the front door jolted Victoria out of her reverie, and she carefully placed the picture on her desk as she stood to go to the door. Benjamin was stepping inside as she came into the room. He put his backpack down, gathered her in his arms, and they shared a warm kiss.

"Hello, my love. How was your day?" Benjamin asked. "I have been on the edge of my seat waiting for the outcome of those test runs," he added, referring to a new machine language algorithm she was struggling with at her workplace, Vectorsonds, Inc.

"That can wait, Benjamin. I want to hear about your encounter with the *Bon Temps*. I was worried about you."

"You really shouldn't, you know," he said. "They were a bunch of well-meaning people amped up by a slimeball journalist. The worst that could have happened to me is them throwing me overboard, and I had John and Shelley along to keep that from happening. It all worked out. The rocket launched, nobody got hurt, and I'm home with you tonight."

"I know I should not worry, but I cannot help it. You know how I am about these things." Victoria smiled. "Now, please tell me what happened."

Benjamin provided the narration of the intercept and seizure of the *Bon Temps* he knew Victoria wanted to hear. With a crowd of civilians and a journalist already involved, there were no secrets to be filtered. She laughed at Bondurant's comment about

Benjamin throwing the journalist overboard, but only smiled on hearing of Shelley's ribald answer to Childress's impertinent question. Despite Benjamin's assurances that the job would not permit any relationship between them, even if Victoria were not in the picture, Shelley was an attractive woman who had a great deal in common with him. Even Victoria was human enough to be a little jealous of her.

"Oh, and the big news is happy and sad at the same time," Benjamin said.

"Bittersweet?"

"Yes, that's the word. Sam has been selected for promotion to lieutenant commander."

"Surely that is excellent news, Benjamin. What could possibly be sad about that?"

"It *is* excellent. He was selected years ahead of normal, which is a huge deal for an officer. Naturally, I think he deserves it; even so, it is nice to see the Coast Guard do right by him. The thing is, they can't leave him on *Kauai* as a lieutenant commander. I guess he would have had to rotate next summer anyway, but I had hoped they could use our special status to keep the band together."

"Oh, I see how that could be sad." In fact, the news was alarming to Victoria. She knew if Samuel left, Joana would follow, and she could no longer hang around with the woman who had become her closest friend. Benjamin picked up on her thoughts at once.

"I know Jo is an important part of your support system here. Will you be OK?"

She hugged him again. "Yes. I am coming to terms with it. Of course, we can still talk and text, but it has been wonderful to visit with her, particularly when you are gone. You warned me this sort of thing is part of military life."

"Yes, hails and farewells. But hey, it will be months before we have to deal with the bitter part. Let's celebrate Sam's good fortune. Do we have any of that cabernet you like? We're both off tomorrow, so we might as well enjoy tonight."

"We do indeed."

"Super. How about I crack a bottle of that while you regale me with your tale of adventure in machine language land?"

Victoria snuggled into Benjamin three hours later as he lay soundly asleep and turned on his left side. It had not been a night of lovemaking, just talking about Samuel, Joana, their work, and their future together. She caressed Benjamin's upper right arm lightly, careful not to awaken him. Like most patrols, this most recent one allowed little time for sleep, and Benjamin had been exhausted when he arrived. *Still, you stayed at it, making sure I was alright at work and with the news that Joana and Samuel were leaving us.* She softly kissed and then rested her forehead against Benjamin's shoulder. *Sleep, my love. I have the watch now.*

Next Generation

State Route 528, eleven miles east of Orlando, Florida
10:02 EDT, 23 October

Haley

Lieutenant Haley Reardon, U.S. Coast Guard, was halfway through the final hour of the two-and-a-half-hour drive from her duty station at the Coast Guard Sector Office in St. Petersburg to a meeting on Patrick Space Force Base just south of Cape Canaveral. The order had come down yesterday from the Seventh District Office—she was to report to a building associated with the 45th Operations Group in her tropical blue uniform at 12:30. There were no other details, and Haley's mind whirled at the possibilities as she drove her blue Miata along the flat and straight four-lane through the alternating open fields and pine woods of the Tosohatchee State Preserve. The oppressive heat and humidity of the Florida summer were finally showing signs of breaking, and she longed to have the Miata's top down in the bright, warm sunshine. But she had spent enough time getting her shoulder-length black hair into a tight regulation bun before leaving the apartment this morning, and she did not want to deal with it again at her destination.

Just past her twenty-ninth birthday, Haley was a taller-than-average five-foot-eight with superb all-around fitness. She had been an all-state track and field star in high school in Rhode Island with scholarship offers from Brown, Bryn Mawr, and Princeton. But she loved competitive sailing growing up. After a visit to Newport by the Coast Guard's "tall ship" *Eagle*, Haley had opted instead for military service via the tiny Coast Guard Academy, to the mild disappointment of her well-to-do father and absolute fury of her socially climbing stepmother. Still, the passion for fitness stuck with her, and, short of being at sea or flat on her back sick, she was at the gym for one to two hours every day.

Haley was two years into her tour in the Law Enforcement Section in the Response Department at Coast Guard Sector St. Petersburg. It was her first ashore job since graduation from the Academy seven years ago, having been assigned first to the large National Security Cutter *Wasche* out in Alameda, California, for two years, then as Operations Officer of the Fast Response Cutter *Joseph Napier* in San Juan, Puerto Rico, for three years before coming to St. Petersburg. Haley appreciated the need for diversity in assignment experience, and, as she freely admitted after two afloat tours, it didn't suck to be ashore on liberty almost every night. But, like most junior officers, she longed for the opportunity of her own afloat command with its associated excitement and a career boost. Haley had been quite successful in her assignments and had plenty of confidence in her abilities. Still, she was anxiously awaiting the Junior Command Screening Panel results, due out later that month, determining whether she would have a chance to wear the moniker "Captain" in her next assignment or stay another junior officer in the mix.

Glancing at the navigation display, Haley noted she would be at her destination with an hour and twenty minutes to spare. She also noted that automated navigation systems tended to go wonky on military bases with their seemingly random building numbers. It was best to have a time buffer to allow for the search at the end. Additionally, her route included a seventeen-mile stretch on Interstate 95, a nexus of stupidity where just about anything could happen. Haley did not know what lay ahead of her, but she infinitely preferred to be waiting around for it to happen to being late.

As it happened, the I-95 stretch was an uneventful fifteen minutes, as was the short drive on 404 through Palm Shores, across the Indian River, and through South Patrick Shores to the Patrick SFB South Gate. After a brief wait in line, she presented her CAC to a Specialist4 in combat utilities and held her sunglasses up while he compared the image on his scanner to her face. Satisfied, he returned her card and said, "Welcome to Patrick, Lieutenant. Are you carrying any weapons today?"

As she always did when asked this question, Haley suppressed a smile and answered, "No."

The specialist rendered a crisp salute and said, "Have a nice day, ma'am."

"Thank you," Haley replied with a nod as she drove through. *I wonder if anyone ever answered, "Why, yes, I am!" to that question.* The navigation system worked this time, and she quickly located the 45th's HQ building and the associated parking. She glanced again at the clock: 11:13. *Where's the Exchange? There's plenty of time for a salad at the inevitable Charley's to hold down the stomach growls.*

After a quick meal at the Base Exchange, Haley returned to the 45th HQ, parked, and presented her CAC at the checkpoint. The Technical Sergeant manning the desk scanned the card and returned it with a visitor's badge. "Please wear this above your waist, ma'am. If you have any smart devices, drop them off before entry, please," he said, gesturing to a set of lockboxes on the wall. "Specialist Jinks will escort you to the room."

"Thank you," Haley said as she attached the badge to the pocket flap of her light blue uniform shirt. After dropping her cell phone, Fitbit, and key fob in a lockbox, she followed the young specialist through the security door. After a short walk, she was shown into a small room with a round table and four chairs.

"Bathrooms are down the hall to the right. Is there anything else I can do for you, ma'am?" the specialist asked.

"No, thank you very much," Haley replied and then sat at the table as the specialist closed the door behind him on leaving. The room had the usual décor proper to the service, in this case, the Air Force: large pictures of aircraft and rockets lifting off on standard military cream-colored wallpaper, with the standard military Berber carpet and 12:19 displayed on the standard military twelve-hour clock in the center of one wall. *Oh, good. At least eleven more minutes to wonder what this is about.*

It was actually eighteen minutes later when the door opened after a brief knock, and a woman in her mid-forties, stoutly built and one or two inches shorter than Haley, with short graying brown hair, stepped into the room. She was wearing the same Coast Guard tropical blue uniform as Haley, except for the four stripes of a captain on her shoulder boards. Haley jumped to attention and said, "Good afternoon, Captain!"

The woman waved her hand and said, "Carry on, please." She held her right hand out and continued, "Lieutenant Reardon? Jane Mercier. It's good to meet you."

"Likewise, ma'am," Haley said, shaking her hand. *The District Chief of Staff? What the <u>Hell</u> is going on here?* She instinctively completed the flash scan of the captain's uniform all officers did on their first meeting. Mercier had aviator wings above a stack of ribbons topped with the Legion of Merit, Distinguished Flying Cross, and Meritorious Service Medal, over her left breast pocket with a Command Ashore pin on the flap.

"Please, have a seat," Mercier said, sitting in one of the chairs. After Haley was seated in the opposite chair, she continued. "I'm sorry for all the close-hold associated with this trip. I imagine you're wondering WTF, am I right?"

"Something like that, ma'am," Haley replied with a smile.

"I think you'll be happy to hear you are being considered for a mid-season transfer to your own patrol boat command. The selection is outside the normal command screening process because of the time element and the unique mission profile of the boat. Is that something you'd be interested in?"

Haley's heart skipped a beat—*a PB command!* "Hell, yes! Oh, I beg your pardon, ma'am."

"No, that's OK," Mercier replied. "You don't have to decide at this moment. In fact, we dragged you over here for some frank talk about this unit and to observe an awards ceremony for the crew. After that, if you have reservations, you can turn this down with nothing going on the record."

Uh-Oh. "Captain, what unit are we talking about here?"

"*Kauai*," Mercier replied, staring intently into Haley's gray eyes.

Ka-thunk! Haley tried to maintain an indifferent expression as her heart fell. *Talk about a poisoned chalice! A beat-up old one-ten consigned to be range safety cutter at the Cape until they could shitcan her? A mid-season assignment, too—they're probably yanking the CO for cause. Awesome!* "Um, ma'am...."

"Hold on a bit," Mercier interrupted. "I can see in your face that you've heard things, and I'll start by saying that there are official and unofficial versions of this boat's history."

"Yes, ma'am?" Haley said. *My God! Could it be* worse *than everyone says?*

"I'll start at the beginning. A couple of years ago, *Kauai* was a troubled unit with a buttload of discipline and operational issues. We finally relieved the CO after he almost lost the boat in a mishap on a routine migrant operation. It was quite a mess, and we considered washing our hands of her and advancing her decommissioning date. But she was in pretty good material shape, and with the FRC deliveries going slower than we hoped, it was killing us to give up a viable hull voluntarily. So, we decided to try something wild. We put on the best guys we could find for CO and XO—the previous exec was injured in the mishap—and let them build a solid team with the good folks they had and swap out the deadbeats.

"After a few months, the new cadre had completely turned things around, and *Kauai* was the go-to boat for any really outside-the-box stuff that could come along. The first test of that capability came last January. I can't give you details of that mission—there are only about a dozen people in the *world* who are totally in the loop on that one. All I can tell you is in the aftermath, both the officers ended up with the Coast Guard Medal, *Kauai* got a serious upgrade paid for by the Director of National Intelligence, and four of her crew got special combat tactical training."

Haley's earlier gloom vanished. "What sort of upgrades, ma'am?"

Mercier smiled at the change in Haley's expression. "She already had a prototype installation of the new Mod 2 Mark 38 twenty-five-millimeter gun we are putting on the FRCs. We updated the command-and-control systems and sensors and rehab-ed the Bridge. The existing diesels were swapped out with a diesel-electric-battery plant that supports the increased electronic load and silent operations for short periods. Round that off with the addition of some light armor and stealth coatings, and you have a hull resistant to everything short of twenty-millimeter with the radar cross-section of a Response Boat, Small."

Haley leaned forward. "So, I take it the range safety cutter stuff is just a cover, ma'am?"

"No, if there's a launch from the Cape, *Kauai* is honestly doing that job. At other times, though, she is doing more-or-less normal PB operations, with the caveat that she must be made available immediately whenever needed for any 'off the books' operations.

As a result, we keep *Kauai* within a radius that will allow us to turn her around quickly onto anything hairy that comes up."

"I see, ma'am. And *has* anything really hairy come up?"

"Yes. Last April, we sent her on a mission off Honduras, another hyper-secret one. You're about to get what details can be shared at the Top Secret level in the awards ceremony. The rest is codeword-classified."

Haley blinked in surprise. Codeword-classified referred to information and programs so secret that access could be granted only to specific individuals on a case-by-case basis after special vetting and read-in. She had worked at the highest classification levels on *Wasche* but saw no codeword-classified material there. The idea of a tiny one-ten caught up in a codeword program was mindboggling.

There was just one more thing, and it could make the difference between Haley stepping into an elite team or a demoralized mess. "Ma'am, why the hurry of a mid-season relief? Is there a problem with the current CO?"

"On the contrary," Mercier replied. "He has just been deep-selected for lieutenant commander and advanced to the top of the promotion list. No, this one is weird because of his and the XO's arrival timing. Do you remember I said they came on together to replace the old command? That would be two years ago in January. We don't want to pull them both simultaneously—we want continuity in the command. We also don't want to leave the XO on there for three or three-and-a-half years because it might hurt him professionally. Finally, the CO has been in commission for eight years, six-and-half at sea and four in command. And the last two years have been hard, first pulling that crew out of the crapper and then putting them in harm's way big time. In that last mission, he had two wounded, one of them the XO, who damn near died and is a close friend.

"In short, we need to give the man a break and a reward for what he's done. We swung a Command and Staff Course slot for him at the Naval War College starting in January. It will do him right professionally, and Newport is close to his and his wife's families, so big win."

Haley was about to respond when there was a knock at the door, and Specialist Jinks poked his head in at Mercier's bidding.

"Excuse me, Captain. You wanted to be informed when the admiral arrived," Jinks said.

"Oh, yes. Thank you, Specialist. We'll be right along." After Jinks departed, they both stood, and Mercier turned to Haley. "Have you met Admiral Pennington?"

"No, ma'am." Haley hadn't thought her mind could spin up any further. *Wrong. The Seventh District Commander traveled from Miami to Patrick Space Force Base to decorate a patrol boat crew for a mission so secret its name could not be spoken aloud? Incredible!*

"Well, he's the real deal. He knows why you are here and wanted to speak with you about this after the ceremony. He wants to make sure that you go in with your eyes open if you take this job," Mercier said as she led the way down the hall. "Oh, and close-hold on everything we have discussed regarding the CO coming off—we have not told him yet. We'll duck out at the end of the presentation, so you don't get buttonholed by anybody."

"Yes, ma'am," was all Haley could say. *Holy Shit!* was all she could think.

****

When Mercier and Haley entered the reception area, two men in Space Force utilities were chatting with a third in a Coast Guard tropical blue uniform with an admiral's all-gold shoulder boards. Rear Admiral Horatio Pennington, U.S. Coast Guard, was commander of the Seventh Coast Guard District, which included all the units in South Carolina, Georgia, the Florida peninsula, and the Caribbean basin. He had only been in the job for a couple of months, taking over when his predecessor had been disabled in a car accident. Haley had not met nor seen the admiral before, but Pennington had a reputation of being one of the smartest and best leaders in the service. In his early fifties, he was of average height and build, with a full head of close-cropped graying hair and brown eyes looking through round, silver-rimmed glasses.

Pennington turned as they approached as said, "Ah, Jane. And you must be Lieutenant Reardon." He held out his hand. "I've read a lot of good things about you."

Haley flushed at the compliment and shook his hand. "Thank you, Admiral."

After introductions between the new arrivals and his Space Force companions, Pennington said, "Gentlemen, could you excuse us, please?" After exchanging salutes and handshakes, the two men departed, and Pennington turned to Mercier and Haley. "I am glad you could attend, Lieutenant. Do you go by Haley?"

"Yes, sir."

"Good. As I was saying, I am glad you're here. My aide is getting things set up right now. Did Captain Mercier tell you I want to chat with you afterward?"

"Yes, she did, sir."

"Right. How do you feel so far?"

"Pretty damn psyched, if you'll pardon me saying so, sir."

Pennington's smile broadened. "You might change your mind once you hear what's involved, but I like the enthusiasm."

Before Haley could reply, a young Coast Guard lieutenant junior grade wearing the gold aiguillette of an admiral's aide on his shoulder came through one door and said, "They're ready for you now, Admiral."

"Thank you," Pennington said, then turned to follow with Mercier and Haley in trail.

After a short walk, the four turned into an alcove leading to a small briefing room where a dozen Coast Guard personnel stood in line in front of a podium. They all snapped to attention as Pennington came through the door when the aide shouted, "Attention on Deck!"

Pennington announced, "Thank you, rest." Pennington continued after the people in line came to parade rest, with feet slightly apart and hands behind them. "The best thing about being a flag officer is the chance to shake hands with courageous people and award them the recognition they deserve, not just for special actions, but for being there every day at the tip of the spear. This is one of those times, and I want to say how proud I am to be here and of you. I'm sorry your families can't be here to see this and hear what I have to say to you firsthand. The nature of your work, important as it was to both the nation and world, is too sensitive to release, and I appreciate your discretion." He turned to his aide and nodded.

"Attention to orders," the young man said, and while everyone else in the room came to attention, Pennington and Mercier walked to and stood before a Seaman at the far left of the line.

After they exchanged salutes, the aide continued reading from a folder. "Citation to accompany the award of the Coast Guard Achievement Medal to Seaman Mitchell L. Pickins, United States Coast Guard. Seaman Pickins is cited for exceptional performance of duty while serving on board USCGC *Kauai* on the night of five to six April in action against armed terrorist forces on the island of Barbello, Honduras...."

The awards were presented by the increasing precedence of the medal and increasing rank of the awardee. Haley noted that the most senior member of the award party, a lieutenant, presumably the CO, was third from the end on the right. To his left stood a diminutive female wearing second class petty officer collar devices and a coxswain's insignia that marked her as a boatswain's mate and a lieutenant junior grade Haley guessed was the XO. Through the award narratives, Haley could piece together the story of the action:

Intelligence sources had detected a weapon of mass destruction on a boat seized by a terrorist drug cartel and moored at their island stronghold off the coast of Honduras. The nature of the weapon and its origin were not revealed, which Haley deduced was the codeword information. The need to secure the device before it was moved and maintain secrecy prevented the assembly of a strong military force—the job fell to *Kauai*, supported by a small SEAL team and air force reconnaissance aircraft.

While the SEAL team stealthily seized control of the vessel, *Kauai* penetrated the harbor under the cover of a rainstorm. The XO led a boarding team of four to rig a towline and manage the boat under tow during the escape. The rain had passed by the time of *Kauai*'s egress, and the cartel forces detected and engaged the cutter with rockets and machine guns. *Kauai* was hit by a rocket, causing minor damage and wounding one crewman. Shortly afterward, the towed boat was hit, parting the towline and imperiling both vessels. The female boatswain's mate went into the open during the firefight to cut away the towline wreckage with an ax, saving the cutter.

Meanwhile, the XO's boarding team restored and started the seized boat's engines, which the cartel had disabled. They safely cleared the island, but the XO was felled when a stowaway cartel member emerged and opened fire as the vessel was about to be scuttled in deep water. The officer had suffered a near-fatal brain injury and had to be evacuated by helicopter to a Miami hospital.

Bronze Star Medals were awarded to a boatswain's mate first class who took over the boarding party after the XO was wounded, the chief operations specialist who helped plan the assault and conned *Kauai* during the action, and the CO for his leadership during the raid. The boatswain's mate second class and the XO each received the Silver Star Medal for their efforts, and the XO and a boatswain's mate third class received the Purple Heart Medal for the wounds they suffered.

Haley was amazed by the citations and awards, and for the first time, she was experiencing personal doubts about this assignment. *How in the hell will I have any credibility with these people after what they have been through?*

As Pennington gave his closing remarks, Mercier turned to Haley and said, "Why don't you push off back to that conference room? The admiral and I will join you as soon as I can pry him away."

"Yes, ma'am," Haley said, then stood and quietly left the room. She had never been as conflicted as she was at this moment. Haley wanted this command more than anything in her life, yet, could she lead this elite of the elite teams? She had fifteen minutes to stew on it before Pennington and Mercier arrived in the room.

After they were seated, Pennington smiled at Haley and said, "Now's your chance, Haley. You have the complete picture now, and if you would like to pass on this, it goes no further than this room."

"Admiral, may I speak freely here?"

"Of course."

"I really want this command, but I am not sure I am the right one for this."

"Your record disputes that, but I'm interested in why you think that might be the case."

Haley swallowed and pointed at her ribbons, the highest of which was the Coast Guard Commendation Medal. "How do I go in there with this and command people with Coast Guard Medals, Bronze Stars, and Silver Stars?"

"The same as any other lieutenant in the Coast Guard. You go in with orders to command, and you command. If the criteria for selecting a new CO were a personal award as high or higher than anyone else on board, we would be out of luck because there isn't a lieutenant in the Coast Guard with that qualification. Is there anything else?"

Haley shifted in her seat. "There is just one other thing, sir. It's a question of leadership style. I'm effective, but, to be frank, I'm not much for the touchy-feely stuff."

Pennington sat back. "You won't need to be. They needed that personal touch a couple of years ago, but they've grown beyond that. Sam Powell did you a big favor there. Moreover, you don't *want* to be. You can expect the missions to become more, not less risky, and the risk calculus will be based on national defense, not SAR or law enforcement. In those cases, there *are* acceptable losses on a successful mission. Getting too 'touchy-feely,' as you call it, would be too hard for *you*. Do you understand what I'm saying?"

The sobering thought brought a quote from World War II to Haley's mind. "Yes, sir. When they get in trouble, they send for the sons of bitches." Pennington's eyes widened in surprise, and Haley thought, *Oh, shit! Now you've done it.*

To Haley's relief, Pennington laughed and said, "Well, I would like to agree with that in concept, but would not apply that term to you."

"Yes, sir. Not the 'sons of' anyway."

"At ease, Lieutenant," Mercier growled.

"Sorry, sir," Haley said contritely. *Yes, there* was *a line you don't cross.*

"That's alright. So, would you like some time to think it over?"

"No need, sir. I can do the job for you if you still want me."

Pennington smiled and nodded at Mercier. "I guess that's it then. You can expect orders shortly."

"I'll take care of it, sir," Mercier said.

"Excellent." They all stood, and Pennington offered his hand to Haley again. As they shook hands, he said, "Thank you, Haley, and good luck!"

"Thank *you*, Admiral," Haley replied.

After Pennington departed, Mercier turned to Haley and said, "I'll give your CO a call and explain the situation. You should expect orders within a week to kick off the transfer process. We'll do our best to get you out on *Kauai* for at least one patrol for familiarization before the handoff, so be flexible."

"I will. Thank you, ma'am."

Mercier started to leave and then paused. "One more thing. The admiral is a kind and patient man, virtues I do not share. If you pull any of that wiseass shit in front of me again, I'll squash you like a bug, clear?"

Haley swallowed hard. "Yes, ma'am."

****

There was no way Haley would head back home without taking a peek at her prospective command. She punched "Coast Guard Station Port Canaveral" into her GPS and was immediately rewarded with a display of the route up A1A via Patrick's North Gate. Haley put the top down on the Miata and headed out. Traffic was heavy through Cocoa Beach, and she was cursing her poor judgment for not opting for the longer, but probably quicker, I-95 route when the traffic thinned. She followed A1A in a gradual left turn to the west, then took the exit for 401.

After passing the cruise ship terminals on her right, 401 curved to the east, and she exited on the side streets leading to the Coast Guard station. As Haley pulled up to the sliding security gate, she had a clear view of the station's pier. One of the new Fast Response Cutters was moored, but she could not see a one-ten.

Huh. Where the hell is she? Haley pressed the call button on the gate's control box.

"Quarterdeck, Seaman Davis, may I help you?" said a disembodied female voice from the speaker.

"This is Lieutenant Reardon. Could you tell me where to find *Kauai*, please?"

"Yes, ma'am. She ties up in the East Basin now, and you'll need to go through the gate at the Space Force Station. It's just half a mile east on 401."

"I see. Thank you," Haley said. *I should have known there'd be some sort of Batcave for a secret squirrel unit like that.* She backed out of the driveway, hit the accelerator, and headed to the highway with dust kicking up from her spinning back wheels. The pantomime at the Space Force Station Cape Canaveral security checkpoint was the same as Patrick's gate. After avowing the absence of weapons, Haley proceeded through and onto the station.

About one thousand feet past the gate, Haley turned right onto South Petrol Road and, a few seconds later, cleared the trees on her right, revealing the East Basin of Port Canaveral. There, moored with her port side to the north end of the massive Trident Submarine Wharf, lay the Coast Guard Cutter *Kauai*. Haley's pulse quickened at first sight of the white-painted patrol boat, and she slowed to a stop on the roadside and stepped out to look, pulling on her white and blue combination cap.

There was no activity visible on the boat, just the U.S. flag drooping lazily from the flagstaff at the stern and the union jack similarly lolling on the bow's jackstaff. Haley could not see any significant difference in appearance from conventional one-tens resulting from *Kauai*'s special modifications, although she admitted it had been years since she had seen one of the older patrol boats. She longed to go aboard for a close look inside and out, but was still bound by Mercier's instruction to avoid disclosing her status as the prospective CO.

Haley was lost in thought, staring at her new command, when a voice from behind startled her.

"Ma'am, please keep your hands at your sides and turn around slowly."

Haley momentarily froze, then pivoted slowly to see a man in combat gear, hand resting on his sidearm, his partner standing behind him next to their vehicle with his M4 carbine unslung in the ready carry position. Between her captivation with *Kauai* and the harbor noise, she had not even heard the security vehicle arrive.

"I'll need you to pull out your ID, ma'am. One hand and nice and slow, please."

Haley reached into her left breast pocket and held out her CAC. The guard stepped forward, took the card, and scanned it with his handheld scanner. After verifying the image on the card and his scanner matched her face, he handed the card back.

He saluted and asked, "Can I help you find something, Lieutenant?"

Haley returned the salute and replied, "No, thank you, officer. I'm just looking at the boat."

"Ma'am, there's parking at the docks. Please don't stop along the roads unless you want to draw attention to yourself and a visit from us."

"I'm sorry, officer. I should have known better. Won't happen again."

"No problem, ma'am. You have a nice day."

After another exchange of salutes, Haley pocketed her CAC and turned to her car. The two security guards watched as Haley climbed into the Miata and started to the station exit. After clearing the station boundary, she pulled off onto the asphalt apron next to the rocket launch viewing area, shifted into park, and laughed until she was almost in tears. *That would have been the shortest command on record.* She tried to picture Captain Mercier getting a call to bail Haley out of a Space Force jail just an hour after smacking her down for being a smartass in front of a flag officer. *Hell, even I would say, "Just keep her!" and hang up.*

Haley wiped her eyes, shifted to drive, and headed out on the first leg of the long return drive to St. Petersburg.

588

Part II—Transition

Atlantic Ocean
The Bahamas
Turks and Caicos
Cockburn Town
Cuba
Guantanamo Bay
Windward Passage
Haiti
Dominican Republic
Caribbean Sea

Where There Is Life

Motor Vessel *Miho Dujam*, North Atlantic Ocean, sixty-two nautical miles northeast of Cockburn Town, Turks and Caicos 07:22, 16 November

Anca

Anca Cazacu snapped awake as she lay on her mattress on the floor of the dimly lit room. She sensed it was morning from what she could hear outside the walls of the makeshift holding area she and eleven of her fellow captives shared. It was difficult to tell night from day in the windowless cargo hold of the ship in which they had been confined since their departure from Dubrovnik. *Days or weeks ago?* Anca honestly did not know. Time had no meaning waiting in this dark, stinking, awful place for a fate that would probably be worse.

It was only a month ago that Anca was in a different world, mid-way through the fall semester of her third year of medical school at Victor Babeş University of Medicine and Pharmacy, Timişoara, enjoying the challenges of school and the excitement of city life. Although brought up in a small town in the northern pastoral region of Romania known as Maramureş, Anca was no fool. She knew dangers were lurking beneath the façade of joy and sophistication of Timişoara, particularly for a young and attractive female college student. She took personal safety precautions when going out on the town: she stuck to public places, avoided drinking and drugs, and stayed with the group.

She did not expect to be betrayed by another woman.

Anca had befriended a barista in one of the coffee shops near the university campus. Karla was a city girl, funny and enjoyable to be with, who knew the ins and outs of Timişoara. Unlike many of her classmates and most campus locals, Karla did not look down on Anca for her provincial origin. Anca looked forward to the time she and Karla spent together. She did not think twice when Karla invited her to drinks and a meal at her apartment after several rendezvous at local restaurants and clubs.

Anca knew something was off as soon as Karla answered the door and invited her in. Once she stepped inside, powerful arms gripped Anca from behind and clamped a cloth over her nose and mouth that smelled of chloroform. The last thing she remembered seeing before passing out was the satisfied smile on Karla's face.

The indoctrination into the hell of sex slavery followed. Anca's captors hurried her out of Romania, from site to site in Bosnia and Croatia, where, even if she escaped, she would stand out and quickly be recaptured. There were no beatings, nothing that would mar her highly marketable body. Her captors were veterans of secret police goon squads with abundant tools and skills to inflict extreme pain while leaving no marks. Anca quickly realized the futility of resistance and instead concentrated on surviving, watching in the hope of the chance to escape, contact her parents, and hide out until they came to retrieve her.

That hope ended two weeks ago when she was handcuffed, hooded, and taken by van to Dubrovnik and loaded aboard the *Miho Dujam* with twenty-one other captives. No one knew where they were going, but the fact they were aboard a ship and not in the back of a van or truck told Anca they were likely being transported out of Europe. None of the guards spoke; they just showed the same icy contempt and demanded compliance, enforcing it with pain positions and electrified batons. The possibility of what awaited them filled her with dread.

Anca did her best to bond with her fellow captives when they were locked up. Meals comprised what Anca supposed were Russian army rations in boxes with Cyrillic lettering and water in plastic bottles. They were only allowed out of their confinement in small, easily controllable ones and twos for exercise and toilet use. Still, she learned there were twenty-two of them altogether, dispersed between the two rooms in the cargo hold. They were from several countries in central and southeastern Europe, and a network of translators evolved among the women to cope with the many languages and dialects in play. Some of Anca's fellow prisoners had been forcibly kidnapped, as she was, and others had been lured into servitude with promises of employment in housekeeping or au pair positions. The most tragic cases were the two young Moldavian girls, aged fourteen and fifteen, who their parents had sold to local pimps.

The two girls were the focus of the event that broke them all. Four days into the trip, one guard had cornered and was sexually assaulting the youngest of the girls when a young Polish woman intervened and physically struck him. The reaction was immediate—she was seized and held. After the women were assembled in the hold, the unfortunate woman was brought forward and given a paralyzing injection. Then, one by one, the seven guards raped her as the other women were made to watch.

After the ordeal, the head guard spoke in Russian, and he paused while his words were translated into the several languages spoken among the shocked and whimpering women. "The drug we gave her left her paralyzed but awake and able to feel everything. We will give her the antidote, and she will recover quickly. Know that we can repeat this with her or any of you as many times as we like without the risk of physical injury or death, although I am sure she and you would rather die. Do as you are told. Do not resist us, or you will suffer the same."

After the ghastly ritual was complete, the guards returned the women to the two rooms. The guards deposited the Polish woman on the floor in Anca's room, gave her an injection, left the room, and locked the door. After a minute, when none of the other women had moved, Anca stood and went to see if she could help. The head guard was wrong. The antidote may have counteracted the paralysis drug, but the woman had not "recovered." Instead, she lay unmoving, staring at the ceiling in a near-catatonic stupor.

Anca called over two other women, and together they moved the Polish woman to one of the sleeping pallets near the side of the room. She remained there, unmoving, since the ordeal. Anca became her caregiver, and she and the other women did their best for her, bringing her food and water and cleaning up after her since she could not use the toilet on her own. After a few days, Anca was convinced the woman would not recover without dedicated treatment, but she feared telling the guards. She knew they would simply throw the poor woman overboard. At least she was eating and drinking—as long as she was alive when they reached their destination, there was a chance, however slim, that she could be saved.

As hellish as their treatment had been, things became far worse once the weather turned. Unable to see outside, Anca sensed a change in the ship's motion that suggested they had moved into a different body of water. Remembering her high school geography, she speculated they had sailed the length of the Mediterranean and passed through the straits into the Atlantic. However, she could not guess where they were ultimately headed.

A couple of days after the sea change, the storm struck.

The ship's motion had been lively in the Mediterranean, a rolling that made it difficult to eat and walk, and the pitching up and down made some women sick for a day or two. In the Atlantic, it was different—the rolling and pitching were still there but slower. That changed when the storm arrived. As the motion increased, Anca and her companions tied down the Polish woman to keep her from being thrown around and then held on for dear life themselves. Everyone was deathly sick, and soon, every container in the room was filled with vomit.

After the second day of unrelenting violent motion and sickness, the guards stopped coming. Anca deduced they must be sick too, but their absence presented a fresh problem. No one was interested in eating, of course, but from her limited medical training, Anca knew she and her fellow captives were becoming dehydrated. Without water, death was certain. She stood, made her way to the door, and started pounding on it whenever the deck was level enough for her to stand.

After what seemed like hours, the voice of one guard called out in slurred Polish, "Be quiet, bitch!"

Anca responded in rudimentary Polish, "We need water!"

"Fuck you, bitch!"

"We will all die without water! How will you profit from that?!"

There was a muffled response, then nothing. Anca huddled in despair beside the door for another half hour when she heard the lock removed. The door flew open, and the burly guard pushed two cardboard boxes into the room and slammed the door shut. Anca tore open the closest box, found three dozen water bottles, and shouted, "Thank you!"

Anca took two bottles out of the box and offered them to the women huddled on either side of her, getting dulled looks in return. "Drink! You have to drink, or you will die!" Finally, the two women took the offered bottles, and Anca moved on, dragging the box behind her. After handing each woman a bottle, she took one herself. Her stomach roiled as she drank the water, but she downed the entire bottle without vomiting. Anca turned to the Polish woman and, assisted by another captive, raised her into a sitting position and got her to drink.

The storm lasted for two more days, then the ship's motion settled to a still lively but tolerable level. The seasickness had passed, but Anca had to breathe through her mouth to avoid the nauseating smell of the room. Eventually, the door opened again, and two guards pushed in buckets and mops. One woman said something about being hungry, and the Polish guard said, "Clean room, then eat!"

Anca could not argue with the logic—she doubted she could keep any food down inside that room in its present state. Two women grabbed the mops and started swabbing the floor as Anca and another captive moved the Polish woman aside. Half an hour later, the guards returned, took out the buckets and mops, and pushed in boxes of food and water. Anca was ravenous by this time, and even the poorly made Russian rations tasted delicious.

The rest of the trip was the struggle of eating and sleeping, with occasional trips to the toilet being the only exercise. There was no night and day in the sealed, dark hold, but Anca could eventually make out the time of day by listening to the sounds around her.

On the fifth day after the storm, the routine suddenly changed. The ship's motion had settled down to almost nothing, and Anca supposed they must have moved into sheltered water. The ship's engine, which had been a low and steady thrum, became louder and picked up speed. Anca heard excited shouting but could not make out what was said. She had a glimmer of hope a naval or customs ship would stop the *Miho Dujam* and find them. Then she shook her head. There would be no rescue—if the inspectors could not be bribed to ignore them, their captors would simply kill them and drop them overboard.

The engine ran at high speed for a couple of hours when there was a tremendous bang, and it ground to a halt. There was more shouting and then silence. After several minutes, one woman shouted something and got to her feet. There was water leaking into the room from beyond the wall. Anca stood, dipped her hand in the water, then sniffed and tasted it. Saltwater! The ship was sinking! Anca stepped to the door and started beating on it as the other women cried out in panic.

Anca's terror grew as the water level crept higher in the room. She frantically pounded on the door, then stopped when she heard a voice on the other side. She could not understand what the voice said, but she kept pounding on the door, shouting in Romanian, "We are in here! Please save us!" She heard the lock being smashed off, then the door flew open, and the light of a powerful flashlight blinded her. Anca stepped back involuntarily into the mass of huddling and whimpering women. She did not know who the men with the flashlights were, only that they were not the guards. For the first time since she left Romania, Anca dared to hope.

USCG Cutter *Kauai*, North Atlantic Ocean, twenty-three nautical miles north of Cockburn Town, Turks and Caicos 10:23 EST, 16 November

Ben

Ben was over halfway through his morning watch as the officer of the deck, also known as OOD. It was a typical mid-autumn day in the area, warm and humid with bright blue skies and puffy clouds over an azure sea. *Kauai* was gently pitching and rolling in the light seas as she motored along at a speed just high enough to hold a comfortable course.

Kauai was two weeks into what was euphemistically referred to as a "stretch patrol" at a location well off their usual beat between Florida and the Bahamas. They were holding a blocking position to intercept an expected uptick in illegal smuggling traffic skirting along the eastern side of the Lucayan Archipelago from the Caribbean to the southern U.S. It was a job better suited to a larger medium endurance cutter whose radar and embarked helicopter could surveil much more area per day, but these were in short supply.

There was a Coast Guard surge operation working to cope with a considerable upswing in illegal immigration from Haiti to the

United States. On those rare occasions when economic conditions were particularly desperate in that miserable country, people sallied forth in every maritime conveyance available, from coastal freighters to rafts, even hollowed-out trees. The hope was to slip by unnoticed to land their human cargo in South Florida. Few made it. Some died en route, and the rest were intercepted by the Coast Guard and repatriated to Port Au Prince. With their ample flight deck space and more plentiful food and water, the larger cutters could readily support the hundreds of migrants interdicted each day while they awaited repatriation, and they were soon diverted from other duties.

Because of this migrant surge, the regular smuggling routes via the Windward Passage and Mona Passage on the western and eastern sides of Hispaniola were saturated with ships and surveillance aircraft. As the humanitarian crisis persisted, intelligence held that surpluses of illicit drugs would eventually push an increase in traffic along the longer but less crowded routes to the east. *Kauai* and other patrol boats had to pick up the slack with every available large cutter involved in surge operations.

Ben completed a round with the binoculars and stepped over to check the radar. They were idling about twenty miles north of Grand Turk Island, close enough to pick up any illicit traffic skirting the islands from the Lesser Antilles plus any Windward or Mona leakers sneaking through the Turks Island Passage. Commercial ship traffic was light through this area. The shortest routes from Europe to the Panama Canal were east of here through the Mona and Anegada Passages, and those from the Continental U.S. were west via the Windward Pass and Yucatan Channel. Anything passing where they were was either a local freighter or a target of interest.

Ben glanced at the left-hand console seat, where Chief Deffler monitored the UAVs. The UAV capability was limited—no radar and a narrow field of view camera that Deffler likened to "looking through a soda straw"—but it was far better than no aviation support. Ben, Hopkins, and Deffler had worked out a picket fence tactic with one or two UAVs orbiting at the edge of *Kauai*'s visual horizon, with cameras trained southeast along the threat axis. It was a simple solution that effectively quadrupled the ocean's width they could scan, allowing them to pick up anything between the shoreline and twenty-five miles seaward. But contacts were scarce, and some watches, like Ben's current one, had none. Warm, not hot weather, clear blue skies, and mostly calm seas made for a pleasant, uneventful watch. It was boring, but Ben would take boring any day over the soul-crushing grind of alien migrant interdiction operations.

Ben turned to look as Williams came through the door. "Joe, what's up?"

"I'm meeting Ms. Reardon to do soup-to-nuts on fire control, XO," he chirped. Williams was the expert on the integrated fire control/command and control or FC3 system. It was unique to *Kauai* in the Coast Guard but was being evaluated for retrofit in some form on the newer FRCs. Williams loved working on the system and showing it off.

"Right. Well, don't scare her off with the details. OK?" Ben said with a wink, returning to his watch.

Williams walked over to Electronics Technician Third Class Darryl Bunting, who had the navigation watch and was sitting at the console, and tapped him on the shoulder. "It's going to get crowded up here, bud. Let me take the watch for you, so you're not just standing around."

"Thanks, Joe!" Bunting said with a smile, then began a handoff brief.

The stretch patrol was an excellent opportunity for Haley to learn the ins and outs of the new command and get a feel for the boat. Ben felt odd working closely with Sam's replacement on an operational mission, but he liked what he had seen of her so far. She was leaning into Williams, Hopkins, and Drake, soaking up knowledge of the new systems while she was just another officer and not yet the skipper.

Haley was close to Sam in terms of seniority, having graduated from the Academy about six months after Sam's graduation from OCS, but was closer to Ben in age. Despite this, their first meeting was a little awkward: it took several minutes for them to work out how to address each other to avoid hiccups after she took command. But they then settled into detailed discussions on Ben's unique dual role of second in command and tactical lead. Ben found her pretty different from Sam in terms of personality. Friendly enough, but not much for small talk, even when off the Bridge. Ben understood—working into a close-knit team like *Kauai*'s had to be difficult.

Haley arrived soon after Williams. She wore the same dark blue operational utilities as everyone else, but still wore her Sector St. Petersburg ball cap. She scanned the Bridge, then came straight over to Ben. "Good morning, XO. How's it going?"

"Another quiet one, ma'am. No contacts."

"That's how it goes sometimes. If you have no objection, I asked Williams to give me the FC3 one-oh-one this morning."

"Not a problem, ma'am. If you like, I can clear it with the captain to spin up the main gun for dry runs."

"I'd appreciate that, thank you."

"No worries, ma'am." As Haley stepped over to Williams, Ben called Sam.

"Captain," Sam answered after two rings.

"OOD, sir. Nothing to report on the watch. Ms. Reardon is going through fam on the fire control, and I'd like your permission to power up and exercise the main gun."

"That's a good idea; permission granted. Anything else?"

"No, sir."

"Right. See you at chow."

"Yes, sir." Ben hung up the phone and turned to Williams. "Joe, the captain has OK-ed powering up the gun. Make the usual announcements."

"Will do. Thanks, XO." Williams nodded and went back to his instruction.

As Ben was relaying the permission to Williams, he noticed Haley giving him what he thought was a cool look. *I wonder what that's about?* He decided it was just his imagination and continued his rounds with the binoculars.

Deliverance

USCG Cutter *Kauai*, North Atlantic Ocean, twenty-two nautical miles north of Cockburn Town, Turks and Caicos 11:37 EST, 16 November

Ben

Deffler straightened suddenly in his chair on the left-side station of the FC3 when an alert popped up on his screen. The artificial intelligence scanning the video feed from one UAV detected what it evaluated as an anomaly. It was a group of pixels different from its surroundings of sufficient size and duration that qualified for a notification to the human operator, who was otherwise unlikely to notice. Deffler switched to manual on the camera and activated the zoom. These were often items of no interest—a flock of seabirds or a patch of seaweed.

At first glance, Deffler could see nothing. He cranked the zoom using the vernier knob until the image became pixilated, then backed off slightly. "Ah, there you are," he murmured. It was a ship, alright, but it had a light-blue painted hull and dull white masts, making it challenging to pick out in the bright sea haze. He looked across the Bridge at Ben and said, "OOD, I have a visual contact with Bird Two. It's definitely a ship, but too far away right now to classify."

Ben walked over, looked at the screen, then smiled and said, "Well, that broke the monotony. Can you close on the target for a better look, Chief?"

"We have some margin, sir," Deffler replied. The UAVs had to stay within a certain distance of *Kauai* to maintain contact with their line-of-sight radios. At their current altitude, combined with the height of the ground control antenna on *Kauai*'s Flying Bridge, this distance was around twenty-one nautical miles.

"Right. Break the pattern. Close to the safety limit, and then we'll see if we want to move over," Ben said.

"Very good, sir." Deffler manipulated his controls. The UAV banked right and headed for the target, accelerating from its maximum endurance speed to its forty-five-knot long-range cruise speed.

"Are you going to call the captain?" Haley asked. She and Williams had paused their conversation on Deffler's first call to Ben.

"I can hold off for a couple of minutes, ma'am," Ben replied. "No sense pulling him off something important for what could be a supertanker. I've been down this road before."

"I see."

After a few minutes, the UAV closed sufficiently to significantly firm up the electro-optical picture. "OK, sir, I classify this target as a coastal freighter, heading southwest, twelve to fifteen knots."

Ben gazed intently at the image on the screen. Although it was still difficult to make out much detail, he agreed with Deffler on the classification: it was a small ship, not much over one-hundred-fifty feet long, with the pilothouse aft, clearly heading southwest. But that course made little sense for a ship of that size—a coastal freighter should parallel the shoreline. This ship's course was consistent with a transatlantic crossing, which you did not want to do with a small coastal freighter. Besides getting beat to hell in any rough weather, you could not carry a large enough cargo to make such a long trip worth the expense in fuel and time. He eyeballed a rough intercept course and then turned to Pickins on the helm. "Right ten degrees rudder, steer one-five-zero."

"Right ten degrees rudder, steer one-five-zero, aye, sir."

Ben picked up the phone and dialed Sam.

"Captain."

"OOD, sir. Could you come to the Bridge, please? A UAV has spotted a coastal freighter I am classifying as suspicious, and I have changed course to intercept."

"I'm on the way. Go ahead and spin up."

"Aye, aye, sir," Ben said, then dialed the engineering watchstander in Main Control.

"Main Control, Brown."

"Brown, OOD. Put one and three online. We're heading for a target."

"Put main engines one and three online, sir. Estimate two minutes."

"Very well, thanks." Ben hung up the phone. With the electric motors running at their slow patrol speed, there was only a small power demand on the ship's electrical grid. One of the three diesel generators was sufficient, and the other two were shut down to conserve fuel. With the high speed and maneuvering expected during an intercept, they needed the power from all three. Ben saw Sam coming through the bridge door and announced, "Captain on the Bridge!"

"Thank you. Carry on, please," Sam said. He stepped over next to Ben at the console and asked, "What have you got, XO?"

"Captain, we have a small coastal freighter, ID unknown, estimated bearing one-one-three at twenty-two point five, estimated speed twelve. This is still based on EO from UAV Two; the target is not above our radar horizon yet. MDEs one and three estimated online in one minute." As if in response, a muffled whirring followed by the grumble of a diesel engine sounded below.

"All good. Recommendations?"

"We'll need to increase speed to reach him before he enters the pass, sir, but I don't see a problem pacing him. I recommend having Bird Two light off Ghost and park it overhead when he's within twenty."

"That's good too. Make it so. Also, move the other bird in that direction at max endurance."

"Very good, sir." Ben bent over Deffler and gave the order as Sam stepped back and sat in the command chair.

Haley leaned close to Williams and whispered, "What is Ghost?"

"It's an active camouflage system, ma'am," Williams whispered. "It senses the brightness and color of the sky above the UAV and projects it on the underside. The bird is almost invisible with a clear sky like we have now or a solid overcast."

"Cool!" Haley whispered.

"Yes, ma'am. There's a lot of stuff like that around here," Williams said with a nod.

The phone buzzed, and Ben answered. "Bridge, OOD."

"Main Control, sir. All MDEs are online, full power available on the grid." It was Drake's baritone voice.

"Thanks, COB. You're pretty quick to the scene today."

"When there are no guns, I ride to the sound of the starter, sir."

Ben chuckled. "You take what you can get, I guess. Thanks again." He hung up the phone. "All MDEs online, Captain. Full power is available, and I'm coming up to twenty-four knots."

"Very well," Sam said with a smile. "I hope this one is interesting—I would hate to see all this enthusiasm wasted on another dud." He nodded at Williams and said, "Very fortuitous for you, Ms. Reardon: you get to see our top guy run through a suspicious contact procedure."

Kauai's bow lifted a few degrees as she started planing when approaching twenty-four knots. Fortunately, the seas were light, and they only had an occasional thump as the boat sped through the water. An alert notice drew Williams's eye to the navigation panel. "Radar contact, sir, at one-one-five and twenty point three. Running a plot now. Negative AIS." The target was not transmitting the Automatic Identification System, known as AIS, information required by international law.

After sharing an eyebrows-raised glance with Ben, Sam said, "Chief, I want to get a name and homeport as soon as possible. Coax the bird toward the stern, please."

"Will do, Captain," Deffler said. "Shouldn't be more than a couple of minutes now."

"Very well."

"Captain, target's course is two-four-zero, speed thirteen knots. He's heading for the center of the Turks Island Passage," Williams said, then turned to Ben. "Recommend one-five-two at twenty-four knots, XO."

"Very well. Helm, steer one-five-two."

"Steer one-five-two, sir."

"Ship's name coming into view, sir," Deffler said. "Um, not sure how to pronounce it. I spell: Mike, India, Hotel, Oscar, space, Delta, Uniform, Juliet, Alpha, Mike. Homeport says Dubrovnik. Where the hell is Dubrovnik?"

"Croatia," Haley answered. "He's a *long* way from home."

Sam leaned forward. "Agreed. Let's not take any chances. XO, sound Condition One, please."

"Aye, aye, sir," Ben said, then stepped over, grabbed the microphone, and activated the public address system known as the 1MC. "Now, General Quarters, General Quarters, set Condition One throughout the ship. This is not, repeat, not a drill." He hung up the microphone and pressed the paddle switch on the red general alarm box, starting a loud ringing gong sound over the 1MC lasting twenty seconds.

Williams stood, walked to and opened the locker at the rear of the Bridge, and took out Lightweight Helmets and Modular Tactical Vests. Haley appeared at his side and asked, "Can I help?"

"Yes, ma'am. Could you take these to the captain and XO, please?" Williams said, handing her two pairs of vests and helmets.

"On it."

Williams took out four more sets, handed one to Haley when she returned, stepped across the Bridge, and handed one each to Deffler and Pickins. Then he donned the last one himself and sat in the center seat of the console. Hopkins appeared next to Ben, pulling on a vest and helmet she picked up from the locker.

"What's going on, sir?" Hopkins was the OOD for Condition One and, after a quick rundown from Ben on the situation, relieved him of the duty. Ben took advantage of the break to get a good look at the *Miho Dujam* in the UAV video display. It was a small ship, a break-bulk carrier by the look of the cargo booms on the single mast and the size of the hatch covers on the holds. It was an old ship, or old-looking at least, with plenty of rust visible. Ben's suspicions were confirmed—there wasn't a chance in hell that ship would make a profit hauling any legitimate cargo across the Atlantic.

Ben noted the ship had an unusually large boat and davit system on the port side of the superstructure. *That is one hell of a lifeboat.* "Chief, can you get me a tight shot at their small boat, please?" he asked Deffler.

"Coming up, sir."

As the aircraft crossed behind the ship from the starboard side, Deffler manipulated the camera controls, and the image of the stowed boat filled the screen. It was a rigid hull inflatable like

Kauai's RHIB, but far larger, with a wide, flat deck and three outboard engines. Such a craft would have little purpose in the coastal trade in the ship's home territory of the Adriatic and Aegean Seas, but for running illicit cargoes ashore in out-of-the-way coves and bays, it would be perfect.

Haley had stepped beside Sam's chair to get out of the way of the console. She watched the action around her and was clearly impressed by the crew's quick transition from normal cruising to battle-ready. She turned and asked Sam, "Where do you want me, Captain?"

"Right there is good," Sam replied.

Ben stepped up on Sam's other side in his vest and helmet. "I've been relieved of the OOD by Chief Hopkins, sir. The ship has an unusually large RHIB on the port davits—looks like a runner for offloading cargo rather than a lifeboat."

"OK. Get with Zuccaro and set up a SIPR chat with JIATF South," Sam said, referring to Joint Interagency Task Force South, their operational commander on this mission. "Explain the situation and get any intel they have on the *Miho Dujam*."

"Very good, sir," Ben said. He stepped over to the console and kneeled beside Zuccaro.

Zuccaro glanced at Ben and said, "I heard him, sir. I'm working up a SATCOM link now."

He smiled back. "Nice. Let me know when you're ready, and I'll give you the details."

"Roger that, sir. Standby." After a brief period of concentration and furious typing, she said, "Alright, I'm ready, sir."

Ben dictated the details and timeline of the event and requested any information on the *Miho Dujam*. After more typing, Zuccaro uploaded the message and received an acknowledgment from JIATF-S. Ben's previous experience with intel requests was it took hours or days to get a response. *Hopefully, being in hot pursuit of the suspect will light a fire under somebody!*

"Looks like he's on to us, sir," Williams reported. "I'm picking up an increase in speed, now fifteen knots. No change in course; he's still heading for the pass." Ben glanced at the Tactical Situation or TACSIT screen. The red icon symbolizing the *Miho Dujam* included a line segment pointing southwest and a digital course and speed. The latter increased from fifteen to sixteen as

Ben watched. *They can't get much more out of that bucket. She must be at least fifty years old!*

"I'm getting an update from JIATF South, sir," Zuccaro reported. "Nothing on EPIC or EID, and they're still waiting on DoD and Interpol."

Ben breathed a soft sigh of relief. He had expected nothing from EPIC, the El Paso Intelligence Center law enforcement database mainly dealt with drug smuggling from South and Central America—he doubted the *Miho Dujam* had ever ventured into the western hemisphere before now. On the other hand, EID, the Department of Homeland Security's Enforcement Integrated Database, would have any information about a terrorist threat associated with the ship. The fact there were no alerts was not conclusive. *Miho Dujam* wasn't likely to be loaded to the gunwales with suicide bombers, but there could still be a threat. He glanced again at the TACSIT readout and shook his head in wonder as the speed ticked up from seventeen to eighteen. *My God! Does he really think he can outrun a patrol boat?*

It took another fifteen minutes for *Kauai* to draw even with the freighter just as it drew abeam of the northern tip of Grand Turk, eight miles in the distance. Hopkins slowed *Kauai* to keep pace—nineteen knots—and gave minor course corrections to Pickins to maintain their position one-half mile abeam of the freighter. Ben could see no one on deck, just some shadowy figures on the Bridge.

"Incoming message from JIATF South, sir," Zuccaro said. "Negative on *Miho Dujam* from DoD, but Interpol has a TCO alert on them." TCO was the acronym for Transnational Criminal Organization, supranational organized crime groups that had become a plague in Europe after the collapse of communism. "Known association with the 252 Syndicate."

Ben whirled to look at Sam, who shook his head and said, "Damn. Not them again!"

Haley asked, "You have dealt with them before?"

Ben replied grimly, "Yes, ma'am. They're old friends who are always good for a few medals when you run into them. The kind of medals you earn by getting your head shot off."

Sam said, "Zuccaro, tell JIATF South we are keeping station with the subject at one-half mile and request instructions."

"Aye, aye, sir," the young petty officer replied and turned back to her panel.

"What do you think they're doing down here, XO?" Sam asked.

"Arms trafficking would be my bet, sir. It would not be drugs coming from Europe, although they might try carrying a load back. I'm not sure why they still have the pedal to the metal, though. They must know they can't outrun us."

"No, it makes sense. They know we won't stop and board without flag state clearance, and they probably have enough graft or intimidation in Croatia to tie that up until after they make port if they beat feet. After that, they'll be a ship in a bottle, but I imagine the profit from the guns would make it worth the trip. Any load of drugs or whatever on the return would be gravy."

"Sir, reply from JIATF South," Zuccaro said. "Maintain close contact only until further notice. Initiating flag state consultation now."

"Q.E.D.," Ben said with a frown.

"Suits me fine, XO," Sam said. "Let one of the big hulls handle a forced-entry boarding on these guys. Let's stand down from Condition One, but we'll keep an augmented FC3 watch to maintain contact. We may have to massage the OOD rotation—work it out with Chief Hopkins after she's relieved of the OOD."

"Will do, sir." Ben stepped over to the 1MC and announced, "Now, stand down from General Quarters, set the at-sea watch, afternoon watch on deck." Ben met with Hopkins after Lee relieved her of the OOD watch, and they worked out an augmented watch schedule. As it happened, the effort was academic.

A little over an hour later, Sam, Ben, and Haley were crowded in Sam's cabin discussing the morning's events when the phone above Sam's desk buzzed, and he answered it, "Captain. Yes, I'm on the way!" As they stood, Sam said, "There's been an explosion on the contact, and it's coming to a stop." Sam jogged to the bridge ladder with Ben and Haley close behind and strode through the door with the usual announcement. He stepped over to Lee, who was holding binoculars. Ben looked across at the contact and saw it was trailing oily black smoke from its smokestack, creating a large black cloud settling toward the water.

"I'm sorry, Captain," Lee said sheepishly. "It looks like their engine blew. I heard a big bang and saw the black cloud and thought it was a bomb or something."

"No, Lee, you did absolutely right," Sam said quickly, grabbing the binoculars. After gazing at the other vessel for half a minute, he offered the binoculars to Ben. "What do you think, XO?"

"It looks like the *Miho Dujam* just became a search and rescue case, sir," Ben replied with mock concern as he examined the other vessel. "I'll bet they're on the satellite phone dialing someone in the Balkans right now asking for instructions." He checked the TACSIT display—they were roughly in the center of the Turks Island Passage, about eight miles due west of Cockburn Town. "Shall we offer our help, sir?"

"Let them call us. When we go on board, I want it clean to avoid losing any evidence in exclusion. Lee, I want you to do an easy right three-sixty and bring us to about three hundred yards off their starboard beam. Can you handle that?"

"Yes, sir!"

"Good. Make it so. XO, set the Rescue and Assistance Bill. I want you to lead a boarding party with Drake, Bondurant, and Lopez if we can get them to give up without a fight. Have Drake look things over. I doubt he can do anything for the engine, but he can assess her fitness for a tow." As Ben stepped over to make the announcement, Sam turned to Zuccaro and said, "Update JIATF South on what's happening. Be sure to include that the *Miho Dujam* has suffered an explosion and appears to be disabled. Explicitly request direction at the end of the message."

"Aye, aye, sir," Zuccaro replied.

As Lee gave the orders to the helmsman for the slow turn to the right, Sam climbed into the command chair, and Haley asked, "Is this the usual tactic?"

Sam smiled and said, "Usual? Like most things we seem to get involved with lately, we're making it up as we go along."

Zuccaro turned and said, "Incoming message from JIATF South, sir. Stand by vessel until further notice. Do not initiate boarding unless subject requests assistance."

"Now there's a big surprise. Thank you, Zuccaro."

Kauai took ten minutes to complete her circuit and stop alongside the *Miho Dujam*. Ben put on his boarding officer gear in his stateroom and went to the boat deck, where the other three boarding party members waited. Lee trotted over a minute later in her boat crew gear—she would be coxswain for the boarding if there was one.

"Greetings, shipmates," Ben said with a mock stern expression. "I suppose you are all wondering why I called you together here in the sunshine of this lovely Turks and Caicos afternoon." After the chuckles subsided, he continued. "Well, I'll tell you. We are standing by to go onboard that disabled ship over there and help if they invite us. If they don't, we might do it anyway if we are sure they won't try to gun us down. This one looks dirty, and we have solid intel that the 252s might be involved, so the threat level is high."

"You don't think I'm going to be able to fix their engines, do you, sir?" Drake asked with one eyebrow raised.

"What, you don't 'know a guy' for that, COB?" Ben quipped. After more laughs, he continued. "No, I don't expect miracles, but we need to know if she's getting ready to go down from damage or might not take the tow. We'll need more of your damage controlman skill set than the machinery tech."

Drake was about to reply when a call came over Ben's headset, and he raised his hand. "LE-One, *Kauai*, *Miho Dujam* crew is abandoning ship via their RHIB, still no contact. Launch RHIB and board *Miho Dujam* ASAP."

Ben keyed his microphone and said, "*Kauai*, LE-One, roger, out." He then looked at the team. "OK, we are a go. The crew is abandoning ship. Let's get over there and take a look." They stood by as Jenkins craned the RHIB off its cradle and brought it even with the deck. "OK, let's go," Ben said.

Lee jumped on first and took her seat in the coxswain's chair. Once situated, she said, "Come on board!"

Ben stepped aboard, followed by Drake, Bondurant, and Lopez. Lee gave Jenkins a thumbs up, and he craned the RHIB off the side and then lowered it into the water. After starting the engine, Lee said, "Let go the fall!" After Bondurant released the crane hook block and guided it off the side, Lee said, "Release sea painter!".Lopez took the line binding the RHIB to *Kauai* off the cleat on the bow and cast it over the side. Lee revved the engine, swung the RHIB toward the *Miho Dujam*, and then turned it alongside the ship's rusty, light-blue-painted hull.

The ship did not have a high freeboard, but the upper edge of the deck coaming was still at least ten feet above the water. Ben took out the grapnel and climbing rope and tossed the hook over the rail. After pulling it into place and checking it, he pulled himself up the rope, walking on the hull with his feet. After pulling himself over the coaming and scanning the deck, he gave the rest of his crew a thumbs up, then stepped over to the other side and watched as the ship's RHIB sped away with ten men on board. By the time Ben returned to the rope, Bondurant and Lopez were on board, giving Drake a hand over the side. He keyed his microphone and said, "*Kauai*, LE-One, boarding party on board and proceeding with the survey. Observed crew motoring off to the east."

"Copy LE-One, proceed. We are eyes on and in pursuit of the crew," Williams's voice replied.

Ben leaned over the rail and said, "Stay close, Shelley. We might want to get off this tub fast!"

"You've got it, sir!" Lee replied.

Ben turned to his crew. "Alright, let's head down below decks. COB, you take Lope and check out the engine space, and Boats and I will move forward in the hold. Stay paired up, please. I don't want anyone knocked out where we can't find them."

"Roger that, XO. Come on, son," Drake said to Lopez and then turned and walked toward a hatch under the pilothouse. Ben led the way through another door at the forward edge of the superstructure and then pulled off his sunglasses when they plunged into darkness. With the engine gone, there was no electrical power and no lights, so Ben and Bondurant pulled their large flashlights and started down a ladder to the cargo space. At the bottom, they turned and started moving forward in the hold.

With the hatch covers sealed, the hold was pitch dark, and Ben and Bondurant carefully stepped forward around stacks of boxes, many of which were annotated with Cyrillic lettering. He took out his waterproof camera, began snapping pictures every few feet, and whispered, "I don't suppose you can translate Russian, Boats?"

"You must be kidding, sir."

"It was worth a shot." Ben was mildly claustrophobic and joking to knock back the growing anxiety as they proceeded further into the dark cargo space and away from the door. Ben knew he couldn't last long in here between the fear of the enclosed space and the reeking atmosphere of diesel fuel, smoke, and stale vomit. If they were going to do a tow, he would first get those hatch covers open to let in the light and air things out. Then Ben heard a noise as he rounded another corner of a stack of boxes and froze.

It was the sound of running water.

"You hear that?" Ben asked in a normal tone.

"Yes, sir. I think we should get the hell out of here, XO."

"Concur. You lead the way," Ben agreed, and they turned around to make their way back. Suddenly, Ben's team radio squawked.

"Lead, this is COB. I'm encountering flooding in the engine space. Believe the crew has started scuttling!"

"Get topside, now. We are on the way.

"Understood."

They started walking again, and then Ben froze at another sound. It sounded like human voices and knocking. "Hello?" Ben shouted and heard muffled cries in response. "Keep shouting; we'll find you!" He knew it was unlikely the person crying out could speak English, but they'd get the drift. He keyed the team radio again. "COB, you and Lope join us in the hold. We can hear someone trapped."

"On the way, sir, " Drake responded.

The muffled cries were regularly coming now as Ben and Bondurant made their way through the obstructions in the hold. Ben could feel the ship listing to port. If they could hear the water running, the list would increase quickly. Beyond a certain angle, the cargo would shift toward the downward side and capsize the ship. They had to move fast!

They arrived at what appeared to be a temporary room built of wood with a padlocked door. Ben smashed off the hasp and lock with his heavy flashlight, yanked the door open, and shined his light into the dark interior. At least a dozen women were crying and cowering in terror on the other side of the space. Briefly shocked, Ben recovered and said, "Does anyone speak English?" No response. *Dammit, we don't have time for this!* He tried his only other option, his high school German. *"Spreckt jemand Deutsch?"* [Does anyone speak German?]

"Ja, Ich sprecke!" [Yes, I speak!] said a woman on the other side of the room.

"Ich bin Leutnant Wyporek von der amerikanischen...Seepolitzei." Ben stumbled on the correct German expression for "Coast Guard," and opted for "Sea Police," instead. *"Ihr schiffe versinkt schnell. Meine schiffe kommt. Sagen sie es ihnen sie müssen jetzt nach oben gehen!"* [Your ship is sinking quickly. My ship is coming. Tell them they must go topside now!]

"Ja, Ich sage." [Yes, I tell.] Rusty as he was, Ben could tell she wasn't a native speaker, but he was not in a position to complain.

"Wie viele sind sie?" [How many of you are there?]

"Zweiundzwanzig." [Twenty-two.]

Twenty-two! They can't all be in here! Ben shined his light around and found another locked door. "Boats, get that door open! Don't go in until we get this translator over there. We can't be chasing them all over the place!"

"Aye, aye, sir!" As Bondurant turned to comply, Drake and Lopez arrived.

"Holy shit, XO! What are they doing here?" Lopez exclaimed.

"Jesus, what do you think, Lope? As soon as the lady gets done talking, lead them topside. COB, recall *Kauai* as soon as you are clear of hull interference—there's no way we can save all twenty-two with just the RHIB."

"On it, sir!"

The woman had spoken her piece, and the other women were still huddling together and whimpering, but they stood and walked toward Drake and Lopez, except for one who remained motionless on the deck. Ben stepped over and saw she was alive, but her eyes stared upward at nothing. Ben turned to his interpreter. *"Sag es ihr noch einmal. Wir müssen gehen!"* [Tell her again. We must go!]

His translator shook her head. *"Sie hörte. Sie ist sehr traurig."* [She heard alright. She is very sad.]

Ben made a mental note, then said, *"Fräulein, komm mit mir."* [Come with me, Miss.] The woman followed him to the other door and into the room as Bondurant stood aside. *"Bitte, sagen Sie ihnen dasselbe."* [Tell them the same, please.]

"Ich, sage." [I tell.]

The situation was getting critical. There was now a perceptible tilt to the deck, and the ship could turn turtle any moment. When the translator had finished, all the women in the second compartment stood and filed out the door.

Ben said, "John, come with me."

"Yes, sir," Bondurant said as he followed Ben into the first room.

Ben could understand checking out after the horrors these women must have been through, but there was no time for therapy. "John, we have to carry this one. Can you give me a hand?"

Bondurant stepped over and said, "I've got her, XO. You go ahead."

"Thanks, Boats, I'll light your way."

The big boatswain's mate picked up and cradled the woman like a child, and followed Ben and his translator to the ladder and up onto the main deck. Ben blinked on emerging from the hatch and quickly donned his sunglasses. The hatch covers were covered with sitting, huddling, and crying women and girls, all looking down or shielding their eyes from the bright sun. Ben scanned aft and saw *Kauai* inbound about a mile away at full speed, her white bow wave spreading quickly from each side—she would be alongside in less than two minutes. He walked over to the grapnel and rope and called out to Lee. "Shelley, take Lope and stand off. We need you to pick up any leakers."

"Yes, sir!" Lee said, then moved the boat under the rope.

"Lope, get over here." After the young petty officer arrived, he said. "Get back on the RHIB and help Lee in case someone goes overboard."

"Yes, sir," Lopez said. Then he grabbed the rope, climbed over, and lowered himself into the RHIB. Once he was seated, Lee goosed the engine to clear the side for *Kauai*'s arrival.

Ben keyed his headset microphone. "*Kauai*, LE-One."

"LE-One, *Kauai*, go ahead."

"One survivor is catatonic. We'll need the litter to get her off."

"Understood, LE-One. Keep everyone clear—we're coming in hot." It was Sam's voice.

"Roger that, sir," Ben said. He looked around and caught the eye of his translator, who trotted over when he beckoned her.

"Vielen Dank für Ihre Hilfe, Fräulein. Wie heissen Sie?" [Thanks much for your help, Miss. What is your name?]

"Anca Cazacu, Herr Leutnant." [I am Anca Cazacu, sir.]

"Sehr gut, Anca. Das ist wichtig. Sag ihnen, dass sie zurückbleiben und darauf warten sollen, dass meine Männer ihnen an Bord helfen. Sie müssen sich aus dem Weg gehen und dürfen nicht versuchen, sich selbst zu hinübergehen. Verstehen Sie mich?" [Very good, Anca. Now, this is important. Tell them to stay back and wait for my men to help them aboard. They must stay out of the way and not try to cross over themselves. Understand?]

"Klar, Herr Leutnant," [I understand, sir,] the woman replied, then turned and trotted back to give instructions to the other women.

Ben keyed his microphone again. "*Kauai*, LE-One."

"Go ahead, LE-One."

"I'm down to three onboard, including me. Recommend we bring lines two and three straight over to the cargo deck."

"LE-One, roger that. I have everyone not on watch headed to the foredeck now. What's your status?"

"She's going fast, sir. We're already listing about ten degrees to port. The cargo is not loose, but it is in high stacks in the hold. If the bindings pop, she'll capsize in a heartbeat. Even if they don't, the water's coming up fast on the port side, and it will be all over when it tops the main hatches. I have the RHIB standing by if we have to jump for it, but the survivors have had it if they go in the water."

"Copy, LE-One. Have your guys stand by the hawseholes you want to use, so we have a reference."

"WILCO, sir."

Ben looked down the deck and could see Bondurant moving toward the aft hawsehole, the reinforced hole in the side they needed to pass *Kauai*'s mooring line through to tie the ships together. He had overheard the conversation and was moving to where he was required. Ben stepped over to Drake. "Try to keep them together, COB. John and I will handle the lines."

Drake smiled. "Roger that, sir. After all this time, my dream finally comes true—a SAR case with dozens of pretty young women."

"Yes, damn shame you're old enough to be their grandpa now."

"Watch it, XO," Drake smiled.

Ben turned and strode to his hawsehole, the smile fading quickly from his face.

Even if everything went right, it was going to be close.

Calculated Risk

USCG Cutter *Kauai*, Turks Island Passage, eight nautical miles west of Cockburn Town, Turks and Caicos 13:07 EST, 16 November

Haley

What had started as just another low-key day on a quiet patrol had turned into the most exciting operation Haley had ever experienced. She was impressed with both the competence and confidence of the crew as they dealt with what Sam had said was a new challenge for all of them. She wanted to pitch in but realized that anything she did would disrupt the rhythm and likely hurt more than help.

Haley had been nervous as they closed on the fleeing cargo ship. If, as Ben speculated, they were smuggling arms, they could include man-portable rocket launchers that stood a good chance of sinking *Kauai* with one or two hits at her waterline. Sam admitted as much when she asked him about it privately in his cabin.

"That's a fact, but it wouldn't have come to that," Sam said with a completely blank expression.

"How so? I don't see the twenty-five-millimeter or the fifty-caliber being able to respond effectively in time," Haley said.

"We had eyes on with both the UAV and the EO camera. If I had seen anyone carrying anything looking like a launch tube, I would have green-lighted Guerrero on the Flying Bridge." During General Quarters, Gunner's Mate Second Class Deke Guerrero was stationed in a fortified position on the Flying Bridge. He was trained and equipped with a fifty-caliber M2010 enhanced sniper rifle. Anyone using a rocket would have to step into the open because of the backblast, and Guerrero could hit any target center mass from up to a mile away under the conditions they had today. Haley had not realized that kind of capability was in play.

The dispatch of the boarding team and the chase after *Miho Dujam*'s crew had also surprised Haley, who doubted she would have assumed that risk. She said as much to Sam on the Bridge as *Kauai* drove at full speed to cut off the crew's escape. Sam also had his worries, but answered frankly.

"It took me some time to accept it, but this is the job. The 252s are already a plague in Europe and are trying to establish themselves here with a ready narcotics supply and arms market. We have to keep them or any other TCO like them from linking up with the cartels, or we will have a war on our hands in our own backyard. This pushes beyond the standard law enforcement risk calculus.

"Ben and his team are combat-trained and can handle anyone left behind. They'll do a quick sweep and bail if they see anything sketchy. But if we can grab something, anything that leads us to whomever the 252s are working with over here, it'll be worth it. As for these mooks," Sam said, pointing at the fleeing boat on the video screen. "They're obviously not kamikazes, or they would have shot it out with us from a more defensible position."

The old expression that a stern chase is a long chase was coming true today. Even loaded down with ten people, the *Miho Dujam*'s RHIB was only a few knots slower than *Kauai*'s top speed. But they were closing the distance and were within minutes of heading off the villains' escape when the call came from Drake on the *Miho Dujam*.

"*Kauai*, COB, request immediate assistance."

Sam bolted out of his chair and grabbed the microphone. "COB, *Kauai* Actual, what's going on?"

"Sir, they set up scuttling before they beat feet. They also left twenty-two female trafficking victims and no PFDs or rafts."

"COB, we're on the way." Sam turned to Hopkins, "Chief, return to the ship. Fast as possible, please."

"Aye, Aye, sir," Hopkins replied and turned to the helmsman. "Left full rudder."

"Left full rudder," the helmsman repeated. "Chief, my rudder is left thirty degrees."

"Very well, steer two-six-five," Hopkins added as *Kauai* heeled to the right in reaction to the hard left turn.

Sam followed the fleeing RHIB with his binoculars after *Kauai* steadied on her new course, then slammed his right hand on the bridge railing. "Dammit! I should have known they would have done something like this." After a few seconds, his face returned to its regular calm expression, and he grabbed the microphone and switched to the 1MC. "All hands not on watch, don life vests and helmets and muster on the foredeck for rescue and assistance operation. Health Services Technician provide." He hung the microphone and called out the port bridge door, "Hebert!"

"Yes, Captain!" Hebert replied from his post on Mount 52, the port machine gun.

"Secure the mount, get to the foredeck, and take charge! We will have twenty-plus survivors coming on board in a few minutes!"

"Aye, aye, sir!"

Haley saw a chance to contribute and pounced. "Captain, those women have probably been through hell, and it can't hurt to have a female face down there."

Sam glanced at her, smiled, and said, "Go!"

Haley ran to the main deck, grabbed a boat helmet and life vest out of the ready locker, and continued to the foredeck. Hebert was already briefing the crew and turned to her. "Ma'am?"

"You're still in charge, Petty Officer Hebert. I'm just another pair of hands."

"Yes, thank ya', ma'am." Hebert nodded and then turned to the other crew.

Haley looked across the water at the *Miho Dujam*. There was wispy black smoke still drifting upward from her smokestack, and the bright colors of individual clothing were just becoming visible on the decks. Haley estimated about a mile to go. Two pairs of line handlers detailed by Hebert were already laying out mooring lines and attaching heaving lines to the ends, and Hebert himself was suspending three large fenders over the side.

Bryant stepped beside her, carrying a litter in one hand and his medical kit in the other. He placed both on the deck next to the superstructure and said, "Ma'am."

"Petty Officer Bryant." Haley stood silently for about half a minute. Bryant was one of the few people aboard *Kauai* who seemed less interested in small talk than she was. "Have you handled any human trafficking before?"

"When I was in the army, ma'am. Not here."

"I imagine communication might be a challenge. Do you speak any foreign languages?"

"Some German, Czech, and Polish, ma'am."

"Really, how much?"

Bryant turned to face her. "Enough to do the job. Do you speak any foreign languages, ma'am?"

"A little Spanish," Haley answered.

"Won't do much good with this crowd. Here's what you need to say: *Komm mit mir* is 'Come with me,' and *bleib hier* is 'Stay here.'"

"You think they speak German?"

"Enough of them will, ma'am," Bryant nodded and handed her a travel-sized jar of Vicks Vapor Rub.

"What's this for?" Haley asked as she looked at the jar.

"The smell, ma'am. Those gals have been locked in a box on that tub for two weeks on a North Atlantic crossing in November. I prescribe a swipe of that under your nose if you don't want to be hurling yourself."

They were within a quarter-mile now. Haley could clearly see the deck was crowded with individuals, and the ship had a visible list to port. They were still charging at full speed. *Hopkins had better hit the brakes if she doesn't want to overshoot.*

As if reading her mind, Hopkins's voice came over the 1MC, "All hands, prepare for crash-back!"

Haley observed the deck crew kneeling and grabbing a handhold. As she did the same, the bow suddenly dipped down, and the hull began the shudder Haley recognized as engines going full astern with a high forward speed. She almost fell forward in the deceleration as *Kauai* came to a halt about thirty feet off the *Miho Dujam*.

"Heaving lines, let fly!" Hebert shouted, and two small lines with weighted balls at the end streaked across the water to where Ben and Bondurant were standing. They hurriedly pulled over the two mooring lines, threading them through the hawseholes on the ship and giving a thumbs-up to show they had been attached. In the meantime, Hopkins was working motors and rudder to walk *Kauai* sideways into the larger vessel, with the crewmen pulling in the slack from the mooring lines. The two vessels came together with the loud squeak of compressing fenders. "Hold all lines!" Hebert shouted. "Second men, report to me!"

The second man at each position dropped his mooring line and trotted over as Hebert said, "Help Doc get the litter over there." As they assisted Bryant, Hebert turned to Haley. "Ma'am, it's gonna get mighty crowded mighty fast. Can you take them to the messdeck when we gather half a dozen? I have water bottles laid out for them."

"No problem!" Haley answered.

"Thank ya, ma'am."

The litter with the catatonic woman came across first, with Drake and Bondurant on each side handing it carefully across to their counterparts on *Kauai*, followed by Bryant. The men carried it aside, laid it on the deck for Bryant to do his work, and returned to their place on the rail. Like the litter, Drake and Bondurant handed off each survivor to the crewmen waiting on the patrol boat while Ben was herding the others into a single file for the transfer. Haley beckoned over each new arrival to keep the path clear. The fear they showed of the male crewmembers and the contrasting expressions of gratitude on their faces when they saw Haley almost made her tear up. As they huddled close to her, Haley was grateful for Bryant's gift—even in the open air and through the Vapor Rub smear she applied under her nose, the stench of waste and old sweat and vomit was almost overpowering.

When she hit the required critical mass of six victims, she led them aft to the open messdeck, sat them in the chairs, and handed out water bottles. There was concern among the women when she turned to leave, so Haley smiled, waved her hand, and said, "*Bleib hier.*" as Bryant suggested. Those who had stood sat again, although their looks of concern remained until Haley returned with the second half dozen survivors. Some faces were more expressive than others, but the new arrivals brought signs of relief and hope.

On her second return to the foredeck, Haley noticed Ben was no longer herding the remaining women in line. In fact, he was nowhere to be seen, and she wondered if he had returned on board while she was shuttling survivors to the messdeck. After her third run, she remained on the foredeck and watched as the last survivor came aboard, followed by Drake and Bondurant after they cast off *Kauai*'s mooring lines. As the two vessels drifted apart, Haley walked directly to Drake and asked, "Chief, where's the XO?"

"He's inside looking for evidence, ma'am," Drake replied.

"He's *what?*"

"The XO told us to cast off and return on board after the last survivor crossed over. He's taking the RHIB back." Drake and Bondurant shared a worried look.

"How much longer will that ship last?"

"Ma'am, I'm surprised she's still upright."

Haley hated stepping in, but things seemed to be getting out of hand. "Chief, call the RHIB!"

"*Kauai*-One, COB, is the XO with you?"

"Negative," Lee's voice replied.

Drake lifted his radio again, but before he could speak, a series of loud bangs erupted from the *Miho Dujam*, and she quickly rolled to the left. He keyed the radio and shouted, "*Kauai*, COB, XO is still on board!"

The ship continued to roll with a cacophony of bangs and crashes and, within twenty seconds, had completely capsized with only her hull bottom visible. Haley, Drake, and Bondurant were transfixed in shock until the 1MC jolted them into motion.

"Man Overboard Port Side, repeat Man Overboard Port Side! This is no drill!"

Ben

Ben ducked as the heaving line came over, then grabbed it and started pulling over the mooring line. He seized the eye as soon as it came within reach and secured it to a nearby bitt after leading it through the hawsehole. Ben then returned to the crowd of women and, with Anca's help, herded them into a single file for the crossover. By the time he finished, the first few women had already transferred to *Kauai*.

Ben looked down the line of fearful women with despair, realizing that even if any of them were to come forward, their credibility in any American court would be almost nil. He had to get some tangible evidence of the 252's involvement. He strode over to Drake and said, "COB, I'm going to the Bridge to see if they left any logs or charts. If I'm not back when the last survivor goes over, cast off the lines and get aboard. I'll get off on the RHIB."

"Yes, sir," Drake said in distraction as he helped another woman over the rail into the hands of the crewman on *Kauai*.

Ben trotted over to the superstructure and darted inside. A series of cabins led to the Bridge, and although all were disorderly, he couldn't find any personal items, not even clothing. *Well, no one said these guys were dumb—they must have either taken everything with them or dumped it in weighted bags.* Ben stepped into the pilothouse and looked at the navigation table. No charts or notebooks were laid out, so he went through drawers. A quick scan revealed nothing with any marks. *They must have taken the ones they marked up.* He paused for a second. *And left the ones they weren't going to use!*

Ben started pulling open drawers looking for plastic trash bags and found some, along with an old laptop computer. They probably hadn't used it in a while and forgotten about it when they left. Ben wrapped the laptop in two trash bags and tucked it between his chest and life vest. He was stuffing charts into a trash bag when his world turned upside down and dark with a sudden lurch and bang.

Ben was floating and breathing and still inside the pilothouse. He knew he had not been swept anywhere by the water he could feel and hear rushing in. Ben grabbed the flashlight off of his belt and turned it on. Shining it upward, he could see the deck he had been standing on and the bottoms of the helm and binnacle. Everything else was floating around him or resting on what had once been the overhead. He was trapped inside a capsized, sinking ship.

Ben closed his eyes and took a deep breath to control the panic. The situation was literally his worst nightmare, and, between the shock and his claustrophobia, he was having great difficulty thinking. *OK, there's an air pocket, but it won't last. At least I'm not hanged up.* He shined the light around and estimated about two feet between the surface of the water and deck, and the water was rising fast. Continuing around, he saw the bridge door and swam toward it. He tried to push it open, but it wouldn't budge. He briefly panicked, then realized the pressure differential would hold it closed until it was completely underwater.

As he did the last time he had faced death, Ben closed his eyes and thought of his first sight of Victoria on their first date. The memory of her smile in that beautiful green dress calmed him enough to think clearly. *When the door fully submerges, I can push it open and swim out. But the ship is above me now, and I have to swim far enough out that I don't get hung up under it. How far?* He closed his eyes again and tried to picture the ship in his mind. *Door on the starboard side, not much more than a walkway to the edge, almost no tumblehome. About ten feet should do it. Pull clear, swim like hell horizontally while counting to ten, then pop the inflation bottle and head toward the light.* He laughed. *No, DON'T head toward the light—float to the surface!*

The water finally closed over the former bottom, now the top of the door. Ben took and exhaled two deep breaths, then held the third, ducked underwater, and pushed on the door. It didn't move. Panic was returning when he realized hadn't turned the knob. He felt around, found and turned the knob, and pushed for all he was worth. The door opened slowly against the inrush of water—it was surprisingly cold this far beneath the surface. The pressure increase was tremendous, and Ben felt the pain he experienced in diving to the bottom of a swimming pool, only far more intense. It was like knives jamming in his ears, and it was all he could do not to cry out. Ben got the door open enough and pulled himself through the opening. He immediately collided with something, a lifeline. He felt his way around it, pushed off the ship, and began swimming. *One thousand one, one thousand two....*

He could see light now, sunlight attenuated and blue-tinted through the water. *One thousand nine, one thousand ten!* He reached for and pulled the tab for the CO2 bottle and felt his vest inflate. It was pulling him up through the water. The stabbing pain in his ears was subsiding, replaced by the agonizing burning of his lungs. He knew he had to exhale, coming up from deep water, and started puffing air out his nose. The light got brighter, and he could now see the waves in the water as he looked upward. Then the light faded to gray and finally, black.

****

"Sir! Sir! Give me your hand!"

Ben opened his eyes and looked up in confusion. It was Lopez, reaching for him from the RHIB. Lee suddenly appeared beside Lopez and also reached for him. Ben put up his hand, then felt himself being pulled into the boat. He lay flat on his back, looking at the bright blue sky, and could hear Lee's voice as the engine revved and the boat turned and sped toward *Kauai.*

"*Kauai, Kauai* One. XO is aboard and alive, returning to ship. Have Doc meet us at the rail with oh-two. Over."

It was hard to hear, and his ears hurt. *What's happening? What am I doing here?* Gradually, his confusion receded, and he could remember. *The ship, upside down, swimming out.* In a sudden flash of panic, he brought his hand over and felt for the laptop—it was still there, pressed against his chest by the inflated vest. He tried to sit up, was overwhelmed by dizziness, and slumped.

"Stay flat, XO," Lopez said as he rested his hand on Ben's shoulder. "We'll be on board the boat in a minute, and Doc can check you out."

Ben looked at Lopez, whose face was a mask of concern, and tried to nod. They were pulling up to *Kauai* now, and Lopez left him to tend to the sea painter while Lee grabbed and slammed the crane fall onto the RHIB's lift frame. Ben felt the boat lift from the water, and as it pulled even with the rail, Bondurant jumped in, and Ben was lifted out.

"Put him in the litter, John." It was Bryant's voice.

After being set down, Ben felt a plastic mask placed on his face and cool airflow. Someone was taking his pulse.

"OK, let's get him to his room." Bryant's voice again.

Ben felt himself being lifted and carried in the litter. He looked over and saw Bryant walking beside him, holding the mask on his face. They entered the boat, and after a couple of quick turns, they were in his stateroom, and he was lifted onto his bed. "Doc, what's happening to me?" Ben asked.

"You are pretty messed up from that deep dive of yours, XO. How do you feel?"

"Dizzy, and my ears hurt."

"Yes, I'm not surprised. You had what is called an ascent blackout. You were unconscious when Lopez and Lee found you. It has to do with the partial pressure of oxygen in the blood decreasing as you ascend from deep water. As for your ears, you have two ear blocks from the pressure underwater. It's the worst I've ever seen and might even be an eardrum rupture. That's probably the source of your dizziness too. I'm confining you sick-in-quarters until a real doctor can see you in Gitmo."

Guantanamo Bay, known as Gitmo, was the U.S. Naval Base on the island of Cuba and the closest resupply base for their operation in the Turks and Caicos. It would not be a long trip, only ten hours at their fast cruise speed of twenty-four knots. "Doc, where is the laptop I brought with me? It's important."

"Yes, we figured it had to be if you were willing to go down with the ship to get it. It's right here on your desk."

"Good, good," Ben said, then frowned as the old worry kicked in. "Will this deep dive blackout affect, you know, the other thing?"

"I'm sorry, sir, I don't know. I can tell you that the dizziness you are having now is far more likely from your inner ear mess than from your earlier injury, and that should mostly clear by tomorrow morning, as long as your eardrums aren't perforated. But they're going to have to do another no-shit neurological workup on you, I'm afraid."

"I figured as much," Ben said with sadness. He hated constantly hanging on the edge of losing his career.

"Try not to worry about it, XO. I can't run the whole battery, but your pupillary response is fine, and you don't have a headache or any other symptoms. As for your ears, I'd be worried if you had bleeding, but you don't, so surgery probably won't be necessary. No promises, though."

"Yeah, there never are. Thanks, Doc."

"Sure. Get some rest, sir," Bryant said as he stood.

Ben drifted to sleep shortly after Bryant had left and was startled awake by a knock on his door. He glanced at the clock on his wall—16:15—over two hours had passed. "Come in," Ben said.

Sam poked his head in and said, "How are you doing? Feel like talking?"

"Of course, sir." Ben started to rise, then settled when Sam waved his hand. Sam came in, shut the door, and sat in Ben's chair.

"You know, laddie, you really are doing your best to help me get over moving on from this job. If you weren't flat on your ass right now, you'd be braced-up in my cabin," Sam said with a warm smile. "Care to explain to me what you were thinking?"

"I'm sorry, sir. When I saw those women and what they were going through, I couldn't let those bastards get away with it. I figured I'd grab some charts or logs or something, but the laptop was all I could find."

"I saw those women too, and believe me, I'm as mad as you are. In fact, I'm glad I didn't know it during the chase—I'd have been tempted to blow their asses away with the twenty-five. That said, your decision is worrisome. Tell me something: if you had been unable to go yourself, would you have sent Bondurant, Lee, or Lopez?"

Ben dropped his head. "No, I wouldn't," he admitted.

"Why not?" He continued as Ben stayed silent. "Never mind, the question was rhetorical. The answer is because gathering evidence, even in this case, was not worth risking their lives." He paused for a second. "You took that decision out of my hands, but not the responsibility. Here's some CO perspective for you. It would've been devastating enough to have had to make a condolence call after Barbello or the *Aurora Mist*. Can you imagine what it would have been like for me telling Victoria or your parents you died trying to recover a *logbook*?"

Ben looked Sam in the eyes and tried to think of something worthy of the remorse he was feeling. "I don't know what to say, sir."

Sam reached over and squeezed his shoulder. "I won't say, 'forget about it.' Never forget about it. Let's take the W and consider ourselves lucky."

"Yes, sir. What's the plan? I understand we're headed for Gitmo."

"Yes, we need to get those survivors some attention. There are no English speakers among them, and, near as we can tell, they're from at least six different countries. Doc might be able to conn them through first aid and head calls with the German, Polish, and Czech he has, but he can't conduct a proper interview, and we wouldn't want him to, anyway.

"They have all been abused beyond human endurance sexually, psychologically, even hygienically. They're all scared shitless of any male right now. Thank God for Haley—she was spot on about a female face being therapeutic. She's keeping things calm on the messdeck right now. When we get to Gitmo, we'll hand them off to the people who can give them the proper care first and gather the facts later.

"As for you, the flight surgeon down there will also give you a going-over."

"Well, at least I didn't have to be medevac-ed off again."

"Not an option. Doc said any flight would blow out your eardrums if they aren't already. You're on the slow boat for the rest of this trip."

"Yes, sir."

"Also, that laptop is generating interest. We will be met at Gitmo by our buddies in the DIA, who will take possession.

"Pete Simmons again?"

"No, I'm happy to say we will not be renewing our acquaintance. Somebody named Frankle."

"Art Frankle?"

"I guess. His name is listed as Arthur."

"Yeah, that's Art. I met him on the Resolution Key op. You'll like him—very by-the-book."

"That will be nice for a change." Sam stood. "You rest easy. If you need anything, let me know."

"Thank you, Captain."

Beginnings

USCG Cutter *Kauai*, moored, Pier B, Naval Station Guantanamo Bay, Cuba 14:18 EST, 17 November

Frankle

Arthur "Art" Frankle, Senior Case Officer, Defense Clandestine Service, Defense Intelligence Agency, stopped for a moment to take in the view down Pier B of the Naval Station. Frankle was tall for a field agent at six-foot-one and still remarkably fit for a man in his late fifties. Only his graying hair and the deepening wrinkles on his face hinted he was approaching the time for retirement. He had done his time in the field, trained dozens of junior agents, and still mentored many of them. His current assignment was mainly desk work, a well-earned break from stress and fear. Still, he enjoyed getting out of the building, even if it was only courier work.

It was feast or famine here at Gitmo: either the ships were few or, like today, the harbor was a beehive of activity. With the latest mass migration from Haiti in full swing, it was beehive time. Unlike the grim days of the Cold War, the ships crowding the docks were not haze gray-painted frigates and destroyers, but white-hulled Coast Guard cutters with their red "racing stripes" ducking in for fuel, replenishment, and what passed for recreation inside the forty-five square mile navy base parked on the coast of a hostile communist country.

Several smaller patrol boats were among the larger ships, sleek and fast compared to their larger sisters, but with shorter legs. The large, blunt ships were built for endurance and could hang offshore for two to three weeks at a time without replenishment. The most the patrol boats could endure was one week, and that was stretching it. In a high-tempo operation like this, darting back and forth at high speed in response to migrant vessels spotted by aircraft, their cycle time diminished to only three or four days.

Still, Frankle liked the patrol boats better. Their looks and speed appealed to him more as a former U.S. Marine Gunnery Sergeant than the larger ships. And, he admitted to himself, he was biased, having worked with one of those boats before. He scanned the dockside and picked her out. Her name was not visible from this perspective, but the number 1351 painted on her bow marked her as *Kauai*.

He had never set foot on the patrol boat, just seen her from a distance at the end of that near fiasco in the Florida Keys last January. Pete Simmons, a former mentee of Frankle's in the DSC, had sold the bosses that a Russian nuclear-tipped cruise missile accidentally fired after a midair collision between a Russian bomber and U.S. fighter hadn't flown harmlessly off into the Gulf of Mexico, but crashed somewhere in the Keys. The subsequent hunt for the live nuclear warhead overlapped a 252 Syndicate narcotics smuggling operation. After spending several days on *Kauai* during the search, Pete shifted ashore with the boat's young XO, Ben Wyporek, in tow as a liaison. The 252s launched a dandy snatch operation to grab Pete, tying down his backup in another location while they cornered him and Ben on the northern tip of Resolution Key. If it hadn't been for *Kauai*'s skipper driving the boat at flank speed through fog and shoal water to arrive in the nick of time to provide gunfire support, Pete and Ben would have been killed or captured. As usual, Pete's luck paid off, and, besides finding and securing the nuke, they disrupted a 252 scheme to import narcotics to the U.S. and wiped out a team of killers.

Frankle had only associated with Ben on two occasions on that operation, for a couple of hours during the first meeting after he and Pete had come ashore and for a few minutes after the fight on Resolution Key. He liked what he saw that first meeting—a bright, modest, and earnest young man. Frankle's esteem jumped an order of magnitude after Ben stood shoulder-to-shoulder with Pete in a fight to the death against five times their number of 252 soldiers. And when he saw how close Ben and Victoria had grown, he respected the man even more. Frankle and Victoria had worked together for several years, and he admired the woman's smarts and intuition. Since her resignation, he missed working with her and was delighted that Ben had seized the crucial laptop he had come to Gitmo to retrieve. Frankle looked forward to sitting with him to get the story and catch up with Victoria's life.

The TCO Section of the DIA, in which Frankle headed the 252 desk, had picked up a significant increase in chatter involving the setup of a major syndicate hub somewhere in the western hemisphere, but the location was a mystery. The chance meeting of the *Miho Dujam* with the Coast Guard confirmed these suspicions. It was regrettable that the crew could destroy the ship and its arms cargo and escape while the Coast Guard was occupied with saving the embarked sex trafficking victims. Frankle could not argue with the decision—although he would gladly break the rules to wipe any 252 member out of existence, he would not sacrifice innocent lives to do it. Saving twenty-two young women from death, or even worse fates, was a good day's work in anyone's book.

Frankle had arrived that morning on the daily logistics flight the Coast Guard ran from their air station at Miami-Opa Locka to Leeward Point Field across the bay from the piers. A twenty-minute ferry ride had brought him across to the deepwater part of the bay and resurfaced memories, good and bad, of the time he was posted here as a Marine. He had hated it then, like everyone else stationed here. Now, it was a nice, warm place to visit while Washington descended into winter.

After arriving, Frankle's first stop had been the base hospital, where the women rescued by *Kauai* were being treated for their ordeal and processed by Immigration and Customs Enforcement. A couple of his people had come with him and were waiting to interview the women about their 252 captors. Frankle wasn't hopeful—even if they knew something, they were unlikely to share it out of fear for themselves or their families. The initial report from the ICE people was that the victims, some as young as fourteen, came from various backgrounds in Poland, Moldova, Croatia, Romania, and Bulgaria. Some had been abducted, others duped into thinking they were going to housekeeping or au pair jobs. Heartbreakingly, the two youngest girls had been sold to traffickers by their families. Frankle pulled his agents aside and directed that those two girls and anyone else in a comparable predicament be classified as government witnesses and detained in foster care. It was not by the book, but he was damn sure not going to let them be deported straight back into the situation that brought them here.

After reviewing the situation of the victims with the ICE agents and his people, Frankle drove his government vehicle loaner the four and a half miles over the rough base roads to the docks. He could not contact the ship and hoped the officers were not ashore, seeing to the many needs of turning around a warship during a short port break. He walked over to what passed for a quarterdeck, a small standup desk with a phone manned by a young seaman, and presented his ID. Within a minute, Ben and two other officers stepped out of the boat's superstructure and walked over to meet him.

"Art, it's good to see you again," Ben said, offering his hand.

"Likewise, Lieutenant," Frankle said, shaking his hand firmly.

"Senior Case Officer Arthur Frankle, this is my CO, Lieutenant Sam Powell, and our incoming CO, Lieutenant Haley Reardon," Ben said, introducing his companions.

"How do you do, Captain, Ma'am," Frankle said, shaking hands with each.

"Welcome aboard," Sam said. "It's pretty tight in my cabin for all of us. Will we be discussing anything too sensitive for the messdeck?"

"That should not be a problem, sir," Frankle said. After they were inside and seated at one of the mess tables, he continued. "I wanted to congratulate you on a magnificent piece of work yesterday. I stopped by the base hospital this morning, and those poor gals are still being treated and cleaned up, but their outlook has improved tremendously since yesterday."

"Yes, we were lucky we ran into them. That area is not regularly covered," Sam said with a nod. "Was it as bad as it looked?"

"At least. Some were near to losing their minds. Several of them were raped, that one you guys brought off on the stretcher repeatedly. She is still just staring at the ceiling right now. It seems she pushed back when one guard started getting fresh with the children, so they shot her with their paralysis drug. You know the one I'm talking about, Ben."

"Yes, that I do," Ben replied, his face darkening.

"As soon as she locked up with the drug, they took turns raping her while the other women were made to watch. No one pushed back after that. I didn't think I could hate those 252 guys any worse than I already did—I was wrong. Well, that's a few off their hook." He shook his head. "OK, I know you're busy, so we might as well get to it. What can you tell me about yesterday?"

Sam and Ben took turns relating the story, leaving out the details of Ben's near-fatal experience in the *Miho Dujam*'s capsizing. As they finished, Frankle said, "Yes, it's a pity they got away, since they had plenty of time to sanitize the boat before you guys got on board. Still, the laptop could be a gold mine for us."

"I'm not so sure," Ben said. "Given how thoroughly they were clearing up their personal items, it is surprising they would leave behind a PC. Could it be a red herring?"

"Possibly, but I think and hope they tucked it there at the beginning of the trip and forgot about it. Even if it is a ruse, the metadata in the files could offer opportunities for us to penetrate their networks, email, finances, *et cetera*. I'll get this over to the cyber-ninjas as soon as I get back to DC," Frankle said.

"I am surprised by the interest and quick response," Haley spoke for the first time. "What is going on that puts a senior DIA guy on a plane from DC?"

Frankle smiled in response. *This one is sharp. Good looking too.* "Good question. We've been picking up chatter that the 252s have worked a deal with someone over here to arrange a permanent depot for the transshipment of drugs and arms. That crowd you picked up yesterday was the staff for a new brothel there. After the Barbello deal, they realized they needed a base of their own to play over here. Our challenge is finding it.

"The problem for the 252s is that after they annihilated the Salinas Cartel, none of the other established outfits want to touch them. If they try to grab some territory of their own, the other gangs will do what it takes to evict them, even if it means working together to do it. So, we think they might try to work through one of the corrupt governments in the region. That's about all I can say outside of a secure space."

Haley nodded. "It seems strange that they didn't resist us, given what they had at stake on that ship. They could have caused actual harm during the boarding, maybe even sunk us if they carried any rockets."

"Not really," Frankle said. "Knocking you guys off would make it a whole new ballgame. Right now, they are a big law enforcement problem for Europol and a minor national security issue for us. They sink a Coast Guard cutter or other warship, and that's war. We would not only come down on them kinetically and financially but also put them on the Terrorist List and mess up everyone they do business with. They may eventually decide that's worth the risk if they can work a major government to cover for them, but not right now."

"Man, I hope I don't live to see that," Sam said, shaking his head.

"You and me both, brother," Frankle agreed. After a pause, he said, "I might as well grab the box and get going. Any chance of getting a tour while I'm here? I haven't seen the boat since Resolution, and that was from the beach."

"Not a problem," Sam said. "Haley and I will excuse ourselves to resume our handoff discussions if you don't mind. Ben can show you around and give you two a chance to catch up. It's worth your time—we've had quite an upgrade since Resolution."

"Excellent!" Frankle said as they all stood. After shaking hands with Sam and Haley, he turned to Ben and said, "After you, sir."

Frankle was surprised by what he found on the tour. He knew *Kauai* was among the last in her class still in commission and expected to see an aging, patched-up set of diesels in the engine room. With its clean and modern diesel generators and Ben's description of their new diesel-electric battery drive capabilities, *Kauai's* powerplant was more like a modern conventional submarine than an obsolescent patrol boat. Now the account of the Barbello operation he had read made much more sense. The Bridge was another wonder, with capabilities beyond even the newest patrol boats coming into service. "I thought the Coast Guard was the mendicant of the federal government. How did you guys manage to get all this?" Frankle asked after Ben finished his presentation of the FC3 system.

"The DNI dug our performance at Resolution and wrote the Coast Guard a big check for upgrades; Barbello was the first payback."

"Wow. The DNI wasn't stingy, was he?"

"Nope, the total was at least four times what the Coast Guard originally paid to build the boat, even adjusted for inflation. Still, it was less than they're paying for the new ones."

"Nice," Frankle said. This was good information in his pocket, and he would know for whom to ask if they were ever facing another challenge like Resolution. "Well, this was fascinating. On a personal note, how are you doing? I heard you got roughed up at Barbello."

"Just shot in the head—no damage to anything of value," Ben joked.

"You're shitting me," Frankle said with astonishment.

"The bullet didn't penetrate my helmet, but it did mess me up badly enough that my parents almost got the dreaded 'we regret to inform you' call. On the whole, I was lucky, considering the DEA guy standing next to me was killed," Ben said, his smile disappearing.

"Man." Frankle shook his head. "That's rough."

"Yes, I *do* draw a lot of fire whenever I'm with you DIA guys."

"Hey, that's Pete. Most of us go our entire career without shooting outside of the gun range. Heard from him lately?"

"Not since I got hit at Barbello. Victoria says he's been detailed to the DNI's staff. Is that a promotion for him?"

Frankle shook his head. "More of a place of refuge. He tangled with the DIA director over how Barbello was run in front of the JUBILEE committee, and she does not forgive and forget. The DNI is giving him cover until she moves on to another job. It's a nice gig, but he can't wait to get back in the field."

"He seems to have a bug up his ass about the 252s."

"Yes, well, when it's that personal, even the hardest among us can get obsessive."

Ben looked at him with a raised eyebrow. "Personal? How so?"

"You know about Julie, right?" Frankle asked.

"His fiancée? She was Victoria's big sister. They've only mentioned that she died."

"Not exactly. The 252s murdered her."

"*What?*"

"Yep. Julie was 'collateral damage' in a car bomb assassination they pulled in Paris. Pete wasn't even in the service then, just a smart-alecky postdoc at Princeton with a talent for martial arts.

It crushed him. He'd probably have killed himself if it hadn't been for Victoria. Pete hung on, but he's been on a crusade to eradicate them since joining us."

"He didn't tell me, and neither did Victoria, which is surprising considering she's an open book. I guess I should have asked about Julie, but I didn't want to dredge up painful memories for her." Ben said, hanging his head.

"Don't beat yourself up, kid," Frankle said as he patted his arm. "When she feels the need to talk about that, she will. We're all pretty happy she got hooked up with you, you know. Real-life Dudley Do-rights are rather rare these days."

Ben cocked his head and said, "I can't figure out if I should be pleased or insulted."

"Take your pick," Frankle said with a grin. "Now, how are you and Victoria doing? We sure miss having her around, both personally and professionally."

"I'll share that with her. Actually, we're awesome. She seems happy, and I can't believe my good luck."

"Better and better. So, will you make an honest woman out of her?"

"What, are you relieving Pete of the 'Dad Watch' or something? Please pass the word to call off the hit squads—I'm working up to it."

Frankle smiled warmly. "Good for you. And I mean that. Now, how about you hook me up with that laptop, and I'll let you get back to the regular job?"

"Suits me," Ben said.

After retrieving the laptop from Ben's safe and signing an evidence receipt, Frankle followed Ben to the quarterdeck and stepped ashore. Shaking hands with the young officer, he said, "Thanks again, Coast Guard. Take care of yourself and our girl."

"I will, Art. Stay safe."

As Frankle turned and started walking along the pier in the warm sunshine, he glanced at his watch: 16:18. He had time for a round of Gitmo Golf before sunset. Not that he was an avid golfer, he just wanted to tell the tale when he got home. The naval base had a nine-hole course of sorts. Its only grass was the artificial greens around each hole. The rest was rocky dirt—golfers carried a piece of Astroturf on which to drop and hit the ball for "fairway" shots. Gitmo Golf, iguanas, and the up to two-foot-long gray

Hutias, known locally as "Banana Rats" wandering around, were part of the storied charm of Guantanamo Bay.

The truth was that Frankle needed the distraction before returning to the grind of Washington. The women from that 252 ship got to him, particularly that poor Polish woman who was raped into madness simply for standing up for a child. Maybe the laptop could provide something that would make a difference in the fight against the 252s, or maybe not. All he knew was that he needed to seriously consider pulling out of the game once this case concluded. He was beginning to hate too much, which can get you and your teammates killed.

USCG Cutter *Kauai*, Atlantic Ocean, twenty-three nautical miles north of Grand Turk Island
19:21 EST, 19 November

Haley

They had been on station for a full day, with three more to go. This time, it would be back home to Port Canaveral, not just another fuel, water, and food top-off at Guantanamo Bay. This first day had been as uneventful as their patrol had been before the *Miho Dujam*'s arrival. Haley had used this respite to complete the last of her technical familiarization. A few frank, one-on-one discussions with Sam about individual crewmembers remained, a vital part of the handoff on a unit this small. The talks gave her essential insight into the strengths and weaknesses of each individual and how they understood, anticipated, and played off each other, much like a championship basketball squad.

Haley also used these sessions to benchmark herself against Sam, professionally and personally. Although they had come to this common point in their careers from different paths—Sam via the enlisted ranks and OCS and Haley through the Academy— they shared a similar worldview and upbringing. Both were highly intelligent and came from wealthy families who disapproved of their career choice. They were also aligned in their love for the Service and a desire to stay operational on ships if possible. But that was where the similarities ended.

Sam was a devoted family man, married with two young children, and, thanks to a very understanding wife, he successfully balanced the competing demands of job and family. His wife had been a navy brat and served as a navy petty officer before completing her bachelor's degree—Joana understood and embraced the nomadic life associated with being a military spouse and was Sam's partner in every sense. Haley could see that Sam missed his family terribly when he was on this long patrol, as much as he enjoyed the job and the company of his crew.

Haley could not have been more different in this respect. She'd had relationships at school and after getting her commission, but determined that the benefits did not cover the costs. Haley found out early that you didn't hook up with other officers in the Service—the job was too competitive for any relationship to work, and the wreckage afterward was bad for everyone, not just the couple. Likewise, she had no success with men outside the Service. The interesting ones moved on when they learned what her career entailed, and those who did not move on were inevitably needy. Haley was single and comfortable with the choice—the occasions when she missed having someone to unload on were rare. She treasured the freedom to go after opportunities wherever and whenever they presented themselves without worrying about pulling kids out of school or her partner's job or preferences.

In their two weeks together on this patrol, Haley grew to admire Sam and was impressed by his leadership talent and history. The crew liked and trusted Sam as a man and the captain. Haley suspected his having made his way up to chief petty officer before being commissioned lent him more credibility in their eyes than the typical junior officer. But it clearly went beyond that. Her brief exposure led her to believe Sam was one of those rare people possessing the total package: knowledge, judgment, experience, and "people sense." It wasn't just the crew—it was clear Ben's admiration for Sam was unbounded. The two men were the closest of friends, despite their superior-subordinate positions in the military hierarchy. Haley thought their talks would reveal insights into whatever secret sauce Sam used to build this much personal power.

Haley had hoped to get some detail on what was behind that last operation, but Sam had to decline, citing the codeword restrictions. He did share that the Resolution Key mission culminated with him driving *Kauai* at flank speed through fog and the shoal water north of the Florida Keys to rescue Ben and DIA Agent Simmons from a deadly 252 trap. Sam shared his intense dislike of Simmons for his recklessness that endangered Ben and his crew and warned Haley to be very wary whenever the agent was involved in an operation.

"I'm not saying he's corrupt or evil or anything like that," Sam said in summation. "He just has a different calculus for risking the lives of the people around him. You need to keep that thought in your mind whenever you work with him."

"Not much chance of that, is there?" Haley said.

"*Au contraire*," Sam replied. "He was behind the Barbello mission, too, although he wasn't responsible for the damage or injuries we suffered. Keep in mind this boat was practically rebuilt using DNI money, and the Intel Community will be looking for a return on investment. Simmons is one of those people."

"I see," Haley said. "So, does Ben share this view?"

Sam smiled sadly and said, "Yes and no. I think Ben was awed enough by Simmons to go along with some decisions he came to regret. That fight he was dragged into on Resolution scared the bejesus out of him. He's been much more cautious since then. I have to admit that I miss the old happy-go-lucky Ben sometimes." He paused and grinned. "But I treasure the new Ben."

Haley nodded. "Off the record; tell me about him."

Sam sat back and put his hands behind his head. "He's the XO of your dreams. Super smart and capable, but he doesn't seem to know it. At least, he is extraordinarily modest. Ben has an amazing grasp of what's needed and makes it happen with patience and humor. There isn't a member of the crew, from Drake on down, who wouldn't follow him straight into a hurricane. And he is as courageous as they come. Let me tell you a story that captures Ben to a tee.

"When he was on his way from Virginia during his transfer from *Dependable*, he called to tell me he had been held up by a traffic accident. His vehicle was not involved, but he was set back for a few hours. I told him to play it safe and report in the afternoon rather than driving all night. Good headwork, right? So he reports in the next day, and we're off to the races. Well, a few weeks later, the Sector Commander comes knocking to pin a Commendation Medal on him. He saw the accident alright, then climbed into an SUV about to fall off a cliff to rescue an unconscious woman and her two little kids. He stuck around long enough to give a statement to the cops and make sure the kids were safely in the hands of their aunt, then got back on the road. The only reason the Coast Guard learned of it was that the woman's husband was an army officer—he found out Ben was in the military and put him in for an award."

"What was Ben's reaction?"

"He was surprised and embarrassed. Ben saw the act as something that needed to be done, so he did it. He did not want to call attention to it because he did not want to admit how scared he was. It was the same way on the Resolution and Barbello deals—said all he did was get himself shot."

"Still off the record. Can Ben make the tough calls?"

"Yes," Sam said, then tilted his head. "Why would you ask that?"

"He strikes me as being too friendly for an XO, first names, touching, that sort of thing."

"Hmm. Ben plays by the rules in the ballpark. If you want to step things up, he'll make it happen.

"You disagree?"

"No, Haley. Even if I did, it will be your boat, not mine. We *have* been a little loose with things because of where we started and the lack of risk with the people here. I would probably play it tighter if I came on board now."

"I'm relieved it's not just me, and I'll break it in gently. Is there anything else I should know, as in personally?"

"Again, why would you ask that?"

"I have heard his girlfriend has 'issues.' Have you had any concerns about his focus?" She hated bringing this up, but Zuccaro had used the word "creepy" regarding Victoria in an informal discussion Haley had had had with the women a few nights ago.

The meeting was one of those "seemed like a good idea at the time" mistakes. Haley wanted to get a read on the gender relations climate before her ascension to command would make that impracticable. The atmosphere had turned decidedly frosty when she asked point-blank whether any male crew had done anything to make them uncomfortable. Zuccaro had been the only one to say anything but an emphatic negative. Haley suspected it was cattiness based on the silent death stares Zuccaro received from Hopkins and Lee, but she had to be sure.

Sam leaned forward with a frown. "I won't ask who suggested that, but I recommend you consider them unreliable sources. Victoria is, I guess the polite word is 'neurodiverse.' She is a fully functioning adult with a genius IQ and an eidetic memory. I mean, this woman is world-class smart. She is also the warmest, most charming individual I have ever met. She does have an unusually formal way of speaking, and an intense curiosity about whomever she is talking with that some may find a little odd. Victoria is the one net positive from our involvement with Simmons—she was his protégé, and Ben first met her on the Resolution op. About her effect on Ben, he is a better, more mature man because of her. Believe me; I've seen the before and after versions."

"Thank you. I suspected as much, but I had to make sure."

"I understand. There is one other thing I'll tell you off the record related to this topic. I hate doing it, but I'd prefer you get the straight story from me instead of someone spreading scurrilous rumors."

Uh-oh. Haley leaned forward. "OK, let's have it."

"Hopkins has hugged Ben on two occasions; both were as he was heading into those two fights. There was nothing sexual, just her matronly instinct overruling convention in extraordinary circumstances. I saw no harm in it and did not feel the need to make it an issue. If it would make you more comfortable, I can write a formal statement you can keep on file that I dealt with the matter appropriately."

Haley blinked and said, "No, that won't be necessary. I am going to put a stop to that, though."

Sam shrugged and said, "Your call. Is there anyone else you want to discuss?"

"No, I think that will do. If I come across anything else, mind if I pick your brain again?"

"Anytime. Please grab me for any questions. I've been at this for so long that there's stuff I don't even think of anymore that might be important."

"Thanks, Sam. Good night."

"Good night, Haley."

Haley closed her notebook and stepped over to Ben's stateroom. She and Ben were "hot bunking"—alternating occupying the room for sleeping on this patrol. It was awkward, both in terms of the gender mixing and their soon-to-be respective positions.

This latest revelation regarding Hopkins was a particular concern. Haley was shocked that Hopkins found that kind of behavior appropriate, even more, that Ben did. And yet, Sam did not have a problem with it. *Is it just me? Am I "that guy," the one looking for an excuse to throw his weight around?* Haley shook her head. *No, I get now why Mercier wants to move Sam along. He's gotten too close to everyone. If he can't put a stop to something like this, how will he make the hard choice when the time comes?*

She spread her sleeping bag out on Ben's bunk and checked her watch—she needed to be dressed to turn the room over to Ben in just under six hours. As she disrobed, her mind went to how she would manage the transition from the current situation on board to the one that needed to be. *I'll break it in gently. Easier said than done.*

Change of Command

State Highway A1A, Port Canaveral, Florida
09:18 EST, 1 December

Haley

It was shaping up to be a beautiful day, one of those late fall days in Central Florida when everything was perfect for an outdoor event. It was warm but not hot, with moderate humidity, a light sea breeze from the east, and a bright blue sky with just a few small cumulus clouds. Haley was smiling as she drove the blue Miata with the top down along the causeway bridge crossing the Banana River—she could not help smiling as this was the day she had trained and hoped for across her eleven years in the Coast Guard. When she crossed this bridge on the return trip to her apartment today, she would be the commanding officer of the Coast Guard Cutter *Kauai*.

Haley got off at the cruise ship exit and followed route 401 to the Coast Guard station on the West Basin. Unlike her earlier visit a little over a month ago, the gate was open and manned by two Coast Guard seamen in tropical blue uniforms to check for official identification or, for those without official ID, whether they were on the approved guest list. Haley had her CAC ready and presented it to one seaman, who saluted and directed her to the parking area. On her way to her parking spot, Haley passed *Kauai*, moored here instead of her usual berth on the Trident Wharf. The festivities were held here rather than on the Space Force station because it was far easier to get the guests through the more moderate security and the venue was more aesthetically pleasing than the shipyard-like grounds around the wharf. Haley almost teared up when she saw the boat in the full sun, gleaming white and "full dressed" with her signal flags hung in the prescribed rainbow pattern from a temporary cable leading from the jackstaff on her bow to the crosstree on the mast and then back down to the flagstaff on the stern.

Haley parked in her assigned spot, climbed out of the Miata, and donned her combination cap, running her eyes over her uniform for the hundredth time today. She was in dress whites, as were the other officers taking part in the ceremony. Haley hated the white uniform for its fragility—you could not bump into anything without leaving a glaring mark, and the need to avoid doing so distracted from everything you were doing. She retrieved her sword from the car boot and attached it to the belt hook protruding from her jacket. The sword was another anachronism Haley did not care for, but it was useful in that wearing one took skirts and pumps off the table.

Holding the sword loosely with her left hand to keep it from swinging around, Haley strolled to the grassy softball field, where a broad canopy covered a wooden platform on which a microphone-equipped podium and several folding chairs already stood. Hopkins was busy arranging items on a folding table to the side of the platform and came to attention and rendered a salute when she saw Haley approaching.

Haley returned the salute and said, "Chief, the boat looks wonderful. You've done a great job."

"Thank you, ma'am, but it was a team effort."

"Well, I appreciate it." Haley glanced at the table. "Anything I can do?"

"No, ma'am, we are pretty much ready to go."

"Right. I'll get out of your way then. See you later."

"Yes, ma'am."

Haley turned and walked toward the station's admin building, where the officials and guests gathered before the ceremony. Hopkins's cool demeanor made her uneasy—it had been that way between them throughout Haley's familiarization patrol. She wanted to attribute it to the natural wariness of someone new who was about to take over as CO, but the other enlisted personnel did not seem to share it, at least to that degree. Even the quiet Bondurant was downright chatty when compared to Hopkins. *I need to figure out what's going on there and fix it; that and the hugging thing.* She smiled again as she walked. *But that's for later. Now live for the day!*

Haley reached the admin building, stepped inside, and followed the "KAUAI COC" signs to the dayroom, where people were huddled in small groups and talking. Ben and Sam stood with Drake in one corner, chatting over various details of the ceremony. Ben had the harried, intense countenance that junior officers and XOs always had going into any highly choreographed ceremony. Drake towered above the two officers, calm and fatherly-looking, politely attentive and nodding in his tropical blue uniform. Sam was smiling at the interchange, confident and relaxed as ever.

Three women stood in another corner with Chief Deffler, talking and chuckling. Haley recognized Ben's girlfriend, Victoria, from the pictures on his stateroom wall. She was petite, with long auburn hair pulled back into a ponytail to reveal a heart-shaped face with large green eyes. Victoria was an attractive young woman, with a girl-next-door look in her sundress and sandals masking a formidable intellect.

Joana, Sam's wife, stood in a conservative white blouse and dark blue skirt to Victoria's left. She was a stunningly beautiful woman—the pictures in Sam's cabin did not do her justice. She was a couple of inches taller than Victoria, slender, with lightly tanned skin, dark eyes, and wavy raven-black hair cascading over her shoulders. Sam had related in passing they met when he was in OCS, and Joana had been the sister of one of his classmates. She was a work-from-home computer graphic artist who shared Sam's gregarious nature and sense of humor.

Haley did not know the third woman, a medium-sized forty-ish woman with short, light brown hair, but guessed she was Drake's wife. Deffler's presence was curious—he was not a regular crew member, although Haley knew he deployed with them whenever they had a UAV detachment on board. She supposed he was invited and had accepted as a matter of courtesy.

As Haley walked over to the other officers, Ben and Drake came to attention, and she and Ben shared salutes. "Good morning, ma'am," Ben said.

"XO, Captain, Chief, good morning," Haley replied. "Everything going OK?"

"Same as usual, ma'am," Drake answered. "I'm keeping things running, the XO's sweating the small stuff, and the skipper's sitting back enjoying the day."

Ben smiled, and Sam rolled his eyes as Haley laughed and said, "That's one tradition we need to keep."

"Very sensible decision," Sam said. He glanced around the room and added, "Do you have any guests coming?"

"A few classmates and my parents," Haley said, glancing at her watch.

"I'll see they get seated in the front, ma'am," Ben said.

"Thank you," Haley replied with a neutral expression. She had mixed feelings about her father's and stepmother's attendance. Haley adored her father, Bradford Reardon, and, for that reason alone, tolerated her stepmother. Haley was an only child; her mother died of ovarian cancer when she was just ten years old. A few years later, Bradford met and married Margot Treadway, a beautiful and vibrant Newport socialite. She and Margot had the usual stepmother/stepdaughter friction, but Haley supposed it could have been worse. Over time, they settled into a truce for her father's sake, more or less ignoring each other as long as Haley kept her grades up and stayed clean.

They hit a rough patch when Haley joined the Coast Guard. Margot Reardon looked down on the military as she did any laborers and was convinced Haley had selected the Coast Guard Academy over Brown or one of the other civilian schools just to spite her. Haley thought the notion that anyone would endure the rigors of the Academy and subsequent privations of military service simply to irritate someone else ludicrous and told her as much. After Haley completed her obligated service and elected to stay in the Coast Guard, Margot was finally convinced that this was neither a spiteful jab nor a passing whim, and the two resumed their peaceful coexistence. Haley had to admit that Margot loved her father dearly and made him happy; for that, she could forgive a lot.

Sam broke into her thoughts. "Let me introduce you to everybody." After they had walked over, he continued. "Chief Deffler, you already know."

"Ma'am," Deffler said.

"Lieutenant Haley Reardon, this is Trudy Drake, the long-suffering spouse of our beloved chief of the boat," Sam said.

"Don't get me started," Trudy joked as she shook hands with Haley.

"I'm pleased to meet you," Haley said.

"And this lovely lady is Ben's friend Victoria Carpenter," Sam said.

"How do you do?" Haley said, extending her hand.

Victoria took her hand and said, "I am doing quite well, thank you, Miss Reardon. I am pleased to meet you."

Haley wasn't sure what surprised her more, the formal language or the deep husky voice coming from such a slight young woman. "Um, likewise," she said awkwardly.

"And, of course, my wife, Joana. This is Haley Reardon," Sam said.

"Haley, I don't know how to thank you for prying Sam loose for us," Joana said with a warm smile as she shook hands.

"Happy to take the hit for the team, Joana," Haley replied, drawing a puzzled look from Victoria and chuckles from everyone else.

The small talk continued until Lopez appeared in the doorway and hurried over to them. "Sirs, ma'am, Captain Mercier is coming through the gate now." Mercier would officiate the ceremony today, and the three officers were expected to greet her on her arrival.

"Thanks, Lope," Sam said, then turned to the others. "Folks, please excuse Haley, Ben, and me. We've got some eagle-stroking to do."

"Carry on, my brave captain," Joana said with a grin.

As the three officers followed Lopez out toward the parking lot, Haley felt her first pang of dread at the thought of encountering Mercier. They had had no occasion to speak since their last meeting, which ended with Mercier upbraiding her for being a smartass. *If she held a grudge, I wouldn't be here now. Right?* Haley thought, hopefully. A car pulled up, and Mercier and a lieutenant stepped out.

Mercier and the young officer returned Sam, Ben, and Haley's salutes as they walked up, and Mercier held out her hand to Sam. "Congratulations, Sam. How are you feeling this fine day?" she asked as she shook Sam's hand.

"Too many emotions to list, Captain," Sam replied.

"Yes, I know. It's always that way." She turned to shake Haley's hand. "Haley, last call to duck and run."

"Not a chance in Hell, ma'am," Haley replied with a smile. *OK, we're through that.*

Mercier turned and shook Ben's hand. "What do you say, Ben? Think you can get through the ceremony without getting banged up?"

Ben smiled and replied, "As long as your companion is not a closet DIA guy, I should be safe, ma'am."

Mercier chuckled and turned to the lieutenant. "Doug, you're not moonlighting with the DIA, are you?"

"I wouldn't dream of it, Captain."

"That's a relief. Everyone, this is Doug Liggett. He had the misfortune of not having enough work on his plate back home, so he gets to carry the box and listen to me trash talk ship drivers for three hours each way." After introductions and handshakes, she continued. "Doug, I'm sure Ben would like to get back at it, and he can show you where to put the stuff."

"Yes, ma'am," Liggett replied as he opened the car's boot. He handed Mercier her sword, hung his own on his belt, and grabbed a small cardboard box before closing the lid.

"Sam, Haley, how about you take me on a quick walkabout on the boat so I can impart some senior officer-type wisdom on you," Mercier said as she hung her sword on her belt.

"After you, ma'am," Sam said as they turned and began walking toward *Kauai.*

After crossing the parking lot out of earshot, Mercier said, "So, Sam, psyched for the move to Newport?"

"Not for the move, ma'am," Sam replied. "They seem to get harder every time, and I am trying to get my head in the frame for classes and paper writing after a fifteen-year hiatus. Jo is walking on air, though—her folks live only an hour away in Gales Ferry."

"Yes, well, you've both earned a breather after the last few years. Isn't Newport near your family as well?"

"Um, yes, ma'am. Enough said."

"Oh, sorry."

They reached the quarterdeck, exchanged salutes with the seaman on duty, went on board, and then up to the Bridge.

Mercier sat in the captain's chair, then gestured to the seats at the FC3 console. After the two junior officers sat, she said. "It looks like something's brewing regarding the laptop Ben looted from that smuggling ship. We got a warning order from the National Command Authority to put *Kauai* in readiness for an operation sometime in the next two weeks."

"What sort of operation, ma'am?" Sam asked.

"Unknown. The good news for you, Haley, is that you will not be headed to the Windward for migrant interdiction for a while. We need to keep you close."

"Does that mean we don't sail tomorrow, ma'am?" Haley asked.

"No, we'll put you to good use on the Bimini run. As you might imagine, things have picked up there since we've thrown nearly everything we have at mass migration out of Haiti. This op might come to nothing; if I had a dollar for every WARNO that got canceled, I could retire in splendor right now. But we need to go through the motions—cancel leaves and defer maintenance availabilities, yadda, yadda."

"Yes, ma'am," Haley said.

"I'll bet you're relieved you don't have to deal with another DIA-sponsored op, Sam."

"Again, ma'am, mixed emotions," Sam replied with a rueful smile.

Mercier glanced at her watch and said, "I guess we should get back before Ben and Doug melt down." She stood and said, "You two go ahead. Just be ready to catch me if I trip over this damn sword going down the ladder."

****

The trio broke up to mingle among the guests as they approached the venue. Haley saw her father standing in a dark three-piece suit chatting with one of the other guests and hastened to him. Bradford Reardon was a tall man, six-foot-one, lean with a full head of sandy, close-cropped hair, graying on his temples. He grinned as soon as he saw her, and they hugged warmly, and Haley kissed him on his cheek.

"You look wonderful, sweetie," Reardon said as he held her at arm's length and looked her over. "I am so proud of you."

"Thanks, Dad," Haley said, trying not to tear up. "It means everything to have you here." She looked around and asked, "Where's Margot?"

"She's inside arranging dinner."

"Yes, I'm sure it's quite a challenge to find one exclusive enough this side of the Hudson." The quip came out involuntarily, as if Haley had heard it spoken by another person. Her regret was instant, and the change in her father's expression from beaming to sad was the worst rebuke imaginable.

"That's a little uncalled for. You know she didn't have to come, but she wanted to, for you."

Actually, I think it was for you, not me, but that earns her just as much credit. "I know. I'm sorry, Dad. No more bitchiness today, I promise. Can I get a reset?"

"Sure." His proud smile returned, and he looked and nodded toward *Kauai.* "Your first command. She's a beauty! Can you show us around?"

"Let's do it after the ceremony, when we have more time. Besides, I want to be able to describe her as *my* ship!"

"Fair enough." They both turned as Margot Reardon arrived. She was Haley's height and still strikingly attractive, with graying brown hair and hazel eyes. Her stride and dark purple blouse and skirt radiated power. "Everything set, my dear?" Reardon asked.

"It took time, but I found a suitable place in Orlando," Margot answered, then turned and gave Haley an approving nod. "You look magnificent, dear!" After glancing at her uniform, she added, "A little late for white, isn't it?"

Haley grinned in return. "Perhaps, but it's Florida, Margot, not Rhode Island. The seasons are different here."

"Yes, I suppose they are." She looked around. "This is very...quaint. Will we have any role in the ceremony?"

"No, you get to sit back and enjoy it. Even my role is limited— the ceremony is mostly a celebration of the previous command."

"Oh, I see," Margot said with slight disappointment.

Haley glanced over at the stage and caught Ben's attention, motioning him over. As he stepped up, Haley said, "Dad, Margot, I'd like you to meet Lieutenant Junior Grade Ben Wyporek, Executive Officer, who will be my second in command. Ben, these are my parents, Bradford and Margot Reardon."

"Ma'am, Sir, I'm very pleased to meet you," Ben said as he shook their hands. He then said to Haley, "We're set to begin in two minutes, ma'am."

"Thanks, Ben. Carry on, please."

"Ma'am," Ben said, then spun on his heel and trudged off to the next crisis.

Haley turned back to see her father's smile had been replaced by a look of concern. "That young man, Haley. He was wearing the Silver Star and Purple Heart. Did he earn those on *Kauai*?"

Haley was stunned that Reardon recognized the medals, more so that he appeared to know what they implied. "Um, yes, he did." She gave him a look that said, "We can talk about that later."

As Reardon nodded, Margot piped up, "Don't worry, Bradford, I'm sure Haley will have just as many medals before long!"

The accidental humor of the well-intentioned comment struck both Haley and her father, and both smiled. "Thank you, Margot," Haley said. "I appreciate your confidence."

"Not at all, dear." Margot looked approvingly at them.

"Let me get you seated," Haley said, then led them to two folding chairs in the front row before the stage. "Please have a seat, and I'll see you again after the ceremony." Her father squeezed her upper arm, and then he and Margot sat. Haley turned, stepped up on the stage, and stood next to the chair on which she was to sit. *Kauai*'s crew was already standing in ranks next to the stage, and Sam gave Joana a last kiss, then stood beside Haley.

The ceremony began with the formal arrival of Mercier, then the presentation of colors—the honor guard parading the National and Coast Guard flags before the assembly and then off to one side. Ben narrated the purpose of the change of command ceremony and a brief history of Sam's tenure. Mercier presented the Coast Guard Unit Commendation jointly to Sam and Seaman Apprentice Nichols, the most junior crew member.

Next, Drake stepped forward and presented Sam with *Kauai*'s commissioning pennant. When Sam made to return to the stage, Drake said, "But wait, there's more." Joana was invited onto the stage, and Drake and Hopkins presented her with a small round mahogany navigator's box with an inlaid compass. Joana was reduced to tears and hugged the box to her chest after reading the inscription aloud: "To Our First Lady, Love Now and Always,

Your Crew of *Kauai.*" After Joana returned to her seat, Drake and Bondurant presented Sam with a beautifully framed collage of photos of each crew member during a funny moment. Sam was blinking back tears himself as he returned to his seat carrying the picture.

Sam's personal award came next—the Meritorious Service Medal pinned on by Mercier, with Ben reading the citation. His ceremonial "frocking" to lieutenant commander followed—he would not actually be promoted and paid until the summer, but could wear the insignia and be addressed by the higher rank. Per Sam's request, Ben and Joana stepped onto the stage, and each replaced one of his two-stripe lieutenant shoulder boards with a new one having the two-and-a-half stripes of his new rank.

It was time for Sam's farewell speech. He had carried some papers Haley guessed held his prepared speech, but instead folded them up and placed them in his pocket. He then held the picture Drake and Bondurant presented and talked briefly about each crew member and the story behind their photos. It was a profoundly moving and personal tribute to his crew, and Haley was close to tears for the second time that day.

The big moment had come, the formal handover of command. Haley, Sam, and Mercier stood. Haley faced Sam, saluted, and said loudly, "Lieutenant Commander Powell, I offer my relief."

Sam saluted and replied loudly, "Lieutenant Reardon, I stand relieved." He grinned, shook Haley's hand warmly, and said quietly, "Congratulations, Captain!"

"Thank you, sir," Haley replied with scarcely concealed excitement. As Sam returned to his seat, Haley stepped over to the microphone. It was her chance to make a speech, but it was good form for the incoming CO to keep it short, and Haley intended to do just that.

"I want to thank you all for coming today, particularly my parents, who have made this wonderful day perfect for me by their attendance. I also want to thank Captain Mercier for her officiation today and for the trust she and Admiral Pennington have shown in selecting me for this command. Last but certainly not least, I would like to thank Commander Powell for his outstanding leadership and attention to duty that have made *Kauai* and her crew the finest unit in the Coast Guard. No one could improve upon his eloquent expression of the crew's quality, and I can only endorse it with admiration. This is the proudest day of my life, and I will do my utmost to live up to the outstanding legacy of Commander Powell and *Kauai*." Haley turned to face Ben. "Executive Officer, all standing orders remain in effect until further notice. Dismiss the company at the conclusion of the ceremony."

Ben saluted and loudly replied, "Aye, aye, ma'am!"

The ceremony concluded after the formal retiring of the colors. After shaking hands with Sam and Mercier, Haley stepped off the stage to meet with her father and Margot. Reardon's beaming expression had returned, and he said, "Congratulations, *Captain*! What a day!"

Even Margot was red-eyed with the emotion of the event. "I have to admit the ceremony and the stories the commander told were quite inspirational. I think I begin to see what you find so compelling about all this, dear."

Margot's comment genuinely moved Haley. "Thank you, Margot." She said, "I know you would like to see the ship, but we need to attend the reception inside for a bit of schmoozing first."

Margot grinned. "Schmoozing is my strong suit, dear. Lead the way."

****

After an hour into the reception held in the station's dayroom, Mercier bade everyone farewell, and she and Liggett departed. It was the signal to wind down the reception, and as the crew and other guests filtered out, Haley bade farewell to Sam and Joana, then went to gather her parents. She was surprised to find Margot in a deep conversation with Victoria, with Reardon and Ben looking on. "Ben, Victoria, I hope you will excuse me, but I promised my parents a tour of the boat."

"Yes, ma'am," Ben said. "Will you be needing me to accompany you, or would you prefer I waited here?"

Haley blinked. *Duh! They're all standing around waiting for me to grant liberty. Pull your head out of your ass, Haley!* "Neither, XO. Please grant normal liberty. And by that, I mean you too. Beat feet, and I'll see you tomorrow."

"Very good, ma'am, and thank you," Ben said. He turned to Victoria. "Ready to go?"

"Yes, Benjamin. Mr. and Mrs. Reardon, it has been a distinct pleasure talking with you. I hope to do so again soon."

"Same here, Victoria. Good luck with your coding project," Margot said with a warm smile. After they had walked out of earshot, she turned to Haley and said, "What an extraordinarily charming young woman! I can see why your second is so taken with her."

Haley continued to be surprised by Margot's geniality toward everything going on. *Maybe we* have *turned a corner here.* "Yes, I haven't talked to her myself, but she seems to have many fans. Shall we go now?"

"That would be fine. Will I be alright in these clothes?"

Haley hadn't even thought about that. "I wouldn't recommend going down into the engine room in those spike heels, but we should be OK everywhere else."

The tour was an eye-opener for Margot and her father, particularly her cabin, which, while the largest berthing space on the boat, was less than half the size of Margot's closet back in Newport. "Oh, Haley, you are expected to *live* here?" Margot asked in wonderment.

"Only when we are underway, Margot. Remember, *Kauai* is a patrol boat, not a large ship—space is at a premium here."

"Heavens!" Margot exclaimed, shaking her head.

As they completed the tour, Margot said to Reardon, "Will you excuse me while I make a few calls, dear? There are some things back home I need to see to."

"Yes, of course. I'll follow you soon."

Margot turned to Haley. "We'll see you for dinner, dear? I have a wonderful spot picked out."

"I am looking forward to it, Margot," Haley said.

After Margot had walked off, Haley turned to her father. "OK, Dad. What did you put in her coffee this morning?"

"I told you things have changed. She really was impressed by everything today."

"Well, it makes me feel even worse about my snotty comment earlier, but I'll take it."

"Glad to hear it." His smile faded. "Now, I think you owe me some honesty about what you will be doing here."

"I'm sorry, Dad. I would have shared more with you had I known you knew anything about this. Frankly, it comes as a surprise."

"What, you think I'm some sort of lefty brahmin? Maybe I was, but that changed when my little girl went into the service. Did you think I wouldn't learn all I could about your life? If you become a parent, you'll learn that you can't just send your kid off to college and not worry about them anymore. Now come clean—your XO and your predecessor have combat medals. Even I know that differs from the run-of-the-mill Coast Guard stuff you have been doing."

"Dad, the details are classified, but there is more to *Kauai* than meets the eye. I'm sorry, I can't elaborate, but what we do is vital."

He sighed. "And I thought I couldn't be prouder of you—wrong again. I hate employing such a cliché, but you will be careful, for me?" Although he did his best to conceal it with a forced smile, Haley could feel the concern in his voice.

"Dad, I will do my very best to take care of my crew and my ship." Haley smiled. "That covers me by default. Please don't worry about me."

"Sorry, can't comply. It's in the job description. But I guess I'll learn to live with it." He hugged her again.

"Alright, alright. Let's get back to the cars before I get weepy," Haley said. "I need to get back to the apartment and change before heading out on the town with you two."

Evolutions

Scotts on Fifth Restaurant, 141 5th Ave, Indialantic, Florida 19:13 EST, 1 December

Victoria

Victoria was troubled, even though they were sitting in this lovely little restaurant and eating some of the most delicious food she had ever tasted. They had a small two-person table in a relatively quiet corner of the dining room, next to the wall decorated with photos of some of the more famous people who had dined there. Although it was crowded, Victoria's agoraphobia was mostly dormant, overcome by the positive diversions around her. And yet something was going on with Benjamin, and she was frustrated by her inability to read him.

After the change of command event, Benjamin suggested they go out for a nice dinner. Victoria welcomed the distraction—the ceremony, moving as it was, was another step toward the transition of Joana out of her life. They had grown close over the past six months, and although they did not see each other every day, the thought that Joana was nearby was a great comfort to Victoria, particularly when Benjamin was at sea. She worried about how the loss would affect her, much as Benjamin was over the departure of the man who had become his best friend over the last two years. Victoria was grateful Benjamin recognized the need to step out of their routine, especially when he would head to sea again on *Kauai* the next day.

Benjamin had requested she wear the green dress she had worn on their first date but that she need not bother putting her hair up as on the earlier occasion. She reminded Benjamin this was a "hair up" dress, according to her friend Debbie. Like his uniform, it was essential to have things in proper order. He had smiled, raised his hands in mock surrender, and said, "I'll never resist a lady doing extra for me." She knew he liked the look and didn't mind the extra work it took. Still, something was off in Benjamin's unusually solicitous behavior—he was always thoughtful and accommodating of her unique needs, but this increased level usually preceded bad news.

She and Benjamin had had, what was for them, a fight after he returned from his last patrol. Victoria had been appalled by the risk he took that nearly killed him and told him as much. She was not buying the excuse that he sought justice for the women they rescued. Victoria knew from her DIA days the 252s had enslaved scores of women before these and were sure to enslave many more afterward—his sacrifice would make no difference. Then she foolishly demanded a promise that he not take any more chances with his life.

Benjamin was contrite—he admitted he had miscalculated the level of danger—but reminded her that his job entailed some risks. He could not make that promise. As they did with all their disagreements, they talked it out, then went to sleep in each other's arms. But Victoria feared Benjamin might rethink their relationship as a result.

Victoria was finishing her meal of Orange Ginger Salmon, baked potato, and sauteed zucchini served, she was delighted to see, on separate plates. She knew her need to keep her food separated was an irrational obsession, but she could not help it: the food items tasted better when they were not touching each other. Victoria observed that Benjamin's meal and everyone else's she could see in the restaurant was served on a single plate—he must have discreetly insisted her meal be served this way, perhaps even paid extra to make it so. She loved him even more for his cheerful acceptance of this and her other compulsions, but was worried compassion fatigue might appear at some point. This worry was magnified tonight, as Benjamin had repeatedly been lost in thought.

Their dinner plates had been removed, and they were enjoying an excellent dessert wine when Victoria finally decided to press the issue. "Benjamin, you seem distracted tonight. Is there something wrong?"

Benjamin smiled and said, "You are getting better at reading my moods, Victoria. I'm sorry. I was just working myself up for this. We have been living together for almost six months without a firm commitment. I know you did that to spare me from what you thought were personal quirks that I couldn't tolerate. At the same time, I know I put you through a great deal of uncertainty and worry about my job. I guess the change of command finally brought everything into focus, and, as much as I love you and treasure what we have, I need something more."

Victoria felt faint. *No! No, no, no! He is leaving me! That is what all this is about—he is trying to let me down easy.* She took a deep breath to calm herself, then asked, "Benjamin, are you breaking up with me?"

Benjamin's eyes widened in surprise, and he said, too loudly, "*What?*" He looked around self-consciously, then leaned forward and whispered, "My God! No, Victoria!" Then, he scrambled to his feet, came around the table, kneeled, and took her right hand in his left. "I know you set a condition that I would not ask for six months, and it won't be six months until next week, but we will probably be underway next week. You might say no, I hope not, but I could not wait any longer than necessary, and I needed to do this in person, not over the phone." He shook his head as if to clear it, then gave her a pleading look. "I'm screwing up the moment here, sorry. What I am saying is I love you, Victoria, and everything about you. I can't imagine being apart from you. Would you please consider marrying me?"

Victoria put her left hand to her mouth and gasped in shock. Her mind tumbled as it went between the extremes of emotion. She felt like she was about to cry and could only open, then close her mouth, saying nothing. Benjamin's expression became more desperate.

"Victoria, I realize this is a surprise. If you would like time to consider it, I'll understand."

No, I do not need time to consider it! I have been dreaming of this moment since we moved in together. What is wrong with me?! "No, Benjamin."

"No?" Benjamin asked, his face falling.

Oh no! He thinks I am turning down his proposal. "No, no, no! I mean, I do not need more time!" She took another deep breath before continuing. "Yes, yes, yes! Of course I will marry you, Benjamin!"

Benjamin's face flashed relief, and then he kissed her hand. He reached into his blazer pocket, brought out a black velvet ring box, and opened it to her, revealing a white gold ring with a pear-shaped emerald in a diamond halo setting. "I guess I should have had this out from the beginning, but I was worried it might put on too much pressure."

Victoria's eyes were fogging with tears that she blinked away quickly as she offered Benjamin her left hand. Now everything made sense: the subtle questions a few weeks ago on which gemstones she favored, his request for her to wear the green dress, and the quiet, romantic restaurant. He had cleverly created her most perfect vision of a marriage proposal. They had both comically blundered through the communication phase, making it even more special. She gazed at the gorgeous ring as Benjamin slipped it on her finger, then held it close to her heart. Only then did she notice the entire restaurant had fallen silent, and all the other diners were staring at them.

She saw Benjamin, still kneeling and smiling at her. She tilted her head toward the others, and Benjamin turned, noticing that they were the center of attention for the first time. Continuing to hold her right hand, he lifted his left hand over his head with a "thumbs-up" and shouted, "She said yes!"

Victoria jumped in her seat as the restaurant erupted in applause and cheers. Normally, she would have been frozen in terror to be the center of attention of so many strangers. Instead, she stood and pulled Benjamin into a long, passionate kiss. She knew she would be safe with Benjamin for the rest of her life, and the noise and attention accompanying this moment seemed to be just about right.

Twenty minutes later, Victoria was still catching her breath. Several other couples had come to their table to congratulate them. Chef Scott himself came out from the kitchen in his cordon bleu uniform to wish them well hand consented to a photo of the three of them the server took with Ben's phone. When they sat at the table again, Victoria held out her arm to gaze at her beautiful ring. "It is so wonderful, Benjamin. Everything you did was so perfect!"

"Everything but the comms." Ben looked guilty. "It's amazing that after researching to find the most romantic restaurant in Brevard County and all the other preparations, as soon as I opened my mouth, I convinced you I was giving you the heave-ho. Are you sure you still want to marry me?"

"Considering I have been dreaming of this moment for months, and my first response convinced *you* I was declining your proposal, I suggest we both have work to do."

"Well, Victoria, we'd better get on it. We only have the rest of our lives to get it fixed."

"I have every confidence we will succeed, my love!"

****

Victoria lay next to Benjamin, tucked under his arm with her head on his chest as he slept. She listened to his slow and rhythmic heartbeat as her head lifted and fell with his breathing. She had been far too excited to sleep, but Benjamin had to report early in the morning for another patrol. He had been game to stay up with her, but Victoria did not want him to start another fatiguing patrol with a sleep deficit. She used a massaging technique she had researched, which, along with the wine from the dinner and the glass they shared on their return, put Benjamin to sleep.

They hardly talked after their return, just cuddled on the couch for an hour as Victoria admired the new ring on her finger. Although it was a simple design, she was captivated by the shape of the stone and its exquisite green color. As a rule, she did not wear jewelry other than a simple gold-inlaid pearl pendant her sister Julie had given her as a birthday present just before she died. She now had two treasures.

They had shared the news with Joana and Sam by phone on the way home from the restaurant. Both were ecstatic, and Victoria agreed to have dinner with them the following night to give Joana a chance to see the ring and talk about the future. After the call, she and Benjamin had a brief discussion, agreeing at once to ask Sam and Joana to stand as best man and matron of honor at their wedding. Victoria would ask them tomorrow.

There was much to plan and set up—at least Joana would be there at first to help her get started. Then there was communicating the news and sending out the invitations. *I have not even met Benjamin's parents yet. What will they think of me?* The thought they might disapprove disturbed her, and she turned her head slowly to look at Benjamin's face. He was sleeping soundly with a slight smile. It brought back the memory of when he was still in the hospital and, unsure of his future, asked her to reconsider her commitment to him. When she made it clear that would never happen, he had teased her that she was foolish, but they would figure things out somehow. *And here we are, dearest man! We will figure it out somehow, as we always do.*

Victoria nuzzled Benjamin's chest, careful not to wake him. She knew she would miss him while he was away, now more than ever. And the ever-present worry for his safety would be there as well. But that lingering background of fear that somehow she and Benjamin would not work out was gone. The happiness she had known for the past year would continue forever. It was with that sweet thought that Victoria finally fell asleep soon afterward.

USCG Cutter *Kauai*, moored, USCG Station, Port Canaveral, Florida
10:23 EST, 2 December

Ben

Ben was finished with the pre-patrol preparations. The crew was on board and hard at work, the fuel and water stores had been topped off, the container holding the squid projector had been moved from the storage building to the foredeck, and various systems were spooled up and tested. Haley requested a meeting with Ben and the two chiefs before setting the special sea detail and mooring stations. She had not told Ben the purpose, but he suspected it was to lay down the ground rules for the new command.

Ben was still riding high from the events of the previous night. He had been genuinely afraid that Victoria would have reservations about getting engaged, based on how upset she was about his last adventure with the *Miho Dujam*. His heart almost stopped when he mistook her no about not needing more time for a no to the engagement. His relief and joy were palpable, and the commitment, for some strange reason, made him less sad about leaving her for this patrol. There was no actual change in things, yet he felt a confidence in his future that before had been absent.

There was a knock, and Ben turned to see Drake and Hopkins standing in his doorway. "Ready for the big meeting, XO?" Drake asked.

"Damn straight. Let's get it done," Ben replied.

As they stepped over to the captain's cabin, Hopkins said, "You look like you just won the lottery, XO. What gives?"

"Big news. I'll share it when I get an opening," Ben replied as he knocked on the door.

"Yes?" Haley's voice called.

Ben opened the door and stuck in his head. "COB, Chief, and I are here as you requested, Captain."

"Excellent! Please come in and take a seat, as best you all can, anyway."

The three filed in, Ben grabbed the spare chair, and the two chiefs sat on Haley's bunk. Once they were all situated, Haley continued. "I wanted to get together to go over a few things before getting underway. First off, I'll repeat that it is an honor for me, and I'm super excited to be here. Considering where you all started, you have done a magnificent job, and you should be proud of everything you have achieved. We have all talked before, so you know my history and where I am in the power curve. I know I still have some learning to do, so if any of you see something you think might be a problem, you give me a nudge.

"By and large, I really like how everything is running here. I only have a couple of changes in mind. Chief, I want to get back on the Bridge to sharpen the edge a bit. I'd like to take the midwatch as OOD for this first patrol. Can you make that happen?

"Certainly, Captain," Hopkins replied.

"OK. The second thing might sting a little. I want us to tighten things concerning decorum. While I get why Commander Powell was a little looser, given the relief for cause and all, I am confident that everyone here is beyond that, and we can switch to a more conventional approach."

"Ma'am, can I ask you to specify what you mean by decorum, please?" Ben asked.

"Yes. No more first names when on duty, and we need to avoid unnecessary physical contact between the officers and enlisted. By that, I mean the occasional handshake is fine, and obviously, if someone needs help, you do what you need to do, but the other stuff is out. In particular, XO, I can't have officers hugging enlisted members under any circumstances."

Ben felt like he had just been punched in the stomach, but maintained a neutral expression. "Understood, ma'am. It won't happen again."

"Captain, I don't know what you heard, but I hugged Mr. Wyporek, not the other way around," Hopkins interrupted.

"Chief, I'm sure Mr. Wyporek doesn't need a translator," Haley said coolly.

"No, ma'am," Hopkins said equally coolly.

"Good. Now that's settled, how do we look to get underway, Chief Hopkins?"

"FC3 is warmed up with all codes loaded. The main gyro is spun up, and all sensors are checked and correct. Operations is ready for sea, Captain."

"Very well. Chief Drake?"

"Fully topped off with fuel and water, all main diesels blown down with the lube warmed up, ready for start and power grid cutover any time. Engineering ready for sea, Captain."

"Very well. XO?"

"All personnel on board. Full load of ammunition for the main gun, the fifties, and small arms. Squid projector is on board and ready for mounting. All lines singled-up. Deck, Weapons, and Ship ready for sea, Captain."

"Very well." She glanced at her desk clock. "Let's set the special sea detail in fifteen minutes. Questions?"

"No, ma'am," Ben replied.

"Thank you," Haley said and nodded.

Ben and the two chiefs stood and filed out the door. Once it was shut, Hopkins nodded toward the messdeck, and they turned and silently followed her there. Once out of earshot of the cabin, she turned to Ben and said, "I am so sorry, sir!"

"No harm done, Chief." Ben nodded. "I'm still on the Lieutenants List. This will take getting used to, for me, anyway. If I slip up, please give me a nudge, or throw something at me as needed."

"Will do, sir." Hopkins smiled warmly. "Oh, what is your big news?"

"Victoria and I got engaged last night."

"That's fantastic!" Hopkins took a step forward with her arms out, then stopped and dropped them to her sides. She held out her right hand and said, "Congratulations, sir."

Ben shook her hand and said, "Thank you, Chief."

Drake offered his hand. "That's wonderful news, sir. Congratulations!"

Ben shook his hand. "Thanks, COB. I guess we should go get'r done. Gotta send one last FIM, then I'll head out."

"FIM, sir?" Hopkins asked.

"Fiancée IM." Ben grinned.

"Oh, how the mighty have fallen!" Drake quipped as he turned to leave.

"See you on the Bridge, sir," Hopkins said.

"See you in a few," Ben said as he headed for his stateroom.

Haley

Haley looked at her hands folded in her lap. *Well, that sucked.* She had gone back and forth in her mind as to the best way to carry out the change and decided that ripping off the bandage would be the least painful. She knew Ben was an honorable man who probably never realized he was even giving all those back pats and arm squeezes or how an unscrupulous person could use that against him. *He just doesn't think like that.* Haley smiled. *I bet he's also a lousy poker player—he looked like I had slapped him when I gave him the hugging proscription.*

She was sure Ben would recover quickly and not show any effects in the meantime. Hopkins was a different story. Haley was caught off-guard by Hopkins's leap to Ben's defense, and her response to that had been unartful, to say the least. *Now Hopkins is madder than Hell at me. Sam was right: she does have a mother thing for Ben.* Haley shook her head sadly. *At least I don't have to worry about hugging anymore—she'd die before she put Ben on the spot again for that. I have to find a way to reach common ground with her.*

Haley looked around the cabin, which was stark except for a plaque with the ship's crest mounted on the wall opposite her small desk. She thought of decorations for the room. She had a picture of her and her father that she treasured, but she would never hang it in public view—it would be too weird. Margot had offered to help decorate the cabin when they were eating dinner last night. It was a kind offer, and Haley was tempted to accept, if for no other reason than to continue their sudden rapprochement. But chances were that Margot would find something proper for a cottage at the shore, but unacceptable for the CO's quarters on a warship. Haley did not want the risk of having to reject the suggestions and set their relationship back.

As the pipe to set the special sea detail came over the 1MC, Haley stood, grabbed her ball cap, brand new with a small "CO" embroidered with yellow thread above the back strap, and headed out toward the Bridge. The thought of Mercier's reaction if she heard of Haley and Margot "girly-ing up" the cabin brought an amused smile. Fortunately, she could be sure Drake and Hopkins would convey via the Chiefs-Net that it was quite the reverse—a true SOB had taken command of *Kauai*.

One of Our Own

**USCG Cutter *Kauai*, Atlantic Ocean, twenty-three nautical miles east-southeast of Hollywood, Florida
01:14 EST, 3 December**

Haley

Kauai idled at her picket position, halfway between the Florida coast and the Bimini Islands. It was a high-tempo operation, and Haley was on the Bridge, standing a regular one-in-three OOD watch rotation with Ben and Hopkins, allowing Bondurant and Lee to rest when they were not involved in boardings. Haley supposed she would eventually tire of watchstanding and settle into the more traditional CO role of being on call, but not now. She was delighted to be back on the Bridge, conning the boat on this beautiful cool, calm night. There was no moon, only the stars and the soft yellow glow of the Miami-Fort Lauderdale-West Palm Beach metroplex stretching across the western horizon.

It had started as a coordinated multi-unit interdiction operation designed to counter the increased fast-boat traffic between Bimini and the Florida coast. Smuggling gangs assumed a weakness in the Coast Guard coverage of the eastern approaches to Florida's Atlantic coast because of the ongoing Haitian migrant surge operation. They were taking advantage of this by pushing through more shipments of drugs and people by go-fast boats across the forty-five-mile strait between Miami and Bimini.

This assumption was in error. Operations south of the Bahamas *were* absorbing a considerable amount of the larger cutter resources. However, the patrol boats and the speedy response boats at the individual Coast Guard stations were still present and available. The challenge lay in the eighty nautical miles of vulnerable coastline between Homestead and West Palm Beach; almost any point could be used to land an illicit cargo of contraband or illegal entrants.

Among the tactics in use this night was the classic "Hounds-to-Hunters" funnel operation, oriented east to west. Two patrol boats anchored the top of the funnel on the northern and southern ends, acting decidedly un-stealthy in their operations, liberally using radios and lighting to make their presence known. Unladen scout boats sent by the smuggling organizations to reveal the positions of the Coast Guard patrols—places to be avoided during the actual smuggling runs—did their jobs. The locations of the two patrol boats were noted, as was the large coverage gap between them, and passed along to the coordinators who fed the routes to smuggling craft. Smugglers could scurry through the gaps without being detected for a quick run to shore, drop off the load, and make a carefree return to the east.

They did not know that five Coast Guard response boats were concentrated at the western end of the funnel, close enough together to be mutually supporting and well-covered from the air. The smuggling boats were faster than the patrol boats but slower and less maneuverable than the response boats. Those smugglers not stopped and apprehended would dump their loads in an attempt to escape. Either outcome counted as an interdiction, a win for law enforcement, although arrests and prosecution were preferred.

The smugglers knew there was a significant element of risk associated with the trade and losses of cargo. Even the loss of the occasional boat and crew was considered acceptable—part of the cost of doing business passed on to the customers. On the rare occasions they were found, the crew's modus operandi was simple: evade capture if practicable and submit to arrest without resistance otherwise. There was no advantage to fighting back, as the charges, if they could even be proven, were usually pled down to brief incarceration, provided resisting arrest was not included. If you fought back, the gloves came off and the prospect of hard prison time or being killed outright became a genuine possibility. Everyone understood that as long as this "gentleman's agreement" held, short-term consequences were mild and long-term prospects were unaffected.

On this night, someone did not get the memo.

A thirty-five-foot open panga with three outboard engines and a cargo of baled cocaine had launched from a boat landing in Alice Town on North Bimini, heading for a drop-off on Key Biscayne. The operators had been fed the latest intel on their Coast Guard opposition: two patrol boats separated so that only a slight course change was needed to evade them. Besides the usual three crew, a heavily armed drug gang member rode along to ensure delivery. This was not the standard procedure; customer ridealongs increased the risks if they were stopped, but the gang indulged no arguments.

The crew followed the planned track to evade the patrol boats, using GPS for navigation and keeping a moderate speed of twenty knots to conserve fuel. They breathed a sigh of relief upon clearing through the picket line and made a slight course change to the south.

Unbeknownst to the crew, they had been picked up by a U.S. Customs and Border Patrol long-range patrol aircraft shortly after they cleared Henry Bank and tracked throughout their journey. Based on the plane's information, one of the response boats from Coast Guard Station Miami Beach closed to intercept within territorial waters. It should have been easy: light up the target, and they either surrender or run. Everyone knew the rules; everyone but the gang member.

When the response boat's spotlight flooded over the panga, the gang member panicked and opened fire with his AK-47 on full automatic, wounding a coastguardsman and drawing return fire from the boat's 0.30 caliber machine gun. The panga's master, convinced they were about to be gunned down in a vicious crossfire, gunned the throttles to ram the stern of the response boat, hopefully crippling it enough to enable an escape. He smashed one of the boat's outboard engines, taking it out of the fight, but in doing so, the wounded crewman was thrown overboard and struck and killed by one of the panga's propellers.

Word went out instantly. The crew of the fleeing panga had attacked a Coast Guard boat with gunfire and ramming and had murdered a coastguardsman. The customs plane stuck to the boat like glue now, constantly relaying position, course, and speed to the other units on the net as the panga fled to the northeast. A Coastie had been murdered, one of their own, and all law enforcement in the area was determined to make sure this night did not end well for the panga crew.

Onboard *Kauai*, Haley had completed a round with the binoculars when the alert was received. Bunting had the FC3 watch and took the initial call from LE chat. "Emergency message, Captain," the young petty officer said.

Haley stepped over and read the chat message. "OK, Bunting, fire up all systems." She stepped over to the 1MC box and grabbed the microphone. "Now set Law Enforcement Condition One-Alpha, repeat set Law Enforcement Condition One-Alpha." She then pressed the buzzer used on *Kauai* for a law enforcement alert. Condition One-Alpha was law enforcement, where the suspects were considered armed and dangerous. It was essentially the same as General Quarters Condition One in terms of manning and equipment, but the law enforcement use-of-force continuum was still in play. *Kauai* could not engage a target with deadly force unless fired on or granted a statement of no objection from the command center.

Ben was on the Bridge within two minutes, followed by Hopkins and Williams, all grabbing body armor vests and helmets. Williams sat in the center seat of the console while Ben and Hopkins looked at the radar picture and the chat traffic. After a minute, they shared a grim glance, stepped over to Haley, and saluted.

Haley returned the salute and said, "You've seen the board. Do you have any questions about the situation?"

"No, Captain," they both replied.

"Alright. Coast Guard 28167 reported one shooter. We will assume that this is still the case. If it is still the one active shooter, I'll order the sniper to take him out. If it is multiple shooters, we will engage with whichever fifty caliber is unmasked until the gunfire is suppressed and proceed appropriately. Questions?"

"We need to make a general announcement about what is going on, ma'am," Ben replied.

"I intend to. Anything else?"

After both responded with head shakes, Hopkins saluted and said, "Captain, I offer to relieve you of the Deck and Conn."

Haley returned the salute and said, "I stand relieved." She then announced, "On the Bridge, this is the captain. Chief Hopkins has the Deck and Conn!"

After everyone on the Bridge responded with, "Aye!" Haley took the 1MC microphone again. "All hands, this is the captain. A thirty-five-foot panga believed to be carrying narcotics has just fired on and rammed a response boat from Station Miami Beach about twenty-three miles southwest of our current position. One Coast Guard member is confirmed dead. The suspect vessel is now under direct observation, heading zero-eight-eight at twenty-five knots. We will intercept this vessel, stop it, and take all persons onboard into custody. These suspects are considered armed and extremely dangerous.

"I know how you must feel about this. Believe me, I feel the same. Nonetheless, this remains a law enforcement mission, and we will observe the continuum of force rules of engagement. No one is authorized to fire without my direct order." Haley hung up the microphone, walked to the captain's chair, and sat.

Ben said, "All stations manned and ready, Captain. Mounts 51 and 52 are manned with rounds in the chamber. Mount 25 is ready with bore clear and HE in the chute. Overwatch is posted."

"Very well," Haley replied. "Williams, I need a course and time to intercept at twenty-eight knots."

"Aye, Captain," Williams said, typing in the query. After three seconds, he continued. "Recommend course one-eight-three at twenty-eight knots, estimated intercept time twenty-four minutes, ma'am."

"Chief, twenty-eight knots, please. Initial heading is one-eight-three."

"Very good, Captain," Hopkins said as she pushed the thrust levers forward to full speed. "Helm, come right, steer one-eight-three."

"Come right, steer one-eight-three," Pickins, the helmsman, replied. After about ten seconds, he reached the new course and reported, "Chief, steady on one-eight-three."

"Very well. Navigation, are there any contacts with a CPA within two miles?" Even in the pre-dawn hours, this was a heavily trafficked area, and Hopkins's principal responsibility was to keep *Kauai* from colliding with another vessel. Rather than get a series of reports on the dozen-odd targets on the scope, Hopkins requested those with a Closest Point of Approach, CPA, of two miles.

"Negative, Chief," Zuccaro responded. "The nearest CPA on current targets is three-point-eight."

Haley turned to Bunting, who had moved to the left FC3 seat, shifting communications to his screen. "Bunting, report to the command center. We are on an intercept vector for the suspect vessel. Estimate visual contact in thirteen minutes."

"Aye, aye, Captain," Bunting said and then began typing.

Haley turned to Ben. "XO, assuming we stop this target without sinking it, I want you to lead the boarding. Who do you want with you?"

"Bondurant and Lopez, ma'am. Lee on coxswain. Everyone with sidearms and Lopez with a shotgun."

"Agreed. Head down, make your assignments, and brief them. Boarding and deck crew to stay on the messdeck until we call all clear. Get back here as soon as you're done."

"Very good, Captain. By your leave?"

"Go."

Ben turned, stepped to the bridge ladder, and disappeared below.

Haley keyed her headset microphone and said, "Overwatch, Actual."

"Actual, Overwatch. Go ahead, ma'am," Guerrero replied from his sniper position on *Kauai*'s Flying Bridge.

"Overwatch, I don't know how this will play out, so I will give you a conditional. You are weapons tight unless you see someone firing directly at *Kauai*. In that case alone, you are cleared for deadly force on the shooter only. Copy?"

"Copy all, ma'am."

Guerrero was a skilled sniper, trained to hit targets on one moving boat while shooting from another. Sea and weather conditions were ideal, so he could theoretically kill any exposed shooter within seconds, provided the other vessel was not jinking too erratically.

"Alright. Post-shooter now. If needed, can you take out his engines?"

"Should be doable, ma'am, but the time of flight will be critical. I can't promise anything beyond seventy-five yards."

"Understood. I'll do my best to get you inside that."

"Copy, ma'am."

"Mount 51, Actual," Haley said, calling Hebert on the fifty-caliber machine gun on the starboard bridge wing.

"This is Mount 51. Go ahead, ma'am."

"Mount 51, you are weapons tight. Stay low unless you get the order to open up."

"WILCO, ma'am."

"Mount 52, Actual."

"Mount 52, ma'am," replied Fireman Connally, manning the counterpart to Hebert's gun on the port bridge wing.

"Mount 52, same deal for you. Stay low, weapons tight."

"Aye, aye, ma'am."

Haley looked at the bridge clock: 01:29—six minutes before the panga would come over the visual horizon. "Chief, let's darken ship."

"Aye, aye, Captain," Hopkins said. "Bunting, shut down navigation lights."

"Shut down nav lights, aye, Chief." Bunting flipped the switches labeled "Mast," "Side," and "Stern" to off and said, "Lighting off, Chief."

"Very well."

Running at twenty-eight knots without navigation lights was not something done lightly. In the event of a collision, the liability would be substantial, regardless of the other vessel's culpability. But the risk in this situation was negligible, and the gain from not alerting the panga of their presence was considerable.

Zuccaro leaned forward. "Radar contact, two-one-eight, eight-point-six, constant bearing decreasing range. Track position, course, and speed correlate with the suspect vessel, Chief."

"Very well." Hopkins did the math in her head: about forty knots closure, two and a half miles to go. "Williams, train the camera out to zero-three-zero relative. You should see them within three minutes."

"Yes, Chief," Williams said as he slewed the Electro-Optical Infrared camera around to that bearing. The monochrome screen showed the horizon and brightly glowing stars, but nothing else.

Haley leaned forward in her chair, scanning between the sensor/fire-control and navigation panels. *Now the wait. Is there anything I have overlooked?* She turned as Ben arrived beside her. He was decked out for the mission with body armor, a lightweight combat helmet, and an equipment belt with a holstered Sig P229 pistol.

"Deck and boarding parties are ready, Captain," Ben said.

"Thank you, XO. We should have a look at them in about one minute."

"Yes, ma'am."

Haley glanced at him. "Any advice, XO?"

"Ma'am, this is new for all of us. What's your plan?"

"Loop in to parallel him on his quarter at one hundred yards."

"Sounds right, ma'am. Recommend his port quarter. Hebert is steadier, and we'll be masked when we launch the RHIB."

"Good points. We'll do that. Thanks, XO."

"Yes, ma'am. And how do you intend to stop him, assuming we don't end up in a total shootout? I wouldn't plan on using the squid."

"Concur. I'll hit him with the locator light and put a burst over him with the fifty. If he doesn't heave to, I'll turn Guerrero loose on his outboards."

"Recommend you skip the light up and warning shot, ma'am."

Haley sat upright. "That's the protocol."

Ben shook his head. "With respect, ma'am, screw the protocol. Those bastards shouldn't get a reset just because they escaped the first boat they shot up. A warning shot will only tell them to start jinking if they haven't already, or worse, that they have nothing to lose by firing back. Same thing with the light. The engines on those outboards will glow like hot coals in Guerrero's night sight—he doesn't need any light."

Haley sighed. "I hate this, but you're right. We'll do it that way."

Ben nodded sympathetically. "Helluva break-in patrol for you, ma'am."

Haley nodded as she turned back to the panels. "Yea, verily."

Nicholas

Kenton Nicholas was a frightened man. There were three bullet holes in his windscreen from the firefight with the Americans. The closest was just to the right of where he stood at the helm. He had felt that bullet go by as it passed within an inch of him. His younger brother Nathan crouched beside him, staring straight ahead as the boat sped as quickly as possible with the bow partially caved in after the collision with the American.

His deckhand Jayden Wilson was forward, watching the makeshift patch plugging the tear in the hull. At least they had stopped taking on water—the hole in the hull was above the waterline, but gallons of seawater had poured in through the gap every time the bow dipped. The engines screaming at full power should push them at forty knots, but Nicholas would have been surprised if they were even reaching thirty, given the drag from the damage and the hundreds of pounds of seawater sloshing back and forth in the bilges. Fuel was also a worry; they were burning through it fast while traveling at a speed half of what they should be, thanks to that cargo, that damned cargo! Close to a ton of cocaine bales they had failed to deliver. What the hell good was it now? They were running for their lives on a damaged, overloaded boat, yet they could not jettison a ton of deadweight because of *him*.

That La Cantaña cartel monster was standing behind them, his AK-47 in his hands, ready to murder them if they stepped out of line. The man was not afraid, just stood there staring at them with gimlet eyes, his face and shaved head covered with tattoos. He was smoking a cigarette, *smoking*! Their only hope was to make it back to North Bimini without being spotted by aircraft searching for them, and the fool was generating a glow that could be seen for miles! Nicholas had told him to put it out, and the man's only response was to flip the fire selector of his assault rifle off "safe."

He had warned his boss back home that they should not be dealing with these animals. They would bring what up to now had been a lucrative family business to ruin. But the boss would not listen; the money was too good. Then the customers insisted on including one of their men to oversee the trips—they had lost too many loads and wanted to ensure the crew did their job. Nicholas had pointed out how dangerous that was, but at this point, nothing mattered. The cartel owned the boss, and therefore, they owned them all.

Nicholas had tried his best for success this night. The scouts had nailed the positions of the American patrols; all he had to do was get past their picket line by crossing through a wide gap they had left. They didn't even have to land, just pull within twenty-five yards of the beach and dump the load for the La Cantaña cartel men to retrieve. They were still a mile off the coast when, out of nowhere, came a blinding light and the call to heave-to.

It was unfortunate, but hardly the end of the world. Nicholas would turn away from the light and run while Nathan, Wilson, and the cartel man threw bales overboard. They were faster than the Americans when empty—they just had to stay ahead during the dump. The Americans would follow until they were confident the cargo was jettisoned and then stop to retrieve it. Even without arrests, it was a win for them, and no one wanted bloodshed. Lose cargoes? Even a boat or crew? No problem—part of the cost of doing business. He had explained this to their passenger before they left Bimini, and the man simply nodded without expression.

Nicholas was startled when the light hit them—there should not have been any Americans here. He recovered quickly and put the helm over when the cartel bastard started shooting. The Americans reacted at once, and the space between the boats was crisscrossed with 7.62-millimeter tracer fire. Nathan and Wilson flattened on the deck, and Nicholas instantly realized this was a new game. Their survival depended on getting out of range of the machine gun on the American boat. Even if they put down the cartel man, they would not stop shooting. Nicholas had to cripple them somehow and decided a glancing blow to the stern could take out one or both of the American's outboards without leaving his panga crippled. Then he had to run like hell.

It worked. After the jarring crash, they sped off into the night without pursuit. The Americans had stopped firing after the impact, perhaps with damage to their gun mount. Nicholas breathed a preliminary sigh of relief and ordered Wilson and his brother to dump the cargo. The cartel man turned his gun on them and said, "No!"

"You don't understand," Nicholas shouted over the engines. "We have to go fast to get home! This cargo slows us down!"

"No dump!" the man shouted back.

"What good is it when the Americans catch up with us?"

"They catch up, I shoot them too! No dump!"

That was thirty minutes ago, and Nicholas could see from the GPS they had at least another half hour before they reached the shoals of Henry Bank and safety. At least they had not seen any other boats. Nicholas thought luck might see them through when suddenly there was a bang, and the panga lurched to the right. He looked back to see the right-hand outboard spewing smoke. *Damn! Of all the times to blow an engine!* He put in some port helm to compensate for the loss of thrust and keep them on course and shouted, "Jayden, see if you can do something with it!"

The man was making his way back to the stern when there was a second bang, and the boat started drifting left. "It's been shot! They're shooting the engines!" Wilson shouted.

Nicholas's eyes widened in fear, and he spun the helm to the right—too late. There was a third bang, and the center engine, their last, ground to a halt. The boat, already slowing before the previous hit, coasted to a stop. Where only moments before the crew had to shout to be heard over the racing engines, wind, and water sluicing past, there was near silence, only the lapping and occasional thud of a wave striking the hull and the hissing and soft pings of the cooling engines. Nicholas looked around frantically in the darkness; there were no lights or sounds anywhere. The cartel man was training his AK-47 from beam to beam, searching for a target, any target.

Nicholas was dumbfounded. He had expected to hear the whine of a helicopter, one of those the Americans used to shoot out the engines of go-fast boats. At least he should hear boat motors if they were close enough to take out the engines with single shots. But there was nothing at all. Finally, a male voice pierced the darkness from their port quarter.

"This is the United States Coast Guard! You will surrender immediately or be fired upon!"

Nicholas, Nathan, and Wilson ducked behind the stacks of cocaine bales while the cartel man stood and began firing blindly in the voice's direction. There was a loud "crack," and the man's head snapped back, his arms spread out, and he collapsed backward with his assault rifle clattering to the deck beside Nicholas. *Now they'll kill us. That fool has done for us all!*

A moment later, the panga was bathed in a blinding white light originating from the port quarter. Nicholas looked at the sprawled cartel man, his mouth and eyes open and blood seeping from a large hole in his forehead. *Good riddance!* Nicholas reached out, grasped the AK-47, and clutched it against his chest. He had absolutely no idea what to do next.

"This is the United States Coast Guard! This is your last warning. You will discard all weapons and stand with your hands above your head. Anyone holding a weapon or not standing still with both hands in plain sight will be shot without warning."

"You are going to kill us anyway!" Nicholas shouted.

"No," the voice replied. "If you surrender peacefully, you will be placed under arrest and transported safely to the United States to stand trial. If you continue to resist, you will be killed."

"Kenton, what do we do?" Nathan whispered desperately.

Nicholas looked at the assault rifle in his arms, then over at the dead cartel man. *It's hopeless. Try to save Nathan and Jayden if you can.* "Coast Guard, it was the dead man that shot at you! None of us have fired a gun tonight!"

"If that is true, it might work to your advantage at trial. But you must surrender NOW!"

Nicholas tossed the AK-47 aside and shouted, "Coast Guard, we agree to surrender! Don't shoot!"

"Very well. Stand slowly with your hands in the air."

Nicholas nodded at the other men, and the three put their hands in the air and stood.

"Good call," the disembodied voice continued. "Now, stay exactly where you are with your hands in the air until the boarding officers direct you to do otherwise."

Now, Nicholas could hear a boat engine off the port side, and an orange RHIB emerged from the darkness and nudged gently into the panga. Three men in combat gear scrambled on board, two holding handguns, the third a shotgun. The men carrying the handguns had them pointed at the deck, Nicholas was relieved to see, but the man with the shotgun pointed it in the general direction of Nicholas and his crew.

The shorter handgun-holding man stepped over to the cartel man, picked up the AK-47 from the deck, repositioned the fire selector to safe, and then put the sling over his shoulder. He looked at Nicholas and said, "Are you the vessel's master?"

"Yes, sir," Nicholas answered.

"I am Lieutenant Junior Grade Wyporek. You are under arrest for violation of United States law. You have the right to remain silent, and you have a right to have an attorney present during questioning. If you desire an attorney and cannot afford one, the court will appoint one before questioning. Do you understand these rights?"

"Yes, sir."

"Very well. For our safety and yours, this man will search your person. Do you understand?"

"Yes, sir."

The officer nodded at his companion, a large black man who holstered his weapon and began a head-to-foot search. When that was complete, he leaned over and said, "I'm going to handcuff you now. Please put your left hand back." After placing Nicholas's hands in flex cuffs, the big man said, "OK, sit down."

The arrest process was repeated on the other crewmen, then the officer called back the orange RHIB, and the three panga crew were helped aboard. The officer and the large black man followed, and the shotgun man remained aboard the panga. It was a quick trip to get alongside the white-colored Coast Guard ship. When the RHIB had been craned to deck level, Nicholas and his crew were helped on board. Two crewmen took them to a side area on the ship's deck where their flex cuffs were removed, and they were manacled to the deck. The three men sat silently, watched carefully by another Coast Guard man holding a shotgun.

The Coast Guard crew rigged a hawser to tow the panga into port. By the time they had completed the linkup and started the tow, the eastern horizon was already aglow with the coming sunrise. A short time later, two Coast Guard men unshackled Nicholas and brought him into what looked like a dining area. The officer who led the boarding was seated at one of the two tables, some papers spread out before him, and Nicholas was brought to the table and seated opposite the officer. After reading him his rights again, the officer asked if Nicholas wished to answer questions or make a statement.

"Will this help me at my trial?" Nicholas asked.

"I can't promise that," the officer replied.

"Very well, I'll talk," Nicholas said with resignation.

The officer pushed a piece of paper and pen in front of him. "This is a written explanation of your rights and a statement that you are waiving them. You may reassert those rights at any time during the questioning. If these terms are agreeable, please sign on the line. Nicholas nodded and signed the paper, which was then signed by the officer and one of the other coastguardsmen.

"Thank you," the officer said. "Now describe in detail, please, your actions of last night, starting with your departure from Bimini."

Nicholas provided a lengthy commentary of the panga's activity and his role as the master, emphasizing the duress he and his crew felt from the cartel man. The officer nodded, took notes, and uttered an occasional acknowledgment throughout the interview. Finally, Nicholas completed his narrative and said, "That's all I know."

The officer nodded and said, "I have a few questions for clarification. You said the cartel man started the gunfight during your first encounter with the Coast Guard. Is that correct?"

"Yes," Nicholas answered.

"And you did not participate in the gunfight because you were driving the boat, correct?"

"That is correct, sir. Only the cartel man had a weapon, and he is the only one who shot at the Coast Guard."

"And you drove your boat into the Coast Guard boat, correct?"

"Yes, sir, but just to get away from the gunfight. I was not trying to sink the boat, only to keep it from chasing me."

"Very well. Is there anything else you wish to add?"

"No, sir. That is all."

"Very well, thank you," the officer said, then nodded toward the other crewmen. As they took Nicholas's arms and helped him from the seat, the officer said, "Oh, one more thing. Were you aware that a Coast Guard seaman was killed during your incident with the boat?"

Nicholas felt faint, took a breath, and said, "No. I am very sorry to hear that. But as I said, the cartel man did the shooting, not me."

"You just drove the boat."

"Yes, sir."

"As it happens, the man who died was wounded by gunfire…in his arm, a non-fatal wound. When you rammed that boat, deliberately, by your admission, he was thrown overboard. And when he was helpless in the water, one of your propellers took off the top of his head."

"Oh, God!"

"That man had a young wife and a baby girl at home. Now they are going to have to bury him. Most of him, anyway. All because you wanted to help import poison into this country *for money*. You think about that, you son-of-a-bitch!" He turned to the crewman. "Get him out of here and keep him separated from the others."

"Yes, sir," the crewman holding his right arm said. As they walked out on deck, he whispered to Nicholas, "Go ahead and try something. *Please!*"

Haley

Haley was still in her chair on the Bridge. She was tired, but far too keyed up to get any sleep or even eat. The tow of the panga was going well; they were making a steady eight knots toward the Coast Guard base in Miami Beach, where the vessel and their prisoners would be handed over to the appropriate authorities. It was slow going, as the northern set of the Gulf Stream reduced their speed over the ground to a plodding four knots.

Haley turned at the sound of footsteps on the ladder and saw Ben walking through the bridge door. He stood by Haley and saluted. "Interview complete, Captain."

Haley returned the salute and said, "How did it go?"

"About what we figured, ma'am. The dead guy was the only shooter, and the elder Nicholas was the driver. I must regretfully admit to being remiss in not having informed the suspect of the victim's cause of death prior to his admission of guilt in the act that caused it." Ben smiled.

"I'm shocked, SHOCKED at your inattention to detail, XO!" Haley grinned in return. Her earlier concerns about her ability to connect and get sound advice were gone. Ben, in particular, had come through quite well, standing up to her when he felt it was needed and delivering practical and effective suggestions. "Seriously, awesome job today. When we tracked the *Miho Dujam*, Sam told me you guys were often creating tactics on the fly. I'm a believer now."

The jury was still out on whether their not strictly by-the-book tactics would meet with official approval, but it would be hard to argue with the results: three arrests, one cartel shooter dead, a vessel seized along with what looked to be just under a ton of cocaine. And, hopefully, eventually, justice for Seaman Justin Demarest, the young man killed in the ramming. It warmed her heart that Drake had already hit her up to contribute to the collection he'd started for the seaman's young family. The crew and she were in the right hands.

Part III—The Mission

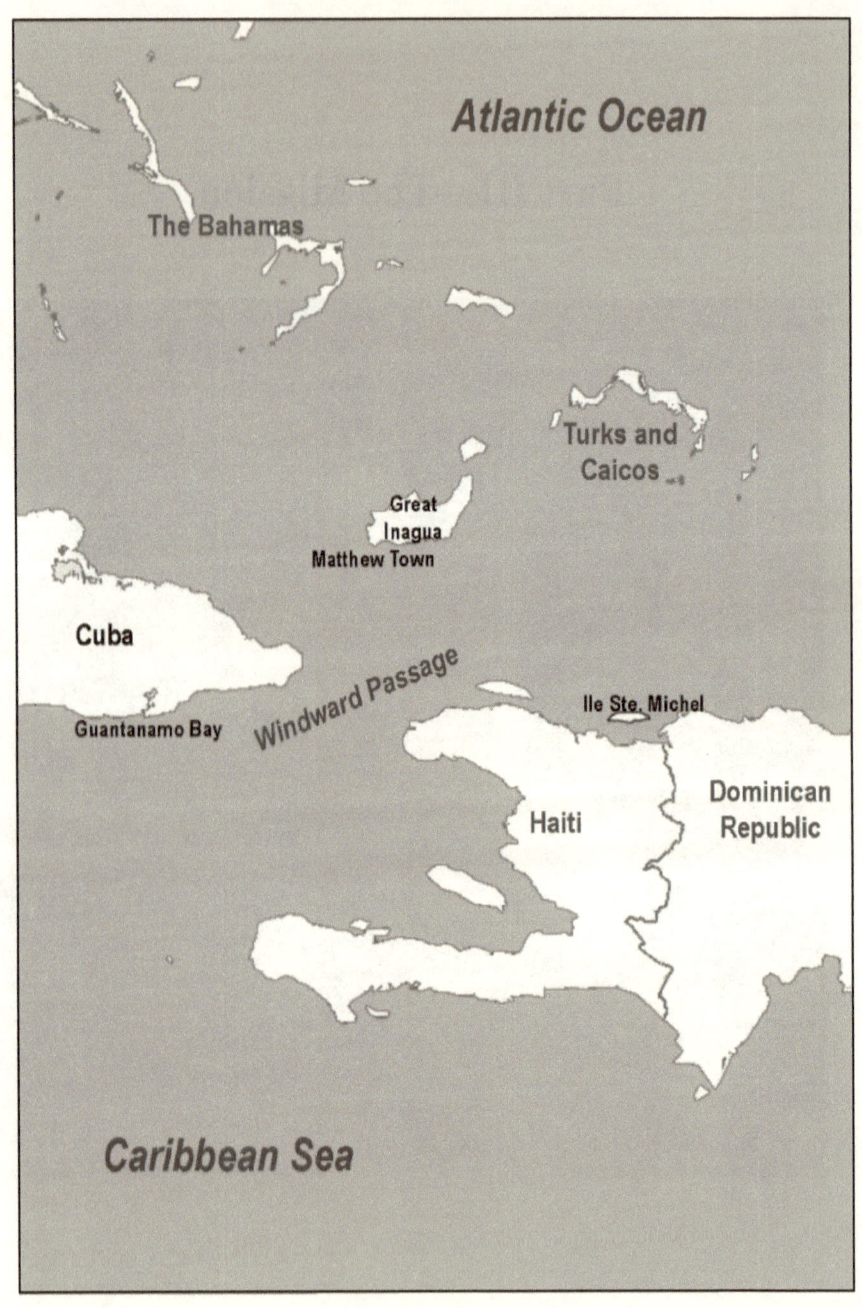
Atlantic Ocean
The Bahamas
Turks and
Caicos
Great
Inagua
Matthew Town
Cuba
Guantanamo Bay
Windward Passage
Ile Ste. Michel
Haiti
Dominican
Republic
Caribbean Sea

Realpolitik

Office of the Commander, U.S. Southern Command, Doral, Florida
0922 EST, 3 December

Pennington

Pennington had a sense of déjà vu as he sat at the conference room table. He had been sitting in this room when he was briefed on the Barbello mission last April. Pennington was the Director of JIATF South then. Army General Lamont Miller, Commander of SOUTHCOM, was sitting at the head of the table now and led that earlier meeting. Vice Admiral Jennifer Irving, Director of the DIA, had been sitting across the table as she was this morning. Captain Mercier, sitting to his right, was also present at that meeting, where she had introduced Pennington to the upgrades the Coast Guard had made on *Kauai*.

"Well, Harry, here we are again," Miller said with a soft southern accent, echoing Pennington's thoughts. Miller was a tall, solid man at six-foot-four and 220. The only changes between his appearance now and back when he was a middle linebacker for the University of Tennessee were his shaved head and the wrinkles he had gathered from years of standing in the sun in the commander's cupola of M1A1 Abrams tanks and M2 Bradley fighting vehicles. "I'm coming cap in hand to borrow that nifty little patrol boat of yours."

"Yes, sir. I thought as much." Pennington nodded. He had a genuine fondness for Miller, acquired when he worked for the general during his last job. Pennington did not have the same affection for Irving, whom he regarded as a callous and conniving asshole. He turned an icy stare at her. "I presume this is another DIA operation?"

"Correct, Admiral," Irving replied with an expressionless face. She was an average-sized, graying blond woman in her early fifties. Like most career intelligence officers, she was nondescript, wearing conservative business clothing rather than her U.S. Navy uniform. "We need the ability to insert and retrieve a team covertly onto foreign territory, and *Kauai* is our best option."

"What country?" Pennington asked.

"Haiti."

"You're joking," Pennington scoffed. "The country is an end-to-end basket case. You could land the entire 82nd Airborne in the middle of Port Au Prince with no one noticing."

"Not all of it is a basket case," Irving responded. "The island of Ile Ste. Michel, for instance."

"The one with the Chinese mine?" Pennington asked. "I suppose I would agree with that. As far as we know, the Chinese miners are the only living things on the island. I can see the irritation associated with a Chinese foothold in this hemisphere, but my understanding is that mine has been a bust. Am I in error?"

"Yes and no. You are correct that output is meager, but that is only because the Chinese need it to be. If they wanted, they could produce more out of that location than the rest of the world combined."

"They are leaving profit on the table? Why would they do that?"

"Admiral, you'll need some background. I brought my expert, Dr. Gregg Kenan, who can explain exactly why we are in a situation here. Doctor?"

Kenan stood and took a handheld remote control from the table. He was a balding, shorter-than-average man wearing a plain charcoal gray suit with a blue tie—more-or-less the stereotypic image of a college professor. He clicked a button on the remote and said, "Good morning, General, Admiral. I have a PowerPoint briefing prepared if I can direct your attention to the screen. I need to open by stating that this presentation is classified Secret, No Foreign."

"Understood," Pennington said.

"Thank you, sir," Kenan nodded. "I'll begin with a brief history leading to the current situation."

Kenan briefed that for most of human history, Ile Ste. Michel had been forty square miles of lifeless, windswept rock north of Cap Haitien on Haiti's north coast. It had no reliable water sources, and thus, none of the forests or arable land possessed by many of the islands in the area. There was no indigenous animal life; only mangroves and the hardiest rock-dwelling plants survived on the island. Neither did it have any natural harbors—even the pirates common to the region in the late 17th and early 18th centuries shunned it. It remained nothing more than a hazard to navigation until the late 1970s, when surveys detected one of the richest rare-earth elements deposits known. Even this elicited little interest at the time.

As electronic engineering evolved and the role rare-earths played in the manufacture of innovative technology burgeoned, the potential value of the Ile Ste. Michel deposit grew. Unfortunately, the upfront costs, which included the construction of a port and harbor, roads, housing for the workers, and fuel and water storage, were considerable. Several private corporations in North America and Europe examined and rejected the project as too risky with a government as unstable as Haiti. Government backing and financing were required, and no western government was willing to risk taxpayer funding on an engineering project principally benefitting a private corporation and Haiti.

However, the Chinese were game and made an agreement with the Haitian government to develop the island on a profit-sharing basis as part of their Belt and Road Initiative, or BRI. Western observers were puzzled by the move. China already controlled nearly all the rare-earth mining. Even on a profit-sharing basis, opening a vast new source in Haiti would only drive down the global market and cause significant pain to their suppliers at home. The true motive behind the Chinese move was revealed only after the mining operation opened.

Production from the mine was very low—less than a tenth of what most analysts and mining engineers had predicted, even after the construction was complete and the site was fully staffed. Observers wondered if the deposit was not as rich as initially thought, and they rechecked the surveys and samples but could find no errors. Worry that the mine was a cover for constructing a strategic base by the Chinese military spurred a CIA effort that "acquired" the documentation behind the deal. The terms of the agreement in these documents were astonishing.

The Chinese agreed to loan Haiti the funds required to build the mining facility and all supporting infrastructure in exchange for a thirty-year exclusive lease on Ile Ste. Michel by the Sino-American Mining Corporation. SAMC was one of the many Chinese Communist Party-owned companies working on engineering projects under the BRI aegis. By the lease terms, SAMC would share fifty percent of the profits from the mining activity with the Haitian government *after extracting whatever funding was required to service the debt.* The Haitian government also agreed to the presence of a small People's Liberation Army security force and to allow the port to service People's Liberation Army Navy warships without restrictions or even notification. The only caveats the Haitians insisted upon were that the port could not be used as an advance base for offensive military operations or any other activities contrary to international law. They did not want to get drawn into any wars or diplomatic sanctions.

The agreement was the most ingenious debt-trap diplomacy operation ever devised. Keeping mine production low artificially kept down the global supply of rare-earth elements, maintaining the profitability of China's domestic industry. It also allowed just enough profit to service Haiti's loan debt interest, keeping the nation servile in China's regional efforts. In effect, China had conned Haiti into funding both a mining operation that maintained China's near-monopoly on rare-earth elements and a Chinese military base on Haitian soil. The Haitian government officials familiar with the agreement's details either quietly went along in exchange for a generous stipend or suffered an unfortunate death in the endemic violence of the capital.

The details of the Sino-Haitian agreement were a closely guarded secret within U.S. diplomatic circles—the embarrassment of an agreement establishing a Chinese base practically in their backyard was too profound for any public release. Diplomatic efforts to induce Haiti to void the deal came to nothing. Although it proved a terrible bargain for Haiti, it was entirely legal under international law, and there was little incentive within the Haitian government to impose their sovereign rights on the island.

"That concludes my briefing, sirs. Do you have any questions?" Kenan asked.

"Yes," Pennington replied. "I'm as outraged by this as anyone else, but I cannot see what the U.S. can do about it, much less the Coast Guard. Why am I here?"

"That is outside my purview, sir. I'll need to refer you to Admiral Irving."

Pennington turned to Miller. "I have no more questions of the doctor, General."

"Neither have I. Thank you, Dr. Kenan," Miller said with a nod. After Kenan returned to his seat, Miller continued, "OK, Jenn. Now, what the hell *are* we doing here?"

"General, we think we might have the opportunity to show the Haitians the Chinese broke this agreement, which will allow us to come in, pay off the debt and open that mine for real. With that mine operating at full capacity, the breakeven point for the profit to pay off the investment would only be a few years. Then it's pure goodness: profit for both us and Haiti, removing a strategic threat from our hemisphere, not to mention a blow to the Chinese rare-earth monopoly and their international standing."

"Sounds fantastic. Exactly how do Harry and I fit into this opportunity?" Miller asked.

"A little more background is in order, General. You recall the last time we gathered together? It was to deal with a threat created by the 252 Syndicate."

"How could I forget?" Miller answered.

"We have a laptop seized from one of their smuggling vessels." Irving nodded toward Pennington. "Thanks to the boldness of an officer from the very patrol boat that carried out the last operation, I might add."

Pennington nodded in return. He had been briefed on the rescue of the sex-trafficked women and the seized laptop.

Irving continued, "Our crypto techs went through it and found evidence of a linkage between that organization and the Chinese. There is nothing we can take to court yet, but the collateral information and metadata have allowed us to penetrate the 252's communications and data at a pretty high level. We know from these penetrations that a senior member of the 252s will come to

Ile Ste. Michel for direct consultation with the Chinese director of mine operations about three days from now. He will fly by private jet into the Holguín airbase in Cuba, then to the Chinese port facility by seaplane. We intend to crash that meeting, grab the 252 man and any documents of the syndicate's collusion with the Chinese, and get out."

"Seems a little fishy to me, a higher-up taking that kind of risk when he can send a flunky. Are you sure this isn't some sort of spoof to embarrass us?" Pennington asked.

Irving nodded. "We thought of that too, but we think the probability is very low. We would see other indicators if that were the case. Why send a boss? They are building a brothel there to service the miners and a depot for arms smuggling. Those facilities were constructed at a sufficient distance from the Chinese port to maintain plausible deniability. The boss wants a look, plus check the feasibility of shipping cargo there by air to avoid our surface patrols, particularly the human cargo. The intercept of their freighter cost them a substantial amount of arms besides twenty-plus sex slaves, and he's on the hook to fix that supply chain for the next run."

"OK. I get why you want to grab him at the crime scene, so to speak, but why do you need *Kauai*?" Pennington asked.

"We can't use a helo in there without blowing the mission, and the ground is too rough to risk a parachute insertion. The narrow waters and shoals around the island make it too big a risk for a sub, even if we could get one there within three days. Our only chance is to close the coast and insert the team by small boat the night before in a remote cove near the 252 depot and then retrieve them by the same means after the snatch. *Kauai* can get in closer to shore than any gray hull and not attract any attention, given all the Coast Guard activity in the area."

Miller leaned forward. "How many do you intend to insert, and what opposition will they have?"

Irving replied, "We will have a team of four. We also have a special operations boat and cradle from Little Creek in the air now. It is a lightweight design that can carry the team plus three to four of your crew without overloading *Kauai's* crane. Our best information is that the 252s are running light right now, about a dozen thugs with the usual small arms."

"And what about the Chinese?"

"One of their reinforced security platoons, about fifty men, supported by two VN-4 light armored personnel carriers. No other vehicles or aircraft that we are aware of."

"And their sea forces?" Pennington asked.

"A couple of tugs and small service boats and one Shanghai-IV class gunboat."

Pennington asked, "And what support will *Kauai* have?"

Irving glanced between Miller and Pennington. "None."

Pennington's jaw dropped. "*None*? Admiral Irving, I presume you know the capabilities of a Shanghai-IV. Do you know what a one-ten, even a souped-up one like *Kauai,* brings to the fight? One twenty-five-millimeter popgun." Pennington was familiar with the Chinese Shanghai-IV from his war college days. "The Shanghai-IV is faster and has radar-directed, twin thirty-seven-millimeter mounts fore and aft that can rip *Kauai* to shreds a mile before she can get in range with her twenty-five."

"We aren't sending *Kauai* into a fight with the Chinese. The operation will be miles from their base, and they are unlikely to rush to the defense of a criminal gang. We evaluate the chance *Kauai* would encounter Chinese forces as near zero. If we move a large support force down there, we will alert the opposition. We might as well not bother running the op."

Pennington was having difficulty controlling his fury. "If that's the level of backup we can expect, maybe we shouldn't!"

Irving's eyes narrowed. "I have my orders, Admiral Pennington. Soon, you will too."

Pennington put his hands on the table and began to stand when Miller reached over and gripped his arm. When Pennington glanced over, Miller shook his head, and he sat.

"Alright, Jenn," Miller said. "When do your boat and team arrive?"

"Their C-130 should land at Miami International in two hours. The boat is containerized for a tractor-trailer, so offload and hook up will be quick. Figure four hours tops to pier side at Base Miami Beach."

"Very well. We'll take it from here," Miller said.

Irving said, "I think I should be involved in the planning."

Miller stared back coldly. "I disagree. You delivered your tasking, and your role is at an end." When she returned the stare, Miller continued, "That will be all, thank you."

Irving stood and turned toward the door, with Kenan scrambling to his feet to follow. Once they had departed and the conference room door closed, Pennington turned to Miller. "My God, General! She really doesn't give a damn! I didn't think a human being could be that cold-blooded. You can't expect me to dish those kids up with no backup."

"Harry, I'd send a task group there if I had one, but I don't. She's right in that we need to take a shot at this if we can, but I have no intention of sending your folks in with no support." He pressed a button on his phone. "Chief, I need to talk to General Ryan at Air Combat Command ASAP. Thanks." He hung up the receiver and turned to Pennington. "Mick Ryan owes me a favor or two, and I'll get you some electronic attack backup and TACAIR if I can."

Pennington closed his eyes and shook his head. After a moment, he looked up again and said, "Thank you, sir. Are you going to tell Irving?"

"Are you kidding? Why do you think I booted her ass outta here? This is still my command, and if she wants to rat me out to the bosses, fine. I'll go out clean."

"Thank you, sir," Pennington repeated. "If you can excuse Jane and me, we need to get orders to *Kauai* to get this goat rodeo set up."

"Absolutely! Captain, coordinate rendezvous times and locations with my J3 staff as soon as your people have the op sketched out."

"Will do, General," Mercier replied.

"Good luck, you guys. You've got my number if you need me to knock any heads together."

"Thank you, General," Pennington said as he and Mercier got to their feet and shook hands with Miller. As they walked to the car after leaving the office, Pennington asked, "How long before *Kauai* pulls into BMB?"

Mercier checked her watch and said, "An hour, sir."

"Pass them a message for the CO, XO, and Ops Chief to report to my office by fourteen hundred. Tell them to bring the DIA team lead with them."

"Very good, sir."

USCG Cutter *Kauai*, moored, Coast Guard Base Miami Beach, Florida
12:47 EST, 3 December

Ben

Ben watched in deep concern as *Kauai*'s crane took the load of the special operations boat parked on the trailer next to the ship. It was engineered to be lightweight rather than durable but still weighed about twenty percent more than the cutter boat, medium *Kauai* customarily shipped. Drake had assured Ben the new crane could easily handle the load, but as XO, he needed to see for himself. The new crane was a significant improvement over *Kauai*'s original unit, cut in half by a rocket hit at Barbello. They had already installed the boat's cradle, actually more of an adapter to the existing cutter boat cradle.

The crane groaned slightly as the boat lifted from its trailer and rose to the height of the boat deck. Bondurant was operating the crane, his face frozen in concentration, watching the pivot and swing of the boat as the crane turned to bring it over the cradle. Drake stood behind Bondurant, scanning the crane and hydraulic connections. The boat descended onto the cradle, and Drake turned to give Ben a thumbs-up.

Lee, standing next to Ben throughout the evolution, grunted. "Looks like a real pig, XO."

"Need a pig to haul around nine guys, Petty Officer Lee." He turned toward her and added, "Think you can drive her?"

Lee turned toward Ben with a raised eyebrow. "*Really*, sir? Puleeze!"

Ben nodded. "Just the same, we'll get you some time on it before the mission to get the feel. Get together with the DIA guys to match pointers as soon as possible."

"WILCO, XO. Have fun downtown with the grownups."

"Yes, I'm sure," Ben said as he turned toward the ship and boarded. A short walk brought him to Haley's cabin, where she and Frankle conferred. "Special boat is safely aboard and being secured, Captain. There were no problems with the crane."

"Excellent," Haley said, then turned to Frankle. "Might as well push off in case there's traffic or other Miami B.S."

"Suits me," Frankle said. He was still wearing his suit and tie, forgoing a change to more casual clothes until after the meeting.

"I'll grab Chief and meet you at the car," Ben said, then started toward Hopkins's stateroom. He knocked on the door and stood as Hopkins emerged. "Ready for the fun, Chief?"

"Semper," Hopkins replied with a smile. "Lead on, sir."

It was a short drive to the Brickell Plaza Federal Building housing the Seventh Coast Guard District offices. After a brief delay through the metal detectors at the entrance, the three Coast Guard members and DIA agent made their way to the Chief of Staff's office to await their meeting with Pennington. Mercier smiled, stood from her desk as she saw them, and said, "Come in, please!" She shook hands with Haley and added, "That was a four-point-oh job with the panga, Haley."

"Thank you, ma'am," Haley said, beaming.

Mercier then moved to Frankle. "Agent Frankle, I'm Jane Mercier. It's a pleasure to meet you."

"Thank you, Captain," Frankle replied.

Mercier then turned to Ben and shook his hand, "Ben, seems you're teamed up with the DIA again."

"Yes, ma'am. I just updated my next of kin notification and servicemember's life insurance data."

She turned to Hopkins with a grin and shook her hand. "Chief, it's good to see you again. Are you keeping these two on the right path?"

"I'm doing my utmost to rise to the challenge, Captain."

"The world is in the right hands then. Please take a seat. The boss will be available in a few minutes. So, Agent Frankle, have you briefed them on what's going on?"

"No, ma'am. I had no orders to do so, and, as you might imagine, we're a fail-passive organization."

"Oh, my," Mercier said with a frown, then looked over at Hopkins. "Chief, could you shut the door, please?"

"Yes, ma'am," Hopkins replied, then closed the door and returned to her seat.

"Thank you. OK. Ben, that laptop you took off the *Miho Dujam* gave us a lot of information on the 252 organization and created quite a stir at the highest levels. In short, we're sending *Kauai* to the Haitian island of Ile Ste. Michel to seize one of their top guys and transport him here for interrogation. You'll close on the island, insert the DIA team, then wait offshore until the following night and return to pick them up."

Haley leaned forward and said, "Captain, I infer from the fact we are meeting with the District Commander that there is more to this than a snatch and grab of some criminal kingpin."

"Yes. The island is under the control of the Chinese."

Yikes! Ben thought, then said, "What kind of control, ma'am? Are we looking at a fight?"

"No, Ben." Mercier shook her head. "We'll discuss this in more detail in the meeting with the admiral, but our intention and belief are that we can avoid contact with the Chinese forces on the island." At that point, the phone on her desk buzzed, and she answered. "Yes, sir, they're here. Yes, sir." She hung up and said, "OK, we can go in now."

They all stood, and the four visitors followed Mercier into a conference room where Pennington was already standing. After introductions, they sat at the conference table with Pennington at the head, Haley, Ben, and Hopkins on one side, and Mercier and Frankle on the other.

"Thank you all for coming," Pennington said. "Agent Frankle, do you go by Arthur?"

"Art, Admiral," Frankle replied.

"Art it is. OK, folks, I know you're wondering why this is such a big deal. The fact is, we have an opportunity to not only nip a 252 incursion in this hemisphere in the bud, but maybe root out a Chinese one to boot. I'm not sure how into geopolitics you all are, but Ile Ste. Michel was a real black eye for us. While we were dithering over whether to invest in development and how much the taxpayers should be willing to risk, the Chinese swooped in and got a lock on what is probably the richest rare-earth element source in the world. At the same time, they built a port that could double as a small navy base right in our backyard.

"They have a thirty-year lease on that island they are maintaining using a debt-trap they laid on the Haitian government. The agreement is rock solid legally, but it has a provision we hope to exploit. Namely, the Chinese will not engage in any violations of international law. We have good intelligence that the Chinese are in cahoots with the 252s, at least locally on Ile Ste. Michel. What we need is evidence, and that is why we are having you take Art's team down there. There's no way to insert them by air and not enough time to develop the networks and cutouts to go in-country in Haiti to pull this off. So, we will send you down there to blend into the AMIO crowd during the day and insert and retrieve Art's team at night. This is the type of mission we designed *Kauai* to do. Any questions of me so far?"

"No, sir," all three of the *Kauai* personnel replied.

"Good. OK, Art, I'll turn it over to you for the next part."

"Thank you, Admiral," Frankle said as he stood and grabbed the remote. He clicked a button, and a topographical map of a landmass titled "Ile Ste. Michel" appeared on the large screen. Frankle put the remote down and walked over to the screen. He then hooked his left thumb in his belt and pointed at the far-right edge of the landmass on the screen with his right hand. "The Chinese constructed the port here on this headland. They concentrated all the admin buildings, warehouses, fuel and water storage, and residences in this area. Their method is to erect temporary buildings where they are actively processing to house the heavy equipment. As you can see, all Chinese activity is concentrated on the island's eastern half right of this ridge." He pointed to a zone of higher elevation, roughly bisecting the island.

"The 252s, with Chinese help, constructed a second site over here, west of the ridge, with residences, warehouses, water storage, and power generation. The site also includes a barracks serving as a brothel catering to the Chinese miners. Morale has been an enormous problem, and the Chinese are paying the 252s a premium to staff that brothel with European women as a worker perk." He glanced over at Haley, Ben, and Hopkins. "That group of women you intercepted was the first contingent.

"The *Miho Dujam*'s loss was a significant hit in terms of prostitution revenue, so the 252s are trying a more secure route by smuggling the women in by air. The 252 boss will pioneer this, flying by private jet into Holguín in Cuba and seaplane to the Chinese port. He plans to stay overnight to inspect the operation, confer with his Chinese counterpart, and return by the same route. We intend to grab him that night."

Frankle pointed at an indentation near the southwest corner of the island. "There is a small cove here, masked from both facilities by intervening high ground we can use for landing and pickup. You have good water to about two hundred yards from shore—I propose we launch the boat from five hundred just to be safe." He traced a path northeast on the map with his finger. "We have high-res satellite shots showing this as an optimal path to this high ground west of the 252 site. It has suitable cover for us to observe their pattern of life during the day and close to engage that night. Once we penetrate, we grab the big cheese and anything that looks like documentation and egress. If we're lucky, we can grab one of the SUVs they use to run around the island. If not, we should still have plenty of time to hoof it to the beach before first light." He turned to the group. "Any questions, Admiral?"

"Yes, Art. What are your rules of engagement?"

"Sir, we will kill any 252 members we meet other than the bigwig. If we run into any Chinese, they will be stunned and sedated, and the only one we take with us is the 252 bigwig. Do you have any other questions, sir?"

"Good here," Pennington answered.

"I have a question," Haley said. "What forces do the Chinese have, and what's the likelihood we will tangle with them?"

"They have a security force of about fifty men, supported by two VN-4 light armored personnel carriers, but no aircraft. The VN-4s have mounted 7.62-millimeter machine guns, but their armor is intended to protect against small arms—armor-piercing rounds from your twenty-five-millimeter will have no problem penetrating. There is a naval threat in the form of a Shanghai-IV class gunboat; its thirty-seven-millimeter guns will do you in before you can even get in range. That's the bad news. The good news is that we do not see them engaging to protect the 252s. As long as we stay west of the big ridge, we think they will leave us be."

"And what if they don't?" Haley asked.

"Um...." Frankle began.

"I'll take that one," Pennington interrupted. "SOUTHCOM is arranging for electronic warfare and tactical aircraft to cover your retreat if necessary."

"I see. Thank you, sir. And what are our rules of engagement?"

"Unless otherwise directed, you will operate independently under the national defense mission code. You will not engage in any other mission activity, even search and rescue, until this mission is complete. You will not engage or fire on any Chinese forces unless fired upon. Do you have any questions about that?"

"Yes, sir. What do we do if the risk of engaging the Chinese elevates during the retrieval phase?"

Pennington looked at her coldly. "You will use your best judgment informed by the principle of calculated risk, and you will not take *any* action likely to result in engagement with Chinese forces. Is that clear?"

"Very clear, sir."

Ben watched Haley exchange a glance with Frankle across the table. Pennington had just ordered her to abandon Frankle's team to their fate if she thought it necessary to avoid contact with the Chinese. The revelation appeared to have no effect on the agent's countenance. *Holy shit, he's OK with that!*

Pennington's face softened. "I want to emphasize that I have every confidence in you and your crew. I appreciate this is a hairy one, but I would not have agreed to it if I were not convinced you and your people would come back safely."

"Thank you, sir. To quote my XO, it is one helluva break-in patrol."

Approaches

USCG Cutter *Kauai*, Old Bahama Channel, sixteen nautical miles north-northeast of Guardalavaca, Cuba 08:12 EST, 4 December

Ben

Ben and Hopkins sat in the messdeck with the four DIA team members for detailed planning of the expeditionary operation kicking off that night. As soon as the last breakfast meals were consumed and the remnants cleared away, the messdeck was placed off-limits, and Frankle and his team covered the tables with a large topographical map of Ile Ste. Michel and the latest satellite photos. The distance from the cove where the team would land and the high ground overseeing the 252 facilities was about two miles as the crow flies and probably half-again that distance over the intervening broken ground. The return route was shorter and more direct, thanks to the unimproved roads the Chinese had graded around the island's periphery and to the 252 facilities. Still, Ben couldn't imagine fleeing nearly two miles on foot while carrying an unconscious man.

The messdeck planning session reminded Ben of the special operations course he attended at Quantico the previous March. One exercise was an overland trek to a surprise assault on an insurgent position. The same types of terrain maps and satellite photos were employed, and the common considerations of time-distance, terrain, and contingencies had to be considered. That was where the comparison ended. Unlike Ben's group of novices fumbling through planning with instructors rolling their eyes or giving prompts ranging from "have you considered…?" to "are you really this stupid?!", Frankle and his team moved briskly through each step on the land op without hesitation or uncertainty.

Besides Frankle, another familiar face was at the table, his partner Lashon Bell. He had been on the DIA land team in the Resolution Key operation in January and had been present when Ben first met Victoria. Bell had been grievously wounded in a firefight with the 252s a day-and-a-half later and had been restored to full duty only months ago. He was very much like Bondurant, mid-thirties with a shaved head, powerfully built and quiet, although not as tall. Bell and Frankle were in their element in the planning meeting—they were both originally in Marine Corps recon units before being recruited into the DIA.

The other two members of Frankle's team were also involved in the January operation, but at a remote location. William "Billy" Gerard was a forty-ish, well-built man about Ben's height with light brown, close-cropped hair and a full, short-trimmed beard. He had also shipped aboard *Kauai* with Simmons on the Barbello mission. Steve Kelly was in his mid-thirties, a couple of inches taller, slim like Ben and clean-shaven, with black hair, close-cropped like Frankle and Gerard. This was the first time he and Ben had met. Unlike Frankle and Bell, Gerard and Kelly were not military veterans, but entered the clandestine service shortly after graduating from college.

After accounting for the route and terrain and the fact that they would navigate using GPS and night-vision equipment, the team calculated they would need between two-and-a-half and three hours to walk from the cove to the observation post and another half hour to dig in and camouflage themselves. They would need to be in place no later than first light, 05:17, meaning *Kauai* had to drop them off no later than 01:45. After observing the numbers and positions of the 252 personnel around the site and their patterns of patrol and movement, they would await the top dog. According to the itinerary, he would arrive at the Chinese port around 14:00 and, after a brief meeting with the lead Chinese administrator, leave for the gang's facility around 17:00. After spending the night, he was due to fly out on the seaplane around 09:00 the following day. Sometime between sunset, 17:09 local time, and 01:00, Frankle and his team would creep forward, silently kill any sentries, seize one of the gang's vehicles while disabling the others, grab the top dog and run to the beach to meet with *Kauai*. They would be over the horizon with their quarry by first light—a piece of cake.

The Chinese were the wild card. Everything depended on them staying put in their facilities across the ridge to the east. Several high-endurance reconnaissance UAVs had overflown the island in recent days, building a pattern of life. Everything seemed as expected—the Chinese were keen to avoid any apparent contact with their criminal neighbors and thus ran no land patrols or surveillance across the ridge. The gunboat showed no sign of movement during the observation period. Frankle was sure that a single sortie by the gunboat would burn through two to three months' worth of the diesel fuel used by the generators, vehicles, and equipment at the facility, so routine patrolling was unlikely.

Ben had no illusions about the gunboat—*Kauai* would be no match for her in any straight-up fight. Their only hope of survival was to avoid contact, and stealth was the order of the day. There was no sign of any radar facilities on the island beyond those organic to the gunboat. Any portable sets used by the Chinese or the 252s would have difficulty picking up *Kauai* beyond one mile. Within three miles of the shore, *Kauai* would maneuver on battery power only to avoid any dedicated or incidental listeners. The special operations boat they were carrying also had a low-power/low-noise signature mode if speed was not at a premium.

The four DIA men finished their discussion and noted the routes and timing in their notebooks. They all turned to Ben and Hopkins, and Frankle said, "OK, folks. You've heard the plan, and we're interested in your views and critiques."

Ben and Hopkins shared a glance, and then she said, "The shoreline is almost open, and the cove's position on the leeward side of the island pretty much guarantees a suitable sea state for operations. I don't see any problem from the maritime side. I'll leave any comments on the land ops to the XO—he's got the training, not me."

Ben turned to Frankle. "Art, you seem pretty confident you can grab a vehicle and knock out the rest. What happens if that doesn't work out? What if you miss one? These guys aren't idiots; they'll know you had to come by boat, and they'll move to cut you off from the only viable landing site: the south shore."

Frankle nodded. "Yes, that's probably the riskiest factor in the op. But we've seen nothing on the overflights indicating they're dispersing the vehicles or running any active patrols."

"Alright," Ben said as he reached for the topographical map and one of the aerial photographs. "I get you can get off the beach through this cut here," he said, pointing at the map showing a gentler slope off the beach to the shallow plateau that formed the island's base. "But looking at these photos, I don't see any way to get a vehicle through here without cutting a bunch of trees. What happens if you have armed pursuit?"

"Any chance *Kauai* could pick them off for us?"

"Nope. We can only do direct fire, and that foliage is too thick, and we can't just hose it down with the fifties without hitting you guys." Ben looked between the map and the photo. "What about this spot here?" he said, pointing at a gap between two copses of trees. "Good cover for an ambush and good fields of fire. A couple of us can set up and take out anyone on your tail after you pass. Once we stop them, we can hightail it to the boat. If your plan works and there's no pursuit, no harm done."

Frankle bent over, looking closely at the map. "What do you think, Billy? Can you find that hole while on the run?"

Gerard shook his head. "Not in the dark. At least, not without a marker." He looked at Ben. "You guys OK with chemlight markers?"

"Should be OK if we hold off lighting them until you get here, about five hundred yards away. It will serve them as well as you, but we want them coming into the crossfire, anyway. We'll set up with Mark 48s—that will cut through anything without armor. We want to be sure we stop them." The Mark 48 was a lightweight thirty caliber machine gun of Belgian design carried by special forces operators. Its larger round packed around twice the impact force of their standard M4 carbine bullets. Ben, Bondurant, Guerrero, and Lopez had special training to use the two carried by *Kauai*.

Frankle stared at Ben. "That will do it, alright."

After a pause, Ben asked, "What?"

"I don't know. Something this hardcore is a little out of character for you."

"I'm not itching for a fight, Art. I'd be a happy man never pulling a trigger again off the range. But Resolution and the *Miho*

Dujam taught me these guys aren't playing soft and cuddly, and neither should I. It's their choice."

"Roger that." Frankle nodded.

"One more thing," Ben said. "You heard our orders. If the Chinese weigh in, the boss has no choice but to leave you behind. Are you OK with that?"

"That's the way it is sometimes."

Ben shook his head. "Amazing. I'll take a hurricane rescue any day over your world of work."

Frankle grinned. "Oh, it's not that bad. We wouldn't be going if the odds weren't right."

Ben pushed the chart and photo away. "OK, I've got enough to brief the boss. Do you need anything more from us?"

"No, good to go here."

Ben checked his watch. "We'll be approaching Great Inagua in about two-and-a-half hours to train with the boat. You're welcome to watch."

"Thanks, I think we would," Frankle said.

Haley

Three days. Haley wondered at the realization that she had held this command for only three days. Her ship had pursued and stopped an armed and dangerous drug smuggler with gunfire during that time, killing a murderous suspect. Now, her XO and chief operations specialist were laying out plans for a covert operation on foreign soil that included the terms "ambush position" and "fields of fire." Haley stared at the chart while her brain came to grips with the reality of it.

"Ma'am?" Ben asked, snapping Haley out of her thoughts.

"Wha…. Oh, I'm sorry, XO. I guess I'm having difficulty taking it all in."

"Yes, ma'am. This is the worst case, naturally. If Frankle's team disables all the other vehicles, we'll be able to get out without firing a shot."

"No, XO, that isn't the worst case by a long shot. The worst case is that damn Chinese gunboat pins us to the shore."

"Yes, Captain. But nobody thinks that's going to happen, me included. Why would they stick their necks out for the 252s? It wouldn't make any sense."

"Crazier things have happened. Let's hope I don't have to make the hard choice. Now, as far as personnel, what are your recommendations?"

"Lee, Lopez, and me in the boat."

"If you are taking the Mark 48s, wouldn't it be better to have Guerrero with you?"

"We are all better off with him as Overwatch, ma'am. Lopez is fully up to speed on the gun."

"OK, why you instead of Bondurant?"

"That's kinda my job here, Captain," Ben answered with a tilt of his head. "Also, I'm pretty sure we're better off with him working the crane, and I'd rather have him around to pull someone out of the boat than the reverse." After a pause, he added, "Besides, he has a wife and two kids."

"That's true, but it's not the principal consideration. What happens if I go down?"

"I can't picture a scenario where you go down, and there's anything salvageable left behind, ma'am."

Holy shit! Are we really *talking like this?* "Very well. Do you see any problems with this new boat?"

"I don't think so. Lee thinks it's a pig, but she's trading a sports car for a family van in her view. The practice runs will definitely help; at least she can get a feel for it. With your permission, I'd like to do a full load-out dress rehearsal at Great Inagua. I know COB said the crane would be fine, but I'd like to see it work before getting into dangerous waters."

Haley nodded. "Concur. You think we can get the DIA team to go along with it?"

"I don't think that will be a problem. Frankle has already expressed an interest in watching the tryouts. In any case, I can be *very* persuasive," Ben said with a grin.

"Very well, make it so." Haley smiled back. Ben's grin was infectious, and she was seeing why Sam had such faith in him. "Is there anything else?"

"No, ma'am, that about covers it."

Haley turned to Hopkins, whose face remained devoid of expression. "Chief, anything to add?"

"No, Captain," Hopkins answered.

OK, it ends here. "XO, this is a scary place, but you've made it easier. Thank you. Now, if you'll excuse us, I'd like to have a word with Chief Hopkins."

"Very good, ma'am," Ben said as he stood, then closed the door as he left.

Here goes. "Chief, Commander Powell said you were his ace in the hole, that he could count on you to give him straight advice and feedback. I'll be frank that I'm not getting that vibe from you."

"I'm sorry to hear that, Captain," Hopkins said.

"Perhaps you are. In any case, whatever this is between us, we need to get it sorted out before we go in harm's way. So, I'm offering you a free shot. For the next few minutes, no rank exists here. Lay out your issues with me, and I'll listen."

"Captain, I am a professional, and I will do whatever it takes to get through the mission and bring the crew and boat home safely. If I think you are making a mistake that threatens that outcome, I'll let you know."

"Good to hear. Now, I'll take a straight answer to my original question, if you please."

Hopkins raised her left eyebrow. "Right. Two issues, the biggest one first. It chaps me royally when someone else gets jammed up for something I did."

"You're referring to the XO?"

"I am. He's one of the finest men I have ever known. The dressing down you gave him in front of COB and me was just wrong, ma'am."

"Chief, Mr. Wyporek is not 'jammed up,' quite the contrary. And it was not a dressing down—I would have handled anything like that privately. My purpose was so that you and COB could help him with the transition. I'm pretty sure he would never dime me out to the crew or you as the reason he turned formal all of a sudden. You helped with that, I presume?"

"Yes, ma'am," Hopkins replied.

"Good. Mission accomplished. Now, what's the other beef?"

"That 'Girl Power' session you held before the change of command. I hope you don't plan on that being a regular thing."

Haley was surprised by both the subject and Hopkins's term for it, but kept a poker face. "No, that was not my intention."

"I'm relieved to hear it, ma'am. I realize you meant well, but it backfired badly. In case you haven't caught on to this already,

Zuccaro is a troublemaker, and that little session empowered her. Don't get me wrong; she's good at her job, but I've had to come down on her before for being too flirty. Now she's smug, and the rest of the junior crew is wary of her, except for Lee, who, given a chance, would throw her ass overboard."

"Point taken. Is this an issue I need to take for action?"

For the first time, Hopkins smiled. "No, Captain. This one has two stops before it gets to you. I just needed to know I had support for a chief's intervention."

"Always. What's the second stop?"

"The XO, ma'am. He's young and amiable, but he's not a soft touch. You're really the last resort."

"His stock continues to rise. So, is there anything else? Now's the time to clear the air."

"That will do for me. Thank you for the chance to...."

"Bitch?"

"Yes, that's the word for it, Captain."

"Happy to oblige. Please keep us straight, Chief," Haley said as she stood and offered her hand.

"*Semper*, ma'am," Hopkins replied as she shook Haley's hand.

USCG Cutter *Kauai*, Atlantic Ocean, five nautical miles southeast of Matthew Town, Bahamas
13:27 EST, 4 December

Ben

They were cruising at an easy twenty-five knots in the special forces boat. Lee was at the helm, Frankle and his team distributed forward of the helm console, Ben and Lopez sitting aft, and five ten-gallon containers filled with seawater to simulate the weight of their arms and equipment, plus their expected passenger. The heavily loaded boat maneuvered as sluggishly as Lee expected, but its powerful engines still delivered a good turn of speed.

Ben keyed his radio. "*Kauai*, *Kauai*-One, stability checks complete. Ready for the high-speed run."

"*Kauai*-One, *Kauai*. We're ready here," Williams's voice replied.

"Petty Officer Lee, feel like opening her up?" Ben shouted.

"Hell, yes!" Lee replied. "In the boat, prepare for a speed run!"

Lee turned the boat to run parallel with *Kauai*, then pushed the throttle levers forward. The boat picked up speed slowly in the calm waters in the lee of Great Inagua island, creating a pleasant cooling breeze and dazzling rainbows of spray as it slammed through the small waves. Ben looked aft, briefly watching their cream-white wake spreading on the dark blue sea behind them. The DIA men were grinning and looking out over the boat's sides, enjoying the warm sunshine. Ben remembered that just the previous day, the men had left the freezing temperatures of Washington, DC behind—for a while anyway, this was like a tropical vacation to them. Ben's smile faded when he remembered what they faced this evening. He checked his watch—three minutes—and keyed his radio again. "*Kauai*, *Kauai*-One. How's it looking?"

"*Kauai*-One, *Kauai*, thirty-four point six knots," Williams replied.

"Roger. Are you ready for practice approaches?"

"Affirmative. Cleared for approach and hookup."

"Petty Officer Lee, that's all we need—thirty-four point six! You can head back now!"

"Aye, aye, sir!" Lee brought the throttles to the twenty-five-knot cruise speed and then turned the boat to port to head for *Kauai*. Once the boat was steady on a heading to the ship, Lopez stood and made his way to the bow to handle the sea painter, a line from *Kauai* the boat would ride on while the crane falls were attached.

They were approaching *Kauai* quickly, too quickly, in Ben's opinion. He was about to say something when Lopez shouted, "Coming in a little hot, don't you think?"

"I've got this, Boot!" Lee replied as she took the throttles into reverse. The boat's waterjet engines, optimized for forward propulsion, dutifully went into full astern but lacked the thrust to save this approach. Lee realized they would not make it, took the right engine out of reverse to provide enough helm control for a turn, and shouted, "Hang on, everybody!"

The last-second correction was enough to alter the impact to a glancing blow, and, with a tremendous "squeak" and lurch, the boat caromed off *Kauai*'s port side.

"Jesus, Shelley!" Lopez shouted.

"OK, sorry about that, everyone!" Lee shouted as she brought the other throttle up and continued turning to the left. She glanced at Ben and said less loudly, "I'll have a hard time living that one down, sir."

"Don't worry about it. That's why we're here."

The next approach was flawless, and after hooking up the sea painter, Lopez grabbed the fall when it came within reach and slammed the hook onto the boat's lift frame. Lee killed the engines and gave a thumbs-up to Bondurant on the crane controls. As the crane took the load, its hydraulic motor screamed as the boat lifted slowly out of the water. The noise was unnervingly loud— Ben would have been concerned if Drake had not been monitoring the pressure gauges on the side of the crane and giving a thumbs-up. As the boat reached the main deck level, Bondurant held while the crew stepped out, carrying the water containers. He then lifted it onto the cradle.

Lee pulled off her helmet and said, "Got a little cocky. Sorry again, sir."

"Forget it, Lee," Ben replied. "That one is still a distant second compared to the 'Smurf Boat' incident!"

Lee rolled her eyes and said, "Yeah, I'll always have that one going for me. Thanks, sir!"

"Anytime. I'm all about morale, you know." Ben chuckled. The "Smurf Boat" event occurred when they were doing operational tests with the Squid, with Lee driving the RHIB in a series of tactical trials. One test squid canister detonated early and doused the RHIB and crew with blue paint. No one was hurt, but the video recording of the event and aftermath remained a crew favorite.

As Lee turned to head inside, Ben noticed Frankle was waiting for him forward of the crane. "You need anything else from us, XO?"

"No, that will do."

"Any changes to the plans?"

"Just for us. I didn't anticipate how loud the crane would be under this load. I'm going to recommend we launch at least a mile and a half offshore and ride the sea painter in and out. It should affect nothing you guys have planned."

"Cool."

USCG Cutter *Kauai*, Atlantic Ocean, one nautical mile south of the western end of Ile Ste. Michel, Haiti
00:18 EST, 5 December

Ben

It had been night for almost six hours. Ben looked at the cloudless and moonless sky, the stars painfully bright through his Night-Vision Goggles, called NVGs for short. The low growl of the boat's muffled diesel engines and the soft hiss of the water as they crept northward at twelve knots were the only audible sounds while *Kauai* was running on batteries. Ben glanced at the shoreline, then around the fully loaded boat, riding the sea painter as *Kauai* completed her approach to the island.

Their approach was later than planned—a result of a delay in the launch of their supporting UAV surveillance flight. They remained in position twelve miles offshore until the reconnaissance confirmed both the Chinese and the 252s occupying the island were tucked into their respective compounds, and the cove was clear. The boat held the same crew as the previous afternoon's foray, but the DIA team had all their equipment and were dressed out for expeditionary operations. Lee, Lopez, and Ben were dressed in full combat gear, body armor, and helmets with mounted NVGs. The three carried sidearms, and Lopez and Ben also carried M4 carbines.

Lee kept her eyes on *Kauai* and adjusted the helm and throttles to keep pace with the patrol boat. The sea painter was a tether only—it would part if they tried to use it to tow the large boat. When they received the visual signal from the Bridge, an NVG-visible infrared light flashing the letter "L" in morse code, they would cast off and proceed independently to the shore. After dropping off the DIA team, the boat would rendezvous with the idling *Kauai*, and the two would proceed in company silently back offshore to the two-mile point, far enough that the crane could not be heard from shore. After craning the boat on board, *Kauai* would proceed offshore to her patrol box and await the team's signal to return.

Ben looked from the boat over to the shoreline—it was quite close now, and he could make out the outlines of individual trees through his NVGs. Finally, a pencil-thin beam of light shined down from the Bridge: dot-dash-dot-dot, the signal for launch. Lee said, "Release sea painter."

Lopez cast off the line, and Lee brought the boat into a left turn, crossed *Kauai*'s wake, and headed to shore at the slow speed of twelve knots. The quarter-mile journey took less than a minute. Lee cut the engines to idle as the boat gently nudged onto the shelving beach and said, "Go." The DIA men slipped over the side into the knee-deep water, and Ben and Lopez handed them their equipment. Once the handoff was complete, Frankle turned to Ben and reached out with his right hand.

"See you when we see you, Coast Guard," Frankle said as he shook Ben's hand.

"Godspeed, Art," Ben replied.

The DIA man gave the bow of the now floating boat a shove to help Lee pivot it around, then turned and began wading toward the shore. Ben scanned the shore with his finger near the M4's trigger until the four men passed into the tree line. He then turned to Lee. "OK, return to ship."

"Aye, aye, sir," Lee replied and pushed the throttles to ahead slow.

Ben looked away from shore, over the boat's bow, and noted that *Kauai* had already turned toward the open sea. She would hold bare steerageway until the boat caught up, then speed up to twelve knots to the recovery point. The journey and recovery of the boat took fifteen minutes. As *Kauai* continued offshore under battery power, Ben climbed to the Bridge, crossed over to the captain's chair, and saluted Haley. "Ingress complete. No issues, Captain."

Haley returned the salute. "Nicely done, XO. Now get some sleep. I expect tomorrow will be another interesting day."

"It is certainly trending that way, ma'am. Good night."

"Good night, Ben," Haley whispered.

Ben was slightly startled at Haley's use of his first name on the Bridge, but headed down without comment. He was suddenly exhausted, too tired to think about anything. Guerrero met him at the bottom of the bridge ladder.

"I'll take the heaters, sir," he said.

Ben had forgotten the M4 and the Sig pistol he was carrying—both would need to be locked in the armory. "Thanks, Gunner," he said as he handed them over, then took the short steps to his stateroom. As he stripped out of his combat gear, Ben heard the whirring of the diesel engine starter, followed by the low grumble as the engine turned over and started supplying power to the grid. Now that they were far enough offshore to be unheard, there was no further need to run on batteries.

He stared briefly at Victoria's green dress picture, smiling at the memory of her face when he slipped the ring on her finger. "Good night, my love," he said, touching the picture. He then flopped on his bunk and was asleep within a minute.

Surveillance

**Ile Ste. Michel, Haiti
00:25 EST, 5 December**

Frankle

Frankle took a last look at the boat as it swung around and headed away from shore toward the larger patrol boat. They were committed, and the team's fate would depend on the accuracy of their intelligence, their choices and guesses during the planning, and their skills as operators. They arranged their equipment on the sand between them. During the offload from the boat, there was no time to ensure each man had the correct equipment items—they just needed to grab everything and sort it out on land. Each man removed his floatation vest; they were a useless encumbrance now and could be hidden within the tree line for use during the return trip. *Hopefully.*

Frankle grabbed the satchel he needed and slung it over his shoulder, then picked up and shouldered his personal weapon, in his case, a suppressed Uzi machine pistol. On his belt, he also carried a holstered Sig Sauer P228 and the Ka-Bar fighting knife issued to him when he was in the Marines. Bell also carried a Sig and Ka-Bar, but he favored a SOPMOD Block II-equipped M4 carbine that allowed for long- and short-range fighting. The other two men had standard M4s and Glock nine-millimeter pistols.

Frankle took out the Garman handheld GPS navigator pre-programmed with their route and slipped on the special hood as the others sorted themselves out. The screen would only light up when pressed to his eyes, which would prevent detection if anyone was looking their way. He turned the unit on and looked into the hood. The unit calibrated itself and then displayed a rough topographical map showing their current position and intended route. The Coasties did well: they were within a hundred feet of their planned drop-off point. Frankle looked from the navigator and, through his NVGs, located the gap in the trees that marked their route. He glanced at the others, standing ready with their equipment, and whispered, "Right, let's go."

The four men set out slowly with Frankle in the lead, walking from landmark to landmark, guided by the navigator. The lack of moonlight was a blessing in remaining undetected, but it forced them to find their way among the rocks using NVGs. Progress was slow but steady as they progressed north and climbed the sloping high ground to the west of the 252 facility. They reached the rally point three hours and forty-five minutes after landing, a good hour before first light. They each disbursed to their observation points and donned the ghillie suits that would camouflage them through the day.

As Frankle settled into his nook, he placed his Uzi in the satchel and, as the horizon grew light with the coming dawn, also tucked in his NVGs. He had binoculars and a rangefinder scope in the bag, and he would not use those until later when the chance of light reflecting off their lenses was eliminated. There would be plenty of time to make the final observations needed to complete the mission. Frankle adjusted his position to be as comfortable as possible and put his head down to get some sleep. Gerard had the first watch on the compound and would alert them via their encrypted headset radios if it looked like anyone was approaching their position.

As Frankle laid his head down, he noticed for the first time how quiet it was. With the lack of open freshwater sources, there was almost no non-human animal life on the island, so the usual crescendo of bird and terrestrial animal calls that came with the dawn was absent. Likewise, no mosquitos, Frankle thought with satisfaction—there was no blood to be had and nowhere for them to breed. *Always with the silver linings, old man*, he thought as he fell asleep.

Aeropuerto Frank País, Holguín, Cuba
09:38 EST, 5 December

Edward M. Hochsmann

Rostov

Yevgeny Vladimirovich Rostov adjusted his sunglasses and descended the stairs of the Gulfstream Five business jet leased to a Croatian shell corporation belonging to the 252 Syndicate. It had been a long flight from Zagreb, over ten hours, but an agreeably smooth one. Rostov yawned and stretched, taking in the wonderful warm sunshine under the cloudless sky, tempered by the cool breeze of the easterly trade winds blowing in from the Atlantic, thirty kilometers to the northeast. Not quite a sea breeze and no pleasant odors from the sea or flora, just the familiar stink of diesel and burned jet fuel.

Rostov glanced at the hangar about a hundred meters away and noted a white and green painted CD2 twin-turboprop amphibious seaplane being towed out. A former security officer in the *Voyenno-vozdushnye sily Rossii*, or Russian Air Force, he was familiar with most aircraft types, particularly those built in Russia. Still, this was the first example he had seen of the late production Chinese version of the Dornier Seastar. This would be the plane that would ferry him and his three companions the remaining hour and a half of their journey to the Chinese base on Ile Ste. Michel. It would be far less comfortable than the luxurious business jet he'd stepped out of, but after a busy night of drinking and sex, he was looking forward to getting some sleep on the way.

Rostov was one of the young turks of the 252 Syndicate, joining after being drummed out of the Air Force for *excessive* corruption. The founders, the first generation of secret police plotters and torturers turned out when the Warsaw Pact collapsed in the early 1990s, had largely passed from the scene, either through retirement or death. The present ruling cadre, the second generation, were the junior backroom heavies and assassins who rode in behind the founders to fill out the middle ranks of the new syndicate. Young and hungry movers and shakers like Rostov were moving up in the organization, searching for opportunities to shine, be recognized, and move into one of the coveted territory governing chairs. Rostov's chance came when he got close to Xiaotong Chen, a senior Chinese Communist Party official administering the BRI effort in Moldova. Each recognized a kindred spirit in the other: a rapacious and power-hungry sociopath with a knack for sensing and seizing opportunities for promotion. Their early partnership had cleared several bureaucrats out of the way of BRI projects via the go-to 252 tools of bribery, extortion, and murder.

Chen had been rewarded with a promotion and assignment to clean up a problem with morale on Ile Ste. Michel. The high rates of discipline problems and suicides among the miners assigned there were unacceptable. His predecessor employed the usual, often brutal, disciplinary actions but had failed—the mine was falling well short of even the artificially low targets set to keep the Haitians on the hook. Chen deduced that unrelenting boredom and physical isolation from normal civilization were to blame and evaluated that providing relief in recreational drugs and submissive women was the path out of the problem. He naturally turned to his erstwhile Moldovan partner, Rostov. The latter was quick to respond, negotiating not only an additional revenue stream for the syndicate but a strong base in the western hemisphere under the aegis of the BRI's Haiti project.

The *Miho Dujam*'s loss had been a significant setback, both in terms of the loss of revenue from the arms shipment and a blow to the syndicate's prestige in the late delivery of services to their new Chinese partners. At least the fools running the ship had sunk it rather than letting the cargo or any evidence linking it to the syndicate fall into the Americans' hands. The chief of the Croatian arm of the syndicate, who had been singing Rostov's praises before the loss, made it clear his future success in the organization, if not his very life, depended on him cleaning up the mess. Rostov got the message. The women could be delivered by air as soon as they were gathered, and the heavy cargoes of arms and drugs would come later, once the sex services were functional.

Rostov had seen to this first delivery himself, from selecting the women to the transport to the island. Knowing Chen's fondness for blondes, Rostov had scoured the syndicate-controlled brothels and, unable to find candidates of sufficient "purity," expedited a couple of ongoing abduction operations to obtain two worthy candidates, one each from Poland and Latvia. He oversaw their indoctrination into their new life and gave each a "test flight" on the trip across the Atlantic. They were still aboard the Gulfstream with his bodyguard, awaiting the call to board the CD2. Rostov was certain Chen would appreciate the personal touch he had put on this first delivery.

Rostov glanced to his right, where his assistant Dmitri was locked in an intense discussion with a local official beside a dated Peugeot sedan with "PNR" lettering. Two soldiers with shouldered AK-47s, also with the *Policía Nacional Revolucionaria,* watched from the side. Undoubtedly, the advance bribe the organization had paid for a smooth transition through Cuban jurisdiction proved insufficient. Rostov was used to corruption in government—it was a leading tool in the syndicate's business model—but Cuba was truly in a league of its own. Fortunately, a large cache of currency, both in Euros and U.S. Dollars, was locked in a concealed safe in the Gulfstream. After an appropriately vigorous but futile resistance, Dmitri would re-board the plane, supposedly to collect all the money the crew was carrying on their persons. He would grab a pile of odd dollar and euro bills from the safe and return to the official to learn the amount just happened to be the exact shortage in the pre-paid arrival tax. It was comically venal and part of the cost of doing business.

After a few minutes, Dmitri turned, shook his head, and walked over to Rostov. "Time for some theater, Boss," he said.

Rostov affected an annoyed expression and put his hands on his hips. "Well, we'll make it look good, Dmitri," he said, shaking his finger in his assistant's face and getting a shrug in return. After a good show of indignation, Rostov took a wallet out of his pocket, pulled out 223 Euros in assorted bills, and, after handing the money over to Dmitri, made a significant gesture of shaking it upside down to the smiling Cubans. Dmitri took the bills, then trudged to the Gulfstream to complete the collection effort. Five minutes later, the official pocketed the money Dmitri handed him, and he and the soldiers climbed into the Peugeot and drove away.

As Dmitri stepped over, Rostov said, "Well done, my friend. You can tell the pilots it's safe to come out now." The CD2 pilots hid in a hangar storeroom to avoid getting caught up in the impromptu tax collection. They were Cubans running a charter service as a front for one of the 252's partners. The men were well-paid, and there was no risk of their blackmailing Rostov for more cash—the 252s were reluctant to risk acting against Cuban government agents but wouldn't hesitate to kill citizens and their families in brutal fashion. Dmitri returned with one man while another walked toward the plane.

"We are ready to depart whenever you wish, *señor*," the man said.

"No reason to delay," Rostov replied and turned to Dmitri. "Get them on board."

"I should come with you, Boss," Dmitri said.

"No, my friend, I need you to look after things here. Besides, Comrade Chen is a nervous man—the fewer of us there are, the better."

"Yes, Boss," Dmitri said, turning to walk to the Gulfstream.

Rostov followed the Cuban pilot to the CD2 and climbed aboard. It was configured for VIP transport, and Rostov had just sat in a comfortable rear-facing seat in the cabin's front when his bodyguard Vasili arrived, each of his massive fists with a firm grip on one woman. They were both lovely and well-dressed, but they were cowering in terror as Vasili dragged them on board and pushed them into two seats in the back. Dmitri followed with two suitcases and handed them to the pilot, who stored them in a baggage compartment, closed and locked the entry door, and then made his way to the cockpit.

As the CD2's two engines completed their start sequence, Rostov waved out the window at an obviously concerned Dmitri. He regretted leaving the man behind—Dmitri was a clever negotiator, and though Rostov did not expect any issues with Chen, you never knew. Neither man knew the decision had saved Dmitri's life.

The flight to Ile Ste. Michel took the advertised one-and-a-half hours, and with the beautiful weather and keeping over water absent of heated land updrafts, it was smooth enough for Rostov to nap the entire way. He was startled awake by the touch of the copilot, who said, "We are on final approach to the harbor."

Rostov stretched and said, "Thank you." Then he looked out the window to see the island's brown and tan landscape, surrounded by the deep blue of the Atlantic with the lighter shallows rimming the land. The plane descended and made a smooth landing in the sheltered waters just off the docks of the Chinese port facilities, then taxied ponderously to the boat landing, where the engines labored to push it up the incline. Once on level ground, the pilots shut down the engines, and Rostov watched as four armed Chinese men surrounded the plane.

The copilot stood, made his way to the cabin door, opened it, and stepped out onto the tarmac after showing he was empty-handed. After a moment, he poked his head in and said, "They wish to speak to you, *señor*."

Rostov nodded and stood, then walked back and climbed out of the plane to face two armed Chinese soldiers. "Good morning, gentlemen," he said in English. "I'm here to see Comrade Chen."

"Comrade Chen is far too busy with government business to visit with wayfarers," one soldier said. "You may contact your associates to pick you up, but you will remain with the aircraft until they do so. After you depart, the aircraft must as well."

"Very well," Rostov said. The cold shoulder was expected—one of the caveats in the treaty establishing the Chinese presence on Ile Ste. Michel was the prohibition against association with international criminal activity. He respected Chen could not be witnessed meeting with Rostov or any other syndicate members. Chen would make his way to the 252 compound after dark. "It will soon get hot within the aircraft with this sun. May my companions and I wait outside?"

The guard glanced inside and noticed the women for the first time. "Yes, but you will remain within five meters of the aircraft, and anyone straying outside that boundary will be arrested."

"Understood, thank you." Rostov turned and motioned to Vasili, who seized the women and pulled them through the door and under the shade of the CD2's narrow wing. The guards stared hungrily at the women, and Rostov was confident that if Chen weren't looking at them through binoculars from his office right now, he soon would be. Rostov pulled out a satellite phone and contacted the compound for a pickup.

Twenty minutes later, a large blue Chevy Tahoe pulled next to the plane, and, after one guard verified his identity, the driver climbed out and walked over to Rostov. It was Krupin, the supervisor of the compound. "Greetings, Mr. Rostov," the man said in Russian. "Welcome to our little tropical paradise." He glanced over at the women with a smile. "Our first attendants. Excellent choices, if I might say so. There is a considerable backlog of orders."

"They will remain unfilled for the time being, my friend," Rostov said. "These two lovelies are reserved for Comrade Chen and me tonight." He turned to Vasili and nodded, prompting him to move the women into the SUV.

"As it should be," Krupin said, grabbing Rostov's bag.

As they were driving away from the ramp, Rostov heard the CD2's engines start. He envied the pilots—they would fly to Puerto Plata in the Dominican Republic and stay overnight in a resort hotel, while he would have to make do with what passed for a VIP suite in a tropical brothel. *Such are the privations one has to sustain when you are the boss*, Rostov thought. He then glanced at the two women in the rearview mirror and smiled. *Of course, it could be worse.*

Frankle

Frankle stretched and rubbed his neck. He never liked this part of the job, laying prone and still for hours at a time, but at least the temperature was pleasant, not too hot or cold. The cold bothered him the most these days, yet another sign that it was time to hang it up. A glint of sunlight on glass caught his eye, and he trained his hooded binoculars on the road leading from the island's east side. It was the blue SUV returning, hopefully with their quarry on board. Frankle was a little surprised they were returning so quickly—he had noted the passage of a seaplane less than an hour ago he was sure carried Rostov and his bodyguard. He had expected a much longer meeting with the Chinese.

The overflights had tracked three SUVs associated with the 252 compound. Frankle's men had accounted for two, one sitting in front of the generator building and the other returning down the road. Frankle was disturbed by the fact they had not yet located that third vehicle—no other known 252 activity on the island could account for its absence. He supposed it could be off on the island's eastern side, working on some activity involving the Chinese. Another variable to be accounted for among too damn many.

He watched as the SUV continued down the coastal road, turned onto the side road leading to the 252 compound, and pulled to a stop beside the barracks/brothel. He moved his gaze to the forward passenger door and adjusted the focus as a man climbed out. It was Rostov, all right, looking like someone in a Sandals ad with his pastel blue shirt, white pants, and sunglasses. The rear door opened, and his hands tightened on the binoculars as another thug climbed out with two women. *Dammit, there wasn't anything about trafficking in the messages! Maybe they're volunteers; I'd rather be here than in a Croatian cesspool.* The thug answered his question by violently wrenching one woman's arm as he dragged both into the building. *Enjoy yourself, King Kong; you haven't long to live.*

Frankle's headset chirped, and he flipped it on. "Boss, did you see that?" said Bell's voice.

"Affirmative," Frankle replied.

"So, what are we going to do?" Bell asked.

"Our mission. Now get off the air."

Shit-shit-shit! As if it wasn't tricky enough to get into that compound and kidnap a security officer trained to resist. Bringing along two abused, traumatized, and likely hysterical women pushed it into the impossible category. He glanced over his shoulder south of the island. Although she couldn't be seen in the sea haze, *Kauai* was out there, somewhere within their radio range of fifteen miles, making like a typical Coast Guard cutter on a migrant interdiction patrol.

What would they think of a proposed mod to the mission to include the women? He knew what Ben would think, based on his performance on the *Miho Dujam*: Hell, yes! Reardon was another story—she was a cool customer, unlikely to react emotionally in a way that put the crew and boat at risk. Frankle nodded. *Yep, that's exactly what you need in a CO of a unit like this one.*

Frankle took out his tablet and typed a text message for encrypted burst transmission. "To Orchid From Delta, target on-site, observed in company of 2 captive women. Rpt, believe 2 women are prisoners. Unless otherwise directed, will attempt extract of prisoners during egress if willing. Ends." Frankle took the handheld directional antenna out of his bag, plugged it into the tablet, and scanned the southern horizon until it picked up *Kauai's* carrier signal. He tapped the send button, and the tablet did the network negotiation and sent the message in less than half a second. The tablet chat line said, "Msg rec'd OK," showing the checksum variable transmitted was valid for the message.

Frankle held the antenna pointed in the direction yielding the carrier tone and, minutes later, received another chirp in his headset indicating an incoming text. He glanced at the tablet. "To

Delta From Orchid, prisoner extract approved. Window 2000-0030L. Req rndz time when able. Ends."

Frankle smiled, pleased but hardly surprised, as the risk to the boat was the same whether the women came along or not. Although it imposed a constraint, he was pleased to see the "window" times for the extract, for it meant Pennington had got them some air support. *Hopefully, we won't need it.* He put the antenna down and turned back to his observations of the compound. *The boat's big enough to carry the extra two passengers, but can that crane handle the added two hundred pounds?*

USCG Cutter *Kauai*, Atlantic Ocean, fourteen nautical miles south of the western end of Ile Ste. Michel, Haiti
12:05 EST, 5 December

Haley

Haley looked across her cabin at Ben and Drake. There had been minimal discussion about the response to Frankle's request to extract the women. There was no added risk to the mission if they wanted to come off, and Haley could hardly refuse, even if she was inclined to do so. The extra weight in the boat was a concern. During the full-load test, the howl of the crane's hydraulic motors had made her hair stand up, and she wanted assurance it could take the extra weight. "What do you think, COB?" she asked.

"I don't know, Captain," Drake answered. "We were nibbling at the red line throughout the lift, and I sure wouldn't bet a paycheck on it."

It was not the answer Haley wanted to hear. She looked at Ben.

"We could put a Jacob's Ladder over, ma'am. One or two DIA guys and I can climb out before the lift to take some of the load off. It will delay the recovery, but that has to be preferable to risking a complete breakdown."

"Why leave Lopez in the boat?" Haley asked.

"Can't take the chance of leaving Lee with no help in case we need a Plan B, ma'am."

"Agreed. OK, let's plan on that. Rig the ladder and brief your crew."

"Yes, ma'am," Ben replied as he and Drake stood.

After the two left, Haley sat alone in the cabin and contemplated the five-pound ice cube in her stomach. As she had a dozen times in the last couple of days, she went over her decisions relating to the upcoming operation. The message detailing the assignment of the Compass Call C-130 electronic warfare aircraft had been a tremendous relief, and at least they would have a good handle on what the Chinese were doing. It was bad enough to send Ben and Lopez ashore with machine guns *(machine guns!)* to support the extract. Sitting there ignorant of the actions of an enemy that could blow them all to hell would be unnerving.

She had only talked briefly with Lopez during her familiarization patrol, but found him bright and earnest. Sam had said they were lucky to have him, that Mercier had added an ME3 billet so that they could keep him on board after he graduated from the Maritime Law Enforcement Specialist A-school training. He was on the shortlist of crew members she needed to get to know better, and after this operation, she would make clearing that list a priority.

She pulled open the drawer and took out the picture of her with her father, taken on her graduation day from the Academy. He was wearing one of his finest suits, and she was in her dress whites, both of them smiling proudly. It had been the happiest day of her life until four days ago, when she had taken command of *Kauai*. She thought, *Oh, Daddy. Look at what your little girl is doing now!* She stood and put the picture back and closed the drawer.

She stopped on her way to the Bridge to glance in Ben's open door at the pictures of him and Victoria on his wall. Haley had been concerned when Ben told her they had become engaged the night after the change of command and remained convinced that emotional ties to the shore were liabilities officers could ill afford. Yet, despite this, Ben seemed to be as focused as before, if not more so, and Haley was wondering if it might be time to revisit her philosophy.

Final March

Ile Ste. Michel, Haiti
19:07 EST, 5 December

Frankle

The sun had set almost two hours previously, and it was fully dark now. It was a new moon period, but their NVGs were fine in terms of visibility under the stars and clear skies. Not that they would need them for the approach to target—the 252 compound was lit up like Yankee Stadium in extra innings.

Right after sunset, the team had reformed on Frankle's position to compare notes and formulate the final assault plan. With Rostov's arrival, the 252s had stepped up their security patrolling, but Frankle and his men agreed it was more for show than any genuine security concern. The lazy way the guards held their weapons and the shortcuts they took on their rounds reflected complacency. It was not unexpected—there was nothing of value stored here yet, no indigenous population to guard against, and the Chinese were under orders not to deal with them. There was a fixed sentry post where the road entered the compound, but the guards posted there mostly sat around smoking and playing video games on their cell phones.

They debated whether it would be a net positive or negative to hit the powerhouse first and knock out the lights. While that would have the definite advantage of eliminating targeted shots from any of their opponents, it would also sound the alarm at the outset of the operation. Frankle decided there were too many risks in tipping their hand that early, and the powerhouse idea was shelved. The plan that evolved had Gerard and Kelly ambush the roving guard as he neared the vehicle parking area. They would kill the man with the silenced pistols they carried, hide the body, find the keys for one of the SUVs and slash the tires on the others. Frankle and Bell would await the success signal from the other team, then take out the entrance sentry and make their way to the barracks where Rostov and the women were housed. Anyone they encountered on the compound would be dispatched silently.

Finding the keys was another wildcard—given the lackadaisical approach to security, they expected to find them inside the vehicles, probably tucked into the driver's window shade. But they could be elsewhere, and a search for them might take minutes if they could be found at all. This was the worst case, as they would be on foot to the rendezvous, but so would what remained of the 252 staff. Not the preferred outcome, but still acceptable.

The tentative go-time for the assault was 21:00, time enough for whatever air support they were getting to get on station and build the tactical picture. The GO-NO-GO decision hinged upon a coded burst transmission from *Kauai* fifteen minutes before launch that she was in position and ready to retrieve them. If something prevented that, mechanical breakdown or activity by the Chinese, for instance, Frankle had a decision to make. He could either sit tight and let the opportunity pass by with a pickup by *Kauai* the following night or go in gunning to kill Rostov and then withdraw and evade as best as possible in the hope of an alternative rescue mode. His orders from Admiral Irving, known only to him, were the latter. He also had little doubt Irving would cut them loose rather than mount a risky rescue operation, and he was not about to throw away the lives of his team. If they had to abort tonight, he would order his team to lie low for another day, then contact *Kauai* for extraction, grabbing the captive women, if practicable.

Frankle smiled grimly. He knew before he started that this would be his last trip. He had maxed out his federal retirement and only held on as long as it stayed interesting. The past year's events, culminating with this op, had taken the shine off fieldwork. If he returned, *when he returned*, he corrected himself, he would put in for one of the instructor jobs at Quantico, Bragg, or Benning. He was jolted from his thoughts by the appearance of headlights on the coastal road off to his right. He took out his night scope and trained it on the oncoming vehicle. The glare of the headlights prevented him from making out any vehicle details. He would have to wait until it passed him. He knew the vehicle had to be Chinese—they had accounted for all three big SUVs the 252s were using in their work. His heart sank. What if it was one of their SUVs or, worse, one of the VN-4s? *What a time for those assholes to start their own patrols!*

He watched with interest as the vehicle slowed and then turned off onto the side road leading to the compound. As it entered a gentle curve to the right, the headlights were finally pointed away enough for him to get a vehicle profile. *My God! It's a sedan! A high-end one, by the looks of it.* The car stopped at the entry checkpoint, and the guard shined his flashlight in on the driver and passenger, then waved the car through. As it pulled into the bright lights in front of the barracks, Frankle could see that it was one of the latest generation BMW 5 series. He zoomed the scope on the passenger door as the driver jumped out, came around, and opened it. A portly man in a Hawaiian shirt, white pants, and sunglasses climbed out, hurried to the door, and then inside the barracks, his driver hurrying to catch up.

I'll be damned! That has to be Chen, the mine director. Only a high-up CCP prick would insist on having a status car on a Haitian island, and no boss would let a flunky use his wheels for a booty call! He chuckled at the comedic aspect of the entire event. *Dressed like Magnum P.I. and wearing Blues Brothers sunglasses at night for anonymity. Hilarious!* He keyed his microphone and whispered, "Bring it in, boys. We need to talk."

A minute later, the three other men had returned to Frankle's position. "OK, boys, here's the deal," he said. "Confidence is high that the *haole* who just arrived is the big CCP boss himself, which changes the objectives."

"Are we going to grab him instead or cap him?" Kelly asked.

"Absolutely not," Frankle replied. "We have strict orders, which I agree with for a change, that we do not kidnap or kill Chinese nationals. However, there's nothing in those orders about knocking one out and grabbing his biometrics. Please, one of you tell me you've brought a biometrics kit."

"Yo," Gerard answered.

"OK, give it to Lashon. Same plan for you guys as before—grab an SUV and bring it upfront after you disable the rest. You will also slash the BMW tires while you wait for us. Clear?"

"Roger, Boss," Gerard answered.

"Lashon, it's on us. We move in on the barracks, take out any guards and move on to the bedrooms. I'm pretty sure we'll find both our guys *in flagrante delicto*. We stun them, and while Lashon is hooking up Chen and grabbing his vitals, I'll be sedating Tovarisch Rostov and tossing clothes at the women. We load everyone and beat feet. Questions?"

"Yeah. How come you always get the girls?" Gerard asked.

"Two reasons. First, I'm the boss. Second, they will be pretty shook up and probably respond better to a grandpa type than the Incredible Hulk here or two other guys that look like the mooks who grabbed them from home."

"Ouch!" Gerard said, smiling.

"Deal with it," Frankle said. "Any questions?"

"Still want to go with 21:00?" Bell asked.

"Better push it back to 21:30 to give the sex, drugs, and wine a chance to take a firm hold. I'll tell the Coasties. Off you go." After the other three men disappeared into the darkness, Frankle took out the antenna and sent an update. After receiving an acknowledgment from the patrol boat out in the darkness, he tucked away the radio and turned to watch the compound. *This could be huge—documented evidence of Chinese collusion with the 252s at the highest level. All we need now is one damn set of keys!*

**USCG Cutter *Kauai*, Atlantic Ocean, eight nautical miles south of the western end of Ile Ste. Michel, Haiti
20:03 EST, 5 December**

Haley

They had gone to General Quarters Condition One half an hour earlier, with radar shut down, and moved from their daytime patrol position fifteen miles south of the island to half that distance. For now, Ben was on the Bridge, having briefed Lee and Lopez; he could be on the main deck and ready to launch in less than a minute. The FC3 panel was fully manned, Hopkins had the OOD, as usual, and everyone was in full combat gear.

An Air Force C-130 Compass Call plane, callsign Starfish One Seven, arrived precisely on time at 20:00, forty-five minutes after its launch from its forward base at Guantanamo Bay. On its arrival, the converted tactical transport made a slow pass along the island's north side, training its extremely sensitive passive sensors, electro-optical, infrared, and electronic surveillance inland. As expected, these detected nothing along the north shore. As they swung in a wide arc around the island's eastern end on a westerly course off its south coast, the Chinese base was unmasked, and things got interesting.

"Orchid, Starfish One Seven," said the disembodied voice from the UHF radio speaker.

Haley plugged her headset into the microphone jack and keyed her press-to-talk switch. "Starfish One Seven, Orchid-Actual. Go ahead."

"Orchid, One Seven, initial sweep complete. No radars operating. Some encrypted traffic on UHF-FM band in the eight-hundred-megahertz range, probably handhelds. One warship dockside, one cargo ship dockside. Warship is active; we picked up a definite exhaust plume on infrared. Over."

Haley's hand froze briefly, then she pushed the transmit button again. "One Seven, can you tell if they are running generators, or is it the full plant?"

"Orchid, One Seven, unknown. We will pull in closer on the next pass."

"One Seven, Orchid. Roger, standing by." Haley dropped her hand and looked across at the navigation display. The screen showed *Kauai* as a pipper in the center, with a map display of Ile Ste. Michel stretching from directly north to the screen's edge to the east. *Kauai's* radars were shut down to facilitate emissions control—they would navigate using GPS and bearings from the electro-optical camera. The heat plume from the gunboat was terrible news, and Haley hoped they were just running their generators for maintenance or normal engine turnover. None of the earlier nighttime overflights had shown any activity like this, and the conclusion was the ship usually ran on shore power when moored. The ten-minute wait for the following report was the longest of her life.

"Orchid, One Seven."

"Go ahead."

"I'm not an expert, Captain, but that ship is putting out an awful lot of heat for generators only. I've got a large exhaust plume around the stern. Over."

"Roger. Can you maintain contact? Over."

"Affirmative. We will maintain a port delta two klicks south of the island's eastern point."

"Thanks, One Seven. If that sucker moves, I need to know soonest. Over."

"WILCO, out."

Haley unplugged her headset and said, "Chief, the XO and I will be heading below for a minute."

"Very good, Captain," Hopkins replied.

Haley looked at Ben and said, "Let's chat."

"Very good, ma'am."

They stepped into Haley's cabin, and she shut the door. "Have a seat." After they both sat, she continued. "What do you think, Ben?"

"Things just got a whole lot iffier, ma'am," Ben said.

"No shit. All of a sudden, the Chinese are doing things they have never done before."

"We don't know why they are lighting off. I don't think they're expecting us to make a hit. If they thought we had an op going and wanted to intervene, they would be underway already. If I had to make a guess, it's a standing order to warm up the gunboat whenever the boss goes over the hill in case the 252s do something stupid. I imagine their armored car troops are on alert as well. If they roll when the shooting starts, I don't see how we avoid an engagement. But I think they'll try to get an order from the boss first."

"Do you think that would delay them more than a few minutes?"

"No, ma'am."

"Which means an engagement with the armored cars, the gunboat, or both would be likely. Something we were explicitly ordered to avoid."

"I would say so, ma'am."

"So you are saying I should follow the orders?" Haley asked.

Ben looked her in the eyes. "Ma'am, it's not my call to make."

"I know that. I'm asking what you would do if you were in my seat."

Ben's mouth tightened, and he said, "I would go in, ma'am."

"You know we wouldn't have a prayer if that gunboat pins us in that cove. Even if we break out, they have the speed to run us down, eight times our firepower, and the range to out-shoot us. Air support would be the only thing that could save us, and we can't count on that. You would take that risk for some abstract geopolitical gain?"

"No, ma'am, I don't give a crap about the price of rare-earth elements, but I would go in there to save four brave men and two innocent women. This is what we do, ma'am."

"At the cost of all sixteen of us?"

"I don't think it will come to that, ma'am."

"And if it did?"

"I would still go, ma'am. It's a big risk for us, but certain death for them otherwise. The SAR dilemma." Ben nodded.

"Very well, thank you for your candor. I need to think about this for a minute. I'll meet you on the Bridge."

"Yes, ma'am," Ben said, then turned and left.

Haley looked at her desk. *How can this be a choice? I obey orders, save my ship and crew, or disobey orders, and maybe get them both shot to hell. No brainer. But is it? Those four men and two women—can I really leave them to die, or worse, in the women's case? These are the choices you have to make,* Captain.

She looked from her desk and slowly glanced around the bare walls of her cabin. *Cold and sterile, like the mathematics of life and death.* Her gaze stopped on the ship's plaque mounted above her bunk. It was a smaller version of the one that hung on the messdeck, and she had to admit that, unlike the crests she had seen on other ships, she liked the design. It featured the escutcheon of the Kingdom of Hawaii, with a silver-colored fouled anchor in the background and the ship's motto on a golden scroll below: *Fortiter et Fideliter,* "Bravely and Faithfully" in Latin.

As the weight lifted from her shoulders, a sad smile crept over her face. *Of all the things, a plaque, for God's sake!* She stood, reached over to give the plaque a quick pat, then headed for the Bridge. "Carry on, please," Haley said as she emerged onto the Bridge to the usual call to attention. "Chief, start your approach. Secure MDEs at four nautical miles."

"Aye, aye, Captain," Hopkins replied.

Haley turned to Ben. "God help us all, XO."

"Indeed, ma'am. One helluva break-in patrol!"

Ben

The diesel engines shut down as Ben went below to the armory to check out his guns for this foray. The eerie silence that followed gave him the shivers, as it always did. *Kauai*'s battery bank stored enough energy to propel her at twenty knots for two hours and progressively longer times at lower speeds. They had never put this endurance to the ultimate test, although they had come close at Barbello. They had six hours at their twelve-knot approach speed—plenty of time to roll in and out.

Lopez was already at the armory when Ben arrived, and Guerrero doled out the weapons and ammunition. The Mark 48 machine guns they were checking out were a little longer and three times heavier than the M4s they usually carried on expeditionary operations. It was one of the many factors Ben had to keep in mind tonight.

"Do you need a refresh, XO?" Guerrero asked.

Ben went through the standard checks from memory of his training six months ago. "Did I do alright, Gunner?"

"Spot on, XO." Guerrero held out his hand. "Good luck, sir."

"Same here," Ben said as he shook his hand. He slung the machine gun, grabbed the belt holding his pistol and other equipment, and followed Lopez out of the armory.

"Think we'll see action tonight, sir?" Lopez asked as they climbed the ladder to the main deck.

"I don't think you and I will. As far as the boat goes, just a little south of fifty-fifty."

"Right. Better make sure we get back then."

"That's the idea," Ben replied. They emerged on deck and walked aft to the special operations boat, already lifted from its cradle and positioned at the rail by Bondurant. "Gather 'round, folks," Ben said as he stood before them. "Plan is the same as we last briefed. The bad news is something is going on at that Chinese base, and we don't know what it is. This has dialed up the threat and our need to beat feet as soon as possible. So, the order of the day is expedite to the limit of safety—anything we break, lose over the side, etc., is the cost of doing business. Clear?"

"Got it, XO," Bondurant said.

"Any questions?" Ben asked. Seeing nothing but head shakes, he keyed his radio. "Orchid, Oscar-One, ready for launch."

"Oscar-One, Orchid, cleared for launch. Good luck, sir." Bunting's voice replied through his headset.

"OK, let's do it," Ben said, following after Lee and Lopez climbed into the boat. It was the same plan for approach as before, with the boat launched at two miles offshore and cruising silently on the sea painter until a quarter-mile and then on her own to the beach. Ben watched the shoreline through his NVGs as the two vessels approached, trying to pick out the agreed landing point. He looked across the boat at Lopez, who was also looking forward toward the island. He glanced at Lee, coolly scanning between her panel and *Kauai* to keep pace without putting too much tension on the sea painter.

A little under ten minutes after launch, the "L" signal flashed from the Bridge, and Lee said, "Cast off the sea painter."

Lopez pulled the marlinspike holding the line in place and, after it disappeared over the side, said, "Sea painter clear."

"Right, hang on," Lee said as she goosed the engine, scooting the boat forward along *Kauai*'s port side. It was a quick trip to the shore, where, unlike the previous night, Ben and Lopez pulled the boat's bow on the beach after they jumped out.

After slinging the gun over his shoulder with a grunt, Ben turned to Lee. "Now, no beach parties while I'm gone, Petty Officer Lee," he said, extending his hand.

"You are just so *Dad*," Lee replied as she shook his hand. "Come back safe, sir." She then grabbed Lopez's outstretched hand. "You too, Boot."

"See ya in a bit, Shelley," Lopez replied, plodding after Ben through the thick sand.

It took Ben a minute of scanning between the landscape presented in his NVGs and the tablet with the GPS app to find the correct gap where he and Lopez would wait. Ben led them through the low brush to the gap, which extended about one-hundred-fifty yards to a pair of tree copses about fifty feet apart, beyond which was open ground. As they neared the mouth of the gap, Ben said, "Set up behind a good tree over there," pointing to the thicket on the left.

"How will they find us, XO?" Lopez asked.

"I'm going to pop a line of five chemlights running right along the center," Ben replied.

"Won't that bring the bad guys down on us?"

"I won't pop them until our guys are a minute out. If there are bad guys, they'll be following our guys. Anyway, we want them to come here instead of hitting us from the flank. Hopefully, there will be enough adrenaline in play to keep them from thinking too much."

"Hopefully, sir?"

"Hey, hope is my strategy for so many things these days."

As Lopez walked to his position, Ben turned and strolled to his. He found an excellent location to the left of a large tree and set up the gun, relieved to get the heavy weight off his shoulder. Once he had everything in place and a round chambered, he pressed the button on his tactical radio. "Delta-One, Oscar-One."

Seconds later, Frankle's voice replied. "Oscar-One, Delta-One, copy."

"Delta-One, Oscar-One, Uber's here. Call me one minute out so I can string the markers."

"WILCO, Oscar-One. We're stepping off now."

"Good luck, Delta," Ben said, getting a double-click in return. He then sat and tried to find a comfortable position on the hard ground. Like Frankle before him, Ben was struck by how quiet the island was, the absence of distraction leaving him with nothing to do but think about their situation. Ben thought back to Haley's decision to go ahead with the mission. It was a gutsy call—Ben didn't know if he could have made that decision, but he knew they would definitely be on the hot seat when they got back.

A Fighting Retreat

Ile Ste. Michel, Haiti
22:03 EST, 5 December

Frankle

The silent trek down from the observation position had taken longer than the twenty minutes Frankle had expected, but both pairs of DIA men were in place. Bell lay beside him, sighting on the front sentry with his silenced M4 carbine. They would wait for Gerard's signal that he had killed the rover and seized an operable SUV, then pop the sentry to make their way among the buildings to the barracks, avoiding the lights whenever possible. It was no minor relief to hear Ben's voice an hour previously announcing they were in place, green-lighting the assault. *"Uber's here." That kid has a way with words,* Frankle thought with a smile.

Chen's driver had come out minutes after they had gone into the barracks and sat in the car, smoking and doing something with his cell phone. It would be handy if they could surprise him there with a Taser, followed by an ampule of the powerful sedative the DIA men all carried. Like his boss, the driver had to be left alive at all costs, and they couldn't afford to chase him all over the compound. Frankle scanned for any other stray 252s; a task made difficult in the alternating light and darkness of the compound. Nothing. He suspected the gang members not asleep were watching satellite TV in the crew section of the barracks at the opposite end of the brothel.

Not knowing the inside layout of the barracks was a real problem, hopefully one that wouldn't blow up in their faces. There would be no one near Rostov and Chen while they were "engaged" with the women—Chen had already evicted his driver, and Frankle suspected Rostov would have his bodyguard within shouting distance, but no closer. *He's probably near the front door where he could corral anyone blundering in. Hopefully, the "gotta pee" approach will work.*

Frankle's headset chirped. "Lead, I got a ride; others are dead," Gerard's voice said.

Thank God! Frankle clicked his transmit button twice, then reached out and tapped Bell on his right shoulder. After waiting for the guard to present an optimal aspect, Bell's finger tightened on the trigger. After a soft "pop" from the rifle, the guard slumped forward without another sound. Bell switched the fire selector to safe, raised to a kneeling position, and nodded. Frankle nodded, and they both stood and started toward the nearest building.

It took a few minutes to work their way around to the shaded side of the barracks behind the BMW. The Chinese driver was still sitting in the driver's seat with his hand out the window holding a cigarette, and Frankle could see he was still looking at his cell phone screen. When he began tapping his hand on the side of the car, apparently in time with some music or dance video, Frankle crept forward with his stunner handy. He jammed the weapon into the driver's shoulder on reaching the car and pulled the trigger. After a brief convulsion, the driver settled into a stupor, and Frankle injected an ampule of the quick-acting sedative. Within seconds, the driver was unconscious, and Frankle bound him to the seat using the seat belt.

Satisfied the driver was finished for the evening, Frankle stepped to the front door of the barracks and beckoned to Bell. When his partner was in position on the opposite side of the door, silenced pistol in hand, Frankle made what he hoped sounded like a timid knock. After a pause, he knocked again.

Behind the door, a deep voice intoned, "*Chego the khochesh?*" [what do you want?]

Affecting the highest voice he could, Frankle replied, "*Mne nuzno polzovatsya tualetom!*" [I need to use the lavatory].

"*Po'shyol 'na hui!*" [Go screw yourself!]

Frankle knocked again, holding in a laugh. "*Pojaluista, vpustyte menia!*" [Please let me in!]

As expected, the door flew open, and Vasili's huge hand reached out to grab Frankle by the neck. The agent grabbed his arm and pulled the big man through the door in stunned surprise, where Bell killed him with a single shot to the back of his head. The two agents grabbed Vasili as he fell, dragged him into the barracks, and dropped him in an easy chair a short distance from the door.

Frankle nodded at Bell, and they each pulled a Taser, then crept forward to listen and peek in each door in the long hallway. Eventually, each found a target, and as Bell watched him, Frankle counted down on his fingers. Upon reaching zero, Frankle plunged through his door, shot a surprised and naked Chen with his Taser, then pounced on him with flex cuffs and a gag. The sedative was not an option with Chen, as they could not risk the man dying from an allergic reaction. He looked over to find a blond woman staring back wide-eyed and clutching bedsheets across her bare chest. "Do you speak English?" Frankle said. After getting no reaction, he tried German, *"Sprechen sie Deutsch?"* The woman nodded, and he continued, *"Ich bin ein Amerikaner, hier, um dich zu retten. Anziehen sich."* [I am an American here to save you. Get dressed.]

Frankle had just finished tightening the gag on Chen when Bell appeared at the door and tossed him the biometrics kit. The agent took Chen's fingerprints, a blood sample, and digital photographs of his nude body at almost every angle. He flipped him on his stomach, patted him on the shoulder, and whispered in his ear, "Congratulations, Comrade. You are now the most biometrically documented man in history." He stood and gently took the now-dressed woman by the arm and keyed his microphone. "Billy, bring it in."

"On the way."

As the pair stepped out into the hallway, they almost ran into Bell, carrying the unconscious Rostov over his left shoulder, with the other woman following them. Glancing at Rostov's briefs, Frankle asked, "Not that far along, was he?"

"No, I have a weak stomach," Bell replied.

Frankle chuckled and peered out the front door. When an SUV pulled up, and Gerard jumped out, Frankle opened the door and said, "Billy, take care of the Beemer. Steve, help Lashon with Rostov." As Gerard pulled out his K-bar, Frankle led the two women to the SUV and helped them into the rear seat. As Bell and Kelly moved the unconscious Rostov into the middle seat, a shrill alarm sounded across the compound. "Shit! Let's go, let's go!" Frankle shouted, slammed the back door, and jumped into the forward passenger seat. He turned and shouted, "*Alles auf den boden!*" [Everybody, get down!]. Gerard jumped in, and the SUV hurtled toward the road, a cloud of dust spreading behind it. Frankle could hear automatic fire and the thuds of bullets striking the car's body. A burst shattered the rear window, and one woman huddled on the floor screamed. Through the smashed window, he saw headlights behind them on the road. "Billy, I thought you got all the cars!"

"I did! The damn Beemer has run-flats, and I didn't have time to do anything else!"

"Shit!" Frankle said, then keyed his microphone. "Oscar, this is Delta. We're three minutes out, and we've got a tail. Over!"

Ben

Ben was going over the mathematics of the gunboat's ETA when a strange sound got his attention. At first, he could not make out what it was, then came the unmistakable sound of automatic gunfire in the distance. Ben transmitted on his command set, "Orchid, Oscar-One, I'm hearing gunfire from the direction of the compound. Over."

"Oscar-One, Orchid, roger, out."

Ben jumped to his feet, grabbed a handful of chemical light sticks, trotted to the rear of the gap, activated, and dropped one. He ran ten yards up the middle of the gap, activated, and dropped another. After three more similar drops, he trotted back to his gun and reached it as Frankle's urgent call came.

"Oscar, this is Delta. We're three minutes out, and we've got a tail. Over!"

Ben keyed his microphone. "Delta from Oscar, we're ready. The path is lit!"

"Roger, out!"

"Lope!" Ben called across to Lopez.

"Yes, sir!"

"They've got a tail, and we're going to make sure we hit the driver. As soon as the first vehicle passes, open up on the second one with full auto. Aim at the lights, got it?"

"Copy, sir!"

Ben keyed his command set again. "Orchid, Oscar-one. Delta reports en route with pursuit. We are standing by to engage."

"Oscar, Orchid-Actual, roger, act at discretion, out."

Ben could see headlights now, bobbing on the graded road. He could intermittently see the second vehicle's headlights through the dust billowing behind the first vehicle. He watched as the headlights reached the coast road, then turned right toward their position. The second vehicle reached the road and followed, creeping up on the first. The lead vehicle reached a point where the driver could see Ben's chemlights and turned off the coast road, heading toward them. When the second car turned to follow, Ben shifted to the gunsight and watched in fascination as the target closed.

The first vehicle tore past them in a cloud of dust with a roar, and Ben and Lopez simultaneously pulled and held their triggers. After ten seconds of continuous firing, there was an eerie silence. Ben could see nothing through the smoke and dust at first. Then the light breeze from the northeast cleared the obscuration, and Ben could make out the car. Part of the car, anyway—their gunfire had killed the driver, and it had careened into a boulder, crushing the front half. Ben could make out something sticking out the smashed rear window. Ben stood for a better look and realized it was a human arm. The next thing he knew, he was bending over and vomiting. He was still leaning over ten seconds later when Lopez shouted, "Sir, are you OK?"

Ben stood upright, shook himself, picked up the gun, and said, "Yes. Let's go!" He gave the car one last look, then trotted after Lopez down the gap. The SUV had effectively cleared the underbrush down to the beach, making the going a lot easier for Ben and Lopez on the return. They were halfway to the boat when Ben's command set buzzed.

"Oscar-One, Orchid-Actual, warning, Chinese vehicles approaching on the coast road. Expedite departure!"

"Orchid, Oscar-One, WILCO, out!" He turned to Lopez and said, "Move it. The Chinese are coming!" Then the two men took off in a dead run toward the boat where the DIA men and guests were already loading. As they got within twenty yards, Ben shouted, "Push off! The Chinese are coming!" When they arrived, everyone was on board but Kelly. After Ben and Lopez tossed their guns in the boat, the three men pushed it off the beach until they were thigh-deep and then pulled themselves on board. "The hell with stealth, Shelley, haul ass!" Ben shouted.

Lee slammed the right throttle forward with the helm hard over to the left, and the heavily loaded boat turned ponderously toward the sea and *Kauai*. Ben could see two sets of headlights approaching on the coast road. About the time the boat completed her turn and Lee had pushed both throttles to full ahead, the vehicles stopped near the gap with the still-glowing chemlights. A searchlight winked on and traced the path down to the SUV stopped by the water. *OK, you've found the SUV, now let it go, please!*

After pausing for a few seconds on the SUV, the searchlight began sweeping across the water off the beach. It passed over, came back, fixed on the white wake, and followed it up to the boat. When the light reached and settled on the boat, Ben shouted, "Hit the deck!" Two seconds later, the first burst of gunfire struck.

Haley

"Orchid, Oscar-One, I'm hearing gunfire from the direction of the compound. Over."

Haley wanted to jump from her chair but held herself in place and simply nodded at Bunting.

Bunting turned and transmitted, "Oscar-One, Orchid, roger, out."

"Captain, I have a vehicle. Make that two vehicles, moving down the side road from the compound on EO. Contact is intermittent because of land shadowing," Williams reported.

Haley swallowed. "Very well, track them as best as you can. Put it on the screen."

Ben's voice came from the command set speaker again moments later, "Orchid, Oscar-one. Delta reports en route with pursuit. We are standing by to engage."

"I'll take this one," Haley said, then keyed her microphone. "Oscar, Orchid-Actual, roger, act at discretion, out." Haley knew Ben would have done that anyway, but she didn't want him wasting a single thought on whether she approved. *This was what Sam was talking about. This is the agonizing part where you get to watch everything, with absolutely no ability to help. Those are your kids out there, and you have to trust them.*

Williams couldn't hold a fix on the vehicles with the ship's camera until they reached the coast road. Then the picture cleared, and Haley was surprised to see an SUV pursued by what looked like a luxury car—she would have expected the opposite. They lost the picture again when the vehicles turned off the road near the boat's landing site.

"Conn, Mount 52, sound of automatic gunfire, three-zero-zero relative, no visual target!" Connally reported through the open bridge door on the port side.

"Conn aye!" Hopkins replied.

Soon, Connally reported again, "Conn, Mount 52, sound of automatic gunfire has stopped!"

"Conn, aye!"

Lee's voice came over the command set, "Orchid, Orchid-One, SUV has arrived, passengers loading!"

Haley nodded to Bunting, who transmitted "Orchid-One, Orchid, roger, out."

Haley was about to ask for a report from Ben when the UHF speaker barked again. "Orchid, Starfish One Seven, I have movement from the Chinese base. Two vehicles, appear to be some kind of APC. Over."

APCs? Armored Personnel Carriers! It's the VN-4s! Haley changed to UHF on her radio selector and keyed the microphone. "Starfish One Seven, Orchid-Actual, please confirm two APCs headed west on the coast road. Over."

"Orchid, One Seven, confirmed. Over."

"One Seven, Orchid-Actual, roger. Keep an eye on that gunboat, out." Haley switched to the command set. "Oscar-One, Orchid-Actual, warning! Chinese vehicles approaching on the coast road, expedite departure!"

"Orchid, Oscar-One, WILCO, out!" Ben replied.

Haley balled her fists, then took a deep breath. "Williams, train the EO on the coast road from the east. Let me know when the VN-4s come into sight."

"Aye, aye, ma'am," Williams replied.

"Chief, no point in ultraquiet anymore. Light off the mains."

"Aye, aye, ma'am," Hopkins replied. She pressed the intercom and said, "Main Control, Conn, put all engines on line."

"Main Control, aye," Drake's voice replied. Within seconds came the whine of a diesel engine starter, followed by a grumble as the first engine caught and came up to speed.

Haley switched to intra-ship radio. "Overwatch, CO."

"Go ahead, ma'am," Guerrero replied.

"We have two Chinese armored vehicles approaching. Hopefully, they'll just have a look and go home. But, if not, we may have a fight. They have a mounted seven-point-six-two, but it is manually operated and will need target illumination. Your target will be that searchlight, but you will be weapons tight unless they fire on us or the small boat or I give a direct order. Do you copy?

"Ma'am, target searchlight, weapons tight. Engage only if the vehicle opens fire."

"That's correct. Good luck."

"Thank you, ma'am."

"Captain, I have headlights on the coast road, estimate one mile," Williams reported.

Haley turned and gazed at the EO screen. "Load APDS-T."

"Load APDS-T, aye," Williams said, then typed a command into the console. On the foredeck, the ship's gun emitted a series of clanking sounds audible on the Bridge as the automatic loader fed the first armor-piercing, discarding-sabot tracer round into the breech. "APDS-T loaded, Captain."

Haley gripped her chair and said, "Surface action port. Target the lead vehicle."

Williams said, "Target the lead vehicle, aye." Williams slewed the gun camera to the ship's EO, already locked on to the leading VN-4. After he typed in a few commands, the gun mount came alive and traversed left to align with the gunsight. Then the gun elevated automatically to account for the VN-4's height above the water and compensate for the slight ballistic drop over the measured distance. When the computer's AI was satisfied with the gun's alignment, the reticle on Williams's screen turned green. "Target identified. Target selected. On target and tracking, Captain."

"Very well, hold."

"Hold fire, ma'am," Williams said, eyes locked on the screen.

The Chinese vehicle stopped and, as Haley expected, turned on a searchlight and directed it down onto the beach. Williams repeated, "On target and tracking, ma'am."

"Hold."

"Yes, ma'am," Williams said, shifting in his seat. "They're sitting ducks in that boat, ma'am."

"Knock it off, Williams," Hopkins said, to Haley's surprise.

"Aye, Chief."

Haley watched in agony as the light swept out from the shore, and held her breath as it picked up the wake, then settled on the boat. Then the VN-4 opened fire, tracers reaching into the boat.

"Commence fire!"

Williams had already pressed the fire button at the beginning of the command, and the gun barked a loud bang and immediately loaded another APSD-T. The quarter-pound penetrator shed its sabot jacket on leaving the barrel, and its tracer tail made it look like a glowing red streak as it crossed the water at almost four times the speed of sound. At around seven hundred meters to the target, the flight time for the round was half a second. The round punched through the light armor in the empty troop compartment and filled the interior with fragments and dust. Guerrero's first shot arrived almost simultaneously, tearing the searchlight off the vehicle. The panicked gunner shifted from the boat and fired wildly toward *Kauai*'s muzzle flash while the drivers scrambled to put the vehicle in reverse. *Kauai*'s second and third rounds ended all that, cutting the gunner in half and bursting the vehicle's fuel tanks. The second VN-4's commander was no fool, backing away from his burning comrade at full speed without lights or gunfire.

"Second target disengaging, Captain," Williams reported.

"Ceasefire, but stay on him until he is out of sight," Haley said, then keyed her command set. "Orchid-One, Orchid-Actual, report!"

"Orchid, Orchid-One, three down: Kelly, Frankle, and Lopez," Lee replied. "Minor hull damage, but we should make it to the ship. Over."

Haley felt like she had been punched in the stomach. "Orchid-One, how bad? Over."

"Kelly is dead. Lopez is very bad; XO is working on him now. Frankle should be OK. Over."

"Roger, continue to ship. Out." Haley stared straight ahead, her mind reeling.

"Captain, shall I get underway?" Hopkins asked.

Haley turned and blinked. "Yes, minimum recovery speed, heading your discretion."

"Aye, aye, ma'am."

"Orchid, Starfish One Seven."

Haley looked at the UHF speaker and thought, *Oh God! Not now!* She nodded at Bunting.

"Starfish One Seven, Orchid, go ahead," the young petty officer transmitted.

"Orchid, One Seven. Your gunboat has left the pier and is heading your way. Estimated speed thirty-two knots. You need to get out of there, sir."

Haley said, "I'll take it." She switched her radio to UHF and said, "One Seven, Orchid-Actual, we have to recover our boat. Is there anything you can do to help us out? Over."

"Orchid, One Seven, I can jam his fire control radar and call for help. That's about it. Over."

"Do what you can, One Seven. Thank you. Orchid-Actual, out." She switched to intra-ship. "Boat deck, CO."

"Boat deck, ma'am," Bondurant replied.

"Boat deck. We have a Chinese gunboat bearing down on us at full speed. As soon as that small boat hull is out of the water, I need to know so we can start running."

"It's coming alongside now, ma'am. Stand by." Moments later, *Kauai* heeled a few degrees to port. "CO, boat deck, the small boat is clear of the water!"

Haley turned to Hopkins. "Chief, course three-zero-zero, maximum speed."

"Helm, right standard rudder, steer three-zero-zero!"

"My rudder is right fifteen degrees, coming to three-zero-zero, Chief!" Pickins replied.

Hopkins keyed the intercom. "Main Control, Conn. COB, we have an enemy gunboat coming after us at flank speed, and we need every knot you got. Take propulsion control."

"Conn, Main Control, I have propulsion control. I am by-passing safeties."

"Very well."

"Captain, I have the gunboat on EO/IR, bearing one-seven-eight relative, target angle zero," Williams said.

Haley glanced at the navigation panel in front of Zuccaro. It showed the island in the navigation chart function, but no radar overlay with all transmitters secured. Zuccaro was frozen, staring at the screen, and her hands were motionless over her keyboard. "Williams, I want you to ping that gunboat with the rangefinder long enough to get a single readout—don't leave it on."

"Aye, aye, ma'am."

"CO from boat deck." Bondurant's voice came over the intra-ship channel.

"Go ahead," Haley said.

"Small boat is cradled, and the crane is secure. Casualties and passengers have been transferred to the messdeck. XO asked me to pass that he is assisting Doc with the wounded."

"Bondurant, relieve Mr. Wyporek of his medical duties. I need him on the Bridge ASAP."

"Aye, aye, ma'am."

"Captain, gunboat range is six thousand, three hundred fifty yards," Williams said.

"Very well, ping them once every thirty seconds."

"Aye, aye, ma'am."

Now it was a race. Haley hated to drag Ben to the Bridge when all he was likely to do was stand around, but they had to have a standby if she or Hopkins were incapacitated. *What has gotten into the Chinese? Are they going to start a war over a bunch of goddammed criminals?* She stepped over to the ship's telephone and dialed the messdeck.

After one ring, the phone answered, "Messdeck, Jenkins."

"Petty Officer Jenkins, Captain. Is Mr. Frankle able to talk?"

"Yes, ma'am. Standby, please."

After a couple of seconds, Frankle came on the phone. "Frankle."

"Agent Frankle, I've had one shootout with the Chinese, and now that I'm retiring, I've got a gunboat coming balls to the wall to catch us. What the HELL is going on here?!"

"I knew I should have killed that son of a bitch! It's Chen, the Chinese base leader. We caught him with his pants down, literally, in that brothel. He knows if we make it through, he's finished! When the APCs didn't do the job, he must have ordered the gunboat to destroy us at all costs. I'm sorry, Captain, I did not see this coming."

"Right. So much for negotiations. Chief Drake's pulling out the stops below, and maybe we can stay out of reach."

"Yes, ma'am. And again, my apologies."

Haley hung up the phone, turned to see Ben coming onto the Bridge, and was briefly shocked at his ghastly appearance. He was covered with dirt and blood and had the pale, vacant look of shock. She walked over, reached for his upper left arm, and squeezed it. "Ben, I can't tell you how relieved I am to see you," she whispered. "How's Lopez?"

"Doc is working on him, Captain. Bondurant, Gerard, and Lee are doing everything they can to help." He turned to look her in the eyes, then shook his head.

She led him to the command chair and said, "Have a seat."

"No, ma'am, I'll be OK...."

"Sit down. That's an order. We may need you again soon."

"Aye, aye, ma'am."

"Captain! The gunboat has opened fire!" Williams shouted.

Haley's gaze snapped to the camera display, where a line of four glowing balls climbed slowly into the air, seemed to stop, and then descended into the water, flashing when they hit.

"Ranging shot," Williams said. "Starfish has their radar jacked up, so they don't know our range."

"In other words, they're pinging us."

"Yes, ma'am. But they're already inside six thousand yards, and their pings will start reaching us any second."

Haley keyed her intra-ship transmitter. "Mount 51, Mount 52, and Overwatch, secure and shelter inside the Bridge!" Then she turned and stared at the image of the gunboat on Williams's screen. As if on cue, the image emitted another string of four balls. These landed much closer, and Haley could feel the taps from the shock waves of the detonating shells through the balls of her feet, although the sounds of the explosions were masked by the roar of *Kauai*'s diesel generators.

Hopkins stepped beside her and said, "Captain, you should let the crew know what to expect."

Haley looked at her and received a sad smile in return. "You're right. Thank you, Chief." Haley stepped over to the 1MC and picked up the microphone. "Folks, this is the captain. I'm sure you've heard we have a Chinese gunboat on our tail, and he's closing fast. We are within his thirty-seven-millimeter range, and I expect him to start sending HE shells our way, hoping for a lucky hit. We have an electronic warfare bird who has knocked back his radar, so his shooting will be wild until he gets closer. Our bird is calling in air support, and it will hopefully be here before then. Our armor should keep out the shell fragments, so hang tough and stay inside and away from the windows. Good luck to us all." *Yeah, and when he gets close enough for direct fire with armor-piercing rounds, what then?*

Guerrero was coming through the door with his rifle, with Hebert and Connally right behind him as she replaced the microphone. "Hunker down, guys, and prepare for incoming."

"You don't need to tell us twice, ma'am," Hebert said as he and the other two grabbed spots in the Bridge's rear.

Ben stood from the command chair and held it for Haley. She had just taken her seat when Williams said, "Here it comes!" The gunboat had fired a burst of four shells, which landed even with *Kauai* about fifty yards to port and detonated on contact with the water. These were close enough to hear the loud bang of the explosions.

"Chase salvos, Chief!" Haley ordered. *Kauai* was a difficult target at this distance, and the gunboat was trying to conserve ammunition using short bursts rather than continuous fire. Without radar, the gunboat would have to correct its aim based on where the last burst landed. "Chase salvos" meant turn toward that side and foil the correction.

"Aye, aye, Captain. Helm, left to two-nine-five."

"Left to two-nine-five," Pickins repeated.

Another burst landed and detonated off the starboard side, and Hopkins ordered a course change to the right. Haley knew their luck would not hold for long—as soon as the gunboat captain realized what they were doing, he would go to rapid-fire. She selected UHF and keyed her microphone. "Starfish One Seven, Orchid Actual. Where's that help? Over."

"Orchid, Starfish One Seven. I'm on with a flight of F-16s from the 93rd, and they're three minutes out. Over."

"One Seven, Orchid Actual, roger, tell them to step on it! Out."

Hopkins had just altered course to the left again, and the game went on for two more salvos. Then, as Haley feared, the Chinese captain tried a long burst. The twelve shells missed, falling on both sides. Two were close enough to pepper *Kauai* with shrapnel, sharp pings ringing through the Bridge like hail on a tin roof.

Their luck ran out on the next burst: one shell exploded on the left side of the mast, knocking out the EO camera and showering the Flying Bridge with shrapnel. Another struck the special operations boat and started a small fire. The fire itself was not an immediate danger to the ship, but it provided a beacon that brought hell down on them. Shells were bursting on the rear of the superstructure and in the water around *Kauai*. The bridge crew huddled behind what cover they could find as the windows in the rear doors shattered and debris scattered around them. As they kneeled together between the command chair and the FC3 console, Haley looked into Ben's face and, seeing the same fear she had, reached out and gripped his hand.

The bombardment ended abruptly with an ear-shattering double boom that shook the deck beneath them. Haley's first thought was, *Shit! Now they're using rockets!* Then a second double boom shook the ship, and, after a brief delay, another pair of double booms.

"It's the F-16s! They're thumping the gunboat!" Ben cried.

Haley smiled with relief, gave Ben's hand a last squeeze, then let go. They both stood and looked at the chaos of the Bridge. As the others stood, Haley called out. "Chief! Are you OK?"

"Pickins and I are tolerable, ma'am! Still on heading three-zero-zero."

"Thank God. Ben, are you alright?"

"Yes, ma'am."

She glanced at the FC3 crew, Hebert, Guerrero, and Connally. "Anyone hurt?" After getting mumbles of "OK" and thumbs-up from the rest, she nodded and turned to Ben.

"What the hell does 'thumping' mean?"

"They were buzzing the gunboat at a hundred feet and Mach One-plus. My dad told me they used to do it when he was flying F/A-18s in Iraq, and they needed to provide close support but couldn't drop bombs or shoot. That double boom was the shock wave. If it shook us at two miles, you can imagine what it must be like a hundred feet away. It's non-lethal, but you can be sure there isn't an intact window, light bulb, or glass lens on that gunboat anymore."

Haley nodded, plugged into her command chair, and selected UHF. *Please let this be working.* "Starfish One Seven, Orchid Actual.

"Orchid, One Seven, good to hear your voice, ma'am!"

"One Seven, Orchid, Backatcha. We're blind here. What's going on?"

"Orchid, One Seven. Your gunboat is bugging out. He's heading zero eight zero at thirty-four knots. The thumper element has bingo-ed for the tanker, but the two shooters are holding on station until he heads into port."

"One Seven, Orchid, roger. Please pass a huge thanks from us."

"WILCO. And, for the record, none of us were ever here. Copy?"

"One Seven, roger that. Never heard of you. Thanks for everything. Out." She turned to Ben. "Nothing like a 'Back Off or we'll kill you' gesture to give a captain a moment of pause. He probably thought he was chasing some pirates until the attack aircraft showed up."

Ben nodded. "Yes, ma'am. The boat is still burning, Captain. I'll head down to deal with that now."

"Yes, good luck. Call me when you can."

"Yes, ma'am. Hebert and Guerrero, let's go!" Ben said, then turned and left with the two petty officers, their feet crunching on broken glass and ceiling fragments covering the deck.

"Petty Officer Williams, see if any bridge systems are still working," Haley said.

"Aye, aye, ma'am. Bunting, Zuccaro, give me a hand!"

Haley tried the intra-ship radio without a result. She stepped over and pressed the call button for the intercom. "Main Control, CO."

"Main Control, COB here."

"Report, COB."

"No damage in Main Control, ma'am. I have Brown checking the hull forward for leaks."

"Thank you, COB. Carry on, please."

"Yes, ma'am."

Hopkins stepped beside her. "Ma'am, we need to throttle back and post a lookout."

Haley put her hand to her forehead. "Yes, thank you, Chief. Come back to ten knots for now."

"Aye, aye, ma'am. Connally, grab a handheld radio and binoculars and get up to the Flying Bridge. No, wait, it's probably trashed. Go on down to the bow. See if you can remember how to be a lookout."

"On it, Chief!"

Hopkins pulled the throttles back, and *Kauai*'s hull ceased planing and settled back into the water. Haley grabbed the bridge railing for support and shook her head. *Wouldn't that be ironic, surviving two gun battles and then sinking after smacking into another boat?*

Ben

Ben led the two petty officers down the ladder, carefully hugging the ship's side with their boots crunching on broken glass, shrapnel, and other debris. The fire hose nearest the boat deck was shredded, and Hebert had to make two stops before finding one still intact. The fire proved easy to extinguish, as it was confined to the boat, having started when the shell shattered the engines. Ben posted Guerrero as a re-flash watch and did a quick tour around the hull—there were plenty of black marks from blast scoring, but no penetrations from what he could see.

Ben dreaded what he would find on the messdeck. He would never forget that awful moment of chaos on the boat when the Chinese machine gun fire laced across the bow. It was only the one burst that hit home. *Kauai*'s return fire, each round looking almost like red laser fire accompanied by a loud crack from the shock wave, silenced the Chinese vehicle. But the damage had been done.

Ben had cried out when he saw Lopez was down and crawled over to find him bleeding profusely from two wounds—the bullets must have been armor-piercing as they punched right through his vest. Lopez was writhing in pain as Ben pulled open his vest and applied pressure to the wounds with his bare hands. Lopez quickly passed out and remained unconscious for the rest of the boat's return to *Kauai*. Ben looked around the bow to find Kelly face down, unmoving, and Frankle, his arm a bloody mess, being attended by Gerard.

Bryant was waiting with the litter when they arrived, and Ben helped carry Lopez into the makeshift surgery on the messdeck. Bryant worked quickly—he had performed gunshot wound first aid frequently in Iraq and Afghanistan while in the army. Ben bent to the task of assistant, helping with surgical equipment and I.V.s until Bondurant tapped him out.

"You're needed on the Bridge, sir."

"Screw that!" Ben muttered, turning to Lopez.

Bondurant grasped his arm and gently turned him around. "*We* need you on the Bridge, sir."

Ben looked at the big boatswain's mate and blinked. "Right."

That was only twenty minutes ago, Ben thought as he looked at the clock when he came into the messdeck. His gaze fell on the mess table, where Bryant, Bondurant, Lee, and Jenkins were clustered—a bloody white sheet covered Lopez's upper body and head, and no one was moving. Ben blinked in disbelief. His chest tightened, and when he could finally breathe, he blurted out, "No!"

They all turned, and Lee walked over, embraced him, and buried her face in his chest. "No," Ben said again, more quietly, putting his arms around Lee and holding her as she sobbed.

Tristitia Victoriae

USCG Cutter *Kauai*, moored, Pier C, Naval Station Guantanamo Bay, Cuba
13:29 EST, 6 December

Haley

Haley was exhausted, physically and emotionally. She was waiting in her cabin to be called to give her statement to the commander sent by the Seventh District headquarters, who had met them when they arrived at 07:30 that morning. He had eyed the vessel coolly, saluted respectfully when Lopez's and Kelly's bodies were brought ashore, then informed Haley and Ben he was sent to get statements from the crew about the mission. One by one, the senior members of the enlisted personnel had been called in, and Ben was with him now.

Haley expected to be relieved of command by day's end. She had checked every block required: violated orders, banged the shit out of her command, and got one of her crew killed. Haley knew she should go over her account in her head, if not on paper, but she couldn't work up the motivation. She felt empty and, for the first time in her life, utterly alone.

She thought back to last night, shortly after the battle. They were hard at work restoring functionality to the bridge systems when the news of Lopez's death brought everything to a stop. Haley stood in shock, staring silently out into the darkness. She did not know how long she stood there before she felt Hopkins's hand gently laid on her shoulder.

"I'm sorry, Captain, but you need to say something," Hopkins said.

Haley turned to look and could tell, even in the darkness, that Hopkins had been crying. Haley walked stiffly to the 1MC and reached for the microphone. "Attention, all hands. I have just learned that our shipmate Juan Lopez has died from his wounds. If I could give you time now to pause and think of him, I would, but we need to look to the boat right now. I know that is what Juan would have wanted. We will take the time to grieve for him as soon as we are out of danger, but I must ask you to continue with the repairs for now. Thank you." She hung up the microphone, turned, and returned to the command chair.

Williams, Bunting, and Zaccaro quickly restored communications and the auxiliary navigation radar—the primary multi-mode radar had taken a direct hit and was finished. At least, with an active navigation radar, they could travel safely. Haley made her initial report of the damage, Lopez's and Kelly's deaths, and her intent to dock at Gitmo as quickly as possible. Shortly after Ben returned to the Bridge, they received confirmation orders to Gitmo and were informed resources for emergency repairs were being sent.

There was a knock at her door, and Haley called, "Come in."

Ben opened the door and stepped in. "Commander Lewis wants to see you, ma'am."

"Thank you. How did it go?" Haley was almost afraid to ask.

"He's thorough. But he seemed just interested in the facts."

"I see."

As she stood, Ben said, "It's going to be OK, ma'am."

"Thank you for that," she said resignedly.

"No, ma'am, you don't understand. I have been in exactly this situation before, at Resolution. Sam thought he would get canned and came out with a medal. It's the same. You'll see."

Haley gave his shoulder a soft squeeze. "Thank you, Ben. Whatever happens, you sure earned your pay this week."

"Thank you, Captain," he said, then stepped aside to let her pass.

It was a short walk to Drake's stateroom, where Commander Charles P. Lewis conducted the interviews. Lewis was the Coast Guard Liaison Officer for the Guantanamo Bay Naval Base and had been detailed to put together a formal report of the action. Drake's quarters were cramped for such an effort, but the Bridge was under emergency repair, and the messdeck was still being cleaned. Haley knocked on the door and entered when Lewis bade her come in.

"You wanted to see me, Commander?" Haley said with as little emotion as possible.

"Yes, Captain. Please take a seat." After Haley sat, he said, "I apologize for adding to your stress after the hell you all have been through, but orders were to get statements while the events were still fresh in everyone's mind." He then explained her rights against self-incrimination and asked if she wanted counsel.

"No, sir. Let's get it done," Haley replied.

"Good. Now take me through the action from when you put the DIA team ashore on the 4th."

Haley told the story to the best of her recollection and then answered several questions, none of which were the "gotcha" kind she expected. After she answered the last question, Lewis said, "That about does it for me. Do you have any questions?"

"Yes, sir. Will they decide soon? I would like to get my folks home."

"Decide what?"

"Whether I'm to continue in command."

He sat back in astonishment. "*What?* That is not a question on anyone's mind, to the best of my knowledge. I was sent here to help you transfer your 'guests,' get patched up and on your way, and relieve you and your XO of the burden of writing an official report. I apologize if you were given any other impression. The reading of rights is standard procedure for any inquiry."

"I see. Thank you, sir."

"Look, it's not my place to tell a captain what to do on her ship, but I strongly recommend you and your XO get some rest. You've both been through hell. Let us take the load off you while you're here, at least."

"I'm grateful to you, sir."

"Not at all."

USCG Cutter *Kauai*, Port Canaveral Ship Channel, two nautical miles east of the Trident Access Channel, Port Canaveral, Florida
09:03 EST, 8 December

Haley

This was an easy transit for Haley. This time, Lee was doing the mooring, with Hopkins doing the coaching. Lee was a nervous wreck, of course. Haley shook her head in wonder—Lee was fearless when it came to danger and a master with a small boat, but she was almost a basket case on a special sea detail with the CO looking over her shoulder.

Ben was standing beside her, ostensibly assisting with oversight. In fact, he was there so Haley could keep an eye on him. Ben looked like hell, and Haley was sure he had slept little, if at all, since the engagement with the Chinese. Despite her insistence to the contrary, she knew he blamed himself for Lopez's death and was genuinely worried that he would end up another casualty of the action. Haley called Victoria when they came under cell phone coverage and asked her to meet them at the dock. Hopefully, she could reach him and pull him back. At the very least, there was no way Haley would let Ben drive in his current state.

Lee's mooring was flawless, and as Haley was finishing a very positive critique, Ben strolled onto the port bridge wing, as usual, to watch as the deck crew doubled the mooring lines and rigged the brow. Haley followed a moment later and saw him looking at a woman approaching. It was Victoria, walking toward the ship in her white sundress with her red hair pulled into her customary ponytail. She saw Ben and waved.

"XO, aren't you going to wave back?" Haley asked from behind him.

Ben, startled, then waved at Victoria. "How?"

"I called her once I got a cell signal," Haley answered. "I told her you had a rough trip, best discussed once you two were home. She agreed. Now, you are done for this patrol. Beat feet."

Ben blinked away tears and said, "Aye, aye, ma'am."

Haley watched from the Bridge thirty seconds later as Ben strode over the brow and swept Victoria into his arms. *You're a lucky man, Ben Wyporek. Don't screw it up.*

Haley went inside the Bridge, nodded to Hopkins, who was busy securing the FC3 with Williams, and went to her cabin. She was only there a minute when her telephone rang, and she answered, "Captain."

"Seaman Pickins on the quarterdeck, ma'am. You have a phone call on Line 2."

"Thank you, Pickins," she said, then pressed the Line 2 button on her phone. "Lieutenant Reardon."

"Haley, it's Sam Powell. I heard about what happened and wondered if you would like to talk."

"Thank you for your consideration, Commander. I'll be fine."

"It's still Sam, and if you'll forgive me for saying so, I don't see how anyone coming off what you just went through would be fine."

Haley was conflicted, as she really *did* need to talk to someone right now. The clichéd term "loneliness of command" was suddenly very real for her, and her choice to stay unattached was rapidly losing its appeal. Still, she didn't know if she could share with the man who brought this ship and crew through two years of challenging operations when she balled it up and lost a man in her first week.

"OK, Sam. What have you been told?"

"Mercier shared the gist and asked me to call. She's seen this sort of thing before and is worried about you. She knew she couldn't help, so she called me."

"To straighten me out and get things back on track?" Haley asked bitterly.

"Not hardly. She knew you were on your own, going through an experience that would have cracked *me* when I had the two best partners in the world to lean on, Jo and Ben."

"You got everyone through two years. I got Lopez killed before I completed my first week."

Sam sighed audibly. "There, but for the grace of God. I was lucky, Haley, luckier than I deserved. I lie awake sometimes thinking of how bad Resolution and Barbello could have gone, maybe should have gone."

"Maybe, maybe not. All I know is that Ben will have his hands full with transfer requests when he returns. If he returns, that is. You should have seen him this morning."

"Victoria will put Ben back together, and he'll be on board in a day or two—don't sell either of them short. And he won't come back to any transfer requests. Do you think the crew will lose faith in you because you took a calculated risk that didn't work out? With respect, you're wrong. The mistake would have been leaving that DIA team and those two women to their fate, and they would never have forgiven you for THAT."

"And what about Lopez?"

"He would feel the same. And he would have gone, too, even if he knew things would go south. Did Ben tell you the Lopez/Barbello story?"

"No."

"He was coming to the tail-end of his ME A-school when we got the call. He was supposed to meet us over at AUTEC in the Bahamas the following week, so Hoppy called and told him to hang out in PC instead. Not Lope. He wrangled an early graduation and drove a rental down to Key West to jump on with us before we stepped off. There was no way he would sit around while his family was mixing it up."

"Is that supposed to make me feel better?"

"No, just point out what the crew has transcends you and me. They know the risks and are on *Kauai* because they want to be. They don't expect miracles from you, only that you keep the faith, and you've proven that."

"*Fortiter et Fideliter.*" She glanced across the room at the small plaque, but could only see a blur through the tears.

"Exactly. I'm not here to pump sunshine up your behind, just to tell you that you are what and where the crew and the Coast Guard need you to be."

Haley took a breath to steady herself, then said, "Thank you, Sam."

"Not at all. Could you come over for dinner tonight?"

"No, I know you are busy getting ready for the move."

"Nonsense. We need a break, and Jo needs an excuse to whip up her Ropa Vieja. You'd be doing me a favor—she's been on my ass for weeks to drag you over here. Please, take another hit for the team."

"Well, when you put it that way, how can I say no?"

"That's the spirit. Go Bears! See you at six?"

"Sounds good."

"Excellent! 5630 Breakers Lane on Patrick."

Haley jotted the address on her notepad. "5630. Got it. Thank you."

"No worries. You have my number. Any time you need to talk, I'm here."

"Thank you, Sam. I'm looking forward to dinner."

"Take care, Haley."

He really is a good man. She thought as she replaced the phone. She felt rather silly now, thinking Sam would try some cheap psychological bullshit on her. *You haven't been right about anybody lately.* Then she smiled sadly, pulled her cell phone out of her desk drawer, and dialed a number she hadn't in a long time.

"Haley!" the voice said, answering after two rings.

"Hi, Dad."

Victoria

Victoria did not recognize the phone number when the call came at 7:30 that morning, but remembered the area code as one of the two in Hillsborough County, Florida. She knew no one in Hillsborough County and was inclined to let it roll over to voice mail. However, the software on her phone did not indicate spam or a telemarketer, so she took a chance. "Hello?"

"Hello, Victoria? This is Haley Reardon."

"Oh, hello, Miss Reardon!" Then the realization set in. *Why is she calling me and not Benjamin?* "Has something happened to Benjamin?" she blurted out.

"No, no, he's fine," Haley had answered quickly. "Sorry, I should have led with that. And I wish you would call me Haley."

"Very well, thank you, Haley. Is there something I can do for you?" Victoria asked, trying to conceal her relief. She was afraid of appearing "clingy," particularly in front of Benjamin's new commanding officer.

"Yes, we'll be entering port this morning, around nine o'clock. I hope you'll excuse me. I try not to meddle in my subordinates' personal business, but I wonder if you would mind meeting us at the dock when we arrive."

"Oh, I do not mind at all, Miss... Haley. Is there something wrong?"

"Not to worry you, Victoria, but it has been a difficult patrol, particularly for Ben, and I'd feel better if he did not drive himself home this time."

"I am grateful for your concern for Benjamin. Can you tell me anything about what happened? I appreciate there might be things you must hold back because of security concerns."

"No, Victoria, it's not security. It's that I'm pretty far out on a limb just calling you, and Ben should tell you about things in his own way."

"I understand, and I will be there in time to meet *Kauai* when she arrives."

"Thank you, Victoria. I hope to see you soon. Goodbye."

"Goodbye, Haley," Victoria said as she hung up.

For the next hour, ending when she left for the harbor, Victoria scoured the Internet for some clue of what had happened over the past few days that would involve Benjamin. Nothing. She was tempted to call Joana for advice, but decided she had to learn to do these things herself. Her need to focus on her driving as she made her way to the base was a welcome distraction.

She recognized the guard at the gate of the Space Force Station—he was one of her favorites. "Hello, Sergeant Timms. It is good to see you again!" She handed over her ID and the special pass that allowed her on base.

"Good morning, Victoria. Likewise. How's it going?"

"Quite well, thank you. Benjamin and I are engaged."

"Wow, that's terrific! Those Coasties have all the luck," he said as he returned her documents.

"Thank you, Sergeant."

"Take care, Miss."

It was a short drive from the gate to the Trident Wharf. When she cleared the trees, Victoria's heart jumped when she caught sight of *Kauai*, already in the Trident Access Channel, after passing the security barrier. She parked and walked through a gap in the warehouses to watch the mooring. The process involved in the mooring and unmooring of a large vessel like *Kauai* was always fascinating to Victoria. Using asymmetric thrust from the engines, turning moment from rudders and mooring lines, and the direction and speed of the wind were all factors in a delicate ballet that brought *Kauai* into the exact desired spot along the wharf. Benjamin said that Emilia Hopkins was the best at this—Victoria wondered if she was in control just now.

Something was off about *Kauai* this morning. As the ship got closer, Victoria ran her eye carefully over the boat's lines and noted some discrepancies from her memory. Several of the lifelines and stanchions were missing, as was the RHIB. The large radar antenna atop the mast had been removed, and tarps covered the large electro-optical camera below it and the entire Flying Bridge. As the boat pivoted to moor pointed outbound in the channel, Victoria could see the windows in the doors at the rear of the Bridge were also covered. *It looks something like the damage from Hurricane Jacob, but there was no storm anywhere in the vicinity. What could have happened?*

Victoria saw Benjamin come out onto the bridge wing to watch the line handlers, followed by a female officer she took to be Haley. Victoria waved when Benjamin looked in her direction, but he did not wave back at first. Most unusual. He had some sort of discussion with Haley, then disappeared into the Bridge. Less than a minute later, he emerged and crossed over onto the dock. Victoria ran to meet him and pulled up in shock as he approached.

Victoria had never seen Benjamin look like this. His face was pale, eyes red with dark periorbital circles, and he looked haggard. Victoria had seen him fatigued before, but this was something altogether different. He dropped his bag and took her into his arms, and, like always, she squeezed him tightly, feeling the strength of his arms and immersing herself in his scent.

"Victoria, thank God. I'm so happy to see you," he said.

Even his voice seemed drained. It was apparent now why Haley had been concerned. "I need to get you home, Benjamin."

"But my car..." he said distractedly.

"Your car has sat here for five days, Benjamin. One more day will not matter," she replied firmly.

"Yes, Boss," he said with a sad smile.

Victoria reached up to caress his face, gave him a quick kiss, then took his arm and led him to her car. They traveled home in silence. Benjamin knew she did not like to be distracted by conversation while driving, but his complete silence was unusual. He stared vacantly out the window the entire trip, almost without moving.

When they reached the apartment, Victoria led Benjamin inside and over to the couch, sat beside him, took his hands, and said, "Benjamin, I know something is wrong. I can see that *Kauai* was seriously damaged, and even I can tell something is affecting you inside. I know you want to spare me, but we are formal partners now, and you need to tell me when something is wrong."

Benjamin nodded and began a narration of the story from the beginning. This was the first time Victoria had to deal with a serious emotional event with Benjamin—she was terrified of doing something wrong and adding to his distress. She rigorously applied Joana's advice: just listen; don't guide him, inquire deeper, offer suggestions, or tell him he's wrong to feel the way he does. Just let it flow.

Benjamin broke down and started crying when he got to Juan Lopez's death and his sense of responsibility for it. Victoria desperately wanted to tell him he was not to blame and should not feel that way, but held her tongue. She was beating back tears herself—she had talked to Juan at one of the unit gatherings and was fond of him—she would save her grief for later. Benjamin had finished and was quietly sobbing, his face buried in her chest. She leaned her cheek on his head, stroking his back and nape.

The moment had cleared away the last remaining barrier between them. During this terrible time, Victoria knew Benjamin needed her very badly and felt confident at last that she was precisely where she needed to be, doing exactly what she needed to do. *My brave, good, and kind man, I finally have a chance to give back what you have always given me.*

Robbery-Homicide Division Commander's Office, Police Administration Building, 100 West First Street, 5th floor, Los Angeles, California
09:05 PST, 14 December

Haley

The Condolence Call. This was the other hard part they tell you about in CO school, but nobody seemed to know anyone who has had to do it—line-of-duty deaths were that rare in the Coast Guard despite the extreme hazards of the work. Lopez had not listed any next of kin or emergency contact information, and they were at a loss as to what to do with his personal effects. Then Ben remembered Lopez talking about knocking around in the foster care system, teetering on the edge of becoming just another victim or victimizer, when an LAPD detective stepped up and changed his life. Lopez could not say what motivated the detective and his wife to take him on as a foster child, just that they gave him an excuse to do good. Ben pulled Lopez's Servicemembers' Group Life

Insurance forms and found a name—Reuben S. Vasquez—then, after a little more research, found a Captain Reuben S. Vasquez in command of the Robbery-Homicide Division at LAPD Headquarters. There was no doubt this was the same man.

It was cool in Los Angeles that morning, with the typical bright sunshine but a rare on-shore breeze that brought a sense of freshness to the city. The weather was a small blessing during the short walk from the hotel to the Police Headquarters Building in her service dress dark blue uniform. Haley had flown in the night before, a non-stop from Orlando, leaving Ben in acting command of *Kauai* in her absence.

Ben had returned after three days of quasi-convalescent leave, with a worried-looking Victoria dropping him off with a kiss. He was changed, less light-hearted, and more focused than before. Like Sam before her, Haley had mixed feelings about what was arguably a professional improvement. Haley was stunned and moved a couple of days later when he submitted a request to extend for a year as Kauai's XO. "You need looking after, ma'am," he said semi-seriously when she had asked why. It was the most expeditiously approved extension request in Coast Guard history.

Ben had offered to make this trip for her, and Haley had been tempted to accept—Ben had known Lopez for over a year instead of Haley's few weeks. She was also not looking forward to blowing up the lives of Lopez's beloved foster parents with the devastating news. In the end, she knew this was one duty a CO could not delegate.

Haley waited in the outer office with the beautiful mahogany box holding Lopez's personal awards and keepsakes. Haley had been surprised when Drake had brought it in before her departure, expecting a simple cardboard box. Her question of where he got hold of it received the standard Drake reply: "I know a guy." Fortunately, he stepped out before she opened it and found the inscription on the brass plate inside the hinged lid—In Memory of Maritime Law Enforcement Specialist Second Class Juan Lopez, Our Shipmate Forever, the Crew of USCGC *Kauai* (WPB-1351). She had cried for ten minutes after reading it.

"Lieutenant, Captain Vasquez can see you now," Vasquez's administrative assistant said as she held open the office door. After seeing Haley fumble with her combination cap, the middle-aged woman continued, "I can take care of that for you, miss."

"Thank you," Haley replied as she stepped through the door, and it closed behind her.

"Good morning, Lieutenant!" Vasquez said, standing to come around his desk with an outstretched hand. He was a fit and handsome man, an inch or two taller than Haley, with short salt-and-pepper hair and a mustache in his late fifties. Vasquez was in shirt sleeves, tie, charcoal-colored vest, the matching jacket hanging on a clothes tree in the office corner. "I am always psyched to meet another Coastie." He smiled as he shook her hand. "My foster son is a petty officer in the service."

"Yes, sir. I know. I...was Juan's commanding officer," Haley said. Vasquez's hand froze, and his smile vanished.

"When?"

"A little over a week ago. I am terribly sorry, Captain, both for your loss and the delay we had in informing you. Juan didn't list you as next of kin or emergency contact."

"No, that's Juan for you. Please sit down," he said, gesturing to one of the guest chairs by the coffee table. "I'm sorry, I didn't get your first name," he added as he sat in the chair facing her.

"Haley, sir."

"Thank you, Haley. I appreciate you coming to see me. Is there anything you can tell me?" he asked, looking into her eyes.

"Yes, sir. He was badly wounded helping rescue two women from a transnational criminal gang and died on the operating table. Last week, his remains were buried with full military honors at Arlington National Cemetery. Again, I'm sorry we didn't get word to you, but I promise everything was properly done. We have put Juan's awards and some of his personal items we thought you might want in this box," she said as she carefully handed it to him.

"Awards?"

"Yes, Juan was awarded the Coast Guard Commendation Medal with the Valor device for a classified action last April and the Coast Guard Medal for saving a couple and their two little girls during Hurricane Jacob in September at great peril of his life. The others are the Bronze Star and Purple Heart for his last action." She paused when he put his head down, and a tear fell on his lap.

He regained control before he straightened up and gazed into her eyes again. "Is there anything else?" he asked, placing his hand on the box's lid.

"Yes, sir. A few pictures, his collar devices for petty officer second class—he was promoted posthumously—and a beat-up copy of *The Black Echo.*"

Vasquez nodded. "Yes, that was the first book I ever gave him. He wanted stories about what I did—Connelly's novels captured the gist and are good reads." His eyes welled again. "He was a wonderful kid who became one of the best men I've ever known."

"I can name sixteen Coasties who would say the same, sir. I had only known him for a few weeks as I had just taken command, but his loss was the most terrible one I have ever faced. You should know that he thought the world of you and your wife. He said he could have easily gone very wrong. There was so much peer pressure, but you two gave him something he could grab onto and hold close."

He looked down and shook his head. "I wonder why we bother. Medals and no difference to the drugs, crime, and misery. Is that what Juan died for?"

"Sir, if I may, I think you'll find this a more substantial legacy." She pulled an envelope out of her pocket and handed it to him.

Vasquez took a piece of paper out of the envelope, glanced at it, then at Haley.

"Those twenty-eight names are people whose lives Juan had a direct role in saving. The first four are the family I told you of, the next twenty-two were human trafficking victims he saved from a sinking ship, and the last two were the ones from his last action. Those people are alive today because of Juan—he made a difference."

Vasquez read through the sheet, then folded it and put it in the envelope. "Thank you, Haley. That does help."

"I'm glad of that, sir. Is there anything else I can do for you? Anything that you need?"

Vasquez stood, walked over, and placed the box in the center of his desk. "No. Thank you for coming."

They shook hands, and Haley stepped out of the office. She could hear Vasquez quietly sniffle as she closed the door. As

Vasquez's assistant handed over her cap, Haley asked, "Where is the restroom, please?"

"Turn right, then the second door on the right," she said, pointing across the room.

"Thank you, ma'am," Haley said. She barely made it inside before she started crying again.

Coda

Interrogation Room 3C, United States Penitentiary, Administrative Maximum Facility, Florence, Colorado 11:07 MST, 27 December

Rostov

This was his sixth visit to the interrogation room in the three weeks he had been incarcerated. On each previous occasion, he had been frog-marched the two hundred meters by two burly guards and chained to a fixed table and chair in the middle of the room. There he sat for close to an hour awaiting the arrival of a government lawyer, who would read the charges against him and ask him if he wanted to give a statement. He would say no, he wanted an attorney, and then the government lawyer would pack up and leave. He would be returned to solitary confinement in his 3.5-meter by 2-meter cell. Rostov was unfamiliar with this interrogation technique. It was certainly not one he would have used when he was a security officer—the process took far too long and had none of the ancillary benefits of inflicting pain on the victim.

This trip held an immediate surprise: someone was already seated at the table when he arrived. Rostov looked him over carefully as he was brought into the room and shackled to the table. He was of average height and stature in his mid-30s, with a plain face, brown medium short hair, and a scruffy beard. He wore a plain navy blue suit with a white shirt and plain maroon tie. Everything about the man was plain. He was obviously no lawyer—this man was an intelligence officer.

After the guards had secured him to the table, the man said, "That will be all, thank you." The guards departed without speaking and closed the door. He then sat staring at Rostov without speaking or moving for what must have been five minutes. It might have been another novel interrogation technique—bore your opponent into submission—but Rostov decided to bring it to an end.

"Aren't you going to lay a panoply of my alleged crimes before me and threaten me with millennia of incarceration unless I confess and betray all my comrades?" Rostov asked.

"Yevgeny Vladimirovich, why on earth would I waste my time with such a useless gesture?" the man replied in perfect, northern-accented Russian.

"My compliments, you speak passable Russian," Rostov replied in Russian.

"Hell, if one hundred forty-five million Russians can do it, how hard can it be, eh?" the man said in English with a broad grin. After allowing the insult to set in, he continued. "I sense you believe that my government needs something from you, something that we would be willing to make a deal for, perhaps to include your freedom. If that is what you genuinely believe, please let me set you straight. We know everything about your organization, from top to bottom. There is nothing you can tell us about the 252 Syndicate we do not already know. How do we know these things? Let me explain.

"About two months ago, a ship operated by one of your front companies, the motor vessel *Miho Dujam*, was detected and pursued by U.S. law enforcement agents in the Bahamas. The crew scuttled the ship, which prevented the seizure of a large quantity of illegal armaments but failed in the murder of the twenty-two female captives on board who were destined for sexual servitude. I am delighted to say these women have been or soon will be returned to their families or another safe environment. Before the *Miho Dujam* sank, our officers found, aside from the women, a laptop computer containing enough data and metadata for us to penetrate your IT systems at all levels. That is how we learned of your travel itinerary and could position forces to apprehend you.

"Your organization wisely ditched all their current passwords when you were taken, but it was far too late by then—we were in everywhere. As we speak, forensic accountants across the northern hemisphere are tracing every bank account you use, every property you own, and every bent politician and policeman on your payroll. The days of expansion are over for the 252 Syndicate. Now, I'm not saying we can extirpate you. There will always be those countries where most of the ruling class is corrupt, and a vile organization like yours can flourish. You are welcome to them. So, Yevgeny Vladimirovich, there is nothing the United States needs from you to sink the 252s."

"You lie! If that were true, why go to the trouble of kidnapping me? Several of your men were killed, and was that for nothing?"

"Ah, now you *are* thinking, Yev. Yes, we thought you would be of value along with documentation of your organization's involvement with the Chinese government, particularly involving the Ile Ste. Michel operation. So we went after you while you were there. But wait, right in the middle of our operation, the Chinese base's big Lǎo Bǎn himself shows up! There to dip his wick with two more victims you provided, whom we also rescued. We got every biometric known to man from that guy while he was in your brothel. So, once again, your utility to the United States has vanished. Unless...."

The man leaned forward. "Are you familiar with the expression 'icing on the cake,' Yev? No? It means something a little extra on top of an excellent thing. In your case, it means you give a detailed account of your involvement with Xiaotong Chen and any other Chinese officials working the BRI efforts in Europe. We already have a slam-dunk case of conspiracy in international crime that we can use to help the Haitians break out of that God-awful lease they signed. However, the Chinese can tie things up for years in World Trade Organization litigation. It would be nice to drop some hints that the smart play for them would be to let it go, lest *things* get out into the press. Things that make other BRI clients, past and future, stroke their chins and say, 'Hmm, I wonder if....'"

Rostov started to fold his arms, but then the rattle of chains reminded him the gesture was impossible. Instead, he grinned and said, "Sounds like I have a powerful hand to play after all. Suppose I tell you I have quite a dossier on Comrade Chen and several other colleagues. Depending on what I get in return, I might share that treasure. Now, what are you offering *me*?"

The man sat back with a grim smile and said, "Your life."

"My life?"

"Yes, you get to live. You see, Yev, if you don't give us everything you have, you are quite useless to us. It is expensive to keep a prisoner in a supermax facility like this. With no return on investment, why would we? This is your one and only deal, and the offer, if not accepted, expires when I leave this room. You answer every question we ask about the Chinese, wholly and truthfully, whenever we ask, and we'll keep you alive. Otherwise, we'll cut you loose for a public demonstration of the criminal justice system and find out who wins the race to kill you, the Chinese or your erstwhile chums in the 252 Syndicate. My money will be on the latter, by the way—I'm sure they have a stronger presence in our prison system than the Chinese."

Rostov opened his mouth silently, his mind racing. This was the endgame, and he had no cards he could play. Rostov ached to reach across the table and snap this *Amerikanski mu'dak*'s scrawny neck. He looked down at his shackled hands, trying to keep the frustration off his face.

"Tick, tock, Yev. I haven't got all day here. And don't think I have any investment in keeping you alive for a second. I'm sure there will be plenty of action around my office in *your* death pool."

Rostov glared at the smug little man with all the hatred he had. *Someday, I'll pay you back with interest for this. But I must be alive to do it.*

The man shook his head, stood, and said, "So be it. Good luck in Hell, Yev."

As he turned toward the door, Rostov said, "Wait. I agree. What do you want to know?"

The man shook his head. "That's for someone else. No, Yev, our association ends here. Another officer and lawyer will be with you shortly to get your signature on the usual waiver documents and start your interrogation. I will drop these clothes in a burn bag and go for a long, scalding hot shower in bleach to try to get your stench off me."

As the man reached the door, Rostov spat, "Who the hell are you to talk to me like that?"

"Doctor Peter Simmons, DIA," he said, then stepped through and closed the door.

Harbour House, 1901 Highway A1A, Indian Harbour Beach, Florida
20:07 EDT, 20 May

Haley

It had been a beautiful ceremony, with Victoria and Ben standing beneath the floral arch on the beach overlooking the Atlantic Ocean. Victoria was radiant in her elegant white dress, with her hair up and her long veil lightly stirred by the gentle on-shore breeze. Ben looked every bit the dazzling hero in his dress white uniform with medals, sword, and his brand new shoulder boards holding the two full stripes of a lieutenant. The nondenominational ceremony was conducted by a young Air Force chaplain from Patrick, whom Ben and Victoria had befriended shortly after moving to the area. Even the vows were memorable, with the nervous Victoria delivering flawlessly in her beautiful low voice while the confident Ben actually stumbled with emotion in a couple of amusing places. Overall, Haley rated it a four-Awww! performance.

Kauai's crew, past and present, was heavily represented in the wedding party. Sam Powell stood up for Ben in dress whites as best man, and Joana was a resplendent matron of honor in a long, v-neck, cranberry-colored dress. Hopkins and Lee were almost unrecognizable in their matching dresses, with their hair down and, in Hopkins's case, glasses laid aside for the day. The only "foreigners" in the wedding party were the two groomsmen, two of Ben's friends from the Academy, also in dress whites.

Haley attended as a guest, happy to be spared the awkwardness of appearing in either her uniform or a bridesmaid's dress. She had used the event as an excuse to go shopping with Margot on her last visit home. The strapless blue cocktail dress they picked out was rather stunning compared to Haley's usual choice and made the most of her athletic build. It had been a simple, but significant bonding event that had cleared the remaining bad air with her stepmother.

The reception venue was also first-class and conveniently next to the beach altar, while the reception itself was on the low-key side, with about fifty guests and a DJ. The food was excellent for a mass service, and Sam's wedding toast to the bride and groom did not disappoint. Pleasant as the ceremony and reception were, the most exciting factor for Haley was the man standing in as the father of the bride.

Victoria's parents had been killed in a car crash when she was only eight. Her older sister had filled in as a surrogate parent until she died, shortly before Victoria's graduation from high school. Victoria and her late sister's fiancée helped each other through their grief, and then he, a post-doctorate astrophysicist, helped her through her undergraduate studies at Princeton. When he entered the DIA, he arranged for a data scientist position for Victoria, an arrangement of considerable mutual benefit for her and the organization. This was the famous, or, from Sam's point of view, infamous, Dr. Peter Simmons.

She was intrigued by her first sight of the man as he escorted Victoria to the altar. He was only average height, maybe an inch taller than Haley, but he had a nice build—athletic without being over-muscular. He looked a few years older than she was, maybe mid-thirties, with medium-length dark hair, a close-cropped beard, and a youthful face that reminded her of one of her favorite actors, Joseph Gordon-Levitt. Obviously reveling in his current role, he was beaming as he walked Victoria to the altar and shared a warm look and handshake with Ben when they arrived.

The contrast between Ben's dynamic with Simmons and the latter's with Sam and Hopkins was fascinating. Haley knew Sam was not a fan of Simmons from their conversations in the command handoff, but the depth of the animus surprised her. On the one occasion she saw them shake hands, Sam's bearing and expression were what she would expect from a man forced to shake hands with his soon-to-be-ex-wife's slimy divorce attorney. Hopkins didn't even make a pretense of civility, just turned and walked away the one time Simmons approached her. And yet, he and Ben were clearly friends.

Haley got her chance to inquire later in the evening as she took a stroll on the deck outside the venue overlooking the beach. She was gazing at the stars, surprisingly bright in the cloudless sky, when a voice from behind startled her.

"A rather boring selection this time of year."

She turned to find Simmons looking at her with interest. "I mean the constellations, of course."

"Of course," Haley replied, turning again to look. "Good for navigation, though. I can see at least eight first-magnitude stars."

"Six, actually. Antares, Vega, Capella, Arcturus, Spica, and Procyon. Although Castor, Pollux, and Regulus are close. I'm Peter Simmons, by the way."

"Really? I seem to have heard of you."

"And I of you, Captain Reardon. Am I what you had expected?"

"Fewer tentacles and less brimstone than my predecessor would have me believe."

"Well, we all have our supply chain issues these days."

After a chuckle, she said, "You can call me Haley if you like."

"Thanks, Haley. Pete."

Haley nodded, glanced toward the venue, and said, "So, is this a happy day for you?"

His smile became warm. "Honestly, yes, one of the happiest I have experienced in quite some time. The woman I love like a little sister has just married the finest man I've ever known. It would be an enormous challenge to improve on that score."

"I understand you were the one who brought them together."

"Yes, that's true. I would love to claim it as a stroke of genius, but it was dumb luck."

"Sounds like an interesting story."

"You can pry it out of me with a drink."

"I'm game. Let's go."

A short time and several drinks later, Haley got round to the question she had been dying to ask all night. "So, what is the deal between you and Sam? I mean, he and Ben are so tight, I can't get my head around his hostility to you."

"*Mea culpa*. We started badly, and I haven't been able to make it up since. We almost came to blows at one point."

Haley glanced across the room at Sam, sharing a dance with Hopkins. "With Sam? Really?"

"No shit. Ben had to get in between us to prevent a fistfight in the Key West SCIF, of all places. Then I got suckered by the 252s into a kill box with Ben along for the ride, and Sam had to throw away the book to save our asses with *Kauai*. That's how I got added to Hoppy's death list, by the way," he said with a rueful glance.

"Hmm. I guess I can understand the hostility."

He grinned. "And yet, we are still here sharing drinks."

"Yeah, I like to live dangerously. A bad boy geek from the intel community sounds like an interesting way to burnish my badass cred."

"*Bad boy geek?*" Simmons grinned. "Now that's a moniker I can work with." He raised his glass. "Here's to the beginning of a beautiful friendship, the Bad Boy Intel Geek and the Badass PB CO."

Haley clicked his glass with hers and said, "Cheers. One thing, though, before we get too far along on this epic relationship: if you get any of *my* kids in a jam, I *will* kill you."

USCG Cutter *Kauai*, moored, Trident Wharf, Port Canaveral, Florida
08:13 EDT, 31 May

Haley

It was Ben's first day back from his and Victoria's honeymoon to Yellowstone, an interesting choice for a venue, although understandable given Victoria's curiosity for anything and everything scientific. The trip was apparently quite a success, as the man who returned was much more like the original Ben she had met. It was another tally on her personal ledger's "time to hookup" side.

Haley herself had had a long sojourn with Simmons—three days and nights. He was a remarkable man, entirely unlike anyone she had ever been with before in many respects. Besides his physical prowess, he had an exceptional intellect combined with a wonderful sense of humor that made him exciting and fun to be around. She looked forward to the next time they could get together.

There was a knock on the door, and Haley turned to see Ben standing there with a smile. "Come in, XO. Let's catch up. Tell me about your trip." Ben settled in his stateroom/office to plow through the physical and electronic inboxes for an hour after the initial hello. As usual, Hopkins had monitored things in Ben's world of work to make sure nothing important was overlooked in his absence, so it was not a heavy lift coming back.

"It was a wonderful time, ma'am. We ended up with quite an adventure, although not exactly what we planned."

"Really? What, the flights didn't work out or something?"

"No, we got there all right. But instead of touring for a week as we planned, we pitched in on a no-shit mystery."

"No way!"

"Way. They had never met a data scientist before, much less employed one. Victoria was over the moon. And I can cross 'run with a posse' off my bucket list."

"You're serious?"

"Yes, ma'am. On the whole, they were pretty happy with our contributions, and the sheriff said they more than made up for the squad room windows."

"The squad room windows?"

"Yes, ma'am. And the gazebo."

"The *gazebo*. XO, is this a story I want to dig in on?"

He paused, deep in thought. "No, come to think of it. You probably don't. How about I just say we had a fantastic honeymoon and leave it at that?"

"I'm very OK with that, XO."

"Very good, ma'am. I've gone over the check-off lists on all the work orders. There are some outstanding items on this availability, but I think I can get those knocked out today."

"Super. No problems heading out to AUTEC next week?"

"None, ma'am."

"OK, let's get it done, then."

"Roger that. Excuse me, Captain."

After he stood and headed to the door, Haley said, "XO?"

He turned and said, "Yes, ma'am?"

She smiled warmly at him. "I'm glad you're back, Ben."

"Thank you, ma'am. Me too." He nodded and closed the door on his way out.

Extract from the Canadian monthly periodical *Financial Journal*, published 5 June.
"Canada-U.S. Joint Venture to Take Over Haitian Mine Lease."
By: Edmond L. Peterson

TORONTO. Quesnel Mining & Development Corp [QMD | TSX] revealed the formation of a joint venture today with the American firm Penobscot Engineering Ltd. [PEL | AMEX] to succeed Sino-American Mining Corporation [SMC | SGX] in the long-term lease of Ile Ste. Michel, Haiti, for Rare-Earth Element (REE) mining, effective 1 July. The new venture, called Pan-Antilles Development Ltd., headquartered in Toronto, is scheduled to begin operations within 60 days of the lease transfer. The announcement coincides with the formal approval of financing by the U.S. Export-Import Bank (EIB) to clear the outstanding balance of the Haitian government's debt to the Silk Highway Fund, a state-owned investment fund of the People's Republic of China, headquartered in Shanghai. This financing will be repaid via profit sharing between the EIB, Pan-Antilles, and the Haitian government.

Industry experts were surprised by both the formation of the new enterprise and the swift approval of financing by the U.S. government. The annual outputs of the REE mining operations on the island of Ile Ste. Michel, located 25 miles north of Haiti's northern coast, have consistently fallen far below predicted levels, leading to speculation that original assessments of the richness of the REE find were flawed or fraudulent. The rapidity with which the lease was terminated by mutual consent of the Haitian government and SAMC has further stoked the speculation that China is seeking to cut its losses.

Responding to inquiries on whether filings estimating output at 8-11 times the current levels might be overly optimistic, Pan-Antilles CEO Lloyd Dunnington-Smith cited next-generation equipment, techniques, and management as making these forecasts readily achievable....

Notes from the Author

None of the characters in this book represent any particular person (you got that, all you lawyers out there?). However, some of the best qualities of the fictional crew members of *Kauai* were inspired by many of the fine people with whom I had the honor and pleasure to serve while I was a part of the Coast Guard.

USCGC *Kauai* is fictional. There is no "D Class" of the 110-foot patrol boat series, and the last of those built was USCGC *Galveston Island* (WPB-1349). I created a fictitious D-Class to buy some extra margin of verisimilitude and get the nit-pickers off my back. The cutters *Dependable* and *Joseph Napier* are genuine and still in service as of this writing.

The island of Ile Ste. Michel, Haiti, is fictional. The geography illustrations at the beginnings of Parts II and III of this story were altered to show it off the northeast coast of Haiti.

The lethal encounter between the panga and the Coast Guard response boat is based on an actual event occurring on 2 December 2012. USCGC *Halibut* was operating in the Channel Islands off Ventura, California, when it detected a Mexican panga loitering off Santa Cruz Island. A boarding party led by Chief Boatswain's Mate Terrell Edwin Horne III was dispatched in the cutter's RHIB. When directed to stop, the panga rammed the Coast Guard RHIB, ejecting Chief Horne, who was struck by the panga's propellers and died of his injuries. Horne was posthumously promoted to Senior Chief Petty Officer and awarded the Coast Guard Medal. The new Sentinel-Class cutter USCGC *Terrell Horne* (WPC-1131) is named after him. The suspect vessel was pursued by other Coast Guard units and stopped four hours after the ramming, and the two men on board were arrested. They were convicted in the death of Chief Horne on 5 February 2014.

****

I had a devil of a time getting this book off the ground. Many ideas were already on the table after the first two books in this series, and it was hard to weave in stuff that would be both fresh and yet still believable. I decided early on that I needed to bring some new blood into the command, so I contrived a way to replace Sam without killing him (early promotion and transfer). Bringing in a female CO was almost a no-brainer as it opened some doors beyond the "new boss tribulations" trope regarding conflict with Chief Emilia Hopkins that would not have been possible with another male as captain. Once I launched on the story, it came together amazingly quickly—in fact, I wrote the story in less time than it took to think up and decide on it.

I agonized over the vignette involving the captive women aboard the *Miho Dujam*. I needed something to remove the reader's doubts that the 252 Syndicate were irredeemable, sociopathic monsters. My reading of the horrors of real-life human sex trafficking offered a much starker and more personal moral cause than the abstract damage caused by arms and drug trafficking or even assassination. Still, even in the toned-down form I used in the book, the scene disturbed me to the point that I nearly ditched it entirely. Dark as it was, I decided to leave it in for its value, along with the hurricane scene and the climactic action, as a "Why We Fight" item.

When I was writing the first novel in this series that eventually became *Dagger Quest*, I took a break to clear my mind and doodled up a notional ship's crest (most warships have a unique crest, sort of a coat of arms). I thought having some meaningful Latin phrase to include as a ship's motto might be classy, so I set to work in Wikipedia. My first stop was *audere est facere* (to dare is to do) which I thought was quite cool. Unfortunately, it was also trademarked by the Tottenham Hotspurs Football Club across the pond in England. I tried to see if they might be interested in a minor sharing arrangement. Then, when they did not respond, I thought better of it and moved on. The next one that caught my eye was *fortiter et fideliter* (bravely and faithfully), a common but non-trademarked phrase and also very cool—USCGC *Kauai*'s motto was born.

It did not occur to me at the time that this phrase could play a significant role in a story, certainly not to the degree that it furnished the title for a novel. However, as this book evolved, the overriding theme of the responsibility of command and the grim mathematics of calculated risk became more dominant. "Bravely and Faithfully" becomes more than just a motto for a crew whose courage, competence, and faith in each other is such that they will take the most extreme personal risks to save the lives of strangers. It ultimately describes the mettle of two captains, each of whom must decide whether to take on a mission where anything that goes amiss could result in the horrible death of these people you honor, respect, and even love.

This book is about a group of ordinary people whose association with each other allow them to meet extraordinary challenges. It is quite true to life in the technical sense and illustrates that you do not have to be a superhero or a supersoldier to make an enormous difference.

MAYDAY, MAYDAY – Request Assistance!

First of all, thank you for purchasing *The Kauai Sea Adventures*! I know you could have picked any number of books to read, but you chose this book, and for that, I am incredibly grateful. I hope it gave you what you were seeking, be it a little extra enjoyment or just a chance to escape the trials and tribulations of life for a while. If so, it would be really helpful if you could share this book with your friends and family by mentioning it on Facebook and Twitter.

If you enjoyed these stories, I'd like to hear from you and hope you could take some time to post a review or at least a rating on your bookseller's website. Your feedback and support will help me as I work on future projects, and I am very interested in hearing your thoughts. Please visit my website when you have the time to provide your feedback, find out what is new, and grab the occasional freebie:

 https://www.edwardhochsmann.com/

Very Respectfully,

Ed